SHADOWFALL

BOOK ONE OF THE GODSLAYER CHRONICLES

SHADOWFALL

BOOK ONE OF THE GODSLAYER CHRONICLES

JAMES CLEMENS

A ROC BOOK

ROC
Published by New American Library, a division of
Penguin Group (USA) Inc., 375 Hudson Street,
New York, New York 10014, USA
Penguin Group (Canada), 10 Alcorn Avenue, Toronto,
Ontario M4V 3B2, Canada (a division of Pearson Penguin Canada Inc.)
Penguin Books Ltd., 80 Strand, London WC2R 0RL, England
Penguin Ireland, 25 St. Stephen's Green, Dublin 2,
Ireland (a division of Penguin Books Ltd.)
Penguin Group (Australia), 250 Camberwell Road, Camberwell, Victoria 3124,
Australia (a division of Pearson Australia Group Pty. Ltd.)
Penguin Books India Pvt. Ltd., 11 Community Centre, Panchsheel Park,
New Delhi - 110 017, India
Penguin Group (NZ), cnr Airborne and Rosedale Roads, Albany,
Auckland 1310, New Zealand (a division of Pearson New Zealand Ltd.)
Penguin Books (South Africa) (Pty.) Ltd., 24 Sturdee Avenue,
Rosebank, Johannesburg 2196, South Africa

Penguin Books Ltd., Registered Offices:
80 Strand, London WC2R 0RL, England

First published by Roc, an imprint of New American Library,
a division of Penguin Group (USA) Inc.

First Printing, July 2005
10 9 8 7 6 5 4 3 2 1

Maps provided and drawn by Steve Prey. All rights reserved. Used by permission of Steve Prey.

ROC REGISTERED TRADEMARK—MARCA REGISTRADA

LIBRARY OF CONGRESS CATALOGING-IN-PUBLICATION DATA:

Clemens, James.
Shadowfall : book one of the godslayer chronicles / James Clemens.
p. cm.
ISBN 0-451-45994-6 (trade hardcover : alk. paper)
1. Goddesses—Crimes against—Fiction. 2. People with disabilities—Fiction. 3. Knights and knighthood—Fiction.
4. Wilderness areas—Fiction. 5. Witnesses—Fiction. I. Title.
PS3553.L3927S53 2005
813'.54—dc22   2004027360

Set in AGaramond
Designed by Leonard Telesca

Printed in the United States of America

To Charles Mack

Welcome to the family

ACKNOWLEDGMENTS

This new world of Myrillia grew too vast to tread alone. So I put together my own fellowship of companions, allies, coconspirators, trailblazers, and general muckrakers to keep me on the straight and narrow. First, thanks to Carolyn McCray, who red-inked every page before anybody else, and my posse of critique-group members who hide behind the infamous title of "The Warped Spacers": Judy and Steve Prey, Chris Crowe, Michael Gallowglas, David Murray, Dennis Grayson, Dave Meek, Royale Adams, Jane O'Riva, and Caroline Williams. And for all help with the map that fronts this book, a special thanks to Steve Prey for his artistry, skill, and insight. Finally, thanks to the three people whom I respect for their friendship as much as their counsel: my editor John Morgan, and my agents Russ Galen and Danny Baror. And as always, I must stress that any and all errors of fact or detail fall squarely upon my own shoulders.

ᵐᒥᑦᕠ ᐃᕘᒍᐱ ᓂᐅ ᑕᐱᕐᑭ ᑎᑕ ᕐᒍᓪᓗ ᐃᕁᑕ ᐅᕅᕁ.ᓄ ᕈᑕᐃᕁᕁ,
ᵐᒥᑦᕠ ᓗᑕᐃ ᕆᑕᕘᒎᑦ ᕁᕠᑦᐳ ᕴᒍᑎ ᑕᕁᕉᐸ ᑦᕁᕁᓘᐳ
ᒎᕠᑦ ᑎᕈᕠ ᑕᓗᑕᑕᑦᑦ ᕆᕁᑦᑦ ᕴᕚᒍᕁ, ᓗᓂᕁᕁᑦᑦ ᐊᓂᑎᕁ ᑕᑕᕁᕉᐳ
ᕴᒎᕠᑦ ᕴᕁᑎᕴᒎᓗᐳ, ᓗᓂᕁᐳ ᕴᒍᑎ ᑕᕁᕉᐳ ᑎᑕᕁᐳ
                         ᒎᓗᕁᕁ
ᵐᒥᕋᐅ ᓂᐅ ᑕᕁᕁ ᕴᕚᒍᕁ ᕋᒥᕟ ᒪᕟᐳᑎ ᐃᕘᒎᓗ.ᓄ.
ᕼᕟᑎ ᕋᕋᕟ ᑎᕈᕁ ᕋᕁᓗᕋ ᕋᕁᕁ.

The way is open to all who seek power,
The low road ends at one's heels
And the bloodred path, lined with bones and petals, lies at
one's toes
                      Alone
This is the path one must walk.
But not the only way.

                                 —the last spoken words of the Tongueless God

ᕈᕋᕟᕁ ᐅᕟᓂᕋ.ᓄᐅ
ᕼᕟᑎ ᕌᕆᑕᕋᕃ ᓂᑎ ᑕᓗᑕᑕᕃᐅ ᑎᕈᕁ ᒪᑕᐅᑎ
ᕌᕴᕚᒎᕧᕚᒎᕠᕟ ᕆᕋᐅᕁᐳ.

All shite stinks
But from it blooms the most fragrant roses.
                             —an unsubstantiated proverb from a rogue god

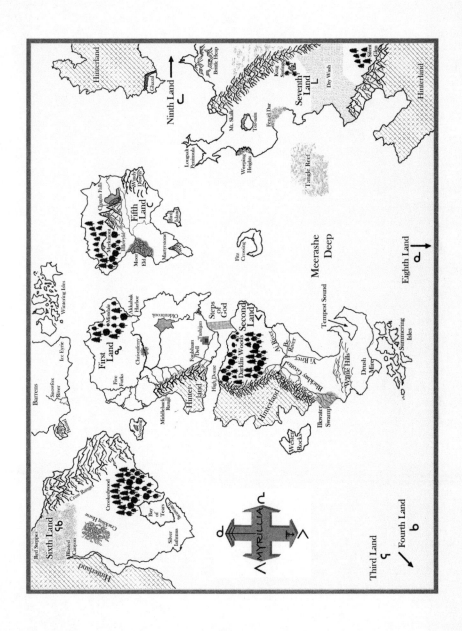

In Darkness . . .

IT GLIDES, A SHADOW SEEKING THE LIGHT.
Its true name cannot be spoken within the logics of flesh and breath. It is no more than a trembling, a dark vibration along the plane that lies beneath rock and storm. It has no form, no shape, no substance.

Naethryn.

That is its being, but not its name. It is a creature of the naether, that vast and empty void.

It glides up to one of those rare places where its existence overlaps into the world of substance. Few know of these moiety points. But they exist. Just as the sea rides up onto a rocky shore, so do the tides of the naether roll against the world above.

The naethryn finds a hidden estuary, an opening where its world and the upper world blend and shift. Rising, it swims up a choked channel, silty with substance, into the world above.

Abandoning the naether far below, it enters the depths of a black sea, birthing into the icy waters. Light never reaches these depths. Here is eternal darkness, blurring where one world ends and another begins. But the naethryn knows its way. It's been told, instructed, willed.

The shadow creature rises through the cold, dark sea. It shudders and gains form, drawing bits of luminescent life from the ocean. The deaths are small, but they thrum through its being, vibrations of pleasure. It sails upward. More and more life is drawn. Substance builds, layer by layer, like barnacles on a ship's keel.

Form and shape bloom out of nothingness.

Pressure lifts as aquamarine moonlight bleeds down, bathing the naether creature's new form. As it nears the surface, schooled fish flee in clouds of scale. Even a monstrous rill shark flicks its muscular tail and vanishes.

Unconcerned, it allows them to escape. It has all the structure it needs for this world. It tests its black limbs, its long snaking tail, and swims upward out of the dark womb.

At last, the naethryn breaks the waves with a crested head and breathes the night's salt-soaked air, testing its lungs. Lidless eyes shine with a light that does not belong to this world. It stares across the foam-limned waves toward the distant shore.

Islands breach the waves: shoals, reefs, atolls, volcanic peaks.

An archipelago.

The Summering Isles.

A hiss escapes the broken fish bones that make up its teeth. It swims toward its destination, the largest island of the archipelago. Eyes reflect the flickering lights that sparkle from the isle's crowned peak and spill down its slopes to the sea, describing homes, streets, and ramparts. A few lamps even skip out into the waters, marking moored fishercraft and masted deepwhalers.

The naethryn ignores all, knowing its purpose.

As it crosses the ring of reefs, none note its undulating passage. Even the lesser moon hides her face behind fog and cloud. The naethryn moves through the seawater as easily as through the insubstantial reality of its home.

Land rises beneath the waves. The naethryn resists touching such solidness, gliding through the shallows, remaining in water for as long as possible. But soon, force and blood and promise drive it from the waves.

Clawed feet dig into sand. Climbing upright, it balances with a long tail. Though it wears flesh and bone, edges blur with the shadows of the dark beach. It does not belong here.

It steps forward.

It must.

Water sluices from the assassin's shoulders as it lurches forward. Steam rises from its scales. Claws drip with more than water. It moves across the sand, turning each step to molten glass behind it.

It has come here to slay.

To slay a god.

FIRST

FALL FROM GRACE

Hu.mour, u mêr, <u>n</u>. [Old Littick ⌁ΓLσΓρ, to be moist.] (1) any functional fluid of an animal (2) one of the quadricals of greater bodily fluids (blood, sweat, masculine seed, feminine menses) or quintrangle of lesser bodily fluids (tears, saliva, phlegm, yellow and black bile) (3) the blessed fluids from which flow the nine Graces of Gods.

—Annals of Physique Primer, ann. 3593

I

PUNT

SOME NIGHTS SIMPLY NEVER END.

    Tylar de Noche rolled to one knee atop the broken cobbles and wiped blood from the scrub of dark beard under his chin. A moment ago, tossed out of the Wooden Frog, he had landed hard on an arm that was more club than limb. His support had given way, slamming him face-down onto the unforgiving street.

As he kissed the stones, he was reminded of an old adage concerning the Summering Isles: *A good night can last forever, but a bad night lasts even longer.*

On his knees now, Tylar prayed for this particular evening to end. Forget raising a pint and acknowledging, if only to himself, the thirtieth pass of his birth year. He wished only for his lone bed in the garret over the fishmonger's shop.

But that was not to be. He would be lucky to see sunrise.

Tasting blood from his split lip, he swept his gaze right and left as he sought any means of escape.

Upstreet spread the terraces, *palacios,* and gardened heights of those with enough wealth to enjoy the cooler breezes of the isle's cliffs, leading up at last to the white castillion that blazed atop the Summer Mount. Guarded heavily, there would be no escape in that direction.

Nor downstreet. That direction led to the crooked alleys, whored corners, and dark narrows of Lower Punt. Safety *never* lay in that direction.

So, trapped in the middle, he faced his adversaries.

Bargo and Yorga.

The pair of bulky Ai'men bore matching tattoos on their shoulders. Two halves of the same slave ring. Once bonded and linked combatants in the blood circuses, they were now freemen.

Only their sport hadn't changed.

Yorga fingered ebony guild beads woven into a lock of his mud-brown hair. Tavern shield beads. Marking him as a hired guardsman to the ale-house.

At his side, Bargo, the one still with his tongue, barked, "Goodly Master Rind don't take to Punt scabbers crawling into his tavern a'beggin'."

Tylar, his eyes narrowed, kept his post in the street, knowing better than to protest his innocence. He'd come to the tavern with two brass pinches, plenty for a pint. But it seemed he had chosen the wrong tavern. He knew better than to risk the establishments of the high city. This wasn't his place. Yet sometimes he forgot himself. Sometimes he simply sought some memory of a different life.

He shut out such thoughts and crouched on the cobbles as a warm black rain misted from the dark skies. It was not the pleasant, cleansing downpour of a true storm, but more of a fog that trapped the day's heat and held it to the islands.

Still, it wasn't the weather that pebbled Tylar's brow with sweat and made his ragged clothes suddenly seem too tight.

Yorga balled up a fist, and a garbled sound flowed from his scarred throat. Laughter.

The pair of Ai'men strode out from under the creaking sign of the Wooden Frog. Tylar was to be their amusement this night.

❖

Yorga came first, all fist and muscle. Little finesse. But skill was not needed against Tylar—at least not any longer. Once a Shadowknight, Tylar previously could have taken both with hardly a wind.

But the Graces had been stripped from him, along with rank and title. Additionally, the empty vessel left behind had been broken by a half decade spent in the slave rings of Trik. His sword arm was a callused club, numb from the elbow down. His legs had fared no better—one knee was a knot of locked bone from an old hammer blow, the other slow and painful. Even his back was crooked, tightened by scars from the whip.

He was no knight.

Not any longer.

Yet his Shadowmaster at Tashijan had taught him not to depend on the Graces. A cuff usually accompanied his instructor's gruff words: *Remember, the deadliest Grace comes not from a God, but from the heart and mind of a cornered man.*

It seemed a small lesson compared to the size of the combatants here.

The hulking Yorga, bare chested and sweating of ale, outweighed Tylar by half.

"When we're done with you in the streets," the Ai'man warned, roughly grabbing his crotch, "we're going to finish you in the alley. We always wanted to bugger a Shadowknight."

Tylar narrowed one eye. Finally it was clear why these two had chosen to harangue him. It wasn't his shabby attire, nor even his broken form. It had been the stripes tattooed on the sides of his face, running in jagged lines from the outer corner of each eye to ear, heralding his former rank, forever marking him. Three stripes. One for page, one for squire, one for vowed knight. What he had once borne with pride was now a mark of disgrace.

A fallen knight.

He kept the stripes hidden as much as possible, letting his black hair grow long and ragged, hanging over his storm-gray eyes. He kept his head bowed away from the sight of others.

Still, anger burned deep behind his ribs, a fire that never dampened. Though it might smolder to embers, it was always there. Always ready to flare.

Yorga lunged an arm at him, meaning to grab a fistful of hair.

A mistake.

Tylar rocked out of the way, pivoting on his clubbed arm. He lashed out with his other, swiftly, bringing his elbow around to strike the bridge of Yorga's nose as he leaned down.

Bone crushed.

Tylar didn't feel it—but he heard it, along with the howl that followed. It wasn't a cry of pain so much as outrage. Yorga lurched backward, blood spraying from both nostrils.

Bargo roared, coming around his partner's side.

Tylar rolled to his scarred back, kicking out with his legs. He knew where to strike. The heels of his boots smashed into the larger man's knees. Bargo's legs flew out from under him. He toppled forward, toward Tylar, arms outstretched, face a mask of rage, spittle flying.

Tylar, still on his back on the cobbles, rolled to the side, wrapping himself in his tattered cloak. Bargo crashed to the stones beside him, landing as Tylar had a moment before, face-first.

But the slave fighters knew how to work together.

Yorga's fingers clamped onto Tylar's ankle. With blood flecking from his snarled lips, Yorga hauled Tylar toward him. As a squire, Tylar had once fallen off his horse, tangling a boot in the stallion's stirrup, and had been dragged behind the beast. Yorga was stronger.

With a grunt, Tylar flipped from his back to his stomach. The Ai'man had a grip on his mangled leg, the one with the frozen knee. It was like holding a bent shepherd's crook. The twisting forced Yorga to loosen his grip, lest his own wrist be broken.

Partially free, Tylar slammed his boot heels together, catching three of Yorga's fingers between them. Yorga half-lifted Tylar and tossed him away.

He rolled on a shoulder and allowed the momentum to put distance between himself and his attackers. He stopped in a half crouch, back to his enemies, glancing over his shoulder. He ached everywhere, his small reserves of strength ebbing.

Yorga helped up Bargo. Fire burned in both men's eyes. Tylar had caught them by surprise. That was over. Together the Ai'men approached, stepping to either side to flank him.

"*Hold!*" The voice froze them all.

It came from farther up the street.

Bargo and Yorga parted to reveal a single figure in a black surcoat trimmed in silver, with a matching cloak, standing still. No chain, no armor, no shield. Only a sheathed sword hung at his waist. The black diamond on the hilt's pommel glowed with its own light. That was all the protection needed here. The figure had been blessed in Grace.

A Shadowknight.

The same light from the diamond shone in the eyes of the warrior.

Tylar could not match that gaze. He turned askance.

A wind caught the edge of the knight's cloak, willowing it out. Maybe it was a trick of moonlight, but as the cloak swept across the knight's form, darkness consumed the figure, vanishing him half-away.

Tylar knew it was not a trick of the light . . . but a blessing of shadow. The Grace of such knights: to move unseen, to shirk into darkness and away. At night, there was no greater foe.

Bargo and Yorga knew this and bowed out of the way, heads lowered, backs bent. Yorga dropped to a knee as the knight stepped past him.

"What is the mishap here?" the knight asked, his heavy gaze settling on Tylar.

Rather than looking up, Tylar maintained a focus on the knight's boots. There was much to tell from a man's boots. Calfskin and mullerhorn. Fine tooled leathers from the Greater Coast. Worn well at the arch from riding hundreds of reaches in the stirrup. Since none of the Summering Isles were more than five reaches across, the knight must be an outsider to this sea-locked realm. Perhaps a blessed courier from another god-realm. Or perhaps a new conscript called in service to the god here, Meeryn of the Summering Isles.

Either way, he's new to his cloak, Tylar concluded, *or he wouldn't scuff his boots on such a petty street brawl.*

Bargo finally coughed loose his tongue. "This scabber were a'beggin' in Goodly Master Rind's tavern house. We were bending his arm a bit to send him back down to Punt."

"Is that so?" the knight asked. Tylar heard the wry amusement in the other's tone. "From my vantage, I'd say he was the one doing the bending."

Bargo blustered.

The boots Tylar had been studying stepped closer. "Your name, sirrah?"

Tylar remained silent. He didn't bother to look up. There was no need. The knight's features would be hidden behind a wrap of masklin, a facecloth cut from the same blessed material as the knight's cloak. All that was ever seen of a knight's face were the eyes and the triple stripes that blended into the masklin.

"Is what they claim true?" the knight continued. "You are aware, sirrah, that begging of coin is not allowed after sunset."

As answer, Tylar reached into his pockets and tossed the pair of brass pinches on the cobbles before the knight's toes.

"Ah, so it seems the scruff here has a coin or two. Sirrah, perhaps your pinches are better spent in a tavern of the lower city." A toe nudged the bits of brass back toward Tylar.

Such rare kindness earned a curious glance toward his benefactor. The knight was tall and lithe, a willow switch in a cloak. His face was indeed wrapped in masklin. Eyes glowed at him. Tylar saw them pinch in surprise. A step was taken back.

"He's a stripped knight," Bargo said. "A shiting vow-breaker."

Tylar pocketed his coin and gained his feet. He stared the knight up and down, anger burning away shame. He read the disgust in the other's stance. He met the other's gaze fully for the first time. "Fear not. Disgrace is not contagious, ser." He turned swiftly away.

But not swiftly enough . . .

"Ser Noche . . ." The knight spoke his name with raw shock. "*Tylar* ser Noche."

Tylar's step faltered. A thousand reaches from his homelands and he still could not escape his cursed name.

"It is you, ser, is it not?"

Tylar kept his back to him. "You are mistaken, ser knight."

"Curse my blessed eyes if I am!" Boots scuffed closer. "Face me."

Tylar knew better than to disobey a Shadowknight. He turned.

Beyond the knight's shoulder, he spotted Bargo and Yorga slinking back to the Wooden Frog, happy to escape the knight's attention. They knew their game had ended, but Bargo stopped at the threshold. He wiped blood and snot from his lips and cast a murderous stare toward Tylar, a promise of pain to come, a debt he meant to collect. Then the brawlers pushed back into the tavern.

Tylar's attention focused back to the fellow before him. "As I was saying, you mistake me for someone else, ser."

As rebuttal, the knight reached to the clasp at his throat. A shadowy waft of masklin fluttered free.

Tylar instinctively glanced down. Only a knight was allowed to see another knight's features.

"Face me, ser." Command lay thick on the other's tongue.

Tylar trembled and obeyed.

He found a familiar countenance framed within the cloak's hood. Tylar knew those features: high cheekbones, white-blond hair, amber eyes. The young knight was all sunlight and autumn fields, in contrast to Tylar's stormy and dark countenance. Time sailed backward. Tylar recognized the peach-faced boy behind the bearded man who stood before him now.

"Perryl . . ."

The last time he had seen this face there had been only two stripes. Perryl had been one of his three squired lads back in Tashijan, under his tutelage before . . . before . . .

He glanced away, his heart aching.

The Shadowknight dropped to one knee before him. "Ser Noche."

"No," Tylar refused. "No longer *Ser* Noche. It is simply *de* Noche."

"Never! To me you will always be hailed as *ser*."

Tylar twisted and stumbled away. "Get off your knees, Perryl. You shame yourself and your cloak. It seems even in this small task I have failed the Order . . . training you so poorly for your station." He continued down the street.

A scuffle sounded behind him as his former squire gained his feet and fled abreast of him. "All that I am, I owe to you."

The words cut like poisoned daggers. Tylar hurried on, knowing he could never flee a blessed knight, but perhaps he could escape his own memories.

Perryl kept beside him. "I would speak to you, ser! Much has changed back at Tashijan. If you will meet with me on the morrow—"

Tylar stopped and swung toward Perryl. His chest heaved on swells of shame and misery. "Damn your eyes! Look at me, Perryl." He held up his crooked arm. "The knight you knew is gone, long buried. I'm a scabber out of Punt. Leave me to my hole and seek me out no more."

His outburst thrust the other back a half step.

In the knight's face, he saw the boy again, wounded and at a loss for a response. The young man stared up at the lesser moon's glow. "I must be away," he mumbled apologetically, fixing his masklin back in place, then met Tylar's eye firmly, a knight again. "Whether it bring you pain or humiliation, I would still speak with you."

"Leave me be, Perryl," he begged with all his heart. "If you ever loved me, leave me be."

"For now . . . only for now." He swung his cloak and backed into shadow, blending away. Only a pair of eyes glowed back at Tylar. "A dread and perilous time is upon us . . . upon all of us."

Then Perryl was gone, moving with the speed born of Grace.

Tylar stood a moment longer. His fingers clutched the pair of brass pinches in his pocket. Would that he had a silver yoke to drown away this night. But he doubted that even a pouch of gold marches would wash this pain away.

He let the pinches slip between his fingers into his pocket as he continued down the street. He skirted around the darkest alleys of Punt, aiming roundabout for the docklands and his lone bed.

On the morrow, he would seek a boat to another island. He did not want to be known or remembered. He would lose himself again, sinking into the solace that came with anonymity.

Still, Perryl's words stayed with Tylar as he hobbled along. *A dread and perilous time is upon us all.* A streak of dark humor cut through his pain and shame. *A dread and perilous time?* That fairly summed up his state of affairs since he was stripped five years ago. How was any of this a new tiding?

With a shake of his head, he shut out such thoughts.

It was none of his concern.

❖

As the night wore thin, Tylar walked from streets lined in cobbles to those simply worn from the natural sandy rock. Here the houses were shuttered and dark, hiding their faces.

Off to his left, the alleys and narrows of Punt echoed with cries, shouts, and sounds to which it was best to be deaf. But one could not escape Punt's smells. It shat and sweated and pissed like a living creature, ripe with corruption, pestilence, and decay.

One never developed a nose for it. It was too changeable—by day, by season, by storm, by fair weather.

Tylar kept his shoulders hunched, skulking through pockets of gloom. One learned the value of being inconspicuous in the lower city. He crept along shadows. Though now Graceless, he was not without skill at moving unseen.

He rounded past Gillian Square with its empty gallows and cut through Chanty Row with its tanners and dyeworks.

Still, he could not fully escape Punt's gaze. It leered at him as he crawled home. It screamed and laughed and watched him from a hundred dark windows.

He hurried over Lumberry Bridge as its stone spanned the stagnant canal that drained the upper city, carrying away its refuse and bile. Beyond the bridge, the canal dumped into Lower Punt, the island's chamber pot.

Past Lumberry, Tylar had his trickiest traverse. Here the boundary between Lower Punt and the more stable dockyards blurred. Taverns and wenchworks occupied every corner. Dark alleys crisscrossed blindly.

Tylar entered the gloom, and while shadows had always been his home, here there was no safety. The very air was heavy and thick, moving sluggishly, a fetid exhalation from Punt. It was a common lay for thieves seeking a quick slice and run or hard-pricked roughers looking for a bit of alley rutting, willing or not. Neither was much threat to Tylar. He seldom carried enough coin to be worth the effort, and his bent, scarred form hardly fired anyone's loins.

So he hurried through these last alleys, already picturing his straw-filled bed. But as he rounded the darkest patch, entering a small square of derelict buildings, his feet suddenly stopped as surely as if he had run into a wall. A waft of scent had almost dropped him to his knees. Not foul, but the sweetest bouquet, lavenders and honeybloom, bright against the darkness.

It was silk and a child's laugh.

Tylar stood, planted on the sandy stone of the square. How could he walk away? He doubted he could even be forced away. Tears welled in his eyes. The darkness scintillated with the sweetwater scent. All he could do was search for its source. What beauty could bloom in such shite?

Then a scream shattered the night, startling him back to the dangers that lay in the shadows of Punt. It was a man who cried out, and Tylar had never heard such terror, not in all his years.

There followed the bright sound of sword on stone. Shouts accompanied in chorus. Panicked. Close. The neighboring alley. Footfalls echoed, running away—

No . . . *toward* him.

Tensing, Tylar twisted around. He was momentarily unsure where to flee. Then a figure unfolded from the darkness before him. A silvered sword, held aloft in his hand, split his dark form like lightning. Above the blade, eyes matched the shine.

A Shadowknight.

Instinctively, Tylar knew it was not Perryl. The form was too broad of shoulder. The man dropped to his knees—not in supplication as Perryl had moments ago, but in prostration.

Tylar stepped toward him, a hand rising in aid. But he was too late.

As the knight's body struck the street, his head rolled impossibly from his shoulders, bouncing obscenely to Tylar's toes.

Slain . . .

Gasping, Tylar stumbled away.

Other bits of darkness fell out of the shadows. More knights, wrapped in masklin and cloak, appeared. They fared no better than the first, seeming to come apart at the seams. Limbs dropped away, bloodless but dead. Innards burst, pouring in tortuous loops from bellies. One knight collapsed in on himself as if his bones had suddenly jellied.

Horrified, Tylar fell back. What deadly Grace was at work here? He found his back pressed to the mortared stone of a burned-out structure. He huddled into a doorway's alcove, seeking refuge inside, but the entrance was boarded tight.

Trapped, his eyes widened, seeking any clue, any answer to the slaughter. Something shared the shadows with the knights—but what?

Across the alley, a fog of light swelled between two soot-painted buildings. A glowing vessel flew into the square. It was a mekanical flutterseat, an open carriage held aloft by a pair of blurred wings. It bore a lone woman, crouched on the single seat. Other knights flanked the carriage and trailed it.

But one after another, they fell, afflicted like the others, until there were none.

Alone and unguarded, the carriage canted, struck the cobbles, and spilled over. Broken wings shattered against stone. The passenger, a wisp of a woman, flew free of the wreckage and landed spryly. She twirled in the center of the shimmering mist. A dance of panic and wildness.

Tylar was again struck by a swell of sweet-water scents, stretching from some distant spring. But now it held a touch of winter's frost, too.

Fear.

Tylar knew the woman was the very bloom of this bouquet. She was also the source of the glow, a living lamp. The cold sheen of terror on her skin cast its own light. She must be richly blessed in Graces to shine with such power. Perhaps a noblewoman, or someone of an even higher station . . . Her dress was snowy finery and lace, her hair loose to the shoulder, as dark as her skin was pale.

Somewhere deep inside, he knew he should go to her aid. But he remained in place. He was no longer a knight, but a broken man. Shame burned as bright as his fear.

The woman fled to the center of the dark square, still dancing warily, eyes flashing with glowing tears. She was indeed powerfully blessed, rich in humoral Graces. The blessing of the gods flowed from her every pore, misting from her body as she whirled. But with whom was she dancing?

The answer was not long in coming. Darkness took form at the edge of her glow, coalescing out of shadow.

It stood upright like a man—but was no man. It was scale and snake and shattered teeth. A crest trailed from crown to whipping tail. As it approached, a mist of Gloom steamed from its skin, a contrary Grace to the bright glow of the lone woman.

She faced her enemy, stopping her dance. "You will not win," she whispered.

As answer, a hiss of fire licked from its burned lips. There were no words, but a sound accompanied the flame, distant, yet still reaching clearly to Tylar in his hiding place. It pierced and ate at his will. His legs shook. He knew it to be a voice, but no throat could utter such a noise. It was not a sound that belonged anywhere among the Nine Lands, nor anywhere across all of Myrillia. It was a keening wail, crackling with lightning, laced with the scurry of dark things under the ground.

Tylar covered his ears, but it did not help.

The woman listened. Her only response was a paling of her snowy skin. Bone shone through. Her eyes dimmed. She uttered one word: "No."

Then the beast lashed out, moving faster than the eye could follow. Darkness crested like a wave over the bright well of Grace that shielded the woman. Lightning flashed across the darkness, lancing out and striking the woman.

She fell back, arms outstretched, momentarily impaled between her breasts by the stroke of brightness. It was not lightning, Tylar realized, but something with substance . . . yet at the same time not completely of this world.

Pierced through the chest, the woman cried out, a wail of a songbird, sharp and aching.

The beast pursued, leaping. Darkness swallowed the woman away, rolling over her. Both vanished in the steaming gloom of the creature's shadow.

Tylar held himself clenched.

Then like storm clouds roiled away by swift winds, the blackness swirled outward, becoming a tempest trapped between stone walls.

It struck all around, tearing at mortar. Glass shattered.

Tylar clutched the walls of his alcove, nails digging for purchase. He fought to hold himself in place, but he also felt a tug on all that held his spirit in place. His sight was taken from him—or perhaps it was the world that had been stolen away. He teetered at the edge of an abyss. His skin both burned and iced. His heart stopped beating in his chest. He knew his death.

Then he was let go. He fell back against the boarded-up door. Before him in the square, darkness roiled into a great vortex as if draining away down some unseen well. The darkness whirled, growing smaller—then it swept down and away.

Across the ravaged square, the beast was nowhere to be seen.

All that was left was the woman's form sprawled in the center of the square. Her limbs still glowed, only weaker now. Rivers of brightness ran and pooled out from her form. Blood, shining with the richness of powerful Graces, flowed from her. She did not move.

Dead.

Tylar stumbled from the alcove. He sensed in his bones that whatever had entered Punt had vanished away. Still he dared approach no closer. He headed away, past the bodies of the slain. Sprawled in their blessed cloaks, the knights seemed like ghosts, blending with the shadows. Though the wearers were dead, the cloth still maintained its Grace, working to hide its owner even in death.

As Tylar skirted the square, the scent of flower petals and warm sun swelled around him. He turned, knowing the source. The pale, misty beauty remained unmoving on the stone. From this angle, he spotted the black hole pierced through her chest, as wide as a fist, blackened and wisped with curls of smoke.

He sensed it was down that hole that the darkness had vanished away, the well through which the enemy had escaped.

Though the forces at work here had nothing to do with a fallen knight, nor a broken man, he found his feet walking him toward the woman.

As he approached, he attempted to keep his feet from her glowing blood, but there was too much. He moved into her light, careful of the slick stone. She surely was a noblewoman of high stature. It was seldom someone was blessed with such a degree of Grace. Perhaps she was even one of the eight handservants to Meeryn, the god-made-flesh of these islands. Such servants dwelled in the god's castillion, harvesting and preserving the humours from the god they served.

Tylar eyed the castillion blazing atop the isle's highest point, Summer Mount, the seat of Meeryn. If he was right, if the lass had indeed been in service to this realm's god, he pitied the hand behind this attack. A god's vengeance knew no pity.

He reached the woman's side. He stared down into the wan beauty, brought low here. She was young, no more than eighteen. Her face glowed with a fading brilliance, gone to embers. The blank eyes, as blue as the seas, stared skyward.

Then those same eyes twitched in his direction, seeing him.

Tylar clenched back a step in shock.

She did indeed still live! But surely not for long . . .

"Child," he whispered, not knowing what words he could offer at this last moment.

He crouched, soaking his pant leg in blood. As the dampness reached his skin, he realized his mistake. The blood burned his flesh—not like fire, but like spiced wine on the tongue, as much pleasure as pain. It was a burn to which he was well familiar.

Crying out, he fell backward.

Fingers latched onto his wrist, holding him, squeezing like the iron manacles that had bound him for five years.

He gaped in horror. The woman was not dead. Then again, how *could* she be? She was not a *woman* at all.

Tylar knew who lay before him now, who clutched him.

It was not a handmaiden.

It was Meeryn herself . . . the immortal god of the Summering Isle.

Fingers squeezed and drew him closer. Her other arm rose and reached toward him. The palm was bloody. Tylar had neither the strength nor the will to fight.

The reaching palm struck his chest as if to push him away, while the clutching fingers pulled at him. The blood on the outstretched hand blazed through both the rough-spun cotton of his shirt and the soft linen of his underclothes. It touched the flesh over his heart. This was no spiced wine. He smelled the smolder of seared skin. The pain was excruciating, but at the same time, he never wanted it to end.

It didn't.

The god at his feet pushed deeper, stretching for his heart as it fluttered, a panicked bird in a bony cage. He gasped out fire as burning fingers entered his chest. The stone of the square vanished from his eyes, snuffed away like a pinched candle. The small sounds of the night blew out. The hard grind of stone fell away under his legs.

Only now did he understand the lack of substance behind reality.

Yet sensations remained.

A palm pushing at his chest, a hand dragging him down by the wrist.

He spun in these contrasts, but here, where there was no substance, both were possible. He felt himself shoved up into a brilliance that blinded, while dragged down into a darkness that was somehow just as bright. Where a moment ago he had stood at the edge of a bottomless abyss, now he hung over the same. But as he spun, he recognized his mistake. There was not one abyss, but *two*—one above and one below.

Both stared at him as he hovered between, his bones burning like a torch.

This was more than death.

I am undone, he thought, knowing it to be true.

Then a wash of coolness drenched his form, drowning him, driving him back to the slaughter of the square, back into his own body. He struck it like he had the broken cobbles outside the Wooden Frog: hard and abrupt.

Sensations filled him again—but the palm on his chest no longer burned. From the god's hand, a chilled wash spread out and through him.

He knew this sensation, too.

In a different life, he had bent a knee to the god Jessup of Oldenbrook. Then, too, he had been filled with Grace. And like Meeryn, Jessup had borne the aspect of water. To many, this aspect was the weakest of the four. Most of his fellow knights had sought out gods of fire, loam, or air. But not Tylar. He had been born as his mother drowned aboard a sinking scuttlecraft off the Greater Coast. Water was his home as much as shadow.

So he knew what filled him now.

"No!" he gasped. Grace flowed into him, drowned him, a hundredfold richer than when Jessup had ceremonially blessed him. He didn't deserve this honor. He could not face it. But he also could not escape it.

Grace swelled in him, stretching him.

No . . . too much . . .

His back arched. He remembered his birth, shoved brutally and lovingly out of the warmth of his mother's womb and into the cold seas of Myrillia. Then, too, he had breathed water, momentarily one with the sea—until salt burned and lungs fought to cry. He would have died had not the net of a lobsterman hauled him from the waves.

But who will save me now?

Water surged through him. He could not breathe. He craned, stretching for air.

Too much . . .

Something gave way deep inside him. The swell of water spouted up and drained down, spewing from him in racking spasms. He felt part of himself given away with it, released, stolen, shared—and at the same time, something entered, swimming up the flowing channel and into his chest, settling there, coiling there.

Then the water finally emptied from the broken vessel that was his body. Tylar collapsed in on himself, spent and drained. The momentary blessing was gone.

The hand on his chest fell away. His wrist was released.

He stared down again into Meeryn's face.

Her soft skin no longer glowed, but her eyes still stared at him as dawn finally broke over the island, taking the edge off the gloom. Meeryn would recover. Like all the gods, she was immortal, undying, eternal.

Her lips moved, but no words were spoken. He thought he had read the word *pity* on those perfect lips, but maybe it was just something in her eyes. What did she mean?

"Lie still," he urged, leaning closer. "Help will come."

A small movement. A tiny shake of the head and a sigh. Her lips parted again. He cocked his head, bringing his ear closer. Her breath was cherry blossoms on a still lake.

"Rivenscryr," she whispered. It was not a fragment of thought, but a simple command.

Tylar's brow pinched at the strange word. *Rivenscryr?* He faced her, a question on his lips. "What—?"

Then he saw the impossible before him. It took all breath from him.

Meeryn lay as she had a moment before, but now all light faded from her—not just the glow of her Graces, but *all* that separated the living from the dead. Her eyes, still open, went empty and blind. Her lips remained parted with her last word, but no breath escaped them.

Both as a Shadowknight and as a slave, he had come to know death. But here it was not possible.

Gods do not die.

A strident burst of horn startled him, driving him to his feet. He twisted around to find a dark shadow sweeping at him with the swiftness of a black gale. He fell back, fearing the beast had returned.

But glowing eyes stared down at him; shape took form, a familiar one. The cloak billowed out, then settled to narrow shoulders.

"Perryl," Tylar said, relieved that his former squire had not been a part of the slaughter here. In the distance, the horn blared again. Shouts now could be heard. The castillion guards were closing in.

The young knight took in the scene. "What have you done?" he asked in a rush.

Tylar frowned at such a strange question. "What do you mean?"

Tylar glanced down at himself. He was covered in blood—Meeryn's blood. In the center of his chest, a perfect palm print had been burned through his shirt and linens. The skin beneath was as black as the scorched edges of his clothing. He touched the flesh. No blistering. Just a black stain.

He was marked.

Tylar lifted an arm. "You can't think I—?"

"I saw you earlier."

"And I you . . . so?"

Perryl eyed him from head to toe. "Look at yourself."

"Why—?" Further words died as he finally understood. Perhaps he had been too numbed by the events. Or perhaps it was like a pair of well-broken boots, easy to forget once donned. Either way, he finally noted the straight hold of his back, the breadth of his shoulders, the strength in his arms and legs.

"You're healed."

Before he could react, castillion guards pounded into the square, bearing pikes and long swords. Cries arose as the bloody sight struck them. Many fell immediately to their knees; the stronger fanned out to shield the square and attend to the night's victims.

A full complement surrounded Meeryn, driving Tylar away at the point of a blade.

"Do not say a word," Perryl hissed in his ear, staying at his side.

Tylar stared at the many drawn weapons and obeyed.

A fresh cry erupted from the crowd around the fallen god. "She's dead!" one man shouted.

Another, bearing the oak sprig of a healer, stumbled free of the group. His face had drained of all color, his eyes bright with shock. "Her heart . . . her heart is gone . . . ripped away!"

All around, guards stared hard at Tylar, many weeping, others swearing. He knew how he must look: the lone survivor, covered in Meeryn's blood, her palm print burned into his chest as if she had attempted to thrust him away.

And on top of it all, he was healed, cured, made new again.

A cadre of castle guards approached with swords drawn, murder in their every step.

Perryl stepped before Tylar, facing the men. "Under the edict of the Order, this man is arrested under my name."

Shouts met his words, angry.

Perryl yelled to be heard. "He will not be harmed until the matter here is attended and the truth be known."

The guards stopped, hesitant. Swords remained drawn.

Their captain took another step forward and spat in Tylar's direction. He uttered one word, both curse and accusation: "Godslayer."

2

DART AND PUPP

S HE NEVER LIKED CABBAGE.

Half a world away from the Summering Isles, Dart stared at the plate covered in a soggy bog of boiled leaf. She fingered through the pile, searching for a bit of carrot and maybe, if she were lucky, a chunk of raven's egg. She liked raven, believing the keen senses of the aerial hunter would flow into her if she ate enough eggs.

As she bent to stare under an especially large leaf, something slapped the back of her head, bouncing her nose into her meal. She yipped in surprise.

"Enough!" the matron of the Conclave screeched at her, sounding like one of the feathered residents of the rookery at the top of the tower. "Eat or I'll boil you into the next batch!"

Dart straightened, wiping cabbage drippings from her nose. "Yes, mum . . ."

The other girls seated along the two tables of the third floor commons laughed behind their hands. Fingers pointed.

Dart kept her face lowered. She was the youngest of the thirdfloorers, barely thirteen birth years, but she already stood a head taller than the eldest. In fact, Dart had been named after the dartweed, a hardy plant that sprouted stubbornly between the cobbles of the courtyard, growing fast enough for the eye to follow, shoving its yellow head up after the sunshine. Even her unruly thatch of straw-blond hair matched the weed's hue. And like her namesake, she was considered a nuisance here, an eyesore, something to be trampled underfoot.

The Conclave of Chrismferry was one of the most distinguished schools for training gentle boys and gentle girls in the art of proper service to a god's household. The finest families from the Nine Lands fought, bribed, and prayed for one of their offspring to be granted admittance.

Dart, on the other hand, came here by chance. She was not even from the blessed Nine Lands. The prior headmistress had discovered her among the hinterlands, where only rogue gods roamed, an unsettled and barbarous country. Dart, as a newborn, was to have been sacrificed to one of the rogue gods. But the headmistress, a willful and pious woman, had stolen her away, whisking her out of the hinterlands and into the Conclave. And though the woman died only three years later, Dart had been allowed to remain out of respect for the memory of the esteemed headmistress.

Unfortunately none of that respect had rubbed off on Dart.

"Finish your breaking fast!" the matron said, stalking away. "By the time I pass through here next, your plate had better be empty. That goes for all of you!"

Murmurs of dutiful assent followed in the woman's wide wake until she left the room.

Dart pinched a leaf, studying its limp form with resignation. Sighing, she glanced under the table to where Pupp lay curled at her feet. "How about helping me with this?"

Pupp stirred. He cocked his head in her direction.

Dart frowned, knowing he couldn't help. She popped the cold wet leaf into her mouth, attempting to chew without breathing. Every fiber in her being fought her valiant effort, but at last she succeeded and swallowed the slimy lump.

With a renewed determination, she set upon her plate, working down through the mountainous pile of boiled fare. Almost finished, she stared at the remaining leaves, disappointed.

Not even a sliver of raven's egg.

Movement drew her attention back across the table. Sissup and Jenine shifted and allowed Laurelle to push between them. The eldest of the thirdfloorers reached over and dumped her load of cabbage atop Dart's plate.

"What are you—?" Dart began to complain.

Laurelle straightened. "Did anyone see me do that? I'm sure they didn't."

Laughter followed from the other girls.

With a flip of her long ebony hair, freshly washed and oiled by her family's servitors in residence, Laurelle glanced back to Dart. "Eat up, Dartweed. Maybe you'll fill out that boy's body you're wearing." Laurelle leaned a hand on the table and stuck out her chest, posing like some harlot.

More laughter met her antics.

At fourteen, Laurelle was already rounding into a woman. Boys in the school dogged her footsteps, pining for a nod from her, a wink. All the girls worshipped her, too. Laurelle was from a well-to-do family out of Welden Springs. She had her own servitors and showered small presents of honeycakes and cloth dolls to those in her favor. But of even more significance, rumors abounded that Laurelle would surely be handpicked at the next full moon's gathering, only eight nights away.

It was an honor they all craved: to be chosen as a handmaiden to one of the hundred gods of Myrillia. The best the remainder could hope for was to be assigned in some small measure to the court of a god, to bask from afar in such Grace. Yet worst of all, many would simply be sent back to their families, humiliated and rejected. This was the worry they all shared.

And even more so for Dart—she had no family and no other home. All that she possessed, her only family, lay curled at her feet.

Still, the Conclave of Chrismferry lay in the very shadow of the elder god's castillion and, of all the Conclaves, this school produced the most handmaidens and handmen. The teachers stressed this fact daily, imposing hard rules and firm teachings. The matrons and masters were proud of their school, the foundation stone of which had been blessed four thousand years ago by Chrism himself.

Laurelle straightened with another flip of her flowing black hair. Dart smelled the sweet-water oil in it. She truly felt like a weed before a flower.

Suddenly Laurelle yelped. She danced from the table.

"What's wrong?" Sissup asked. Jenine was already on her feet.

Laurelle shifted up the hem of her skirt, revealing an ankle in white stockings. A bloom of red spread out across the white lace. "Something scratched me!"

Sissup fell to her knees, searching under the table. "Maybe a nail?"

"Or a sliver!" Jenine said. "These cruel benches are as old as the stones."

Dart knew better. Though no one could see Pupp, she motioned her secret friend closer to her. She ducked lower, pretending to search for what injured Laurelle. "Bad dog," she whispered.

Pupp lowered his head, wincing, glancing back toward the bloody ankle. He gained his clawed feet and shoved between Dart's legs, passing ghostly through the flesh of her thighs as he sought a place to hide under her skirt. The only sign of his passage was a slight chill on her skin. His face appeared from her hemline, poking through the fabric as if it were air. His head cocked up toward her, eyes mournful with shame.

She felt bad scolding him. He was simply too ugly to be mad at for long. His features were dreadful, all hard planes of beaten copper, with iron spikes in a mane around his face. His eyes were faceted jewels above a muzzle filled with sharpened blades; his tongue was a lap of flame. The rest of his body, squat and bulky, was a mix of armor and chain mail, with four thick limbs ending in steel claws. All of it glowed ruddily and seemed to flow and melt in swirls, subtly reforming her friend at every moment. Pupp was like a sculpture fresh from the forge, still molten from the flame's touch.

She reached down to reassure him, but as always her hand passed through Pupp. He wasn't real. Still bent over, she glanced to Laurelle's bloody ankle. Dart knew Pupp scratched her. At odd times in the past, he had done such things, affected the real world. Dart didn't understand how this could happen. In fact she had no idea *what* Pupp was. Only that he was her friend, her companion for as far back as she could remember. She had long given up trying to convince others of his existence. Only she saw him, and no one could touch him.

"It looks like a deep scratch," Margarite said, coming to the aid of her best friend. Though Margarite's family was from the opposite end of the Nine Lands, she could have been Laurelle's twin with her sleek fall of black hair, snowy skin, and full lips. She even dressed in the same finery of blue velvet and white stockings. "We should fetch Healer Paltry."

Though Laurelle's cheeks were flushed and her eyes moist with tears, she waved such a thought away, struggling for a dismissive demeanor. "I'm not a piddling firstfloorer." She bent and ripped her stocking, which earned a shocked cry from Sissup, who was not from such a rich family. Laurelle used the snatch of lace to bind her wound, which had almost stopped bleeding already.

It truly was not a deep scratch. Pupp had barely nicked her.

Laurelle inspected her handiwork, then nodded and stood.

A smatter of applause rewarded her effort. "She's so brave," Jenine murmured to Dart as Laurelle left with Margarite in tow. The nigglish prank on Dart had been all but forgotten.

Almost . . .

Matron Grannice appeared at the doorway, ringing a small bell. "To your classes now, gentle lasses! No dawdling. Don't keep the mistresses and masters waiting." She worked down the two rows, adding her usual litany of warnings. "Sharyn, make sure you keep your ankles covered when climbing the stairs. Bella, if you stain your petticoat with ink again, I'll make a washerwoman out of you. And Hessy . . ."

The scolding continued, trailed by a chant of "Yes, mum" as the girls fled the commons, heading to the morning teachings.

Dart held her breath, staring at her laden plate.

Matron Grannice stopped behind her. Though Dart kept her back turned, she sensed the sour look. "Why are you always such a stubborn and willful child?"

From under lowered brows, Dart glanced to the door and saw Laurelle standing there, staring back. At her side, Margarite waggled fingers toward Dart, smiling at her predicament.

"Answer me," Grannice barked.

Dart met Laurelle's eyes and mumbled, "I don't know, mum."

"And why do you always speak as if you're carrying a cheekful of nuts?"

"Sorry, mum." Dart watched Laurelle nod back to her. Satisfied that the prank would not be laid at her feet, Laurelle left with Margarite, but not before Dart noted a glimpse of something deeper in the other girl's eyes. It was not satisfaction, nor shame. It made no sense, but Dart could not dismiss what she had seen. Always off to the side, Dart had learned to read the subtleties in another's features: the narrowing of an eye, a pursed lip, a flush of color on a cheek. But what she saw in Laurelle still made no sense.

Why would Laurelle envy me?

Matron Grannice interrupted her reverie. "It seems there is only one way to straighten this arrogant bent. And that is to learn from those even more willful than you."

"Mum?"

"It's off to the rookery with you! Perhaps a morning of scooping droppings, scrubbing floors, and spreading hay will temper your demeanor, young lass."

"But classes?" Dart sat up straighter. "We're to practice for the moon's ceremony."

Grannice let out an exasperated sigh. "You can practice with the ravens." Dart's ear was grabbed and she was hauled to her feet. "You know where the pails and brooms and brushes are. Now off with you."

Dart hurried from the room with a rush of her skirts. She saw the last few of the other girls heading down the stairs, giggling and laughing, clutching books to their bosoms. They were fifth- and sixthfloorers heading down to the courtyard and classes in the neighboring towers. She watched them disappear, then faced the spiraling stair that led upward.

"To me, Pupp," she mumbled and began the long climb toward the rookery in the roost atop the tower. Her companion clambered past her, trotting a few steps ahead. The flow of his molten body seemed agitated. Pupp was clearly excited by the adventure.

They climbed the fourth and fifth floors, then past the levels that quartered the mistresses and matrons and healing wards, then up past levels vacant and dusty. At last, she reached a door at the top of the tower.

Beyond it lay the rookery.

Pupp nosed the solid squallwood door, then passed through it as if it were mere smoke. The only material that ever seemed to thwart Pupp was stone.

Continuing after her friend, Dart tugged the latch and hauled the way open for herself. She had to lean out with her slight body to fight the door's weight and ancient hinges. The door squealed open, setting the ravens inside to flapping on their hundred perches and nests. Screeched complaints echoed across the cavernous stone chamber.

She ducked through and pulled the door behind her, leaving it cracked open to allow the outer hall's torchlight to filter in. The only other illumination came from the twenty guano-stained windows high up the walls. The remainder of the room was cloaked in gloom. Large eyes reflected the meager light, stared down at her. The birds did not like their slumber disturbed.

When not aloft, carrying messages, the residents here kept busy at night, keeping the Conclave grounds clear of mice, rats, and voles. The birds were also a source of eggs and meat for the kitchens.

Crinkling her nose at the stinging smell of the place, she crossed to a small cupboard inset against one wall. She would stink like the rookery all day. Inside the cupboard were buckets, brushes, and brooms in their usual places.

She tied her skirt around her knees and set to sweeping the old hay and dried droppings. It was mindless work.

As she swept, Pupp chased after the broom's straw bristles, biting playfully, his razored jaws passing harmlessly through the bristles. Still, his determined efforts drew a smile from her.

"Stupid dog . . ." she mumbled with a grin.

❖

With the floor finally swept, Dart still had to give the planks a good scrubbing on her hands and knees, then break one of the stacked bales of hay and spread fresh straw as she had done so often before.

Wiping her brow, she crossed to the corner pump and cranked the plunge handle. It was hard work drawing water up from the midtower cistern. As she labored, something warm and wet slapped against her cheek. Scowling, she wiped it away.

Raven shite.

She glanced up toward the rafters. "Thank you for your blessing, Lord Raven." With a shake of her head, she set to the pump again, hauling its handle up and down. Sweat trickled down her back. The day was warming out of morning toward midday.

She could only imagine her fellow thirdfloorers practicing their curtsies and bows for the ceremony, learning the proper responses, and reciting the Litany of Nine Graces. She sang out as she pumped, naming each Grace as she pulled and its property as she pushed.

"*Blood*... to open the way, *seed or menses* to bless, *sweat* to imbue, *tears* to swell, *saliva* to ebb, *phlegm* to manifest, *yellow bile* to gift, and *black* to take it all away."

As she finished, water flowed from the spigot into the bucket. She allowed it to overflow. She'd need an entire bucket to wash the floor.

With her pail full, she straightened. Hot and moist from her effort, she crossed to a ladder and pushed it toward one of the high windows.

Just a little breeze and a bit of freshened air ... then I'll get back to the chore.

She climbed the ladder. Once at the opening, she shoved her head through. Only now did she notice how much her eyes and nose burned from the reek of the rookery. She took deep, gulping breaths.

All of Chrismferry lay sprawled below her. The city spread in walls, canals, and roofs all the way to the horizon. It was split in halves by the mighty Tigre River, shining silver in the sunlight. It was said that the city was so wide that it took a man on foot ten days to cross from one end to the other. There was a common response when one spoke about its vastness: *The world is the city, and the city is the world.*

Gazing from the window, Dart saw it was true.

Set like a jewel in the heart of the first of the Nine Lands, Chrismferry was the hub around which the world turned. The entire surrounding countryside, from shore to shore, fed the city, barging up from the coasts, carting down from the fields, flown in on the potbellied flippercrafts. The city was insatiable.

And at the center of it all stood the great castillion of the eldermost god, Chrism. Dart, resting her chin on her fingers, stared at the walled and towered fortress. A vast thousand-acre garden spread out from its southern side, shadowed by the castillion itself. Wooded, it looked more like a forest than a garden, fitting for a god of the loam.

And like Lord Chrism himself, his castillion was both noble and humble. Its walls were thick white granite, quarried locally, and unadorned. The main keep had been built on the site of the original ferry bridge that once forded the Tigre River. The structure rose up from both shores and spanned the waterway in between. The center halls were held above the river by giant, ancient pillars, all that was left of the original bridge. Even its nine towers, the Stone Graces, shared the river. Four rose from the north bank, four on the south, while the last and tallest rose above the river itself. These towers were the same white stone, simple, yet reassuring in their solidity. The only bits of decoration anywhere were the carved silver gates to the castillion, depicting the great Sundering, the moment when the kingdom of the gods had been shattered and they appeared among the lands of Myrillia.

Dart sighed, dreaming of stepping through those brilliant gates someday. Until then, there were floors to clean.

As she turned, the sharp creak of hinges startled her, loud in the stone space. Ravens stirred and squawked in complaint.

Dart hopped down from the ladder, fearful of being caught idle. She found the gloom of the rookery suddenly oppressive. The door lay cracked open, wider by a handbreadth. But no one was in sight.

"Good morrow!" she called. "Is anyone there?"

There was no answer. Slowly her straining eyes began to pierce the darkness. Shadows retreated. She saw no one. *Must have been a crosswind . . . tugging at the door.*

She turned to gather her pail and brush. As she bent away, the tower door crashed shut.

Ravens screeched. A few took wing, crossing from one perch to another. Plops of guano rained around the room.

The loss of the filtering torchlight from the hall drew the shadows toward her again, eating away the room.

"Is anyone there?" Her voice was meeker this time, her throat tight with fear. "Please . . ."

Footsteps answered, crossing toward her.

She fell back against the stone wall.

"There's no need to fret, little kitten." The voice was soft and deep. A figure appeared out of the gloom, large and broad shouldered.

Dart recognized the voice as Master Willet, a scholar of the Conclave. As he stepped into the patch of sunlight flowing from the window, she saw he wore the usual sashed black robe of the Conclave, his hood thrown back. As was customary for the mistresses and masters, his head was shaved to the scalp.

Dart stepped from the wall and curtsied with a half bend of a knee. "Master Willet."

He waved her out of the gloom under the window and into his patch of sunlight. "Come, child. What are you doing up here all alone?"

Dart slumped forward. "Punishment, Master Willet." She curtsied again, in case he hadn't seen her first one.

"So I've been told."

Dart felt a rush of heat to her cheek. Her humiliation knew no end.

"It seems you've been a slovenly pupil. Needing additional tutoring. I was sent up here for a private lesson."

"Ser?"

He stepped closer. A hand rose swiftly to her cheek. The back of his knuckles slid along her skin.

Startled by his sudden touch, she fell back a step—but fingers snatched on to the collar of her shirt. She was yanked toward him. His other arm encircled her waist and pulled her tight against him, lifting her onto her toes.

"Master Willet!" Tears rose to her eyes, confused, terrified.

"Not a word, little kitten." He leaned down to her ear, his voice suddenly savage. "Not now, not later, not ever."

She struggled. Lips found her throat, pressing and hungry. She smelled garlic and spiced meats on his breath.

"No!" she cried out.

A hand struck her across the face, stinging, shocking. She tasted blood in her mouth.

"Not a sound, little kitten." His words were both angry and strangely thick. He shoved her to the wall, pinned her between the stone and his heavy body.

She knew what he intended. Here at the school they were trained in all the humoral fluids, including the handling of a god's seed or menses. As such, they were instructed in the private ways of men and women. It was no great mystery.

But it was a mystery forbidden to them. To serve a god, a handmaiden must be pure, untouched. Once bedded, all hope of such honor was gone. Just last year, a secret tryst between a young man and woman, both fifth-floorers, had been discovered. They had been whipped, then banished from the Conclave.

"Not a word," he growled again, fingers at her throat. His other hand reached down between her legs, under the tied edges of her skirt. Fingers tore at her undergarments, ripping and pulling.

Tears ran down Dart's face, burning with shame and horror. She couldn't breathe. She stared over the master's head as he panted and pawed. A hundred pairs of eyes stared down at her from the rafters. Silent witnesses.

And there was one other.

Pupp ran in circles at her feet, passing through her flesh, biting at her attacker, but his razored teeth found no purchase. The bit of energy he had used to scratch Laurelle must have wasted his reserves.

Dart felt just as helpless.

Below, fingers found what they had been searching for, cupping against her skin. She had been touched like this in the past only by healers testing her virginity. But now it was rougher, horrific. A scream built behind her ribs.

Then the hand moved away.

"Now for your lesson," he groaned at her. "To show you how to please a god."

She was forced to the floor, on her back. He straddled atop her, pulling up his robe. He wore nothing underneath.

He kneed her legs apart and shoved her skirts above her hips.

She fought against him, but this only seemed to make him grunt harder and his eyes glint more feral. She sobbed and choked and even tried to bite at him. She would lose more than her virginity here on this floor. She would lose all her hopes for herself, for her future, for the only home she knew.

But there was no stopping him. He was huge, outweighed her by ten stone. All she could do was cry and sob. Terror had taken all her strength away.

She turned her face. Pupp lay near her head. His eyes glowed with fury. Though forever silent, Dart imagined him whining, sharing her pain and terror.

Then she felt Willet shove inside her, ripping her, breaking her. Blood flowed. The scream burst from her lips, but he was ready even for this. A fistful of her own skirt was shoved into her mouth, gagging her.

"I am your god!" he moaned.

Pupp was again on his feet, diving through her body, his touch cold. He shoved down between her legs, his frigid wake ebbing some of the pain. When he reached her belly, ice flared. The momentary agony vanished, washed away. She felt nothing below her waist.

Still, Willet continued to rut into her, pounding and pushing, grunting and panting.

Dart squeezed her eyes closed, wishing herself away. But there was no escape. She could smell him, hear him, feel his lips on her neck.

Then the monster arched back from her, gasping out through clenched teeth. Dart cringed, but Master Willet's cry of pleasure suddenly transfigured into a scream of pain. He fell back from the cradle of her thighs.

Dart opened her eyes in time to see an arc of blood spout from the man's groin, fountaining up like a stream of piss.

But the man no longer had anything with which to piss.

Nothing lay between the man's legs.

The same was not true of Dart. Still numb, unable to move her legs, she watched Pupp crawl out of her belly, rising up between her thighs, covered in her own blood. The small creature spat out a limp chunk of flesh: the man's prick and sack. Pupp had bitten it all off from inside.

"Pupp . . ." she moaned. Feeling returned to her, agony flaring, as her friend climbed free of her.

Only then did she notice Willet's eyes grow wide with horror. He was staring at Pupp, seeing her monstrous friend for the first time.

It was the last thing he ever saw.

Pupp leaped at the cowering man, becoming a blur of blade, spike, and razored teeth. He drove into the man's belly, burrowing straight through. But Pupp was no longer a ghost. Flesh sizzled and burned with the touch of his molten skin. Curved spikes tore through flesh and bone.

A horrible howl accompanied the slaughter.

On hands and knees, Dart fled to the far side of the room. She had worked in the kitchens. She had seen meat ground into sausages, metal churning organ to pulp.

This was the same.

In moments, butchered to scrap, nothing remained of the man.

Pupp crawled free of the pile, shaking blood and bits of gore from his spiked mane, coughing up gouts of scorched meat. With a final shudder, his body blazed into brightness, a burning ember blown to life.

In that moment, Pupp shone with a terrible and fierce beauty. An intelligence beyond her friend stared into this world as a keening wail filled the chamber.

Shadows thickened and billowed outward from his form, sweeping through the room. Ravens, silent sentinels until this moment, shattered from their perches in a panic of wings and feathers. As a flock, they dove out the windows and were gone.

Alone now, Dart cowered, trapped between horror and panic.

But no further harm came to her.

The shadows fell under their weight, sinking to the floor and vanishing away. The piercing wail vanished with them.

Pupp remained in the center of the room, his blaze doused to its usual ruddy hue. He was now clean, unsoiled—as was the rest of the rookery.

Numb, Dart watched Pupp cross the spotless floor, trotting to her side as he had done all her life. He sat at her feet and groomed himself with a flaming tongue.

Dart reached a trembling hand out to her friend. But her fingers passed through him. He had gone ghostly again. How?

She took a step away, suddenly fearful. But as she moved, her legs shuddered, her knees jellied. An ache throbbed throughout her belly. She felt a fresh trickle of blood flow down her thighs. Sobbing, she fell to her hands. The room spun. She vomited boiled cabbage all over the floor.

Pupp was there, nosing her, concerned.

It was all too much. She fell on her side and curled herself on the floor, crying, sobbing, and shaking. She stared across the chamber. There was no sign of Master Willet, not even a stain of blood. All had vanished into the darkness.

Had it happened? Had it *all* happened?

A fist lay curled between her thighs, holding back the ache. She tugged her hand free. Her fingers were covered with blood.

Pupp belly crawled to her bosom. She reached to him again. Her bloody hand found warm flesh to touch. Pupp pushed into her, rubbing into her stained palm. She could feel him! He was hard and warm, like an agate stone of a fire god, freshly blessed in blood.

The answer was clear.

"Blood," she whispered.

The effect was brief. As the heat dried the dampness from her palm, her fingers fell through Pupp's form. He was gone again.

Allowing the mystery to distract her, she sat on the floor and pulled her knees up to her chin. With her arms wrapped around her shins, she shivered and shuddered, rocking slightly. Occasional sobs broke through, but she focused on merely breathing. *In and out.* The Litany of Nine Graces echoed in her mind: *blood to open the way, seed or menses to bless, sweat to imbue, tears to swell, saliva to ebb . . .*

But she kept coming back to the first.

"Blood to open the way . . ." She stared at Pupp, now curled at her side, and wondered the meaning of it all.

A bell rang out sharply, rising from the courtyards below, announcing the ending of lessons.

Only now did she notice the brightness of the western windows as the sun settled toward the horizon. She had been lost to the world for most of the day.

One last sob shook through her. The reality of where she was and her situation could not be ignored. She carefully stretched her legs, rolling slowly to her feet with a groan. She stood for another long spell, dazed, at a loss in which direction to move.

Who could she tell? What could she say? How could she explain?

As these impossible questions and a thousand others rattled through her skull, her feet took over. She found herself at the bucket she had filled in another life. She bent and picked up the scrub brush. She stared down at it, knowing her body had already settled on an answer.

She was no longer pure. No one would believe the truth here. All that would be understood was that she was now spoiled, fouled for any god, unfit to walk these halls. She would surely be cast out.

But not this night.

After what happened here, she could not survive banishment.

Not this night.

Dart knew what she must do.

She shed her clothes and used the cold water and brush to clean her body. At first, she worked in a half panic, fearing being caught. Her hands trembled. But slowly her fingers gripped the brush more securely. She concentrated on the simple act of bathing, falling back on ritual. The cool water helped calm her.

Once clean, she dried herself with rags. She still bled, so she padded herself with her ripped undergarments and climbed back into her outers. She carefully inspected her skirts and rubbed dust and dried guano over any bloody spots, hiding all evidence.

She washed her hands in the pail and stared at her shattered reflection in the rocking waters. The girl who had climbed these steps was gone, vanished into the darkness as surely as Master Willet's butchered form.

She stared at the spot on the floor. She would never return here.

Her eyes settled next on Pupp, sitting diligently, patiently. Like her, he had been transformed in this room, becoming a deeper mystery. She understood less about him, only that he had stood by her, protected her.

For now, that was enough.

Though an ache still lay buried deep inside her, where no scrub brush could ever reach, Dart put away her bucket and broom and broke open a bale of fresh hay. The smell of summer and pasture filled the room as she kicked a fresh layer around the chamber. She spread it thick to fully cover the floor.

By the time she was done, the windows to the east had gone dark and the sun was but a weak glow to the west. She could no longer hide up here.

She crossed to the door and pulled it open. The torchlight was blinding. As she blinked away the glare, laughter echoed up from far below, bright and cheerful.

It sounded brittle and brought an ache to her head.

Supper was already being served. No one seemed to remember the little girl up in the tower. No one missed Dart.

She headed down the stairs. Each step hurt, reminding her of something she hadn't wanted to face.

Someone *had* known she was up here. Someone had let Master Willet pass up the stairs, had let him know a girl was alone in the rookery.

Something darker than anger filled her. Whoever it was, they would pay. The dartweed that grew in the courtyard, her namesake, developed woody thorns as it aged . . . thorns that were seldom seen until they pierced the flesh.

"To me, Pupp," she said quietly. "To me."

3

DUNGEON

"I**T AREN'T THAT BAD IF YOU IGNORE THE FLIES.**"

Tylar studied the moving feast that was his meal. Flies coated the stew of gristle and fat. The crust of bread atop it looked to be milled more from mold than flour. But he'd had worse. He soaked the hard bread into the broth, trying to soften the crust enough to chew. Tiny worms used the bread as a raft, climbing aboard.

"What about these maggots?" he asked sourly, shaking the crust clean of the squiggling stowaways.

"Nothing wrong with 'em. Them's the only thing that gives this stew any taste."

Tylar bit into the bread and glanced to the ragged rat of a man who had joined him in his cell that morning, tossed in naked and striped with whippings across his back. A head shorter than Tylar, he was all bone and beard. He set upon the meal like a hinter-king upon a feast. From the gray hairs laced in his red beard, he was not a young man, but what little muscle on him was still hard. *About a decade older than myself,* Tylar judged.

The prisoner noted his attention. "Name's Rogger," he mumbled over the edge of his bowl.

"Tylar."

"So how's a Shadowknight end up here?" The man touched three fingers to the corner of his eye, indicating Tylar's tattoos.

"Apparently I killed a god."

Rogger choked out a gobbet of gristle. "You! So you're the one!"

Tylar glanced up to the barred window high on the stone wall. He had been imprisoned here seven days. He'd not had one visitor until now.

"No wonder there were so many guards in the halls," Rogger continued, his face buried in his meal, spitting out pieces of bone as punctuation. "I even spotted a pair of bloodnullers at the end of each hall, reeking and covered in shite."

Tylar nodded. Bloodnullers were smeared in a god's black bile, their soft solids. Such a blessing granted the power to vanquish the Grace of a person or object with the mere touch of a single finger. They were stationed to keep Tylar in check, in case he attempted to use Dark Graces to escape. Their continued presence seemed a waste since they had already run their hands over his entire body when he first arrived here in shackles. If he'd had any hidden Graces, they would have been abolished at that time.

Still, Tylar understood their worry. While occasional rogue gods had been killed, never had one of the Hundred been slain. No one was taking any chances.

Rogger coughed a piece of gristle loose from his throat and nodded at Tylar. "It seems they must crowd all their god-sinners into the same damn cell on this cursed island."

Tylar returned his attention fully to the man. "God-sinner? You? What did you do?"

He laughed. "I was caught sneaking into ol' Balger's place, trying to nick a bit from the bastard's vault."

"At Foulsham Dell?" Tylar asked, eyebrows rising. Balger was one of the seven gods that shared the First Land. His settled realm, Foulsham Dell, lay at the foot of the Middleback Range, bordering the wilds of a hinterland, where rogue gods roamed and no law governed. The Dell was a place of murderers, pirates, and scoundrels. And the god Balger was the worst of the bunch, known equally for his debaucheries and his cruelties. He was as close to a rogue as any of the hundred settled gods. His entire realm made Punt seem a tame and civilized place.

Tylar eyed the man, wondering what sort of thief tried to steal from such a god's larder.

"And I would've made it out of there," Rogger added, "if it hadn't been for some handmaiden coming to the vault to deposit a jar full of her lord's blessed piss."

"A jar? You mean a repostilary?" Shock rang in his voice. Repostilary jars were vessels of a god's humoral fluids, sacred beyond measure, handled only by handmaidens and handmen.

Rogger nodded and laughed again, spraying spittle out his beard. "Apparently ol' Balger has trouble holding his bladder throughout the night."

"So you were caught?"

As he ate, the man tilted to the side, baring his right buttock. A brand, long healed, had been burned into the flesh:

Tylar eyed the sigil. It was ancient Littick. "Thief," he read aloud. "I don't understand. How did you end up in a dungeon on the Summering Isles, a thousand reaches from the Dell?"

Rogger finished his bowl and gingerly settled back against the wall, wincing from his whipping. "Because of you, now that I crank on it."

"Me?"

Rogger lifted his arms and exposed the undersides. More Littick sigils lay burned into the thief's skin, aligned in neat rows.

From his training as a Shadowknight, Tylar recognized them: all names of gods. "Balger's punishment . . ." he mumbled, sickened.

"A pilgrimage," Rogger conceded sourly.

It was a cruel judgment, and not unexpected coming from a god of Balger's ilk. As punishment, Rogger had been marked and exiled, forced to travel from god-realm to god-realm, sentenced to collect a certain number of brands. Only after you were properly marked could you return to your home and family.

"How many gods were you assigned?"

Rogger sighed, lowering his arms. "Remember. It was against *Balger* I sinned."

Tylar's eyes grew wider. "He didn't . . ."

"A full pilgrimage, no less."

"*All* the gods?"

"Every blessed one of them. All one hundred."

Tylar finally understood why Rogger was imprisoned here. "And with Meeryn dead, you can't complete your punishment."

"Once I learned of her death, I tried to escape, but that's hard to do when you're standing between two guards, knocking on the damn gates to Meeryn's castillion. They snatched me up, whipped me thrice for the rudeness, and tossed me in with you."

"What're they going to do with you?"

"The usual choices I imagine: hanging, garroting, impaling."

They were the three standard punishments meted to a pilgrim who failed in his journeys and tried to settle somewhere else.

"I think I'll go with hanging. Garroting is too slow, and as for impaling, I'd prefer not to have anything shoved up my arse." He shifted uncomfortably. " 'Course, I have a couple days to think about it. They're still attending Her Highness up there, seeing if she's truly dead."

Tylar sat up straighter. "Is there hope?"

"Hope is for the rich. All we have is shite and piss. And speaking of that . . ." Rogger climbed and crossed to the pail that served as the room's privy.

❖

As the day wore on and his thievish companion stretched on the floor snoring, Tylar considered his companion's words. Could Meeryn still be alive? If so, she could clear his name, attest to his honor, what little he still had left. But in his heart he knew better. He had seen the light fade from her eyes.

Voices echoed down the dank hall of the dungeon. Guards arguing, then the stamp of boots sounded on the stone floor. Tylar climbed to his feet, hearing them approach. Rogger continued to snore in his corner.

Shadowed faces appeared at the small barred window. "Open it!" a familiar voice ordered.

The bar was slipped with a scrape of wood, and the door swung open. A cloaked and masked figure filled the threshold.

"Perryl," Tylar said, trying his best to stand tall when naked and covered in filth. Healed of his hunched back, Tylar now stood a fingerbreadth taller than his former squire. He kept his arms folded, not in defiance but to half-hide the black palm print, Meeryn's mark, that rested in the center of his chest.

Perryl's eyes narrowed at his condition and turned to the dungeonkeep at his side. "I thought I left orders for the prisoner to be treated with care."

"Aye we have, ser knight. We've not beaten him once."

Perryl pointed to Tylar, his eyes never leaving the guard. "Give him your shirt and breeches."

"Ser!"

"Do you defy the word of a blessed knight?" A hand settled to the diamond pommel of his sword, aglow in the sooty torchlight.

"No, ser . . . right away, ser." The dungeonkeep hurriedly stripped down to his underclothes and passed the outerwear to Tylar.

"I think I was less soiled when I was naked," Tylar grumbled as he pulled the sweat-stained jerkin over his head, but it did feel better to have some clothes on his body.

His former squire waved away the dungeon guard and waited until he was gone. Rogger had grumbled at the commotion, then curled away and was already snoring again.

Alone and private, Perryl freed his masklin, exposing a worried face. He eyed Tylar up and down, the glint of Grace bright in his gaze.

Tylar crossed his arms again. "I heard there was a deathwatch."

Perryl nodded and paced the floor, parts of him slipping into and out of shadow as his cloak reflected its owner's agitation. "Seven days. It ends this night, when the lesser moon's face touches the greater moon."

"And there is no hope of her reviving."

Perryl shook his head. "Her heart is gone. The finest alchemists have tested her remaining fluids. There are no signs of Grace in any of her humours. She is as empty as any man or woman. Even decay and corruption have set in, bloating her body."

"Then she is truly dead."

Perryl stopped his pacing and stared hard at Tylar. "This story of some Darkly Graced beast . . . you swear this is the truth?"

"Yes, but I have nothing left to swear upon except the filthy body I'm wearing."

"An unbroken body." A twinge of suspicion laced Perryl's words.

"Unbroken and *marked*." Tylar parted his jerkin enough to expose the black fingers on his chest. "This is not a curse. Meeryn blessed me for some reason known only to her."

"But why?" Perryl began to pace again. "It's all impossible."

"As impossible as a slain god?"

Tylar read the dismay in the other's eyes. For four thousand years, ever since the time of the Sundering, none of the Hundred had ever died. Every child knew the history of Myrillia, of the madness and destruction that followed the arrival of gods to this world. It lasted three centuries until the god Chrism chose the first god-realm and imbued his Graces into the region, sharing his powers to bring order out of chaos. Other gods followed, settling various lands, bringing to bear their unique Graces.

Thus the Nine Lands were formed.

Beyond these god-realms lay only the hinterlands, spaces wild and ungoverned, where rogue gods still roamed, as untamed as their lands. Occasional rumors and stories spoke of the death of gods out there, stories of great hinter-kings who slew maddened rogues, raving creatures of dark power.

But never had one of the Hundred been slain . . . until now.

Perryl stared up at the lone window. Night fast approached. "Already the Isles have judged you. The word *godslayer* rings through the streets. Only my cloak protects you from the gallows or worse."

"And I thank you for that."

Perryl turned back to Tylar. "But that protection cannot last forever. A single knight's cloak is only so thick. As the sun sets, I will board a flippercraft headed to Tashijan, to seek the counsel of the full Order on your behalf."

"You waste Grace on such an effort," Tylar scoffed. "The Order has no love for a fallen knight, especially me."

"I know of your past crime. Selling repostilaries to the Gray Trade, lining your pocket with gold marches. All preposterous lies."

Tylar shook his head. "The accusations were true."

Perryl blinked, looking a surprised boy again. "What? How . . . ?"

"I had my reasons. But I did not kill that family of cobblers on Esterberry Street."

"Your sword was found there."

Tylar faced Perryl. "Do I look a child killer to you any more than a godslayer?"

"No, but then again, I never imagined you a trafficker in repostilaries."

Tylar turned his back on the Shadowknight. With even that one crime, he had broken his knightly vows. It was reason enough to have been stripped of his Graces and cast out of the Order, but the crime of murder carried a heavier sentence: to be broken on the wheel, then sold into slavery.

"The caste of Gray Traders at Akkabak Harbor knew I was about to expose them. They sought to discredit me." He glanced back to Perryl. "And they succeeded."

"So you claimed before the adjudicators, but the soothmancers said you spoke falsely."

He lowered his head.

"And they were not the only ones," Perryl whispered. "Kathryn—"

Tylar swung around sharply. "Do *not* speak her name in my presence, Perryl. I warn you."

The young knight did not back down. "She said you were gone from your bed that night and returned bloody to the sheets. And when asked if she believed your claims of innocence, she denied you, a fellow Shadowknight and her own betrothed."

Tylar hardened. "I will not speak any more of this. I've paid for my crimes and won my freedom in the rings as was my right."

"And what of the slaughter you're accused of now?"

"I expect no fairer justice in this matter. I know how it must appear, so let them have me."

"I can't." Perryl balled a gloved fist. "A god has been slain, not some cobbler's family. If for no other reason than to find out how you succeeded in bringing down one of the Hundred, the Order will intervene. The truth will be known."

"I have no faith in the Order."

"Then have faith in me."

Tylar saw the pain in the other's eyes. He touched the man's elbow. "You've soiled your cloak enough already, Perryl. Stay away before you're dragged down with me."

Perryl refused to move. "There is much you don't know. As I warned you on the streets, these are dark and perilous times." The young man sighed. "Have you heard about Ser Henri?"

"What of the old man?" Tylar asked cautiously.

Henri ser Gardlen was the warden of the Order, the leader of Tashijan for as long as Tylar could remember. He ruled the Order and its council with a firm but even hand. It was only through Ser Henri's intervention that Tylar had not been hanged for his crimes.

"He died . . . most strangely and suddenly."

"By all the Graces, how?"

"His body was found on the stairs leading up to his tower, his face a mask of horror, his fingertips burned to the first knuckle. Tashijan is keeping the details shuttered. When I left there a half-moon ago, the Order was still in chaos. Factions war behind closed doors, vying for the seat of succession. I can only hope matters have settled to deal with the tragedy here."

Tylar stood, stunned.

"But that is not all. Strangeness abounds across all the lands. Over in the Fifth Land, Tristal of Idlewyld has gone into seclusion on his peak, cutting off all Graces to his sworn knights. Talk is that he raves. Ulf of Ice Eyrie has frozen his entire castillion, locking his court in hoarfrost. None can enter or leave. And across the Meerashe Deep, rumors abound of a mighty hinter-king rising on the Seventh Land, threatening to break out into the neighboring god-realms."

Tylar shook his head. "I've heard none of this."

"Few have. The tidings are scattered and scarce. Perhaps they are merely a spate of bad fortune, but now this." He glanced to the doorway. "Ten days ago, Meeryn sent a raven to Tashijan and requested a blessed courier."

"You?"

Perryl nodded. "It was my honor."

Tylar touched his brow in thought. Once gods settled to a land, they were rooted to it, requiring intermediaries to carry their messages between them. Only the most important messages were born by the sworn couriers of the Order.

"I don't know how Meeryn's death ties to all this," Perryl continued. "But I sense dark currents in the tides of the world. Something is stirring down deep, out of sight."

"And you think it struck here? To silence Meeryn?"

"It seems an extraordinary coincidence that she summons a courier, and on the very day I step on this island, she is slain." Perryl reached to Tylar, touching his hand. "If you spoke the truth about that awful night, then Meeryn blessed you for some reason, healed you with the last of her Grace. She must have championed you for some purpose."

"I don't know. Perhaps it was simply a final kindness for the man who comforted her during her last breath." He remembered the swell of Grace into him. His fingers wandered unbidden to the center of his chest, where she had touched him.

"Did she say anything to you in those last moments?"

Tylar dropped his fingers and shook his head—then realized he was mistaken. "Wait." He focused back to Perryl. "She did say one thing. But it made no sense."

"What was it?"

He struggled to remember the exact pronunciation. "Riven . . . scryr."

Perryl's eyes pinched.

"Does that mean anything to you?"

Perryl shook his head. "I . . . I've never heard of such a name." He backed a step, looking slightly paler. "But perhaps the scholars at Tashijan or in Chrismferry will know better. I should be going. There is much to arrange before I leave, much to ponder."

As Perryl turned away, Tylar reached out to the edge of his friend's cloak, but he dared not let his fingers soil it. The young Shadowknight fixed his masklin in place and studied his former teacher. "Be safe, ser."

Tylar let his arm drop. "And you," he mumbled.

"Until our cloaks touch again," Perryl said, then vanished away.

These last words were a common farewell among knights. Tylar turned to face his dank cell with its steaming chamber pot and snoring guest. Even fit and hale again, he felt like no knight.

The door slammed behind him, and the bar was shoved in place. The dungeonkeep grumbled something about his clothes, but he didn't dare ask for them back. Tylar wondered how long such protection would last once Perryl was gone.

Rogger groaned and rolled to face Tylar. "Talkative fellow, that tall dark one." The thief must have been feigning sleep the entire time. "A friend of yours?"

Tylar settled to the mound of lice-ridden straw that was his bed. "Once . . . and maybe still."

Rogger sat up. "He had much to say . . . and little else of real worth to offer."

"What do you mean?" Tylar's attention drew sharply toward the bearded and branded fellow. He spoke more keenly than earlier. Even his manner seemed more refined.

"As a pilgrim, I've journeyed far and wide. I've heard, too, of the dark tidings of which the young knight spoke. And not only in halls and castillions through which your once-and-maybe-again friend walked, but in those many places where the sun doesn't shine as bright."

His speech suddenly thickened again, his manner roughened, hunching a bit. "Th'art many a low tongue that'll wag to a whipped dog that won't speak to a lordling or maid."

Tylar knew this true enough himself. The underfolk kept many secrets unto themselves.

"Then again," Rogger continued, "there are many in high towers who speak freely at their castillion door, blind to the ragged pilgrim on their doorstep." A sly glint blew bright in his eye. "Or on the floor of a cell."

It seemed sleep was not the only thing this thief had been feigning. There was more to the man than first impressed. "Who are you?" Tylar asked.

Rogger started to wag a finger at him, then thought better of it and used it to dig a flea out of his beard. "Just a thief and a pilgrim." An eyebrow rose as he paused in his scratching. "Or rather should I say I'm as much a thief and pilgrim . . . as you are a *knight?*"

Tylar's head hurt from trying to riddle meaning out of these strange words. "Are you truly on a pilgrimage? Was your story of Balger's punishment true?"

"Alas, as true as the stripes on my back, I'm afraid. But one story does not make an entire man, does it?"

Tylar had to agree. "You mentioned hearing other grim tidings on your journeys. What sort of happenings?"

"Rumors, whispers in the night, tales of black blessings and ilk-beasts stirring from the hinterlands. Your young friend has barely nicked the flesh on what's really going on, but he still hit the heart of the matter. Something is indeed stirring out there."

"What?"

"How in the naether should I know?" Rogger rolled back to his straw billet. "And now that I finally have a bit of quiet, maybe I could get some true sleep. I doubt we'll get much rest this night."

"Why's that?"

"The bells, ser knight, the bells."

Tylar had almost forgotten. Meeryn's deathwatch ended with the rising of the Mother moon. The death bells would announce her passing. They would surely peal all night.

He settled back to his own bed and pondered all that had been told him. But his thoughts kept returning to one moment—or rather one *word*.

Rivenscryr.

What did it mean? Why had Meeryn blessed him, healed him? Was it for him to be her champion, as Perryl had suggested? Was this word supposed to mean something to him?

Tylar sensed something unspoken in Perryl. The young man had paled with the mention of Rivenscryr. But if Perryl knew more, why hadn't he spoken?

There could be only one answer.

Perryl must have sworn an oath. While the young knight might show his face to a man who had once been his teacher, even protect him, he would never break an oath.

Perryl had learned that much from Tylar.

Rolling to his side, Tylar tried to stop thinking, stop remembering.

It hurt too much.

❖

Tylar startled awake in his bed, sitting up. He vaguely remembered dreams of being crippled again . . . and now waking to his hale body, he felt oddly disappointed. His broken body had sheltered him, hidden him these long years, requiring nothing of him but survival. But now Tylar had to face the world again, a whole man.

He groaned.

From beyond the lone window, hundreds of bells pealed, ringing and clanging. The noise was deafening.

He glanced upward. Full night had set in. Evening mists flowed in through the high barred window, pouring down like a foggy waterfall. His eyes grew accustomed to the gloom and spotted Rogger across the cell. The thief was standing under the window, bathed in mists.

"It's all over," Rogger said, noting him stir. "The Hundred are now ninety-nine."

Tylar stood, joining him. He had heard the sorrow in the other's voice. Despite the thief's calculating and dismissive demeanor earlier, the man understood the loss, felt it deeply.

"This is just the beginning," Rogger mumbled. "The first blood spilled. More will flow . . . much more . . ."

Though the night remained hot and muggy, Tylar shivered. Bells rang and rang, echoing out to sea and beyond. Cries could be heard rising in the night, mournful, pained, angry, frightened. Prayers were sung from a tower top, cast out to the skies.

The pair in the cell remained silent, standing under the window for a long stretch. Rogger finally turned away, staring at Tylar. "You talk in your sleep, ser knight."

"So? What does it—?"

Rogger cut him off. "You were speaking in Littick, ancient Littick, the old tongue of the gods."

Tylar found this claim doubly odd. First, he was hardly fluent in Littick. And second, how did a thief from the Dell even recognize Littick, especially ancient Littick? "What did I say?" he asked, expecting no real answer.

"You were whispering. It was hard to make out."

"Yet you're sure it was Littick."

"Of course. What I did make out was clear enough. You kept saying, *'Agee wan clyy nee wan dred ghawl.'* Over and over again."

Tylar pinched his brow. "What does that mean?"

Rogger pulled on his beard in thought. "It's nonsensical."

"Then it's probably nothing. Dream babble, nothing more."

Rogger seemed not to hear him. *" 'Agee wan clyy'* . . . break the bone. *'Nee wan dred ghawl'* . . . and free the dark spirit."

Tylar waved the words away. "As I was saying, dream babble."

"Then again," Rogger continued, *"clyy* could mean *body,* rather than bone. Depends on the emphasis." The thief sighed. "And you *were* whispering."

"How do you know Littick so well?"

Rogger dropped his hand from his beard. "Because I once taught it."

Before Tylar could inquire about such an oddity, voices arose from the hall, right outside the door. The peal of bells had covered the sound of approach.

Both men turned as the door was yanked open.

Castillion guards filled the hall, including the captain who had spat at Tylar days ago and named him Godslayer. The dungeonkeep backed aside to let in two others: one cowled in a bloodred robe that glowed ruddily in the darkness, rich in Graces, and one dressed formally in gray with silver rings on each finger and ear.

A soothmancer and an adjudicator.

Their eyes fell on Tylar.

The gray figure stepped forward. "Tylar de Noche, you are to present yourself to the Summer Mount Court to be soothed and judged."

Guards sidled in with swords drawn. The captain followed, carrying clanking iron manacles for wrist and ankle.

Rogger backed aside, mumbling, "It seems your friend's cloak was thinner than even he supposed."

Tylar did not fight his manacles, even when they were snapped too tightly, pinching. Perryl was leaving as soon as the deathwatch had ended. These others must have come for him as soon as he boarded the flippercraft and was away. So much for respecting the command of a Shadowknight.

Poked in the back by the point of a sword, he was led out of the cell.

"Bring the pilgrim god-sinner," the soothmancer commanded from under the cowl of his red robe. "His guilt is as plain as the brands on his flesh. On this mournful night, we will cleanse our house of all who have blasphemed. The way must be pure to grieve the loss of the Brightness of the Isles."

The adjudicator nodded and waved to the guards.

There were no additional manacles, so Rogger was simply grabbed and hauled.

They were led roughly down the rows of cells and up the long winding stairs into the central keep of Summer Mount, rising out of the dank darkness of the island's natural stone and into the sunbaked brick and tapestried walls of the castillion. The odors of piss and blood were replaced by the scent of braziers smoking with incenses: sweetwood, dried clove, and sprigs of thistledown.

The scents of the isles . . . in memory of Meeryn.

The deeper into the castillion they traveled, the more cloying the odor became. Braziers burned everywhere, as if death and grief could be smoked out and away. Every mirror they passed was shattered to hide the faces of those mourning. Black drapes covered windows to hold back the sun.

And over it all, bells rang and rang. Children dressed in black finery ran the halls, even among the guards, carrying small cymbals, clanging away, meant to chase away ghosts. It was supposed to be an act of grief, but spatters of laughter trailed the wake of the little ones. Death was not their concern, not even the death of their god.

More somber figures stood at doorways, bearing witness to the procession through the castillion. Tylar was cursed, spat at. Many carried silver bells, ringing them violently toward him as if trying to beat him with the noise.

At last, they reached the doors that led into the central court. They were flung wide, and Tylar and Rogger were led into the spacious hall beyond. The heavy doors closed behind them, rows of guards falling into place. The great hall, muffled from the bells beyond, seemed deadly silent.

Tylar stared at the court. It was plainly adorned, unlike some gods' courts. The walls were painted white, simply decorated with frescoes of twining vines and small purple flowers. Eight windows, thickly draped in black, lined one wall, facing the sea.

Aligned against the opposite wall stood seven figures, draped like the windows. They might have been statues, except for slight movements, the turn of a head, the shift of an arm. Tylar guessed who they were. The Hands to Meeryn, men and women in service to the late god, numbered eight, one for each bodily humour. But only seven stood here now. One was missing.

Rogger noted them, too, and whispered under his breath, "They'll all need a new trade now."

Tylar remained focused ahead. A high bench crossed the breadth of the court. Only two figures sat there, dressed in gray like their fellow adjudicator. Past their shoulders, a tall seat rose. Meeryn's throne, empty now, but seeming to bear her presence still.

The group was led before the high bench. The adjudicator who had collected Tylar from the dungeons climbed the steps and took his seat with the other two adjudicators. An old woman sat in the center, hard-eyed and stoic.

"Tylar de Noche," she said. "You know why you are brought before this court. To be soothed and judged for the death of Meeryn, the Brightness and Light of the Summering Isles." Her voice cracked slightly upon naming her god. "How do you speak?"

Thrust forward, Tylar stumbled toward the lone chair. Painted red, it stood before the high bench. He knew the procedure well enough, having attended such trials before from both sides. "I swear to all assembled here that I had no hand in the death of the god Méeryn. I am innocent."

"So you have claimed before," the other adjudicator said. He appeared even older than the woman, heavy with weight and age, sagging in his seat. "The honorable Perryl ser Corriscan has informed us of your past and your fall from grace. He also vouched for you, asking for a stay in this court until the matter could be attended in Tashijan."

"The Shadowknights have always served the gods and the realms," Tylar pressed, hoping that Perryl's request might still be honored. "I would bow to the Courts of Tashijan in this matter."

"As you have once before," the adjudicator that brought him here said. "They let you live when you should have been slain for murder so foul. If they had attended their duties without sympathy to one of their own, Meeryn might still live."

Tylar held back a groan. They thought Tashijan had been lenient upon him. If anything, the opposite was true. But his word would not be believed. The folk here had no faith in far-off Tashijan.

He tried another tactic. "A court of this import must be attended by those of the Order." Shadowknights were required to be present at trials of murder or serious offense.

"Then it's good fortune I returned from the outer islands this very night," a new voice interrupted. Shadows shifted near the back wall and a figure unfolded from the darkness, revealing himself. A Shadowknight. Cloaked and featureless behind his masklin. "My name is Darjon ser Hightower, the last of those sworn to Meeryn, the last still living. And before I see my duty done among these islands, I will see her avenged. So fear not, the Order *is* represented here."

Tylar's heart sank. No wonder Perryl's command to stay this trial had been ignored. They had their own knight, newly arrived, to argue otherwise.

"Let him be soothed," the woman said from the bench. "The truth will be known."

Tylar was pulled back into the single red chair. His manacles were unlocked and he was roped in place.

The red-robed mancer, his face cowled and shadowed as was custom, stepped before the bench. He bowed deeply, arms crossed and folded in his sleeves. As he straightened, he pulled a small silver bowl from one sleeve and a glass repostilary from the other. The latter vial glowed with an inner fire, a mixture of blood and other humours, an alchemic blend known only to the soothmancers.

Kneeling, he placed the silver bowl on the floor, whispered prayers of thanks, and poured a few drops into the basin. He stoppered the repostilary, and it vanished up a sleeve. With his hands free, he dipped his fingers into the bowl, wetting each tip with the glowing crimson mixture.

The mancer stood and crossed behind Tylar's chair, his robes sweeping the floor.

"Are you ready to put him to the word?" the mancer asked the court.

"We are," the trio at the bench responded.

Tylar braced himself. He hated being soothed. It was a violation like no other.

Wet fingers reached from behind and touched him at temple, forehead, and behind the corner of his jaw. The touch was fire, searing into him, seeming to reach into his skull. He gasped at the burn. The guild of soothmancers bowed to the gods bearing the aspect of fire. The unique blend of alchemies required the blood of such a god.

As the Grace-fed fire burned through his will, winding to the center of his being, the mancer spoke. "Put him to the word. Let the truth be judged."

Near blind from the pain, he heard the first question. "Did you slay Meeryn?"

"No!" he gasped out.

There was a pause as the adjudicators turned their attention to the soothmancer. Tylar had no trust in such a one. He had been soothed before, questioned upon the murder of the cobbler's family. His answer had been the same: denial. But the mancer had stated he was lying to the court. It had made no sense. Tylar knew the soothmancer to be a good and honest man. He had served the court of Tashijan for many decades. How could he make such a mistake?

Only much later did Tylar understand. In his heart, he had indeed felt responsible for the death of the cobbler and his family. They had been slain by the Gray Traders to discredit him. So in a way, he had been the cause for their bloody deaths. The soothmancer at Tashijan must have sensed this deeper guilt in Tylar's heart and answered honestly.

Still, it was a mistake. Truth was more complicated than what was written in one's heart. Justice could not always be found so easily there.

But he felt no guilt for Meeryn's death. "No!" he repeated to the court before the mancer could even respond.

"How do you find?" the lead adjudicator asked.

The soothmancer responded slowly, strained. "I . . . I am having difficulty reading this one's heart. There is a well of darkness beyond anything I've ever soothed before, beyond anything I could burn through to the truth. The corruption inside this man has no bounds, no depths. He is more monster than man."

Tylar squirmed under the other's fiery touch. "He lies! I am no worse nor better than any other man."

Fingers broke from his skin, releasing him. "I cannot read this one. His very touch sickens me. I fear he will corrupt the purity of Grace I bear." The mancer fell away, legs trembling with true horror.

Tylar stared at the accusing eyes. The soothmancer's words doomed him, claiming him evil beyond measure. Only such a corrupt spirit could slay a god.

He saw the judgment firm in the eyes of the adjudicators.

"We must find how he killed Meeryn," the Shadowknight said.

"How?" the elder woman asked. "How without the guidance of a soothmancer?"

"There are other ways to loosen a stubborn tongue." Darjon ser Hightower shifted closer, his cloak billowing outward. "Older ways, cruder ways. He has slain our Meeryn, murdered our realm into a godless hinterland. Let him face the tests of truth from those same barbarous lands."

"What do you propose?"

"Let me put him to the torture, make him scream the truth."

Tylar closed his eyes. He had worn this healed body for such a short time, and it was already going to be taken from him, broken again.

"So be it," said the woman behind the bench.

4

BLOOD MOON

Now it ended.

On the seventh floor of the Conclave's tower, Dart sat in a chair, hands folded in her lap. She tried not to stare at the row of girls seated in chairs along one side of the hall, and especially not at the dwindling number of girls that stood between her and the closed doors at the end of the hall. The sigil of the healers, an oak sprig, was carved into the door's lintel.

In preparation for the night's ceremony, they were to be tested, and examined, judged whether or not they were pure enough to kneel before the gods' Oracles.

Dart already knew her fate.

Tears threatened, a mix of terror, guilt, and sorrow.

The door opened again, releasing another girl, a fourthfloorer, who fled along the rows of chairs like a frightened sparrow. But from the smile on her face, it was not fear, but delight that was the wind under her wings. On her forehead, she bore a smudged blue cross, a mix of oils and dyed unguents, marking her as pure by Healer Paltry. She could attend the ceremony this night, opening the way to being chosen as a handmaiden.

Matron Grannice appeared in the open doorway. All the seated girls stood. Dart did the same, well aware of the ache in her loins, a dull bruise of the former pain.

Matron Grannice waved for the next girl, seated nearest the door. "Come, Laurelle. We've a long day ahead of us."

Laurelle curtsied. On this day, she would be the first of the thirdfloorers to be tested. As was custom, the sixthfloorers were checked first, then the fifth and fourth, leaving the thirdfloorers for last. It would be the first time for Dart's class to be presented before the Oracles, the blind servants of various gods, who arrived with the first full moon of summer to pick handmaidens and handmen for their gods.

Draped in white silk, her feet slippered in snowy soft velvet, Laurelle crossed to the door. She was the embodiment of purity. While it was a rarity for a thirdfloorer to be picked, what Oracle, blind or not, could fail to see the perfection that was Laurelle mir Hothbrin?

Pausing at the threshold, Laurelle glanced back at the line of remaining thirdfloorers. The powder on her face could not hide the blush of heat in her cheeks. Nervousness. She tried to smile bravely at the others, but it came out sickly.

All eyes, including Dart's, followed Laurelle as she disappeared into the healer's chamber. The door closed.

Now one girl sat between Dart and the door: Margarite. Like Laurelle, Margarite was dressed in white finery, down to the flowered tassels on her slippers.

Dart fingered the simple white shift and sash she wore, trying to pluck some semblance of beauty from it. Still, no amount of linen, silk, or the finest embroidery could make her pure again.

"Quit fidgeting!" Margarite spat under her breath, quick-tempered from her own anxiety.

Dart's hands settled back to her knees.

For the past seven days, she had hidden all signs of the attack. But it had not been easy. Ripped and sore, she had continued to spot her underthings and bedsheets for the first three days.

On the second night, it came to the attention of Matron Grannice. Dart had hurriedly told the third floor matron that the bleeding was from her first menstra. With a frown, the portly woman had pulled Dart into her private study.

Panicked, Dart had expected her corruption to be bared, but Matron Grannice had merely sat her down and spoken kindly and gently. "The bleed is nothing to be ashamed of," she consoled. "It is your first step into womanhood." She then went on to instruct Dart in how to control her seepage and keep herself clean. Afterward, the matron had given her a long hug, a rare showing of warmth and affection from the large woman.

Dart had cried. It was not just relief that drew out her tears. Wrapped in Matron Grannice's bosomy embrace, Dart was reminded how much she was about to lose. It was more than the roof over her head and the warm meals in her belly. It was the familiar faces she had known since a babe, the everyday routines of the only life she knew. Here was her home, her family.

She had cried for a long time until finally Matron Grannice had gently shushed her, wiped her tears, and sent her back to her bed.

A few days later, here she sat, awaiting the end. She would be stripped and spread on Healer Paltry's bench. Experienced fingers would touch her shame and find her broken and spoiled, unfit for a god, too corrupt to even walk the halls of the Conclave. She would be whipped and cast out to the streets, spurned by all.

Master Willet had ripped away more than her virginity and innocence on the floor of the rookery. His rutting had torn down the very stone walls around her, broken her home into a bloody ruin. Had the monster known this? Had this been part of his black pleasure?

Master Willet's disappearance had not gone unnoticed by the Conclave. Talk, rumor, and innuendo had quickly spread: that he had been waylaid by brigands outside the Conclave and his body dumped in the Tigre where it was washed away; that he had taken a whore for a wife and fled the First Land; that he had been practicing some Dark Grace and been sucked into the naether, never to be seen again. The less fanciful supposed he simply took service with some other caste and had left before his current contract was contested. But there were three in the Conclave who knew the truth: Dart, Pupp, and the person who had sent Master Willet up the stairs to attack a lone girl.

This last remained hidden, as much an accomplice in that dark play as those up in the rookery. No one came and pulled her aside, accused Dart in private or public of the crimes in the high tower. But someone knew.

Dart's eyes settled to the hall's stone floor. Pupp lay curled, his body steaming gently, his molten brass surface glowing brighter with each breath, then dimming as he exhaled with a wheeze of flame. She had experimented with him in solitary moments, testing various humours to see if anything besides blood would allow her to touch his phantom form. Nothing did, not saliva, yellow bile, or even tears.

Only blood.

In the dark, she had planned horrible strategies upon the body of the one who had sent Master Willet up the stairs. But now she would be cast out before her vengeance was complete.

The door at the end of the hall opened again. Laurelle strode out, back straight, eyes flashing. None needed to see her satisfied smile or the blue cross on her forehead to know she had passed judgment. "Margarite!" Matron Grannice called from the doorway, startling them all. "Don't drag your heels, child! Get in here!"

All the girls popped to their feet. Margarite hurried through the door.

Dart moved two steps over and took the girl's abandoned seat. It was still warm from the fear of each girl who had sat there before.

The door closed.

Laurelle stood a few steps down the hall, basking in the envy of her fellow pupils. "It was nothing," she consoled the others. "It is no more frightening than the yearly physique. Only much more *thorough.*" She spoke this last with the authority of a master to apprentices, then pressed the back of her hand to her forehead. "I have never felt so completely tested, so sure of my purity and readiness to be a handmaiden."

Murmurs of approval and assurances that she would be chosen wafted down the line of seated girls.

Her words awakened the terror in Dart's heart. As she stared at the closed door, her eyes traced the oak leaves and acorns on the lintel. Normally the sigil signified the art of healing: soothing balms, calming teas, all the gentle Graces to ease a body. But now the meaning had darkened; beyond that door, her life ended.

A touch on her shoulder made her jump. She turned to find Laurelle bent before her. All the girls watched, ready to see what new mischief Laurelle meant to inflict on Dart for their amusement.

Pupp was already on his feet, passing through Laurelle's gown, his molten skin roiling with agitation.

"I know your secret," Laurelle whispered, so softly no other could hear. "I know about the blood."

Dart tensed, her vision darkened at the corners.

Laurelle continued. "I overheard Matron Grannice. Having your first menstra is frightening enough, but to have it mere days before the full moon ceremony . . ." Her fingers found Dart's hand and squeezed ever so gently, then let go. "You'll be fine."

The sudden kindness caught Dart unprepared.

Laurelle straightened. "It's not like you have any chance of being chosen this night anyway."

Snickers and giggles met her words.

But Laurelle seemed deaf to the others. As she turned away, she carried a haunted look to her eye, and a touch of something else, the hint of envy again.

Studying her closely, Dart watched Laurelle struggle for a more confident smile. Dart had always been the invisible one, the girl in the shadows, as much a phantom as Pupp at times. For the first time, she wondered how much of a burden it was to always stand in the light.

Laurelle moved down the line of girls, offering little words of encouragement and praise. But Dart saw how her shoulders trembled slightly, burdened by the weight of all the expectations placed upon her. Not only by the girls, Dart suspected, but by her family, too.

The creak of hinges drew all their eyes back around. Margarite appeared, head high, a blue cross shining brightly on her brow.

"Margarite!" Laurelle cried, rushing to embrace her. "You passed!"

The girls laughed, dancing in each other's arms.

Matron Grannice shooed them farther down the hall. "Dart, you're next. Let's not keep Healer Paltry waiting."

Dart stood, but with her first step, she came close to falling. Her knees had turned to porridge, her thighs to rubber. Only a quick hand to the wall saved her.

"It's not a walk to the gallows," the matron grumbled and helped her stand straighter with a grip on her elbow.

Dart was half-led, half-dragged over the threshold.

"Why does she even bother?" Margarite said behind her. "Who would pick such a weed when there are flowers like us to choose?"

Matron Grannice closed the door behind Dart, shutting out the rest of the thirdfloorers. Dart wondered if she'd ever see them again.

Behind her, Pupp pushed through the door, trotting to Dart's side. The healer's illuminarium was bright with candles and smoky with burning stems of dried herbs. The scent of witchweed and briertail almost made her swoon.

"Come, child." Matron Grannice led her past the cramped antechamber and into the illuminarium proper.

The room was circular in shape with small cots aligned along the wall like the markings on a sundial. The beds normally comforted the ill, but they had been emptied for this hallowed day. Privacy was necessary to adequately judge the potential servitors to the gods.

In the center of the room, a single bench rested, shaped like a reclining figure, arms and legs spread. Dart had never seen such a bench, but she had heard of it.

Along with the four sacred illuminaria that surrounded it.

Above the bench, a chandelier blazed with fist-sized bulbs; the glass globes held small drizzles of a fire god's humour, burning brightly. Below, a crystal basin brimmed with water, its surface stirring in a constant whirlpool, blessed by a single tear from a god of water. And to either side rested the remaining two illuminaria: a small glass terrarium containing a full-grown, miniature oak tree, perfect down to its pin-sized acorns, and a lightning box that held a billowing cloud behind glass, flashing and roiling. They represented loam and air respectively. Each aspect was represented to verify the purity of the supplicant.

As Dart stood at the threshold, she sensed her doom. Even if she could somehow hide her shame from mortal eyes, the four illuminaria would reveal her corruption.

"Off with your clothes," Matron Grannice said with a trace of impatience and boredom. "Pile them on the bed over there, then return to the bench and lie down."

Dart undid her buttons with shaking fingers. "Mistress . . ." she began, sensing she might fare better if she revealed all now.

"Shush, Dart. Now is not the time to speak. Here comes Healer Paltry."

The head of the Conclave's healing caste entered through a back door. He was dressed in a simple robe of blue silk with a hatching of oak leaves around the collar. He was not a tall man, barely Dart's own height. His eyes were the deepest blue. His hair, long to the shoulder, was as dark as any raven's feather. Though barely thirty years past his birth, his skills in the Arts were known throughout Myrillia. It was said he even ministered to Chrism himself at the Grand Castillion. And here at the Conclave, there was many a girl who feigned fever or stomach churns just to be near him.

Even Matron Grannice tugged a loose strand of hair into place behind an ear, smoothing it down as he strode to them.

Though busy, Paltry still offered Dart a tired smile. "Be welcome, child. There is nothing to fear here."

Nodding despite the lace of terror around her heart, Dart shimmied out of her outers. Then after a moment's hesitation, she stripped bare of all, even her scuffed slippers. There was no reason for shyness with Healer Paltry. Twice yearly, the man gave the girls their physiques, confirming their intact virginity. He was always gentle, teasing with light words, his hands always warm.

"Onto the bench with you, child," Matron Grannice said with a nudge, bumping her back to the moment.

But Dart found herself frozen in place, knees locked together. "Mistress . . ."

Paltry cupped her chin. "This will be quick."

His calming touch released her from the spell of her fear, and she stumbled stiffly to the bench. With gentle directions, she lay back, spreading her arms out and her legs along the joists. Her hands nearly touched the illuminarias of loam and air. Overhead, the fire globes blazed hotly, and below, unseen, Dart felt the stir of the basin's waters in her own stomach.

Now it would all end.

Paltry leaned over her, holding four thimble-sized jars. "This unguent is made of the blood of the four aspects. You might feel a little tingle, and the corresponding illuminaria will shine brighter if you are accepted. You must pass all four. Do you understand?"

"Y-yes." She squeezed closed her eyes. In her ears echoed the cries of ravens.

A finger touched her brow four times: top, bottom, left, and right. The points of a cross. Only if she passed would the marks be connected with blue oils, sealing her purity.

Dart shook, knowing that would never happen.

As the fourth mark blessed her forehead, Paltry spoke near her ear. "Now to judge the purity of your spirit and—"

Glass exploded with a shatter. Dart cried out, curling in a ball. Overhead, shards rained down from the chandelier. Dart felt impacts rattle the underside of the bench. Slivers cut into her back and arms and thighs, like a thousand bee stings.

Matron Grannice yelped, ducking away. Pupp raced in circles around the bench, eyes ablaze, jumping and leaping, as startled as any of them.

All around light blazed from the four illuminaria, near blinding in their brilliance.

Paltry stood, bleeding from lacerations on his face. His eyes were huge. "By all the gods . . ." he swore under his breath. The light quickly faded from the four exploded illuminaria. "I've never seen such a response."

"What happened?" Matron Grannice asked, accusation in her voice, her eyes fixed on Dart.

"I didn't . . . I couldn't . . ." Dart said. "I'm sorry."

Paltry wiped his face, picking out glass, then did the same for Dart. "It's not her fault. While normally the illuminaria wax only slightly brighter, I've witnessed more brilliant displays over the years. Yet nothing of this magnitude. The strength and clarity of her spirit is without question." Finished with his ministrations, he glanced up at Grannice. "From this radiant response of the illuminaria, I see no need to perform a physique."

Dart felt a surge of hope. Without an intimate exam, her terrible secret would remain hidden. Perhaps for another half year, until the next physique.

But such hope was dashed with Matron Grannice's next words. "You must, Healer Paltry. A supplicant before the Oracles must be cleared spiritually and physically."

Paltry stared at the ruined illuminarias. "Of course, you're right. But let's be quick about this. I must study in more detail what happened here." He waved for Dart to stretch back on the bench. He examined her with swift efficiency, hurried, with none of his usual gentleness.

Dart trembled under his touch as he checked her body from brow to toe. Lastly, he crouched between her spread legs and reached toward the ache in her loins, probing toward the root of her shame. "She's been bleeding," he said.

"Her first menstra," Grannice explained, arms folded.

By now, tears rolled down Dart's cheeks. She awaited the end of her life.

With a clearing of his throat, Paltry straightened and gained his feet. "Everything appears fine," he said, patting her inner thigh. "She can attend the night's ceremony."

Dart gasped in shock, struggling to speak.

"Up with you then, child," Matron Grannice said. "Into your clothes."

Dart stared between the portly woman and the healer as he marked her forehead in blue oil. "I . . . I passed?"

She could not keep the incredulity out of her voice. Was she healed? Maybe the attack in the rookery had been just some horrible nightmare. She could almost believe it, wanted to believe it. At times over the past days, it had even felt that way. Or had some Grace secretly blessed her, made her pure again?

"Pure," she repeated aloud. In her heart, the word also meant home and family.

"Yes, yes," Matron Grannice scolded, "it's indeed a blessed miracle. Now get yourself dressed. You've much to do before the full moon rises." The matron turned to Paltry. "What of the other girls? Those still in the hall?"

Paltry shook his head. "I can test no others. It will take some days to acquire another four illuminaria. As such, they will not be able to attend this moon's ceremony."

Grannice hurried Dart into her clothes. "See what you've done, child! Ruined it for all the others!"

"But I didn't mean to—"

"It's truly not her fault," Paltry pledged in her defense.

Dart nodded vigorously, tugging on the last of her clothes. She could only imagine the anger of the remaining thirdfloorers. There would not be another choosing until midwinter.

Frowning deeply, Matron Grannice led the way to the door. Dart hopped after her, trying to get her foot into her last slipper. Pupp, thinking it a game, jumped and nipped at her loose footwear. She shooed him away.

The matron reached the door and tugged it open. As Dart pulled into her slipper, she heard the matron's announcement and the shocked responses that followed. Wincing, she stood in the shadows, sheltered behind the large woman's bulk.

Healer Paltry placed a reassuring hand on her shoulder and leaned to her ear, speaking low and urgently. "I don't know what you did with Master Willet, but I promise you I'll find out."

Dart gasped. Understanding struck her immediately. She had passed the healing wards on the seventh floor on her way to the rookery. The room tilted, and her vision darkened. *Paltry* was Willet's partner. The healer had lied about her purity a moment ago. She remembered his fingers . . . in her, probing . . . possibly even appreciating his partner's bloody handiwork.

A shudder passed through her. She felt violated all over again, her momentary hope dashed into ruins. She felt unmoored, terrified, trapped.

"I'll be watching you, Dart." His voice was as gentle as ever, but his fingers dug deeper, painful, threatening. "In the meantime, it seems we both have secrets to keep."

Matron Grannice spoke above the babble of shocked voices from the hall. "Come, Dart. Night won't wait on you forever."

With a small cry, Dart fled the healer's grasp and into the passageway. Forty pairs of eyes narrowed at her in angry rebuke. None came to congratulate her on the blue cross on her forehead. She felt a bone-deep urge to flee to the nearest privy and scrub the mark off. But for now the cross was all that stood between her and banishment.

She continued down the hall, refusing to look back. She had won back her home for a short time—but was it even worth it?

Laurelle and Margarite met her at the end of the hall. They stared at her as if she had been freshly dredged up from the muddy bottoms of the Tigre.

"What happened back there?" Laurelle asked.

Dart shook her head. She had a more important mystery to ponder: What was she going to do now?

❖

Night came much too quickly.

Dart huddled with the crowd of other supplicants in the hall below the High Chapel. In the center of the room, a spiral brass staircase wound up to the sacred domed chamber above, but the way remained locked, awaiting the rising of Mother moon's full face and the chiming of the oracular bells.

Earlier, after sunset, Dart and the others had been sent here to prepare themselves. Small altars dotted the walls of the hall. After fasting the entire day, the supplicants to the Oracles were required to burn a stick of incense, sending their prayers up into the aether, while dropping leaden weights into deep watery troughs to shed their sins into the naether below.

With this final purification complete, only the waiting remained.

Dart stared around her. Off by the staircase, in a place of honor, the young men and women of the fifth and sixth floors gathered, stubbornly struggling to look calm or bored, but Dart saw their terror. Time ran short for members of this group. It was the very last ceremony for some of them, the last chance to be chosen.

On the other side of the hall, the fourthfloorers chattered merrily, wide-eyed and still fresh to the ceremonies, excited by the pageantry of it all.

Closer at hand, a sea of boys surrounded her, all thirdfloorers, dressed in the traditional black breeches, tucked into gray boots with loose gray shirts. The likelihood of being chosen was slim for those of such tender age. As such, their attention was focused away from the spiral staircase and toward the odd trio of small girls in their midst: Laurelle, Margarite, and Dart.

Word of the incineration of the illuminaria had spread rapidly through the Conclave. A few glared at Dart with murderous intent, others seemed merely intrigued, while most simply found it all too amusing.

"So they blew up?" Kessel asked, motioning with his hands and whistling. "I wish I could have seen poor Healer Paltry's face!" The boy screwed up his own face into a mock of outraged shock.

His young attendants almost burst from trying to stifle their laughter, patting him on the back, holding their sides, and trying not to make too much noise.

"It was not funny!" Laurelle huffed at him, pinning the others with a baleful glare. "The . . . the accident ruined the chances for the other girls. Now they have to wait half a year, until the midwinter ceremony."

"That only leaves more chances for all of us!" Kessel said with a shrug. "We should be thanking that girl."

The gathered gazes focused back on Dart. She tried to shrink away.

"Don't worry," Margarite said heatedly. "The other girls will be *thanking* her later up on our floor."

"That's if she isn't chosen first," said a boy in the back. Dart did not know his name, but she had noticed him before. He was new to the Conclave, arriving only last year. He was taller than the others, his skin a deeper bronze than theirs, suggesting he came from one of the lands far to the south. But he never said exactly where, not even to his fellow third-floorers.

"She'll never be chosen," Margarite shot back. "Look at her, wearing hand-downs from storage. She smells of mothguard and mold."

Dart kept her arms crossed over her black dress, tucking down her frayed gray half cloak. Even her boots were mottled white with age, not like the rich gray leathers of Margarite's and Laurelle's footwear.

"It is not the cut of one's cloth that will be judged here," the bronze boy said, turning away dismissively.

Dart appreciated his support, but it was futile. Despite the blue cross on her forehead, she was not pure enough to kneel before the Oracles of the Myrillian gods. It was not only mothguard and mold that would be sniffed out by these blind seekers of handmaidens and handmen. They would surely know of her corruption. The servants in the High Chapel were not mere boxes of old humour, like the illuminaria. They were the very senses of the gods.

The best she could hope was not to be exposed. And if she did indeed escape such ruin, what then? The punishment that would surely be inflicted upon her by the other girls was nothing compared to the terror that awaited her in the empty halls, where Healer Paltry would be waiting.

She had only one other hope.

Pupp appeared out of the crowd of boys, winding around some, passing straight through others. The crowds had him all excited. He pranced to her side, glowing brightly, his brass-plated muzzle steaming, a tongue of flame lolling from his razored mouth. At her side, he shook out his mane of copper spikes, ruffling them like real fur.

As she reached a hand to him, chimes began to ring overhead.

The oracular bells.

The room immediately went silent. Laurelle and Margarite grabbed each other's hands and pulled in close.

At the top of the spiral staircase, double doors were thrown wide. The musky scent of darkleaf flowed down from the open doorway, accompanied by bright moonlight. The beaten silver doors shone like shields of pure light.

The ceremony had begun.

The fifth- and sixthfloorers headed up the brass stairway, winding around and around. They would be presented first, followed in order by the other floors. As everybody waited to mount the steps, tension in the room grew thicker. Many were already in tears, wiping them away quickly lest they appear weak. One boy from the third floor ran to an altar stone and emptied his belly with a splash of fluid. None derided him. All felt the same.

Now was the moment when dreams were either lost or fulfilled.

As the last fifthfloorer disappeared into the vast vault that was the High Chapel, the fourth floor's group headed up the steps, their earlier chatter strangled away by the austere moment.

At the base of the staircase, the boys from the third floor had already gathered. Their faces craned upward, bathed in moonlight. Only one remained bowed, eyes on the floor: the bronze boy who had come to Dart's defense. His lips moved in silent prayer.

Dart found herself staring at him. In the moonlight, his skin appeared even darker, a bronzed sculpture in prayer. Then his group began the winding climb to the High Chapel. He unclasped his hands and followed.

Dazed, Dart continued to stand there, frozen in place, a statue, too.

A small hiss drew her attention. Laurelle motioned to her. She and Margarite, still hand in hand, were heading for the stairs. Pupp followed after them, sniffing at the edges of their dresses.

Dart found her feet moving on their own. She hurried to the girls, finding comfort in the familiarity of her fellow students. As she joined them, Laurelle reached out with her free hand and gripped Dart's. All past sins forgotten in the terror of the moment. Even Margarite nodded to her, eyes wide.

The last thirdfloor boy mounted the stair.

The girls stared at one another. Who would go first? Laurelle took a deep breath, steeled her grip upon her two companions, then let go. She crossed stolidly to the stairs and climbed them. Margarite was right at her heels.

Pupp planted his forepaws on the lowest step and wagged the stump of his brass tail. He stared back at Dart. For the briefest flicker, she again saw a strange, dark intelligence shining from his eyes, studying her. Then it was gone, snuffed away by unseen winds. Dart headed to the stairs. Laurelle and Margarite were already two steps ahead. She hurried to close the gap. Her boots clanged on the brass stairs. The rail was ice to her fingers.

She stared at the line of boys vanishing away through the blindingly bright doors overhead. Nothing could be seen beyond. The line of supplicants continued to be swallowed away.

At last, Dart and the other two girls reached the top of the stairs. The open doors lay ahead. Laurelle glanced back to them, her face drained of blood. Tears brimmed her eyes.

Words came to Dart's lips. It was the first she had spoken since entering the hall below. "Be strong," she whispered.

Laurelle closed her eyes for a breath, opened them, and nodded. She turned and strode through the smoky doorway. Margarite ran after her. Dart moved more slowly, led by Pupp.

The group marched through the clouded nave. They passed braziers piled with dried darkleaf, the leaves crisping and curling in flame, roiling with thick, acrid smoke. In the chapel beyond, a single greatdrum beat in slow rhythm, guiding their steps forward. The sonorous beat thrummed against the rib, against the heart.

Once past the braziers, the smoke cleared as the domed chapel opened before them. It was like stepping out of a tunnel and into open air. The High Chapel stood atop the tallest tower of the Conclave. It was said that the only higher tower was Chrism's own keep.

Dart's gaze immediately drew upward to the glass eye in the domed roof. The full face of the lesser moon shone down at them. The greater moon had long set, leaving the night sky to the beauty of its pregnant sister.

The illumination of the moon limned the entire room in silver. There was no other source of light. Then again none was needed. It was nearly as bright as midday.

Dart trailed the others into the chamber.

Tiered rows of seats and balconies circled the High Chapel, climbing half the wall. The highest tiers had long gone rotten and were blocked off from use. Shadowy shapes filled the lower benches and balconies: the mistresses and masters of the Conclave, the cloistered entourage that accompanied the great Oracles from far-off lands, and the families of supplicants with wealth enough to be here.

Dart noted Laurelle searching around, a hopeful glow on her face.

But there was not much time to scan the gallery. Already the other students were filling the supplicant stoops. The kneeling benches were raw squallwood, arranged in an oval, facing inward. Dart kept in step behind Margarite, but with her eyes on the chamber, Dart's foot knocked into the corner of a stoop. She flew forward, arms outstretched. She bumped into Margarite, who kept her feet.

Dart was not as fortunate.

With a startled yelp, she landed on her hands, skinning her palms raw and landing flat on her belly. Dart quickly pushed up amid small sounds of amusement from those in attendance, but it quickly hushed. Dart scrambled to her feet, ignoring her stinging hands, and hurried after the two girls.

Margarite glanced back at her, mortified. Laurelle simply covered her mouth. Dart motioned them forward. They hurried after the last boy and took the three stoops beside him. Dart noted it was the bronze boy. He glanced at her, then away, his face unreadable.

Dart gratefully sank to her kneeling bench, resting her elbows on the rail. There were many empty stoops, as vacant and dusty as the upper balconies, more than could be accounted for by the missing thirdfloor girls. The school must have been more populous in the distant past.

Before Dart could consider this oddity, the bells chimed one final peal. From a door opposite the supplicants, a row of white-draped figures drifted into the room.

The Oracles.

A small red-liveried servant attended each figure, guiding their blind masters. As each Oracle entered the chapel, their snowy cowls were tossed back. They bore red strips of silk across their eyes, or rather where their eyes should have been. From her studies, Dart knew that the Oracles' eyes were burned to empty sockets by the blood of the god they represented. Emblazoned on their foreheads was the sigil of the god they served.

No one knew how many Oracles would show up at each ceremony, seeking replacements for their lieges' handmaidens or handmen. It was a matter of utter secrecy. Even the Oracles themselves had no foreknowledge of how many or what manner of servants were needed in other gods' households. Handmaidens and handmen, called collectively Hands, lived exultant but short lives, exposed to powerful Graces that slowly altered their bodies. Replacements were needed regularly by the households of the hundred realms.

The Oracles were led into the center of the chapel, surrounded by the supplicants' stoops. They faced the hopeful group, abandoning their red servants for the moment, concentrating on the circle of young men and women, boys and girls.

Dart noted the sigils: Yzellan of Tempest Sound, Isoldya of Mistdale, Dragor of Blasted Canyon, Quint of Five Forks, Cor Ven of Chadga Falls, and on and on. The number of Oracles was not large, but they represented some of the finest houses.

A small murmur spread through the assembly as the last Oracle entered the chapel and revealed himself. It was a very old man, borne by two servants and still needing a cane.

Dart squinted at his sigil on his forehead—ᔕ—and gasped with recognition.

Chrism.

Here was the Oracle of Myrillia's eldermost god. It had been three years since Chrism had called for a new servant.

As this elderly Oracle took his place among the others, another servant ran in from the hallway. He searched the room, then hurried to one of the Oracles. The two bent in whispers. As the Oracle straightened, his cowl was drawn back over his head. He withdrew with the new servant, leaving the chapel amid fervent murmuring from the gallery.

Dart had read the sigil on the departing Oracle. *Meeryn of the Summering Isles.* How odd. She could not recall an Oracle ever withdrawing in the middle of a ceremony. Something drastic must have transpired in Meeryn's household.

As Meeryn's Oracle left, the greatdrum began to beat again, slow and solemn. It filled the vast space, making it seem larger, yet at the same time more intimate.

It was the signal to begin the choosing.

Dart knew what to do from here. Kneeling, with her elbows already on the rail, she pushed out her hands, palms up, and bowed her brow to her forearms in the posture of supplication. As she did so, she was acutely aware of the sting of her abraded hands. It was shameful to offer such soiled palms, but then again, it was somehow fitting, considering the corruption of her body and spirit.

With her head bowed, she saw nothing. Still, she closed her eyes to staunch the hot tears that threatened. She heard the shuffle and brush of robes as the Oracles spread out among the supplicants, searching with the senses of the god they represented, seeking the perfect match to fill their need.

Dart's hands trembled. The stoop was all that kept her upright. Around her, she heard startled cries from the other students as they were chosen.

After so much pageantry, the selection was a simple matter. The Oracle would simply place a small gray slate stone, the size of a dol-jin tile, into a student's upraised palm, claiming the supplicant for their god.

There was no appeal or argument allowed. In the High Chapel, under the first moon of summer, the Oracles *were* their gods.

The chosen would then be raised from the stoop by the red-liveried servant and brought to stand by his or her new master. Only then could they look upon the tile and know which of the nine Graces they had been assigned. The primary quadricles were the most exalted: blood, seed, menses, sweat. But none would shun any of the secondary quintrangles: tears, saliva, phlegm, yellow and black bile. It was an honor to be chosen at all.

The choosing stretched painfully long. Dart heard Oracle after Oracle pass her station with a brush of robes. Her palms stung worse and worse. No cool tile was placed there to numb the pain.

Then the beating of the greatdrum ceased on one resounding crash, and it was over.

Dart raised her face, noting the empty stoops. Margarite still knelt beside her. But beyond was an empty station.

Laurelle had been chosen.

Margarite began to sob with the realization. Both of them searched the gathered Oracles to see who had chosen her best friend. Already the servants were pulling up their masters' cowls, preparing to leave.

Dart was the first to spot Laurelle. She covered her mouth in shock and delight. Laurelle stood in the shadow of the elderly, bent form.

"It's Chrism . . ." Dart whispered in awe.

Margarite sobbed harder, a bitter sound.

Noting their attention, Laurelle nodded to them and touched the corner of her eye. She was signaling the Grace to which she had been chosen.

"Tears," Margarite half-wailed, shedding her own for her friend and for her own loss.

It was the best of the secondary quintrangles, an honor for one so young.

Dart simply kept her mouth covered. She allowed the pleasure of the moment to well through her, happy for Laurelle. She read the bright expression of relief on her face and could not help but be delighted.

"All of our sisters should have been here to witness this," Margarite hissed, grief quickly firing to anger, needing a target.

Dart's momentary happiness dimmed. Margarite was right. It was a success the entire floor should have shared.

The Oracles began to file out of the room with their charges. Dart noted the bronze boy leaving with the Oracle who represented Jessup of

Oldenbrook, a distinguished house of the First Land. The dark boy did not seem to notice her attention, but she followed him with her eyes as he departed. No other thirdfloorers had been chosen.

With her attention focused elsewhere, Dart barely noted the slow, assisted passage of the ancient Oracle. He and his entourage crept past Dart's station. Laurelle waved to her and Margarite, wisping a kiss in their direction, tears running down her face. But Laurelle's eyes also spent a long time searching the tiers and benches.

Dart noted her lack of discovery. Her family was not in attendance.

But Dart had her own concerns. With the ceremony over, she had to face the ruins of her own life. How long could she stay hidden here? What of Healer Paltry, lurking in the halls?

The bent-backed Oracle stopped before Dart's station, leaning heavily on his cane, resting a breath. Servants supported him on both sides. His head swung in her direction, blind and swathed in silk. But Dart sensed him staring at her, like a weight upon her heart.

A crooked finger rose and pointed at her.

Another servant rushed to her side and grabbed her by the shoulder.

Dart pulled away, knowing she had been found out, her inner fears heard by the blind seer. Weak from dread, she did not fight as her arm was yanked forward.

The Oracle stepped heavily toward her, stabbing his hand out at her. She stared wide-eyed, taking in every detail: the yellow nails, the parchment-thin skin, the spiderweb of veins. It was more claw than hand.

A cry built up inside her. All eyes were on her. She would be debased before the entire assembly.

Then a stone dropped into her palm. Reflexively she caught it, closing her fingers. Her arm was released.

Murmurs of shock and surprise echoed from the gallery.

"You are chosen," the servant at her side spoke solemnly. "Rise and take your place."

Dart could not. She simply trembled. "I can't . . . mistake . . ." She tried to push the tile back toward the Oracle.

The ancient one ignored her and stepped away.

Laurelle took his place. "Be strong," she whispered, returning Dart's words to her. She offered a free hand.

Slowly, on wobbling legs, Dart stood. She slipped around the stoop and stepped to Laurelle's side.

Margarite looked on, her face aghast and drained of all color.

"What Grace have you won?" Laurelle asked.

Dart numbly glanced to her closed fist. She opened it and stared down at the painted Littick sigil:

$$H_{\circ}$$

Her hand trembled, almost dropping the slate.

Laurelle steadied her with a hand. "Well?"

Dart could not speak. She showed her tile to Laurelle. The disbelief on the other girl's face matched her own.

It was the one Grace above all others.

Blood.

5

BROKEN BONES

"I . . . I DON'T KNOW ANYTHING," TYLAR MOANED, HATING HIMSELF FOR the sob that racked through him.

"Again," commanded the masklin-wrapped Shadowknight.

Tylar no longer had the strength to tense. He heard the crack of the whip, then felt the lancing sting as a long stripe of flesh was sliced to bone. His body jolted against the whipping post. The flesh on his wrists tore against the unforgiving iron. He hung by his manacles, looped over a hook high on the post, his toes brushing the dirt of the courtyard.

He was stripped to a loincloth. Blood ran down the back of his thighs and calves, dripped from his toes. Tears trailed through his sweat. He stared up at the full face of the lesser moon shining down on him.

He had lost count of the strokes. Eighteen lashes? He wasn't sure. He had slipped away once, the pain driving him into oblivion. But a splash of cold water had mercilessly revived him, along with a crumpled cloth soaked in bitter alchemies shoved under his nose. Apparently it was rude to sleep during one's own torture.

Dazed, he slumped against the post, lolling in his manacles. Crowds packed the courtyard stands to watch the spectacle. The trio of adjudicators sat in seats, a silver tray of pomegranates and kettle cakes beside them. The red-robed soothmancer stood at their side, arms crossed. At least he had the decency to look sickened. The group of black-draped Hands clotted in one corner, consoling one another in low whispers, barely noting the festivities.

And a festival it was. The balconies and parapets were crowded with lords and ladies of the high city, servants of the castillion, even some drabbed underfolk who must have bribed their way to a viewing seat. Laughter and shouts for more blood rang off the walls. Black ale flowed along with spiced wine. Somewhere a minstrel played bright tunes, while hundreds of bells rang from the lower city.

The Shadowknight, Darjon ser Hightower, leaned closer to his face, one gloved hand resting against the whipping post. "Tell us the truth, and your death will be swift."

Tylar tasted blood on his tongue as he attempted to speak. "So you keep promising . . . but here I keep hanging, though I keep telling you the truth."

The eyes of his torturer narrowed. "We've barely begun here. I can make this last more than a single night."

Tylar closed his eyes. "You want the truth . . . ?" He took a deep breath, though it pained him to do so.

Darjon bent nearer.

Tylar opened his eyes and spat with the last of his strength, catching the knight square in the face. "There is your truth!"

With a roar, the Shadowknight reared back. He waved an arm to the whipmaster.

The crack of flying leather answered, and Tylar was slammed into the post. His back flashed with fire, his agony darkening the world to a pinpoint. He did not fight it, but instead sank away.

Somewhere far off, he heard a shout. "Keep that up, y'art going to kill him."

Tylar recognized Rogger's voice. The thief, bound in ropes off in one corner, seemed to be his only defender. Of course, his pleas for clemency might be self-serving. Once Tylar confessed and was killed, Rogger was due to be impaled next to him, both destined to be bits of decoration for Meeryn's tomb. So the longer Tylar held out, the longer the thief drew breath.

As Tylar drifted farther away, acrid vapors suddenly assaulted his nostrils. He struggled to get away from them, tossing his head. Cold water flooded over him, shivering over his flesh. He gasped as the world shook back into foggy focus.

He saw the healer's face hovering at the tip of his nose. "Here he comes," the man said, pulling away the crumple of stinking cloth. He glanced to Darjon at his shoulder. "He's lost a lot of vital humour, ser. Next time I might not be able to revive him."

Darjon swore. "The whip's not loosening this one's tongue anyway. We'll try other tortures that aren't so bloody. Cut him down!"

A guard rushed forward and unhinged the hook. As the manacles slipped free, Tylar's body felt tenfold heavier. He collapsed, facedown, into the bloody mud under the post.

The healer dropped to one knee. "I could put some firebalm on his wounds. It stings mightily, but it'll staunch the bleeding."

"Do it! I won't have him dying on us . . . at least, not yet."

The healer rummaged in a satchel.

Darjon twisted a fist in Tylar's hair and pulled his face up. Limned against the full moon, his countenance was entirely shadow. Only his eyes glowed with Grace. "Before this night ends, I will discover what you did to Meeryn."

Tylar sensed Darjon's ferocity. And something darker. There was more to this man's determination than mere vengeance. While punishments could be cruel, torture was not the way of the Order. But Tylar was too tired to curse the man, so he told him the truth in his heart. "You . . . You disgrace your cloak."

Darjon shoved him away.

The healer pulled free a tiny clay pot. "This will sting," he said under his breath.

Tylar steeled himself, though it had done him little good so far.

The healer's shadow fell over him. Fingers touched his shoulder. The spread of balm on his flesh did not burn. Not at all. Instead, it was like the sweetest nectar on the tongue, a soothing caress on a fevered brow.

Tylar moaned in relief, unable to keep it bottled in his chest. It was as if every scrap of torture-inflicted pain was being repaid in kind by rapturous pleasure. It rippled over his flesh.

A small surprised gasp escaped the healer. "By all the gods!"

"What?" Darjon asked, stepping around.

"He heals with just a touch of the firebalm." The healer slathered his back with more salve as proof and demonstration. "Look how the lash wounds glow under the balm, and the skin closes over."

As Tylar shuddered with the pleasure of the balm, Darjon stumbled back a few steps. "The glow . . ." He swept out with his shadowcloak to command attention. "It is Grace . . . the Grace stolen from Meeryn! Here is the proof we've sought all night! He heals with Meeryn's own dying Grace!"

Despite the soothing touch of the balm, Tylar groaned.

Figures closed in to witness the miracle. Guards held off all but those who had been in the hall earlier. The adjudicators watched as the healer repeated his demonstration, treating the last of the lash marks. Sounds of amazement rose from those gathered.

A black-gowned figure fell to her knee beside Tylar. She raised her hands to her face, lifting her veil. She was ashen-skinned, her lips daubed black. "It's blood Grace!" she gasped. "I would know it anywhere . . ."

Another of the entourage spoke, a man dressed also in black. He placed a hand on the woman's shoulder and explained, "Delia was the maiden who handled Her Brightness's blood."

Tears rose in the young woman's eyes. "It is indeed Meeryn!"

"Can there be any doubt of his guilt now?" Darjon said boldly. "I say we put him to more vigorous tests. Grind the truth from his very bones."

Fervent agreement met his words. Only the kneeling woman looked confused. "Why does he bear her blood?" But no one heard her.

She was helped to her feet by the man who had spoken on her behalf. The crowd dispersed, making room.

Tylar turned.

Darjon led two men. One hulking fellow carried a stump of wood. The other, even larger than the first, carried an immense iron hammer.

As the stump was dropped in the mud at his feet, Darjon bent closer. "There is more than one way to break a man, Godslayer."

In this instance, the knight was speaking literally.

"Undo his manacles. Drag his right hand onto the wood."

Tylar balked, understanding what was intended. They meant to pulp him. He fought the guards as his manacles fell away. *Not my sword hand.* He had regained his dexterity only days ago. He had not even the chance to hold a hilt again.

"First the one hand, then the other, then we'll start with your knees." Darjon seemed to take particular delight in his prisoner's thrashing, but Tylar couldn't stop himself. It was not just the pain he feared.

"No!" he begged. "I've told you the truth."

"Your own blood betrays you. What the whippings have hinted, the hammer will reveal."

Tylar was too weak to resist. Two guards gripped his arm and thrust his hand atop the stump.

Darjon leaned closer. "Tell us how you slew her!"

"I didn't—"

Even before he could finish, Darjon signaled the giant with the hammer. Swung from the shoulder, the fist of iron arced high and plunged down toward the stump and its pale target.

Tylar cried out. He heard Rogger do the same: *"Agee wan clyy!"*

The words made no sense.

Then the hammer struck. Tylar felt the rebound all the way up his arm. It shuddered past his shoulder and into his chest. A wave of agony followed on its heels. Blinding . . . a thousandfold worse than a single lash.

He screamed, arching back, his face bared to the moon overhead.

Then he felt something loosen deep inside. He had already pissed himself, and if he had anything to eliminate, he would have done it long ago. This was something deeper, something beyond bowel and flesh. He could not hold it back, even if he wanted.

From the black palm print on his chest, something dark wrested out of him and into this world. It gutted him, tearing out of his chest, taking all pleasure from him and leaving only pain.

The torment in his hand spread throughout his body. Other bones broke and reformed, callused, then broke again.

He screamed anew, as much in anguish as agony.

Somewhere far away, Rogger answered him: *"Nee wan dred ghawl!"*

In the heart of his torment, Tylar now remembered those words. *Agee wan clyy . . . nee wan dred ghawl.* Ancient Littick. *Break the bone . . . and free the dark spirit.*

His vision cleared somewhat. All he saw was the moon. His body was still arched back. Something rose from the center of his chest, a trail of black smoke against the bright moon.

Screams erupted around him.

The font of darkness climbed high, taking the last of his strength. Tylar collapsed back into the mud. The cloud took shape, still trailing a dark umbilicus to the black print on his chest, like some newborn babe to its mother.

The pain in his body ebbed. He tried to move, to crawl from the shadow above. He found his limbs uncooperative. One knee refused to bend, the other was slow to respond. His arms were no better. Tylar realized his state. He had returned to his broken form, unhealed. Even the freshly pulverized hand had returned to a mere claw of old, scarred bone.

He was back in his same crippled body.

A cry of despair escaped him.

He stared up at the apparition still linked to him. What had first appeared to be smoke now seemed more a pool of midnight waters, flowing and taking shape. Wings unfurled and a neck stretched out, bearing a beastly head of a wolf, maned in black flames. Eyes opened, shining like lightning, unquestionably Graced with tremendous power.

Those eyes glanced to him, narrowing dismissively, then away, out to the screaming folk fleeing in terror. The adjudicators and soothmancer had retreated under a phalanx of guards. Lords and ladies scrabbled with common folk to every doorway and gate. Several were trampled underfoot.

A squad of castillion guards, led by the same captain who had first named Tylar godslayer, rushed forward with pikes high and swords low.

"Kill the daemonspawn!" the captain yelled and chopped an arm through the air, a signal.

Archers let loose from the parapets, while longbowmen in the courtyard fired from bended knee. Bolts sliced through the air, passing into the beast and out the far side, aflame.

The burning arrows struck into the thatched barrack roofs and set straw to flame. Others shattered brilliantly against stone or hard dirt.

Tylar sought meager refuge behind the stump.

To their credit, the guards did not balk, continuing their headlong rush toward the shadowbeast. Swords flashed in the moonlight.

Black wings folded, and the beast, the size of a horse, settled silently to the yard to meet the attack. Pikes plowed into it first, but they fared no better than the arrows, spiking out the back of the creature, flaming like torches and crumbling to ash.

The shadow daemon reared up, snarling a spit of bright flame, and slashed out with its forepaws, catching the two nearest pikemen. With its mere touch, the men tumbled back, collapsing in on themselves, boneless yet still alive, mewling like misshapen calves born sickly.

Other guards fled from the horror.

Tylar had seen such foul work before . . . in Punt, upon the Shadowknights guarding Meeryn.

So had others.

The captain shouted a retreat. By now, those under the house guards' protection had fled the courtyard. The captain's eyes found Tylar, still hiding behind the stump. "Godslayer!" he shouted. "You show your true form at last!"

Tylar had no words to defend himself, not after what had ripped from his body, not after what now lay dying in the yard.

The guards retreated to the keep, forming a protective shield for those who had fled inside. In the center of the yard, the shadowbeast stalked before Tylar. Eyes afire with lightning watched all, wary.

It's protecting me, Tylar realized. He stared down at the snaking black umbilicus that still trailed from Meeryn's mark to the beast. *I didn't ask for this.*

He waved a hand, trying to sever the connection, to push it away, but his fingers passed harmlessly through the cord.

"Tylar!" a new voice shouted, closer at hand. It was Rogger. The thief had freed himself from his ropes with a loose dagger. He pulled a muddy cloak over his bare shoulders while waving his dagger toward the main gates. "Tether your dog, and let's get our arses out of here!"

Moving on instinct, Tylar gained his legs, hobbled as they were, and stumbled away from the castillion's central keep. He headed toward the open gates. The few defenders still at their posts noted his approach and fled wildly, panicked, abandoning the gate. They had no desire to keep the daemon and its supposed master here.

As Tylar worked across the yard, the shadowbeast kept pace with him, only steps away, tethered in shadow.

One of the gate's defectors loosed a lone arrow at Tylar, but the shadowbeast's wing snapped out and turned the bolt to ash before it could strike.

Tylar hurried his pace, limping and shuffling across the yard.

As he neared the gate, a lithe form fled from the shelter of a doorway. A woman, draped in black, one of the Hands. Rather than running away, she fled toward Tylar and his beast, blocking his path.

"Stand back!" Tylar shouted, fearful of harm coming to the young woman. With her veil missing, Tylar had no difficulty recognizing her. It was the handmaiden who had knelt beside him earlier.

She came to a stop under the very shadow of the daemon. The beast hunched menacingly. Ignoring this threat, she slipped out a small glass jar, dark ruby in the moonlight and glowing with soft effulgence.

Tylar knew what she held.

A sacred repostilary.

She poured the humour from the jar into one hand and held it out toward the beast.

The creature reared up, wings sweeping out.

"Meeryn," she whispered. "It is you, is it not?"

With a shudder, the daemon settled back down, stretching its neck toward the woman, seeming to sniff.

Tylar caught the faint whiff of summer's bloom and bright sunshine. It was the bouquet of Meeryn, distilled within the repostilary.

The daemon dropped, kneeling upon its forelimbs, head bowed.

Delia reached with a hand, bloody and aglow with Grace. As her fingers touched the darkness, light flared out, coursing over the black surface of the beast like fire across an oily sea. The brilliant cascade crested over its body.

Tylar watched in amazement as the beast's form lost focus.

As the scintillating wave finished with the beast, it fed along the only channel left open to it: the snaking umbilicus that led to Tylar.

It spiraled down the tether toward him. He stumbled away, trying to flee the fiery attack. But he could not escape.

The Grace-fed flames leaped the distance and struck him square in the chest. It felt like a mule kick. He flew backward, landing arse down on the dirt.

He rolled immediately to his feet, crouched, ready for another attack.

Delia remained where she was, eyes wide.

The daemon had vanished, vanquished with a touch.

Tylar stared down at his body. He flexed his sword hand. What was crushed under iron was new again. He was healed. Entirely and wholly. As if he'd never been injured.

He fingered the mark on his chest.

Something stirred deep inside, something too large to be held in a cage of bone.

The daemon.

It had not been vanquished, but simply returned to the hale body that was its roost.

Rogger reached them, panting. "I'd say from the looks of you that you're fit enough for a bit of running. Something I think we should be testing 'bout now."

Tylar glanced back across the courtyard. With the shadowbeast gone, the guards would not wait. Already shouts rose from the castillion guard. Tylar turned. Ahead the gate lay open and, for the moment, unguarded.

He pointed. "Off with us then!"

As they ran, the woman followed.

Tylar waved her off. "Begone. This is none of your concern."

"No! Where you go, I go!"

"Why? What madness is this?"

"I don't know how or why," she gasped at him as she ran, "but you carry Meeryn's blood in you. I saw it shining from your lash marks. And in the eyes of the winged creature, the glow of Grace . . . It was Meeryn, too!"

"And you would go with the man accused of her slaying?"

She countered, but less surely, "No man can kill one of the Hundred."

Tylar shook his head and mumbled, "You could've voiced that sentiment earlier."

Rogger laughed as he reached the gate. "That's a woman for you. A fickle lot, the bunch of 'em."

They passed under the empty archway, Rogger leading the way. The moonlit streets of the high city opened ahead. The thief pointed. "I have a few friends in Lower Punt who—"

Before he could finish, a fold of shadow fluttered from the archway to Tylar's left. He caught a flash of silver slashing down toward him. He leaped headlong, reacting with old instincts. He landed in a roll and jumped back to his feet. He twisted around, now crouched in the cobbled streets outside the archway.

Rogger fled to one side, Delia to the other.

From the gate, a figure of flowing shadows stepped into the moonlight, forsaking its hiding place. The Shadowknight held a length of silver in his grip. His blessed sword.

Rogger swore. "It seems we bottled that beastie of yours a natch too soon."

Tylar kept to the brightness under the moon, praying the knight's shadow-borne speed would be dulled in the light. He waved the others back, but kept his eyes focused on the Shadowknight.

"Godslayer," Darjon hissed, stepping forward. "At last the hammer revealed the truth you hid so well. You are no man! But I've seen you bleed—and what bled once can bleed again!"

Before Tylar could answer, the knight leaped with a fury-driven speed, fast even in the moonlight.

Tylar spun from the stroke. The stabbing blade passed under his arm, grazing his side with a slice of fire. He ignored the pain, continued to twist, and brought himself under the knight's guard. He slammed an elbow into the knight's midriff, knocking him back a step.

Darjon used the force of Tylar's blow to fall backward, rolling cleanly in his shadowcloak and back to his feet, sword at the ready.

Tylar knew this was a battle he could not win. Though his bones had been healed, he was still weak from blood loss and fatigued from all that had transpired.

Darjon's eyes narrowed above his masklin. His cloak billowed back to the waiting shadows. The edges of his form blurred as the Grace of shadow flowed into the knight, building toward a power that Tylar could not match.

Rogger noted the same. "Tylar! Here!"

From the corner of his eyes, Tylar spotted the flash of silver. The thief's dagger. Without turning, Tylar lifted a hand and caught the flying knife. He flipped it to his other hand, keeping it low. A dagger was a poor weapon against the blessed weapon of a Shadowknight, but it was better than bare hands.

Tylar attempted to watch every muscle of his combatant, but shadowy Graces blurred lines and edges, fogging detail, making it difficult to anticipate an attack. Tylar had worn such a cloak for many years. It had been a second skin, as much a weapon as the sword.

But every weapon had a weakness.

Shadows built up behind Darjon, filling the archway. Beyond, shouts from the castillion guard grew louder. The stamp of boots hurried along the parapets, approaching fast. Darjon merely had to hold Tylar here for a few moments longer.

But the Shadowknight would not settle for such a victory.

Darjon leaped forward with a surge of shadows that made it hard to tell where darkness ended and form began.

Tylar squinted, aimed, and tossed the dagger with the full strength of his arm. It flew true, but shadows shifted out of the way, too swiftly. The flash of the small blade passed harmlessly over the knight's shoulder and away.

Unchecked, Darjon continued his lunge, sword leading the way, propelled upon a wave of darkness.

A distant *thunk* sounded as the dagger struck wood.

Tylar allowed a grim smile to form as he hurdled straight back, the sword's point scribing his chest.

Then the plunge of the blade simply stopped, jerked to a halt.

Darjon's charge turned into an uncontrolled tumble. He landed hard on the cobbles, tangled in his own cloak, betrayed by the very weapon that served him.

His sword bounced from his fingers and skittered across the stone to Tylar's toes. Bending, but never taking his eyes from the knight, Tylar retrieved the weapon.

Darjon twisted, staring back toward the archway as shadows collapsed around him, dissolving under the weight of moonlight. Impaled into the gate's wooden frame was Tylar's dagger—and pinned beneath the blade was a snatch of cloth, the edge of Darjon's shadowcloak.

Still entangled, Darjon swore and tugged, attempting to free his cloak, but it held securely.

Blessed or not, cloth was cloth.

Horns blared stridently from the castillion walls and were answered from the courtyard.

Tylar backed away, carrying the knight's sword. The diamond-hilted blade was granted to a Shadowknight upon receiving his third stripe of knighthood. It was bonded in blood to the wielder, a cherished emblem of the Order. Darjon would miss it as much as his own right arm. Tylar motioned with his stolen sword toward the empty streets. "The guards come swiftly. We must be away."

Rogger and Delia closed the distance between them, and as a group, they fled the heights of Summer Mount.

❖

Tylar led the way swiftly, slipping along alleys and narrows, heading down from the high city and into the lower. The night stretched ahead of them, but dawn could not be far.

Mourners still crowded the lower streets, ringing bells, lifting tankards of ale. Tylar and the others slid among them, becoming harder to track. Here, any word of daemons and escaped prisoners fell on drunken ears, deafened further by the countless bells.

Even the horns chasing them grew distant, their blaring cries slipping farther and farther behind. Tylar suspected more than one guard was happy to let them escape, unwilling to challenge a godslayer and the daemon he could summon.

As Tylar donned a cloak stolen from an ale-soaked mourner, Rogger spoke in quiet tones. "You should've killed that knight back there. He'll not rest until one of you is dead."

Tylar scowled, picturing the bald fury in the knight's eyes. "Mistaken or not, the man was doing his duty. I will not cut him down in the streets for that."

Rogger shook his head, scratching his beard. "You may live to regret such mercy."

"I'll settle for living until the morning."

As they continued through the lower streets, a sharp cry drew Tylar's attention to a side alley. His step slowed. It was a woman's cry. Two large men clutched a girl between them, their rough intentions clear. She struggled, sobbing.

Tylar knew these assailants. Frowning, he glanced to the sign hanging above the neighboring door—the Wooden Frog.

It was Bargo and Yorga.

Rogger stood at his shoulder. "Why have you stopped?"

"Stay here." Tylar strode into the alley, sword low. It was time someone put an end to this pair's tyranny over the weak.

Yorga held the girl in a thick-armed hug, while his partner fumbled with the ties to his breeches. Bargo was having trouble, too drunk to make his fingers work. But he blearily noted Tylar's approach. "Wait your turn," he slurred thickly. "You can have 'er after we're done."

Tylar recognized the lass, one of the Frog's tavern wenches, no more than sixteen. She met his eyes, terrified.

He moved from the alley's shadow into a slice of moonlight, keeping his sword beside his leg. "Should I be jealous?" he asked, stepping around. "I thought those pinpricks of yours stiffened only for me."

Yorga focused on him. His mouth opened. Without a tongue, he could only gurgle his surprise.

Bargo swung around, half-teetering. He had finally managed to free his waggling manhood, flopping at half-mast. His eyes traveled up and down Tylar's form. "You! The . . . the scabber knight."

Yorga shoved the girl away. She landed on her hands and knees, crawled a few steps, then jumped up and fled in tears.

The two Ai'men bunched together, filling the alley, blocking the exit.

"There's no Shadowknight to protect you now," Bargo grunted.

"No," Tylar agreed and lifted the blade into view. "But I do have his sword."

The brawlers paused, clearly recognizing the black diamond on the hilt.

He leaped at them, moving with a swiftness borne not of shadow, but of fury and retribution. If it weren't for these two, he wouldn't be in his current predicament. None of this would've happened. All he had wanted was a pint of ale to celebrate his birth year.

Bargo tried to swat his sword aside, but Tylar parried and stabbed at the man's flesh. Tylar sliced where it would do the most good, proving there was more than one way to cut a man down.

Bargo yowled, falling to the side.

Tylar spun on a toe and slipped between the two brawlers. Yorga grabbed at him as he passed, but Tylar easily ducked, escaped the pair, and backed to the exit.

Yorga swung around as Bargo continued to moan, sliding down the wall.

Tylar waved his sword in clear warning at the tongueless man. Unless Yorga foolishly pressed, no more blood needed to be shed. As a knight, Tylar had been schooled to use his head as much as his sword.

Yorga was clearly subservient to Bargo, his lack of tongue binding him by need to his partner. And with Bargo's brutality plainly fueled by lust, it required only one keen cut to end this pair's tyranny, altering their relationship forever.

"I've found you a new tongue," Tylar called to Yorga, pointing to the severed manhood lying in the alley's filth. "I don't think Bargo will be needing it any longer."

Bargo clutched his groin, blood welling between his fingers. Yorga stood, dazed.

"You'd best look after your friend," Tylar finished and joined Rogger and Delia in the street. Horns could be heard in the distance. "Let's go."

Rogger glanced a final time down the alley. "Remind me never to get on your sour side."

❖

After another stretch, the trio left the streets and pushed into the black warren that was Punt. It greeted them with its reek, dark laughter, and sudden cries.

"You have friends down here?" Tylar asked Rogger.

"Aye . . . as well as anyone could have friends in Punt."

Delia slunk closer to them. Dressed in her finery, she was as out of place as a diamond in a sow's ear. Throughout their long flight, he had tried to get her to flee, to head back to Summer Mount.

Her answer was always the same: "I have nothing back there. All I cherish is tied to you."

He hadn't pushed too hard. He had a thousand questions he wanted answered, and she seemed to know more than she let on.

But the handmaiden wasn't the only one with secrets.

Tylar watched as Rogger led the way now, heading toward whatever low friends he knew down here. He remembered the thief's shout as his sword hand was pulped under the hammer, repeating words supposedly spoken by himself in ancient Littick.

Agee wan clyy . . . nee wan dred ghawl.

Break the bone . . . and free the dark spirit.

After what happened, the truth of those words could not be denied. There was clearly more to this bearded thief than lice and larceny.

Rogger wended down byways and crawl throughs. Here the walls ran thick with black mold, and the buildings tilted drunkenly. Windows, when not broken, were shuttered tight against the night. The trio had to fight through piles of refuse, chasing rats and dire vermin from underfoot. The air reeked of fetid humours, blood and bile of every ilk.

As they marched, Delia paled even further. With her black-daubed lips and dark hazel eyes, she looked like some risen ghoul, fresh from the grave. Her dress was soiled and clung heavily to her. She had long shed her lace cap, revealing black hair, lanky and loose to her shoulders.

Occasionally some scabber would spy at them from afar, but Tylar kept his sword in plain sight. None could mistake the weapon . . . nor the stripes on his face.

Let them think me a knight if it will hold the worst at bay.

But Tylar suspected there was a clearer reason they passed the narrows unmolested. The underfolk had an uncanny ability to pass information from one mouth to another. The creatures of Punt knew a godslayer walked their streets and stayed away.

Delia spoke at his side, her voice soft and concerned. "Are you hurt?"

Tylar glanced to her as he walked, the confusion plain on his face. Was she asking if there were any repercussions from his torture?

"You're limping," she said, nodding to his gait. "And hunched oddly."

Tylar straightened. Distracted, he hadn't even noticed himself falling into old patterns, moving as if his body were still broken. He continued onward, forcing himself to walk more evenly.

Rogger cocked an eyebrow at him. "Your bones may be healed, but I 'spect it'll take a bit longer for your mind to catch up."

Tylar scowled and waved him onward.

At last, Rogger ducked along a dark alleyway and marched up to a low door made of rusted iron. "Here we are." He knocked.

A small window opened, enough to peer through.

"Show yourself," a dark figure spat at them.

Rogger turned, lifted the edge of his pilfered cloak, and bared his naked arse to the doorman.

Delia covered her mouth at such a rude introduction.

Rogger, still bent over, noted her response. "Have to prove I'm a thief."

Tylar recalled the sigil branded on the man's buttock. A sliding bolt scraped, and the door swung open on oiled hinges.

"What is this place?" Tylar asked.

"Guildhouse of the Black Flag," Rogger answered, straightening and covering himself.

"Black Flaggers?" Delia lowered her hand. "Scuttlers and pirates? These are your *friends?*"

Rogger shrugged. "Now's not the time to be choosy, my dear. We need a way off this island."

Tylar couldn't argue with that.

"Besides, I'm owed a favor here."

"A favor?" Tylar asked.

Rogger waved a hand. "From another life, ser knight . . . one life among many." He glanced significantly at Tylar. "Truly, who lives only one life?"

Tylar motioned with his sword. "Let's get this done."

Rogger climbed down a narrow passage, surprisingly clean. Tiny braziers blazed merrily at corners, scented with thyme and honeythistle to drive away the worst of Punt's odors.

After crossing several side passages, the main chamber opened at the end of the corridor. A pair of men, faces blackened by ash, flanked the entry. They dwarfed Bargo and Yorga, clearly loam-giants, young men blessed in the Grace of loam. They leaned on heavy axes, looking bored, but Tylar knew how swiftly such giants could move.

Rogger nodded to them, good-naturedly. They followed his passage as if he were a scrabbling ant.

The same could not be said for the room's lone occupant. A voice boomed from beyond a desk. "Rogger! I can't believe it!"

A tall figure rose, dressed in a fine cut of black leather, from boots to cap. The man's face was ash blackened, a custom among the Flaggers, making them harder to identify, even among their own guild.

But no one could mistake this pirate. His hair was snowy white from years of salt and sun. The length was knotted and hung over one shoulder, striking against his black leathers.

Rogger pulled on his beard and crossed to shake the man's hand. "Krevan! It is good to see that no shear has come within a lick of you! Before long you'll be tripping over that rat's nest."

"The same could be said of that beard of yours."

They clasped hands.

The sun-crinkled eyes of the pirate traveled past Rogger to Tylar and Delia. "I see you brought the godslayer with you."

Tylar started, his fingers tightening on his sword.

Rogger merely shrugged.

Krevan released the thief's hand with a short laugh. "Then again, you always kept the strangest companions. I remember that blood witch from Nevering who—"

"Please!" Rogger interrupted. "There is a lady present."

"Of course." Krevan broke into a soft smile, gentle and respectful. "My lady, be welcome."

Delia offered the smallest curtsy.

Rogger opened his mouth, but Krevan cut him off with a lifted hand. "Yes, a boat. I know. Arrangements are already underway. The Flaggers know how to repay a debt, even one owed as long as yours. But . . . ?" His smile faded into harder lines.

Rogger nodded. "To cross ships downline, many palms will need pressing."

Krevan sank back to lean on his desk.

"We have this sword to trade," Tylar said, stepping up.

Rogger shook his head at the offer.

Krevan leaned back. "He is amusing. Wherever did you find him?"

Rogger shrugged. "Dungeons."

"Ah, same as the blood witch."

The thief scratched his beard thoughtfully. "You'd be surprised what can be found abandoned with the rats and chains."

Tylar flipped the sword hilt up. "What about this diamond on the pommel? It must be worth a handful of gold marches."

Krevan sighed. "Aye, but you'll need ten times that to press the proper palms."

Tylar's eyes widened.

Rogger explained, "To silence the passage of someone of . . . well, of your *reputation,* does not come cheaply. We'll need to hide your trail in gold." He turned to Delia. "But luckily we brought with us something of considerable worth."

Delia paled and backed up a step.

Tylar put up a protective arm. "I will not trade in flesh."

Rogger raised an eyebrow. "Do I look a slave trader? Remember I'm a thief . . . specializing in certain sacred objects."

Tylar suddenly understood, remembering what Rogger had been caught stealing in Foulsham Dell. "Repostilaries."

Delia gasped, growing even more pale.

Tylar remembered the crystal vial she had used to douse her hand and send the daemon back inside Tylar. A repostilary bearing the blood of Meeryn.

"I cannot give it up," Delia said, clutching the vial hidden in a pocket over her heart. "It holds the last drops of her blood."

"Can you just imagine its worth?" Rogger said to Krevan. "The blood of a dead god?"

The pirate's eyes had grown large, plainly yearning for such a prize. "The price it would fetch among the Gray Traders . . ."

"Enough to book passage safely away?" Rogger asked.

Krevan slowly nodded, unblinking.

Delia still clasped tightly to the pocketed vial.

Sighing, Tylar knew the trade was the only way. "I'm sorry," he whispered to her. "But if we're to ever solve the mystery of what's inside me . . . ever to learn the truth about Meeryn, we'll all have to pay a stiff price." He parted his cloak to reveal the black palm print. "If you would serve your god still, then it must be done."

She closed her eyes and bowed her head. Her fingers reached into her pocket and removed the single repostilary. She held it out to Rogger.

He gently took it and passed it to Krevan, who handled it as if it were the most precious jewel.

"I will arrange everything," the pirate said. He held the vial up to the flame of a wall torch. Fingers gently touched the crystal. Oddly, tears rose in his eyes. His next words were softly spoken but as hard as iron. "If I thought you had really slain Meeryn, Tylar de Noche, you would not be walking out of here."

Krevan rose and crossed to a glass cabinet shelved with books, a few scrolls, and several boxes.

As he hid away the repostilary, Tylar whispered to Rogger, "Can this fellow be trusted?"

The pirate heard him. "I am not the one who broke my vow. I know how to swear an oath." Krevan turned back to the torchlight and used his wrist to rub at the corner of an eye, smearing away the ash.

Three dark stripes were tatooed on his skin, the same as on Tylar's face. Tylar choked on his words. "You . . . you're a knight."

Krevan turned away. "Rogger, take your guests to the east wing. They can rest until the morning tide, when your boat will be leaving."

Rogger waved them back toward the two loam-giants.

Tylar whispered to Rogger. "A fallen knight heads the Black Flaggers?"

Rogger glanced back to the tall figure. "Who said he had *fallen*?"

Tylar cast a sharp look at the thief.

"Not every knight breaks his vow," Rogger said firmly, staring Tylar in the eye. "Some simply walk away."

With his brow pinched in thought, Tylar left the room, bearing more questions than when he entered. He had thought himself wise, but now he felt like a swaddling babe, new to the world.

As the sun rose over the Summering Isles, Tylar stood at the rails of the deepwhaler. The ship had ridden the tide out and now swept toward the deeper seas. At midnight, they were to change ships in the waters off Tempest Sound, then again at Yi River, hoping to shake any hunters from their trail.

A scrape of boot heel sounded behind him. Rogger stepped to the rail. He looked a new man, in the fresh clean clothes of a whaler and his beard neatly trimmed.

He noted Tylar's attention and ran a hand through his clean beard. "That Delia knows a thing or two about brushes and shears. Makes me almost want to lead a better life."

In silence, the pair watched as the ship escaped the morning fog and sailed under open skies. Behind them, the misty isles appeared ghostly, more a dream of land than real.

"What now?" Tylar asked.

Rogger shrugged.

Delia was belowdecks, ill already from the roll of the ship in the swells. She had refused to remain behind, casting her fate along with Tylar, sensing in him a way to still serve her god. Tylar wasn't sure why he had allowed her to come. It was something in her eyes, a pain and longing he could not deny.

Rogger's motivation for accompanying them had been far simpler: "I have nothing better to do." Sentenced as a pilgrim, he had been punished to wander the lands until he had collected all the branded sigils. But now, tied to the story of the godslayer, he figured his best chance of survival was to "walk beside the fellow with the big black daemon." Still, despite his flippancies, Tylar sensed Rogger, like Delia, left much unspoken and unexplained.

Like that snippet in ancient Littick.

Tylar repeated it now, fingering his chest. *"Agee wan clyy nee wan dred ghawl."*

"Break the bone," Rogger whispered to the waves, "and free the *dred ghawl,* the dark spirit. I think that's an apt enough description of the beastie."

"What was it? A daemon? Some naether-spawn? Its attack was similar to the creature that killed Meeryn and her Shadowknights."

"Outward appearances can fool the eye. As you well know, *Godslayer.*" He stressed the last word but offered nothing more.

The silence grew heavy between them.

Sighing, Tylar flexed his sword hand and held it up. "Break the bone," he mumbled, switching to the first part of the phrase, to something easier. "What about that?"

"Aye, it seems I was right back in the dungeon. *Clyy* means *bone,* not merely *body.* The *dred ghawl* appeared only when the bones of your hand were crushed, not while you were whipped to the edge of your life. I find it interesting that Meeryn healed all your bones at the same time she blessed you with the spirit creature. It was as if she had made a cage out of your healthy bones, requiring only one crack, one broken bone, to set it free."

"Leaving me crippled again until it returned," he added sourly.

"There's always a price . . . I seem to recall you saying that to young Delia earlier."

Tylar shook his head. So much remained a mystery. Again silence settled around them. The deepwhaler caught a stiffer breeze, sails swelling. The islands faded behind them, sinking into the horizon.

After a long while, Tylar quietly asked, "Do you think we'll make it?"

"Not a chance," Rogger answered, pulling a pipe from a pocket.

Tylar turned, leaning an elbow on the rail.

Rogger filled his pipe from a pouch of blackleaf. "Don't look so surprised. The Summering Isles will never let you rest. That Shadowknight, Darjon ser Hightower, will hunt you throughout the Nine Lands. And then there are all those other gods out there. Ninety-nine, at last count. They're not going to let the murder of one of their own go uncontested. They'll pool all their Graces into finding you. But even they're not the worst threat."

"What do you mean?"

Rogger paused to light a taper from a lamp on the deck, then set the flame to his pipe, puffing in and out until he had a good fire to the leaf.

"What could be worse than vengeful gods?" Tylar asked.

Rogger perked one brow. "Whoever really slew Meeryn, of course. The true godslayer. He'll need you dead lest you prove your innocence. And whoever could kill a god . . . ?" He shrugged and chewed on his pipe, leaving the obvious unsaid.

He could surely hunt a lone man.

"So what do you plan to do?" Rogger finally asked, eyeing him.

Tylar rubbed his brow. "The only thing I can, I guess."

"What's that?"

"Follow the one clue left to me. Meeryn's final word."

Rogger glanced to him. *"Rivenscryr?"*

He nodded. "Meeryn healed me, gave me a daemon to protect me. All to deliver one word, a riddle I must solve if I ever hope to prove my innocence."

"So where are we headed first?"

"To a place where I'm even less welcome than those cursed islands." Tylar turned his back on the Summering Isles and stared far to the north, half a world away. "To Tashijan . . . the Citadel of the Shadowknights."

SECOND

TANGLED KNOT

god-realm, god-relm, *n.* [old Littick ⸜ᴐᴄ˥ᴐˢᴅᴄ⌐L, kingland] a region, domain, or land settled by one of the hundred Myrillian gods; a section of territory into which the unique Graces of a God are imbued and blessed; *as the humours of a body course through a god, so they do its land.*

—Annals of Physique Primer, ann. 2593

6

FIERY CROSS

SHE HAD NEVER THOUGHT TO HEAR HIS NAME AGAIN.

Kathryn ser Vail stood near the mooring docks that topped the highest tower of Tashijan. Though it was midmorning, the light remained a twilight gloaming. Black clouds stacked to the horizons on all sides, whipping and rolling in from the seas to the south.

Tylar . . .

As she waited, cold winds flapped her cloak and tugged at the masklin pinned across her face. As a Shadowknight, she had to keep her face hidden from the laborers here. Her breath blew white into the frigid, thin air. Ice frosted the parapet stones and made the mooring ropes crack as they were run across the stones by line handlers and dockmen.

Clutching her arms around her, she fought to trap the fleeting warmth carried up with her from the bowels of Tashijan. The mooring tower of the Citadel thrust fifty floors into the sky, a thin spire built three millennia ago under the guidance of Warden Bellsephere. Aptly named Stormwatch, it took the humours of a hundred gods to build this one tower.

"There she is!" her companion shouted into the teeth of the wind.

Gerrod Rothkild was encased in bronze from head to toe, oblivious of the wind. He was squat of form, typical for a hillman from Bitter Heap. But unlike his barbarous, uneducated countrymen, he was of sharp intellect and even sharper wit. Under his helmet, he bore the tattoos of fifteen disciplines, all masterfields. "That tub'd better have a skilled pilot to strike the docks in this gale."

Kathryn watched the salt-scarred flippercraft lower out of the sea of clouds overhead. It was a wooden whale, blunt at both ends but flaring into a wide keel at the stern. At the prow, a thick window of blessed glass

stared down at the mooring docks. Shadowy movement could be seen behind the glass: the ship's frantic landing crew.

On the port and starboard sides, the score of balancing paddles battled
the winds, some turning, others stationary, some extending out from the
ship, others retracting. It took an experienced pilot, one ripe with air, to
finesse the craft.

"He's burning blood," Gerrod commented.

Kathryn saw he was right. From the top of the flippercraft gouts of
smoke choked into the skies from the exhaust flue, furthering the craft's
image of a flying whale. "Why does he hazard the storm? Why waste humour on such a risky landing?"

"His need must be urgent," Gerrod answered gruffly. "And such urgency seldom heralds fair tidings."

Kathryn suspected the same. Could the news be anything but foul, especially as of late? The sudden death of Ser Henri, the warden of Tashijan, had left a hole in the Order. And like a drain plug pulled from a tub,
the warden's vacancy had created a maelstrom of opposing factions seeking to fill it, whirling and churning the once calm waters.

And now worse tidings still: the slaying of a god. An impossible death.
And tied to such a tragedy, a name from her past, a name that both stirred
her and quickened a pain long since buried.

Tylar . . .

She shuddered and concentrated on the skies, pulling her cloak tighter
about her shoulders.

Overhead, the ship foundered in the crosswinds that swept around the
tower. Its bulk rocked and teetered, lowering toward the waiting mooring
cradle, paddles flapping frantically. The stern planks glowed from the over-
worked aeroskimmers. Kathryn could imagine the mekanism's brass pipes
and mica-glass tubes shining as bright as the sun, channeling and pumping raw humour through its belly, an alchemy of blood from one of the air
gods. She watched the tortuous twist of inky smoke from the stern flue.

"It's madness," she whispered.

Steel fingers touched her hand. "There must be a reason—" Suddenly
those same fingers clamped on her wrist and tugged. "Down!"

Overhead, the ship dropped like a stone. It heeled over on one side,
paddles sweeping toward the tower top. The line handlers and dockmen
dove and scattered.

Kathryn and Gerrod flattened to the ground.

The flippercraft righted with a scream of wind and crack of wood as one paddle struck a parapet and shattered into splinters. The ship tilted nose first, plunging for a sure crash into the granite mooring cradle.

Then miraculously it bucked up at the last moment, and the ship's keel slammed roughly but securely into the cradle. The jarring impact popped a few rib planks and a tracery of fractures skittered across the glass eye of the wooden whale.

Immediately the mooring crews were back on their legs, yelling into the winds, tossing ropes and tethers about the grounded flippercraft. A few cheers of appreciation rose from the workers.

Kathryn rolled back to her feet smoothly and quickly, sharing no such appreciation. "Nothing is worth such a risk of vessel and folk."

The rear hatch of the flippercraft winched open. A single figure leaped out before the hatch even thudded against the stone. He was a swirl of darkness, a shred of shadow cast into the wind.

"I believe that would be young Perryl," Gerrod said at Kathryn's side.

Perryl hurried toward them. His eyes were sparks of fury, his manner full of wildness. He reached them as the first mooring line was secure—and didn't stop.

He offered only one word as he passed: "Below."

Caught in his wake, Kathryn's rebuke for his reckless haste died in her throat. She and Gerrod Rothkild followed at his heels. Perryl strode to the tower door and fought the storm winds to open the way. He calmed enough to wave them through first.

Kathryn ducked past the threshold to the stairs beyond. As Gerrod followed, a spat of hail burst out of the sky, pelting stone and wood with balls of ice the size of goose eggs. Yells and shouts echoed. Perryl caught a blow to his cheek, ripping his masklin loose.

He slammed the door and turned to them. His face was deathly pale. "Tylar's escaped . . . fled . . ."

The silence that followed was punctuated by a barrage of hail against the wooden door, sounding like the strikes of a hundred mailed fists.

Kathryn attempted to digest this information. She unpinned her masklin and shook back her cloak's hood. She had failed to braid her hair into its usual fiery tail and finger-combed it away from her pale face. Never a beauty, she was still considered fair of feature, though nowadays a certain hard edge frosted her blue eyes. She stared stolidly at Perryl, demanding elaboration.

"A raven reached the flippercraft while I was en route," Perryl continued. His eyes would not meet Kathryn's, and his tongue stammered.

"Against my orders, the fools attempted to execute Tylar, but he somehow called forth a daemon. Several guards were killed as he fled."

"A daemon?" Kathryn asked.

"That is all I know. But the message was sealed with the mark of the Order. Darjon ser Hightower. The only Shadowknight to survive the slaughter." Perryl finally met Kathryn's eyes. "I didn't know there were any of Meeryn's Shadowknights still alive after the attack upon her. Our brother leads a force in pursuit. Word suggests the Black Flaggers abetted Tylar's escape to the sea."

Kathryn turned. "Pirates and daemons . . ." As she stood on the steps, time slipped backward. She had watched the man she once loved hauled in chains onto a slave barge, headed across the Deep, a knight no longer, face bared to all, an oath breaker and a murderer. Tylar's eyes had searched for her on the river docks, but she had remained hidden in the shadows of an alley, ashamed that her own words had doomed him. But she could not lie to the court, not even if soothmancers hadn't been present. He had to know this. Then he was dragged onto the barge, gone from sight—but not from her heart, never her heart.

"I thought him innocent," Perryl said from the top of the stairs.

Kathryn started down the stairs. *As did I once . . . long ago . . .* She cleared her throat. "Castellan Mirra must be informed of all that transpired. She awaits your attendance." They began the long hike down to the main keep of Tashijan. Ser Henri's old castellan had assumed the duty of governing the Citadel until this evening's winnowing, when a new warden would be chosen by a casting of ballot stones.

Gerrod Rothkild kept pace with her down the stairs. His voice was soft, meant for only her ears. "Save judgment for now. Not all is as plain as it first appears, little Kat."

"Then again, some is," Kathryn answered. She had to bite back a sharper retort. She knew Gerrod sought only to comfort her. But even Gerrod, with all his mastered disciplines, could not fathom the emotion that welled through her with Perryl's damning testimony.

It was not despair that filled her—only relief.

Though ashamed, she could not deny it. Tylar was clearly guilty, a godslayer of one of the Blessed Hundred. *If he could kill a god now, then oath breaking and murder were not beyond him in the past.*

Tears rose. Tylar had to be guilty. Her past words had banished him, broken him. Over these past years, the only way she had survived her betrayal was to place all her faith in the justice of the Order and the Grace of her cloak.

Tylar *had* to be guilty.

Still, she remembered the touch of his hand on her cheek, the brush of lips on her throat, the whispered words in the dark, dreams and hopes for a future . . . together. A hand found her belly, rested a moment, then fell away, cold. There was one last betrayal even Tylar had never learned.

By all the Graces, he *had* to be guilty.

❖

Castellan Mirra's private hermitage lay in the north wing, overlooking the Old Garden and shaded by the twisted branches of the lone wyrmwood, a tree as old as Tashijan itself.

Kathryn found herself staring out the window, watching a tiny tick squirrel hopping from limb to limb among the dark, sodden leaves, searching for any nut yet unfallen. But already the spring buds hung from stems, heavy yet still folded. All the nuts had long since fallen. Still, Kathryn appreciated the creature's dogged determination.

Especially in the rain.

The storm that had swept Perryl here had broken into a steady downpour, falling like a veil across the view.

Off to the side, Perryl continued relating the events and tragedies that had befallen the Summering Isles. Gerrod Rothkild had already left to gather the Council of Masters.

Two steps away, the castellan sat with her back to the window by the room's hearth, wrapped in an old furred cloak edged in ragged ermine. Her feet rested almost in the hearth's flames. Some said she was as old as the wyrmwood tree outside her window. But the passing of winters had not dulled her sharp intellect. She stared into the flames, nodding. Occasionally one finger would rise from her armrest with a rare question, asked in a firm, unwavering voice.

The crooked finger lifted again. "Boy, tell me about this Darjon ser Hightower, the one who sent the raven messenger."

Perryl, clearly irked by the condescending manner of Mirra, glanced to Kathryn, drawing her attention.

Kathryn's frown deepened, warning him to simply answer her question. One did not cross Castellan Mirra, especially when she was in such a harsh mood. She had almost refused to see them. The death of Ser Henri had struck the old castellan hard. She had retreated to her hermitage, leaving Tashijan to rule itself until the night's ballot stones were cast and a new warden was chosen.

Perryl continued. "Ser Hightower is well respected, Your Graced. He was second in command at the Summer Mount."

"Yet he wasn't at Meeryn's side when she was murdered."

"No. Duty had called him to another isle on that dreadful night."

Mirra nodded, studying the dance of flames in the hearth. "And now he seeks vengeance."

"He leads a contingent of castillion guards aboard a fleet of corsairs. They scour the southern seas for Tylar's track. They believe he's escaped into the Deep."

Kathryn spoke softly. "If he's reached the open ocean, then there is no telling where he might head. All the Nine Lands will be open to hide him."

"But he will be welcome among none of them," Perryl said. "Word has spread among the Hundred. All the god-realms know of his crime."

"He could always flee to one of the hinterlands," Kathryn contended. "He could hide forever in one of those godless lands."

"Perhaps," Mirra said. "But even within the hinterlands, there are gods."

"Mere rogues," Kathryn answered. "Vile creatures, maddened and raving."

Mirra stared into the hearth. "Such were our own Hundred . . . before they settled the various realms so many millennia ago."

Kathryn cocked an eyebrow. *What is the castellan implying? There seems some hidden meaning hinted here.*

Silence settled around the room.

"Tylar must be found," the old castellan finally stated, as if she had decided something to herself.

"He will be," Perryl said. "Already Ser Hightower is closing a net over the southern seas."

"A net that will surely drown our godslayer," Mirra said. "That must not happen. He must be protected."

"Why?" Perryl asked, as surprised as Kathryn.

"Tylar is not guilty," Mirra said with rasping authority.

Kathryn stepped closer, unable to hide her shock. "I don't understand. He fled his accusers, he called forth a daemon . . . pirates shield him. Are these the actions of an innocent man?"

Mirra shifted in her seat. Her eyes locked on Kathryn's. "They are the actions of a man accustomed to betrayal and false accusations."

Kathryn went cold inside. "What are you saying?"

Mirra settled back to her chair. It was a long time before she spoke, and when she did her tongue was slow with regret. "There are words I fear to share . . . but I see no other course. I am too old for this burden alone. It broke Ser Henri, and he was stronger than I."

Kathryn crossed gazes with Perryl, but neither spoke, allowing Mirra the space to reveal what troubled her.

The old castellan fixed each of them with her sharp gaze, weighing their resolve. Her eyes settled on Kathryn, softening slightly. "Do you still love him?"

"Who?"

"Your former betrothed."

Kathryn's brows pinched. "Tylar . . . I . . . no, of course not. That was buried long ago."

Mirra turned away and whispered to the flames, "What's buried is not always lost . . ." She stared into the fire for several breaths before speaking again. "What I tell you next is no kindness. In many ways, it is a cruelty that shames me, and worse still, shames the memory of Ser Henri."

"Nothing can make me think ill of Ser Henri," Kathryn said. In many ways, the old warden had been the father she never knew. She had been born to and abandoned by a sell-wench on the streets of Kirkalvan.

Mirra seemed deaf to her. "Shame no longer matters. Time runs too short for pride. I tell you these words now on the eve of the winnowing, on the last day I will wear the emblem of the castellan." Mirra fingered the diamond seal pinned under her chin. "By midnight, a new warden will be chosen and, as you well know, the outcome is almost certain."

Though Perryl looked confused, Kathryn understood. As of the past two days, the faction supporting Argent ser Fields had become firmly entrenched in the lead, pinning down a majority through old ties, pacts, and bonds. He was a fit leader and a strong spokesman, having served on many and varied boards. Even Kathryn had chosen to cast her ballot stone in his direction.

"What does any of this have to do with Tylar?"

Mirra's eyes took on a faraway glaze that was both tired and angry. "Half a decade ago, your betrothed had been a minor piece in a larger game, tossed aside after he was no longer of use. And while Tylar was not entirely blameless for his actions, neither was he guilty of the bloody crimes for which he was accused. He set in motion—blindly though it might have been—a series of events that almost brought down Ser Henri. To preserve the Order of Tashijan, to protect it from darker forces, Tylar had to be sacrificed."

Kathryn's legs went weak with her words. As thunder echoed through the castle walls, she found herself leaning on a table for support. "Then the murder of the cobbler's family . . . ?"

Mirra shook her head. "Their blood does not stain his hands."

Kathryn felt the room's walls close in. Darkness oiled the corners of her vision. *Innocent . . he was innocent . . .*

Mirra sighed. "Now, I don't understand Tylar's role in this new gambit. Was it mere chance, a twist of fate, or are there darker currents at play? In any case, it proves even a broken pawn can arise again and shake the board, rattle the play of the game."

Kathryn shook her head, trying to clear her mind. "What game are you talking about?" Anger flared, hardening her tone. "Tell me!"

Mirra remained unmoved, a stone against Kathryn's fury. "Even I don't know all the plots and contrivances. I doubt even Ser Henri knew, and he was the wisest of us all. But he believed the struggle waged behind the walls of Tashijan was only an echo of a larger war brewing outside."

"Then start here first," Kathryn said.

"For the past decade, Ser Henri has fought to weed out a secretive faction within the Order. A faction that calls itself the Fiery Cross."

Kathryn glanced to Perryl, then back to Mirra. Rumors of such a group had been bantered about for as long as Kathryn could remember: secret rites performed in the dead of night, hidden passages and chambers built into the walls, rogue members of the Order practicing the Dark Graces. But it was considered more myth than reality.

Mirra nodded. "They exist and have grown stronger and more open. Their goal: to turn the Order into more than servants to the gods and arbiters of peace. They seek to mold the Shadowknights into a warrior force, mercenaries for hire, assassins for those with enough coin."

"But that goes against all our oaths," Perryl said sternly.

"Oaths can be changed," Mirra answered simply and added cryptically, "as they have been in the distant past."

Kathryn found her legs and moved to the hearth's edge, needing the warmth. "And Tylar became embroiled in this struggle?"

"He was caught between the Order and the Cross, blind to the forces around him, and crushed. The murder of the cobbler's family was laid at his feet, and in order to prove his innocence, Ser Henri would have had to expose agents loyal to him who had infiltrated the Cross, risking even more deaths. So Tylar was sentenced to banishment and slavery. All Ser Henri could do was beseech the overseer of the trial to keep your betrothed from the gallows, sparing his death."

Kathryn laid a palm on her belly. *Not all had been so generously spared . . .* She lowered her hand, swallowing down the rage that burned through her. "Then *who* murdered the cobbler family?"

Mirra's voice dropped to a whisper. "The same person who murdered Ser Henri."

Perryl fell back. "It cannot be . . ."

Ser Henri's death was the cause of much speculation and rumor. His body had been found on the tower stair, his face locked in pain and horror, each finger burned and blackened to the knuckle. But murder? Ser Henri dabbled in alchemies, often dealing with volatile mixtures. An experiment gone awry was the Council of Masters' judgment on the death, though they still left the inquiry open.

Kathryn bit back her shock, fingers clenching. "Is what you say true?"

The castellan continued her vigil upon the flames. Tears shone in her eyes. "The murder cannot be proven, but I know the truth nonetheless."

"Who was behind it?" she asked.

Mirra pulled her ermine cloak tighter around her thin form. "It was the head of the Fiery Cross . . . either upon his order or by his own hand. I'm sure of it."

"And does this monster have a name?"

Again the barely perceptible nod. "Ser Henri had his suspicions, nothing that could be proven."

Kathryn refused to accept defeat so easily. "Who was it?"

The old castellan's next words were frail with despair. "The next warden of Tashijan . . . Argent ser Fields."

❖

Kathryn shared her evening dinner with Gerrod Rothkild. It was a somber meal of diced boar in potatoes and turnips, whetted with a poor vintage red wine. They partook their meal in Gerrod's quarters in the master's wing of Tashijan.

He kept his room as orderly as his own mind: a small hearth aglow with coals, plain and heavy woolen drapes over slit windows, and simple furnishings of greenwood and hammered copper. The only adornments were fanciful iron braziers in shapes of woodland creatures—eagle, skreewyrm, wolfkit, and tyger—at each corner of the room, cardinal points of a compass. Even these had their practical uses, simmering now with sweet myrrh to scent the air, though more often they burned rare alchemies to focus the mind and thoughts.

"And that was all Castellan Mirra could tell you?" Gerrod asked.

There was no need to answer. It was the fourth time that question had been asked. But Kathryn nodded anyway.

Gerrod stabbed a fork into a chunk of meat. As usual, he wore his bronze armor, shedding only his helmet, indicating a level of comfort and familiarity with his dining companion. Though no older than Kathryn, he was as bald as his helmet, his scalp tattooed with symbols of his fifteen masterfields. His skin was pale to the point of translucency, even his lips. Only his eyes remained a rich brown, a match to his bronze armor.

The soft *whir* of his armor's mekanicals was loud in the silence as he brought the forkful to his lips. The armor sustained his frail form. After showing promise as a boy, he had been ripened with alchemies of air and fire to ready his mind for his studies, but he had been pushed too far. Mastering fifteen disciplines had cost him the strength of bone and muscle, leaving him dependent on the armor to move his limbs.

"I can't bring this to the Council of Masters," Gerrod said. "Not without proof. Especially with accusations involving Argent ser Fields." This last was said with a sad shake of his head. "It seems unbelievable, unfathomable."

"Castellan Mirra seemed certain of her claim."

Gerrod's brow furrowed into pale lines. "And the old castellan definitely is not a person prone to fits of fancy."

"As it was, she was loath to inform us of even this. She wished to consult with those still loyal to Ser Henri before explaining more. I think she told Perryl and me only because of our ties to . . . to Tylar. She is convinced he is of some importance to the struggles here and abroad. Whether he is a willing player or not, she was not sure."

Gerrod sighed, wheezing like his armor. "And you've taken me into your counsel, spreading the word. Do you think this is wise? I did not know Tylar."

Kathryn reached forward to touch his bronze hand. "If I can't trust you, then who within the walls of Tashijan can I trust?"

His metal glove cleaved open like a clam, exposing the skeletal fingers within. She did not flinch from touching them. A small smile formed on his lips. Like all Masters of Discipline, he had forsworn women, but that did not keep him from loving. Kathryn knew his feelings for her and hers for him.

Five years ago, after Tylar's trial and banishment, something had broken inside Kathryn. She had retreated for a year into the monastic levels of Tashijan, to the underground lair of the masters with its libraries, illuminariums, and alchemy laboratories. There, she lost herself in study and meditation, burying herself under the keep as surely as in a grave.

And she would still be there if it hadn't been for Gerrod. Newly arrived to Tashijan and blind to her past, his eyes had not looked upon her with accusation for her damning testimony against Tylar, nor did they glance away with sad sympathy for her loss.

Gerrod simply saw her.

Over the next months, he drew her out with his wit and plain wisdoms. *You're too much a flower to hide from the sun . . . leave such places to mold and mushrooms.* He helped build back her strength, find her center once again. It was holding this same hand that she left the subterranean levels of the masters and returned to the Order of the Shadowknights above, where she resumed her place as a knight. Though they could never be together, they were forever more than friends.

And it was enough for both of them.

A knock at the door interrupted. Kathryn stood as Gerrod's armor snapped back over his fingers. "Who is it?" Gerrod called out.

"It's Perryl, Master Rothkild!"

Kathryn hurried to the door as Gerrod climbed to his feet with a whirring protest from his mekanicals. He snapped his hinged helmet back over his head.

She opened the door, and Perryl hurried in. Like most knights, he had shed his shadowcloak while within the main keep and wore plain black breeches, boots, and a gray shirt, buttoned formally. He had oiled and combed his straw hair straight back as was custom for a Ninthlander. Free of his knight's wear, Kathryn was shocked by his boyish appearance. It was easy to forget how young he was, so new to the cloak.

"The count is almost finished," he said in a rush of breath. "They expect to announce the new warden in the next quarter ring."

"So soon?" Kathryn asked. It was still well from midnight, the expected time for such a pronouncement. All ballot stones had been cast with the ringing of the eighth bell. It should have taken until the middle of the night for all the stones to have been tallied.

"That's why I hurried here. Word is that the vote was so overwhelming that the outcome was plain from the first spill of the stones."

Kathryn wore a worried expression. There had been five main candidates for the seat of Tashijan, each represented by a different colored stone: red, green, blue, yellow, and white. During the secret ballot, Kathryn had chosen none of them, selecting instead a black stone, a vote against all the candidates.

"What stone leads?" Gerrod asked, though there could be only one answer.

"White," Perryl confirmed. "Ser Fields's color. Word whispering from the council hall is that the other colors were but a few daubs against a sea of white. No count will be necessary to declare the victor."

"Then it's over," Kathryn whispered. She faced the others. "We should bring the news to Castellan Mirra. See what she has to say."

As a group, they vacated Gerrod's rooms and climbed out of the Masterlevels buried under the central keep of Tashijan. The floors above, the Citadel as it was called, were the domain of the Order of the Shadowknight. The Citadel and the Masterlevel composed the two halves of Tashijan, one aboveground, the other below. And the loftier the level in the Citadel, the more esteemed the residents. A castellan was second only to the warden. That meant a climb of twenty-two flights to reach Castellan Mirra's hermitage.

They climbed in silence, lost to their own thoughts and worries. But they were not alone. Young squires and pages sprinted up and down the central staircase as it wound through the heart of the keep, voices sharp with excitement. A few knights marched the same steps, mostly heading down toward the Grand Court. Word of the early pronouncement had spread quickly.

Kathryn nodded to her brothers and sisters as they passed.

"Have you heard?" one called to her. "Argent's color rides high. Looks like ol' One Eye will be leading us from here!"

Kathryn attempted a smile, but it felt crooked on her face. Then the other knight was gone, vanishing around a turn of the stairs.

They climbed the rest of the way up to the proper level and crossed down the resident halls of those who ruled Tashijan. By morning, there would be new occupants in all of these rooms as Argent ser Fields picked those who would work beside him. A new warden meant an entire upheaval for those in power. Kathryn glanced to the doorway that led to Ser Henri's private rooms, the Warden's Eyrie, as it was called. Soon it, too, would have a new resident, an eagle replaced by a blood vulture.

Perryl reached Castellan Mirra's door first and knocked. The sound was unnaturally loud in the stone hallway. They waited for a response, but there was none.

"Perhaps she's already heard," Gerrod said. "As castellan, she'll have to make an appearance at the Grand Court when the pronouncement is made."

"Or perhaps she's asleep," Perryl added. "Her hearing is not as keen these last years."

"Try again," Kathryn urged.

Gerrod shifted past Perryl and knocked an armored fist on the door. Though he didn't pound hard, the strike of bronze on wood startled Kathryn with its clangor. Even the stone deaf could not fail to hear his hail.

A small, frightened voice finally sounded from beyond the door. "Who is it?"

Kathryn recognized the shaky tone. It was the scrap of a girl that served as maid to Castellan Mirra. She tried to remember her name and failed. "Child . . . it is Kathryn ser Vail."

There was a long pause. "Castellan Mirra . . . she's not in residence."

Kathryn frowned at her two companions. Perhaps Gerrod was right . . . she'd gone already to the Grand Court.

The maid spoke again. "She's been gone the long day, since the mid-day break."

Kathryn's lips hardened further, her eyes sparking toward the others. Surely the old castellan would return to her rooms to freshen herself before appearing before the court. The maid's name snapped into her mind. "Penni, did she say when she would be back?"

"No, ser. I can't say. I left to fetch some fresh water and hard coal, but when I returned the mistress had already left. I don't know when to expect her back."

Kathryn did not trust such strange tidings. Not on this day. "Penni, please let us in. I would rather not discuss this out in the hall."

Another long pause stretched.

"Penni . . ." Kathryn's tone grew more firm.

"I'm not supposed to allow anyone in when the mistress is away."

"It's important. You know we were speaking with Castellan Mirra only this morning. You know your mistress's trust in me."

"Still, I . . . I dare not disobey. The mistress does not like her word to be ignored."

Kathryn sighed. She couldn't argue with that. Few disobeyed the old castellan. Her tongue could sting sharper than a whip's tip.

Perryl stepped closer. "Let me try," he whispered, then turned to the door. "Penni, it's Perryl. I'm with Ser Vail and Master Rothkild. You need not fear. On my word and honor, I will assert your honest and firm guardianship of her rooms. But it is of utmost importance that we attempt to find some clue to your mistress's whereabouts."

Kathryn glanced to Gerrod and rolled her eyes. Since when had Perryl developed such a sweet tongue? When last they were here, Kathryn had noticed how the maid had glanced from under heavy eyelashes at Perryl before being dismissed. He did strike a strong, willowy figure. Who said a knight's strength lay only in his cloak?

The door swung slowly open. A small face framed in brown curls tucked under a lace cap peeked out at them. The cheeks reddened as her eyes glanced over them, settled on Perryl, then swept away again.

"Thank you, Penni," Perryl said with a half bow. "You have done your mistress no disservice."

She returned his bow and waved them inside.

The hermitage was uncomfortably warm after the unheated halls. The thick drapes had been drawn over the balcony windows, shuttering out the storm and making the room seem smaller. Tiny lamps dotted the room, wicked low to conserve the oil until the castellan's return.

The wool rug muffled their footsteps. Nothing seemed out of the ordinary. The room simply awaited the return of its master.

"Your mistress left no message, no note?" Perryl pressed the maid, whose head remained bowed, hands clasped together at her bosom.

"No, ser."

Gerrod had crossed to the room's center and searched slowly, standing in one place. Only his eyes could be seen through his bronzed armor. "The castellan's cane is still in its stand," he noted aloud.

Kathryn glanced in the direction he indicated. A tall ebony walking stick, swirled in silver filigree, rested in a brass stand. Castellan Mirra's legs were not as stout as once they were. She required either a supportive arm or a cane.

The maid stepped forward again, bowing slightly as she spoke. "That is her fancy stick, Master Rothkild. Her regular one is gone from the wardrobe." She pointed an arm, not looking up.

Kathryn nodded. Castellan Mirra was not one given to show. She usually hobbled on a greenwood stick knobbed in bronze. Kathryn waved a hand, turning away. "That one is used only for ceremonial occasions."

"Like the passing of wardenship to a new hand," Perryl said. "Would she not have taken it to the Naming Ceremony?"

Gerrod mumbled inside his helmet, "Unless it was her way to insult the proceedings. A jibe against those who would succeed her."

Kathryn crossed to the hearth, ruddy with coals. Mirra was supposed to have met with those loyal to Ser Henri and herself, those who had set themselves against the Fiery Cross. Had she met with them? Had they all decided to flee?

Kathryn felt an ache behind her eyes. She was not used to thinking in terms of such intrigues and machinations. She turned from the hearth, her eyes settling on the chair where Mirra had sat earlier. The ermine-edged cloak still lay over its back. Like Mirra herself, it was old, ragged at the edges, but still retained a certain beauty.

She crossed to finger the cloak. As it shifted, an edge unfolded, revealing a blackened and singed corner. She pulled the cloak up and brought the edge up into the light. "Look at this."

Penni cried out. "Oh, dear! The corner must have been too near the hearth when I freshened the coals! Mistress Mirra will be furious with me!"

As Perryl attempted to calm the maid, Gerrod stepped to Kathryn's side. His voice was a whisper. "There are ways of telling what sort of fire burned the robe. I can take it to one of the alchemists for study." He stepped around, blocking the view of Perryl and the maid.

Kathryn slipped a dagger from her belt and cleanly cut away the burned swath. She passed it to Gerrod. It vanished into a compartment in his armor, one of many hiding places on his bronzed form.

Before anything else could be made of the matter, a loud ringing echoed up from below. Slow and ponderous. It was the Shield Gong of the Grand Court, calling all knights and masters of Tashijan to gather.

"The Council of Masters is done with their tallies," Gerrod said. "It seems a new warden has been chosen."

Perryl crossed to them. "What now?"

"We join the court," Kathryn said. "As we must."

"And Castellan Mirra?" Perryl eyed the empty chair.

Gerrod answered, ever practical, "If she's still within these walls, she'll have to respond to the summons."

That is, if she's still alive, Kathryn added silently.

Bodies pressed and jostled outside the western entrance to the Grand Court. An air of celebration rang through the crowd of knights, squires, and pages. After the gloom and uncertainty that pervaded the halls since the death of Ser Henri, the choosing of a new warden promised a return to order and the beginning of a new era for Tashijan.

Following the ceremony, ale would flow from the top of Stormwatch down to the subterranean bowels of the masters' dens. Already, servants and maids festooned the passages with flower petals; incense burners smoked cheerily. But before the revelry could begin, there was one last observance to attend.

The Naming Ceremony.

Kathryn worked through the crowd toward the packed entrance. The banter and excited talk had faded to the steady drone of an overturned beehive. The doorway was framed in black onyx stone, surmounted by a massive crystal of dark quartz, representing the black diamond that marked the hilt of every Shadowknight's sword.

She passed under the arch with Perryl in tow.

Once through, the way opened as the crowds dispersed to the gallery seats. The excited chatter in the outer hallways faded, both from reverence for the chamber and simply because the voices were lost in the vast spaces overhead.

In ancient times, the Grand Court was a natural amphitheater worn into the stone cliffs that towered over the Straits of Parting. It was said that human kings once held court here, before the coming of the gods. As such, the revered place was chosen for the site of Tashijan, hallowed ground where mind and might became one, the Shadowknights embodying the purity of muscle and reflex, the Council of Masters epitomizing all the learned studies and meditations. Over and around this ancient amphitheater, the Citadel of Tashijan had been constructed. The natural granite hollow had been carved into tiered benches with balustrades and stairs leading from one level to another.

Kathryn crossed to the stone railing that circled this level. She stared down toward the floor far below. An arc of eight seats, hewed from the granite itself, stood before a deep central pit, the Hearthstone. Flames licked upward out of this stone well, smoking with alchemies and lighting the seats in a ruddy glow. Various leaders of the Order and Discipline already sat in their seats, leaning toward one another in whispered conversations.

"She's not here," Perryl said.

Kathryn's fingers tightened on the balustrade. Ser Henri's old seat, the tallest, stood vacant, as did the one to its right, the castellan's chair.

"What now?"

Kathryn imagined much of the whispering below centered on that empty chair. She searched the lower levels of the court, the tiers reserved for the masters. It did not take long to spot Gerrod down there. His bronze armor stood out among the robes. He was gazing up at Kathryn. He shook his head.

Around the nearer tiers, the various knights, pages, and squires took their seats. As in Tashijan itself, the upper levels were their domain.

"We should get as close as possible," Perryl said. "Watch for any sign of the castellan."

Kathryn nodded and led the way down into the thick of her fellow knights. She found two seats just above the masters' tiers. She hurried to them.

Following their passage, Gerrod climbed upward and traded spaces to occupy a seat directly beneath them. He stood, his head at their toes. "I've listened upon the masters and knights. No one knows what keeps Castellan Mirra away. But they've agreed they can wait no longer."

Kathryn glanced behind. Most of the crowd had shuffled in and seats were packed up to the edge of the domed roof. A majority of knights, like Kathryn herself, wore their shadowcloaks, casting vast swaths of darkness over the tiers.

Gerrod continued. "There is no law requiring the castellan to be present at the ceremonies. Most seem settled that she has taken ill. They plan on proceeding as soon as—"

His words were cut off as the deafening reverberation of the Shield Gong echoed off the roof and across the open space, silencing all in a breath. Its voice also traveled along a series of echo tunnels behind the gong, to be heard throughout all of Tashijan, above and below.

"So it begins," Gerrod mumbled as he took his seat.

Kathryn sat straighter, tense.

The head of the Council of Masters stood from his seat to the left of Ser Henri's old chair. Master Hesharian was as wide as he was wise, his girth swelling the brown robe of his standing. Firelight shone upon his bald pate, tattooed like Gerrod's own. He bore eleven disciplines, second only to Gerrod in number.

His voice boomed across the hall, carried upon the natural acoustics of the amphitheater and accentuated by the Graces smoking from the Hearthstone pit. "We are gathered here where ancient kings once stood to carry on the traditions of Tashijan, to raise high one of our own to lead us."

Murmurs of excitement met his words.

"We stand upon the cusp between the old and the new, the past and the future. As throughout time, stones have been cast and counted." He nodded to the circle of seats on the lowest level, the Council of Masters, who had tallied the ballots. "And a new warden will rise this night!"

Clapping met his words. Calls for a name were raised as was tradition and spread throughout the galleries. Master Hesharian simply stood, bathed in the cheering and chanting. Finally he raised an arm, and the swell died down.

"A name you ask for! A name you will hear!" He raised his other arm high. "Stand and greet your new warden."

As one, the crowd gained their feet. Kathryn did so reluctantly.

Master Hesharian searched the tiers, though clearly he had to know where the victor sat. He pointed an arm. "There stands the one cast in stone by your own hands! *Warden Argent ser Fields!*"

Cheers erupted before the announcement was past Hesharian's lips. Argent's name was shouted and chanted. And a few among the crowd, those already into their cups, called out, *"One Eye! One Eye! One Eye . . ."*

Flogged by the pounding enthusiasm of his brethren, Argent ser Fields climbed down out of the knights' tiers and past the masters' levels to finally reach the floor, greeted by hand and a kiss upon each cheek by Master Hesharian. He was led to the center chair. He acknowledged the warm reception humbly and with a generous smile.

Argent ser Fields was two decades older than Kathryn, but he could pass for her younger brother. His deep auburn hair, worn long to the shoulder, bore not a hint of gray. And age had done nothing to his strength or skill. For as long as Kathryn had been at Tashijan, he had not been bested at swords or daggers. But that was only half the man. His face was hard, but more often than not, softened by good humor. He was known to be generous with his well wishes, yet justly firm in rebuke when affronted. As such, he had earned the respect of all, master and knight alike.

The only blemish to his striking figure was the patch worn over his left eye, a small plate of bone taken from the skull of a raving hinter-king, the same fiend who had blinded him during tortures meant to loosen the knight's tongue. The flaming poker had taken the sight from his eye, but it never weakened his will. Freeing himself, he eventually slew the king and opened the way for victory during the Bramblebrier Campaign.

Kathryn stared at him, wondering if this same hero could truly be the head of the Fiery Cross, Ser Henri's murderer. She began to wonder if Castellan Mirra was mistaken. Just this morning, Kathryn herself had been planning to cast a white stone in his favor.

Argent ser Fields raised a hand to quiet the crowd, but they were slow to respond. He kept his arm raised, patient, still smiling. Finally the crowd broke to his will, and quiet spread over the hall.

Argent stood straighter, lowering his arm. His smile faded to a more serious and austere countenance. "I accept this mantle with a heavy heart. For it is tragedy that brought me to stand before you, opened this seat that I must take. But take it I will!"

Clapping met his words, but he waved for silence.

"Troubled times face Tashijan, the Nine Lands, and all of Myrillia.

Strange and dire tidings rise both from our neighbors and from afar. Rumors of skirmishes and raids along the fringes of the hinterlands. A surge in the practice of Dark Graces. And now one of the Hundred slain in the south."

Argent shook his head. "We stand at a moment in history like no other. And Tashijan must be the beacon that rallies all. We must be at our strongest, at our most united. We will be the light to lead the way! The flame in the darkness!"

More clapping and cheers met his words. It was what they all wanted to hear, an end of the uncertainty, a firm path to follow.

Still, for Kathryn, those same words trailed an icy path through her: *a light to lead the way . . . the flame in the darkness.* The imagery was too strong to be mere chance. Were they hints of his ties to the Fiery Cross?

She noted Gerrod glancing back at her. The same worries had not escaped him.

Argent continued, booming over the clapping, "Tashijan will be a new beacon to the future! We cannot, *will* not fail!"

The crowd stamped boots and pulled swords. Argent's name was shouted to the roof. He settled back to the seat, hands on the granite armrests. He waited for the crowd to tire itself.

Gerrod twisted toward her. She leaned in closer. "He has won them surely," Gerrod said. "Both heart and mind. Even if what Castellan Mirra stated is true, there may be nothing we can do about it. It may be too late."

Kathryn refused to accept that. She stared down at the man sitting in Ser Henri's seat. Around her, the crowd slowly settled.

Argent remained seated, but he spoke again. "It seems there is an order of duty required of all new wardens. The naming of a new castellan to serve on my right side."

There was a stirring of surprise through the Council of Masters. Such an important decision was usually made a few days after the Naming Ceremony.

Argent stood again. "We dare not delay. As the chair to my right is currently unoccupied, we should fill it this night, so we can be united from this day forward."

Kathryn fought a sneer, struggling for a dispassionate expression. She searched the ring of masters. It was tradition for one of the Council to be picked. She wondered which had plied Argent enough to gain this coveted seat. Even Master Hesharian stirred his bulk uneasily. Though he already occupied the seat to Argent's left, the right held more power.

Argent stared at the empty castellan's seat for a long moment. "As we face a new time, it is time for a bold move on this first day of my service to Tashijan. We must not be blinded and ruled by the past and its conventions."

He turned from the chair and faced the Council of Masters and its many hopeful faces. "If we are to be a beacon in the dark days ahead, let us look to a new path to the future." His eyes drifted upward, past the ring of masters.

Kathryn tensed. What new treachery was afoot?

Argent's eyes settled, turning her blood to ice. "I name my right hand this night. Rise and join me, my new castellan—*Kathryn ser Vail*!"

A hushed shock spread through the gallery. Kathryn felt herself falling back into her seat, but Perryl's hand clutched her elbow, holding her steady.

"I don't understand," he whispered as tentative clapping arose and grew firmer. Her name was called out . . . then again and again.

She glanced down at Gerrod. His armored face was unreadable, but his eyes were bright with shock and worry.

She stared back toward the floor. Argent fixed her with a steely, one-eyed stare. There was no enmity there, only open invitation. He lifted his arm and beckoned.

"You must go," Perryl urged at her shoulder.

Around her, others added the same encouragement, but more exuberantly. Kathryn found herself half-carried down the aisle to the stairs. Perryl followed, sheltering her as best he could. But once they reached the steps, she was on her own.

On numb legs, she mounted the stairs and began the long descent toward the floor. Her welcome among the master's level was polite, but not nearly as enthusiastic. The castellan position was always filled by one of their members. She felt like some thief slipping through them.

But for the moment, they were the least of her concern. She reached the central floor. She had stood here only twice before: first when she had been granted her cloak and sword, then when she had given testimony against Tylar.

This final memory gave her pause. Did any of this have to do with Tylar, with her connection to him?

Before she could ponder it further, Argent crossed and grasped her hand in his. He leaned in close as if to kiss her, but he merely whispered, "Welcome, Kathryn . . . or should I say, *Castellan Vail.* It seems we have much to discuss."

He led her to the seat that neighbored his, still holding her hand. Once in position, he raised their joined arms to the roar of the gathering. She searched for her friends—Perryl and Gerrod. They were lost in the masses. She was alone.

Finally, he allowed her arm to drop, giving her hand a final squeeze. She felt something hard between their palms, something he held. It was left in her grip as his hand slipped from hers.

She stared down at it. It was a balloting stone. A *black* balloting stone.

Kathryn knew it was the same one she had cast earlier. But in the firelight, she noticed it had been defaced. Upon its dark surface was etched a perfect circle, bisected by two perpendicular lines, all painted a flaming crimson.

The symbol of the Fiery Cross.

7

FATHOM

"WE'RE BEING HUNTED."

"Have you spotted sails?" Tylar asked as he hurried after Rogger up the ladder to the open deck. It was the fourth ship they'd ridden since leaving the Summering Isle—from a deepwhaler, to a sea barge, to a limping frigate—only one step ahead of their pursuers. They'd been three days aboard the *Grim Wash,* a wavecrasher out of Tempest Sound.

"Not a ship," Rogger answered as he shoved through the hatch out to the stern castle of the ship.

"What do you mean?" Tylar asked, climbing after him.

Rogger didn't answer as he led the way to the starboard rail. Tylar craned around. The wavecrasher's crew scrambled in the rigging, working sail lines. The black-skinned captain of the *Grim Wash* stood by the great wheel, flanked by a pair of steersmen at the lesser wheels. All their faces were etched in stern lines.

"Haul your arses, ya blooding bastards!" the chief mate screamed across the middeck, rousing the sailors to a quicker pace.

"What's happening?" Tylar asked.

"See for yourself." Rogger pointed an arm out toward the empty seas behind the ship.

Tylar shaded his eyes against the achingly blue sky. Clouds scudded in vague smudges. Sunlight glared off the rolling seas. The waters of the Meerashe Deep lay empty. "I don't understand what—"

Then he saw it. Words died as horror iced through him.

A wide wake surged toward them, a V-shaped churn of white water, cutting through the blue swells like a sword through a sow's belly. It was still a full reach away, but it was rapidly closing the distance. A massive pale form hummocked up momentarily, breaching between the arms of the wake, corpse bright against the blue seas. Its surface flailed with fleshy appendages and tentacles. Then it was gone again, rolling below, leaving only the wake of its passage as it flowed below the surface.

"A miiodon," Tylar gasped out at the impossibility.

"Jelly shark," Rogger agreed, using the more common name.

"But they don't hunt these cold waters." From all Tylar had been taught, miiodons lived only in the equatorial seas, below even the Summering Isles. "What's one doing all the way up here?"

"Maybe you'd best jump in and ask 'im," Rogger said, tugging at his beard.

Tylar felt the deck buck slightly as the wavecrasher's speed increased. New sails snapped into the steady breeze. He watched the crew's frantic efforts, their eyes tight with fear. Their only hope lay in outrunning the beast. The *Grim Wash* was not outfitted with the Chilldaldrii ice harpoons necessary to defend against such an attack. The beast would tear the ship apart, snatching free what bits of flesh it could glean with its poisoned tentacles.

"She's diving deep!" a cry called from the crow's nest atop the center mast.

"Below!" shouted Captain Grayl, a black-skinned Eighthlander whose shipping-guild tattoos were bright crimson on the nape of his bulging neck. The crew obeyed their captain without hesitation, sliding down ropes and leaping to the deck. Hatches crashed open as the evacuation commenced.

The captain waved off his two steersmen. "I'll man the wheel. Try to keep her in the wind as long as possible."

Rogger tugged Tylar toward the open hatch, but Tylar shook free of the old thief's grip and marched toward Captain Grayl.

"What are you doing?" Rogger asked, heeling after Tylar.

The captain noted them. "Get below!" he shouted.

"You'll need someone to guard your back," Tylar said, sliding free the sword he had stolen from Darjon ser Hightower.

Grayl eyed the sword, then grunted. "It's your hide."

Rogger stepped to Tylar's other side and nodded to the sword. "That'll do you little good against a jelly shark. But what about that smoky beastie of yours? Mayhap it could defend the boat."

Tylar had already guessed that this was the reason Rogger had called him out on deck. He fingered the loose shirt that covered the black palm print centered on his chest. He sensed the savage beast lurking behind the stain. Since their escape, he had not dared attempt to call forth the black daemon . . . the *dred ghawl.*

Still he balked. On every level of his being, he feared what dwelled inside him. He remembered the crush of his fist under the torturer's hammer, the pain as his body broke apart, crippling once again. But that was not the worst. He also sensed the bloodlust, savagery, and raw hostility in the daemon, along with a foreignness to this world that felt deeply *wrong*, an affront to the very existence of wind and stone, blood and flesh. And while connected by the dark umbilicus that tied palm print to beast, Tylar had felt himself drawn into that wrongness.

He was loath to feel it again . . . even if it meant his own death.

Past the ship's stern, the waters remained empty. Tylar was not deluded enough to believe the miiodon had fled. It had simply dived deep, tight on the trail of its quarry, preparing to launch its dramatic attack.

At the great wheel, the captain grumbled, "I'd give my left stone right now for an ice harpoon."

Rogger shook his head. "You'd have a hard time making that deal. One stone doesn't sell as well as it used to. You'd probably have to give them a matched pair."

"Aye, I'd if I still had the other," the captain bantered grimly, one eye on the seas behind them, one on the sail. "My first wife still has it in a glass jar on her mantel."

"That's why I always stick to sell-wenches," Rogger said. "While they may lighten one's pocket, they take little else." The thief kept his stare fixed on Tylar, awaiting his decision.

Tylar took a deep breath. It wasn't only *his* life in danger. Belowdecks hid an entire ship's crew, with families in ports scattered across the Nine Lands.

"How . . . ?" Tylar had to clear his throat. "How do I loose the daemon? I don't have a hammer handy."

Rogger kept his voice low. "I wager it takes only a single broken bone to unlock the cage that holds the beast. Like a snapped finger. It'll break free on its own from there."

Tylar watched the seas. *Break free on its own . . .*

"Here it comes!" the captain shouted.

Beyond the ship's stern, a flurry of bubbles preceded the miiodon, boiling up from below as if a deep-sea volcano had opened on the ocean floor. Then it appeared, shooting straight out of the depths.

The miiodon's roiling tentacles had fused, narrowing its form to a sleek arrow almost half the size of the *Grim Wash* itself. As its bulk cleared the waters, the mass of tentacles unbraided from its streamlined form and billowed out around it. Tylar had witnessed fire-sky displays exploding above nighttime festivals. This was the same—only instead of fire and lights erupting, here exploded a horror of flesh and poison.

A plume of water showered the deck as the creature sailed over the stern masts. A trailing tentacle, its *footpad,* struck the mast's sailcloth. Poison burned through, allowing it to reach the mast's wooden pole. It latched on and used this toehold to bring its bulk crashing into the middecks.

The sudden weight drove the boat deep into the waves. Seawater sloshed across all decks. Screams rose from below, echoing up through the planks. The center mast cracked with a thunderclap and went toppling sideways, a tangle of sailcloth and ropes.

Tylar fought to hold himself upright by gripping one of the lesser wheels. The captain hugged the central great wheel and kept the ship from swamping completely. It was a skilled effort. The *Grim Wash* bobbed back up, lolling back and forth.

But the boat could not escape its new passenger.

The miiodon lay spilled across the middle of the ship, filling the space between the stern and forecastle. It was a forest of snaking tentacles around a central mound of pale, watery flesh. A pair of black globular eyes, as large as pumpkins, gazed from deep within the translucent mass, protectively buried in the center.

Tylar felt those eyes gazing toward the trio of men. Tentacles wormed in their direction. Easy meat.

"Below!" Grayl bellowed. He waved them toward the hatch in the stern castle.

As they retreated, Rogger tossed an oil lantern at the nearest tentacle. Fire splashed across its skin.

The captain shoved the thief toward the hatch. "Fool, you'll burn my ship to the waterline before you even warm its hide. Ice is all that can harm a jelly shark."

Rogger glanced at Tylar, his meaning clear. Act now, or see the ship sunk.

Tylar stopped a few paces from the door. "Get the captain below," he whispered through clenched teeth.

Rogger nodded and hurried to the hatch with Grayl.

Tylar turned his back on the pair.

Tentacles squirmed over the stern deck's rail and roiled toward him. He smelled the bitter tang of their poison in the salty air. Channels of oily yellow venom flowed beneath translucent skin. A mere touch would melt flesh to the bone, creating a liquid feast for the tinier, sucking tendrils that fringed each tentacle.

"Skags," he swore and sheathed his sword. He needed both hands free.

"What is the fool doing?" the captain grumbled by the hatch.

"What must be done!" Rogger answered. "Now give the boy a bit of privacy."

Tylar heard a scuffle and assumed Rogger was forcing the stubborn captain away. It was not his concern. As a questing tentacle snaked toward him, Tylar grabbed the smallest finger of his left hand. If this didn't work, at least he'd have his right hand, his sword hand, to fend off the miiodon's attentions. He bent his small finger backward to the point of pain. Just one fast snap, he told himself.

"Stop!"

The sudden shout almost did the job for him, but he released his strained finger and swung around. "What in all the gods' names are you doing up here?" Tylar barked.

Delia strained to push past Rogger, but the thief had a grip on her upper arm. Here was the source of the scuffling. The captain stood behind the pair, clearly bewildered by his strange passengers.

"Let me go, you damnable oaf!" Delia yelled, finally shaking free. Her cheeks were fetchingly rosy against her snowy skin, but now was not the moment to notice such things.

Tylar danced closer to his companions as a persistent tentacle scented his blood. Delia hurried to his side with Rogger in tow. The captain kept guard at the hatch.

"When you all didn't come below," Delia said in a rush, "I knew what you were going to do."

"We have no other weapon against the jelly shark." Tylar glanced past his shoulder to the captain, careful of his words.

Only now did the young handmaiden seem to notice the *Grim Wash*'s new passenger. Her eyes widened and the rosy color fled her cheeks.

The miiodon, now settled and secure in its middeck roost, began its assault in earnest. Muscular tentacles ripped planks loose with loud pops. A foredeck hatch was torn free and flung through the air. It struck a flap of sail and tumbled into the sea. Closer, the roil of tentacles that had been sniffing over the rail of the stern deck now surged toward the gathering before the doorway.

"Get your arses down below!" the captain ordered. "I must seal this hatch."

Rogger simply kicked the door closed in the captain's face. "Then bolt the damn thing already!"

Delia reached a hand to Tylar's elbow. "If you free the *dred ghawl*, there's no way to bottle it back up. We don't have any of Meeryn's blood."

Tylar knew this. They had traded the repostilary bearing the last of it to book passage and cover their escape. But what choice did they have now? He'd simply have to find another way to get rid of the daemon . . . or live with it. And *living* was the key point of it all.

"I have no other course," he answered and grabbed his small finger again.

Delia kicked him in the shin. Unfortunately it wasn't hard enough to shatter bone, but it did get his attention. "Miiodons fear icy water!"

"So we've been told," Rogger said, urgency entering his voice as they were forced away from the hatch by the approach of snaking tentacles.

Tylar paused enough to listen. That was the strange part of this attack. Jelly sharks liked warm equatorial waters, not the cold of the Meerashe Deep. "What are you getting on about?"

Before Delia could answer, the sound of a hatch crashing open drew all their attention across the ship. Upon the foredeck, a lone sailor appeared with a raised sword. His eyes were wild, his gait wobbling. Drunk. It seemed some sought courage in a bottle, but found only stupidity.

He crossed to the rail that overlooked the miiodon. He cursed and shook his sword.

"Get back, man!" Tylar yelled.

The drunken sailor took his warning as encouragement and sliced at a tentacle that wandered too near. He cleaved clean through it, but he was rewarded with a spray of blood and venom to his face.

A scream tore from him as his flesh boiled and smoked. He fell to his knees, blinded. He clawed at his face in agony.

Delia cried out and turned away.

She needn't have hidden her face. The miiodon surged toward the man, sensing the blood. Appendages crested over the foredeck rail and fell upon the sailor, covering him completely. In a heartbeat, poison silenced his cries.

"At least his death bought us some deck space," Rogger said, ever practical.

With the jelly shark distracted by its meal, only a single tentacle still probed their deck.

Tylar drew them all to the rear rail.

"Maybe now's the time to let loose that shadowy beast of yours," Rogger persisted.

"No," Delia said, rising from her shock. A hand darted into her robe, searching a pocket. "There's another way." But her voice had dropped in timbre, her confidence in whatever drew her up here clearly waning.

Tylar touched her shoulder and spoke softly. "What is it?"

Delia's eyes were watery with fright, but she finally freed a crystal jar from a pocket. She held it out to Tylar.

It was an empty repostilary, like the one that had borne Meeryn's blood. But it was not blood Delia wanted.

"We need your water."

Tylar gaped at her. "What?"

"You want the man's piss?" Rogger echoed his confusion.

Delia shoved the glass bottle toward Tylar. "Trust me! Please!"

Confused, he accepted the repostilary and glanced to Rogger.

The thief merely shrugged. "My mama taught me never to refuse a lady."

Shaking his head and biting back a curse, Tylar swung away. He loosened the strings to his trousers and freed himself. He held the glass jar. Never in all his trials as a Shadowknight had he even been in such a dire predicament. If the jelly shark didn't kill him, humiliation would.

He stared down at himself, at the priceless crystal repostilary. He hated to foul such a vessel with his own water, but like a good and noble knight, he kept his aim true. The repostilary was soon filled.

Before he could even tuck himself back into his trousers, Delia was there. She grabbed the crystal vessel and lifted it to the light. Her lips parted in relief. Lowering her arm, she held the repostilary out toward him again. "Blood."

"What?"

"Just a drop . . . quickly."

Tylar was beyond asking. The miiodon's tentacles were showing a renewed interest in their party. He simply did as she told him and nicked the tip of his left thumb on his sword. He held forth the bleeding wound.

Delia kept a warding hand over the repostilary. Her eyes met his. "Think of ice. Water so cold it freezes with its mere touch."

He nodded as she uncovered the jar.

"Concentrate hard!" she ordered.

He did, picturing in his mind's eye a font of frigid water. He knew cold. He had once traveled to Ice Eyrie in winter, to hunt down a nasty band of bloodrunners. He had spent eight days on the frozen tundra. He remembered the frost that rimed his cloak, the ache of wind across his bare skin. Then he had stepped wrong, broken through a crust of ice, and fallen headlong into a blue tarn. He allowed the memory of that icy dunk-ing to wash through him.

A drop of blood fell into the repostilary.

Delia replaced the stopper, shook the vessel, then held it out. "Throw it." She pointed to the middeck. "Toward the bulk of the creature."

Tylar took the glass vessel. He was shocked to find the crystal had gone ice cold in his hand.

"Throw it!"

He arched, bringing his arm back, then flung the repostilary through the air. It sailed in a perfect arc and shattered against the broken mast stub, spraying the contents over the undulating flank of the jelly shark.

The miiodon reared up. Convulsing waves coursed outward across its skin from the site of the splash, darkening along the way. Tentacles con-tracted back toward their wellspring, curling in on themselves, leaving behind trails of sizzling poison like so much snail slime. The tang of venom choked the air.

"Seems the beastie don't much like your piss," Rogger said. "Not that I can blame it, having shared a cell with you."

"It isn't Tylar's water the beast shuns," Delia said, awe tracing her words. "It's the Grace held within."

The jelly shark writhed upon the middeck, rocking the ship with its mass. The dark stain upon its flesh continued to spread, as if the beast were being cooked from the inside.

"What's happening?" Rogger asked.

Delia watched, her eyes studious. "A miiodon's digestive venom is kept from consuming its own flesh by the beast's body heat. That's why the Chilldaldrii ice harpoons can fend off the creatures. A wound from an ice spear activates the jelly shark's own poison around the point of contact, causing the venom to eat the beast's flesh. The pain drives the creature back into the sea where it eventually heals."

Tylar watched the darkened sections of the miiodon begin to melt and slough. If Delia was right, the miiodon wasn't *cooking* from the inside out. It was *eating* itself from the inside out.

Finally, the jelly shark's thickest tentacle, ending in a footpad, lashed out to the starboard rail. It grabbed hold and heaved its bulk over the side, seeking to escape the agony. The miiodon crashed gracelessly into the sea and sank away.

"Will it survive?" Rogger asked, leaning over the rail and watching the bubbling fade to empty seas.

"Doubtful," Delia answered. "That was no mere harpoon that struck the beast, but the full Grace of a god's blessing."

Tylar remembered Delia saying something similar a moment before. "What are you talking about?"

She faced him. "You cast a blessing upon the beast, a charm of icy waters."

"A charm from his piss?" Rogger interrupted.

She nodded. "And blood."

Tylar remained very still. He was no Hand, trained in the art of Graces, but having been a Shadowknight he was not ignorant of how a god's bodily humours functioned. Only the flows from a god could bless or charm.

"What are you saying?" he whispered hotly. "That my fluids have the same potency as a god's?"

"Not any god's," Delia answered. "Meeryn's."

"Impossible," Rogger muttered.

Delia kept her focus on Tylar. "I saw it the day you were whipped in the yard. I recognized the glow of Graces in your blood. When Meeryn died, she not only gifted you with the *dred ghawl.* She somehow granted you her power as a god. It flows through *all* your humours, not just your blood."

It seemed impossible, but Tylar had only to stare at the empty decks as proof. He remembered the icy touch of the repostilary in his hand. Could it be?

First a shadowy daemon, now the very Graces of a god . . .

Before anyone could question further, the crash of a hatch drew their attention around. Captain Grayl appeared, followed by a cadre of sailors, all armed with swords.

The boulder of a man gaped at the empty decks. "By all the gods, it's true! The jelly shark . . . it's gone!"

"Back into the sea," Rogger said.

"How . . . why . . . ?"

Rogger shrugged. "Mustn't have liked the taste of your fine ship. Too salty, I'd guess." The thief leaned toward Tylar and Delia, and whispered through his beard. "Perhaps we should continue this *other* discussion below."

Tylar risked a slow nod.

The captain's attention had focused elsewhere. His ship had been saved, but it was far from unharmed. The center mast was gone, and what was left of the middeck still steamed with poison. It would take some time to get her seaworthy again.

"You and you!" the captain yelled. "Get new planks from the bilge deck! You! Hoist up buckets of scrub salts! Where the naether is my first mate?"

Behind the captain's back, Rogger motioned to the open hatch.

As a group, they retreated to the doorway leading to the lower decks. Tylar had his own questions.

But was he ready for the answers?

❖

In a short time, the trio gathered in the cabin shared by Tylar and Rogger. It was no more than a cupboard with stacked beds against one wall and a single wardrobe. There was no window, only a lone lamp burning blubber from a leechseal. The smoky flame cast little light but plenty of stench.

Rogger sat on the bed, rubbing his bare feet, while Delia stood by the closed door, stiffly, as if unsure she should be in such close quarters with two men.

Tylar paced in front of the wardrobe.

Rogger spoke, picking at a blackened toenail. "So the boy here is crammed full up the arse with godly Graces."

"I'm certain," Delia said.

Rogger nodded. "Then I'm beginning to fathom how Tylar's able to hold a daemon inside him . . . with that much Grace running through him."

"There certainly might be a connection," Delia agreed. "I hadn't considered that."

Tylar was less interested in such ponderings, but he kept silent.

Rogger scratched his beard. "Let's start at the beginning. Meeryn was one of the water gods, right?"

Delia nodded. All the gods had varied talents and abilities, but all basically were categorized as one of four aspects: air, water, loam, and fire.

Rogger raised one eyebrow. "And you just *guessed* that Tylar had the ability to freeze the jelly shark. That he could pass on an ice charm with his piss and—"

Delia cut him off. "We prefer the phrase *yellow bile.*"

"Yes, and shite is *black* bile. Pretty words for what can be found in a chamber pot. But tell me how you knew Tylar could perform such miraculous acts."

"As I said, I suspected from the Grace glowing in his blood."

"And so you just took a gamble with the jelly shark, hoping his piss was blessed with Grace, too."

A bit of color flushed Delia's cheeks. "Not so large a gamble as you might suppose. Who do you think has been emptying the chamber pots from your cabin?"

Rogger blinked a moment, glancing to the bedside, then laughed. "By all the gods, Delia, you little secret alchemist! You already *knew* Tylar's humours were rich in Grace."

"I didn't want to say anything," she mumbled. "Not until I was sure."

Tylar studied his body as if it were a stranger. He spoke, turning his face to Delia. "You were a Hand to a god. Tell me what I can expect." Her eyes grew sympathetic. "I can tell you only what I know of gods. A mortal man has never borne such power. You have good reason for caution."

"Tell me of the gods, then."

She nodded. "Each god holds eight humours. Blood is the key to all, but you must learn how each of the others serves. You've seen how your water could pass on a Grace, but it lasts only a short time. It would take . . . well . . ." She motioned to her waist.

"His seed," Rogger filled in.

She nodded. "It would take such a humour to *permanently* pass on a Grace to a living person or animal."

"While my sweat could do the same to an object, something inanimate," Tylar said. "Like blessing a Shadowknight's cloak." He knew that such sacred garb was anointed in the sweat of gods from all four aspects. It was this charmed blessing that granted the cloth the ability to shift shadows.

"Exactly," Delia said. "All the remaining humours are what we call qualifiers, refiners of a charm." She touched the corner of her eye. "*Tears* hold the ability to enhance a blessing or charm already laid." She touched her mouth. "While *saliva* contains the ability to weaken the same. But such an effect's duration depends on the quantity applied."

"That still leaves two others," Rogger said, ticking off with his fingers.

She nodded. "*Sputum,* or phlegm, is more complicated, used more in the field of alchemy. Such a humour can combine the Graces from various aspects, such as a fusion of fire and water. The combinations are myriad and would require a skilled alchemist to explain in more detail. I don't fully—"

"Yes, whatever," Rogger said. "And we all know what the last does. Black bile. We ran into a pair of bloodnullers in the dungeons."

Tylar held back a shudder, remembering their fetid touch. Black bile, the soft solids of a god, wiped all blessings away, turning the charmed back into the ordinary.

"Yes," Delia said. "Bloodnullers are smeared in the bile of all *four* aspects, fused with an alchemy of sputum. That is why they can wipe all blessings away."

Tylar shook his head. "But I was cleansed by nullers in the dungeons of Summer Mount. Why wasn't I stripped then, made normal?"

"Because you are not just superficially charmed or blessed. You *are* Grace. Like a god. It forms continuously in your humours."

Tylar felt sickened by this thought.

"What about his blood, then?" Rogger continued. "You said it was the key to all."

Delia glanced away. Tylar noted the tears moistening her eyes. She had been the blood servant to Meeryn. It had been her honor . . . and now it was her loss.

They waited in silence.

"Blood," she began softly, "is indeed the key to all. It is tied to the will of the god. They are one and the same. It takes blood and concentration to bend the general properties of an aspect, like water, into a specific charm."

"Such as the charm of *ice*," Tylar said. He remembered her request earlier to focus his mind on cold water as he dripped his blood into the repostilary.

"Yes, even such a simple charm requires blood to make it so. It is the key to granting all blessings."

Thoughtful silence fell among the party, until Rogger added his own bit of wisdom. "Well, in the jelly shark's case, it was more a *curse* than a blessing."

The ship suddenly lurched under them and canted to the port side. Delia fell against the door with a small cry. Tylar grabbed the edge of the wardrobe. Overhead, booted feet pounded across the deck, accompanied by muffled shouts of alarm.

"Seems we're not out of bad luck yet," Rogger commented calmly, still seated on the bed.

"What's happening?" Delia regained her balance, though the floor remained tilted. "Has the miiodon returned?"

"Let's pray not." Tylar joined her at the door and forced it open. He stumbled out, followed by Delia and reluctantly by a barefooted Rogger. They climbed the stairs to the stern hatch.

Tylar was the first out. The smoky confines of the lower decks brightened to the fresh breezes of the open sea. The air smelled almost sweet.

But Tylar's attention focused on the chaos atop the deck. The crew ran ropes and climbed rigging. Orders were shouted along with brittle curses. The frenzied activity bordered on panic.

A few steps away, Captain Grayl stood at his post by the great wheel, flanked by his two steersmen. All three men clutched their wheels, leaning their full weight to turn them farther.

"Another four degrees, damn you!" Grayl bellowed.

The *Grim Wash* listed to the port side. Clearly the crew fought to turn the ship, attempting to angle her sharply against the prevailing wind. But with the central mast and mainsail gone, it was a futile struggle.

Tylar crossed to the captain's side. "What's wrong?"

The captain's face had purpled with the strain. "Tangleweed dead ahead! Have to avoid it, or we'll be bogged down and trapped!"

Tylar shaded his eyes—and saw the danger immediately. Filling the ocean beyond the ship lay a mat of thick green vegetation. A smattering of stalky white flowers bobbed in the wind and current. He now understood the source of the sweetness to the air. Tangleweed was the curse of the Meerashe sailor. Such patches floated with the currents and tides. They were unpredictable and could snare careless ships, snagging them up and holding them for days until they could be chopped free . . . if they could be chopped free. Many ships met their end within the embrace of tangleweed.

Rogger spoke beside Tylar, his voice dry in his throat. "That's no ordinary scrap of weed."

Tylar glanced to the thief.

"That's Tangle Reef."

The captain heard Rogger and spat on the deck. "Turn this damn ship, you bastards! Now!"

"Are you sure?" Tylar asked.

Rogger bared his arm with the branded sigils. He pointed to one of the scars.

"Fyla," Delia said, naming the symbol for the god of this watery realm.

Rogger lowered his arm. "I've already been here."

Tylar shook his head at their cursed misfortune. At sea, they had hoped to avoid all the god-realms of the Nine Lands, to never touch soil. Now they had stumbled upon the one realm that had no *land.*

Fyla was a solitary and reclusive god. Even her own handmaidens and handmen were born here—which, considering the unusual nature of her realm, was not surprising. She and her citizens lived beneath the sea in a city formed from tangleweed. They were hunters, fishermen, and sea farmers. Their realm, like the weed in which they made their home, roamed throughout the seas of Myrillia.

Rogger said, "While I consider bad luck my constant companion in life, I must say that running into Tangle Reef right now is beyond pure chance."

Delia nodded. "The gods are on the move. They know of Meeryn's death and have joined the pursuit. Tangle Reef must've been sent to hunt you down."

Tylar sensed his doom, a stony weight sinking deep into his chest.

Rogger continued. "We now know who sent the jelly shark after us."

Tylar stared over to the carpet of undulating weed. The ship, tilted in a frozen turn, continued its plowing course toward the tangling trap, driven by relentless winds and current. The miiodon had been used to cripple them, herd them into the waiting tendrils of the tangleweed. Such was not beyond Fyla. The ocean was her domain, the creatures at her command.

Rogger sighed. "And if she uses a jelly shark like a sheeper's mutt, there's no telling what else might be waiting for us."

8

CHRISMFERRY

DART SCRUBBED THE STONE FLOOR WITH A HORSEHAIR-BRISTLED BRUSH. Her knuckles were raw, both from the rough surfaces and the stinging lye soap. Her simple shift of rough-spun wool clung to her damply. Sweat rolled from the tip of her nose.

Laurelle fared no better, in the same shapeless dress, hair in a drab bonnet. Using both hands, she scrubbed her brush across the stone floor of the Graced Cache. Though little more than a drudgery maid, she seemed content in her new role.

They were handmaidens-in-waiting.

This was their duty. To perform chores, lowly though they may seem, that not even the highest nobles of Chrismferry would be allowed to observe. Like now, scrubbing the floor of the Graced Cache, a vault that contained and preserved all of Chrism's repostilaries.

"In this manner," their matron had extolled, "you'll know your place here. While you were raised high by the touch of an Oracle, chosen from many, here in the Lord's castillion you are mere servants. You must never forget your place."

And so, on their knees, they learned this first lesson.

Pupp was their only company here, sniffing about the floor, his molten body aglow in the dim chamber. He kept near Dart's side, perhaps wary of the power and wealth in this room. While Chrismferry was a rich city, grown fatted over the four millennia since its founding, its true wealth lay here.

Here was the heart of the city.

Dart sat back on her heels and wiped the sweat from her nose with the back of her hand. She stared across the vast vault.

The Graced Cache was located deep underground, where the quarried stones of Chrism's castillion became natural limed stone. Its ceiling hung unusually low. Even Dart had to keep her head bowed from the roof.

"The better to know your place," Matron Shashyl had instructed. "To honor what is stored here with bended back."

Still, despite the low ceiling, the Cache did not feel confining. Its space covered an area larger than the central courtyard of her old school. Most kept their voices whispered because of the chamber's unnerving habit to echo and amplify. It was as if there were a ghost haunting the room, mocking their words.

The Cache reminded Dart of a wine cellar. While there was a certain dankness to the air, a pleasant sweetness lay beneath it, like the spirits distilled from aged wine casks—though no barrels had ever been rolled into this vault.

All around, rows of ebony weirwood shelves marched to the four walls of the subterranean chamber. Resting upon the shelves, small crystal repostilaries glittered in the torchlight, like a thousand stars in the night. The Cache was divided into eight areas, each representing one of the eight blessed humours of the god they served, a god neither Dart nor Laurelle had yet set eyes upon.

"What are you thinking about?" Laurelle asked, shifting closer to her. The ghost in the room echoed the word *thinking*, bouncing it back and forth.

Dart noted Laurelle's eyes flitting about, attempting to follow her fleeing word. She kept her own voice a breathless whisper. "I was wondering when we'd be granted an audience with His Graced, Lord Chrism."

Laurelle sighed, a flicker of a smile. "I hope soon. But I expect it won't happen until those who we are to replace have faded completely."

Dart nodded. They were indeed handmaidens-*in-waiting*. The two handservants, representing blood and tears, those whom they had been chosen to replace, were ailing but not yet gone, and continued in their duties, as was their honor.

In the meantime, Dart and Laurelle were placed under the daily tutelage of Matron Shashyl, the matron superior of the handservants. While not a *Hand* herself, she had served the castillion for over five decades and it was said only Chrism himself ever questioned her or went against her wishes. She personally instructed Dart and Laurelle in the finer points of their specific duties and oversaw the practices of the proper rituals. Some lessons had already been taught to them back at the school, but much had not.

"I wish Margarite could see all this," Laurelle said.

Dart surprisingly felt the same way. Though Margarite had mostly been cruel to her at the old school, the girl would have been a welcome reminder of the only home she had ever known. Alone here, strangers to the castillion, Dart and Laurelle had grown much closer together. They even shared a bed in the dormitories; apparently it was rare to have two handservants-in-waiting arrive at the same time. Still, Laurelle clearly pined for the crush of friends that had always surrounded her.

"I even miss Matron Grannice," Laurelle sighed. "She was so kind. She once read to me when I was fevered . . . do you remember that?"

Dart felt tears well in her eyes. She wiped them brusquely. The matron had been as close to a mother as she had ever had. Now she would never see her again. Dart's defilement would not long go unnoticed here. She would surely be banished . . . if not worse. She felt a sudden urge to blurt out her fears to Laurelle, to unburden her heart. If there was anyone she could trust . . .

"Laurelle, can I tell you something?" The words were out of her mouth before she could stop them. The next spilled out in a rush. "Something you'd swear to tell no one else."

Laurelle shifted closer with a rustle of skirts. "What is it, Dart?"

She reached a hand to her friend. Laurelle grasped it, her eyes bright in the torchlight.

"I . . . the day that I was sent to the rookery . . ."

Laurelle squeezed her fingers. "After I teased you," she said. "I'm sorry. Sometimes I forget myself and do silly things to make the other girls laugh. I shouldn't have. It was mean and petty."

Laurelle's brow crinkled—not in shame, but with a weary knowledge of her own foolishness. For a moment, Dart saw the woman her friend would grow into: sharp-eyed, with a keen mind and a beauty that would weaken men. Dart suddenly felt too small to speak.

"What is it?" Laurelle encouraged softly.

Dart opened her mouth, ready to confess all.

Then a crash and tinkle of shattering glass startled them both. They swung around.

Dart spotted Pupp, balanced up on his hind legs, nosing one of the upper shelves. A broken repostilary lay at his paws. She watched him sniff at another vessel, setting it to rocking.

"No!" she cried out and leaped to her feet.

Her exclamation was taken up by the ghost and echoed throughout the room. Pupp glanced at her, eyes squinted in chagrin, tiny brass ears tucked back in shame. He lowered himself to the floor. She hurried to him and shooed him back from the shelf, keeping her motions hidden by her skirts.

Laurelle joined her. She stared down at the broken jar and the spilled humour. "How . . . ?" She glanced around the room nervously. "Why did it fall?"

"We have to clean it up!" Dart declared, panicked. "If Matron Shashyl finds out . . ."

"But we didn't do anything wrong," Laurelle said, just a girl again, one who was convinced that the world was just and fair.

Dart knew better. "I don't know what knocked the jar off the shelf. Maybe a groundshake."

"I didn't feel—"

"Maybe a small one, too mild for us to notice, but enough to rattle one of the repostilaries."

Laurelle nodded, needing to believe something besides the mischievousness of an echoing ghost.

"But will anyone believe that?" Dart crossed back to their abandoned bucket of sudsy soap and brushes. "What if nobody felt the groundshake? We'll be blamed."

Laurelle's eyes grew round.

"Perhaps even cast out for such an abuse."

Her friend covered her mouth with a small hand. "No!" she whispered through her fingers. "My father would flay me . . ."

Dart recognized the true terror in the other's eyes. From the time Laurelle was a babe, her family had groomed her for this position and would not tolerate any other role for her. Since their arrival here, Laurelle had received a single congratulatory letter from her parents, along with a small basket of snowy lilies. Dart had read the note. Though it was mostly kind, there was an undercurrent of disappointment. Laurelle had been chosen for one of the five *lesser* humours: *tears*. That night, Laurelle had shed many of her own tears, weeping at her failure, while pretending they were a joyous outpouring.

Dart had not been fooled. Looking at the raw fear in her friend's eyes now, Dart wondered if being an orphan was truly the worst outcome for a child.

"We'll clean it up," Dart promised. "None will be the wiser. There are thousands of repostilaries stored down here."

Dart bent and carefully picked up the shards of glass. The tang of yellow bile, the god's water, wafted. At least it hadn't been his blood, the most valuable of all the humours. She dropped the sharp bits into the sudsy water, hiding Pupp's crime. She would cast the broken pieces out when she dumped the bucket.

Laurelle steadied herself with a deep breath. Again proving her inner strength, she dropped to her knees and set about cleaning the spilled humour and rinsed the brush in the water.

In short order, the floor was clean, all evidence scrubbed away.

"We mustn't tell anyone," Dart warned.

"Our secret," Laurelle answered. The last word was echoed by the ghost. It seemed all were in agreement.

With her heart finally calming, Dart glanced over to Pupp. He had his tail tucked low, nose close to the floor. She took a moment to frown at him. How had he knocked the jar off? Was it just another of those chance pushes into this world? Like when he had nipped at Laurelle? But he had done such things only when he was agitated, worked up, and protective of her.

She stared at her hands, remembering the one other time, when her blood had allowed her to touch him. She shied away from that memory and glanced back to the empty spot on the shelf. It made no sense. Unless it had something to do with the power contained within the repostilary, the Grace-rich humour.

As she pondered the mystery, a booming voice called out to them, one not even the ghost dared to mock. "Maidens! Please put up your buckets and brushes!"

Matron Shashyl.

"She knows," Laurelle bleated in panic.

Dart shushed her with a stern look. "She's just here to collect us."

Without windows, time ran strange down here, but Dart was sure it was about the end of their morning shift. That meant a short meal of bread and hard cheese, washed down with a bit of tea and honey. Then it was on to their lessons for the remainder of the day.

Laurelle stood on shaky legs, clutching her brush to her bosom. Dart collected the bucket, knowing that Laurelle would be unable to carry this burden, while Dart was well accustomed to the weight of secrets by now.

She held out the bucket for Laurelle to toss her brush into the water. Their eyes met. Dart read the plain relief in her face.

Laurelle touched Dart's fingers. "You're the bravest girl I know."

Dart took no pride in the praise. She knew the true source of her courage lay not in a stout heart, but in simple despair. With no way of knowing how long her impurity of flesh would remain hidden, she took

each day with a roof over her head and a warm meal in her belly as a blessing. But it could not last. She knew this.

She led the way with the bucket and brushes. What did it matter if
they were caught? She could only be banished once.

Dart wended the way through the shelves, trailed by Laurelle and
Pupp. The light from the pair of torches grew brighter as they neared the
door.

A dark shadow filled the threshold.

Matron Shashyl was a large woman, with a substantial bosom and
wide hips. There was nary a bit of flab to her, though. Her legs were as
stout as a draft horse, and her face could easily be mistaken for the same
in the dark.

"Hurry, girls. We've a big day ahead of us."

Laurelle curtsied as they reached the door. Dart tried to repeat her
smooth motion, but with the bucket unbalancing her, it came out more
as a bumbled parody. She came close to spilling the bucket's sloshing contents upon Matron Shashyl's shoes, exposing their crime.

Matron Shashyl didn't notice, clearly excited. Her cheeks were flushed
as she turned away. "We have so much to do! Neither of you are ready!"

Dart sensed a twinge of misgiving.

"Ready for what, Matron?" Laurelle asked, following her out.

"You're both to be presented to Lord Chrism!"

"When?" Dart gasped, almost dropping the bucket again.

"This very night!"

❖

Dart tasted nothing of her midday meal. It may as well have been made
of paste and sawdust. She ate it nonetheless, for it was surely the last meal
she'd be offered here.

Laurelle picked at her bread like a nervous crow. She lifted her cup of
tea, then set it back down. She didn't seem to know what to do with herself since Matron Shashyl's announcement.

"We're going to meet our god," Laurelle said for the hundredth time,
followed by her usual sigh. "I may just faint . . . simply swoon away."

Dart kept quiet and poured more honey into her tea. She couldn't
seem to make it sweet.

The girls had been served their meal on the grand southern terrace that
overlooked the walled Eldergarden of Chrism. It was one of the oldest
botanicals in all the world, or so they had been told by Jasper Cheek, the

magister who oversaw the castillion grounds and towers. "First seeded and planted when Chrism chose this spot for his grounding," Jasper had said with pride. "He was the first god to marry himself to the land and share his Grace with all. His own hand laid the first seed, watered with his own blessed blood."

Dart stared across the garden to the millennia-old myrrwood in the center. It appeared more a grove than a single tree. As a myrrwood spread its branches outward, roots would drop from the tips, which upon reaching the fertilized soil would form secondary trunks supporting the tree as it reached out yet again with new branches, growing wider as it grew taller. It now covered a thousand acres. A single tree had become a forest.

"Besides marking Chrism's land," Jasper had instructed, "the myrrwood also represents the Hundred. Lord Chrism was the first to place his roots in the land here, grounding and settling. And by his example, other gods followed, spreading new roots across the Nine Lands of Myrillia."

Dart had walked under the edges of the famous tree. It was gray barked with leaves so darkly green as to appear black in all but the brightest sunshine and so dense that she imagined one could walk beneath its woven branches in the fiercest storm and still stay dry. Under its canopy, she discovered a natural colonnade of arched bowers spreading deep into the garden, a place where lovers met for secret trysts and whispered promises were always kept. It was said that at the center, near the tree's true trunk, the Heartwood, the bower lay in eternal midnight, lit only by glowing butterflits that nested throughout the branches. But no one could say for sure. It was sacred to Chrism himself. A private sanctuary. None but the first god was allowed near it.

Dart dreamed to see such a place. But now it would never be. She forced her eyes away, upward, denying herself even the view of the garden.

Last night's storm had passed, leaving behind an achingly blue sky with only the occasional high cloud. Even the air was warm with the promise of winter's end and the beginning of spring. But all Dart felt was a numbing cold, cheerless and dank, that seemed to have settled at the base of her spine. She shivered where she sat.

"You'll be fine," Laurelle said, reaching over to pat her hand. "We'll both be fine."

Dart could sit still no longer. She stood up abruptly, startling Laurelle. "I'm going to take a bit of air," she mumbled apologetically. "Before Matron Shashyl coops us back up in her lessons chamber."

"We won't have much time . . ." Laurelle began to climb to her feet.

"I think I need a moment alone," Dart said, backing up a step. "Do you mind?"

Laurelle could not keep the wounded look from her face, but she nodded and settled back to her seat. "Shall I wait for you here . . . so we'll go together to meet the matron?"

Dart nodded. "I won't be gone long." She turned to the curve of stairs that led from the terrace to the gardens. It felt good to be moving, even if it was aimless.

And she wasn't entirely alone. Pupp crawled from beneath the table, passing ghostily through Dart's abandoned seat. He had sensed his mistress's mood and kept himself scarce. But where Dart went, he must follow.

Dart felt a stab of irritation. Though she loved Pupp with all her heart, a part of her wanted to flee from him, to run as fast as she could from all of this.

She reached the edges of the Eldergarden. Cobbled paths wended throughout the vast botanical. Dart strode under an opening arch of ginger roses smelling sweetly with their early blossoms. She chose a path framed by low hedges, keeping to the sun. She passed manicured patches of purple sylliander and wild sprays of rosy-pink narcissus. Small wooden bridges forded stone streams, the waterways dotted below with green lily pads and heavy-lidded flowers. Flashes of aquamarine could be seen in the water, small minnowettes and a few larger carp.

Dart found her footsteps growing ever faster. She hurried along paths, crossing one way, then another. Pupp kept with her, but it was not her ghostly friend from which she sought to escape. It was her own skin. Tears rose to her eyes, blurring her vision.

Her steps became a stumbling trot. The edges of her skirt snagged upon the occasional thorn or snatching bramble, but she ran faster. Sobs shook through her.

She wanted only to keep running. She would not even let the garden wall stop her. She would continue. Banishment was certain. Or even worse punishments: dungeons, chains, whippings. But her worst terror was that the violation in the rookery would be repeated. Even now, the certain doom of this day felt the same. She had no control over her fate.

Her flight through the gardens was not so much an escape as a way to grab back some semblance of power. She could flee, keep running, disappear into the low, shadowed streets of Chrismferry, and never be seen again. It was banishment . . . but it would be by her own hand, not another's.

She raced along a path that was gravel rather than cobbles. It was one of the older sections of the garden. Here, the beds ran wilder, overgrown, and the occasional fishpond or stream was coated with green and moved sluggishly, if at all. Trees reached higher, spanning the path. Shadows thickened.

Her feet began to slow. She passed a crumbled line of stone that bisected her path. One of the old garden walls. Over the many centuries, the Eldergarden had grown, spreading south from the river and castillion, requiring old walls to be knocked down and new ones to be raised farther out, continually consuming a part of the central city. It had happened twenty-two times over the four millennia, according to Jasper Cheek.

Dart crossed through the stone row and entered an ancient section of the garden. She was surprised to find the branches of the myrrwood stretching over her. She glanced behind.

The castillion's nine towers, the Stone Graces, formed a half-moon, cupping the vast Eldergarden within the palm of their battlements. Each tower rose twenty stories, yet only the tops could be discerned between the trees.

Dart found herself frozen in place, pulled in two different directions. A part of her heart begged for continued flight, to escape while she could, but a part of her felt drawn back, to face her responsibilities, to not abandon Laurelle without even the kindness of a good-bye. But deeper still lay a fear of what awaited her beyond the walls of the Eldergarden. The city was an unknown that still terrified her. Would she toss herself to its mercies without hope of redemption?

Before she could make her choice, voices intruded, drawing her attention back to the shadowed bower of the myrrwood. They were accompanied by laughter, as merry as the dappled wood. A small party approached.

Though Dart had broken no rules, she feared being spotted. She searched quickly for a hiding place. Pupp merely sat on his haunches, tongue lolling, his stumpy tail wagging.

She retreated through the broken wall, finding a tumble of blocks on the far side to shelter behind. A few steps away, Pupp nosed through a bit of fiddleleaf shrubbery, hunting a scrub mouse that had scampered from Dart's toes.

The voices drew nearer, two people, a woman and a man. Laughter continued to trail them. Lovers on a picnic, Dart imagined. Oh, to live a life where such simple pleasures were allowed. She hunkered down lower as they came to the breach in the wall.

They stopped. Dart peered through a crack in the rockery. For a moment, Dart thought it was Laurelle. Wrapped in a brown velvet cape, the girl bore the same fall of ebony hair, the same creamed skin. But as she turned her face into the sunlight, she was clearly a few years older, and not as fair of features, though her beauty still far outshone Dart's. Her lips parted as she tilted to accept a kiss from her companion.

He, in turn, could have been the young woman's father. Older by far, his black hair was touched by white at the temples and in a narrow streak, like a lightning strike, across his crown. He was dressed in a brown riding cloak with knee-high boots, coat open at the collar to reveal a deep burgundy silk shirt. Nobility, for sure.

They kissed for several breaths. The woman leaned against the wall, only an arm's length from Dart's cubby. The man ground into her, one hand reaching beneath the cloak to grope. He found what he sought and suddenly broke the embrace, stepping back.

His hand came free from the woman's cloak. A long dagger lay in his palm. "Did you think us so easily fooled, Jacinta?"

The woman gasped, then crouched slightly.

The man examined the weapon in the sunlight. Its blade was black, a shadow given substance. It ate the light, rather than reflected it. "A blade blessed in Dark Graces . . . brought here of all places. To the heart of Chrismferry. And you thought we wouldn't know?"

Jacinta straightened, but her voice lowered to a poisoned edge. "We'll stop you . . . all of you, by any means, foul or fair."

Her words built storm clouds upon the other's brows. He leaned closer to her. Even hidden behind rock, Dart sensed a font of power in the man. His eyes snapped with lightning. "Who sent you? Who supplied you with this?" He shook the dagger at her.

She laughed, but not the merry sound from a moment ago. She sounded much older than she appeared. "That you will never know!"

Before he could answer her challenge, Jacinta lunged at the man, grabbing for the dagger. He misjudged her intent. She snatched at his wrist, not to wrest the weapon away, but to hold his grip firm. With a kick off the wall, she hurled herself forward, onto the blade.

"Myrillia will be free!" she shouted as the dagger struck home, into the hollow above her collarbone.

Dart saw it all, biting on a knuckle to keep from screaming. She watched the man fall away, yanking the dagger free. Blood shot out—and a spat of flame, chasing the retreating blade. The woman fell to her knees and then face forward to the ground.

As her body struck the path, her cloak collapsed in on itself. A billow of ash and smoke swirled up, filling the gap in the wall. It was all that was left of the woman named Jacinta. Flesh turned to dust.

Dart didn't escape the backwash of ash. In one breath, it filled her nostrils—what was once the woman's flesh.

A racking gag escaped her. She could not stop her revulsion.

Knowing her presence could be hidden no longer, she fled back to the path. The empty cloak lay in the wall's breach, the gap still smoky with the cloud of ash. A dark shape moved beyond it.

The man with the dagger.

If she couldn't see him clearly, there was a good chance her features were shaded, too. Perhaps she could escape unknown.

A shout chased her. "Stop!"

She ignored the command, thumped over a small bridge, and dodged behind a hedge. Ducking low, she ran to the hedgerow, attempting to keep out of direct light.

A pounding of boots on the bridge sounded behind her. He was closing fast, having no need to hide. Dart straightened and sprinted down the row. From behind, dressed in her plain bonnet and skirt, she would appear no more than a scullery maid. She prayed it would be enough to keep her unknown.

"Fear not, lass! There is no reason to flee!"

Mayhap the man was right. From the exchange, it was hard to say who might be the wronged party. Had it not been the woman who had thrown herself on the dagger, her own dagger, one blessed in Dark Graces? Was such a death *murder?* Still, Dart sensed dread matters afoot in their dealings, matters in which she had no wish to become embroiled. She had enough secrets to bear. A single more would break her back.

She searched for a crisscrossing of paths, praying for some fast turns to lose her pursuer. But she had fled back to the younger sections of the garden, to the cobbled paths. Here the shrubs were low, and the trees spindly and still leafless from winter. Her heart pounded in her ears . . . or was it the man's boot steps?

The garden flew in a blur around her. The path took a sharp jag to the right, away from the castillion. Dart felt a sob build in her chest. She was lost. The castillion loomed before her, but she could not find the set of paths that led back there. Cutting straight through would only get her trapped by hedges or bogged down in the deeper ponds. She had to stick to the paths.

With her skirts flying around her ankles, she rounded past a whistle-down bush. A shape suddenly loomed into the path before her, a dark shadow.

She screamed, but her momentum was unstoppable. She crashed into the figure. She scrambled and kicked to be free of the other's arms as they sought to catch her up. He held something in his hand. The cursed dagger!

She cracked a knee up into the man's groin.

A loud *oof* followed, and she was free, stumbling backward.

Only now did she truly see her attacker. He was as tall as the man who had accosted the woman in the gardens . . . but much younger. No more than five or six years older than Dart. The young man was dressed in simple rough-spun breeches and shift, gripping a small spade—not a dagger.

"Skags, girl, what the naether is wrong with you?" he asked, half-hunched over. "You came close to unmanning me there."

Dart balanced between relief and shame. It was one of the groundskeepers. His hair was cut to the shoulder, deep brown, like the rich loam of the gardens. His eyes were as green as its ponds.

"I'm sorry," she said, stepping closer and half-turning to check the paths behind her.

They were empty. Only Pupp danced on the cobbles, bouncing a bit, ready to run some more, his molten skin shining bright in the sunshine.

"I . . . I thought someone was . . ." Dart let her words die and shook her head. "I think I got myself lost. I was trying to find my way back to the castillion."

"I can take you back to the maid's drudgery, if you'd like." He carefully straightened. "That is, if I can still walk."

Relieved at his offer, Dart glanced down at her stained and scratched skirts. She must appear to be a low maid. "Thank you, but I need to reach the overlook terrace."

He studied her up and down, one eyebrow cocked. "Truly . . . the overlook?"

"Yes," she said, more sharply than she intended.

He shrugged and stepped around her. He reached for her elbow. She sprang away, having to force herself not to swat at his hand. She didn't want to be touched.

"It's back this way," he said, letting his arm drop.

She followed him from a couple steps away. He smelled of the plants he had been weeding, a spicy musk that bordered on sweet. She found herself moving closer, studying him. His back was broad, his shift clinging to his muscular shoulders. He could probably carry her all the way back to the terrace without raising any sweat on his brow.

She pushed such thoughts aside and turned her attention to the gardens around her, watching for any sign of the dark man. But the sun seemed to have warmed all menace from the Eldergarden. Pupp trailed them both, eyes fiery, a lightness to his step.

They continued down a maze of paths. The keeper spoke quietly, a comforting sound, relating details about various plants. "The jackawillows will be blooming in another moonpass," he said, pointing to a small tree leaning over a pond, branches weeping to the water's edge. Small buds hung from tiny stems, like the heads of drowsy children. "They open as large as fists and appear in every hue of a rain's bow."

He sighed.

By now, Dart had crept up even with him. She found his voice comforting.

"You never did tell me your name," he said. "If I might be so bold."

She considered lying but found she could not. "Dart," she finally said.

"Ah, like the dartweed," he said with a deep laugh. "I've punctured a finger or two on that thorny, yellow-headed invader."

She bristled, reminded of the teasing back at her old school.

"You have to respect that weed," he continued, oblivious. "It appears a tender, fragile shoot, but at its heart, it's as tough as the strongest stranglevine and blooms despite adversity."

He glanced over to her. Tall for her age, she stood only a couple fingers shorter than him. His voice cracked with wry amusement. "A fitting name, I'd say."

Unbidden, a blush rose to her cheeks.

"Ah, here we are," he said, turning away, saving her from embarrassing herself. He pointed a hand forward.

Dart spotted the familiar arch of ginger roses. Beyond the garden's edge, up on the terrace, Laurelle stood at the rail . . . alongside Matron Shashyl. The matron wore a deep scowl as she searched the gardens below. With sudden trepidation, Dart realized how late she was. And in all the terror of the gardens, she had forgotten what lay ahead of her on this day.

"There you go, lass," the groundskeeper said. "I hope to see you again sometime."

Dart doubted that would ever happen. She would surely be cast out before the sun rose on the next day. She hurried forward. "Thank you," she mumbled as she passed.

He followed her to the arch of roses. She hurried up the curving staircase, holding her skirt's edge up to keep from tripping. Laurelle and Matron Shashyl had noticed her approach. They crossed to await her at the top of the steps.

"Child, do you know how long we've been waiting?" Matron Shashyl asked, fists on her wide hips. She grabbed Dart by the elbow and hauled her up the last step. "And on this day of all days!"

Laurelle hovered on her other side. "Dart, what happened to you?"

Her friend's words drew the matron's attention to the condition of her skirt. Its hem was stained and wet. Tiny rips frayed its edges.

"Is this how you care for items left in your charge?" Matron Shashyl shouted. "I should strip you bare right here and march you straight down to the laundress, have you explain to Mistress Tryssa how your clothes came to such a sorry state."

Tears rose to Dart's eyes. She hated to show such weakness, but the day had worn her too thin. First the broken repostilary down in the Cache, then the revelation that she was to meet Lord Chrism, and now the terror of the gardens. "Leave the girl be," a familiar voice said behind her from the stairs. "She's had a bad fright."

Matron Shashyl's grip on her elbow snatched tighter. Before Dart could turn, the matron dropped to her knees, tugging Dart with her. Dart fell amid a tumble of skirt. She landed on her hands.

Laurelle looked confused until the matron waved her down, too. With her brows knit together, she lowered slowly, careful of her own skirt.

Matron Shashyl bowed her head. "Lord Chrism."

Laurelle's eyes flew wide—then she, too, dropped her head, fingers folded at her bosom.

Dart, still on hands and knees, found herself unable to move. Horror dried the earlier tears. She knew that voice. Only now did she connect the man in the gardens to the face carved and sculpted throughout Chrismferry. Who would've expected the eldermost god of the Hundred to be found without his guards, walking the gardens?

A weary sigh sounded behind her. "Enough of this foolishness. Please stand."

"Of course, Lord Chrism," Matron Shashyl said, obeying him, but keeping her head bowed. She waved up Laurelle and Dart. "These are your two chosen handmaidens-in-waiting."

Laurelle gained her feet smoothly, a flower rising toward the sun.

Dart, tangled in her skirts, had to crawl a bit, struggling.

A hand reached to her arm and helped her up. "There you go, lass."

On her feet, Dart turned and stared up at the god she had mistaken for a groundskeeper. She remembered crashing into him, striking him with her knee. Her gaze tore away, unworthy, horrified at how she had treated him.

Lord Chrism lifted her chin to face him. "It seems my Oracle chose well indeed."

9

GLOOM

"A RE WE STILL SUPPOSED TO BE PANICKING? ROGGER ASKED. "BECAUSE I'm getting sores on my arse from all this waiting."

Tylar shrugged. He had no idea why they hadn't been attacked yet. He and the thief, along with Delia, sat on a shadowed bench under a fold of sail and watched the seas.

The *Grim Wash* lay mired in the tangleweed, like a bottlefly in a spider's web. The slack sails fluttered weakly with the occasional gust of wind, as if trying to fly free. But escape was impossible.

Tylar stared at the entwining growth. The field of tangleweed undulated with the ocean swells, surrounding the ship in all directions. It took a spyglass to see the open water now.

Earlier in the day, they had crashed broadside into the edge of the choked patch. While they foundered there, the tangleweed flowed past the ship's flanks, encircling the boat, its passage marked by a ghostly scritch-scratching against the planks, like drowning men clawing to board the ship. Captain Grayl had attempted to keep at least the keel clear by lowering a man on ropes with an ax, but with every chop, more weed writhed up from below. It was futile. The weed was relentless. Even the galley cook reported tendrils sprouting through the boards of the galley, twining inside.

With the ship mired, there was nothing the crew could do but watch the sun crest the sky and begin its slow fall toward the western horizon, baking the ship beneath it.

Eyes narrowed at Tylar. "We should just throw his arse over the rail," he heard a sailor mumble to another. "Give the watery god what she wants."

Tylar had heard similar rumblings all day. Only the captain's goodwill

protected him from attack. But how long would it last? Gold bought only
so much loyalty, especially among the ilk that bartered with the Black
Flaggers.

As the day wore on, the heat continued to rise, damp and salty,
smelling of wet weed. It didn't help the crew's temperament. The occasional gusts brought a bit of movement to the air, stemming the heavy
heat and wafting upon them a sweetness from the fields of blooming
spore heads. The thorny flowered stalks pushed above the roll of weed,
jostled sluggishly by the current. They looked like white-haired old men,
skeletally thin, shaking their heads at the sorry state of the wooden intruder into their midst. But these flower-headed men remained their only
companions. The weed hid all else below.

"Are you certain this is Tangle Reef?" Tylar asked for the hundredth
time.

Captain Grayl spoke behind them, where he oversaw the repair crews.
"It be the Reef, surely. I've never spotted a patch of tangle so large. It can
be no other."

As confirmation, Rogger tapped the brand on the underside of his
right forearm, reminding everyone that he had been here before. "The
good captain is correct."

Tylar motioned to the spread of weed. "Then where are all the trading
barges, the supply ships, the floating dockworks that service the city
below the waves?"

Delia answered, waving a small silk fan before her face. "The Reef is
as changing as the seas it rides on. It is a living creature whose heart is
Fyla." She touched her chin with the back of her thumb, respect for letting a god's name pass from her lips. Though the young woman had
nailed her fate to theirs, she was still a handmaiden and would not speak
harshly of another god, even one meant on capturing them, most likely
killing them.

Delia continued. "The weed moves through the Deep by Fyla's will,
but it still requires preparation. Once the hunt began, she would have no
choice but to unfetter the Reef's support ships, to withdraw her surface
docks below. There are limits even to the tangle's reach."

"It reached us fair enough," Rogger grumbled, glaring down the length
of the *Grim Wash*.

The wavecrasher listed about four hands to port, tilting the crowded
decks. Most of the ship's crew had come topside, standing, sitting, pacing,
all eyes on the horizons. Some attempted to keep busy under the baleful
eye of Captain Grayl. Others stood by the rails in supplication, rubbing

prayer beads between palms, spitting into the sea to add their waters to the Deep. But most, like Tylar, Rogger, and Delia, stared listlessly at the weed, awaiting certain doom.

"So why isn't Fyla attacking?" Rogger asked, keeping his voice low. "She must know you're here."

Tylar shook his head. "Perhaps she's consulting with the other gods."

Rogger spat over the rail in irritation. "It's not like our watery mistress of the weed doesn't have the time to dally. We're certainly not going anywhere. There's no swimming to freedom, not through this snarl. It'll pull you under before you're past the ship's shadow."

The chief mate crossed by them, headed for his captain. He had come up from below. His leggings were soaked from the knees down. Not a good tiding. He tapped Grayl's shoulder.

"Captain, we're taking on water in the bilge. I have men working the bellows pumps, but it's a lost battle."

"Maybe Fyla means to sink us," Rogger said, leaning back and stretching. "Why dirty her hands with air breathers when she can drown the lot of us?"

Delia stirred. "No. Fyla would want to face Tylar at the very least."

"Face a godslayer?" Rogger asked doubtfully. "Would she take such a risk?"

"For Meeryn, she would," Delia answered. "Fyla and Meeryn were close. Both were water gods of the warm seas. Once a decade, the Reef would sweep into the Summering Isles. And though Meeryn could never leave the islands to which she was bonded, the two gods would meet near the Tumbledown Beaches. Fyla would ride in upon a woven carpet of weed, pulled by a pair of silverback dolphins. I saw such a meeting once with my own eyes. Two gods within arm's reach of each other."

Tylar could only imagine such a sight. As the Hundred were bound by blood to the lands they settled, it was rare for one god to meet another. Occasionally those who shared neighboring realms would meet at the borders, but even that was rare.

"Some say," Rogger began, lasciviously cocking up an eyebrow, "that the two were once lovers. Before the Sundering. Now I'd slap down a silver yoke or two to see those two together."

Color rose darkly to Delia's cheeks, but before she could reprimand him, shouts burst from the port side.

"The weed is opening!" a man in the high riggings called down. He pointed an arm.

Those gathered atop the deck rushed to the port rail. Tylar was pulled along with them, trailed by Rogger and Delia.

A lone sailor left on the starboard side rubbed prayer beads together. "Everyone on your knees!" he yelled to his shipmates. "Beg forgiveness from she who moves beneath! Cast the blasphemer from our sight!"

A few glanced to the crazed supplicant until someone in the rigging threw a tin cup at the man's head. He cried out and went silent.

Captain Grayl stepped to Tylar's side, plainly worried the tense crew might mutiny against his sworn charge. "Stay close," he warned. "No telling when the lot of 'em might forget how you fought off the jelly shark and saved their filthy hides."

Grayl cleared a way to the port rail. Tylar stared at the rolling spread of weed. Its sweet scent wafted stronger now.

"Something's rising!" the crewman in the nest yelled.

They all saw it a moment later. Through the gap in the weed, a huge black bubble rose from below. It surfaced, sluicing water from its iridescent smooth sides.

"A deepwater pod," Rogger said.

The top of the bubble peeled open like the petals of a nightshade. Cupped within the center were six men, tall, muscled, hairless from crown to heel. They were naked, except for snug loincloths that blended with their skin, a fish-belly paleness striped in swatches of gray, brown, and ebony.

In their right hands, they carried spears that glinted in the sun. Traceries of green phosphorous crackled along the shafts. Weapons blessed with Grace.

Tylar knew who stood before the ship. The elite guard of Fyla. The Hunters of the Deep. The Shadowknights of the seas.

Their leader stepped forward onto the closest edge of the folded petal of the pod. "Tylar de Noche!" he called to the ship. His voice was oddly nasal, but still rich with authority. "You are ordered by she who moves below to present yourself to her court, to address the heinous acts of which you are accused."

Captain Grayl gripped Tylar's elbow and whispered fiercely. "It is certain doom."

"No doubt, but we have no choice here."

"We can still fight. I have archers in the riggings, ready on my word. I owe you my ship, my life."

"And I would have you lose neither defending me." Tylar freed himself from the captain's grip.

"Then what will you do?"

Tylar found Rogger and Delia staring at him. "I will go. Once you're all safely out of harm's reach, I'll seek another way to escape." He had little hope for such a possibility. He barely understood the Graces that ran through his blood and bile, let alone how to use them. And the daemon inside could not save him from drowning.

Delia shook her head. "I'm going with you. I can speak on your behalf. Fyla might listen to words coming from Meeryn's blood servant."

"And where you go, I go," Rogger added.

Tylar sought words to argue. He wanted to bravely cast aside their loyalties, but in his heart, he found strength in their companionship.

Before he could settle the matter, a shudder passed through the ship. Sails shook, ropes rattled in their stanchions, planks trembled underfoot. Cries arose throughout the ship.

"What's happening?" Delia squeaked.

Captain Grayl answered, "We're sinking!"

Leaning over the rail, Tylar saw the waterline climb the flanks of the ship. "It's the skagging tangleweed!" Grayl spat. "It's pulling us under!"

The leader of the Hunters called out again. "Tylar de Noche! Show yourself or the ship and all aboard will be drowned!"

The *Grim Wash* continued its shuddering descent into the choked seas, pulled from below. There was no more time for discussion or debate.

Tylar raised an arm high. "I am here! Spare the ship and I will come freely!"

With his words, the tremble in the ship stopped.

The eyes of the Hunters narrowed on him. The *Grim Wash* remained half-submerged, awaiting his cooperation.

"I must go," Tylar said.

Captain Grayl wore a determined but resigned expression. "I'll drop a rope ladder."

It was all done hastily. The crew was anxious for Tylar to abandon the ship. A few looked ready to simply push him overboard. As he swung a leg over the rail, Grayl grabbed his arm and twisted his wrist.

"What—?"

"Here," Grayl said. "A return for the remainder of the journey not sailed." Three gold marches were dropped into his palm.

Tylar shoved them back. "Where I go, I have no need for coin."

The captain refused to accept them, and the marches fell between their fingers and bounced on the planks.

Rogger set upon them in an instant. "Who says we won't need coins? You sound like a man heading to the gallows."

Tylar frowned at him.

"Trust me," the thief continued. "I've lived enough lives to know that the future is never fixed to one path. And no matter which course opens, a bit of gold never hurt." He jangled his pocket and waved Tylar over the rail. "Now get going before I change my mind about following someone so lacking in good sense."

Tylar mounted the ladder and descended while Rogger helped Delia over the rail. They didn't have far to climb. The water's edge was three-quarters of the way up the ship's side.

Tylar reached the last rung, ready to jump into the seas and swim to the awaiting Hunters. He turned to get his bearings and found the deep-water pod floating toward the boat, petals extended toward Tylar's group. The weeds parted before its path.

After a moment, the lead petal's edge bumped against the ship. Tylar stepped out onto it, wary of his footing. He needn't have worried. What appeared delicate was firm and steady. Thick veins ran through the leafy petal, supporting it. It was a living thing, a part of the mass of tangleweed.

He stepped away, allowing room for Delia and Rogger. Up at the rail, Captain Grayl raised a hand in sad farewell.

Tylar nodded, mystified by the simple nobility of someone tied to the notorious Flaggers. He had always known that the world was more gray than black and white, but he had never imagined that gray came in so many shades.

Rogger spoke as he stepped onto the petal, his eyes focused on the pod's center. "Let's hope these Hunters are half as hospitable as our good captain has been."

Tylar turned to face the gathered guards. Closer now, he spotted the ribbed lines that shadowed either side of the Hunters' throats. Gill breathers, like all who lived in Tangle Reef. They could live for short spells above the waters, but it was uncomfortable, and after a day's time, they would sicken and die unless they returned to the seas.

Tylar led Delia and Rogger forward. The points of five spears tracked them. Only the leader kept his weapon by his side.

"I am Kreel," he said when they were a step away from him. "Know that you will die on my spear if you attempt any misdeed. She who we serve has blessed me with the sight to see any flows of Grace, whether dark or bright. Cast any charms or summon your daemon and I will know it within a breath, and you will die on the next."

Tylar noted a glint in the other's eyes that had nothing to do with the sun overhead. He spoke the truth. There was power hidden there. Tylar refused to flinch from his gaze. "I swear that I will bring no harm to anyone in Tangle Reef unless provoked. As you protect your god and people, so I will my friends here."

Kreel nodded and stepped back, opening the way to the pod.

They gathered into the center of the pod. The Hunters stood at the edges, spears pointing at them like the spokes of a wheel.

"What about the ship?" Tylar asked.

Kreel nodded. "They will leave unharmed."

As proof of his word, the *Grim Wash* suddenly bobbed up amid small cries of distress from the crew. The boat had been set free. Tylar watched as a lane opened in the weed behind the ship's stern. He heard Grayl's gruff voice bark orders. Sails climbed up the masts. Even before they could be unfurled, the ship began to move, gliding down the open space in the tangle.

"The weed's pushing 'em," Rogger said. "Shoving them out of here."

Tylar watched. "At least they're honoring their word in this regard."

"I suspect it's not so much *honor* that grants this boon."

Tylar glanced to the thief.

He nodded to the retreating ship. "There goes all hope of ever escaping Tangle Reef."

With those words, the petals of the pod folded up and over their heads, forming a seamless seal. Instead of darkness, the space glowed with a soft green luminescence, filtered sunlight through leaf.

As they began their descent, Tylar was reminded again that the pod was a living part of the weed . . . and they'd just been swallowed up.

For a long silent stretch, they continued blindly into the depths, pulled smoothly by a stalk underneath the pod. Tylar, standing in the center, sensed tiny vibrations through his boots.

"Look," Delia whispered, drawing his attention to the walls.

When they had first begun their descent, filtered sunlight from the surface had slowly faded to eternal darkness. A small glass lamp—a *fire lantern* blessed with a single drop of blood from a fire god—had been shaken and bloomed with a tiny flame to light the darkening space.

Now, like an onion peeling, the outermost layer of the pod's walls had begun to fold back. Translucent walls transformed to fine crystal, opening a clear view to the seas beyond the pod.

Tylar gaped.

All around, a vast forest spread through the dark waters, lit by glowing globes that hung from arched branches. Slender trunks rose in fanciful spirals, while giant fronded leaves waved everywhere. Currents wafted entire sections in slow, undulating dances, moving to a music beyond their hearing.

Rogger spoke. "Who would've guessed that snarl topside would look so handsome from down here?"

"I thought you'd been here before?" Tylar said.

He hitched a thumb upward. "Only to the surface docks. I was branded under the sun. To travel down more than a handful of fathoms is forbidden to all but a select few. The mistress here likes to keep the true face of Tangle Reef turned away from sunlight and wind."

A sudden storm of luminous pinpricks swept up the pod, swirled in eddies like a snowstorm, then rolled away.

"Sea sprites," Delia said, amazed, following their flight as they fluttered away. "They're the tiniest bits of sea life, more energy than substance."

Other larger denizens came swimming up with flicks of tails or writhes of bodies: sharkrays, nibblecray, mantai, and a monstrously large gobdasher. This last curious visitor dwarfed the pod and stared in at them with one baleful yellow eye, then the other. Its mouth cracked enough to reveal three rows of palm-sized teeth, razor edged. But a school of puffer crabs chased it off, jetting through the water with little bursts and nipping claws at the gobdasher's tail.

Tylar watched it flee through the forest. Farther away, movement caught his eye. Something shifted as the gobdasher passed. It made their recent visitor look like a minnowette. Tylar caught a brief glimpse of flailing tentacles, falling upon the gobdasher; then the sight vanished away as their pod descended farther into the depths.

Tylar knew what he had seen.

A miiodon . . . very likely the same one that had attacked the *Grim Wash*.

Kreel stirred from his place by the fire lamp. "The Reef," he announced.

Tylar turned. A starscape sprawled below. Glow globes, fire lanterns, and natural phosphorescence mapped out small homes, towering villas, terraces, and courts. Crowning it all, a vast castillion blazed, appearing on fire from the number of lamps lining its parapets and towers.

Their pod dropped toward the tallest tower, dragged by a winding stalk that disappeared down its open throat.

As they drew nearer, figures appeared, limned in the city's glow. They swam or floated among the buildings, which seemed to be constructed of the same sturdy material as their pod. A lone girl, arms laden with an empty net, glided through the waters with small flicks of her ankles and twists of her torso. She swept up to the pod.

Kreel noted her approach and made a keening sound that set Tylar's teeth to throbbing. In response, the girl spun in place and with a swift kick of her legs sped away.

The pod reached the tower's top and continued down its throat. All sight vanished to the sides. Overhead, the glowing opening retreated as they dropped into the depths of the castillion.

Heading to the dungeons, Tylar thought sourly.

After another moment, a rough bump shook the pod and almost knocked him on his backside. They had stopped. He glanced to his companions but found only worry in their expressions.

Tylar searched upward. The tiny circle of light vanished as a hatch pinched closed just overhead. Once sealed, a gurgling vibrated through the pod.

"They're draining the water," Delia whispered.

Bubbles danced all around the pod. In only a few breaths, the waterline trembled down the sides and disappeared away. As the gurgling ceased, a light bloomed to the right, outlining an open doorway. One of the pod's petals peeled toward the new glow.

An empty passage awaited them.

Two of the Hunters hurried ahead and flanked the entry.

Kreel pointed his spear. "She awaits in the grotto."

Tylar stepped out of the pod, leading his companions. The low passage was tubular with curving walls, lit by a vein of phosphorescence that ran along the ceiling. The air was damp but surprisingly warm, smelling of salt crust and algae.

They proceeded down the passage. Kreel kept a step behind them. Tylar felt his eyes on him, a dagger tickling his neck. He studied the pair of Hunters ahead of him.

One Hunter scratched a finger along his gill flaps, fluttering them, clearly dry and irritated. Their escorts had been out of the water a fair amount of time.

Tylar could not fathom why someone would choose this life for a child. The denizens of the Reef drank a special elixir when heavy with child, an alchemy of Graces from Fyla herself. It touched the growing babe in the womb, blessed its development. And though there were other folk that chose similar paths by imbibing godly elixirs when with child— producing loam-giants, fire walkers, and wind wraiths—at least these offspring still lived in the world of land and air. Why abandon the world above for such an isolated life below?

The passage ended at a translucent door. Brighter light from beyond set it aglow, but details remained murky. As they neared, the door parted, splitting in a perfect star pattern and withdrawing away in five sections.

A sweet billow washed over them. Tylar recognized it immediately.

The aroma of the tangleweed flower.

The two Hunters stepped through the open portal first, dropping to their knees just past the threshold. Kreel nudged Tylar with the tip of his spear.

Tylar entered a grotto of breathtaking beauty.

The space opened under an arched dome, large enough to hold all of Summer Mount and festooned with hanging plants, vines, and bright flowers. Light blazed from a single colossal fire lantern as wide as a man's outstretched arms. It floated in the center of the dome's space, unsupported, rolling and drifting gently over the landscape below.

Lit beneath it, pools and waterfalls graced walkways lined with flowers unlike any seen under the sun. Rather than growing from soil, their beds were streams and sculpted puddles. Flowers of every hue grew riotous among trees and leafy bushes. Some he recognized: honeybloom, jasper's heart, wyldpetal, sea-dandle, and ghost palm. Most were unknown. Strange fruit hung from one fronded tree, appearing like yellow vipers, twisting and hanging from branches. Another tree's leaves twinkled with a soft violet radiance.

Every glance held a new wonder.

Delia spoke at his shoulder, a whisper of a whisper. "The Sacred Grotto. It is said Fyla collects her botanicals from all over Myrillia, some even from the hinterlands."

Tylar simply stared. He had never imagined such beauty under the seas.

Kreel waved them forward, never taking his eyes from Tylar.

They were led down the central path that wound into the heart of the grotto. The guards maintained a ring around them, Kreel at their backs.

All about, the babble and tinkle of water echoed. Passing over one bridge, Tylar happened to glance down and saw another of the Reef's Hunters glide along the channel below. The spear in his hand was plain to see.

Rogger noted the same. "I have read of this place." He waved an arm over his head. "This is but half of the garden. The other half lies beneath our feet, a maze of waterways and flooded caves. She could hide an entire army down there and we'd never know it."

Tylar's sense of wonder dimmed as his anxiety rose again.

They mounted a long bridge, one that arched in a graceful curve over a wide pond. The waters below teemed with sea life: from tiny tick eels to the sweep of giant mantai. Schools of fish silvered the waters as they shimmered and danced.

In the center of the pond rose a tall island surrounded by a white sand beach. The fire lantern hovered directly over its peak, shining upon the rich flora flowing over the cliffs and slopes. From its very top, a frothing spring jetted high into the air, then raced down its sides in rivulets and cascades back to the pond. The most dramatic course was a wide waterfall in front: a flow of molten silver fell sheer from the peak's top into a small rocky basin at its base.

As they reached the bridge's end, the two lead Hunters crossed their spears, barring the way onto the island. The green phosphorescence of their blessed weapons flared brighter.

Kreel called out, "We have done your duty, Mistress of the Reef. He who has been named Godslayer stands before you for judgment."

The island remained quiet, except for the chatter of falling water. After several breaths, a voice finally answered, "Let him come forward."

Delia dropped to her knees. "Fyla . . ."

The guards uncrossed their weapons.

Tylar stepped from the bridge to the sandy beach. Rogger moved to follow.

The voice stopped them both. "Only the godslayer."

Tylar glanced to the thief. He saw Rogger's hesitation and waved him back. "I'll be fine." He even felt a bit of confidence in this statement. He didn't feel like he was going to die.

Still, a finger of dread traced his spine. He had met only two gods face-to-face in his short life: Jessup of Oldenbrook, to whom he had bent a knee in service as a Shadowknight, and Meeryn, who had died in his arms. But he had heard stories of various gods. Shadowknights talked among themselves after a few cups, sharing tales and stories. The personalities of the Hundred were as varied as their number. Some were reclusive, others gregarious, most were benevolent, a few iron fisted. Yet one fact remained consistent: *They were not to be crossed.*

Tylar stepped onto the sandy strand. "I am here. Not as a godslayer as I've been falsely accused, but as a man."

Behind the sheer screen of the silvery waterfall, movement met his words. A figure stepped forward through the fall. The cascade of waters fell about her: over her head, past her shoulders, along the swell of her breasts, through the flat hollow of her belly, and down her long legs.

She was naked, yet somehow carried a fold of the cascade along with her. Shimmers of water coursed over her body, forming a gown and cloak. She stepped into the pool at the peak's base. She was hairless, smooth as her Hunters, her skin pale white with a single black spiral from neck to right ankle. Her eyes were limpid pools of ocean blue.

Tylar could not meet her gaze and bowed his head.

She crossed over to him, stepping free of the pond and onto the sand.

"Mistress . . ." Kreel whispered, warning in his strained voice.

"Silence, Kreel." She continued toward Tylar.

He began to tremble, unable to stop. He could have been blind and still known she approached. Her Grace sang to his blood. Something stirred deep inside him, and he began to fall to his knees in the sand.

But a hand touched his cheek, freezing him in place. Fingers traced the three black stripes on his face.

"A Shadowknight . . . so it is true."

A finger lifted his chin. He found eyes blazing with Grace. Her two hands slipped to either side of his face. He sensed her strength. She could easily crush his skull, yank his head from his neck.

Instead, she pulled him up to her and kissed him deeply.

For a moment, Tylar felt himself falling into darkness, but a strong tide drew him back. Lips pressed his; breaths were shared. Strange memories flooded through him, warming him. A moan arose between his lips and Fyla's, a mix of sadness and loss. Then after an untold time, he was released.

He dropped to his knees, gasping, all strength gone.

Fyla lowered to him, cupping his cheek with a palm. "It is truly you, Meeryn, my love."

Before another word could be spoken, a violent tremor shook through the grotto. Sand danced on the beach. The sheer waterfall trembled and sprayed. The wide pond sloshed far up its banks, while cries of surprise arose from Tylar's companions.

Fyla straightened.

Tylar still knelt.

More Hunters swept up out of waterways, rising with spears at ready. Kreel hurried over from his station by the bridge. "Mistress . . ."

"A naether-quake," she said, her voice going cold. Her eyes, still ablaze with Grace, turned upon Tylar—not with accusation, but concern. "You must leave. As I had feared, it is not safe for you . . . even here." She motioned him to stand.

"What's happening?" Tylar asked.

Rogger and Delia were led to his side.

Fyla lifted her arms high, then brought them down in a sweeping gesture. Similar to the deepwater pod, the outer layer of the arched dome crinkled back, revealing the open ocean beyond.

Tangle Reef glowed on all sides, but now it appeared as a living organism. The entire city writhed in the quake, thrashing along with the weeds, as if a storm raged through the forest. Schools of fish darted in maddened patterns, flashing through the waters.

Yet more disturbing, throughout the Reef, strange clouds billowed up from below, blacker than the dark water. Lances of brilliance flashed among them like undersea lightning. Where they touched weed, green life charred into black death. Frightened fish entered clouds and tumbled back out as white bone.

"They sent a Gloom," Fyla said hotly.

"A Gloom?" Tylar asked, sickened by the sight.

"A bloom of the naether into this world. Deadly to all in its path." She crossed to Kreel. "I must protect the Reef."

Kreel bowed on a knee, holding forth his spear. She gripped its bare blade. With a nod from his mistress, Kreel drew the spear from the sheath of her fingers. Blood followed, flowing from her sliced palm.

She turned to the basin at the foot of the waterfall and allowed her blood to run into the crystalline waters. The stain swirled down and away. "This should ward the Reef against the Gloom for now. But I cannot say for how long. As long as you are here, all are at risk."

A sudden crash drew all their attention to the far side. A creature had latched on to the dome. Tentacles writhed against the surface.

"The jelly shark," Rogger gasped.

"It's gone mad again," Fyla said. "I'd thought my blood brought it back under control."

"Mad *again?*" Tylar asked.

Her gaze remained on the miiodon as its venoms attacked the dome's clarity, trying to eat through. "It was never supposed to have boarded your ship, only driven you to me, so I could see you for myself. But something broke my control, allowing it to attack your ship."

Delia grabbed Tylar's arm and pointed at the jelly shark. It slid down the side of the dome, leaving behind a trail of acid-etched marks.

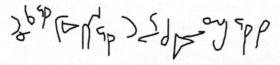

"That's ancient Littick," Delia said.

Rogger nodded. "She's right."

"What does it say?"

Delia glanced to Tylar, her eyes frightened. "It says *give us the god-slayer.*"

"They know you're here." Fyla waved them all to follow. "Hurry." She led them around the rocky basin and through the shaking waterfall to a cavern hidden behind it. At the back, a smaller pod awaited, tucked in an alcove. "We must get you down to the wetdocks."

Tylar stood his ground beside the pod. "What is going on?"

Fyla stared hard at him, eyes aglow. "The naether is searching for you. I was foolish to bring you so deep. But . . ." Her bloody hand rose and touched his cheek, a loving gesture. A tingle ran along his skin. "I had to know the truth, to touch you myself, to feel her in your blood. All that is left of my Meeryn. The naether must sense it, too . . ."

"I don't understand," Tylar said, stepping back. "The naether? It hunts me?"

The naether was a place meant to scare children, an underworld of eternal darkness and damnation, plagued by daemons and monsters. It was no more real than the *aether,* a bright land of ethereal spirits, those unseen beings worshipped by the faithful throughout Myrillia.

Fyla waved them to the pod. "I'll tell you what I know, but not here. We must go."

Tylar allowed himself to be herded inside the pod, along with Rogger and Delia. Fyla joined them, accompanied by Kreel with a fire lantern. It was tight quarters as the pod closed.

Fyla touched the wall and the pod dropped, falling swiftly away through tunnels. The descent was rough, bobbled by the shaking.

Rogger held to the walls for balance. "What is this naether-quake?"

Fyla stared overhead. "In a few places in the world, where sunlight never reaches—deep underground, in the midnight depths of the sea, in tombs sealed for millennia—the walls between Myrillia and the naether grow thin. It can be breached, allowing the naether to influence our world for a short time. I felt such a rupture on the eve that Meeryn was slain. Nothing escapes my notice in the seas of Myrillia. I followed it to its source, off the coastlines of the Summering Isle. I am certain something came through."

"The black beast," Tylar said, remembering the lizard creature ripe with Dark Graces that had attacked Meeryn.

"A naethryn," she said with a nod.

Delia gasped at this name. "Impossible. How . . . ?"

Fyla seemed to finally notice her. "I'm not sure. Such a thing has never happened."

"A naethryn?" Rogger asked, parroting the question in Tylar's own mind.

Fyla sighed. "What do you know of the great Sundering?"

"What all know," Tylar said. "How the kingdom whence the gods came had been shattered, bringing you to Myrillia."

She nodded. "But it was not just our kingdom that was shattered." She glanced to Delia. "We were shattered ourselves. Into three parts. That which you see here, gods made flesh, but also two others. A part of us was thrust into darkness, into the land you call the naether, and another into brightness."

"The aether," Delia whispered.

"Correct. What was once *one* became *three*, separate yet still weakly connected. I can sense my other selves, in the other planes. The dark and the light. But only here do we have substance. Or so we thought." Her eyes flashed with fear, a sight that would chill the stoutest man.

What could scare a god?

Fyla answered his silent question. "The naethryn are the undergods, our counterparts in the naether realm, dark shadows of ourselves."

Silence settled over the pod as it glided through the heart of Tangle Reef. The tremors of the quake continued.

"One of these naethryn came to slay Meeryn?" Tylar mumbled. "Why?"

"I had hoped you knew." Her face creased with worry. "For the past decade, there have been stirrings in the deep, strange creatures found rotting on ocean beds. I shared knowledge of these disturbances with Meeryn when last we met. She promised to speak to others across the Nine Lands, to consult with the masters at Tashijan."

"She must've learned something," Rogger said. "Something she wasn't supposed to know."

Fyla shook her head, unsure. "The last message I received from her was cryptic. She had great trepidation about something and wanted to consult with the Court of Tashijan before speaking of it."

"She had called for a blessed courier," Tylar said, recalling Perryl's summons to the Summering Isles. "She was slain before he reached her."

"Which is cause for more worry," Rogger said. "She was slain after she contacted Tashijan—it makes one wonder if someone betrayed her."

"Someone at Tashijan?" Tylar could not hide his disbelief.

"You of all people should not place so much confidence on the folk that banished you into slavery."

Tylar shook his head, deeply troubled. Though he had been sourly treated, a part of him knew his punishment had not been unwarranted. He had bargained with the Gray Traders . . . and it had cost the life of an innocent family. Though it wasn't his sword that slew them, he was still to blame.

"There are black tidings all across the Nine Lands," Fyla said. "Corruptions and bouts of madness. Who can say if Tashijan has been spared?"

"That was where we were heading," Tylar grumbled.

Fyla glanced at him. "Why journey there?"

"To seek answers from its libraries."

Rogger nodded. "And now we have another reason to continue there. If someone at Tashijan betrayed Meeryn, then therein may lay your salvation, Tylar. Expose the scabber and prove your innocence."

The pod shook more vigorously, striking the sides of the tunnel. Everyone fell against the walls.

"Before any journey can be undertaken," Fyla said, "I must get you safely away. The naether is too strong down in these dark depths. You must escape to the sun, back to land."

The pod bobbled again. Tylar sensed they were corkscrewing through a winding tunnel. "Where are we heading?"

"Even deeper," Fyla answered. "To the bottom of the Reef."

They continued their descent to untold depths, each lost to their own thoughts. But at least the quakes seemed to have subsided for the moment. Tylar finally spoke. "There's a question I must ask you."

"I will answer if I can," Fyla said.

Before he could speak, the pod halted with a final shudder. A petal peeled open on to a curving hall, flooded to the level of their knees. Water rushed in—cold, but not icy.

"The wetdocks," Fyla announced.

"Well named," Rogger said glumly as Kreel waded into the water. The others splashed after him.

One side of the passage was honeycombed with large half-submerged alcoves. Some were empty, but most sprouted tails of strange-looking craft.

Fyla waved to one of the nearest occupied alcoves. "Here we dock the Fins, the bloodships of the Reef."

The Fins appeared to be made of the same ubiquitous dark green material as the pods, but in this case, it was elongated and pinched at either end, surmounted by a prominent fin. Along the belly ran a pair of smaller fins, like runners on an ice sled.

Kreel showed them how to open the top hatch and climb inside.

"Looks like the inside of a tiny flippercraft," Tylar noted, inspecting the four seats: two in front, under a crystalline dome, and two in back. The inside walls were lined with mica tubes, all leading to a central crystal sphere full of gently glowing crimson liquid.

"It's fueled by a similar alchemy as the flippercraft," Fyla conceded, still standing in the outer passage. "But rather than the Grace of an air god, this is fueled by my own blood. It will speed you through the seas faster than any ship."

Kreel checked the levels. "There should be enough blood to reach Fitz Crossing."

Tylar nodded. Fitz Crossing was a rim island in the middle of the Meerashe Deep, a god-realm of Dain, the domain of orphans and runaways.

Rogger sighed. "I know some folk in Scree, on the far side of the island from Dain's castillion. From there, we should be able to book passage to the First Land." He jangled a pocket. "I guess it's lucky we still have Captain Grayl's gold marches."

"But the island is still a far ways off," Fyla warned. "You must be wary of the Gloom. It will sap the ship's reserves if you travel through the naether bloom for very long. Flee upward as soon as you leave, away from the deep."

Tylar nodded. Kreel gave them a fast lesson on the Fin's controls. They were simple enough. Tylar took the captain's seat. Delia took the neighboring chair, guarding the spherical tank of alchemies. Rogger sat behind her. The Fin rested at a slight angle, nose aimed down a short flooded tube to the open sea.

Kreel climbed back out and prepared to seal the Fin's upper hatch. Before he could lock it down, the Reef shook with a new quake, more violent than the others. Tylar was thrown from his seat. He stared back up at the hatch. A wall of water swept along the hall outside.

Kreel clung to the Fin's tail. "We're breached!"

Fyla stood on the far side, water climbing her form. "Be off! I must see to my city!"

"I'll get the hatch," Rogger said, swinging back to the stern.

Tylar remembered the question he had meant to ask before landing at the docks. "Wait! Fyla! Does the word *Rivenscryr* mean anything to you?"

She froze, half-turned. Her eyes flared with Grace, her whole manner hardened with fury. Ice formed over her body.

Before she could answer, seawater began to pour into the cabin from the flooding docks.

Delia opened the flow of alchemies. "We must go!"

"Fyla!"

She stirred. "It is a forbidden name, one known only to the gods."

"What does it mean?" he asked frantically. "What is it?"

Rogger sputtered under the hatch, seawater flooding over him.

"Your people gave it a different name." She stared through the rushing water.

"I must close the hatch!" Rogger choked, pulling it down.

Tylar pleaded with his eyes.

As the hatch clanged shut over the flood, her words reached him, "Though it is neither, you call it the *Godsword.*"

More confused than before, Tylar fell back to his seat. The water sloshed over his ankles. The only light came from the glow of the mica tubes as the alchemies raced through them.

Delia twisted the valves that controlled the flows. "Now, Tylar!"

He grabbed the wheel with one hand and pushed the plunger with the other. Grace surged out into the fins and the ship jetted forward, flying down the dark chute and out into the bright sea.

Once free, he concentrated on using the foot pedals and wheel to control the craft. The Fin raced through the water, carving a path beneath the Reef above. Against the city's glow, the patches of Gloom were easy to spot as steaming columns of blackness. Scintillations of lightning crackled through their hearts.

Tylar sped around the trunks of tangleweed, many now blackened and leafless from the touch of the naether.

"Once we're clear of the Reef," Rogger said, "we should angle both up and away, make for the open water beyond the weed. We don't want to get snarled up in the surface tangle."

Tylar nodded. They were almost at the city's edge, where the central corona cast off spiraling arms leading to sea plantations and hatcheries. Tylar aimed between two such arms.

As they shot upward, water sloshed to the back of the cabin. The shift threw off Tylar's balancing of the controls. The Fin spun in a fast spiral as he struggled to rein it in. They crashed through some branches of tangle-weed, jarring their ship.

"Maybe you should slow," Delia suggested.

"Watch your starboard!" Rogger yelled from the back.

Tylar spotted it too late. What had first appeared to be shadow was a smoking column of Gloom. He slammed the right rudder. It was too much. The Fin spun completely around, sweeping through the cloud of Gloom. All the mica tubes flared to a bright fire, protecting the ship. Then they were clear of the Gloom.

Tylar straightened the Fin, raised its nose toward the sky, and sped away. The glow of the Reef slowly faded below them, disappearing amid the thickening forest. Soon, only the luminescent globes that dotted the tangleweed's branches lit their path. Somewhere far above, the sun waited for them.

"How are the reserves?" Tylar asked shakily.

Delia measured the tank with her palm. "That single brush cost us a good fifth of our alchemies."

"Let's not do that again," Rogger suggested.

"I wasn't planning—"

The miiodon attacked from above, dropping upon them like a fisher-folk's net. Tentacles swallowed the Fin completely. The weight of the jelly shark rolled the ship. They were tossed about the cabin. Tylar sensed them dropping, tumbling back into the inky depths, to where the naether waited. The rolling stopped as the Fin stabilized, upside down in the clutches of the jelly shark. Tylar and the others lay sprawled upon the cabin's roof, the controls overhead.

Delia spoke near the bow. She crouched with her face pressed to the crystalline dome. "There's a space here between two tentacles. You can see through a bit."

Tylar joined her. The Reef glowed nearby. They had fallen back to where they had started. He rested his forehead against the dome. A column of Gloom roiled off to the port side. Death lay all around.

"What about loosing your daemon?" Rogger asked. "Maybe it could slay the beastie before we're crushed."

Tylar shook his head. He remembered how back at Summer Mount the *dred ghawl* had turned the guard's arrows to ash. He feared what it would do to their Fin if it tried to pass through the walls to the seas beyond.

"Then charm the miiodon again," Rogger persisted. "With blood and piss like before."

Delia leaned back. "We need to be able to touch it to charm it."

"Maybe not . . ." Tylar had a sudden idea and swung around. "Delia, I need you to man the wheel and rudder. Hurry!"

She knit her brow, but climbed to her feet under the controls, arms raised in hesitation. "Someone has to push the rudder pedals by hand. I can't man the wheel at the same time."

"I'll help," Rogger said.

Tylar pressed his face to the dome, studying the landscape. "When I say *now*, I need you to burn as much alchemy as you can while pulling hard on the wheel and left rudder."

"What are you—?"

"Get ready!" His target came into view. He held his breath. "Now!"

Rogger and Delia worked the controls. A vigorous trembling shook the ship. The mica tubes grew bright and hot as the craft fought the miiodon's bulk. It proved too heavy. Nothing happened. They continued to drop into the depths, unimpeded.

"More power!" Tyler scolded.

"Hang on," Delia gasped. "I'll break the damper valve."

Glass shattered with a small *pop*. The Fin jolted as if kicked by a loamgiant. The mica tubes flared with intense heat. Slowly the miiodon's bulk, clasped around the Fin, began to slide horizontally through the water, dragged by the sputtering ship.

"A little farther . . ." Tylar begged.

As he held his breath, the edge of the jelly shark brushed into a neighboring column of Gloom. The reaction was immediate. Tentacles spasmed, fonts of venom spewed into the surrounding seas. Like the weed and the schools of fish, the miiodon was a creature of this world, not the naether. The Gloom ate through its bulk as it fell farther into the heart of the naether bloom, feeding its substance to the void.

The Fin was dragged with it.

Again the mica tubes blazed sun bright with protective alchemies. Tylar's right hand brushed a cross tube, singeing his skin.

But they were free.

"Release the rudder!" he cried.

The Fin jumped forward, passing out of the Gloom and into clear waters. Shoving to his feet, Tylar took Delia's place at the controls and rolled the ship back into proper position. They regained their seats, and he fought the Fin up at a steep angle.

"With the damper broken," Delia said, "we can't slow her down."

They shot between the spiraling trunks of tangleweed, racing out of the depths, going faster and faster, cleaving through snarls and branches. No one spoke until the midnight waters lightened to twilight.

"The sun," Rogger gasped.

High above, a pool of watery brightness promised fresh air and escape. As the waters brightened to aquamarine, they shot free of the tangleweed forest and into the clear seas. Tylar held white-knuckled to the controls, keeping the ship angled upward.

"Hold tight!" he called.

They breached the ocean, bursting forth from the waves like a monstrous fish leaping into the air. The Fin sailed high for an endless breath, then crashed back to the seas with a jarring splash. For a moment they sank again, but the Fin bobbed quickly back up, jostling and rolling in the swells.

The sunlight through the dome was blinding, even with the sun close to setting by now.

"We made it!" Rogger cheered. "Not that I didn't think we would, mind you." He clapped Tylar on the back.

Delia sighed, not as pleased. She pointed to the spherical tank of bloody alchemies. It was empty. "We ran dry a few fathoms ago. We were climbing on buoyancy alone."

"Let's worry about that later." Rogger crossed to the stern, cracked the hatch, and threw it wide. A clean breeze swept into the cabin. "For the moment, at least we're still breathing." To demonstrate, he took a dramatic chestful of fresh air.

Tylar joined him, glad to face the sun. Still, a dark shadow remained around his heart. He considered what Fyla had given him, a name that revealed nothing but dread and mystery. "The Godsword," he mumbled aloud to the setting sun.

Rogger grunted. "An ominous epitaph indeed."

"Could it be real?" Tylar asked. "I'd thought the sword a fable."

Rogger shrugged. "Maybe it is. But fables often have some seed of truth."

Tylar still found it hard to believe. According to black myths told throughout the ages, the dreaded Godsword harkened back to the lost past of Myrillia, to the time of the Sundering itself, when the home of the gods was shattered. No one knew the true form of this dread weapon, though artists and storytellers dwelled upon this mystery, while philosophers debated its very existence. Only one detail was shared by all the tales: the Godsword was the weapon that shattered the gods' realm and brought about the Sundering.

But what did Meeryn mean by uttering it in her last breath?

He remembered Fyla's cryptic final words. *Though it is neither, you call it the Godsword.* He rubbed at the ache between his eyes. *Though it is neither . . .* What did that mean?

Rogger sighed, sensing Tylar's internal turmoil. "There is only one way to find out more about this Godsword, *Rivenscryr,* and that's in the libraries of Tashijan, where we are already headed."

"And where, if you are right, Meeryn's trust was betrayed."

Delia called up from the cabin. "I see sails on the horizon!"

Tylar and Rogger swung around to stare across the bow. Off to the west, limned against the setting sun, a cluster of full sails climbed into the sky.

Tylar ducked down. "A spyglass!"

Delia found one secured in a cubby. She passed it to him.

Tylar popped back up and pointed the glass toward the ships. The horizon sprang closer. He read the flags at the top of a center mast. A black castle against a silver background. The flag of the Shadowknights. And beneath it flapped a blue flag with a yellow sun emblazoned on it. He had lived under that flag for the past year.

It was the fleet of corsairs out of the Summering Isles.

He shifted the spyglass lower. At the ship's prow stood a figure draped in black. The distance was far, but Tylar knew who watched there.

"Darjon ser Hightower."

Rogger groaned. "And we're sitting in a floating milkweed pod. I don't suppose we can hope for rescue from the *Grim Wash?*"

Tylar focused on something hanging below the corsair's prow. "No," he said with pained sorrow.

Dangling there, hung by his neck, was Captain Grayl.

10

BLOOD RITES

MATRON SHASHYL SMOOTHED DART'S GOWN WITH AN EXPERIENCED hand, pulling hems straight, tucking away a loose gather, ruffling her half cloak so it fell evenly from her trembling shoulders.

"Calm yourself, child," she hushed in warm tones. "You'll shake yourself right out of your petticoats."

Dart nodded, but her trembling worsened. Her knees threatened to betray her at any moment. She could not feel her toes.

Shashyl sighed. "Child, you've already met the Lord. You know he won't bite."

Laurelle stepped to her other side. She moved like a flow of moonlight in her silver dress. She had affixed a diadem of kryst jewels to her ebony hair. The priceless stones, also called God's Tears, sparked in the light from the chamber's lanterns. A single Tear could ransom an entire village, but Laurelle wore the diadem as easily as a crown of woven grass.

Dart's friend touched her cheek. "You look so beautiful."

The words startled Dart out of her terror of the ceremony to come. Her disbelief must have been plain on her face.

"Come see," Laurelle urged, drawing her to the silvered looking glass.

Dart stepped in front of her reflection. She was draped in crimson high silk, a rich cloth that flowed like water. Her gown streamed from her buttoned neck to the stone floor beneath her slippered toes. A gold sash cinched the silk tight around her waist, while the sleeves billowed loosely at the wrist. A fire ruby rested in the hollow of her throat, seeming to flash with her own heartbeat.

Her hair had been scented with oils and combed back from her face, held in place by a gold net that sparkled with tiny fire rubies. Her cheeks blushed at the sight. Such richness could make a fatted sow beautiful.

Still, she found herself staring at the image in the glass, wondering if this was truly herself. Pupp had followed her. He nipped at the trailing edges of her gown, his teeth passing harmlessly through the silk. She ignored him, focusing on the stranger in the looking glass.

"If you two lasses are done admiring yourselves, perhaps we could finish your primping." Shashyl waved them over to her. "The horns will be sounding your summons at any moment."

A knock drew all their attention. The door opened to reveal two figures dressed in similar hues to Dart and Laurelle: a man draped in crimson, a woman in moonlit silver. *Blood and tears.* They were attended upon the arm by two servants.

Dart and Laurelle bent a knee each in a hurried curtsy.

Shashyl simply placed her hands on her hips. "Mistress Huri and Master Willym, if you get my girls to soil their dresses on this filthy floor, I'll not forgive you." Her words were stern, but her face smiled warmly. The woman, Mistress Huri, the Hand of Tears, entered the room, assisted by her maid on one arm and leaning on a cane with the other. "We would not think to spoil such loveliness, Matron Shashyl." Her eyes were milky, near blind, her back bent under the weight of ages. She was only fifty-six birth years, but appeared twice that. Such was the burden of Grace.

She hobbled to Laurelle, guided by her maid. "Come, child, let us speak." Laurelle stepped away with the woman whom she was meant to replace. Dart noted the awe in her friend's gaze.

Next came Master Willym. He was younger. Fifty-two birth years. But he moved as if death had already claimed him. His gold shirt and crimson surcoat hung on a frame of bones. He teetered as he walked, supported by a servant, but he kept no cane. He shuffled into the room toward Dart and lifted a hand. His skin was luminous and translucent, showing blue veins.

"I believe you are named Dart, is that not so?" he asked, his voice surprisingly firm, a remnant of the young man he once was. In his voice, he carried a smile warmer than the feeble curl of his trembling lips. "So you are the young lass come to take my place at my Lord's side."

She curtsied again, unable to speak. This was the first time they had met. The other Hands would be introduced at the ceremony as Dart and Laurelle were formally presented and raised to their place in the court.

She followed him to a small cushioned bench. It took him some gentle maneuvering to settle to a seat. He fell the last handspan with a heavy sigh, leaning back, eyes closed. "Ah, to have a young man's legs and back again . . ."

Dart hovered over him as Pupp sniffed at his pant leg. Willym finally patted the cushion beside him.

She sat on the edge, back straight.

He swung to face her. His eyes were cloudy, but shone with a spark of fierceness that belied his fading body. "It is custom for one handservant to speak words of comfort and reassurance to their successor." He reached and took her fingers between his own. "But I was never one for custom."

He nodded over to Laurelle and Mistress Huri. The pair embraced. "I can only imagine Huri has spoken all the sweet words required with great diligence and earnestness. Such is her way."

Dart stared over at them. Their very poses spoke of comfort.

Master Willym cleared his throat. His hands were cold on hers. "Instead I will share with you the counsel my esteemed predecessor instructed me with some four decades ago when I sat on this same bench." He stared hard at Dart. *"Gods live forever by sucking the life from their servants."*

Dart gasped at such blasphemy, drawing away her hand.

A dry chuckle escaped him. "Do not look so shocked. I saw your face as I hobbled in here. I must have worn the same expression four decades ago. It is one thing to understand the price of bearing a god's Grace, but it is another to see its wrinkled face before you, is it not?"

Dart gulped and kept her gaze upon the stone floor.

"Answer me, child."

She swallowed hard and choked out one word. "Yes . . ."

He struggled to sit straighter, assisted by his servant. "Face me."

She slowly turned.

He took her hand again. "Listen closely. Flesh is only wood, slowly burning to ash as we age. It is green when we are young, resisting the flame, smoking with all the fervency of youth. In the middle years, life's flame begins to lick and devour. And at the end, all will be consumed." He patted her fingers. "Understand, to serve a god is *not* a loss of life span. Our fires are not snuffed out early, but only stoked higher, to burn more brightly. Do you understand?"

Dart nodded tentatively.

Fingers squeezed hers as he leaned back. "Then you are better than I," he sighed. "I think what I said is all so much shite."

She again started.

A true smile formed on his lips. "I guess all I can really tell you is that I do not regret my life and service. Instead, I rejoice in it. As will you. There are no fancy words I can share that can encompass what you are about to experience, to live in Grace, to shine with it, to share your life with a god."

Dart trembled, knowing herself unworthy of such an honor, more so now than a moment ago. She was tainted. All would soon know. Lord Chrism had failed to note her disgrace when they had first met within the Eldergarden—he clearly must have been distracted—but her secret could not withstand his full attention.

A trembling hand reached to her chin, drawing her eyes back to Master Willym. Amusement faded to concern in his gaze. He seemed to be searching for something. After a moment, there was the faintest nod. His eyes flicked away to the room, then back again. Almost a nervous gesture. Strange in one so esteemed. His lips parted as if he were to speak again.

A horn sounded from the larger chamber beyond.

Willym turned, breaking the spell. He lifted an arm for his servant to take. "It begins." For the first time, his voice sounded as tired as he looked. Helped to his feet, he led the way toward the door, joined by Mistress Huri and Laurelle.

Matron Shashyl fussed over Dart one last time before finally letting her go. Dart took her place at Master Willym's side.

He kept his face forward but spoke one last bit of wisdom to her as the doors pulled open before them. "Trust only in blood . . . and your own heart. And all will be fine."

Dart took a deep breath, praying he was right.

Tigre Hall was named after the great river that splits the First Land into halves. It flows through the center of Chrismferry, a township that dates from before the coming of the gods, when the river's raging course had been forded by a ferry bridge here, the only means of crossing for a thousand reaches. Mills were built, tolls collected, and the trading post grew to a village, and the village into a township. It became a central site for trading, commerce, and countless wars. The ancient stone footings of the original bridge became the foundations for Chrism's castillion. The very hall down which Dart now paraded stood over the Tigre River. If one listened quietly, the river could be heard passing below.

Dart gaped around her.

Gentlefolk and those of nobility lined the curving rows of benches that faced the central high dais and the lone chair. It was as yet empty, a seat of carved myrrwood, ebonized, tall backed, arms curling to either side in gentle waves.

Behind the throne, a curve of smaller seats lined the back of the dais, four to each side, places for Chrism's handservants. The seats were occupied—all except two places, of course. Dart eyed the seat to the immediate right of the throne. She knew this was her place. Laurelle's chair awaited her, second to the left. Panic beat about Dart's chest like a loose sparrow. She hated to be even that far from Laurelle, especially now.

The pair trailed behind the two Grace-bled servants, hanging back, allowing the pair one last entrance into Tigre Hall as handservants to Chrism. The pace was gratingly slow. Eyes followed Dart's every step, weighing upon her like lead. She drifted closer to Laurelle, who seemed to take the procession with easy strides. She nodded to the occasional viewer, whether out of simple courtesy or some familial acquaintance Dart knew not.

She hung in Laurelle's shadow. It took every bit of strength to keep her head high, shoulders straight. Her own stride must appear as graceful as a sway-backed pony.

Laurelle caught Dart's eye for a brief heartbeat. Her gaze flicked off to the right, indicating where she should look. Dart followed her direction, but saw nothing. Then out in the sea of folk, a small hand waved a bit of white silk, catching her attention. It was Matron Grannice, from the Conclave, the old school, her home.

Dart fought back tears and failed. The same weakness afflicted the portly marm. The matron had to turn away. Only then did Dart spot Grannice's escort.

Healer Paltry stood at her side, an arm around the woman's shoulder, comforting. His lips moved with what could only be kind words meant to soothe. But his eyes drilled toward Dart, cold and unreadable.

Dart's feet moved faster, a reflex to escape. A hollow pain throbbed in her belly, an echo of her attack. The mere sight of the cursed healer was like a phantom finger prodding a bruise that refused to heal. Warm tears turned cold on her cheeks.

As she hurried forward, her toes struck the heel of Master Willym. His enfeebled pace stumbled. He went down on one knee before his startled manservant could catch him up.

Gasps and shocked exhalations spread outward, like the waves from a pebble dropped into a pond. Dart hurried to his side and helped him to his feet.

"Please forgive me," Dart murmured.

Willym gained his wobbly legs, his face red. Angry? No, just flushed from exertion. He patted her hand and spoke loudly enough for those closest to hear. "Ah, Chrism's Oracle chose well. A young lass with all the eagerness of an unbridled foal. Plainly ready to take my place. Whether I'm willing or not, it seems."

Gentle laughter joined his own.

He took her under his arm in friendly fashion and waved aside his manservant, dismissing concern. But his weight leaned heavily upon Dart. He tilted his head toward her. "Be at peace, lass. But get me to my chair."

"I'm so sorry."

He smiled gently down at her. "There's nothing to fear here."

An arrow pierced his throat, passing clean through. The steel tip of the bolt sailed past Dart's left ear, whistling away, trailing a spray of blood. Master Willym's eyes went wide as he fell upon Dart, collapsing atop her. Blood gouted from his mouth and nose.

They fell together to the floor.

Dart's skull struck the stones with a ringing blow. She felt no pain, only shock.

Screams rose around her like a whirlwind. In a daze, Dart watched Laurelle and Mistress Huri being shoved behind a bench. Nearby, Pupp ran in panicked circles around her, his molten coat as bright as golden sunshine.

Willym lay atop her, choking on blood, bathing Dart's throat with the last beats of his heart. His lips were at her ear, moving, attempting to speak, but all that came out was blood.

"Be calm," she urged him as her own vision wobbled and began to close tightly, the injury to her skull throbbing.

Deaf to her, Willym choked a final flow, then lay still. A last breath sighed from him, bearing forth a single word, as clear as crystal. *"Beware."*

Black-booted guards tromped to their side, circling them. Several passed through Pupp as he continued his blazing vigil. They were too late. Through her chest, Dart felt the last beat of Master Willym's heart.

He was gone.

She was now the lone handservant of blood, properly blessed.

Her vision continued to shrink in on itself, to a pinpoint, then nothing. The single word followed her into oblivion.

Beware . . .

❖

Dart dreamed.

She was a child again, a babe swaddled in furs, being carried in an open wagon. Voices came from all around. A leafy bower flashed past overhead. The scent of torn loam, manure, and decay carried to her. The voices spoke in a tongue she did not understand, but they seemed frantic, yelling.

A flash of silver swept over her face.

A cry. A curse. A shouted call.

Blood fountained from the left, bathing her hotly.

She cried now, wailing.

A face crept into view above her, tiny as a babe's fist, shining brightly under the dark bower, more fire than bronze. He nuzzled into her, panicked, too.

Together they cowered.

The scent of something feral reached her, huffing behind her, rank and musky. A horse whinnied in terror. A wagon jerked under her.

A warning reached her, beyond language, but still clear.

Flee . . .

❖

Dart woke with a startled wail. She fought the hands that held her.

Flee . . .

"Calm yourself, child. We must clean the blood off you."

Her eyes focused upon Matron Shashyl, bent over her, a fouled rag clutched in her hand. Her caretaker turned to rinse the cloth in a bucket of steaming-hot water.

Dart saw that Laurelle was clutched against her, hugging her. Only now did she recognize how naked she was. She was back in their tiny wardroom, sprawled on the same bench where she had chatted with Master Willym.

"Master Willym . . . !"

"Gone," Laurelle answered her. "Murdered most foully."

Dart again heard the whistle of the arrow past her ear. The blood on her face, neck, and chest was not her own. The back of her head, though, throbbed. She reached back and fingered a hard knot.

"You struck your head but good, child." Matron Shashyl nodded toward a kettle on a tiny brazier. "I'm steeping some willow bark and scamptail. It'll take the ache away."

"We thought you dead like . . . like Master Willym." Laurelle's voice dropped to a whisper. Arms hugged her tighter. "All the blood . . ."

Dart sat up and pulled her friend into her own arms. "I'm fine." She spotted Pupp down by the brazier, sniffing at the brewing herbs.

Matron Shashyl waved the girls apart. "Be off, Mistress Laurelle. You'll foul your petticoats. Let me finish the bathing."

Dart allowed herself to be cared for, too weak to resist. She was bathed clean and dabbed with towels warmed by the brazier. Once done, the matron wrapped her in a dry blanket.

"The assassin?" Dart finally asked. "Why did he . . . ?"

Matron Shashyl hushed her. "He escaped into the dark. Whys and wherefores must await his capture. Dawn nears, and guards have been woken from all the barracks. Grace-blessed hounds have already been loosed. None will rest until the fiend is caught." She wiped a tear and turned away. "Who could do this? Master Willym was dearly loved."

Not by all, Dart thought to herself. She remembered his last word. Was it delirium? *Beware . . .*

Beware what? Still, Dart sensed the warning had been meant for her and her alone. Spoken with the last trickle of life. If he had a message for her, why hadn't he spoken it earlier, here on this same bench when they had chatted?

She remembered the attack in the garden. She had told no one of what she had witnessed, trusting in silence, praying to remain unknown to the secretive nobleman. Now a second murder in one day. Were they connected? Maybe she should have spoken to someone about the bloodshed in the garden. Maybe Master Willym's assassin could have been stopped.

Though clean, Dart still felt bloody.

Laurelle returned from emptying the scrub bucket down the neighboring privy. She had stripped off her own dress and wore only her petties and slippers. "Mayhap we should return to our own room."

Dart nodded. She would not sleep the rest of the night, but it would be good to be surrounded by her own things. The small closet she and Laurelle shared as servants-in-waiting was cramped, but now Dart longed for its closeness, to lay with Laurelle in the single bed, under the covers until the sun rose and this long dark and bloody night ended.

Matron Shashyl had composed herself and faced them. "You're most correct. Your rooms are waiting for you. I'll have a maid bring up tea to your chambers."

Dart looked at Laurelle.

"Chambers?" her friend asked the matron.

Shashyl nodded. "Indeed. You are no longer servants-in-waiting. Though the presentation ceremony was interrupted so foully, this night still marks your ascendance to full handservants. Matron Willym and

Mistress Huri had already vacated their quarters in the High Wing. Your personals should already be up there. Come. I'll show you the way."

Dart numbly donned a set of small clothes and slippers, and wrapped herself in a full cloak of warm velvet. Crimson, like her missing gown. Laurelle modestly covered her own limbs with a silver cloak, thick and ruffled at the hems.

"We've a ways to climb," Shashyl warned them.

Dart didn't care. She was relieved they didn't have to head back through Tigre Hall. They left by another door. It opened upon a spiral stair that led only upward, to the High Wing. They mounted the stairs, past a guard at his post at the doorway . . . Dart had been this way once before, late for her studies under the matron. Shashyl had a suite of rooms in the High Wing as was her honor. Besides their tutelage, Matron Shashyl oversaw the maids and manservants that serviced the tower and its nine occupants: Lord Chrism and his eight Hands.

Pupp followed after them, hopping from step to step.

The climb, as warned, was long. Twenty flights. They passed the same number of guards, liveried in gold and crimson, Chrism's colors, one for each level.

Reaching the top, Matron Shashyl recognized the man guarding the double doors to the High Wing. He was older, black hair going to gray, but his eyes were spry and alert. He wore a nasty, tortured scar across his left cheek. "Kyllan, what are you doing posting a mere door? As Master of the Garrison, shouldn't you be overseeing the hunt for the assassin?"

His eyes flashed. He spoke with the terse tones of the fierce Thirdlanders. "I've given my orders. Huntsman Freetile leads the Graced hounds from the bestiary. Guards are on the streets. A pair of wyld trackers have been summoned from the Seer guildtower."

"And you?"

"Master Willym were under my protection when he fell. I led the other guards here. I'll not leave this post. No more of the blessed Hands will come to harm as long as there is strength in these bones."

He rested one hand on the hilt of his sheathed blade and opened the door with the other, bowing deeply. "Miladies, be welcome. Rest with good assurance. None will disturb the last of this sad night."

Laurelle took it all with easy aplomb. "Most gracious, Sergeant Kyllan."

Dart followed after her friend, nodding to the guardsman as she passed. Once the door was closed and secured behind them, Matron Shashyl waved her charges down the hall. Dart stared over a shoulder as she walked.

Pupp had hung back on the stair, sniffing at the guard. He now simply trotted through the closed wooden door, prancing a bit and shaking his molten coat as if he had passed through mere water. He hurried to catch up with them.

It was a wide passage. A four-draft carriage could have been pulled over the tapestried rug that ran down the hall. Tall, arched stained windows lined one side with historical depictions, but the starlight was too dim to illuminate the scenes, making them appear gloomy and menacing. Along the other wall, eight narrow doors awaited, one for each handservant. Lanterns flanked each threshold, but a fiercer rosy light rose from a grand brazier that stood halfway down the hall's length, where the passage widened into a half circle. Its brightness glowed upon a set of golden double doors that opened into Chrism's private chambers.

Dart's eyes remained fixed on those massive doors, fearing they would open. She had not faced Lord Chrism since that humiliating encounter in the Eldergarden, where she mistook him for a common laborer, treated him rudely and roughly.

Oblivious to her fear, the matron led them down the passageway. At the end of the hall lay a complex suite of libraries, studies, dining rooms, meant for the private use of the Hands to Chrism. Dart could not imagine communing with such esteemed personages as the other handservants. She heard voices echoing. A few of the Hands were still awake.

Before reaching the central brazier, Shashyl stopped before one of the doors. "Mistress Laurelle, these are the rooms reserved for the Hand of Tears." She turned and formally placed a thick silver key in Laurelle's palm. "Blessed in Lord Chrism's own tears."

Laurelle gaped at the key in her hand. Dart found some comfort that her normally assured friend was a tad overwhelmed by the moment. Their eyes met. Laurelle smiled almost shyly.

"Go ahead," Dart said, nodding to the door.

Laurelle used her key. The latch snicked, and the door swung open on silent, well-oiled hinges. Beyond, Dart caught a glimpse of a private greeting chamber, appointed in rich silks, thick carpets, and a hearth gone to ruddy coals. Other rooms could be seen opening deeper into the suite.

"I'll introduce you to your maids on the morrow," Shashyl said as Laurelle hesitated at the threshold. "The entire wing was cleared of all but the Hands as a precaution."

Laurelle took a deep breath and stepped through the doorway, eyes forward.

"Come now, Mistress Dart, let me show you to your room."

As they began to turn away, Laurelle swung back around and hugged Dart tightly. "I'm so glad you're here with me," she whispered.

Dart hugged her back, feeling the same.

Matron Shashyl tolerated their display for only a few breaths. "Enough. It's late." She touched Dart's shoulder. "Let's get you settled and some willow bark tea into you before you retire."

They broke their embrace. Laurelle watched them leave.

The matron led Dart past the glowing brazier. It was not ordinary iron, but a cage of petrified bone from some ancient creature. Its heat was like the sun on a summer day. Pupp nosed the bony brazier. His hackles rose as if bothered by the ancient scent of the long-dead beast. Dart tapped her thigh to draw him away.

They circled the brazier, slipping past the wide gold doors that led into Chrism's private abode.

Matron Shashyl walked her to the neighboring door. "Here are your rooms. The Hand of Blood." Again a key was pulled from a hidden pocket, but this time placed into Dart's palm. "Blessed in Lord Chrism's own blood," she said formally.

It weighed heavily in Dart's fingers. Not silver like Laurelle's, but gold. Dart's hand began to tremble. With such shaking, there was no way she could fit the key into the lock.

A hand rested on her shoulder. "Be not afraid," Shashyl whispered with genuine motherly affection. "You would not have been chosen if you weren't able to fill this duty."

Dart had a thousand words for why this was not true, but she merely nodded. Taking a deep breath, she turned to the door.

Pupp pranced a step ahead of her, seeming to know her destination. No lock was needed for him. He simply walked through the door.

Fearing his mischief, Dart hurried to unlock the way. The entry hall beyond was laid out the same as Laurelle's: stone walls warmed with fine Oldenbrook tapestries; floors covered with woven carpets of lamb's wool, freshly brushed and sprinkled with sweet oils; two winged chairs of tufted goose down facing the hearth and standing as high as a grown man. The only difference to Laurelle's room was that the tiny hearth had not died to coals in the absence of stoking, but still blazed merrily with licking flames.

Dart stepped into the room, searching for Pupp as the matron closed the door behind her, leaving her alone.

Dart spotted Pupp's tail wagging from beyond one of the two chairs. She walked around to scold him, only then noting the figure seated in the same chair, the source of Pupp's attention.

Her eyes grew wide with surprise. She was too startled to fall to her knees. "Lord Chrism . . ."

He was no longer dressed in the simple grubbery of a gardenkeep, but in a finery that outshone the hearth's flames. His boots, polished and lavishly tooled black leather, reached to his knees. His breeches were billowed silk, dyed bronze to match his hair. His black half cloak mounted a shirt woven of finely spun gold strands.

Yet still there remained a harrowed edge to him. His hair, oiled and brushed back from his face, lay mussed as if worried fingers had combed through it. His eyes were puffy and shot with red. He appeared no more than a few birth years older than Dart, more a boy than a god—an exhausted, heartsore boy. Green eyes flecked with gold fell upon her, full of sorrow.

Lord Chrism raised a hand, motioning to the neighboring chair. "Sit with me. For a moment."

Dart found his command easy to obey, her legs weakening with every breath. Had he discovered her soiled nature?

"I apologize for intruding into your private spaces," he said. "But it was here that I knew Willym best. I thought to find some comfort."

Dart's voice was as soft as a mouse's. She kept her eyes lowered to the floor. "All that I have is yours. I'm the intruder here. I'll gladly return to the closet reserved for those in waiting."

"No. Please. Stay. There are words I wish to share with you."

She risked a glance up. "Me?" She recognized the true depth of sadness in his eyes. They were reddened from weeping. Each tear shed, rich in Grace, was as valuable as molten gold. But there was no repostilary resting on the small tea table. He shed such riches freely in the memory of Willym.

He sat forward. His entire manner spoke of exhaustion. "You are now my Hand." He stretched an arm toward her, palm up.

Dart stared at it dumbly.

He waited, fingers outstretched, pleading in his eyes.

Dart rested her hand in his. Fingers closed around hers. His hand felt like any other. Warm, slightly moist. There was still a bit of dirt from the gardens in the cuticles.

Beneath them, Pupp lifted his nose, as if awaiting a treat to fall.

Chrism finally spoke. "I did not ask Willym to step down from my side. He insisted, as did my Huri." His voice caught in his throat, thickening with emotion. "A dark time is upon us, and as Willym was wont to say 'A God is only as strong as his Hands.' He and Huri knew it was time to step aside for those stronger and younger. We had hot debates on this very subject."

Dart could not imagine anyone arguing with a god, not even one of his own handservants.

"But Willym was right . . . if only a tad too slow in convincing me. We had thought we had time to train you, to ready you for the war to come."

"War?" Dart eked out.

He waved away her question. "Dark happenings have been cropping up in the lonely corners of Myrillia: a rash of plagues, ravings among lesser gods, stirrings in the hinterlands. But still, we had thought to have more time. Then Meeryn was slain most brutally . . ."

Dart, like all others across Chrismferry, had heard of the tragedy down in the Summering Isles, half a world away: an assassin blessed in Dark Graces had slain the Brightness of the Isles. Like the murderer here, he had also escaped. Her heart beat faster in her chest. Could there be a connection?

"Our enemies grow bolder, showing their true face," Chrism continued. "There can be no mistaking that a great war looms, one that will sweep all of Myrillia. But I never thought it would strike here so soon, in the very heart of the Nine Lands. And at such cost." A tear rolled down one cheek.

"But why murder Master Willym?" Dart asked.

Lord Chrism's hand gripped hers almost painfully. His long gaze focused fully upon her. Only now did she notice the ancient hidden behind the young. "Don't you know?"

Dart shook her head, beginning to tremble.

"It was not dear Willym who was the target of the assassin," Chrism said. "It was *you*."

❖

Dart waited for dawn. It refused to come. Standing at her bedroom window, she stared out past her private balcony that overlooked the breadth of the Tigre River. The High Wing sat atop the centermost tower of the castillion; four others rose from each bank of the river. Their tower was the tallest rising from the river itself, commanding a sweeping view down the waterway. The city spread to either side, sparkling with lamps and torches in the night.

Dart saw none of it. For the hundredth time since Lord Chrism had departed, her mind's eye played out the murder of Master Willym. She had glanced up just as the bolt had sliced through the old man's neck, whistling past her ear.

A bolt meant for her.

Lord Chrism had briefly explained the conclusion drawn by the Watchers of the Court, those men and women blessed with unending sight, tasked with storing all they saw, becoming walking libraries of events frozen forever in their minds. They were rare folk, Graced in the womb with alchemies of air and fire, leaving them weak of limb, requiring air-driven mekanicals to support them. Some said they could speak to each other through their eyes alone.

Dart had spotted one hovering at the back of Tigre Hall, in the shadows, eyes bright with inner fire.

Two others had been present. They had conferred. The bolt was seen leaving the shadowed assassin's crossbow by one, while another witnessed Master Willym bending toward Dart a fraction of a heartbeat later.

Dart remembered the old man's words: *There's nothing to fear here.*

He was so very wrong.

It was that bit of reassurance that cost Willym his life, bending over her at the wrong moment. If he hadn't, he would be alive now, and she would have taken the bolt to her left eye. So said the Watchers, playing the alternate scene out in their minds.

As the shock of this fully struck her, Matron Shashyl had come knocking at her door with the promised pot of willow bark tea. Lord Chrism finally seemed to note Dart's distress and excused himself, leaving her in the matron's care.

Shashyl had remained with Dart while she drank her tea. She had slipped a small bit of folded paper from a pocket and mixed its contents in the steaming cup. "Valerian root," she said as she tapped the teaspoon. "I sometimes take it to sleep when my old joints are protesting the cold nights."

Dart had taken two cups before the steeped water turned tepid and the taste bitter. But at least her limbs finally stopped shaking. The matron had walked Dart to the back room and put her to rest in a canopied bed of carved myrrwood. Before she knew it, she was pillowed in down and wrapped in layers of silk and velvet.

With promises that she would sleep, Dart thanked Matron Shashyl. The old woman had looked down upon her with concerned eyes, kissed her on the forehead, mumbled "poor child," and departed.

Dart had tried to sleep, but no amount of powdered root could settle her fears. Every time she closed her eyes, she saw sprays of blood, shadowed figures with daggers blackened with Dark Grace; even Healer Paltry's face floated before her. In all the bloodshed, she had forgotten about his appearance at the ceremony. Her worry brought it back afresh. At every turn, danger threatened. Punishment, banishment, and now the threat of murder from a new quarter.

But was it *new*? Could Healer Paltry have had a hand in the plot? To silence the girl who knew too much? Or was it the dark figure from the gardens? Had he recognized her as she fled down the twisting paths?

Finally, apprehension forced her from bed. Pupp followed groggily as she paced the length of her bedchamber, wrapped in a thick robe, praying for dawn to arrive, to burn away this long night.

It must not be far off.

Perhaps it was near enough to risk waking Laurelle.

Worry eased with this possibility. Perhaps she could even sleep if she shared her blankets with Laurelle. If only for this one night . . .

Desire became action.

Dart cinched her robe tighter, praying it wasn't unseemly to wander the High Wing in only robe and slippers. But then again, she didn't plan on being seen. Surely the remaining Hands were soundly asleep.

She crossed through her rooms, which included a bathing chamber, privy, and a tiny dining alcove. It felt good to be moving. She reached the entry hall, gathered her key from the table beside the door, and took hold of the door latch. She hesitated, then bent an ear against the door. She listened for any voices, any noises from beyond.

All silent.

She continued her attention for several breaths. Satisfied, she tested the latch and crept the door open. She peeked out. The central brazier continued to cast a warm glow down the hall. No one was in sight.

Dart eased the door open fully. No alarm was raised beyond the hammering of her own heart. She leaned out and peered in both directions.

Empty.

She hurried out into the hall and whispered across the tapestried rug on her slippers. She circled past the glowing brazier, followed by an irritable Pupp, his coat dull with exasperation. She fled to the second door past the brazier. The wall lanterns had been turned down by a maid or guard to the merest flicker. Still, Dart felt exposed standing beside the door.

She tapped lightly, hoping to wake only Laurelle. Her first attempt was no more than a brush of knuckle on wood. She barely heard the rap herself. She tried again with a tad more vigor. The knocking was loud to her own ears, but it earned no response.

Please, Laurelle, hear me . . .

She struck the door again. Three sharp raps. She ducked, hunching close to the door.

Please . . .

A soft sound answered her, sounding like the mild protest of a cat roused from a warm spot on a windowsill. Dart knocked again, more softly.

"Who's there?" a voice asked shyly from beyond the closed door.

Dart's lips brushed the wood as she answered. "Laurelle, it's me."

The sound of a latch being thrown rang out—it came not from Laurelle's door, but from down the hall.

Dart ducked close to the floor, her heart fluttering to a stop. Beyond the brazier, light spilled into the hallway as a door opened. A figure stepped into the hall, features cloaked in shadow. One of the other Hands.

"Is that you, Dart?" Laurelle called quietly at her ear.

She could not answer. The frantic beating of raven's wings filled her ears. She was again in the dark rookery, alone with a dark intruder. Fists clenched, fingernails digging into palms. *No, no . . . this is not the rookery.*

Dart tapped again on Laurelle's door, no more than the scratching of a mouse. Still, the stranger seemed to hear her and stepped in her direction. Features pushed into the brazier's glow, revealing themselves.

No . . .

Dart heard the lock release at her side. The door eased open. Laurelle's hearth had died to embers. No light flowed out.

Dart fell through the opening. Laurelle's mouth formed an O of surprise, but Dart silenced her with a finger to her lips and a hiss of warning. She pushed the door closed with the tiniest click of the latch, grateful to whoever oiled the hinges. She leaned against the frame, close to tears.

Laurelle dropped to her knees beside Dart. "What's wrong?" she whispered.

Dart shook her head, trying to cast out the image. The figure in the hall. *Lanky black hair split by a white lightning bolt.* It was the murderer from the gardens, the one who had slain the woman named Jacinta.

He was a Hand of Chrism.

11

SEA HUNT

ACROSS THE DARK SEAS, THE CORSAIRS BORE DOWN ON THEM. FIVE IN all. Sails abloom and lit by fire lamps in the rigging. They rode across the midnight waters like a storm of flaming clouds.

"Mayhap they'll miss us in the dark," Rogger whispered from his perch atop the Fin. To steady himself, the thief kept one hand on the tall fin cresting along the back of the craft, riding the swells.

Tylar shook his head as he peered out of the hatch. "Both moons already rise. The night will be clear."

Delia agreed from below. She watched from the Fin's window as the tiny vessel rolled in the gentle waves. "And the greater moon is full faced this night. The entire sea will be burnished silver under her glow."

Tylar scowled at their situation.

As the sun had set, all they could do was watch as the fleet spread out in a furious search, scribing a path along the fringes of the floating mat of tangleweed. Captain Grayl must have told Darjon ser Hightower where he had taken the godslayer before being hanged. Or more likely, one of his crew had spilled all. Tylar refused to think ill of the good captain.

Either way, they were doomed. Even now the corsairs swung out in a wider sweep, aiming for where the trio still foundered in the tiny Fin. They lacked even a paddle to maneuver out of the way.

"We have no choice," Delia said. "We must try."

Rogger turned to Tylar. "She's determined to kill us as much as that bloody Shadowknight."

Tylar dropped back into the Fin's cabin. Delia crouched between the two front seats, staring at the glass sphere, now empty of its alchemy. She unscrewed a silver plug from atop the sphere. "I've studied the mekanicals. I think we should risk it."

"Use my own blood to fuel the Fin?"

She pointed the stopper at him. "You carry Meeryn's Grace in you. The Grace of water. Like Fyla. Why shouldn't it power the Fin?"

Rogger spoke as he reentered the cabin. "Because it is not *pure* blood that runs a Fin. It's an *alchemical* mixture. A blend of humours known to those trained in their manipulations. And as I recall, alchemists live very short lives. Blown up by their own miscalculations."

Delia dismissed his concern. "The mica tubing still contains residual alchemy, the last dregs. All we need is a bit of fresh blood to ignite the Grace inside the mekanicals for a brief time. Enough to flee out of reach. It'll take just a little blood."

"A little?" Rogger repeated. "We've had this discussion already. If you're wrong . . . if the explosion doesn't kill us all, any fiery blast will draw the corsairs down upon us."

"They're already upon us, if you hadn't noticed." Delia cocked a thumb toward the window.

Tylar glanced from the lamplit sails back to the open cylinder. She did make a good argument. But it was his blood that would slay them if the works exploded. He found himself staring at his hands, unsure. Was it any better to take their chances with Darjon's corsairs? He had only to think of Captain Grayl to know how his companions would fare. He pictured Delia and Rogger swinging from their necks.

He would not let that happen.

Earlier, Tylar had hoped the corsairs would dock at Tangle Reef and remain unaware of their presence, giving time for the current to drift them out of harm's reach. Yet even that choice had its own difficulties. Adrift at sea—no food, little water—was only a slower form of death. But something had sent the corsairs searching wider. With Fyla distracted by the Gloom, word must have reached Darjon: The godslayer was loose.

Now, as the corsairs bore down on them, hard choices had to be made.

Tylar held out his hand to Rogger. "Your dagger."

The thief backed up a step, the only space left to him. "You're both as bad as blood witches . . . fooling with Grace that you know nothing about."

Delia snapped at him. "I'm a Hand, not a skagging *witch*."

Rogger lifted a brow at her cursing.

Tylar noted how tired she looked . . . and young. It was easy to forget. She had lost her god, seen her life turned inside out, and for what? To be hunted. He recognized the exhausted fear in her eyes, a haunting desperation.

He continued to hold his palm up toward Rogger. He had his own sword sheathed at his belt, but the long weapon was unwieldy in the cramped space, ungainly for the work needed here.

Finally, the thief slipped a tiny steel dagger from a sheath at the small of his back and placed it in Tylar's palm.

This calmed Delia. She nodded, wiping back a stray lock of hair from her eyes. "We'll just try with a few drops. See how the mekanicals hold."

Tylar moved next to her. "Do I need to concentrate? Direct some will into the blood?" He thought back to the curse of ice he cast upon the jelly shark.

"No," Delia said after a moment's hesitation, sounding unsure. "Raw Grace is needed here, pure force."

Tylar poised the dagger across his palm.

"Let me," Delia said softly, touching his hand. "It is my duty."

Tylar opened his fingers gladly.

She took the knife and, with her other hand, turned his palm down, then up again, seeming to study the length of his fingers, the hairs along the back of his hand, the architecture of his bones. Finally, she pointed the tip of the blade at a ropy vein on the side of his wrist. Her other hand latched above it, causing the vessel to bulge. "Hold steady."

Tylar was surprised by the iron hold of her fingers. She had wicked strength. Her middle finger dug into a painful point behind a wristbone. "Take a deep breath."

He'd just begun to suck in air when she stabbed the dagger's tip into the vein. Caught by surprise, he coughed with the bite of the knife—but there was no pain. She pressed her thumb over the wound before it even bled and stepped back, passing the knife back to Rogger.

Delia drew him by the arm to the glass sphere. She positioned the wound over the hole in the tank and released her thumb.

Blood flowed thickly down the inside of the glass.

Tylar watched. With the release of Delia's fingers, he felt a dull ache bloom from the wound. "How did you . . . I hardly felt—?"

"Training," she cut him off and knelt, studying the flow of his humour into the jar, watching it pool at the bottom.

"I thought you needed only a *little* blood?" Rogger commented.

"It is only a little. The bleeding will slow on its own."

Tylar saw she was right. Already the seep of blood thinned to rolling drops.

"A true draining requires a slice deep to wrist, throat, or back of knee. This should be enough." She stood and slipped a silk kerchief from a pocket. She tied a knot in it, placed it over the wound, snugged the ends tight around his wrist, and tied it in place with deft fingers. "Do not remove it for half a day."

Tylar had watched the seas through the window as she worked. "Here they come," he mumbled.

A quarter reach away, the sweep of high prows could now be seen, cutting through the black seas. Men moved in the rigging. Screened fire lamps shone out over the rails, lighting the waters, searching. Off to the left, the greater moon crested the waves, casting a swath of silver over the seas, pointing a finger directly at them. As Delia had noted earlier, there would be no hiding this night.

"If you're going to blow us up," Rogger said, "let's be quick about it."

Tylar made out the swinging form of Captain Grayl from the lead vessel. He felt the accusing eyes of the dead upon him. Then a fierce brightness enveloped the Fin. The path of one of the fire lamps had glanced over the craft—darkness descended again as the blaze swept away.

Had they been spotted?

Everyone held their breath. Even Delia halted her ministrations of the mekanicals.

The blaze swung back, skittered over them again, then fixed in place, lighting the seas around them as bright as the midday sun.

They had been found.

The lead corsair turned, digging deep as it swung about. The macabre decoration swayed from the prow, the dead captain's feet brushing the waves. Shouts echoed across the water, ghostly yet urgent.

"I'm becoming more and more resolved to the blowing up part now," Rogger said as he looked on, one hand raised against the glare.

Delia hurriedly replaced the silver plug in the crystal sphere. "I'd hoped to test it first . . . to leach no more than a drop or two of blood into the mekanicals."

Tylar crouched beside her. "We don't have the time."

Delia licked her lips, taking a deep breath.

Tylar reached over and gathered her hands in his. Her fingers were ice cold. He warmed them by squeezing tightly. "You were Meeryn's servant. She gave you her deepest trust and so do I."

"But—"

"Let the Grace flow."

Delia nodded, her gaze firming. "Everyone hold on to something secure."

Tylar climbed into the pilot's seat and waved for Rogger to sit.

Delia reached to the plunger that controlled the flow. Her eyes glanced at Tylar, questioning. One last chance to change their minds.

He gave her a nod.

She pulled the plunger.

The blood—*his* blood—drained down the bottom of the sphere, feeding into the mekanicals. The effect was immediate. As the fresh flow met the residual alchemies, the mica tubes flared to a brilliance that blinded, white hot and searing.

"Oh, no . . ." Delia mumbled, slamming the plunger home again with the heel of her hand.

White fire exploded outward, tracing the rib cage of mica tubing, passing over their heads, under their feet, sweeping back toward the stern. Tylar tasted the power on the back of his tongue, felt its heat on his skin.

"Hold tight!" he choked out.

The lines of fire converged upon the tapering stern and slammed together. The Fin reacted as if kicked. It bucked forward, throwing them all back.

Half-turned, Tylar's neck jolted. He used his handhold on the Fin's wheel to pull himself around. His ears rang. He stared through the window.

The blood-fired craft had taken flight—or so it seemed. It skimmed the surface of the black sea, riding atop the twin fins that ran along the belly of the craft. The Fin struck each shallow wave with a shuddering impact, rattling teeth. Tylar tried to slow them, to eke out some measure of control with the wheel.

No response.

Like a bolt from a crossbow, they shot across the seas, as straight as a marksman's aim.

The target loomed ahead.

The lead corsair.

Its bulk swelled into a planked wall before them, filling the world.

Tylar yanked the wheel to the right and left. It made no difference. They were headed for a deadly crash.

Rogger grumbled behind him, "Now this is much better . . ."

"Forget the wheel!" Delia cried out. "You have no rudder. The Fin's tail is out of the water!"

Her words awakened Tylar to his mistake. He had only been thinking port and starboard, right and left. In the ocean, there was also up and down. He shifted his feet to the floor pedals.

Ahead, the flank of the corsair rushed toward them, ready to slam them from this world.

Tylar shoved both pedals down to the floor. The Fin dipped its nose and dove down into the waves. The waters, lit by the moon and the fire lamps, swallowed them away, shining a deep aquamarine. Bubbles blew past as the craft sailed deep, descending toward the darker waters.

But escape still eluded them. A monster blocked their path, a black behemoth. It was the submerged keel of the corsair.

The Fin dove steeply, but their speed and proximity blurred their chances of ducking cleanly under it.

The view went murky. Tylar held white-knuckled to the wheel.

The *wheel*! He had forgotten! Now submerged, the rudder was back in the water.

With a sharp twist, he rolled the vessel to starboard, swinging low the fin protruding from the top of the craft.

And not a moment too soon.

The port side struck a glancing blow against the keel as it passed beneath the corsair. But they cleared it. If the Fin had remained upright, the ironwood keel would've cleaved the top fin as surely as any ax, shattering open the tinier vessel.

Free now, they swooped deeper into the darkening waters.

No one made any joyous sounds, too raw with their fright.

Tylar used the moment to test their controls. Wheel and pedals responded with the lightest touch, whetted by their speed. He stopped their descent. "We'll have to turn around, sweep back," he mumbled, more to himself than to his companions. "We're heading south. We need to go north."

Delia rolled out of her seat and checked the glowing tubing. The white-fire brightness had already faded. She ran a finger cautiously along one of the mica channels. "Cracks. Everywhere. The pure blood is too raw, too volatile. It sheds its Grace violently, burning up quickly."

Tylar noted the controls growing sluggish.

"But will the mekanicals last long enough for us to reach safe haven?" Rogger asked. "Somewhere solid enough to plant our feet upon?"

"We must let the tubes cool," Delia said, "then proceed more slowly from here. Only leach blood in drop by drop. I wasn't sure how much would be necessary to fuel the Fin. Now I have some idea."

Tylar swung the Fin around, gliding upward into the moonlit waters. Ahead pools of brighter water marked the corsair's lamps. He aimed for them.

Rogger noted his course. "Are you daft, man? Where are you going? Circle around them."

Tylar ignored him and continued toward the fleet. He aimed for one ship. It lay ahead of the others. He owed someone a debt. He wouldn't leave these seas without settling the matter.

He sailed the Fin up to the pool of light surrounding the lead ship, then ducked into its shadow. He raced under the keel to the bow. Once there, he kept pace with the ship and gently guided the Fin upward, surfacing just under the prow.

"Take the controls," he ordered Delia. "Just keep us steady."

He climbed past Rogger—but not before relieving the man of his dagger. He crossed to the Fin's stern and unhinged the hatch. He opened it enough to pop his head and one arm out.

Death scented the salt air, gagging him with its immediacy. His target hung overhead, limned in lamplight. Close enough to touch one of the dangling feet. Grayl's boots were missing, most likely stolen by one of Darjon's crew. His body appeared sorely used.

Tylar cocked his arm and threw the dagger with all the skill of his training. The blade flew true, slicing cleanly through the rope holding the captain aloft.

The captain had died because of him. He would not leave the man to be picked at by seabirds and to bloat in the sun. Tylar owed him at least this. A burial in the salt of the sea. An honorable resting place for one of the plowers of the Deep.

The body fell heavily into the waves, sinking rapidly away.

The missing body would not go long unnoticed.

Tylar dropped down, reaching out to slam the hatch.

The arrow pierced his outstretched wrist, striking completely through and into the Fin, pinning his arm down. The shock struck him before the pain.

Over the rail, a ragged scrap of darkness swept over the stars, skirting the risen moon. It swooped toward him.

Darjon ser Hightower.

A trap.

The Shadowknight landed on the back of the Fin, cloak swirling, his eyes aglow with Grace. He seemed more ghost than man, fraying at the edges as the night ate the lines of his form.

He spoke no words, had no hesitation. As soon as he landed, his sword swept for Tylar's throat.

Tylar ducked as low as he could, but his arm remained pinned outside, keeping him from escaping below. His shoulder wrenched. He moved too slowly. A whispered edge of the blade sliced across the crown of his scalp, leaving a line of fire behind.

Below, in the cabin, he found Rogger staring up at him, unable to help.

"Go!" Tylar shouted. Hot blood ran through his hair, past his ear, along his throat.

Delia responded. The Fin jolted forward.

Tylar hoped the sudden movement would unsteady the Shadowknight. Using this moment, Tylar leaped straight up and rolled out of the hatch.

At the stern, Darjon had fallen to one knee, but he was already rising, a surge of shadow.

Tylar focused on wrenching his arm free. Luckily, his own flesh had slowed the bolt. It had not struck the pod with much impact. He yanked his wrist free, taking the arrow with it.

Agony blackened the edges of his vision. But Tylar had lived with the daily tortures of a broken body. The pain focused him, reminded him of his fury.

The pair rose as one atop the back of the vessel: Darjon on one side of the tall central maneuvering fin, Tylar on the other. Darjon's sword stabbed with Grace-borne speed, but Tylar anticipated it. He danced forward, using the fin as cover.

Only then did he realize his mistake.

Darjon had intended only to drive him away from the open hatch. The Shadowknight stepped around. He stood now between Tylar and escape.

It was a foolish slip, one Tylar would never have made before. He may be hale of body, but he was far from his former sharpness of mind and reflex. But he knew enough to cast aside the mistake. It was done. A knight had to stay focused on the moment.

The pod bounced regularly as it sped across hummocked waves. Footing was tricky on the wet surface of the craft.

Tylar eyed the open hatch. If he could get below and seal the hatch, the pod could sink away. Darjon would be washed from its surface, forced to swim for his ship.

The Shadowknight read the intent in Tylar's gaze. With a sweep of cloak, he kicked the hatch closed and positioned himself atop it. "Where is your daemon now?" he taunted.

Tylar did not parry words. With his good arm, he slid free his sheathed sword, letting moonlight trace its length in molten silver.

A hiss of recognition greeted its appearance.

Tylar held Darjon's own blood-sworn sword, stolen in the Summering Isles.

Tylar stepped around the maneuvering fin. He cradled his wrist, still impaled by the crossbow's bolt, to his belly. He noted movement through the Fin's window below. Delia leaned forward, a hand pressed to her cheek, her eyes bright with concern as they met his. She reached from her face to the glass, laying her hand on it.

He turned away. It wasn't good-bye yet.

He studied Darjon. Tylar knew it would be impossible to lure the knight away from the hatch. He'd have to go to him, meet him.

Darjon kept his sword low, waiting, ready.

Tylar edged along the Fin, keeping his balance as the waves rattled the craft. Past Darjon's shoulder, the fleet of corsairs continued their pursuit, lamps aglow. Tylar recalled the ebbing power in the Fin. They did not have time to spare.

He stepped past the end of the maneuvering fin, facing Darjon.

They were beyond quips or barbs. A dead stillness lay upon them both. As in a match of kings and queens, the opening move was the most important. Feint or attack. Advance or retreat. Guard up or down.

The matter was settled in a flash of silver, lightning strikes in the night. Neither could tell who attacked first. Both moved swiftly, speed borne of Grace, fury, and desperation.

Tylar turned his wrist, blocking a thrust to his heart. The knight's sword slid down his blade and struck his hilt's steel guard with a resounding blow. Tylar felt the impact all the way to the shoulder. Darjon was damnably strong.

Forced back a step, Tylar shoved the knight's sword up and away. Bringing his own point low, he sliced through a fold of shadowcloak. If there was any flesh beneath it, Tylar did not find it.

Darjon knocked the blade down with a slamming blow from his hilt, then spun on a heel to slip inside Tylar's guard. An elbow struck Tylar in the center of the chest, knocking air from his lungs.

Another misstep in this dance.

With Darjon atop him, Tylar swung out with the only weapon available: the dart impaled through his wrist. He felt the tip graze more than cloth.

Darjon hissed, confirming the strike, and fell back.

With space now, Tylar brought his sword to bear.

An arm's length away, Darjon hunched. The wild lash of the sharp arrow had cut through the masklin hiding his features. For the first time, Tylar saw the face of his adversary.

The knight's paleness struck him first—not a snowy white, but more an absence of any color, bloodless. Had it ever been touched by sunlight? Even the glimpse of hair was too starkly white, brittle in the moonlight. His other features were as sharp as his eyes: thin lips curled in fury, a narrow nose pinched in distaste. A ghost cloaked in shadow.

But it was not his paleness that gave Tylar pause. A more disturbing revelation was exposed. It was not the presence of something, but the *absence*. The fish-belly whiteness of Darjon's features was unmarred by mark or blemish.

He bore no triple stripe of knighthood.

Darjon read the realization in his opponent's eyes.

Angered and shocked, Tylar missed the flash of silver until it was too late. A dagger, thrown from the hip.

"I believe you left this behind," the false knight spat.

Tylar twisted. The blade shot beneath his raised arm, carving a path along the underside of his limb, slicing tunic, skin, and muscle as it passed. It impaled into the tall fin behind him. Tylar recognized its quivering hilt. It was the same dagger he had used to pinion Darjon outside the gates to Meeryn's keep.

Darjon followed the attack with a savage thrust of his sword. Tylar, off balance, parried the blade poorly. He managed only to deflect. He had no footing to counter.

Panic slowed everything, like a nightmare. Darjon expertly trapped Tylar's sword with his own. Tylar, weak from the dagger's cut, could not stop the blade from being ripped from his grip.

His sword flew and struck the curved back of the Fin.

It slid toward the waiting sea.

Tylar lunged for it, desperate—only to see its black diamond pommel slip beyond his fingertips and plunge away. Weaponless, wounded, he rolled around to his back.

Darjon stood a step away, death promised in his eyes as he raised his sword.

Tylar felt the hot trickle of blood down the inside of his arm, pooling around his hand. He tried to scramble backward, but the footing was slick from the slosh of waves. His back struck the end of the Fin.

If he could snatch the dagger . . .

But a fast glance showed it was beyond his reach.

Darjon closed, his sword point scribing a sigil of finality in the air.

Tylar, wiping cold sweat and blood from his eyes, flashed back to Delia, pressing her palm against the glass. He realized it had not been a good-bye, but a warning.

He looked at his fingers. Sweat and blood. As his yellow bile had charmed the miiodon, his perspiration could do the same to the nonliving.

Such as a wooden craft in the middle of the Deep.

Tylar brought his hand down upon the Fin's surface. As before, he willed the world to ice, touching his memories of frozen tundras, snowstorms, and frost fogs.

From his fingertips, runnels of ice shot outward. In a heartbeat, the damp surface of the Fin froze over, sheeted with planes of ice, crystalline and scintillating in the starlight.

Tylar felt the frigid bite through the damp seat of his breeches, freezing him to the deck.

Darjon had hesitated as the Grace flowed. He now took a cautious step backward, confusion plain on his face. His inattention betrayed the heel of his boot on the slick ice. He skated for balance, lost it, arms pinwheeling.

With a distinct lack of dignity, the man's legs flew out from under him. He landed on the slippery surface and continued his slide. Hands scrambled for purchase. But burdened by the sword he refused to abandon, he failed and soon slid over the edge and splashed into the sea.

Tylar ripped himself free of the frozen clutch of the Fin's surface and crawled on hands and knees. He spotted Darjon a few lengths away, fighting the waves and the weight of his waterlogged cloak.

Shivering, Tylar crossed to the hatch. He fought to lift it, but a coating of ice locked it tight. He pounded a fist on the door, trying to break through the crust. He was too weak, left with only a child's strength.

Across the sea, the fleet of corsairs swept toward them, filling the starry world with firelit sails.

A muffled call sounded below. He could not answer.

Then with a crack that sounded like splintering wood, the hatch banged open, coming within a hairbreadth of smashing Tylar's nose. Rogger popped his head out, scanned the immediate area, then settled on Tylar.

"Figured the chill had to be more 'n a sudden change of seasons," he said, his eyes drawn to the nearby splashing as Darjon swam toward the sweep of ships. "Looks like you shook loose that black-robed barnacle."

"For now," Tylar said hoarsely, picturing the murder in the false knight's eyes. "For now . . ."

Rogger finally seemed to note Tylar's bloody state. He helped Tylar below. Tylar bit back a groan when the arrow in his wrist jarred against the frame of the Fin's hatch.

"Ay, take a care there," Rogger said with his usual late concern.

They fell together the rest of the way into the cabin. Out of the sea breeze, the cabin was as warm as a hot bath, heated by the blaze of mica tubings. Rogger reached up and slammed the hatch.

Across the cabin, Delia dove the Fin deep.

Rogger helped Tylar sit up. "You took a foolish risk back there."

Tylar shivered and coughed. "I had no choice but to fight the bastard." He again pictured the unmarked face of the man, a false knight. For the moment, he kept silent, needing time to mull over this newest mystery.

"I meant," Rogger continued, "it was daft going back to free the captain."

Tylar shook his head. "Captain Grayl deserved the effort. My blood was a small price against his life."

"Dead is dead. Debts end with one's last breath."

"Honor does not."

"Spoken like a true knight. I thought you had given up on that."

Tylar let his scowl answer for him. When he'd been a broken scabber in the alleys of Punt, his life had been without responsibility, even to himself. Now hale again, burdened at every turn, he found the need once more to acknowledge honor . . . even in death. Grayl would not have wanted to end his presence here by rotting at the end of a rope. If Tylar could grant him nothing else, he could acknowledge that and act upon it.

Rogger shook his head.

Delia called back. "Rogger, man the wheel. I've taken us under the waves. Just keep us moving straight. I'll ministrate his wounds."

"Ministrate away," Rogger said as they switched places. "But do something about that stubborn streak of righteousness. It'll kill him faster than any sword."

Delia waved him off. Tylar allowed her to free his coat's laces. Blood flowed from scalp, right wrist, and left upper arm. He read the concern bright in her eyes. "I'll heal," he insisted.

"Of course you will. Firebalm will mend the worst." Delia expressed her true concern as she parted his sodden coat and saw his soaked linen tunic, more red than white now. "But you've lost so much blood."

The world swam at the edges, watery and loose. "I'll live."

"That's not my concern." Realizing what she had said, she quickly corrected herself. "Rather that's not my *only* concern. We need pure, uncontaminated blood to fuel the Fin. But we can't risk taking more now. You've wasted so much of it."

"Sorry," he said.

She slipped a fruit-paring knife from a pocket and sliced off his tunic with deft strokes. She used the strips to bind the cut on his upper arm, then had him hold a wadded piece of his own shirt atop his head.

"We must free the arrow."

He nodded. "Break the iron head, then withdraw it backward."

"It'll bleed afresh."

"Then you'd best collect it," he said with a tired smile.

She kept her eyes down. "Sorry . . . after so long with Meeryn. Every drop is precious. To see it spilled to no purpose . . ." She shook her head.

"Then you'd best find a bowl as you work the arrow out."

"Only glass will preserve the Grace. Any other vessel will allow it to seep out."

Tylar focused on her words as she worked the wooden haft behind the head of the arrow with her knife, scoring the wood to snap it clean. Each scrape stoked the pain in his wrist. He felt it in his teeth. He spoke to keep from screaming, his voice strained with the effort. "Why glass? Why not stone or metal?"

"Stone, clayware, bronze, steel, all come from the ground, from the aspect of loam. Grace wicks into it."

Crack.

Tylar gasped out as Delia suddenly broke the arrow's haft. She had given no warning. "But glass comes from sand," he said tightly, riding down the pain. "Is sand not loam, too?"

"Yes, but glass has strange properties."

"How so?" He used his curiosity like a crutch.

"Glass, though seeming solid, actually flows . . . like water."

Tylar's disbelief must have been plain.

She shrugged. "Despite appearances, alchemists insist on the nature of glass. It's this constant flow—too slow to see—that keeps the Grace preserved and protected behind glass." She reached to his wrist. "Now let's see about removing the rest of this arrow."

Tylar waved his bloody wad of shirt toward the bow. "Help me to the Fin's tank. You were right a moment ago. We'll need the fuel to make landfall."

He allowed Delia to wrap an arm around his bared midsection as he climbed to his feet. The world went black for a moment. His heart thudded in his throat. Then after a breath, vision returned.

He hobbled forward, leaning more upon Delia than he had intended. Shame was a useless emotion at the moment, and he was still unaccustomed to his hale form—yet to lose it again discomfited him.

They reached the tank. Rogger eyed him, true worry shining.

"Shall I pull it out?" Delia asked softly.

"I'll do it."

"Maybe you two need a bit of privacy," Rogger snorted, but his humor sounded forced.

Ignoring him, Tylar yanked the arrow free. His knees buckled. He hadn't expected that. But Delia was there, catching him, struggling with his weight.

Maybe there *was* a use for shame. It returned strength to his legs.

He positioned his arm over the open spigot atop the crystal tank. Blood poured copiously into the vessel. He felt it drain from him with each heartbeat.

Again darkness squeezed his vision to a narrow point. He found himself no longer standing, but slouched in one of the rear seats, head lolled back.

He craned back up, assisted by a hand from Delia. Her palm was so warm against the back of his neck. A moan escaped him.

"There he is again," Rogger said.

Delia held a cup in front of his face. "Drink," she insisted.

Water flowed down his throat. He choked on it. Before he drowned, he pushed her arm away. He saw his wrist was bandaged. How long had he been gone? Delia tried to dote on him. He waved her away, more gently this time.

"I . . . I'm better."

Delia sank into the other seat. Her words were for Rogger. "We must get him to a healer."

"Fitz Crossing is closest," the thief answered at the wheel. "We could be there by morning. But no doubt that Shadowknight and his corsairs will guess our course and head there, too. They may even reach the island before we do."

Delia wrung her hands. "We must take the risk."

"No," Tylar croaked. "We make straight for the Steps. We can reach the First Land in two days' time."

Rogger stared back at him. "Of course, there's a third choice. We're free . . . with a boat. Why not head to some distant backwater where no one knows us?"

Tylar met the thief's gaze. A part of him was drawn to this dream. But his mind's eye kept coming back to Grayl, bare toes swinging overhead. He slowly shook his head.

"Why not?" Rogger asked. "Live our lives with no past."

"Or future." He swallowed hard, a bitter taste in his mouth. "I've been there before . . . the place you say you want to go."

"Where's that?"

"Where I came from. Where I'd been hiding. *Some distant backwater.* A place like Punt. I don't want to go back." As he spoke those words, he felt a noose around his own neck cut free. Something loosed in him and dropped away. "We go," he said, putting every last bit of firmness in his voice.

Rogger slowly nodded.

Delia looked less convinced. "More than anyone, I want to expose what happened to Meeryn, but you must rest. I found a cache of supplies, old from the look of them, at the back of the Fin. There was powdered nyssaroot for pain."

"Nyssa? I'll sleep for days."

"Exactly. You'll leave your wounds undisturbed and give your body time to mend. I insist."

Tylar frowned, sensing a core of determination in her that he didn't have the strength to fight. He nodded. The world spun with even that small motion.

"Good. You should be feeling the numbness in a few moments."

"What . . . ?" He glanced to the abandoned cup. "You already—"

The world rolled backward, darkening.

"Sleep," she urged him.

He had no choice.

❖

A timeless span later, Tylar woke to snoring. It was not his own. He turned his head.

Rogger curled on the floor beside him, nestled in a pile of netting. Each breath rattled in and sputtered out, regular as a well-wound clock. The thief smelled ripe—or maybe it was Tylar himself.

He shifted.

The only light in the cabin was the perpetual glow of the skeletal tubing. Beyond the Fin's window, the waters were inky dark, except for the speckling of spinning bits of phosphorescence. Tiny sea sprites chased and harried the stranger in their midst.

Delia stood silhouetted against the window, chewing on the knuckle of one finger as she inspected the tangled mekanical heart of the vessel. She was mumbling, in midargument with herself.

Tylar shifted, aching all over, but it was a wooly discomfort. Not sharp. He tried sitting. The world shivered, but it settled quickly.

Delia turned.

"You're awake."

"I think so . . . Ask me again in a few moments."

"Would you like some water? Do you need to relieve yourself?"

He nodded to both but asked only for water. He couldn't face her trying to preserve his morning humours. Delia helped him up into a seat. The effort was like climbing a mountain with a full pack of rocks. He sat heavily with the cup in hand.

"This is just water, right?"

She smiled and nodded.

"How long have I been asleep?"

"Through an entire day. It's night again. But the rest has done you well. You look good."

"I wish I could say the same about how I *feel.*"

Concern crinkled her brow.

He held up a hand. "No, I'm doing better. Truly. Don't worry."

Her face relaxed. In this moment, her simple beauty shone. A softness and clarity that was pleasing to look upon.

Tylar cleared his throat, suddenly awkward with such thoughts. She was near to half his age. He glanced to the mekanicals. "How is the Fin holding up?"

Delia sighed. "We lost a few tubes. Shattered away. But if we don't press the works, the rest should hold."

"And the blood?"

"We're fine. Plenty. But it'll take another two days to reach the Steps."

Tylar didn't complain. They were moving, safe for the moment. And much of it was due to the woman seated across from him. He was impressed with her resourcefulness and skill.

He motioned to the crystal tank. "How did you come to know so much about alchemy? Were you schooled in it?"

She shrugged, shook her head, then glanced to her knees, pulling into herself. "My . . . my father had an interest in alchemy."

From the hunch of her shoulders, there was more history than the words implied. Something unhealed. Only now did Tylar realize how reticent Delia had been about her past. Then again, he had been no more forthcoming, having been orphaned himself, birthed as his mother drowned, his father dead. His own past had no family stories or histories, so he had not missed the same from Delia . . . until now.

"Where did he practice his alchemy?"

She seemed to shrink further. "He was not an alchemist, only a dabbler. But his interest became mine when I was very young . . . before my mother died of the pox. She was a healer." She added this last quickly, proudly. "She caught the pox during the Scourge, going into places others wouldn't tread for fear of contagion."

Tylar did a quick calculation. That meant she lost her mother when she was only eight birth years.

"After that, something died in my father. He sent me off to my mother's family, a land away, a family who hardly knew me. He took back his name and left me my mother's. I was not the easiest child at the time."

Heartbroken and angry, Tylar guessed. He could relate. He had been bounced around from home to home himself. But he recognized a deeper pain in her. He had never known his family, long dead and buried. Hers had cast her away like so much refuse. A cruelty that surpassed tragedy.

"How did you end up in the Summering Isles?"

She shrugged. "My mother's family could not control me. I was sent to the Abbleberry Conclave, where I was eventually chosen." A small smile broke through the gloom. "One of the happiest days of my life."

"And what became of your father?"

Her smile vanished.

"I'm sorry. I'm intruding . . ."

"No, it's just . . . we haven't spoken since I was sent off. I doubt he even knows what became of me. The only thing I have left from him is my interest in alchemical studies."

"Yet he wasn't an alchemist himself?"

"No." She glanced to Tylar, her voice bitter. She pointed three fingers toward his face, toward his stripes. "He was a Shadowknight. Like you."

Tylar felt a sting from her words, old anger glancingly aimed at him. He fumbled for words. "What was his name?"

Delia shook her head. "I won't speak it."

"What of his family name then? The one he took from you."

She answered leadenly. "It was Fields."

What little blood that still coursed in Tylar's veins drained to his feet. He fought to keep from yelling. "Not *Argent* ser Fields?"

Delia's gaze darted at him, eyes going hard. "You know him?"

Tylar pictured the long bench in the Grand Court of Tashijan, the line of adjudicators, soothsayers, and representatives of the Council of Masters and Order of Shadowknights. In the center of them all reigned the over-seer of the trial. Beyond this knight's masklin, only a single eye glowed, the other covered in a patch of bone, earning him the nickname *One Eye.*

Argent ser Fields.

"How do you know him?" Delia asked again, almost a demand.

Tylar could not face her. "Your father . . . he sent me into slavery."

THIRD LANDFALL

Tashijan ʃ founded in 129 (new ann.) by First Warden Kreier ser Plumas, the Citadel houses both the Order of the Shadowknights and the esteemed Council of Masters, uniting Myrillian might, justice, and wisdom to the service of high and low. It is said of Tashijan: "The Nine Lands are only as strong as the cornerstones of the Citadel. As Tashijan stands, so does Myrillia."

—Historicals, Treatise of Annise, ann. 3291

12

CROSSROADS

"CASTELLAN VAIL!"

The call drew Kathryn's attention around. One hand still rested on the latch to her new rooms, chambers that once belonged to Mirra but were now hers. She turned to find a stick figure of a man striding down the hall toward her. He was dressed in the blue-and-white of the livery staff; as he neared, Kathryn recognized him as the personal manservant of Warden Fields. The fellow reminded Kathryn of the long-legged mantis bugs that frequented the fields around Tashijan: wide startled eyes, arms always moving, jerky motions of the head.

He offered half a bow as he stopped beside her. "Excuse me, Castellan."

"What is it, Lowl?"

"Warden Fields requests your immediate presence for a private counsel."

Kathryn glanced to her door. For the past several days, she had feared and dreaded this summons. Until now, the few occasions when castellan and warden had met were overseen by various knights and masters, when matters of rule and writ had to be decided, matters of succession and appointment delegated. They had yet to meet alone. But at each meeting, Argent had caught her eye, a glint in his own promising further discussions would follow. It was a look laced with menace, almost leering.

And now the summons had finally come.

She glanced down at herself. She was ill suited for such a visit, just back from an early-morning ride, sweat stained and smelling of horse and saddle. "I will see to the warden as soon as I've adjusted myself properly."

Her hand pulled the latch to her door. She would need a few moments to steel herself for the coming meeting with the leader of the Fiery Cross, the man said to have had a hand in the murder of Ser Henri and perhaps

Mistress Mirra. The former castellan still remained missing, despite days of searching. Trackers with black ilk-beasts sniffed throughout the Citadel.

"Mistress . . . Castellan, I must insist you come with me now. I've been searching for you since the full ring of the Sunrise Bells."

"Then a few moments more will make no matter, will it not?"

A heavy sigh escaped Lowl. She had not thought such a weighty sound could come from such a thin man. "The news is most urgent." He glanced up and down the hall, a mantis searching for prey. He leaned closer. Kathryn backed up a step. "It concerns the godslayer."

Kathryn's hand fell away from the door latch.

Lowl nodded. "Warden Fields knew you would want to hear the tidings from his own mouth."

Her heart thudded in her throat, threatening to choke her. If there was fresh word, then Tylar must have been spotted, found, rooted out. And if that were true, he was surely slain. A mighty bounty had been placed upon his head, with or without his body attached; word had been sent by a flock of ravens to all the cities of the Nine Lands, even out into the few semi-tamed areas of the hinterlands.

"What has happened?"

Lowl shook his head. "I've perhaps said too much already, but I needed you to understand the urgency and follow me at once." He turned on a toe and continued back down the hall.

Kathryn was drawn after him. How could she not be?

Lowl led her to the double doors that opened into the Warden's Eyrie, formerly the abode of good Ser Henri, now the lair of his likely murderer. The manservant tapped the silver knocker on the door. The sound reverberated off Kathryn's ribs.

The door opened before the echo faded, opened by the hand of the new warden of Tashijan, Argent ser Fields.

Lowl bowed deeply. "Warden, I present Castellan Vail, as you requested." He sidled back, making room for Kathryn.

Argent filled the doorway, dressed informally: black boots, trousers, gray shirt with silver buttons. His auburn hair had been pulled away from the hard planes of his face and tied up with a spiraling loop of gray leather that matched his shirt. One dark green eye studied her, the other was a blank plate of bone. It was hard to say which was warmer.

Kathryn stepped forward, hands behind her back. "Ser Fields, you summoned me?"

A tired sound met her words—not so much a sigh as an exhalation.

"Here in the Eyrie, Argent will suffice. We can forgo the formalities." He moved aside. "Please come in."

She passed through the doors, unsure what to expect. She held her breath, eyes alert. She still wore her cloak and sword from her ride—no knight left Tashijan uncovered. She had to restrain herself from pulling up her hood and hooking her masklin in place, an instinctive reaction to threats.

The main chamber was vast with its own terraced balcony overlooking the inner gardens. The view of the giant wyrmwood tree matched her own in the neighboring castellan's hermitage. The door to the balcony lay open to the morning sunshine, allowing a freshening breeze into the room. The appointments to the chamber were simple yet elegant: tapestries that dated to the founding of Tashijan, goose-down settees and chairs, a tall hearth still aglow from the prior night's fire. Thick rugs warmed the bare stone, though one had been rolled back in a corner section of the room. There, a stand of swords and staffs stood racked. Plainly it was a small practice space for Argent to keep his skills honed.

Nowhere about the room was there a trace of menace or ill purpose.

Lowl closed the door and crossed to a small table and chair. A bowl of sliced yellow sweetapples and bunched grapes sat beside a copper tray of cheeses and a loaf of bread. The manservant poured two mugs of steaming bitternut from a silver flagon.

Argent nodded to one of the seats. "The stables sent up word of your jaunt. I'd assumed you'd not broken your fast yet this morning. It would be my pleasure to offer you my table."

"How kind," she answered, but she made no move toward the spread.

As Lowl stepped aside, Argent turned to his servant. "That will be all, Lowl."

Lowl bowed himself out, retreating through a side door into the servants' rooms.

Once the door closed, Argent crossed to the table, speared a slice of apple with a knife, and bit a chunk. He settled to one of the two seats, legs outstretched, relaxed. He stared at her.

Kathryn found the gaze somehow too personal, too intimate. She moved to the table to escape his study. She busied herself with slicing a chunk of bread and smearing a baked cheese onto it. Her eyes focused on her task, she spoke as evenly as she could manage. "Your manservant mentioned some word on Tylar."

"Yes. He's been found."

Kathryn could not stop her shoulders from tightening as she glanced toward the man. His eyes—or rather *eye*—remained stone. Unreadable. He waited. She met his gaze and held it. She would not give him the pleasure of hearing her ask.

Argent shifted and finally continued. "A Shadowknight out of the Summering Isles led a fleet of corsairs across the Deep, following bits of trail left behind by the godslayer. He was almost caught, engaged by this knight, but escaped in a vessel stolen from Tangle Reef."

"Tangle Reef? How?" Kathryn settled the knife to the table, ignoring the bread and cheese. *Tylar is still alive.*

A shrug. "Fyla of the Reef has always been reclusive in her watery realm, suspicious of all. She has refused to communicate, even in this dire matter, withdrawing her realm from habitable seas. But in her wake, large swaths of dead tangleweed, singed and smoldering, foul the seas. Ships report a poisonous stench that kills with a mere breath. There can be no doubt that the realm was attacked most foully and now retreats to lick its wounds."

"Tylar . . ."

"The godslayer proves his dark bent yet again." Argent sat straighter, plucking a few grapes from a bunch. "But measures are being taken."

Kathryn frowned. "Measures?"

He waved away her question with his knife. "I called a council. 'Til then we have more to settle between us. Please sit."

She remained standing.

"Do you not wish to know why I chose you as castellan?"

Warily, Kathryn obeyed. She sank to the other seat, too curious to refuse. "Why?"

He leaned forward, elbows on the table. "Because I need you."

The earnestness of his words struck through her.

"In the past, you have demonstrated the ability to place the welfare of Tashijan above personal gain or desire. When I was overseer for your betrothed's adjudication, you set your own heart aside to speak the truth. I watched the pain with which you spoke those damning words of accusation. Yet you did not falter or attempt to obfuscate."

Kathryn looked down. The pain from that day remained with her. She had sat upon the chair of truth and told all how Tylar had come to bed on the night of the murder of the cobbler's family covered in blood, smelling of ale and drink. She had already heard testimony about how his sword had been found among the bodies, how Gray Traders, under the cloak of anonymity, had shown records of Tylar's dealings with them, and how on the night of the murders, a cross-street neighbor to the cobblers had seen a Shadowknight vanish into the night's gloom.

"Each word you spoke destroyed a small part of you," Argent said.

Kathryn forced her hands not to touch her belly. The heartache and anguish destroyed more than just her own well-being. She had been with child, Tylar's child. She had been hoping to tell him the night he vanished, the morning he came home bloody to her sheets. But that moment was lost forever. During and after the trial, heartache wrung her body, finally choking the child from her. She remembered the blood on her hands, staining her sheets again. Strangely, there had been too little pain to take so much from her.

"It is such bravery of spirit that has always stayed with me," Argent said quietly. "It is such bravery that is needed now, during this dark time."

"Still, you chose me against tradition. One of the Council of Masters has always sat as castellan."

"Not always. There has been precedent in the past. During the rule of Warden Gilfoyl, he chose another knight."

Kathryn knew the story. "The two were lovers."

"So it was rumored, but the pair did rule Tashijan for two decades, well and with much accomplishment. And prior to that, for the first three centuries, there was no Council of Masters. Tashijan was ruled solely by knights."

"And is that what you wish again?"

"Of course not. I would not usurp such power. Balance in all things is the best way to govern."

"So again, why pick me over an equally brave and well-spoken member of the Council of Masters?"

His one eye narrowed. "Because you have no equal, Kathryn ser Vail."

Again the intensity of his gaze felt a violation. She reached to the mug of bitternut and warmed her palms upon its hot surface.

"I've waited a long time to have you at my side."

Kathryn heard a hint of something deeper, a trace of huskiness in his voice. She remembered the stories of Warden Gilfoyl and his castellan. Leaders and lovers. Did Argent believe they, the two of them . . . ? She shoved such a thought away, repulsed. Instead, one hand reached into a pocket and removed a black stone, her cast ballot. She placed it on the table. Painted on the stone's surface, the crimson sigil was plain to see, a circle around a slash of crossed lines.

"What of this?" she asked.

Argent leaned forward again. "Ah, yes, the Fiery Cross."

"So you don't deny that you are a member of this order?"

"Not at all," he said. "In fact, I'm the leader and founder."

Kathryn's blood went cold. She couldn't keep the shock from her face.

"But please, don't mistake the rumors and nighttime tales of the Cross. Such a group never existed. We don't practice Dark Graces or blood rites. We don't skulk around hidden chambers. We are merely a faction of knights who wish to see Tashijan function more independently of the rule of gods and men. It is a minor, yet volatile, distinction. Nothing sinister. So we took the old name of the Fiery Cross as our own. The symbol of *fire* was apt. It is only in flame that something stronger can be forged. And with Myrillia standing at a crossroads in history, choices have to be made. Which path to take? Ser Henri looked to the past, to the old ways. We knew such measures had grown stagnant and that a new path was needed. Ser Henri did not agree."

Kathryn attempted to hide any reaction to the name of Ser Henri, but something must have shown through.

"No, I did not slay Ser Henri. We had our differences, but as I said, they were political and philosophical. Nothing to shed blood over."

"And what of Castellan Mirra?"

"Ah, yes, now that is something of a concern." Argent shook his head sadly. "Ser Henri and I had discussions about her. Few would know, but she has been growing more and more addled of mind and reason. Flights of suspicion that had no thread in reality."

Kathryn kept her own suspicions silent. He had all the right answers, but were any of them true?

"Myrillia is faced with a dark time. Unrest and menace grow each day. Darkness has even reached Chrismferry, in the form of an assassin who slew one of Lord Chrism's Hands."

Kathryn, like all in Tashijan, had heard the bloody story.

"And there can be no doubt where the blame lies," Argent said, brow tightening.

"Where is that?"

He stabbed a finger to the table. "Here."

Kathryn glanced sharply at him.

" 'As Tashijan stands, so does Myrillia,' " he quoted. "And, likewise, as Tashijan ails, so will the Nine Lands. For the past century, the number of Shadowknights has been steadily declining, likewise the number of sons and daughters schooled to be Hands to the gods. Across Myrillia, conclaves have closed or crumbled into ruin. Is it any wonder rot has crept into the rest of the landscape? Ill creatures grow in number. The hinterlands grow wilder and bolder with each passing year. And a daemonic godslayer has risen from our ranks, one of our own fallen. Can one ignore the finger pointed at our very heart? Pointed at Tashijan. We've stagnated under the rules and rites of tradition for far too long, grown fatted and lazy. If we are to face the growing dark tide, then we must start here first. The best must lead us. Those who have been tested under fire, whose loyalty and fealty to Tashijan has been forged and honed to a keen edge."

Argent took a deep breath. "We two—you and I—condemned Tylar. We proved our strength of purpose and focus. He should have been killed. But Ser Henri's soft intervention and petitions won him a reprieve, allowed him to live. And see what such weakness has sown. A godslayer who threatens all."

Kathryn found her head spinning from his words.

"I chose you, Kathryn ser Vail, because once again it is up to us to steel our hearts and make the tough choices, to harden Tashijan in a new flame, to face what must be faced without flinching or soft hearts. You have done this in the past. I ask you to take my side and do it again—for all of Myrillia. Can you do this?"

Without willing it, her head nodded. A dark time was indeed upon them. Despite her suspicions, she could not deny Argent's words. A renewed strength, purpose, and focus were needed to stand against the tide.

"Very good. I knew I chose well. Now we must prepare ourselves for what's to come. Time closes like a noose."

Kathryn raised her eyes, confusion plain to read.

"The godslayer must be stopped."

She found her voice. "How . . . ? I thought he escaped into the Deep."

Argent nodded. "But we know where he's heading."

Kathryn frowned.

"The godslayer is coming here . . . to Tashijan."

❖

Kathryn paced before the balcony window. Sunlight streamed down upon her. She felt none of its warmth.

"Impossible!" Perryl declared as he stood by the hearth.

"Why would Tylar be coming here?" Gerrod echoed. He sat in a chair by the window, his bronze armor achingly bright in the light. He leaned forward, elbows resting on his knees. Though his face was hidden, his posture spoke his intense cogitation. "There is no benefit in returning to Tashijan."

"He's coming for me," Kathryn said, biting at the words at they came, repeating what Argent had spoken just two rings of the bells ago. "One of the sailors aboard a ship upon which Tylar had booked passage, a galleon with ties to the Black Flaggers, had spied upon their cabin. He heard their group speak of Tashijan."

"And you?" Gerrod asked.

Kathryn shook her head. She stopped her pacing and stared out at the bower of wyrmwood beyond her window. The light glowed green through the foliage, a cheery day, one ill suited for the black mood in her heart. "Warden Fields supposes Tylar is returning to Tashijan because of me. To risk such a dangerous course, a strong desire must be driving him."

"Desire for what?" Gerrod asked. "To win you back?"

Kathryn turned to the others. "Or for revenge. If anyone hurt him the deepest, it wasn't the faceless Citadel that sent him into slavery." Fingers clenched at her side—not in anger, but to hold back the tears that threatened.

Gerrod seemed to sense her distress and straightened in his seat with a whir of his mekanicals. He turned to Perryl. "You met Tylar. Spoke to him. What can you say of his posture concerning Kathryn?"

Perryl looked lost with all that had been spoken here, his amber eyes too young, his beard too thin. He wiped a hand through his blond hair, his gaze sinking to the rugs. "He . . . he wouldn't let me speak her name."

"And when he told you this," Gerrod continued, "was it spoken with sadness or anger?"

Perryl shook his head ever so slightly. "The streets were dark."

"The manner of a man's speech does not require lamplight to discern," Gerrod pressed.

Kathryn knew the young knight's reticence lay in an attempt to spare her. "Speak plainly, Perryl. It's important."

His eyes flicked up to her, then back to the floor. "He was angry. His words laced with fury. He would hear nothing about you." Perryl glanced fully up at her. Pain and shame mixed in his eyes.

Kathryn took a deep breath. It hurt to hear, but the truth often did.

"So how do we play this?" Gerrod asked. "Do we believe the new warden's explanations—about his lack of complicity in Ser Henri's demise and the rather convenient disappearance of your predecessor, Castellan Mirra? Do we cooperate?"

Kathryn moved into the room, stepping out of the sunlight and into shadow. She still wore her shadowcloak, loose over her shoulder, and felt the tickle of its Grace respond to the darkness. "I have no choice. I swore oaths. And until true evidence of Argent's duplicity reveals itself, I must act accordingly."

"Ah . . ." Gerrod stood and joined Kathryn as she poured a glass of water from a waiting stand. The armored master touched a point on his breastplate and a small pocket opened. He removed a blackened fold of ermine fur. "Castellan Mirra's cloak. I've tested it with various alchemies. It seems the little maid Penni spoke the truth earlier. It is not any Dark Grace that burned the cloak's edge, only ordinary fire, most likely from lying too near the hearth."

Kathryn sipped. "So again, no evidence of misdeed. Nothing to connect to Warden Fields."

"Perhaps," Gerrod answered. "But I did discover a trace of blood amid the fur. Too minuscule to see without an alchemist's lamp."

"But that could be easily explained away," Perryl countered, still looking morose from earlier. "It could have come from any scratch or cut."

"Ah, yes, Ser Corriscan, that might be true if it were human blood."

Perryl's brow knit a neat crease. "Are you saying it came from a beast?"

Gerrod shook his head.

Kathryn stepped closer and retrieved the burned bit of fur. The remainder of the ermine garment still hung in her wardrobe on the chance Mirra would return. "If not man or animal, that leaves only . . . ?"

Gerrod nodded. "Blood of a *god*. The signature of Grace, while faint, was unmistakable."

Perryl stepped closer. "Which of the gods?"

"Now therein lies the conundrum. Like all alchemists, I have a repostilum, a storehouse of preserved drops of humour from all of the Hundred gods."

Kathryn nodded. She had been in Gerrod's study, seen his repostilum, the eight hundred tiny crystal cubes, each no wider than a thumbnail, resting in a special shelving system on the wall. Each crystal die held a droplet of precious humour.

"I tested the signature upon the cloak and found no match among the Hundred."

Perryl frowned. "Surely a mistake. If the blood didn't come from the Hundred . . ." His face suddenly paled as understanding dawned.

Kathryn finished his statement. "Then it must've come from one of the hinterland rogues."

Gerrod nodded.

She had to resist flinging the bit of fur from her fingers. Rogue gods were wild creatures of madness and strife. Unsettled to any realm, their humours defied the four defining aspects of fire, water, air, and loam. A mere touch could rave a man's mind. To traffic in such humours was the blackest of all Graces.

Gerrod took back the scrap of fouled cloak. "There is no danger. The potency of the Grace is long gone, only the signature is left."

"But what about before?" Kathryn asked. "Argent mentioned Castellan Mirra was showing some evidence of addlement. Supposedly Ser Henri and Ser Fields had even discussed it. Could she have been handling such humours?"

The armored master offered a more dire possibility. "Or the blood could've been exposed to her in secret, to weaken the sharpness of her mind."

"Poisoned by Grace," Perryl said with a shudder.

Kathryn had trouble fathoming such a horror.

Gerrod held up a hand. "But in truth, I cannot say how the Grace presented itself here. Whether by Castellan Mirra's own hand or another, further study is needed. I thought to examine the rest of the cloak, to see if any answers could be divined."

"Of course. It's in my wardrobe."

Kathryn crossed to the door leading to her bedroom. As her hand touched the latch, a scuffle sounded beyond the door. She grabbed the handle and jerked the door wide. She found her maid, Penni, scrambling backward out of her way. She carried an armful of folded linen in her arms.

"Mistress . . ." A hurried curtsy helped balance the maid's load.

"Penni, what are you doing here?" Upon assuming the hermitage, Kathryn had kept Mirra's maid for her own. "Were you listening upon us?" she asked, her words harsher than she intended, surprised to find the girl in her bedroom. But then again, Penni was always appearing out of nowhere.

"No, mistress, a thousand times no." She curtsied again, eyes wide with horror. "At least not with good meaning to. I had just finished changing the bed linens to take to the washerwomen when I heard you and Master Rothkild arrive with Ser . . . Ser Perryl." She glanced sidelong into the room toward the young knight, her eyes shy, clearly enamored. "Mistress Mirra did not like to be walked in upon when speaking with guests. So I waited here until you were finished."

Kathryn frowned at her own lack of foresight. Knowing such dire matters were to be discussed, she should have thought to make sure no ears were listening. But she was still ill accustomed to having a maid doting about her rooms.

Penni kept her head bowed, hiding her face behind the brown curls escaping her white lace cap. "I beg all your pardons."

Kathryn reached a hand to console her, but let it drop. "Penni, mayhap it best you went about your chores with the linen."

"Yes, mistress, right away." Another curtsy.

She made room for the girl, but Gerrod stopped the maid from escaping. "Hold there, Penni. I would bend your ear a moment longer."

Penni glanced back to Kathryn, who nodded, then returned her attention to the armored figure. "Yes, Master Rothkild."

Gerrod motioned for Kathryn to collect the cloak. As she stepped around the corner to reach the wardrobe, she heard his question.

"Penni, you've been interviewed about Castellan Mirra's disappearance, is that not so?"

A silent pause answered him. When Penni spoke next, fear lay thick on her tongue. "Aye. I was put to the chair before the redrobers."

Soothmancers, Kathryn knew. They were all put to the question. She herself was no exception, having been one of the last to speak with Mirra before she vanished. Kathryn opened the wardrobe, gathered up the ragged ermine cloak, and returned to the room.

Gerrod raised an arm at her appearance, his hand out for the wrap. Kathryn passed it to him.

"Can you tell me, has anyone else handled Mirra's cloak? Especially in the last quarter moon before your old mistress disappeared."

Penni scrunched up her face.

Perryl crossed to her, relieved her of the pile of linen wash, and took a seat beside her. He folded his arms atop the pile. "No need to be scared, Penni," he said with a warm smile. "You've done nothing wrong. But we need to know the answer."

Penni kept her gaze to the floor. A bit of color flushed her cheeks, and she turned ever so slightly from Perryl, as if he were the sun, too bright to face. "Then I tell you no. Mistress Mirra's furs were aired out upon the balconies at the end of summer. Otherwise, they are kept in her wardrobe." She glanced to Kathryn. "Like now."

"So no one touched them that you know of."

"No, Master Rothkild."

During this exchange, Gerrod searched the cloak, one way, then the other. He turned and pointed to an inner pocket. A dab of reddish brown was plain to see along the inner edge as he rolled it back. More blood. The pocket was otherwise empty.

Penni watched his every move, her eyes plainly drawn by the soft wheeze of his mekanicals. Being a good maid, she recognized the stain. She covered her mouth with a tiny hand, making a small sound of distress. "I must soak that in lemonpress. Mistress Mirra will be most upset with me. I thought I had cleaned it more thoroughly."

Gerrod met Kathryn's gaze and motioned to the girl with his eyes.

Kathryn dropped to a knee beside her. "Do you know how it became soiled?"

Penni chewed her lower lip. When next she spoke, it was a whisper meant only for Kathryn's ears. "Mistress Mirra did not want me to speak of it."

"But now the old castellan is gone, possibly to harm," Kathryn urged, leaning closer. "If you know something, you must not hide it."

Penni glanced up at Kathryn, then Gerrod, then back to the rug at her toes. She kept her words hushed. "A man came one night, well after final bells, muddied and unkempt, carrying a rucksack, led by one of the livery stablemen. Mistress Mirra gave the stableman a gold march to keep him quiet. I was sent from the room, too, but not before I saw the stranger remove a rolled length of oilcloth from his rucksack."

The maid stopped and wrung her hands together at her waist as if kneading dough, clearly consternated.

"And the blood?" Gerrod said softly, his words echoing a bit inside his helmet.

Penni glanced up to Kathryn. "I didn't mean to watch. I feared for Mistress Mirra's safety with this stranger, arriving in such an unseemly manner. So I stayed, the door cracked open a finger."

"It's all right, Penni. What happened?"

"They whispered together for some time. The man unwrapped the oilcloth to reveal nothing but a bloody swatch of linen. It looked fresh, wet in the hearth light."

"Either fresh," Gerrod mumbled, "or the cloth was charmed to keep it so."

"What then?" Kathryn said to Penni.

"A knock on the door. Hard. Angry. Scared me white. Mistress Mirra hides the bloody snatch in her own pocket. The man rolls the cloth and stuffs it away. The mistress opens the door. It is Ser Henri, right mad and full of flush. I know better than to listen any more. So I sneaks the door closed and hide away."

"And you heard nothing else?" Gerrod asked as her words ended.

"No, Master Rothkild."

Gerrod glanced to Kathryn.

Perryl shifted in the chair next to the scared maid. "Penni, do you know anything about this stranger? A name? Where he might have come from?"

"I'd never seen him before. But though he was muddied and sorely kempt, he seemed a high man of some means. He spoke well and his manners were not low."

"How did he appear?" Kathryn asked.

"He was fair of face . . . not as fair as . . ." Her gaze fluttered toward Perryl. A blush rose on her cheek. "His hair was long to the shoulder, black. I don't remember his eyes."

"Any scars? Any marks to distinguish him?" Perryl asked.

Penni thought for a long moment. "No . . . but I heard him speak to the stableman. To ready a fresh horse, a beast blessed in air, a windmare with enough leg to reach Chrismferry in a day."

Kathryn shared a look with Gerrod. Normally, on horseback, it would take three days to reach the outskirts of Chrismferry. There was clearly urgency here to employ the speed of a windmare.

"That's all I know," Penni finished, almost shaking now.

Kathryn touched her shoulder, causing her to start. "Penni, you've done very well. Why don't you collect the linens and see to the washing."

She curtsied, relieved. Perryl passed her the pile, earning a bright blush. She fled out the servants' door.

Perryl waited until the way closed. "So the man was heading to Chrismferry."

"Or *back* to Chrismferry," Gerrod countered.

Kathryn noted Gerrod drawing in on himself, leaning back, folding his arms across his chest. A troubled posture. He stared down at the ermine cloak on his lap.

"What do you make of all this?" Perryl asked.

Gerrod shook his head. It was all the answer they would get out of him for now.

Out in the courtyard, the Sun Tower chimed the sixth bell. Kathryn hadn't realized how much time had passed. The sun was halfway down the sky. "I have a meeting I must attend," she mumbled to the others as the bells ceased.

Gerrod glanced her way.

"As I mentioned from the first," Kathryn answered, "Tylar is coming here. Warden Fields has gathered folk in the field room to oversee the preparations to receive him. I'm to meet with my supposed guardian."

"A guardian?" Perryl asked. "Do you truly think that's necessary? I still can't believe Tylar would harm you."

Gerrod stirred, standing with a creak. "I don't trust our good warden is only concerned about his castellan's security."

Perryl frowned.

Kathryn understood. "Warden Fields strings a tight net around Tashijan. And I'm to be the bait in the snare. Who I meet will be both guardian and hunter."

Perryl's eyes widened, showing too much white. "Who's been chosen?"

Now it was Kathryn's turn to frown. "That I don't know."

"There is much all of us don't know." Gerrod lifted Mirra's ermine cloak. "I'll see what I can discern from this, but it would be prudent to see if the stableman who guided our dark stranger up here could be prompted to divulge what was sealed by gold and a promise."

"I can check the stables," Perryl offered. "It hasn't been too long since I was squired down there."

Kathryn nodded as he made for the door. "Be discreet."

Gerrod remained behind and fixed her with a stolid stare, his eyes bright through the slit in his helmet. His words softened. "And you be careful. Bait is seldom considered of any value after one sets the hook."

Kathryn met his gaze. "By sword and cloak, I'll be careful," she promised.

Gerrod studied her a moment longer, then turned away. "I suggest you keep both near at hand."

Kathryn kept her pace hurried but respectful as she descended the twenty flights of stairs. With each nod to passing knight or courtier, she felt the press of the diamond seal fixed under her chin, the emblem of the castellan. It was not the true seal, but mere paste and artifice. The real diamond ornament had vanished with Mirra. Kathryn felt the same about her role here at Tashijan, more paste and artifice than true authority or command.

She rounded the last flight of the central stair and proceeded to the tall doors of the Citadel's field room. For ages lost to the past, the chamber was used as a place of strategy, planning, and preparation. Over the millennia, the fate of countless hinter-kings and untold armies had been decided behind those doors. Great battles were mapped, wars waged in ink and blood, treaties signed or broken. All of Myrillia had been forged behind those doors.

A pair of Shadowknights, cloaked and hooded, posted the threshold, standing in shallow alcoves. Their forms seemed to flow into the gloom of their niches. The darkness fed their forms, readying them to respond to any threat with the speed borne of Grace. Only the glow of their eyes could be seen above the black of their masklin wraps.

"Castellan Vail," the closest knight acknowledged with a sweep of cloak. "The warden awaits your presence."

The other guard opened the door with a surge of darkness.

"Thank you," Kathryn mumbled. Both were too young, she thought, fresh to their third stripe, too ostentatious with their show of shadowplay, wasting Grace in theatrics.

She stepped into the field room.

The scent of oiled woods and brittle parchment greeted her first— then a familiar booming voice.

"The castellan finally graces us with her presence," Master Hesharian said. The rotund leader of the Council of Masters stood with four others around a central table.

Despite the chamber's significance, the field room was cramped and tight. The rear windows, overlooking the tourney grounds, had been shuttered for this meeting, ensuring privacy and forbidding the sun. To either side, the Stacks—giant wooden shelves that stored illuminated maps of all the Nine Lands, even rough sketches of sections of hinterland—lined the walls, buttressed by ladders. The only other significant feature to the room was the massive wyrmwood table. Its patina had blackened from the passing centuries, its surface scarred and pitted.

Kathryn crossed toward the waiting group. "I apologize for my late arrival. Matters of some importance detained me."

Hesharian raised one brow. "More important than the security of Tashijan?" The large man still resented her assignment as castellan, a post normally held by one of the Council of Masters.

Kathryn ignored his gibe. She nodded to Hesharian's fellow council members. Master Osk climbed down one of the Stacks' ladders, burdened with a large map roll. He was as thin as Master Hesharian was vast, a lesser moon before a greater. As always, he kept his eyes pinched as if fearful of being struck. He nodded back at her and turned to the table, exposing the line of tattoos circling the back of his shaved skull.

"A moment, Castellan Vail," Argent said formally. He accepted the thick parchment from Master Osk, set it on the table, and shoved the roll loose down the table's length. A schematic of Tashijan revealed itself.

Intrigued, Kathryn stepped to the table.

"It's been a long time," Keeper Ryngold greeted her on the right side with a genuine smile. He was the only person present whose head was not adorned by tattooed sigils or stripes of knighthood. Still, he was well respected by all, head of the entire house staff and laborers. If matters of security were to be addressed, he would orchestrate the underfolk of the Citadel.

On her left, she received no greeting and expected none. A knight of few words, Symon ser Jaklar needed no shadowcloak to cast a pall of gloom around him. He strode under thunderclouds even on the brightest days. His hair, shaved to a coarse black stubble, matched his eyes. Formerly squire to Argent, he had continued his duty as knight under the leadership of his former teacher.

Kathryn studied the ancient map of the halls, levels, rooms, and courts of Tashijan. Spread out on the table, the vast Citadel seemed a city unto itself with byways and alleys, crowded places and lonely ones, all centered round the central Stormwatch Tower that stretched as high as the masters' catacombs delved low. How would they stop one man from breeching the vast domain unseen? It was a daunting challenge, but one the new warden seemed ready to handle, having served in dozens of sieges from both sides of a wall.

Argent placed his palms flat on the parchment. "As I was saying, I know the godslayer is on his way here. Perhaps he's already in the First Land. But over the centuries, Tashijan has grown lazy with its fortifications, weakened its foundations. We can't keep the godslayer out."

"Then what can we do?" Master Hesharian asked.

"We can be smarter. What walls can't stop, strategy can." Argent straightened, sweeping his gaze around the room. "We must guide the godslayer to where *we* want him to go. The best trap is one the victim walks into willingly."

Hesharian frowned. "And how do you propose to accomplish this?"

"By controlling what he most desires." Argent's sweeping gaze settled upon Kathryn.

All eyes turned in her direction.

Argent addressed her directly. "Castellan Vail, I'd like you to meet the man set as your personal guard in the days to come." He lifted his arm. A signal.

A scrape of boots sounded behind her and to the left. She turned as a tall man stepped from between a set of the Stacks. She had walked right past him without even noticing his presence. But it was not Grace that hid him. He wore no shadowcloak. Instead, the man was outfitted in furred breeches, knee-high brown boots, and a mud-brown half cloak with hood. All looked well worn and scuffed.

A wyld tracker.

But it was not the clothes that identified the man. Wyld trackers were blessed at birth with alchemies of air and loam, making them preternaturally keen to scent trails and changes in winds. This blessing was plainly apparent from the prominent protrusion of nose and jaw. *Half muzzled*, as it was called, a beastly appearance, made more so by the lack of white to their eyes, leaving them a solid amber.

Argent spoke at the head of the table. "Tracker Lorr has served at my side since before the Bramblebrier Campaign. There is no finer hunter in all of Myrillia."

He offered a half bow toward the warden, arms crossed. Despite the play at civility here, Kathryn sensed a feral edge to the man. His face bore testimony to past battles, rippled with scars, eyes hard as fieldstones. His lanky brown hair, worn past the shoulder, was shot through with gray. But he showed no signs that age had touched him further. His belts, at waist and crisscrossed over his chest, were decorated with sheathed blades of every shape.

"I've informed Tracker Lorr of his duties," Argent said. "He will not leave your side or your door until the godslayer is subdued."

Kathryn rounded on the warden. "And when does his duty commence?"

"At this very moment. I thought it best you both become acquainted with your new routines as soon as possible." His gaze turned to the tracker. "Lorr, are you ready to introduce Castellan Vail to your . . . ah, what do you call them . . . very colorful as I recall? Ah yes, *your right and left hands.*"

With another half bow, the tracker turned toward the door.

Kathryn hesitated. Was she being dismissed from the meeting already? A hard stare from Argent answered her. Clearly he meant to keep her in the dark on further details. Did he distrust her, think she would betray their secrets to Tylar?

With black clouds about her shoulders, she swung away and followed the tracker. He opened the door and continued through, not bothering to see if she kept pace with him. Perhaps it wasn't necessary, armed as he was with his Grace-sharpened senses.

Out in the hall, the two young knights stirred as the pair stormed out. Kathryn imagined the tracker was no more keen to be relegated to mere guard than she was to be kept *under* guard. He continued down the hall, turned down a side passage, and crossed to a barred room.

Turning to her, he spoke for the first time. His voice was surprisingly soft coming from such a gruff exterior. "Best take care a moment. They're easily spooked."

He lifted the bar and pulled the door open, blocking the opening with his body.

Kathryn felt something large stir beyond the door. A shift of boulders.

The tracker growled deep in the back of his throat. He kept his post for another long breath. The door bumped as something heaved against it. Lorr reached a hand inside. "There's a good laddie," he mumbled in his soft voice. "You, too, you big kank."

He straightened and opened the door wider, revealing a sight to horrify even the stoutest heart.

Two massive beasts filled the doorway, standing shoulder height, heads as large as shields. A pair of bullhounds. Meaty, thick necked, ropes of drool hanging from slavering lips. Where such humour dripped, stone etched with a poisonous hiss. Out in the field, the drool was used to wear heavy bone while gnawing. The beasts, native to the most remote areas of the hinterlands, were known to bring down giant sarrians and battle the massive myrlions.

"Barrin and Hern," the tracker said as introduction.

Kathryn could not tell them apart. Both were maned in black, a tad short of shaggy, and striped in thin bands of copper. She backed away as the pair of bullhounds slunk into the hall: snuffling, breaths steaming, crouched low on bellies, stumped tails sticking straight up.

Creatures of black nightmare.

Lorr stood between them. "We'll keep you safe, Castellan . . . even from a godslayer."

13

THE DELL

"WELCOME HOME."

Tylar scowled at the thief. Rogger crouched in the reeds with Delia. Dawn broke to the east, a cheery rose that did nothing to warm the chill from their bones. All three of them were soaked to the skin, muck-deep in mud and boggy silt. Clouds of gnats and bloodsuckers buzzed and whined about the trio. A few surly marsh frogs, as large as platters, croaked their passage from atop a half-sunken log. A kingwader strode past, its head and speared beak taller than a man, spying above the reeds, regal and aloof.

With the rising sun, they had decided to make landfall here, in the Foulsham marshes, where no one would note their approach and where there was plenty of cover to hide the Fin from both the shipping lanes of the Straits of Parting and the few villages that lay ashore. They had selected an empty stretch of coastline and watched for the glow lights from early-morning giggers and fishers.

Once the skies lightened enough to see by and most of the nocturnal marsh predators had slunk back to their lairs, Rogger had led Tylar and Delia toward the shore. The thief promised that he knew some paths through the marshlands, knowledge gained from the time he spent here in Foulsham Dell.

They planned to steer clear of the god-realm itself, edge past its eastern border, and head overland for Tashijan. They had originally thought to make a more direct approach, landing somewhere along the Steps of the Gods, the ancient series of lofty bridges connecting a series of small islands to form a road between the First and Second Lands. But upon arriving among the islands, they found all the shores heavily guarded. Word of the godslayer's escape from the corsairs had flown ahead of them.

So they had kept their craft submerged and passed between two of the islands, sailing into the Straits of Parting that separated the First and Second Lands. Over another full day, they had glided along the southern coastline of the First Land, debating where best to make landfall.

It was Rogger's idea to go through the marshes.

"So when's the last time you placed a foot here?" the thief asked as they slogged toward more solid ground.

"On the First Land?"

Rogger nodded.

"Five years." The thought had been on Tylar's mind since abandoning the Fin. *Five years.* A long time to be gone. But it seemed too short, especially when measured against the span of his pain and hardship. It seemed an entire lifetime had passed, not just five years.

And now he had returned, come full circle. To what end? To clear a name long abandoned? To right a wrong? Despite the stripes on his face and his healed body, he was no knight.

"Of course, I'm not sure *this* is exactly making landfall yet," the thief continued, dragging a foot from the muck with a slurping sound. "More like making *mud*fall."

Delia slapped her arm, squashing a winged sucker. Both Delia and Rogger bore red welts from their bites on arms, face, and neck. Only Tylar was spared.

Delia caught him staring as she flicked away the offending insect. "It's your blood," she said. "Even the suckers smell the Grace flowing there. Like smoke from a fire. They know better than to sip from such a font."

Rogger scratched a bite on his neck. "And you were grousing about being Grace blessed. I'll take your burden 'til we're out of these skaggin' marshes. Or even for—"

"How much farther?" Tylar asked, cutting him off.

"Not far." Rogger climbed a hummock, shoving between bushes of spiny sedge. He stood with his hands on his hips. "Not far at all."

Tylar helped Delia up. The two had spoken little since the night she had revealed herself to be the estranged daughter of Argent ser Fields, the man who had sent Tylar into slavery.

Delia nodded her thanks as she climbed out of the marsh.

But she did not meet his eye.

Tylar followed. As he hauled himself up, he still felt like he carried the swamp with him: dripping water, caked in mud, sand and silt trapped in every crack and crevice. He had at least managed to keep his bandaged wrist dry, but the motion and exertion had set it to seeping blood again.

Joining Rogger, Tylar spotted a thin path through the marsh grasses, no more than an animal track, but it led away. The hummock they stood on was connected to others in a mazelike chain.

"Do you know where we are?" Tylar asked.

"More west than I'd hoped. This is the Middens, if I'm not mistaken."

"The Middens?" Delia asked.

Rogger picked a leaf from his beard. "The eastern border of Foulsham Dell. We'll have to move quickly. Skirt the edge. In these wilds, there's a good chance we'll be long gone before Ol' Balger sniffs us out. Follow me."

They dared not venture too far into Foulsham Dell. Through the morning mist, Tylar could see the shadowy silhouette of the mountains of the Middleback Range to the north. The Dell lay in the crumble of land where the mountains tumbled into the Straits. It was a landscape of steaming bogs, dark marshes, sudden sinkholes, craggy slopes, misty highlands, and in the center of it all, the sprawling, ramshackle city of Foulsham Dell.

The city was the realm of the god Lord Balger. Its western border dissolved into the wilds of the untamed hinterlands that shadowed the far side of the Middleback Range. In the Dell, such boundaries blurred. It was said that the border between settled land and hinterland was as unreliable as Lord Balger's moods.

The god's stormy temper was as legendary as his debaucheries. He reveled in the pleasures of the flesh without restraint. He ate to a belching fullness, growing rotund. He drank to a blackened stupor, pissing from the towers of his castillion, "blessing" passersby with his streaming Grace. He whored with his own men in low places, accompanied by a Hand who would collect his spilled seed. But worst of all, he found pleasure in cruelty. Screams flowed from his castillion as often as song.

It seemed even the lowliest of Myrillian scum needed a god, a land to call their own. Balger offered them such hard shelter.

Tylar paced Rogger as they followed the thin path through the hummocks and hillocks. "Why risk the Dell? Why not wade back into the marshlands and head due east?"

Rogger waved a hand to the left. "The waters around the Middens are treacherous with quicksand. A misstep and all would be lost. We're lucky to have gotten here as it is. To set off in another tack, we'd have to retreat all the way back to the Fin, then circle back in again. I know the Middens. We'll be fine."

Tylar didn't argue. Here at least was dry, solid land.

As they hiked through the thick marshlands, the sun climbed into the sky, visible through the boles and fronded limbs of swamp palms and the skeletal forms of fennwood trees. The day wore warmer, steaming away the layers of fog and mist. The stench of the bog grew, a pungent smell of sulfur gasses and decay.

Still, they marched onward, occasionally leaping from one hummock to another. Frogs plopped away to either side of their path, marking their passage with tiny splashes. A loon called across the waters, a haunted, forlorn sound.

"You're limping again," Delia said softly after a long spell of silence.

Tylar noted how he had assumed the posture and gait of his formerly broken body: right leg stiff, short hobbled steps, back crooked. He forced himself straighter, his step more assured.

Delia moved closer. "Why do you still do that?"

He shook his head.

"Is it that you don't trust this hale form you wear now?"

"What is there to trust?" Tylar said. "The only reason my bones have been mended is to cage the *dred ghawl* inside me. Once I'm rid of the daemon—if we're victorious—then my body will revert to its broken posture. So why lose the reflexes honed from years of crippling? I may need them again."

Rogger grumbled ahead of him, "Cursed with the daemon . . .broken without it. A real corker there."

As they continued marching, the sun climbed directly overhead . . . and still there appeared no end to the marshlands. Tylar searched around him. Hadn't they passed this way already? Wasn't that the same stump of fennwood? Hadn't he already pushed through this bramblebrier tangle before? He searched the mud for the telltale print of his boots. Nothing.

Still, he felt as if they were circling and circling.

Delia voiced a similar concern. "I thought you said it wasn't far to clear the swamps." She dabbed her brow with a pocket kerchief.

Rogger scowled back at her, dripping sweat from nose and brow. "Far . . . near . . . it's all relative. I'll get us—"

With his attention turned, Rogger failed to see the trap. His foot stepped into the snare, it sprang with a sharp *thwip,* and the thief flipped into the air with a cry of surprise. Bouncing a bit, he hung upside down by one ankle.

Tylar crossed under him. *Deer snare.* During their long hike, he had spotted a few long-legged fawns and even an antlered buck, bounding from hummock to hillock and away. Fleet-footed . . . more so than Tylar's thieving companion. He freed a dagger to cut him down.

Rogger caught his winded breath, still bouncing. His eyes were wide, clearly still panicked. "Trap . . ." he gasped out.

Tylar froze, dagger in hand.

He heard the twang of the crossbow and turned to see Delia struck in the shoulder and spilled into the water. Before he could take a step, he felt something crack against the back of his skull—then the ground rushed up at him and struck him in the face.

He heard Rogger cry out.

Then darkness.

❖

Awareness came slowly. But no sight. He heard distant sounds: the clank of an iron door, the rattle of a chain, echoing words, even the drip of water. But closer, by his ear, a voice spoke from out of the blackness.

. . . BE AWARE . . . BEWARE . . .

Tylar had no sense of himself. He hung weightless in a black sea, between consciousness and oblivion.

But he was not alone.

He felt the stir of current around him, something swimming past, under him. He sensed the immensity of its size, a leviathan of the deep. Its scrutiny drew all warmth from him.

. . . THE CABAL . . . HUNTS . . .

The words were not at his ear, but in his head. Tylar found no tongue to express his confusion, but it was understood.

A more frantic stirring spun him in the dark sea. He sensed urgency, a press of time like a lead weight. What did the speaker want of him?

. . . RIVENSCRYR . . .

Tylar shivered in the darkness. He caught the barest scent of spring blossoms, dried and burned on a brazier, sweet but smoldering. A shadow of Meeryn, the scent of her funeral pyre . . . only this was not death. Again the presence swam beneath him. Tylar sensed who spoke to him now. He felt a writhing where his heart once lay, deep within his chest, past bone and blood.

It was the *dred ghawl.*

Awakened inside him.

A single word arose from the darkness:

. . . NAETHRYN . . .

Tylar inwardly shivered. He remembered Fyla expressing her belief that such a being, a *naethryn,* slew Meeryn. Was this further proof? That one of the dread undergods, the dark shadows of their Myrillian counterparts, had broken into this world?

The scrutiny of the daemon grew more intense, swelling into him, through him. Such language was beyond it, but still it struggled.

NOT DAEMON . . .

It sought to clarify, putting all its efforts into one last thought.

NAETHRYN . . . I AM NAETHRYN . . .

Shock shattered away the darkness. Firelight flickered in the cracks and drove the dregs of the black dream away. Still Tylar felt the slither of the daemon behind the bones of his rib cage, fiery with anger.

Not a dream . . .

I am naethryn.

Could such a thing be possible? Did he bear some aspect of an undergod inside him, a creature a thousandfold more foul than any daemon? And if truly a naethryn, could it be the very monster who murdered Meeryn?

Before he could ponder further, awareness of his surroundings finally struck through his shock. He was in a stone cell. Another dungeon. He lay on his back, naked except for a loincloth, strapped spread-eagle on a rack, lashed in rope that stank of shite. Black bile. The ropes had been blessed by bloodnullers, protecting the hemp from Graced enchantments.

He sensed a presence in the cell with him.

"He wakes," a slithery voice said.

Tylar turned his head, making the room spin and his stomach churn queasily. A black-robed figure huddled near an open door, bent in shadow, face cowled. A hand, smeared in filth . . . black bile . . . pointed to him. The stench off the bloodnuller filled his nostrils, gagging him further.

With the nuller's words, a figure stepped into the doorway, limned in torchlight. A tall man of wide girth and broad shoulders. He wore a beard, forked to the middle of his swollen belly. His clothing matched his hair, as black as a crow's tail: boots, leggings, surcoat. Only his shirt seemed woven of silver thread, reflecting the torchlight, like the finest wrought chain mail.

Dark eyes stared down at Tylar's sprawled form. Fire glowed in them, the shine of Grace, *fiery* Grace. Here stood one of the fire gods of Myrillia.

Tylar needed no introduction.

"Lord Balger . . ." he mumbled.

The god nodded ever so slightly, a strange courtesy considering their situation. "So you are the godslayer." His voice was the grumble of a log crumbling in a stoked fire.

Tylar felt the room grow warmer as the god stepped closer. Grace, heated with the aspect of fire, seeped from the god's pores.

"Not much to look at," Balger said.

"I slew no gods," Tylar choked past his sickened stomach.

"So you have claimed, but many disagree." Balger reached a finger to one of his bound hands. The fingertip burned like a brand. Flesh blistered and smoked.

Tylar cried out.

Balger bent and sniffed the charred flesh. "I *do* smell Grace in you. *Water,* if I'm not mistaken." He straightened and glanced to the blood-nuller. "It seems even the skagging touch of one of that ilk does not wipe away all your blessing. Now why is that?"

A voice answered from the doorway. "He carries the full Grace of a god in him, milord. Meeryn's Grace." Rogger leaned against the doorframe, arms crossed, freshly bathed from the look of his damp hair. "It's in all his humours. He walks like a god himself, only perhaps slightly weaker, a paler shadow, yet still not without potency. You saw how his wounds healed with a mere slather of firebalm."

Balger frowned through his beard. "You've brought me quite the trophy from your pilgrimage."

Rogger shrugged. "I knew it would take such compensation to buy back my freedom."

Tylar stared at the thief, aghast. Had he been betrayed? Surely this was some ruse on Rogger's part.

Balger folded his arms across his ample chest, fingers entwined on his belly. "Well done indeed. I wouldn't have believed it if I hadn't seen such strangeness with my own eyes. A human godling. When you sent that message to expect you in the Middens, I thought it a foolish trick."

"No trick. I've learned better than that." Rogger rubbed one of the branded tattoos from his interrupted pilgrimage. "It took a bit of time and pain. The overheated tubes of the Fin stung like a salted whip. I needed most of a morning, while the others slept, to tattoo that new message into my flesh."

Rogger pulled up a sleeve of his starched shirt, fingering a crude, blackened and blistered scrawl on the underside of his arm. "Firebalm is not healing my wounds as quickly as it does your prisoner." He eyed Tylar as if he were some dried-and-pinned specimen in an alchemist's lab and shook his sleeve back over his betrayal.

Despite the dawning horror, Tylar had to acknowledge the thief's cleverness. Of course Balger would know any words burned upon Rogger's flesh. The god had cursed him with the pilgrimage, requiring the sigils of each realm's house to be branded into his flesh. A pilgrim's progress was overseen by the very god who placed the curse, to ensure the pilgrim continued his journey. Rogger had used that blessed link to carve a message upon his own flesh, to deliver word to Balger, knowing the god would sense every brand pressed into him.

Tylar stared at Rogger. Had this been his plan all along? To buy his freedom? Tylar stared hard at the thief. "What have you done with Delia?"

"Safe," Rogger answered. "It was only a sandbag that tipped the crossbow's arrow. Meant to stun. As I warned in my message. The same as struck you in the back of the head. No broken bones." He eyed the bindings. "We can't have you loosing that daemon of yours."

Tylar's head ached. "Where is she? What have you done—?"

"She's being well treated by the bevy of ladies in Lord Balger's private wenchworks. Scrubbed, combed, and sweetened. It's not every night the Hand of one god will lose her maidenhead to another god. She'll be entertaining Lord Balger this very evening."

"You bastard . . ." He struggled in his bonds, but only managed to choke himself against a leather strap securing his neck. He could barely move a finger.

During this discussion, Balger slowly circled Tylar, studying him, rubbing his upper lip with a finger. "No one knows he is here?" the god asked.

"No, milord."

"He would make for an excellent source of Grace, an ever-flowing font of riches. A golden cow to be milked daily."

"Milord, what of the call from Tashijan? Is he not to be delivered to them? The reward for his capture—both in gold and goodwill—would surely be substantial."

A wave dismissed his words. "Such payment would come but once. A living godling would be a treasure without end."

"But there is also the danger. A chance mishandling, a lowered guard, and it would take but the snap of a finger or toe to unleash the *dred ghawl* inside him."

Balger's eyes both narrowed and brightened. "I would see this daemon, fathom its aspect. Surely there is profit to be found in such a creature."

"Be wary. I believe, as does the handmaiden who accompanied us, that this *dred ghawl* somehow maintains this font of Grace. For its own preservation in a man's form. A cocoon of Grace inside a cage of bone."

Through his anger, words echoed in Tylar's head: *I am naethryn.*

Balger leaned closer. "I'll have my alchemists study his body from crown to toe, from mouth to arse." The god reached across Tylar's bare chest. He splayed his hand above the blackened print atop Tylar's heart, hovering, matching his fingers to Meeryn's.

Tylar smelled the fire flaming from the god's pores.

It was said that a god's aspect reflected his or her character. Gods of loam were as patient as a budding seed, as solid as rock and hard-packed soil, while gods of the air were aloof and farseeing, ethereal in mind and grace. Gods of water, like Meeryn and Fyla, varied the most, fickle in temperament and spirits, as changeable as water itself: solid ice, flowing water, misty vapor. Then there were the fire gods, who were as quick to anger as a lick of flame, as volatile as a woodland blaze, as passionate as the heated embrace of lovers. They were the best and the worst of all the gods.

And Lord Balger smoldered among the worst of them.

He lowered his hand to Tylar's chest. Tylar remembered the burning touch of the god's finger a moment ago, the sear of flesh. The smoke of Tylar's charred skin still tinged the air.

Balger pressed his hand down atop Meeryn's palm print.

Tylar winced but found no burn.

Instead, it was Balger who gasped. The god's fingers vanished into the black print as if Tylar's flesh were mere shadow. He probed farther, wrist deep, into Tylar's chest.

Rogger moved closer. The thief, like Tylar, had examined Meeryn's palm print. The print had been no more than a tattoo on his flesh.

"I think you should be wary, milord," Rogger intoned.

Balger's brow pinched. "What is this strangeness here?"

His gaze found Tylar's. He opened his mouth to question further, but then suddenly the god jerked like a fish on a line. A cry burst from the Balger's lips, spittle flying, landing like molten wax on Tylar's skin.

Balger fell backward and yanked his hand from the shadowy pit in Tylar's being. Only his *hand* did not reappear. The stump of his wrist sprayed blood in a fountain of fire, pumping with the beat of the god's panicked heart.

Balger roared, a noise that threatened to bring the roof down atop them. Alarm spread among the guards beyond the cell door.

Tylar writhed in his bonds. His skin burned from the splashes of blood. A crimson pool of fiery humour poured down his breastbone and vanished into the inky blackness over his heart, as if down a stone well. He felt the Grace flowing into him as warm as mulled ale. The daemon inside swelled, pressing against his rib cage, threatening to shatter through.

There was no doubt what had bitten off the god's hand.

The *dred ghawl.*

Balger roared back to his feet. He cradled his severed wrist as guards swooped into the room like a flock of black crows, capes billowing, swords ready.

Balger crossed back to Tylar, destruction in his eyes.

Rogger attempted to step in the god's path, but Balger shoved the thief aside.

The god leaned over Tylar, baring his mutilation. Already the blood had stopped flowing as the wounded wrist healed with a speed of a god. The hand, too, would grow back in the thickness of time. But for now, Balger's entire bearing flamed with fury. His skin smoked with Grace, his eyes flashed with fire, his breath seared with the winds of a pyre.

A bellow of rage formed words. *"You think to kill me, Godslayer!"*

Balger drew a dagger and wiped its blade across his anger-damp brow. Steel, blessed now by the god's fiery sweat, turned as ruddy as a branding iron. Balger touched the tip of the knife to his seeping wound, gracing it with his own blood. The god's eyes narrowed as he cast a specific blessing. The blade went white-hot, more flame than substance.

"A bale dagger," Balger said, holding up his handiwork.

Tylar struggled in his bonds, sensing his doom.

"Milord! No!" Rogger struggled to elbow through two guards.

Balger raised the dagger high, then plunged it into Tylar's belly.

Searing pain shattered outward.

Balger dragged the knife up from groin to rib cage, gutting him.

Tylar cried out, but agony throttled him, turning wail into gurgle. His body arched off the rack, on shoulders and heels, writhing as the room went black. His innards blazed with molten fire.

He fell backward into darkness.

For an untold time, Tylar balanced on the razor edge of agony, sightless and witless. The pain refused to relent, to let him escape. It held him in claws of fire, ripping and tearing.

Then the torture ended. Abruptly.

The sudden cessation of pain woke him like a frigid dive into a snowmelt stream. Gasping, blind still, Tylar collapsed back to the rack. He blinked back his vision, damp with tears.

He watched Balger step from his side, smoking blade in hand.

Tylar stared down at his body, expecting to see intestines spilling from a gaping wound. But his skin lay unmarked. Only the thin course of hair across his belly smoldered, marking the path of the blade.

Balger leaned over him again. He lifted the blazing dagger. "Ripe with my fiery blessing, the bale blade cuts and heals at the same time. I can slice you all day and all night and you will never weaken or expire."

He raised the blade again and plunged it into Tylar's shoulder, striking clean through to the wood beneath.

Tylar screamed, unable to help himself.

Balger straightened, abandoning the impaled dagger. "Or I can leave it here. Cutting and healing continually in one place, leaving only pain, a pain that never dulls, but always remains fresh."

Tylar writhed. He had been struck by arrows and blades of all manner. The sting of impact was always intense, but it dulled as severed nerves retracted. Not now. This agony never relented.

Movement by his toes drew his narrowed vision. Rogger appeared and grabbed his bound foot. "I'm sorry, Tylar." The thief's deft fingers snatched his littlest toe, met his eyes, then snapped his digit cleanly.

Tiny bones snapped.

The pain was small compared to his shoulder, but in a single breath, it spread outward in a growing wave of agony: up his leg and out over the rest of his body. Bones, healed by Grace before, broke anew, shattering his form. The dagger's bite disappeared under the assault, overwhelmed.

Through this agony, Tylar felt something shake loose from the broken cage of his body, snaking out. In the wake of its passage, fractured bones drew back in place, malformed and misaligned, fusing and callusing anyway. His body twisted and joints stiffened, back into his old bent form.

The pain receded, except in his shoulder. Fire continued to blaze outward from the impaled dagger.

In the torchlight, a font of black smoke, darker than shadow, billowed from his chest as if from a baker's chimney. Eyes opened in the darkness, ablaze with lightning.

Guards scattered to the four walls. Several dropped swords in fright.

Balger kept his post. The god's gaze followed the column of smoke to where it pooled like spilled ink across the cell's low roof.

From the black sea, a sinuous column snaked out and downward, forming head and neck. Wings swept out as a pair of flanking waves. Silver eyes blazed brighter with white fire. Hanging upside down from the roof like some shadowy bat, the daemon studied the room. The *dred ghawl*'s wings lowered protectively to either side of Tylar. A keening wail, beyond hearing but felt on every hair on the body, echoed off the stone walls.

A humpbacked guard stabbed a lance at the shadowy creature. Its steel head melted and splashed back at the attacker's toes. Its haft caught fire, falling away to ash. The guard dropped the cursed weapon and fell out the doorway and away. Others followed. Balger's loyalty was earned by fear. A greater fear now overwhelmed his retinue.

In moments, Lord Balger was alone.

The god's eyes narrowed upon the daemon. "I know you, creature. Spawn of the naether do not belong in this world of sinew and bone."

The *dred ghawl*'s mane of smoke bristled, and its muzzle sharpened. It stretched toward the god. Balger backed up as the daemon snaked out to meet the god, eye to eye. The white-fire blaze of the daemon's gaze flashed. The keening in the room focused to a hiss that pained the ears and drew cold sweat from pores.

Tylar recognized that voice, having heard it before, on the streets of Punt, from Meeryn's dark attacker. It was not easily forgotten. Tylar knew what he heard—both then and now.

The voice from the naether . . . the voice of the naethryn.

Balger's eyes grew wider as he listened to the naether daemon. He stumbled back to the far wall. "No!" the god gasped out with a sharp shake of his head. "Not possible . . . Rivenscryr was destroyed!"

Tylar felt a tug on his ankle. He glanced down to see Rogger slicing his leather bonds with a dagger. His right leg was freed, then his left. Rogger shied forward and worked at his left wrist. "Be ready to run."

Tylar's suspicion of the thief flared, but as long as he was being freed, he kept silent. Pain still flamed his right shoulder.

"The bale dagger," Rogger said, moving to his last binding. "Can you free it?"

As answer, Tylar reached to the hilt of the dagger. He grabbed the bone hilt. He felt the Grace fired within it. It helped steady his grip. With an explosion of pained breath, he tugged it from his shoulder. A wisp of smoke trailed the blade's tip, taking the agony with it. Bathed in the brightness of the blade, Tylar's shoulder was unmarred, healed and hale.

Rogger helped him sit up.

The daemon kept the god pinned to the wall.

But Balger's shock waned. The disbelief in his voice hardened to anger. "You lie, naether-spawn!"

Tylar dragged himself off the rack and crouched on the far side. He fell easily into his old form, back bent, left leg stiff as a walking stick. The ache of his joints was as familiar as a warm cloak. It helped center him, despite the horror.

The dark umbilicus flowed out from the black print over his heart, coiling and twisting. Tylar waved his hand through the channel, but found nothing but smoke. He recognized the billowing darkness now. While fleeing out of the depths of Tangle Reef, he had witnessed the same. What the seafolk named the *Gloom*. A penetration of the naether into this world. Only this black font leaked from his own chest. A conduit for the naether-spawn, the naethryn undergod.

He waved his hand again.

Though it caused him no harm, he knew its touch to be as deadly as the marine Gloom. He had witnessed how the guards had died back at Meeryn's castillion in the Summering Isles, left boneless or broken as he and Rogger fled the keep.

Rogger kept low and hissed at him. "Let's go."

Guards shouted beyond the dungeon cell. The alarm spread quickly. Like all gods, Balger had his own Shadowknights . . . though such men who bent a knee to the lord of Foulsham Dell were of low ilk, disgraced knights whose crimes did not warrant full stripping. They, like their counterparts among men, found themselves washed up on these hard shores, lost and without futures. The knights of this realm were as likely to be found in bed with a sell-wench as snoring under a table at a low tavern.

Still, Tylar knew it was best to be away before pieces of shadow sprouted swords and men. He hobbled after Rogger to the door. The daemon continued its guard upon Lord Balger, sensing the greatest danger lay with the god.

Only once they vacated the cell did the daemon flow back with them.

Balger made no move to follow. Only his voice chased them. "If Rivenscryr is here, we're all doomed!" Cruel laughter followed. "One man and one undergod cannot stop the end of all."

Rogger led the way to the end of the short hall. Empty now. An iron door clanged shut ahead of them. The screech of a sliding bar echoed to them. "The cowards are trapping us here." A snort of derision punctuated his words. "Locking a godslayer with their god."

"What can we do?" Tylar asked as they reached the doors.

From its post behind them, the naethryn daemon snaked its neck over their heads and flowed to the iron . . . *through* the iron. Metal poured in rivers of molten slag. Hinges and locking bar melted away. The door toppled and crashed into the far room.

Bale dagger in hand, Tylar led the way, careful to step on the solid iron, using it to ford the pools of fiery slag. The last of the guards vanished out the other side of the dungeon's anteroom. In their haste, no one bothered to bolt the far door.

In the larger room, the daemon streamed fully forward with a billow of smoke and reformed its wolfish silhouette, wings folded to its back, long neck questing up the stairwell beyond.

Rogger collected an abandoned short sword, while Tylar donned an oversized pair of leggings and boots found beside a cot. He kept his chest bared for the sake of the daemon's umbilicus. Once ready, the daemon seemed to sense their desire and flowed up the stairwell.

Rogger and Tylar followed. As they wound up out of the subterranean warren, Tylar confronted the thief. "You sought to sell my life for your own."

Rogger scowled. "So we wanted everyone to believe."

"We?"

"Delia and I. We concocted this ill strategy while you slept these past days. We guessed word would've spread after our escape from the corsairs. Ravens graced with air can outrace any sputtering Fin. We needed a way to make landfall. A way to get you to Tashijan alive. With blessed wards, far-seers, and Graced armies spread along the shores and borders, it would take the protection of a god to keep your skin on your bones."

"And you chose Balger?"

"What better god to know the value of a godslayer? Balger may be vile, but he is no fool." Rogger shook his head. "I must say even I underestimated his cunning. I thought he'd be satisfied with the price on your head."

"So the entirety of your plan was to have me captured by Balger and delivered trussed up and nulled to Tashijan?"

Rogger tugged his beard. "Just about."

"And you couldn't forwarn me of your plan?"

"We couldn't risk you being soothed. You had to be unaware."

"What about you and Delia being soothed?"

Rogger shrugged. "When you have a godslayer in tow, few look elsewhere. As we imagined, we were ignored."

Tylar frowned. Ahead, a warm breeze blew down to them. It smelled of swamp and sea, salt and weed. Sunlight reflected off the sweating stone walls. With each step, the air grew hotter.

They cleared the last flight and found a doorway of rough-hewn squallwood planks. An open iron grating let in the slanting sunlight. Again the daemon pushed through the door. Wood turned to ash. The iron grating dropped and clanked against the top stair.

Out in the yard, muffled screams and shouts grew louder and clearer as the door fell away. Tylar ducked after the daemon. Rogger kept to his shoulder.

With their appearance, arrows and crossbow bolts rained around them, but the daemon's wings spread out, a shield of shadow. Feather, wood, and steel all burned away or were deflected aside.

Rogger kept low. "Seems Balger's men are braver from a distance."

"What of Delia? We can't leave her here." Tylar slowed. He would not abandon her.

"She's already gone. Two bells ago. Her escape was easy to arrange. I am not unknown among the wenches who serve . . . well, let's say *under* Balger. Though sometimes on top, too, I've heard."

Gongs clanged, raising the alarm.

Rogger pointed to the open gate to the courtyard. They fled across the weed-strewn yard.

It wasn't far. Balger's castillion was no larger than a manor house, a graceless jumble of blocks built of stone and wood. It sat in the middle of the Dell, atop a small outcropping of bedrock, a toad on a mound. The township itself was only so much flotsam and jetsam washed up against its rocky flanks: tumbled, chaotic, broken, waterlogged, bloated, rotted. A miasma of woodsmoke and swamp gasses cloyed the air and turned the sun into a continual glare. Beyond the city lay the only bits of arable land. Wheat, barley, and oat grass formed a fringed patchwork around the ramshackle town. And beyond the farmlands stretched endless marshes, bogs, and fens.

Where could they go?

They cleared the gates and spanned a moat that appeared more of a sewer than a defensive perimeter. Rogger led the way into the alleys and streets of Foulsham Dell. Shutters slammed all around. Cries raced ahead of them.

Rogger finally tugged him by the elbow into a cramped alleyway. He waved a hand at the daemon hulking half in shadow with them. "From here, mayhap you'd best rein in your friend there. That beastie of yours attracts too many eyes."

Tylar licked his lips. The daemon seemed to read their intent. Its head snaked back, framed in a mane of smoke. Its fiery gaze burned brighter, angry. Here crouched one of the naethryn.

"How?" Tylar asked warily. "It took Meeryn's blood last time to drive the beast back inside."

"According to Delia, you bear Meeryn's blood. At least the Grace of it. She thinks you'll be able to reel the daemon back into you with a touch of your own blood."

Rogger held out his short sword.

Tylar pocketed the dagger stolen from Balger. Such a dread weapon could not draw blood, only pain. Tylar ran the edge of his hand along Rogger's pocked sword. It was a shallow cut but stung like an adder's bite. Blood immediately flowed.

The scent of it drew the attention of the shadowbeast. The naethryn craned back, muzzle sniffing, eyes shining silver.

Tylar cradled his weeping wound with his other hand. Blood pooled in his palm. Tylar smeared his hands together, coating his fingers in wet crimson. He reached out to the smoky column and throttled it with his hands.

He expected his fingers to pass harmlessly through the smoke again. But shadow gained substance under his bloody palms.

It felt leathery, yet warm.

From his fingertips, a crackling rush of cold flames burst forth. The wildfire flushed out and over the naethryn's form. In a heartbeat, it reached the tip of its muzzle and rebounded back. On its return, the daemon's form vanished, burned away by the retreating fire. The flow of fire fled back along the umbilicus, back over his hands.

Tylar took a hurried breath as the rebound struck him in the chest. A mule kick. He was knocked against the alley wall. A flash of whiteness blinded him, then winked out. The alleyway lay in full shadow again. Darker than a moment ago.

Rogger searched the shadows for the daemon, making sure it was gone. "That's better. I was sure one of those smoky wings was going to brush through and melt the bones from my body." The thief shuddered.

By the wall, Tylar straightened both his legs and his back. He stared at his arms. Hale once again.

Rogger motioned to him. "Let's get moving. Best keep to the shadows and we should be safe."

His words immediately proved false.

From the shadows at either end of the alley, black shapes folded out of darkness. A dozen. Cloaked, swords in hand. Shadowknights all.

Tylar backed into Rogger. Another trap.

The leader of the knights stepped forth, plainly fearless, sword still sheathed. A mountain of shadow. He was too tall and too wide to be Darjon. His eyes glowed with Grace, swinging from Tylar to the thief.

"Again in trouble, Master Rogger?" The gruff voice, though muffled by masklin, could not be mistaken. "Why is it that your plans always go astray?"

Rogger grinned through his red beard. "We're out of the dungeons, are we not? I count that an improvement."

Tylar glanced between thief and knight.

"Here stands the other part of my original plan," Rogger said as introduction, turning back to Tylar. "If Lord Balger had played along, these knights were to have been your border escorts from Foulsham Dell to Tashijan, in service to our cause. Now it seems they must be our rescuers, too."

The knight bowed. "Your handmaiden brought us rumors of Balger's intent to keep the godslayer imprisoned here. It seems Ol' Balger speaks too freely among his wenches."

Tylar sensed the flow of hidden forces at work here. He eyed the tall knight. The last time he saw the man, his face had been blackened by ash, as was the manner of the Black Flaggers. In fact, he was the leader of the Black Flaggers. Krevan the Merciless. Now he had replaced ash for blessed masklin. The tattooed stripes of his former life as a Shadowknight were plain.

Tylar remembered Rogger's earlier words about the man. *Not every knight breaks his vow . . . Some simply walk away.*

Tylar faced the knight-turned-pirate. "How are you here?"

Krevan shifted, stirring shadows like oil. "We don't have much time for such tales. Suffice it to say, we will get you to Tashijan. Our cloaks will help hide you. We have horses waiting in Fen Widdlesham."

Tylar refused to budge. "Why . . . why are you helping? What has all this to do with errant knights and the Black Flaggers?"

Krevan's masked features were unreadable, but his words grew frosty. "All of Myrillia is in danger. It has been for a long time, out in the fringes, where few but the low know. I had thought never to don cloak and sword again, but some duties surpass personal desire."

"What do you mean by—?"

Rogger touched Tylar's shoulder. "Leave it be for now, Tylar."

Something silent passed between the elder knight and thief.

"You've not told him," Krevan said.

Rogger shook his head. "It was not my place."

Eyes narrowed above the masklin, pinching the black stripes tighter. "I bore a name before earning the title *Krevan the Merciless*. A knight's name. I was once called Raven ser Kay."

Tylar glanced to the thief in disbelief, but only found confirmation there. "The Raven Knight?"

Krevan swung away. "We must go."

"But Raven ser Kay died over three centuries ago," Tylar mumbled.

Rogger stood at Tylar's side, watching the knight disappear into shadow. "Yes . . . yes, he did."

14

WHISPERS IN THE DARK

DART KNELT ON A SMALL GOOSE-DOWN PILLOW AND SLOWLY UNROLLED the linen scarf across the stone floor. She then placed the small wyrmwood box onto its center. All the while, she felt the two pairs of eyes scrutinizing her every move.

Matron Shashyl stood with her hands folded behind her back, her lips pursed as she oversaw Dart's preparation for her first bloodletting.

Lord Chrism merely sat upon a chair, his face turned toward the open window of his chamber. He smelled of hay and freshly turned soil. His hair was oiled and combed straight back, making his green eyes seem larger, shining brighter than the afternoon sunlight.

With trembling fingers, Dart opened the small wyrmwood box. Lord Chrism's sigil was inlaid in gold on the lid. Inside, brown velvet protected the contents: a line of silver instruments, a ribbon of tightly braided silk, and a fresh repostilary. The crystal receptacle had been blown by the glass artisans only two days previous. Dart had toured the Guild's shops across the courtyard and watched this very repostilary being crafted.

Her first.

"This will be a full draw," Matron Shashyl said. "So which lancet will you choose?"

It was not a difficult question. Shashyl had schooled her vigorously over the past two days.

Dart reached and pointed to the leaf-shaped lancet. To create a flow rich enough to fill an empty repostilary to the brim, she would need the largest of the silver blades. It was filigreed with gold inlay, again the sigil of Chrism. Dart knew it was an ancient instrument, dating back to the second millennia following the Sundering. Yet the tool was maintained in such delicate fashion that the silver shone without a single pox of tarnish.

Its honed edge looked sharp enough to slice through darkness itself, its tipped point so fine it was hard to discern the end of the lancet without squinting.

"Very good," the matron said. "Let us not keep our Lord of the loam waiting any longer."

Chrism sighed with a ghost of a smile, his attention drawn back upon student and teacher. "Mayhap, dear matron, you should leave my Hand and I alone for this first bleeding."

"But, my Lord, she is—"

The garrulous old woman was silenced with the lifting of a single finger. "She'll do fine," Chrism said in consolation. "This is a private time between god and Hand."

Matron Shashyl quickly bowed, then retreated toward the exit to Lord Chrism's chambers.

Dart kept her eyes upon the floor, upon the spread of her tools. She found it hard to breathe, as if the air had gone suddenly too thick. Pupp lay on the stones, his stumped tail wagging slowly. His fiery eyes were fixed upon the tools, like a dog eyeing a soupbone. She had warned him off with a firm gesture when she first knelt down.

Chrism stirred in his chair by the window. "As much as the good matron may press upon you the import and weight of your duty, it is truly a matter of no great concern."

Dart glanced up at him. His eyes shone with emerald Grace, framed in soft brown curls, a slight stubble of beard shadowed his cheeks and chin. She found comfort in the warmth of his soft smile. She remembered his tears on the night of Willym's murder, shed without collection, a treasure spent in memory of the god's former servant.

"Every man bleeds," Chrism said. "A god is no different. I can't count the times this past winter alone that I've pricked a finger while working out in the Eldergarden."

Dart found such a concept impossible to imagine, but she recalled her first encounter with Chrism among the gardens, mistaking him for some common groundskeep. Looking at him now, she could not fathom how she made such a mistake.

"While my blood may have value in trade and stock, it flows from me like any other man's. Be not afraid. Master Willym and I were beyond ceremony."

Chrism rolled back the sleeve and exposed his arm. His skin was tanned the color of red loam, while soft hairs, bleached blond by the same sun that tanned his skin, curled up the length of his forearm. He turned his arm to expose his wrist. Here the skin shone paler, appearing tender, as smooth as a woman's cheek.

"You must simply stab deep and quick. My beating heart will do the rest of the work."

Dart nodded. She took up the length of braided silk. Pupp lifted his head, tail wagging more vigorously. She waved him down with her free hand. She did not want him interfering—especially not when blood was involved.

Pupp lowered his head but maintained his vigil.

Dart knelt by Chrism's chair and tied the ribbon above the god's elbow. She worked rapidly, having practiced all night. She snugged it, careful not to touch his flesh.

"Tighter," Chrism said. "You can cinch it more firmly."

Dart swallowed hard and did as he instructed. The silk pressed deeply into his flesh. For some reason, she had thought a god's flesh would be more unyielding, more like stone.

"Very good."

Dart sat back and gently lifted the silver lancet from the scarf. Now came the hard part. To stab the god she served.

"Can you see the vein at the edge of my wrist?" Chrism asked. "Willym preferred that one for a deep bleeding."

Dart reached up and cradled Chrism's wrist. His skin was warm, almost hot to the touch.

"A quick jab is all it takes."

She hesitated.

"Be not afraid." His voice purred with patience and concern.

Dart bit her lip and drove the point into his flesh and out again. A ruby drop of blood immediately welled upon his pale flesh, a jewel more precious than any mined from the heart of Myrillia. Here was a treasure mined from the heart of a god.

"The glass . . ." Chrism said with a smile.

Dart stumbled back, realizing she had frozen in place, mesmerized. She reached blindly for the repostilary, knocked it over with her fingertips; its crystal stopper rolled free of the scarf, tinkling on the stones. She grabbed the tiny decanter.

"Calm yourself. There is no hurry."

Blood welled on the god's wrist into a pool. Dart held forth the repostilary, needing both hands to hold it steady. Still the crystal receptacle tremored with each beat of her own heart.

Chrism leaned forward and tilted his wrist with a skill honed over millennia. The pool of blood became a channel, rushing from his flesh into a thick stream. The repostilary caught the flow as it poured forth.

Dart kept her gaze focused on keeping the wide mouth of the receptacle positioned to accept the god's gift. Her trembling continued to bobble the jar a bit, but not a drop was spilled. The repostilary filled.

Chrism studied the flow. "That should do nicely, Dart." She flicked a gaze in his direction. His lids lowered slightly. A glow bloomed softly on his wrist, moonlight through a break in clouds. Chrism had cast a blessing upon himself. The blood stopped flowing, dripping away, healed.

"The bit of linen, please," Chrism said.

Dart let go of the repostilary with one hand and reached for a folded slip of green Kashmiri linen. She snatched it up and held it out.

Chrism turned his wrist toward her. She dabbed the blood from his skin. No sign of her stabbing wound remained.

Clutching the repostilary, Dart finished her ministrations, wiping the last drops away. The bit of linen would be burned upon the brazier outside the chamber, a fire continually stoked for this very purpose. The residual Grace in the scrap of cloth was too capricious, dangerous, unpredictable, apt to be used in dark rites by black alchemists. Such items had to be purged regularly, including Chrism's daily garments after the slightest soiling by sweat or bile, the same with his bedsheets. Even forks and spoons were cleansed in fire to burn off any residual saliva.

Her focus on Dark Graces brought her back to the afternoon in the gardens, to the murder of the woman named Jacinta, turned to ash. She pictured the cursed black blade—and the man who had wielded it, a lord she knew by name now after inquiring discreetly.

Yaellin de Mar. Another of Chrism's Hands.

Dart knew nothing else about the man, avoiding him at every turn. The man oversaw the aspect of black bile, the solids passed by Chrism into a crystal chamber pot, twinned with another pot that collected the god's yellow bile each morning and night.

Dart had gone over the murder in the gardens . . . and Jacinta's final words. *Myrillia will be free!* What did that mean? It was the woman who had brought the cursed dagger onto the grounds. Once exposed, she had seemed to throw herself on the dagger to keep from being captured. Why? And what role did Yaellin have in all this? If innocent, why hadn't word of the encounter in the garden spread, especially here in the High Wing?

Dart had her own secrets, too many already. She wanted no others. So she had spoken to no one about it, not even Laurelle. What could she say?

How could Dart accuse or slander a Hand who had been in service to Chrism for going on his second decade?

Distracted by these black thoughts, Dart missed the roll of a drop of blood from Chrism's wrist. It fell toward the stones. Wincing, she watched the ruby jewel splatter—not against the floor, but upon a bronze nose. Pupp had darted forward, catching the drop in midair.

Rather than passing through her ghostly companion, the droplet found substance. With the touch of blood, Pupp grew momentarily solid. His bronze nails clicked on the stone floor. His molten form settled into ruddy plates and a mane of razored spikes. Dart felt the heat of his presence like a stoked fire.

She froze.

Chrism's eyes had returned to the view out the window as Dart had finished her ministrations, but now he stirred in his seat. Pupp stared up at the seated god. His eyes flared brighter. His tongue, a lick of flame, lolled out.

As Chrism leaned forward, the droplet of blood sizzled on Pupp's nose and burned away. A tiny dance of smoke marked its passage. And Pupp's form turned just as smoky.

"What's that scent?" Chrism asked. He withdrew his arm, placed his palm on the armrest, and shifted upward, staring around the room.

Dart waved a hand through the puff of blood smoke, clearing her throat. Pupp shook his head like a wet dog and trotted back across the room.

Chrism failed to note his passage, but his nose remained crinkled.

Dart quickly bowed her head. "One of the other Hands must be cleansing the utensils from your last meal, my Lord. In the grand brazier outside your doors."

With a worried crinkle of brow, Chrism settled back to his seat, but not before glancing one more time around the room.

Keeping her head down, Dart carefully plugged the repostilary with its crystal stopper and returned it to the wyrmwood box. She then folded the scarf over the box, and though her knees threatened to betray her, she stood smoothly.

"You did very well, Dart." Chrism returned to his watch on the flowing river below his window.

"Thank you, my Lord."

"Take the repostilary to Matron Shashyl. She'll instruct you from here."

"Yes, my Lord." Dart backed toward the door.

As her fingers touched the door's latch, Chrism spoke again, only a mumble, still staring out the window. "We must be watchful . . . all of us."

❖

"So tell me every bit," Laurelle said in a rush of breath and silk, sweeping into Dart's chamber. "Was it terrifying?"

Dart closed the door behind her friend. Laurelle was dressed in a white cotton dress, belted with silver silk, a match to her slippers. Dart had changed out of her own finery and back into a more comfortable shift that fell about her like a sack. She found its plainness a comfort.

Laurelle fled to Dart's bed and perched on its edge. Her eyes glowed in the last rays of the sun. Beyond her windows, the deeper bowers of the Eldergarden already shone with moonglobes and dancing fireflits.

Dart settled to a spot on the bed beside Laurelle. She took a pillow and hugged it to her belly.

Laurelle fell back to the crimson coverlet, arms flung out. "To see a god cry . . ." she murmured. "His tears shone like molten silver. I feared collecting them. How my hands shook! The tiny crystal spoon quavered in my grip."

Dart listened as Laurelle related her own first collection of Chrism's tears. It was a heady day for both of them. Dart still felt a twinge of unease. Pupp had almost been seen, made solid by the blood of the very god she served. It awakened her own fear of discovery . . . not only of her strange ghostly companion, but of her corruption.

Blood . . . why did she have to be chosen for blood?

"So tell me," Laurelle finished, sitting back up. "Did his humour glow with Grace? Did you swoon? I'd heard back at the school that some Hands faint away when drawing their first blood."

Dart glanced to her friend. "Truly?"

Laurelle's eyes widened. She reached a hand to Dart. "Did you faint?"

Dart shook her head.

"Then what happened? You have a great look of worry upon you."

Dart stared into her friend's eyes. Perhaps she could tell all to Laurelle. About Pupp, about the murder in the gardens, about her own defilement. Instead she found herself relating the event in dry tones. She spoke of Chrism's kindness and patience, of her own nervousness, of the successful draw. Laurelle listened to all with rapt attention.

Dart made no mention of Pupp . . . nor of Chrism's final cryptic words. *We must be watchful . . . all of us.*

"It all went well, then," Laurelle stated as Dart finished. "Why the long pout?"

Dart shook her head. "I . . . I'm just tired. It was trying. See . . . seeing the blood and all."

Laurelle's fingers squeezed hers. "But you didn't faint. You should be proud."

Dart offered a weak smile. It was all she could manage.

Her sour mood dulled the shine from Laurelle but failed to subdue her entirely. "Come," she said, standing abruptly and drawing Dart up by the hand. "Matron Shashyl has promised us a special feast to celebrate our first day. It's to be served in the common room. All the Hands will be there."

Dart now felt a swoon threaten. *All the Hands . . .*

The sixth bell rang out in the courtyard. It was answered by a small chime sounding in the High Wing's hall.

"We must get you dressed," Laurelle said. "Matron Shashyl sent me in here to fetch you. She said you were suffering a headache and she didn't want to disturb your rest until now."

Dart glanced to the cold cup of willow bark tea, untouched. She had feigned illness to escape to her chambers after the bloodletting. Shashyl had seemed to understand, nodding and taking her under her thick arm. She must have suspected, like Laurelle, that Dart had been overcome, perhaps swooned.

A part of Dart felt a stab of irritation. She had performed the bloodletting without mishap. Did they all think so little of her ability? Had she not accomplished her studies with dutiful alacrity?

That bit of fire helped steady Dart's legs. If she could stab a god, she could face the gathered Hands. Even the black-and-silver–haired Yaellin de Mar. He had given no indication that he recognized her from the gardens. And why should he? She had nothing to fear.

So she allowed Laurelle to tug free her shift, and together they searched her wardrobe for proper attire.

"Not too fine," Laurelle said. "We mustn't come off too pompous. But then again, we don't want to appear as drab either." Dart soon found herself in a ruffled white dress with a crimson sash. Though only of moderate splendor, it was far better than any of her clothes back at school. She felt like a mushroom masquerading as a flower.

Laurelle gave her one final look, fixing back a few loose curls. "Perfect."

As if timed, a knock sounded at the door. Matron Shashyl called from the hall, "How are you faring in there? Dinner is being brought up to the commons. Master Pliny will not leave a quail's wing to split between the two of you if you keep his ample appetite waiting."

Laurelle hid a giggle behind her fingers. It was a common jest across the High Wing that Master Pliny, the Hand of Chrism's Sweat, was more a servant of his belly than his god.

Dart and Laurelle crossed to the door. Laurelle took her hand. Dart found comfort in the familiarity and support. Laurelle leaned over and gave Dart a fast peck on the cheek. "As long as we're together, we'll always be fine."

❖

Dinner lasted past the eighth bell. Course after course had been marched into the common room: a soup of roasted butternut squash sprinkled with sweet cheese, a sour stew of boar's meat and ale, an oven full of gravy pies, platters of spit-turned rabbit and quails, a huge haunch of roasted boeuf seasoned with peppered apples, and lastly, spun confections of sugar and cinnamon shaped into fanciful creatures of lore.

By the end, Dart's head whirled amid the chatter and flows of wine.

Laurelle kept at her side, bolstering her up. Skilled with a charmed tongue, she had no trouble keeping up conversation. Dart was left mostly to watch, nibble, and sip.

All the Hands were in attendance. It had been many seasons since any new Hands had been brought into the fold. The six other men and women seemed more family than fellow servants. They squabbled, they pointed forks, they laughed, they taunted with jokes that originated in their shared pasts. Dart sensed it would take considerable time to blend in with this bunch.

But Laurelle tried her best. "And when all the illuminaria shattered, the looks on the other girls' faces were shocked to the point of speechlessness. And Healer Paltry, I had never seen him so shook up."

Dart had only been half-listening up to this point, having been caught up in a conversation between Master Pliny and Mistress Naff about the price of repostilaries. It seemed the flow of Grace between borders had been slowing of late, due to growing turmoil and odd behavior among some of the realms. Dart had listened intently, only to be drawn back to Laurelle at the sound of her own name.

"Dart looked the sickest of them all though. So green of face that you could barely note the mark of purity on her forehead."

"I can only imagine Healer Paltry's countenance," Master Munchcryden mumbled. The diminutive man, the Hand of Yellow Bile, dabbed the corner of his lips with the edge of his sleeve. "How I would've liked to have been in that chamber to see that eternal smile of his break."

Laurelle turned to Dart. "You know best. You should tell this story."

Dart felt an icy finger of terror trace her spine. She knew Laurelle was only trying to include them in the table's talk, to share anecdotes of their own shared past. Everyone knew Healer Paltry here, as he served as the High Wing's healer and physik. To gently gibe him seemed to please the table.

Dart found one set of eyes falling with studied intent upon her. No amusement shone in Master Yaellin's dark eyes. He wore a silver shirt with an ebony surcoat over it, adorned with raven feathers stitched into it as shimmering accents. The reminder of ravens unsettled Dart further.

"What reason did Healer Paltry give for the shatter of the illuminaria?" Yaellin asked. The casual manner of his words did not match his eyes.

Dart found all attention upon her. Under such weight, she lowered her gaze, fixing her attention to her wine goblet. "He said such things sometimes happened. That ofttimes the illuminaria would flare brighter with certain testings." She attempted to punctuate her disinterest with a shrug. She ended up bobbling her wineglass and spilling it across the white linen.

A maid quickly scurried forward and dabbed up the pool. The distraction helped divert attention. Other conversations started. Still, one set of eyes remained focused on her.

Yaellin de Mar's.

"Are you all right?" Laurelle asked.

Dart pushed back her chair. "It's just the wine. I'm not accustomed to such richness of fare. I think I should retire to my room."

Laurelle stood, too. "I'll go with you."

Mistress Naff lifted her wineglass to them. She was lithe of form and generous of bosom, dressed in a gown of red and brown silks, matching the drape and braid of her hair. Though rich of cloth, it was also somewhat chaste, laced to the neck. Naff was the Hand to Chrism's seed. It was whispered back at school that some such Hands would occasionally bed their gods to collect the vital humours, but these rumors were mostly told among the boys, amid snickers and rude comments. It was in fact not the manner. Once monthly, a god would spill his seed or her menstral bleeding into a crystal repostilary. Sometimes a Hand would attend, more often they would merely be called in to collect the crystal receptacle afterward. As such rare humours allowed Grace to be blessed upon a living person, they were second only to blood in importance.

Mistress Naff nodded to them. "Sleep well. And welcome to our small family."

Dart gave a half curtsy. She recognized a certain sadness in Mistress Naff's eyes. Did she see her own lost youth in their young faces? Mistress Naff had served Lord Chrism for only eight years, but already Grace had aged her countenance with early lines and sags. The humour she served was said to be the hardest burden to bear. Though handled only monthly, its Grace was attuned to living people, wearing its servant more than the others.

The other Hands acknowledged the departing girls with raised glasses, except for Master Pliny, who grunted and lifted a honeycake, dusting crumbs from his full belly.

Here was their new family.

Master Fairland and Mistress Tre stood up, too, and announced their departure. They were the most silent of the Hands, barely speaking, seldom smiling, a twin brother and sister, both chosen at the same time, representing the humours of saliva and phlegm respectively. They kept mostly to themselves, even shaving their dark heads to match, a custom among the steamy jungles of the Fourth Land. They were also the newest Hands, besides Dart and Laurelle, having been chosen three years ago.

The assembly continued to disperse in the wake of Dart and Laurelle's departure. Dart heard the well wishes and good nights spreading among the others. She glanced over one shoulder as the twin Hands departed toward their neighboring rooms.

In the doorway to the commons, Yaellin de Mar stood, leaning on the frame, his face in shadows. But Dart knew those eyes were on her. Why? He had shown no interest in her before now.

Without a doubt, the damnable story of the illuminaria had piqued some curiosity in him. None of the other Hands had found the story anything but an amusement. Yet Yaellin's attention pinned her like a crossbow's bolt. This last thought drew a shiver. *A crossbow's bolt.* The murder of Master Willym replayed in her head. It had been a murder meant for her . . . or rather the *position* she held, the new Hand of blood. But now Dart wondered. Had it been a more personal attack?

Without turning, she felt Yaellin's eyes still upon her. What did the breaking of the illuminaria mean? Prior to this moment, she had never properly considered it, too caught up in terror and circumstance since that day. If it had garnered the attention of Yaellin, had it also attracted someone else's eye, too? Someone with ill intent? She again pictured the blood pouring from Master Willym, his weight falling on her.

Was there more meaning upon that attempt on her life?

She glanced over her shoulder. The doorway to the commons was empty.

Yaellin de Mar was gone.

She knew she would have to watch him more closely.

If she was ever to get any answers . . .

❖

Sleep came hard. The rich food and wine did not sit well on her worried stomach. Dart listened to each bell's ringing, until the final bell chimed with the rising of the Mother. The greater moon's face shone full, bright even through the sheer drapery.

But sleep did finally come . . . and dreams.

Dart smelled the sea. She was being carried in a woman's arms, a babe again, her bearer's bosom pressed tight to her tiny head.

"We cannot wait the tide," the woman said to another. "They almost caught us in the wood."

The cloaked figure nodded and led the way down a tiny stone quay. He was dressed all in black, even his boots. As he turned to glance behind, she noted his face was masked.

A Shadowknight.

He crossed to a low skiff with black sails moored at the quay's end.

The woman hurried after, bouncing Dart in her arms. Moonlight shone on her face: auburn hair tied in a single braid, green eyes crinkled with lines of middle years, her complexion bled of all color. Dart knew the woman from vague memories of her earliest years, but even more from the oiled paintings that hung in the Conclave. It was the former headmistress of the school, the woman who had rescued Dart from the hinterlands.

She reached the skiff and hopped into its bow. "We must be away."

"What of the others?" the cloaked figure, a man from the timbre of his speech, asked while freeing the mooring lines.

"Gone . . . oh sweet gods above, all gone . . ."

He tossed the ropes into the stern and dropped beside the rudder. He yanked the black gloves from his hands and dropped them in the boat's bottom.

A horrible howl erupted, sounding as near as a stone's throw. It was all blood and bile.

"They're here!"

"And we're away." The knight waved a hand at the sails, and they filled with winds. The skiff sped across the silver waters of a cove, aiming for the open waters.

The beastly howl chased after them.

The headmistress slunk to the floor of the skiff, cradling Dart in her lap. The swaddling fell open. Dart felt a small tug on her belly. Something fiery rose from the edge of her swaddling, where her navel lay. An ugly face of molten bronze, barely formed, only the pair of fiery eyes, glowing agate stones, were familiar.

Pupp . . .

He was no bigger than a kitten, curled on her belly. He lay nested around a blackened knot on her belly, the tied stump of her umbilicus. He attempted to suckle it like a nipple, seeking milk. Again she felt that tug at her belly . . . *no, deeper* . . . coming from beyond flesh and bone. Pupp's form flared brighter. He then settled back to her belly, half-sunken in her flesh, ghostly.

The man spoke as they cleared the cove. "You can still drown the babe. Be done with the abomination."

A shake of the head. "She is no abomination."

Dart was collected back to the headmistress's bosom, her swaddling secured. Neither seemed aware of the suckling Pupp.

"The Cabal wanted her blood," the headmistress continued. "Rivenscryr must not be forged anew."

The skiff reached the open waters, now riding smooth swells. Behind them, the howl echoed.

The Shadowknight guided the craft, one hand on the rudder, the other occasionally waved at the sails. Dart noted the black tips of his raised fingers, dark to the first knuckle. Dried blood. A blessing of air alchemies.

"There will be others," the man intoned.

The woman clutched her tighter. "But they won't have this one."

A strong gust filled the sail with a snap of cloth and rope. The boat sped faster. The man glanced back to the receding cliffs of the shoreline, then forward again. "We're clear. Even their naether-lenses won't be able to track us."

The headmistress relaxed, though her hands still trembled. Her next words were a mumble meant only for her own ears. "What have I done?"

The knight heard. "What you had to. You know that, Melinda."

A sigh answered him. "But have we done the child any kindness?"

The man stared down at Dart, his eyes aglow with Grace above his masklin. "These are not kind times," he said sadly. "And the worst is yet to come. If what we dread comes to pass . . ."

"I know . . . I know . . . but it seems such a large burden for one so small."

The man grunted. "Sacrifices must be made by all. You saved her from the knife, now you must leave her hidden and unnoticed, a buried key."

The woman rocked the baby. As Dart felt her dream self grow droopy, one tiny hand rose to nuzzle her thumb. She struggled to listen, to hold the threads of her dream.

They proved too fragile, more light than substance.

Words began to dissolve. Images, too. Her blood . . . the headmistress whispered as the boat and sea grew darker.

The knight's words faded. It will take corruption to fight corruption. Will she be strong enough . . . ?

She must be.

Oh, Ser Henri, what have we done?

There was no answer, only darkness and quiet as true sleep carried her deeper, both babe and girl, beyond dreams, beyond words.

Dart woke with sunrise. Her tongue felt thick, and her head addled. The light through the drapery felt brittle and sharpened to points. She sat up, thirsty, her stomach churning. Had she drunk too much wine?

She shoved her feet free of the bedclothes and stood unsteadily.

Pupp poked his bronze nose from under the bed, blinked at her, then retreated back into the darkness. He seemed no more pleased with the morning.

Dart crossed to the privy, unsure if her stomach would hold. Every joint ached as she pumped cold water into the carved marble basin. She soaked a cloth and pressed it to her face. The icy chill quickly cooled the slight fever to her skin, her head ached less, and her stomach settled.

Echoes of the night's dream played in her head. A vague remembrance of a boat ride, the headmistress, and a Shadowknight. They had been talking about her, a babe. Any meaning had been clouded, snatches of a conversation, more inference than communication. Chrism's words returned instead: *We must be watchful . . . all of us.*

She knew this to be true.

Dart stepped back to her room. In the light of morning, it was easier to set aside her disturbing dreams.

She crossed to her wardrobe and was struck by an odd odor. She had not noted it before; perhaps she had been too addled. The scent was as faint as a whisper and seemed to fade with every breath she took, making its source difficult to discern. It smelled of sweated horses and the tang of wintersnap.

Halting in the middle of the room, she turned slowly around.

Pupp remained hidden, but his eyes shone from the gloom under her bed. He must have sensed her sudden tension.

Dart moved slowly to one of the four iron braziers that dotted each corner of the room. Each was identical, shaped like a repostilary jar, covered by a tiny grate. She checked the two closest to the window first. Both were cold to the touch.

She moved to the one by the privy. Also cold.

Already the scent faded beyond her senses. Perhaps she had imagined it. Maybe it had been a miasma from her morning illness.

She crossed to the last brazier, by the door. Her fingers brushed its surface.

The iron warmed her cold fingertips. She placed her palm on its side. It was not hot to the touch, but it was not cold either. Whatever small fire had heated the metal had only recently been extinguished.

Bending down, she creaked open the grate and peered inside. The strange scent wafted stronger again, but the brazier was empty, cleaned, and wiped. Yet coals had been burned here. Recently.

Cold dread crept up her spine, drawing her upright.

Pupp slunk from his hiding place and belly crawled to her side.

Someone had been in her rooms last night.

Someone had lit her brazier.

Who . . . and why?

Perhaps it had only been Matron Shashyl. But she always knocked before entering, announcing herself, awaiting invitation. Though the elderly matron might have a sharp tongue for the newest of Chrism's Hands, she had always respected their private spaces.

No, someone else had been in here.

Dart knew this with horrified certainty. She glanced around the room, fearful of discovering an extra shadow, a hand clutching a fold of drapery. She took a few shuddering breaths to calm herself. Whoever had been here had cleaned the brazier, covering their steps. They were surely gone again.

Still, Dart found her chest constricting. Whatever security and solace there had been behind the locked doors of her rooms was shattered. She had no safe place to call her own.

She trembled. Tears rose.

Someone had been in here, perhaps standing beside her bed, looking down on her. Why?

She remembered her disturbed slumber, the restless dreams, the morning queasiness. She could only imagine what dark alchemies had been burned on the brazier.

To what end? By whose hand? Or rather *which* Hand?

Dart pictured the dark eyes of the Hand of black bile, studying her over dinner, watching her. There could be no doubt.

Yaellin de Mar had been in her room.

15

BORDERLANDS

TYLAR STARED INTO THE SMALL CAMPFIRE. THE TINY HEARTH SMOKED more than it flamed, fed with wet wood, but that was all that could be found in the moldering swamps and bogs. The party gathered as best they could around the meager source of heat.

Rogger spit roasted a marsh hare over the pit. Upon the thief's recommendation, they had built the fire in a shallow pit to shield its sallow flame in the night. He had even caked the rabbit's skinned flesh with clay to cut down the scent of its sizzling flesh.

Next to him, Delia huddled in a cloak lined with otter fur. She was bone tired, as were they all.

No one spoke. Their small party, led by Krevan and his band of cloaked knights, had ridden all day, then fled all night through the marshes: punting a pair of skiffs, trekking salt flats, crawling through a forest of vines and creepers. They dared not risk the main road through the swamps, a rutted overgrown path that wound around stagnant stretches of water and forded bubbling rivers with bridges of stout oak.

And it was good they had taken Krevan's advice to abandon the road and seek out old trapper paths and animal trails. Lord Balger had not waited long before sending out his hunters, a mix of his own sworn Shadowknights and swamp trackers. Their pursuit proved dogged.

A full day and night stretched into one endless chase. Krevan set up traps and looped their course to confound pursuit. But the hunters had the advantage: the blessing of the god of the land. They followed with scent hounds Graced in alchemies of air, they bore weapons anointed in fire, and followed in swamp crawlers fueled as much by Balger's fury as the god's blood.

With such pursuit, the party had little chance to rest. But with dawn nearing, they were forced to ground, too exhausted to tackle the rolling mounds that marked the borderlands of the accursed Dell.

"What do you suppose is waiting beyond those hills?" Tylar asked.

Krevan shrugged.

"Will Balger have sent word ahead?" Tylar glanced to the east, where the skies were just beginning to lighten. "Will he have alerted Tashijan?"

Rogger snorted and pulled the spitted hare from the fire. He sniffed at its baked clay surface. "To raise the alarm, Balger would have to admit that he had you and let you escape. The bastard has too much pride for that. He'd lose face among the brigands and sly folk that make up his countrymen. Word won't travel beyond his borders until you're either dead or captured."

Krevan lifted a hand, standing quickly with a rustle of cloak and shadow. "Someone comes."

Tylar's palm dropped to the hilt of his sword, a borrowed short sword with a bone grip.

Krevan stepped back, half-dissolving into shadow. A whistle of skit-swift sounded from his lips. It was answered by another . . . and another. He stepped back into the circle of firelight. "One of the scouts."

As if drawn out by his words, shadows stretched and birthed the figure of a cloaked man. It was one of Krevan's knights. The man stepped into the glow, shedding darkness from his form. Tylar recognized him as an older knight named Corram. While it took a keen eye to discern one masked and cloaked Shadowknight from another, years of living among such men and women had sharpened Tylar's attention: to the cut and color of hair, to the shape and hue of eye, to the subtle scars and wrinkles. Even the manner of movement, rhythm of gait, and a knight's carriage revealed clues.

Despite his advanced years, Corram moved with a stealth few could match. His eyes were ice, his hair a matching silver.

He nodded to Krevan. "The hunters have found our scent again. They move even now to close us off from the border mounds."

"How quickly?"

Corram shook his head. "We have a quarter bell at best."

Rogger swore and began kicking dirt atop the wood coals, dousing the flames. "Then let us not tarry." He lifted the roasted hare and cracked the caked clay. The scent of sizzling fat and flesh wafted strongly. He handed the spitted hare to one of Krevan's men. "Stake this little bait on the raft by the stream. The current will carry her off, drawing the scent hounds away from our path. I never knew a hound that wouldn't follow a bit of roasted hare."

With a nod, the knight stepped away.

The others quickly broke camp and set off.

Krevan again led the way. His ten knights flanked forward and behind, alert for attack. Rogger strode behind the leader of the Shadowknights. Tylar followed next with his short sword and kept Delia close to his side. She met his gaze for a breath. Her face was smeared with mud, a cheek scratched deeply, and her eyes were rimmed with fear.

"Stay with me," he whispered. It was the only consolation he could offer.

It seemed enough. Taking a shuddering breath, she nodded.

The party stumbled through the tangle of bog brier that had been their bower and splashed across a sluicing riverbed, smelling of stagnant mud and root rot. As they climbed the far banks, the mounds rose before them, limned in the thin light of approaching dawn.

These borderlands, named the Kistlery Downs, were chalk-and-flint hills rising from the swamplands, a hard boundary separating the lowland swamps and bogs of Foulsham Dell from the central plains of the First Land. While the mounds were not high, they were steep sided, creating a maze of vales, hollows, and dells. Confounding the matter, the lowest portions remained shrouded in foul mist. It was as easy to get lost among them as it was to be trapped.

"Do you know the way through here?" Tylar asked.

"Rough enough," Krevan answered.

Tylar found little comfort in his answer.

Rogger dropped beside Tylar. "The only known route through Kistlery Downs is the main road. And that will be guarded."

Delia studied the white cliffs on either side of them. They glistened with bits of gypsum and quartz. "I heard that dark alchemists set up black foundries here, dug into the hillsides, spewing corruption and burned Graces from their subterranean chimneys."

Rogger waved aside such worries. "Blood witches and Wyr-lords are the least of our concerns. They may haunt the Downs, but they'll shy from us as much as we might wish to avoid them."

"Why doesn't Lord Balger rid the hills of their foul ilk?"

Rogger glanced back to her. "Where do you think His Largeness gets most of his revenues? More of Balger's humours flow through the black fires here than are traded across borders."

Tylar noted the deepening frown on Delia's face. Sheltered in schools and selected young as a handmaiden to Meeryn, she'd had little chance to understand how trade among the lands was more often black rather than white. Whereas Tylar had direct dealings with the Gray Traders, those who plied the rivers of commerce that flowed beneath all else, traffickers in Dark Graces, stolen humours, and accursed weapons and tools. Tylar knew that the bale dagger he had stolen from Lord Balger, a blade that healed as fast as it cut, would fetch a significant ransom among the Traders.

And one time he would have made that deal.

As a young man, he had thought himself wise in the ways of the world, capable of moving within that gray territory between the light and the dark. He had raised coin through some shady profiteering. And while most of it went to help the orphanage where he had been raised, a fair amount still found its way into his own pocket.

He'd had a wedding to plan . . . to Kathryn.

He shoved this last thought aside.

But memories still flooded through him: of blue eyes looking deep into his own, of hushed breaths in the stillness of a long night, of tender lips, of promises both whispered and shouted aloud. And through it all, laughter flowed, light, yet coming from the heart.

All had been so easy, so very easy.

No longer.

He gripped his short sword, fingers firm and sure. While his body had been healed by Grace, his heart remained untouched. There was no blessing to heal that which had died long ago.

"How far to reach the border?" Delia asked, drawing his attention to his current plight.

"Another six reaches," Rogger answered. "Barring any missteps—which is not hard in this skaggin' place—we'll reach the far plains a bell or two after sunrise. And if the morning sea mists have burned away, we might even catch a glimpse of Stormwatch Tower in the distance."

Tashijan's tallest spire.

"So close . . ." Delia mumbled.

She glanced over to Tylar. Both had listened silently to Krevan's report on the current tidings at the Citadel. Argent ser Fields had been named the new warden. After hearing this, Delia had bowed her head. Tylar kept silent about the familial tie between Argent and Delia, father and estranged daughter. It was not his place to speak of it.

But all knew of Tylar's tie to Argent's new castellan, Kathryn ser Vail. His former betrothed. Eyes had carefully avoided his as this detail was recounted.

Only Delia had the courage to meet his gaze. Both their pasts had become tied together in one place. A place they must explore to solve a riddle uttered by a dying god.

Krevan stopped ahead, his form barely discernible in the fetid fog that filled the hollow spaces between the hills. With his head cocked, he waved them to his side.

"What—?" Delia began.

He shushed her. Silence pressed down upon them—then a wheezing rasp echoed from up ahead. It was not unfamiliar. They had heard the same telltale noise chasing them all night.

"How many?" Rogger asked in a matching wheeze.

"Too many," Krevan answered under his breath.

He motioned them back. A fresh rasping rose behind them. This was no echo. They were being surrounded. From the darkness, Krevan's knights coalesced, closing ranks.

"They've cut us off," one of the knights hissed.

"What do we do?" Tylar asked, raising his sword, firming his stance.

Krevan glanced to him. "Run, fight, or die. Take your pick."

Beyond Krevan's shoulder, a tall spindly shape crept out of the fog. It moved on eight jointed legs, like some bronze metal spider, twice the height of a man. Each leg ended in a sharpened point, perfect for maneuvering through the muck and rot of the swamps, jabbing into logs and tree trunks for purchase, slipping in and out of the mud with ease.

A swamp crawler.

Tylar smelled the blood burning from exhaust flutes behind the mekanical crawler. Its two riders crouched in the central egg-shaped seat. One controlled the swamper, the other squatted with a crossbow. Both were deadly.

A bolt sliced through the fog, ripping through a fold of a knight's shadowcloak. At the same time, one of the sharpened legs lashed out with a burr of mekanicals, nearly impaling the same knight. But a dance of cloak saved the man. Tylar recognized Corram—then the older knight vanished into deeper shadows.

Krevan grabbed his shoulder. "This way."

His cloak billowed out to either side, sweeping out to encompass Tylar and Delia. Corram reappeared on their other side, offering the same protection to Rogger—but not before flinging out a dagger from a wrist sheath. The blade flashed in the misty starlight, slicing through the fog. It struck the lead rider in the eye.

The bronze mekanical faltered as its pilot fell back, dead in the riding sling. The crawler's front legs crumpled, no longer fueled. The mekanical toppled. The second man tossed his crossbow and struggled to escape his own sling.

Tylar never saw the man's fate as he was guided away. A crash and clatter of bronze echoed after them.

They fled back down the misted vale.

A new pair of crawlers blocked their retreat, moving in tandem, half-climbing the walls to either side, legs digging into the flinty hills. More movement stirred behind them.

Krevan led the way off to the side, to a narrow gorge between two hills. They had to proceed in single file. Corram kept to their rear.

"What about the other knights?" Delia asked.

Cries answered her, coming from behind them. The bronze spiders were finding these flies had teeth.

Still, Tylar knew that Balger had sent a full score of crawlers after them. Too many for the Shadowknights to handle. The others were only providing them breath to escape. But how much breath?

Already the baying of hounds carried to them. More hunters. The dogs' keepers would not be far behind, armed with flaming swords and oiled fireballs in leather slings, capable of incinerating entire patches of forest to the ground.

"I guess those hounds weren't interested in my fine rabbit stew," Rogger mumbled.

Krevan suddenly grabbed Tylar and Delia and dragged them to one wall of the gorge. Corram did the same with Rogger against the far wall. Both knight and thief vanished under a wave of shadowcloak.

Overhead, bronze legs crested over the top of the gorge. Another crawler. It stopped, perched above them.

Krevan pulled Delia farther behind him. Tylar felt the tingle of Grace flowing through the Raven Knight's cloth, keeping them hidden.

The seat lowered into the gorge, suspended by the legs. The pilot worked the controls, swiveling the cabin. The archer kept his crossbow fixed to his shoulder and scanned the gorge. He mostly concentrated back toward the valley.

The pilot settled the crawler in place. It looked as though they were staying. They must have been sent here to block this pass, pinching off retreat in this direction. Other crawlers were probably blocking other escape routes. The noose was tightening.

Krevan stirred. If any alarm was raised, they were doomed, trapped between the walls of the gorge.

Tylar closed his eyes, calculating in his head. He felt Krevan begin to step away. Tylar reached out and grabbed his elbow, warning the knight from rash action. Then Tylar slipped a hand to Krevan's belt and relieved him of one of his daggers. He slid the blade through a fist, slicing skin. As blood and sweat anointed the blade at the same time, Tylar pictured flames, the sear of flesh. He felt the blade heat up in his fist.

Balancing the dagger in his fingers, he pushed from the wall, rolled out under the crawler's cabin, and threw the dagger straight up. The blade struck where one of the legs joined the seat.

He dashed back to the wall, enveloped again by shadow and cloak.

"What . . . ?" Krevan asked.

Tylar silenced him with a hiss.

Overhead, the crawler began to spew smoke from its flues. He prayed the strike of the dagger would be mistaken for a burp in the mekanicals. He watched the pilot struggle to hold his crawler. Its movements grew jerky and labored. More smoke billowed, followed by a cough of flame. The crawler lost its footing, tumbling forward. The pilot fought his controls. The cabin seat struck one of the gorge walls, jarring like a struck bell.

"Go," Tylar urged and pointed deeper down the gorge.

With the hunters distracted by their foundering craft, Tylar and the others fled unseen up the gorge and away. Finally, Krevan spoke. "What did you do back there?"

"I cast a blessing upon their crawler. Using blood and sweat."

Delia glanced back over her shoulder. "You cast heat?"

Tylar nodded. "Crawlers are fueled by fire alchemies. They steam hotly. It takes only a little extra heat to push the mekanicals beyond their limits, burning them out. The same can happen if you overwork them. I hoped that flaming out their mekanicals would be taken as simple bad luck."

Krevan nodded. "And now those same hunters will guard our own path. They'll hold their position and swear no one passed them."

"Changing hunters into guardians," Rogger said. "Not bad, Tylar. You're becoming a right good alchemist."

"I had a good teacher." He nodded toward Delia, who shyly glanced forward.

Corram pointed ahead. "Where to now?"

Krevan forged deeper into the narrowing gorge. "Off to strike a bargain."

"Where?" Tylar asked.

Krevan simply scowled.

Rogger answered, struggling a few steps ahead of Corram, his voice thick with distaste. "The Lair of the Wyr."

As the sun rose, Tylar found the dawn brought little light. The cliffs were high and narrow, shrouded in mists, trapping them in eternal twilight. It seemed they had been marching for days. Tylar trudged after Krevan, Delia behind him, followed by Rogger and Corram. All sounds of battle had long grown silent.

No knight had returned, but Krevan had expressed no worry. "They know to lead the hunters astray, away from our path. We'll regroup in Muddlethwait across the border."

"That is, if we ever get out of these hills," Rogger added.

Tylar glanced to the high walls. He was thoroughly lost. Even Krevan seemed to be losing his faith in his sense of direction, slowing their pace, pausing at crossroads among the maze of gorges.

"How much farther?" Delia asked. "Where is this Lair?"

Rogger moved closer, his voice an edgy whisper. "Child, we've been among the Wyr for the past full bell."

Tylar tightened his grip on his sword's hilt.

"They watch us even now," Rogger said.

As if hearing his words, a rock crumbled from the cliff edge and skittered down the wall.

Krevan ignored it all and continued forward.

Tylar now eyed the crevices and side chutes with plain suspicion, sword pointed and ready. He had, of course, heard of the Lair, an assembly of Wyr, those who practiced arcane alchemies upon themselves, seeking some measure of corrupted Grace. It was whispered that an ultimate goal was sought by the Wyr: the creation of a perfect abomination, to birth a god from human flesh, to bring new divinity into the world from mortal union.

But in this quest, they created misshapen creatures, some raving, others wise beyond measure. And ultimately theirs was a mad goal, an impossibility. Even when gods lay down with a man or woman, no child was ever born from such a union. As Grace foreshortened the lives of the

Hands who served their gods, such strong emanations destroyed this earliest spark of life. No child could be born into Grace. It could only be granted by a god.

Still, the Wyr-lords persisted, producing abomination and deformity. Their ilk, while mostly hidden away in the depths of the hinterlands, could be found throughout Myrillia.

And the true heart of all the Wyr was rumored to be hidden here.

The Lair.

At last the narrow gorge opened into a wide hollow, framed by the tallest of the mounds. In the center, a small pond shone in the thin light, rimmed in red algae and as dark as oil. It bubbled slowly and stank of sulfur that burned the nose.

A woman awaited them, carrying a baby in her arms, swaddled in a blanket. Flaxen haired and pale of complexion, the woman was tall, lithe of figure, generous of bust as was fitting a new mother. She seemed unsurprised by the visitors, but her face was uninviting.

"Leave your weapons," Krevan said. He met Rogger's eyes for a moment longer. "*All* your weapons."

Corram tugged free his sword belt and rested it atop a boulder. He shook back his cloak's sleeves and undid a series of wrist sheaths, each housing three daggers, then did the same at each ankle.

And while this was an impressive array of weaponry, Rogger proved to be a regular armory: short sword, throwing daggers, razored stars, a flail, even a blowgun down one pant leg. It was surprising the thief could even walk upright.

Delia had only a single dagger, Tylar the one short sword.

Krevan was the last to disarm, pulling free his diamond-pomelled sword and holding it before him, blade resting in his two palms as if offering a gift.

Tylar stared at the blade, seeing it for the first time. Along its silver length, a winged wyrm had been traced in gold, filigreed and detailed.

"Serpentfang," he whispered in awe. He remembered Rogger's claim that Krevan was actually Raven ser Kay, the Raven Knight of lore. Any attempt to question Krevan earlier had been answered by a cold stare. And Rogger refused to say more after his initial revelation.

Tylar had assumed Krevan was a descendant of that infamous Shadowknight, a man said to have died three centuries ago. But here was the very blade once said to have been borne by the Raven Knight. Serpentfang had been described in song and fable, depicted in tapestry and in oil.

While the blade was polished, any Shadowknight could recognize its age, its steel folded a thousand times. This was no replica given to some young lord upon a birthing day.

Without mistake, here was the very blade that slew the Reaper King.

And if this was indeed Serpentfang . . .

Tylar watched Krevan approach the lone woman by the lake. Halfway to her position, the Raven Knight dropped to one knee, lowered the blade to the chalky soil, and stepped past it, abandoning a prize that could ransom an entire god-realm.

Only then did the woman stir, stepping into Krevan's shadow. The knight towered over her, blocking the view but not her words.

"Raven ser Kay," she said, her voice sibilant and high, full of malice and amusement. "What brings you into the Lair again? Last we met, you swore to kill me."

Krevan kept a wary stance. "Your memory is long, Wyrd Bennifren."

"Eighty years is not long to either of us, now, is it?"

Krevan remained silent.

"Again, what brings you here?" she asked.

"We wish to buy passage through the Lair's burrow."

A long silence answered his request. Then slowly she spoke. "For you . . . and the godslayer."

Krevan attempted a lie. "Don't tell me you believe such nonsense?" He punctuated it with a harsh snort.

"Perhaps not, but Lord Balger certainly does. We know the Downs are overrun with crawlers, scent hunters, and worse. Two of your knights met their ends among the hollows. The rest are hotly pursued. Yet you bring the true prize to my doorstep."

Krevan had not moved, yet a dark cloud of cloak and shadow seemed to swell from his shoulders. "You bear no special love for Lord Balger . . . or Tashijan. To keep this godslayer as a prize would bring the full wrath of both upon the Lair."

"No doubt of that, but I would see this godslayer for myself," the woman finished, "before we settle on a price."

Krevan glanced back to Tylar. He was waved forward.

Rogger hissed at his ear as he stepped away. "Speak with a cautious tongue. Deals among the Wyr are struck upon one's word."

Tylar moved to join Krevan. Stepping around the large knight's billowing form, he again spotted the woman. She leaned her weight on one leg, throwing out her hip, carrying her swaddled babe there. She wore a bored expression.

"So this is the godslayer?"

Tylar's brow pinched. The woman's mouth had not moved as she spoke. In fact, her entire manner—from slack lips to glazed eyes—struck Tylar as dull and mindless.

"Bring him closer." Pale movement drew his eye. He spotted a tiny white arm beckon to him. It was the baby boy. The infant's eyes were fixed on his face. "Tylar de Noche," the babe said, thick with disdain. "Your reputation precedes you."

Tylar found no words, mouth agape.

Krevan covered for him. "May I introduce Wyrd Bennifren, Lord of the Lair and free leader of the Wyrdling clans."

"Be welcome, Godslayer." The baby smiled up at him, a horrible toothless visage, eyes wizened with age. "Let us strike a bargain for your life."

❖

Tylar paced the confines of the small cave. Their accommodations were surprisingly pleasant. Flames crackled in a small hearth carved into the wall, the smoke fluming away through a buried chimney. Underfoot, thick sheepskin rugs warmed the natural stone floor. Torches blazed on all four walls, illuminating the tapestries of Kashmiri silk woven with gold-and-silver thread. He could easily be in the greeting chamber of some lord's manor house, rather than deep beneath the chalk hills of Kistlery Downs.

"How much longer must we wait?" Tylar finally blurted.

"The Wyr will not be rushed," Krevan said. He sat hunched on a bench. The room had no shadows in which to hide or draw strength, and clearly this made him ill at ease and seemed to age him.

His fellow knight, Corram, simply leaned against one wall, rubbing a wrist where his sheathed daggers once rested.

Seated on a chair by the hearth, Rogger chewed a stubby brier pipe, puffing out clouds of redolent smoke through his beard. "Bennifren is actually treating us—or rather should I say *you*"—he glanced pointedly at Krevan—"much more courteously than I would have imagined."

"What past do you two share?" Delia asked. She also sat by the fire, but in a deep, cushioned chair. She had sunk gratefully into it. Tylar had almost forgotten Delia's past as a handmaiden to Meeryn, where such luxuries were easily at hand. She had abandoned so much, a life of comfort and grace, to accompany him on this hard road.

Krevan stared at her, then away. An imperceptible movement of his wrist toward Rogger indicated it was permissible to speak of this matter.

The thief took up the mantle with aplomb. "Now that's a tale." He stood up to warm his backside by the fire. "But before that one could be told, one must tell the story of the Raven Knight. One not sung by minstrels, nor written in the great recountings of history."

Tylar stopped his pacing and gave Rogger his full attention.

"And we should begin such a story at the beginning—with the death of Raven ser Kay. Some three hundred years now, is it not?" Rogger glanced to Krevan, who only glared back, eyes flashing with Grace.

"Yes," Rogger continued. "Raven ser Kay did not die a noble death on some battlefield, but instead met his end in bed, of an affliction of the heart. Or more specifically, a dagger to the heart, wielded by a concubine who shared his sheets. A comely lass of great beauty, I've heard, but one whose family ties could be traced to the Reaper King. An unfortunate discovery made after she used that same dagger to slay herself."

Delia sat straighter. "Such is the tale sung by balladeers."

"A truly tragic end, one embellished with details over the centuries, making it a grand tale of love, revenge, and honor. But where such ballads end, the true story begins." Rogger paused to puff on his pipe, then continued. "For Raven ser Kay was not like other men . . . There was a reason he survived so many battles. He had a secret he kept from the wardens and castellans of Tashijan. A secret that a comely assassin revealed upon the point of her dagger."

"What secret is that?" Tylar asked as Rogger paused again.

"He has no heart."

"What?"

"There is a reason he is titled *Krevan the Merciless*. It comes from his much older but truer name: Krevan the *heartless*."

Tylar shook his head. "What foolishness is this?"

"He speaks the truth," Krevan grumbled from his bench. "I was born with no heart."

"How . . . ?" Delia asked, growing paler.

Rogger explained. "Exposed as a babe in the womb to black alchemies, his blood was corrupted. It is a living thing, flowing on its own through his flesh and organs, needing no muscled pump. It is this same corruption that allowed him to survive the assassin's blow. You can't stab what isn't there."

Tylar stared at Krevan with new eyes.

"But such a wound could not be hidden. His secret was laid bare. He was given a choice by the warden at that time. Be stripped and humiliated . . . or allow the Raven Knight to die."

Rogger glanced again to Krevan. "So he walked away, leaving his past to the balladeers and historians to pick and chew over like dogs on bone. He started a new life—not unlike you, Tylar—among the low and forgotten. Out of the seed of his pain grew the Black Flaggers."

Tylar sensed corners of the story left untold, but he did not press.

"But how did he come to be corrupted in the first place?" Delia asked. "To be born without a heart?"

The answer came from the doorway. Wyr-lord Bennifren entered, carried by the same woman. "Because he was born here . . . in the Lair."

Delia covered her mouth in shock.

"This is his true home," the ancient baby said in that sickly sibilant tone of his. "He is born of the Wyr."

Krevan gained his feet. "One does not choose a birthplace, but one can choose a life thereafter. I renounced this place long ago."

"Blood is always blood."

Krevan spat on the floor. "And shite is forever shite."

The knight's outburst only amused the Wyr-lord. Dark laughter flowed. Krevan seemed to sense he had been drawn deliberately out. He straightened and glared. "What of the bargain? Will it cost me more of my blood?"

"That bought Allison's freedom eighty years ago. You struck a hard bargain. I still miss your mother." He reached up and squeezed the breast of the woman who carried him. There was no reaction. "She had the sweetest milk of all my cows. Whatever did become of her after you left here? Died I heard. Drowned. Was it an accident or did she still have a bit of will left in her? Perhaps she missed her former life."

"What you did to her . . ." Krevan's reaction was not an outburst, but a coldly spoken promise. "I will still kill you for that."

A tiny arm waved away his threat. "She let you flee the Lair. She had to be punished. But I'm surprised it took two centuries for you to finally come looking for her. Who's to blame for that?"

Krevan's eyes narrowed.

Tylar read the pain there, deep rooted and old. He had to end this. He spoke up, drawing the Wyr-lord's attention. "Is there a deal to be struck here or not?"

"To the point," Bennifren said, ancient eyes staring out of the pudgy, soft face. "Very good. The council has conferred. We will allow you safe passage through our burrows."

"And the price?" Tylar asked.

"One you can live with, I believe . . . and that is the point of all this, is it not?"

Tylar smelled sour milk wafting as the Wyr-lord was carried closer.

"For ages upon end," he continued, "the Wyr clans have sought divinity in flesh. We have made many strides toward that end. The black knight who led you here was but one success, a mortal man almost unbound by time. But he does age, like myself, only much more slowly. A century or more and he will expire, as will I. That is, if he does not die sooner of severe wounds or sickness like any man. We have some manner to go before we can breed godhood out of mortal flesh—but we grow closer with every passing birth."

Tylar had seen the results of such *births* over the years: children without limbs, creatures of misshapen flesh, Grace-maddened beasts. But the worst were those like the abomination before him. Twisted by alchemies in the womb, yet wise beyond reason. They were dangerous and cunning.

He would have to tread lightly. He had no misconceptions about the Wyr, and they surely were not blind to his own abilities: from the Grace flowing through his body to the smoky daemon held in check. Yet they allowed him into their Lair without fear. He did not doubt that eyes watched from unseen places, and safeguards were in place to kill them all at the slightest provocation.

"Then what do you want from us?" Tylar asked again.

"As payment for saving your flesh, we ask only that you leave a little of it behind."

"What do you mean?"

The eyes of the babe flashed brighter. "You have been blasted by Grace, had it infused into your being. One such as yourself could help us achieve our ancient goal in a single generation.

"We want nothing more—and nothing less—than a single sample of each of your eight humours. Leave that behind and passage will be granted to all of you."

Tylar considered this offer. It was plain enough. He began to open his mouth, ready to agree.

Rogger mumbled around his pipe, the words barely reaching Tylar's ears, "Bargain, damn you . . ."

Tylar realized he had been too ready to seal the deal. "You ask for much," he stumbled out. "I say my blood alone should buy us passage."

"What you offer so freely we could perhaps take by force," Bennifren countered, eyes squinting with threat.

"But what will it cost you? You know I am not without weapons."

"Your daemon . . ." the Wyr-lord sneered, a disturbing expression on a babe's face.

Tylar nodded. Let them believe he could wield the creature like a sword. "You would never find your way out of our burrows. We have traps that can kill even a daemon-cursed man. And what of your friends? Do you throw their lives away so easily?"

Tylar sighed and countered. "Then I'll offer blood and both biles."

"Shite and piss? That's how you sweeten the deal. I'm not moved."

"Then make a counter."

"I will leave you tears and sweat, and take all else."

Tylar narrowed his eyes. The Wyr birthed abominations in their drive for divinity. They would want his seed more than anything else. He suspected it was this very reason he was still alive. While the Wyr might harvest most humours from his corpse, his seed would die with him.

Yet now that he considered it, this was the *one* humour he would keep to himself. He would not have some twisted child born from the seed of his loins. Not among the Wyr. He had only to consider Krevan's story to know better.

"You may have all my humours except one," Tylar said.

"You wish to restrain your seed from us," the babe said, as if reading his mind. "Is this not so?"

Tylar felt a chill despite the hearth. Dark intelligence shone from the little one's eyes. He sensed a trap being set but had no choice but to step forward. He nodded his agreement.

"We will allow this."

Tylar could not hold back his surprise and spoke too soon. "Then we have a bargain."

"Almost . . . we will allow you to restrain your seed, for now, to keep it safe where it now resides. But we demand a future claim."

Tylar frowned at this.

"Before you die, you must forfeit your seed to the Wyr."

He shook his head. "Death can come suddenly, without warning. I cannot promise time to cast my seed."

The Wyr-lord nodded. "We accept this risk, but in doing so, we require one last concession to seal the bargain."

"And what is that?"

"One of the Wyr will journey with you from here, to safeguard our claim, to keep its bearer secure."

"You wish to send a guard along with us?"

"That is our last and best offer."

Tylar glanced to Rogger. He had remained silent. His only assistance now was a shrug.

Tylar faced the Wyr-lord. He still felt the presence of the noose, but they had no other option.

With a deep sigh, he nodded. "We accept your bargain."

"So it is spoken, so it is bound," the lord finished. The woman turned, obeying some unseen signal, driven and ridden like a barebacked horse. "Meet your guardian."

Tylar prepared himself to face some heaving monstrosity, some muscled mix of loam-giant and Wyr-blasted corruption.

The guardian stepped into the doorway.

Tylar's eyes widened in shock.

She was as tall as Krevan, stately of limb, decked in deerskin from boots to furred collar, cut low between her ample breasts. The curves of her body seemed to ripple as she entered the chamber, moving like some feral black leopard. Her ebony hair fell straight to her shoulders, unbraided, untamed. Her skin was the hue of bitternut: dark, but mixed with cream. Her black eyes bore the slightest narrowed pinch, accentuating her feline grace. Her lips were full, nose narrow.

Her calm gaze swept the room and settled on Tylar. A perfume of crushed lilies carried in with her . . . accompanied by a deeper, muskier scent that quickened Tylar's breath as he attempted to capture it.

"May I introduce Wyr-mistress Eylan," the babe-lord said.

Rogger mumbled behind Tylar, "You'd better keep a close eye on that seed of yours. Something tells me you might be giving it sooner than you expected . . . and willingly at that."

So here was the Wyr-lord's trap.

Tylar watched Eylan bow, moving with such unassuming grace.

A trap baited most beautifully.

Deep underground, Tylar stepped from the steaming chamber where a hot spring bubbled. Smelling of salt and iron, the air had seared and drawn sweat from all his pores. Wearing only a breechcloth, he shivered as he entered the neighboring cell, ready to let his sweat be harvested by Wyrd Bennifren's alchemist.

"Tylar . . ."

The new voice startled him, unexpected as it was.

Delia stood in the chamber.

He half-covered his nakedness as she crossed toward him.

Past her shoulder, at the entrance, he spotted the thick-limbed giant with the bony brow—his guard—and the wizened old alchemist who wheezed constantly. In the company of these two Wyr-men, Tylar had already emptied bowel and bladder. He had spat until his mouth was paste and had sniffed ground nettlecorn until his nose dripped heavily. Everything had been collected in crystal receptacles, ready for some dark purpose, the thought of which unnerved Tylar.

Delia spoke when she reached his side, glancing askance at his body. "I've convinced them to allow me to harvest your last three humours. Blood and tears are especially delicate to collect. And as a chosen Hand, I've the most experience."

He nodded.

She smelled of sweetwater and lemon. Clearly she had been allowed to bathe. Her hair was damp and combed back behind her ears. It looked even blacker, almost oiled. And she had changed out of her muddy wear and into a soft shift of green linen, belted at the waist with a braid of bleached leathers. The shift clung fetchingly to her. He noted how fair shaped she was: apple-sized breasts, slender waist.

So young . . . *too* young, he reminded himself. Still, he could not discount how she shortened his breath, especially now. With the mud of the road washed from her, she came to him less like a fellow companion and more like a woman.

She stepped to his side and unrolled a silk scarf atop a table, revealing an array of silver and crystal utensils. She picked up a glass blade and crystal cup. She waved him to the table. "Lift your arms."

He did as she instructed. "You don't have to do this . . ."

"I served Meeryn," she said. "I will serve her still."

She drew the dull edge of the blade along his heat-dampened skin, from shoulder to waist, scraping the sweat from his body. She deftly collected the runoff into the tiny cup, then continued across his back, under his arms, down his legs, not unlike a stableman brushing down a sweated horse.

But she was no stableman.

As she stepped around to work his chest, he felt himself stir and fought against it, willing himself to distraction. But she continued her work, moving the blade up and down his chest, scraping delicately and smoothly.

Unbidden, a shiver trembled through him.

She finally seemed to note the flush to his skin. She glanced up to his eyes and saw something that widened her lashes. She lowered the blade. "I . . . I think that will be enough."

Gratefully, he slipped into a cloak, covering his half-naked form before turning back to her.

Delia set up for the next harvest, laying out a silver lancet and twisting up a cord of silk.

Tylar cleared his throat, needing to break the silence. "Delia," he began, his voice coming out strained. "You've done much to get me here, given up much, risked more. But now that I've reached the First Land—"

Without looking up, she cut him off. "I'm not leaving your side. Meeryn is inside you. She is still my duty."

"What's inside me is *not* Meeryn," he pressed. "She died."

"No." Delia continued her preparation.

Tylar took a deep breath, glanced to the door, then back to Delia. He lowered his voice. "What is inside me is not spell-cast daemon but one of the naethryn."

Delia glanced up again, eyes narrowed.

Tylar moved closer. "One of the undergods."

"How do you know this?"

He balked at telling her about his dream. "I just know."

Delia motioned for him to kneel before her. He did. Their knees now touched. She sat silent for a long breath, her brow crinkled. "I should have considered that possibility," she finally mumbled.

Tylar frowned. "What do you mean?"

She took his arm and rested his hand in her lap, palm up, then tied the silk at his elbow. "When the gods were sundered, they were split into three parts: the gods of flesh here, and their counterparts up in the aether and down in the naether. Meeryn had spoken of how she could sense her other parts, lost to her, but still there, tied ethereally and eternally."

"Until now."

Delia nodded. "Somehow Meeryn, as she died, must have used this tie to draw a part of herself into you. Her naethryn self."

Tylar glanced down to the black palm print.

Delia ran her fingers over his forearm.

He shivered again. And it wasn't from Delia's touch this time. He considered what lay inside him . . . not just any naethryn, but *Meeryn's* undergod. What did it all mean?

Delia concentrated on her work, a lock of hair hanging over one eye.

Tylar reached up and brushed the stray bit of hair back in place. It was a reflexive gesture, from another time, another man . . . another woman. He quickly dropped his hand.

"This vessel will do," she said, and gripped his wrist, pressing deeply as before, numbing his hand. She slid the lancet into his arm, then caught the flow into another repostilary.

Tylar looked away.

"If Meeryn's naethryn is inside you," Delia continued, "then I cannot leave your side."

"Why? You swore no oath to her undergod."

"I did not serve Meeryn upon oath alone. I loved her . . . as did all her Hands. She died to bring you this gift." A tremble entered Delia's voice. "I will serve its bearer like I served her."

"I asked no oath of you."

A touch of firebalm flared from his wrist, marking the end of the bloodletting. Delia's next words were so soft Tylar barely heard them. "As with Meeryn, it's no oath that binds me . . ."

He stared into her eyes. They glistened more brightly in the torchlight.

"Oy there!" a voice shouted from the door. It was the crook-backed alchemist. "Enough jabbering. Be quick about your harvest. I'm late for my dinner."

Delia placed aside the blood-filled jar and called back to the Wyr-man, "All we have left are tears." She set about preparing for the next harvest, picking up a glass straw to wick his tears, then pinched a bit of salted powder to sting the eyes.

All we have left are tears.

Tylar considered their future, all their futures. He suspected no truer words had ever been spoken.

❖

Tylar stumbled along with the others. They had been blindfolded for over two bells, guided like sheep through the warren of tunnels beneath the Kistlery Downs. He had at first balked at being put at such a disadvantage, but Krevan had voiced his unconcern. "The Wyr will not break an oath once sworn."

Tylar had honored his side of the bargain, giving up his humours. Even now he shied his thoughts from what ill-use they would serve for the alchemists of the Wyr.

Tylar felt a freshening breeze on his cheek, coming from ahead. The end of the tunnels. He found his steps hurrying. The Wyr-man who gripped his elbow and guided his steps forced Tylar to slow. He heard the creak of some ancient wooden gear and the twang of strained ropes. Another trap was being undone. This last must guard the easternmost entrance to the Lair.

Tylar was anxious to be free of the blindfold and free of the tunnels. As they had traversed the Lair, he had heard strange cries, howls, and low mewlings echoing up from the deeper levels of the Lair. During such moments, he was glad for the blindfold. His guide moved him forward again—into the face of the fresh breeze.

In four steps, he sensed the world open around him. The press of stone lifted, filled by the noises of meadow and forest: the twitter of swifts, the cronk of a frog, the slight rustle of water over stone. Somewhere far ahead, a dog barked, echoing up from below.

He was led another hundred steps, moving up and down, stumbling in his haste.

Finally, he was pulled to a stop. The hand on his elbow vanished. He stood for a moment, unsure where to move.

Delia's voice called out. "Tylar . . . Rogger . . ."

Tylar reached toward her voice, bumped into someone, grabbed hold.

"Watch what you're a-grabbing there," Rogger's voice erupted.

Tylar let go and ripped away his blindfold. He blinked back the dazzle. The others were doing the same. Krevan already stood a few steps away with Corram, at the edge of a steep incline. Their weapons were piled at their feet.

Tylar glanced around the sparsely wooded glen. All the Wyr were gone . . . except for Eylan. She stood a few steps back, stoic, staring in the same direction as Krevan and Corram. The others must have retreated to the Lair's hidden entrance, keeping its location unknown.

Tylar crossed to Krevan, along with Rogger and Delia.

The knight pointed an arm.

Ahead stretched an open plain, broken into green pasturelands and patches of crops. A small township lay not far away, by a small freshwater lake. Muddlethwait. It was where they were to rendezvous with any of the surviving knights.

But that was not where Krevan pointed.

The sun, high overhead, shone clear to the distant Strait of Parting. Near the horizon, a steeple seemed to float above the thin layer of sea mist and cloud. Tylar would recognize that sight anywhere. It had called him home many a day.

Stormwatch.

The highest tower of Tashijan.

"How long to reach there?" Delia asked.

"We should have horses in Muddlethwait awaiting us," Krevan answered. "If we ride hard, we'll reach Tashijan in the dead of night. A good time to seek entry."

"Good or not," Rogger said, "it's the *dead* part that worries me."

Tylar stared across the plains. Now in sight of the tower, the enormity of their task threatened to overwhelm him.

Rogger touched his shoulder. "Are you ready for this?"

He had no choice. Both his past and future lay ahead of him.

"Let's go."

16

CHARNEL PIT

"I BELIEVE I'VE DISCOVERED WHO CALLED UPON CASTELLAN MIRRA," Gerrod Rothkild said. "The one who brought her that swatch of linen in the middle of the night, soaked in blood."

Kathryn stood out on her hermitage's balcony, leaning on the balustrade. The day had proven to be warm, the first kiss of true spring. The rains of the past quarter moon steamed from the damp grounds of the courtyard, trapped between the four stone walls of Tashijan. The air was redolent with flowering buds from the giant wyrmwood tree blooming just these last few days, opening honeyed petals of snow-white. The branches of the wyrmwood dappled the balcony with their shadows, while across the courtyard, Stormwatch Tower climbed endlessly upward, basking in the sun like a sword raised on high.

It seemed too pleasant a day for such dark conversations. It should be night with rain falling. She sighed and turned to her friend. Gerrod's bronzed armor sparked in the patches of sunlight, as if on fire.

"What have you discovered?" Kathryn asked.

Gerrod turned from the balcony and strode back into her rooms. Such words were best spoken in private, away from the open courtyard. Voices could carry oddly, echoing from the yard's walls.

Kathryn followed him inside, closing the balcony doors.

Gerrod reached to his neck and retracted his helmet with a whir of mekanicals. His pale features seemed even paler. He ran a hand over his shaved scalp. The tattoos of his mastered disciplines stood out starkly, looking more like wounds than ink. "What I've found is most odd."

Kathryn crossed and poured them each a tiny glass of rose wine. "Tell me all."

"I was able to loosen the stableman's tongue, the one who took the stranger's horse," Gerrod said, accepting a glass. "Though the groomsman proved stubborn. But what was sealed with gold finally broke under more."

"What did he tell you?"

"Unfortunately not as much as I'd wished." His frown deepened, along with the furrow across his brow. "He knew nothing of what the man carried or what his purpose was in coming so late on so road-worn a horse. But he did know that the man had traveled from Chrismferry."

"And as I recall," Kathryn said, "he returned there again after meeting with Castellan Mirra."

Gerrod nodded. "The stableman also managed to note a detail about the man. At the man's collar, he wore a stitching of oak and twig."

Kathryn's eyes widened. "A healer?"

"So it would appear."

"By why would a healer bring something so foul to the castellan and in such a guarded manner?"

"That I can't answer." Gerrod stared at her with those penetrating green eyes, shining with sharp intelligence. "But my gold did buy one additional bit of information." A bit of wry amusement glinted.

"What?"

"A name."

Kathryn lowered her wineglass to the table. "The stableman caught his name?"

"Not exactly. The healer left his ride behind, taking a fresh horse for the long trip back."

"He took one of our windmares," Kathryn said, remembering the man's urgency. He had needed speed to return to Chrismferry, borrowing an air-graced horse.

"And he rode in on the same," Gerrod commented. "One by the name of Swifttail. This detail, of course, the stableman happened to note. He might miss a man's name, but such a blessed bit of horseflesh would not escape his eye."

"And how does this help us?"

Gerrod stepped to the table and picked at a piece of hard cheese left from her midday meal. He raised a brow inquiringly, asking permission.

"It seems what you bought in gold I must pay in cheese," Kathryn said.

He cut a chunk and gingerly used his armored fingers to nibble at its edge. He washed it down with his wine, sighing contentedly, then continued. "It is lucky that Swifttail's heritage was well-known to our stableman. His knowledge of all the First Land's horseflesh is quite extensive. He spent most of a morning reciting Swifttail's lineage."

"And where does this lineage lead us?"

"To a stable as distinguished as our own. A private stable."

"In Chrismferry."

"Indeed . . . at the Conclave of Chrismferry to be exact."

"The school?" The Conclave was the oldest and most illustrious of Myrillia's institutes of training for young handmaidens and -men. Many of the Council of Masters had once taught there or still consulted.

"And the Conclave has only one healer in residence," Gerrod said. "A fellow by the name of Paltry. I did some investigation and found he matched young Penni's description of Castellan Mirra's night visitor: black haired, fair of features."

Kathryn narrowed one eye. "Healer Paltry. Why does that name sound familiar?"

"He also serves as the private physik to the High Wing of Chrism. You may remember hearing how the man saved several of his Hands from the pox scourge that struck the city two years ago."

Kathryn nodded. "Of course. And now you think it was this healer who brought the bloodied swath to Castellan Mirra."

"I am confident he is the one."

"But why? To what end?"

"That's something that will require further investigation in Chrismferry."

"I can send a cadre of knights—"

"And alert all of Tashijan, including Warden Fields." The name was spoken with a thick scowl. Fields had been instituting changes throughout the Citadel, not all well received. He had trimmed control of the Council of Masters, giving Master Hesharian powers to dictate without a quorum from the rest of the council. Power was concentrating into fewer and fewer hands, and all of those under the thumb of Argent ser Fields.

"What do you propose then?" Kathryn asked.

"There is an early-morning flippercraft headed to Chrismferry. I hope to be aboard it. I'll make an excuse of needing to consult the libraries in the city. Once there, I can make some discreet inquiries, see if I can trace the source and reason for this strange visitation by Healer Paltry."

Kathryn shook her head. "I don't want you to go alone. You'll need an escort."

"I can fend for myself. And I am armored." He tapped a fist on his thigh with a clank.

"No." A firm tone entered her voice. "I want a sword at your side and someone who knows how to use it. You'll take Perryl with you. To lessen suspicion, I can send him as courier to the court at Chrismferry. As castellan, I have some authority."

"At least for the moment," Gerrod countered dourly.

She sighed and glanced to the door, sensing the tracker and beast at her threshold. "He keeps me on a short enough tether as it is. And once Tylar is captured"—her voice caught in her throat—"or killed, my use to the warden will end."

"I'm not so sure," Gerrod said more softly. "He eyes you most salaciously at times. I think his plans for you don't end with Tylar's capture."

Kathryn remembered Argent's talk in his chambers, a hint at some possible union between them. *For the good of Tashijan . . . and in turn for all of Myrillia.* Such had been his rhetoric these past days as new laws were posted to doors and common rooms, justifying the concentration of power. And she was no exception.

"Perhaps Perryl should stay at your side," Gerrod said.

Kathryn rested her hand on the diamond pommel of her sword. "I have a blade . . . and know how to use it."

Gerrod reached and took her hand from her sword. "Still, beware. Trust no one, not even your fellow knights. Shadowcloaks are good at hiding one's heart as well as form."

She reached and hugged him. "You should take the same advice in Chrismferry. It seems something foul is at work there . . . something that struck at the heart of Tashijan."

"Not just Tashijan," Gerrod mumbled and broke the embrace. He raised his helmet. "Perhaps its reach extended as far as the Summering Isles."

Kathryn studied the bronze figure. "The slaying of Meeryn? You think it's all tied together?"

"A master's first lesson is to be suspicious of a chain of circumstance. Something stirs beneath all this. It hides behind many faces, but wears only one."

Kathryn felt the chill of certainty in his words.

"Hopefully I'll learn more from Healer Paltry." Gerrod bowed his head. "Step carefully, Kathryn."

"And you do the same."

❖

The bullhound growled, crouched at a cross passage ahead.

Kathryn stopped at an arm raised by Tracker Lorr. "Barrin smells something," the wyldman said. "Stay here."

Kathryn felt no fear. One bullhound or the other was always scenting something. It made for crossing from one end of Tashijan to the other a major undertaking, full of sudden stops and hissed warnings. But she had wanted to hand the courier message to Perryl herself. She carried it in the inner pocket of her shadowcloak, sealed with wax, imprinted with the castellan's mark. She had spent the afternoon composing the letter, addressing it to the one person she most trusted in Chrismferry. He would be able to assist Perryl and Gerrod in their inquiries.

Kathryn glanced to the bit of sky shining through a high window. The sun was close to setting already. At this rate, by the time she got the letter into Perryl's hands, he would miss the dawn flippercraft.

Behind her, the hulking mass of the other bullhound filled half the corridor. Hern kept watch on their trail. How they could smell anything beyond the rangy reek of their own pelts and fetid breath was a mystery.

Lorr moved to Barrin's side. The tracker's amber eyes narrowed. His loose hair was secured behind his ears with a strap of leather. He had a pair of blades out, one in each hand. Kathryn had seen him impale a rat at a hundred paces, a tidbit of fresh meat for his companions. He scouted the crossing of passages.

Kathryn leaned against a wall. There was no use protesting such caution. Tracker Lorr had been given his duty by Warden Fields. He would brook no other authority.

He waved her forward. "Clear." Lorr sniffed the air. Bred to be a tracker in the ancient forests of Idlewyld, he had been blessed with Grace, his senses of smell heightened by air, his skill at woodlore gifted by loam. He cocked his head high, his profile clearly showing the slight protuberance of the lower half of his face as he scented the air.

"There's an old trail of blood through here," he said. "I would've missed it if not for Barrin here. Someone was killed nearby. Murder, I'd say, from the tang of fear in the air."

Kathryn moved to his side. "How old is the trail?"

"No older than the turn of one moon." He glanced back at her.

Kathryn studied the crossroad of corridors. Her first worry was for Castellan Mirra. "Are you certain?"

"Blood is blood," he said and waved Barrin down the hall.

"Can you follow the trail?"

Lorr shrugged. "Certainly, until the blood runs out. Barrin and Hern may be able to follow it even farther. But what of this letter you wanted delivered? The trail is old. It can wait the night."

Kathryn shook her head, sensing a need for urgency. "No, we must pursue it." She nodded for him to follow.

He balked for a moment, clearly wondering if it was wise to lead his charge along such a path. But his eyes drifted to the trail with beastly longing. Blood was in the air. There was a track to follow.

Finally he huffed at Barrin and pointed. The bullhound continued down the new passage, nose close to the stones. This passage led into parts of Tashijan that had seen little use in ages.

Warden Fields had been correct in his assessment of the current state of affairs, here and across Myrillia. The number of knights and those who sought to serve the gods had been slowly eroding over the past four centuries. So slow was the attrition, it was hard to note, like water wearing a path through stone.

They continued into the lonely passages. Rooms were boarded up, even some windows. Dust grew thicker as they wound down a twisting narrow stairway. Older footsteps disturbed the grime, coming and going.

Lorr would stop and finger some of the steps. "Fresher," he said. "Other trackers have been this way."

"So the blood trail has already been followed," Kathryn said, disappointment hardening her words. She pictured the scores of men and women, trackers and knights, even ilk-beasts, who had searched for Castellan Mirra. None had met with success. If this path had already been followed . . .

Lorr straightened. "There are no sharper noses than those of a bullhound. Where others have given up, we may push farther." A hint of excitement rushed his words. "We move on."

As they searched, Kathryn remembered stories told of Chrismferry. The colossal, ancient city was so broad of scope and breadth that vast areas had fallen into disrepair and returned to wildlands within the heart of the city. Most of the city folk seldom traveled past their own four city blocks. The rest was foreign lands.

The same was true here, Kathryn realized. Tashijan was the size of a small city, half above ground, half below, but much had fallen away and was forgotten. Knights and masters stuck to the corridors they knew. Few ventured into those hidden corners. Warden Fields had warned about the impossibility of defending against Tylar's attempt to enter Tashijan. It had too many forgotten battlements, entries, and secret halls. Kathryn saw the proof of that here.

Lorr was finally forced to light a torch as the corridors grew too dark . . . though Kathryn suspected the light was mostly for her benefit. The wyldman's eyes glowed with a trace of Grace.

"The blood trail grows too thin for me to follow," Lorr said, halting at a spot where the corridor branched in three directions. He knelt and studied the stone. "Someone used a blessing of air to breeze away the dust, hiding their footsteps."

"So we can go no farther?"

"We have bullhounds," said Lorr.

Barrin had already wandered ahead and sniffed at the three passages. He grumbled at the one on the left. A rope of drool dripped from one corner of his lip and sizzled on the stone, etching it. Hern, behind them, simply stood on guard, tongue lolling, waiting on his master.

"This way," Lorr said, stepping toward the left passage. "Careful of the drool."

Kathryn followed behind Lorr. The corridors here were low and narrow. Barrin filled the entire passage ahead, Hern behind. Kathryn felt an intense pang of unease. No one knew she was down here . . . and bullhounds had the capability for consuming all, even the bones, of their prey.

Was that how Castellan Mirra had vanished? Into the gullet of such monsters? Kathryn's steps began to slow. Her hand drifted to the pommel of her sword. Had she walked willingly to her own doom?

They continued for another quarter bell, moving in line, slipping from one passage to the next, climbing crumbled stairs.

A hiss from Lorr drew her attention. He pointed ahead. Barrin had entered a cavernous room. Lorr followed next. He waved for Kathryn to stay at the entrance.

With torch in hand, Lorr moved into the room. The firelight danced shadows on the high-raftered room. It looked like a small gathering hall. Tiered benches circled the walls, though one section had collapsed down upon itself.

Barrin hunched over a mound in the room's center.

Kathryn held a fist to her throat as Lorr's approaching torch revealed a sprawled body, naked, white as bone, arms out wide, legs together. The head was blocked by Barrin's shaggy shoulder. Lorr circled the body, eyes on the form.

Kathryn could wait no longer. *Castellan Mirra . . .*

She hurried into the room. Hern shambled after her, always her shadow.

She rushed to the body on the floor. She quickly saw her mistake. The bared loins revealed the slaughtered figure was a man, not a woman, not Castellan Mirra.

Kathryn stumbled to a stop, aghast.

The man's throat had been cut, his chest cleaved open. A trough, hacked crudely from the stone floor, circled his body. His wrists, also slashed, hung over the trough to either side.

Lorr lowered his torch.

Blood, crusted and dried, caked the trough.

"They bled him like a pig," Lorr said, spitting to the side.

Barrin hung back. The great beast mewled softly, almost fearfully. What could scare such a monster? What did its sharpened senses discern that theirs did not?

Kathryn crossed around and knelt by the man's head. Three stripes darkened his features, from the outside corner of the eye to each temple. A knight. She did not recognize the young man, but he must be new to his third stripe. It appeared freshly tattooed, which meant he had just been gifted with the full Grace of a Shadowknight, his blood freshly blessed, ripe and potent. Such knights were often quickly placed among the Hundred, to bend a knee and serve one of the gods. His disappearance could be easily hidden.

She stood up. Hern made a gruff snort off to the side.

Lorr and Kathryn moved together to one side of the room. A well opened in the floor there, an old hearth, similar to the Hearthstone in Tashijan's Grand Court. Only this hole did not dance brightly with flame.

Lorr leaned his torch over the pit. It was filled with broken branches, cracked and charred. Kathryn blinked as a flicker of torchlight revealed a leering skull, blackened by soot, one cheekbone crushed, peering out among the branches.

She instantly saw her mistake.

It was not *branches* that filled the pit, but . . .

"Bones," Lorr said, almost a moan.

Kathryn swung away, her stomach churning. Whatever fire had been lit in this pit had been fueled with flesh. She stared at the prostrate, slaughtered young man. Knights. The pit was full of the bones of murdered knights.

"A lair of Dark Grace," Lorr said with a fierce growl. "Here in Tashijan. We must tell the warden."

Kathryn eyed the dead knight. His arms had been forced wide, legs together, forming a cross, encircled by a ring of blood, once surely aglow with fresh Grace.

A ring of fire.

Horror iced her heart.

The symbolism of the body's position and ring was plain. A similar insignia was worn on many a knight's arm following the ascension of Argent ser Fields. It was the new warden's badge.

The Fiery Cross.

❖

Kathryn hurried with Lorr back into the inhabited sections of Tashijan. Both were glad to escape such a foul place. Barrin still led the way; Hern followed.

"I won't keep my tongue," Lorr continued his tirade, stalking down the halls. "I've hunted with Ser Fields since his earliest campaign. I will not listen to your suspicions."

Kathryn kept pace with the man. "That dark work back there was done by someone in the Fiery Cross. You know I'm right. I can see it in your eyes. Maybe Argent . . . Warden Fields was not involved." She had to force out those last words. She had no doubt of Argent's complicity. "But someone in the Fiery Cross . . . *his* group . . . led that rite. And it wasn't the first."

Lorr sighed heavily. He had seen the charnel pit. His eyes, hard and flinty, still shone with the horror of it all. "Mayhap you're right. But should the warden not be given word?"

Kathryn gripped the diadem pendant at her neck. The diamond, though made of paste, still signified her position. "I am the castellan of Tashijan, second only to the warden. As some part of the Fiery Cross was involved in this most foul murder, it is right for the warden to step aside in the investigation. He's compromised for his involvement with the Cross. So I must step forward."

"And what do you plan on doing?"

"First, swear you to secrecy."

Lorr glanced harshly at her.

She faced him down. "We must not alert the Fiery Cross to our knowledge or all involved will vanish into the shadows, unpunished and unknown. That must not happen, not until we are ready to snare them all."

Lorr marched ahead, shoulders hunched. Finally he grunted a grudging assent. "I will keep silent for the moment."

Kathryn hid her relief. If Argent knew what they had discovered, he would not let them live until the next dawn. She had to avoid the warden until she could determine some plan . . . which meant consulting with her friend Gerrod before he left.

"I must speak to Master Rothkild," Kathryn said. "We'll forgo delivering the letter for the moment."

Lorr nodded.

Reaching the central main staircase, Lorr started down the wide steps, led by Barrin. The large bullhound's hackles still bristled. A few knights and masters gave the beast a wide berth, pressing against the wall.

They wound down deep under the Citadel, leaving the last rays of the sun behind and entering the subterranean domain of the Masters of Disciplines. She prayed Gerrod was still in his chambers.

The answer stepped around the next bend in the stair.

Master Hesharian gasped aloud as he came face-to-jowl with the slavering Barrin. The man's large bulk stumbled back a pace, tripping on a step. Before he fell, his arm was caught in the bronze fingers of his companion, Gerrod Rothkild.

"Skaggin' monsters," Hesharian huffed, steadying himself. He shook free of Gerrod's grip. "What are you doing down here?" His piggish eyes took in Lorr, the bullhounds, and Kathryn.

Lorr opened his mouth to speak, but Kathryn stepped forward. "How fortunate a meeting. I had hoped to discuss a matter with Master Rothkild."

Hesharian glanced to Gerrod, then back to Kathryn. "We've been summoned to the field room by Warden Fields. It seems our godslayer has made landfall."

Gerrod's features remained unreadable behind his bronze helmet.

Kathryn kept her own face calm. "Where?" she asked.

"Where else . . . somewhere off in Foulsham Dell." He spoke the name with clear distaste. "Warden Fields has doubled the night's shift and calls all leaders to the meeting. I'm surprised you did not receive a summons."

"I've been away from my rooms for the past two bells. Perhaps the message awaits me there."

"I'm sure that is so."

Gerrod stirred. "If that's the case, then certainly Castellan Vail should proceed directly to the field room with us."

Hesharian glared at the two bullhounds, clearly not wanting their company. But he could not discount Gerrod's offer.

They all continued as a group back up the stairs. No one spoke. The bullhounds grumbled, but a cuff from Lorr silenced them.

Kathryn slowed her step, allowing Master Hesharian and Lorr to drift ahead, vanishing for stretches behind the curve of the stair. Hern was their only companion, padding after them, eyes wide.

"Why have you been summoned?" Kathryn asked. It was strange that Gerrod was called to this meeting. He was not even a member of the Council of Masters, though it was rumored he was next in line for one of the seats.

"It seems," Gerrod whispered, "that word of my departure at dawn has reached the ears of the warden. He has some duty to request of me when I travel to Chrismferry."

Kathryn felt a chill skate across her skin. How had Argent learned so quickly of Gerrod's plan to leave by flippercraft? And why this sudden summons?

Gerrod motioned back down the stairs. "Why were you coming down here?"

Kathryn did not like discussing this on the open stair, but she feared she might not have another chance. "Lorr and I discovered something of hideous import." She described the body, its mutilation, the charnel pit.

"Strange," Gerrod mumbled.

"What do you mean?"

"The body was left there, sprawled, mutilated, and abandoned. Does that not strike you as odd? Though the rite was clearly performed in a lonely, abandoned corner of Tashijan, why not hide their crime better? At least dump the body into the pit. Why leave it to be so conspicuously placed?"

"You think it was left on purpose?"

Gerrod nodded ahead. "You said that Lorr led you to the body, he and his hounds. Maybe someone wanted it to be found."

Kathryn shook her head. "But why? Lorr is the warden's man. Why would Argent want to implicate the Fiery Cross in some bloody rite?" She remembered the genuine horror on the wyldman's face.

Gerrod stared questioningly at her.

"No," she said firmly. "Lorr had no foreknowledge about what we would find."

"Then perhaps he was set up also. A fresh blood lure tracked in the corridors. Meant to lead him and his hounds to the site."

"But why? To what end?"

"Maybe there is another party seeking to discredit or expose the Fiery Cross. They couldn't operate in the open, so they led someone they could trust to the spot, either hoping you'd take on the burden or to at least warn you."

"But who? Why the need for secrecy?"

"If we're right about Argent's involvement with the death of Ser Henri and perhaps Castellan Mirra, then whoever is left of their trusted circle may be trying to help you now, fearful to approach directly, but knowing you must not fall under Argent's sway. The new warden can be convincing."

Kathryn remembered her morning meeting with Argent ser Fields a few days back. He had an answer to every one of her concerns, calming suspicion with a ready explanation. He had argued that the Fiery Cross was nothing more than an organization of knights and masters interested in returning Tashijan to full glory during this time of world strife. It had seemed plausible.

No longer.

"What about this tracker?" Gerrod said. "Will he speak? If Warden Fields finds—"

"He's promised to keep silent for the moment."

"Do you trust him?"

They wended around another bend in the stairs. Ahead lay the landing that led to Tashijan's field room. Lorr and Hesharian climbed off the stairs, following the massive bullhound. Lorr glanced back at Kathryn, his hard eyes shining. He motioned her forward, while whistling under his breath to Hern.

The bullhound behind Kathryn pushed her and Gerrod forward.

Lorr spoke as she passed him. The field room lay halfway down the corridor. "I'll see to watering Hern and Barrin. I'll meet you outside the field room when you're done."

They stepped away. Gerrod glanced askance at her, his question still unanswered. *Do you trust him?*

She considered, then nodded to Gerrod, surprised at her answer but still sure. "I do."

She had seen how Lorr cared for the great wooly beasts, firm but kind, demanding but patient. She also saw the deep wound in his eyes at finding the slaughtered young man. There was a well of depth hidden behind that hard countenance. He would not break his word.

Hesharian reached the door to the field room ahead of them, clearly glad to escape the company of the bullhounds. He inspected his white robe for bits of stray fur or any hole burned by a spatter of hound saliva.

A pair of young Shadowknights stood post on either side of the door. One swept forward and opened the way.

Kathryn eyed the young men, picturing another, the knight slaughtered and bled. A pang of sorrow and anger fired through her. She strode into the field room.

It looked the same as when last she was there, except the far windows overlooking the tourney grounds were unshuttered, open on the twilit skies. Torches hung at each corner, well away from the racked rolls of maps and documents.

The same men stood around the scarred wyrmwood table. Keeper Ryngold of the house staff, the black-stubbled knight Symon ser Jaklar, whose sneer seemed a permanent stamp, and of course, at the table's head, Argent ser Fields.

The warden straightened from the map of Tashijan pinned to the table's surface. Small silver tokens marked the placement of men throughout the Citadel. His one eye took in the latecomers, settling on Kathryn.

"Castellan Vail," he said with good cheer. "I feared you would not receive the summons in time. My man Lowl has been scouring the Citadel attempting to find you. It seemed strange that someone accompanied by two hulking bullhounds could be so hard to find."

"Tashijan is large," she answered, waving to the map. "Plenty of places to hide."

Keeper Ryngold chuckled, a strange sound among so many dour and black-cloaked figures. His purple surcoat and the silver baldric of his station stood out brightly. "Such is the problem we face now," he said. "How to guard a place with so many secret corners?"

Symon ser Jaklar's sneer deepened.

Warden Fields merely sighed. "But we do have new allies." He stepped aside to reveal a figure limned against the twilight skies, half lost in the darkness, easy to miss. A Shadowknight. He turned to face them, his masklin lying around his neck, exposing his face, as was custom in this room.

Kathryn flinched at the man's appearance, his bone-white features, snowy hair, eyes a silvery red.

"May I present Darjon ser Hightower," Argent introduced. "Formerly of the Summering Isles, now here to lend his service and counsel to the capture of Tylar de Noche."

❖

Kathryn waited for the introductions to finish. Hesharian nodded to the stranger, his arms folded into the long sleeves of his robe. Kathryn used the time to study the newcomer. His expression remained stern and unwelcoming. He seemed disinterested in the proceedings. Something about the man's eyes disturbed her—not the odd color, but something deeper, a coldness that went beyond an absence of warmth.

But more important, what held her transfixed was the absence of stripes on his face. Yet he wore a Shadowcloak and his eyes clearly shone with Grace.

This did not escape the notice of Master Hesharian. "Why are you unmarked, Ser Hightower?"

"It is a long story," the knight said. The only emotion was a crinkling of a brow, irritation.

"He is indeed a sworn and accepted knight," Argent insisted. "It was a mishap at birth, a blessing went awry, that left his skin unable to bear any pigment, natural or otherwise."

Darjon gave Argent a baleful look.

"But enough of these introductions. We have plans to settle now that we know the godslayer has made landfall here."

"In Foulsham Dell?" Kathryn asked.

"So word has come from one of our knights in the Dell. There is some confusion. Tylar de Noche apparently attacked Lord Balger, actually absconding with the god's hand, so the story is told. Balger attempted to apprehend Tylar in the swamps but with no success. The search continues there, but we must not assume the godslayer is still among the swamps. His appearance at our borders confirms his goal. To come here." Argent's eyes fell upon Kathryn. "To come for you."

Kathryn felt another pair of eyes fix to her. Darjon's attention felt like a wash of icy waters.

"But we will be prepared," Argent affirmed. "We have knights coming in from surrounding realms to aid in the capture of the godslayer. Our numbers have swelled to two thousand."

Kathryn now understood why the hallways seemed so crowded of late. It was becoming such that one couldn't turn a corner without bumping into another knight.

"Before we get down to details here . . ." Argent turned his attention to the last member of this council who had yet to be addressed. "Gerrod Rothkild, it has come to my attention that you will be leaving us, to proceed to Chrismferry on a research trip, is this not so?"

Kathryn forced herself not to react. She and Gerrod had decided only earlier in the day to search for clues in Chrismferry. How had Argent known? Kathryn noted Master Hesharian seeming to take particular attention in the dirt under one of his nails. Gerrod also glanced to the head of the Council of Masters. Plainly he must have informed the council to get permission to leave, and word had reached Argent through his fat puppet.

Gerrod bowed his head. "I am indeed heading to Chrismferry at dawn. I wish to consult the ancient library of Nirraborath and to obtain a few alchemic items."

"Good . . . very good. I was wondering if you'd be willing to do a favor for the Citadel. Master Hesharian has assured me you'd be most cooperative."

"If it is in my capacity to comply, I certainly will."

"I have a parcel that I wish carried by a most trusted hand to Chrism's castillion. It may be delivered to the keeper of the house there. Keeper Ryngold has already dispatched a raven to announce your coming. I hope that wasn't presumptuous."

"Not at all. There is an alchemy shop I wish to visit in the shadow of the castillion."

"Thank you. Visit Keeper Ryngold's chambers before retiring to obtain and secure the parcel." Argent's attention swung away, as good as a dismissal. His gaze again fell upon Kathryn. Argent smiled but the warmth did not reach his one eye. "Am I to understand that you need a courier to dispatch a message to Chrismferry? Mayhap Master Rothkild could deliver that also?"

Kathryn stood very still, attempting to keep from letting any sign of shock showing. No one knew about the letter except Gerrod, herself . . . and Lorr. She pictured the tracker. Moments before she had professed her trust in the man. Was it misplaced? But she had only told Lorr about the letter and her wish to visit Perryl when she was ready to leave her chambers. The tracker had not been out of her sight after that.

So how had Argent found out?

She cleared her throat. "That is most kind, Warden Fields, but Master Rothkild and I have already discussed the matter in private."

Then again, did she have *any* privacy? Argent clearly was enjoying this moment. Was that all the purpose of the show here? To illustrate to Kathryn how much a stranglehold Argent had on her comings and goings, on her most intimate moments and plans? He must have spies everywhere.

She refused to let him rattle her. "This matter is best handled by a Shadowknight."

Argent nodded and waved away the question. "So be it. You are the castellan of Tashijan."

Master Hesharian wore a thick smirk at these words.

Argent began to turn away, then swung back toward Kathryn. "If that's the case, mayhap you'd best deliver your letter without further waste. We can handle matters from here on our own. It's all a tedious matter of shuffling knights anyway."

Again she was being dismissed, shut out of the proceedings here. She did not protest this time. She had only to picture the young knight, naked and bloody, to want to flee as fast as she could from the warden's presence.

They spent another few moments bowing out, but soon Gerrod and Kathryn were free of the field room. She found Lorr already awaiting her with Barrin and Hern. The pair of bullhounds sat on their haunches. Stubbed tails wagged at the sight of her.

Lorr straightened with a curry brush. He had been combing down Barrin. "That was nigh quick. Hardly worth the long climb."

Kathryn frowned at him. Argent had only been pulling her string, making sure his puppet would still respond.

"Are you off to your chambers?" Lorr asked, nodding down the hall.

"It is late," Gerrod said. "I could deliver the letter to Ser Corriscan."

"No, I'd prefer to see Perryl myself." Kathryn was in no spirit to be ensconced in her hermitage. The day had been too bloody, too disturbing. She wanted nothing better than to go to the stable, saddle the fastest horse, and ride until she could forget all this. But she'd settle for a bit more walking. Besides, she needed to explain all to Perryl, to see if he knew of any strange disappearances among his young knights. It was a place to begin her own investigations. "I'll accompany you as far as his floor, then," Gerrod offered.

Kathryn smiled her grateful thanks.

They continued back to the stairs, Barrin and Lorr in the lead again. Kathryn felt an odd comfort in the presence of the two hulking bullhounds.

They walked in silence for a long stretch.

Gerrod finally spoke, whispering to keep their words private. "You know what that was all about, don't you?"

Kathryn nodded. "He's flexing his muscles."

A nod. "Our warden grows bolder, more assured of his position and security. And rightly so, I'm afraid. Tashijan bows at his feet."

"Not all of Tashijan," Kathryn said fiercely. "There's us . . . and whoever might have led us to that bloody chamber. You mentioned before that a shadowcloak hid more than just a knight's face. I think there are more folk on our side than is plain to see."

"You may be right, but to fight for Tashijan, it can't all be done in shadows."

Kathryn knew the truth of his words. Eventually swords would have to be raised and sides chosen.

At last they reached the landing to Perryl's floor. It was one of the lowest of the Citadel's boarding levels, for the knights new to their cloak. Gerrod said his good-byes as he continued down to the subterranean levels of the masters.

Once Gerrod was out of sight, Kathryn and Lorr exited the stair and followed through the warren of narrow passages and low doors.

Kathryn remembered her first years in these halls. It had been a happier time, free of subterfuge and heartache.

She heard laughter from some of the rooms and the rattle of bone cups. The characteristic sour stench of stale ale persisted, soaked into the very stones of this hall. Somewhere farther down the hall a brief scuffle of swords, knights challenging one another, testing, competing.

She wended her way through the maze of corridors to reach Perryl's cell. "Over there," she said, pointing out the proper door. She glanced to make sure she had the letter and that the name upon it was not smudged. Satisfied, she crossed to the door and knocked upon it.

Barrin and Hern took up posts on either side, all but filling the hallway. Lorr kept behind her.

There was no answer. Maybe he was gone, off with friends.

She knocked harder.

A scuffle of noise sounded beyond the door. Someone was home.

"Perryl . . ." she called through the planks of the door.

Silence answered her.

"Perryl, it's Kathryn."

A moment of silence, then a muffled response. "Come inside . . . but be quick about it."

Kathryn tried the door. It was unlatched. She shoved it open. A small hearth crackled to one side of the greeting room. Beyond an archway, the bedchamber lay dark.

A cloaked Shadowknight stood by the hearth, facing the flames. "Close the door. Latch it."

She obeyed, though she knew instantly the figure was not Perryl. The shoulders were too broad, the figure sturdier of frame. Even cloaked from head to foot, Kathryn knew the stranger was far older than the young man she had come to see.

"Where's Perryl?" she asked.

"Gone . . . disappeared . . . no one knows where . . . but there was blood on his bed."

Kathryn pictured the slain knight in the Fiery Cross. Fear gripped her. If Argent knew of her letter, did he know whom she planned to send?

"Wh . . . who are you?"

The Shadowknight turned, his face hidden by a wrap of masklin, his stripes plain to see. "Don't you know me?"

Kathryn stared into his eyes. The room spun, her knees weakened. Time slipped from the past to the present.

"Tylar . . ."

FOURTH

GODSWORD

Lo, the skies darkened with heavy clouds
and 'round the last sun, the great fell

          driven, riven, sundered

Lo, the ground shook with a mighty roar
and within the last mountains, the great fell

          driven, riven, sundered

Lo, the oceans boiled with black blood
and under the last seas, the great fell

          driven, riven, sundered

Lo, the fires went cold and died to ash
and in the glow of the last flames, the great fell

          driven, riven, sundered

          —*Canticle of the Godsword,* ann. 103

17

SHADOWPLAY

"**A**GAIN?" LAURELLE ASKED, SEATED BY THE HEARTH TO HER ROOM. She bent over a lace stocking, darning it with silk on a silver needle. "Is your room too cold at night? If we keep bedding together, folks will begin to speak out of turn."

Laurelle's words were softened by a smile.

Dart felt a blush rise to her cheeks. Still, she did not retract her plea to share Laurelle's room. Dart feared sleeping alone since waking two mornings ago, knowing someone had been in her bedchamber. Even now she imagined Yaellin de Mar leaning over her sleeping form, the streak of silver in his black hair aglow in the dark. She hid a shudder.

Laurelle must have sensed her fear. She sighed. "What is this all about?"

Dart glanced to Pupp. He lay in front of Laurelle. His fiery eyes watched with fascination as she knit a hole closed in her hosiery. Firelight danced behind him, but he cast no shadow. Dart tired of all her secrets, so many now she felt near the point of bursting.

She could stand it no longer. The secrets so filled every space inside her that she found herself unable to eat. Sleep came fitful, even while sharing Laurelle's bed. She felt worn so very, very thin.

Laurelle stared at her with genuine concern. She set down her darning and reached over to take Dart's hand. "You're trembling." She scooted over, drawing Dart closer. "What is troubling you so?"

Dart shook her head—not so much in refusal as in confusion.

Laurelle leaned until her nose was almost touching Dart's. "You can speak to me." Fingers squeezed. "Whatever you tell me can stay between just the two of us."

Dart felt something loosen deep inside her, shuddering free. A sob rose to her lips and burbled out before she could swallow it back.

Laurelle pulled her into an embrace. "Dart, what's happened?"

She shook her head, then mumbled in Laurelle's ear, "Something horrible . . ."

Laurelle sat back. "Tell me. What one can't bear alone, two may carry more easily. Share."

Dart stared at her friend. For all her life, she had lived with secrets. She watched Pupp crawl around them, tail tucked, low to the ground, sensing her turmoil but unable to comfort. For so long, she had found security in silence, keeping her true self hidden away. What would it be like to end all that? To live her life openly? She didn't know what distressed her more: to speak or not to speak.

Laurelle waited for her to decide, holding her hands.

Dart knew she had no choice. The secrets inside her had become a great ocean of dread, and Laurelle was a moon, drawing a tide. Dart felt the shift inside her. She couldn't let it all pour forth. To be that empty and exposed was too frightening, too shameful. She could not speak of what happened in the rookery; that was too deep, the darkest part of her inner ocean. But on the surface roiled her most immediate fear.

Yaellin de Mar.

Laurelle seemed to sense the flow before Dart even began speaking. She settled herself as a swordsman might set his footing before an attack. She nodded to Dart, ready.

"It all started in the Eldergarden," Dart began slowly. Her words came out haltingly, then grew in pace as she related the murder of Jacinta and the Hand that held the blade.

"Yaellin de Mar?" Laurelle's eyes had grown wide. A trace of disbelief shone there.

Dart stared back at her friend. She had found strength with the telling of the story. She allowed it to shine forth. With her conviction, the glint of disbelief slowly faded from Laurelle's eyes.

"Why hasn't he spoken of it?" Laurelle asked. "I've heard no whisper of such strange events."

"I don't know. Maybe all were sworn to secrecy."

"And this woman . . . this Jacinta, have you inquired who she might be?"

"I dared not ask. If Yaellin found that it was I who was spying upon them in the gardens . . ."

Laurelle reached out and took her hands again. "And you've kept this corked up inside you all along." Her eyes shone with a mix of awe and respect. "You've more steel in your blood than I."

"I . . . I had no choice."

"You could've told me earlier." A twinge of hurt entered Laurelle's voice.

"I didn't want to involve you. If there was danger, I wouldn't have you come to harm."

Laurelle squeezed her hand. "We're sisters now. Serving here together. What you face, I will face, too. Together."

Dart so wanted to believe her. Hope swelled through her.

"Is all this why you wish to sleep here?" Laurelle asked. "Are you scared of Yaellin?"

"Something else happened," Dart said. She told of her waking two mornings ago and finding a brazier still hot, smelling of strange alchemies.

Laurelle covered her mouth with one hand. "Someone was in your room."

"I think it was Yaellin."

"Why? Surely he doesn't know it was you in the gardens. You've spoken to no one about it."

"It was the dinner, after our first harvests from Lord Chrism. You told the story of Healer Paltry and the exploding illuminaria. For some reason, this drew Yaellin's attention to me. He kept watching me."

Laurelle nodded. "I remember that. I thought he was just infatuated with you. You were looking lovely in that dress."

Dart was taken aback. "Lovely? Me?" She shook her head. That was not the point. "No. It was your story of the illuminaria. He was watching me so intently as we left the dinner. I know it was him in my room. Who else could it be? He works in secret, tells no one, dabbles in dark dealings, like in the gardens. Then the very night Yaellin's attention is drawn to me, someone sneaks into my room, burning strange alchemies."

"But why would he do that? What did the alchemies do? Do you remember anything from that night?"

"Dreams . . . bad dreams." Her voice drifted back to the strange flight and escape from some dark wood, chased by unknown pursuers.

"Nothing more?"

"No."

"Then I don't see we have any choice," Laurelle said.

Dart frowned. "What do you mean?"

"We must tell Lord Chrism all that happened. He'll know what to do."

Dart clutched Laurelle's hand. "We mustn't."

"Why? He should know of Yaellin's strange actions."

Dart feared the attention such an accusation would raise. She would be singled out. She would most likely be soothed to prove her testimony against one of Chrism's respected Hands. And when soothed, how much else would be revealed? Her dark secrets could not withstand such a bright light. To expose Yaellin meant exposing herself.

Laurelle continued to stare at Dart, eyes questioning.

"I cannot." Dart stumbled over her words. She had no way to explain to Laurelle without revealing her deepest shame.

"Well, I can." Laurelle stood. "I'll tell Lord Chrism. I can explain to him it was I who saw Yaellin in the Eldergarden. That should raise enough of a tumult to sanction him. He'll not be able to sneak into your room after that. The truth will come out."

"No. You'll be soothed. They'll find out you were lying."

"And by that time, Yaellin will be under scrutiny. It will be safe for you to come out of hiding."

Dart realized Laurelle had misinterpreted her reticence to expose Yaellin as a fear of reprisal.

Laurelle gained her feet. "We should wait no longer. I noticed that Chrism keeps a light burning in his room till past the ring of the final bells. I could go now and tell him what you told me."

Dart stood. She had an urge to deny everything, to tell Laurelle it was all a fabrication, a fireside story, nothing more. But fear and exhaustion kept her silent. A part of her wanted this secret taken from her. Dart found her voice. "No."

Laurelle pulled a silver robe over her nightclothes. "We must tell Lord Chrism. Yaellin may even be tied to the assassination of poor Willym."

Dart nodded. "I know. But it should be I who tells him. It is my accusation to speak."

Laurelle handed Dart a second robe, a crimson one. "Are you sure?"

She certainly was not. But she had no choice. Laurelle was right. If Yaellin was pursuing some vile purpose, Dart would have to risk herself to expose him. Others, like Willym, might die if she kept silent. With the decision made, she felt a surge of relief. Come what may, it would finally be over.

Laurelle helped her into the robe. "I'll go with you."

Dart found her hand in Laurelle's. Tears rose in Dart's eyes.

"We're sisters," Laurelle said.

Dart quickly hugged her friend . . . *her sister.* She wiped her eyes on the hem of a sleeve. In the distance, the final bells of the night chimed.

"We'd best hurry," Laurelle said, crossing to the door.

Dart went with her, continuing to hold hands. Pupp left his hearth-side roost and trotted after them. They made a strange company, two robed girls, one in silver, one in crimson, and a fiery companion with no substance.

Dart's confidence in her decision persisted, but she sensed she had for-gotten something significant. Something that tickled a warning across her skin. Before she could ponder it further, Laurelle opened the door and stepped out.

The bells echoed away.

But not her trepidation.

❖

The pair stood in front of the golden doors. The High Wing was dark, painted in ruddy hues from the giant iron-and-bone brazier at their back. The few lamps hanging on the walls had been wicked low and half-shuttered.

Silence was complete. No voices rose from the common rooms at the end of the hall. Everyone had retired to their respective rooms.

Including Lord Chrism.

In the gloom, firelight flickered from beneath the jamb of his wide doors.

"Maybe we should wait until morning," Laurelle said, sounding scared for the first time this night. "You could spend the night in my room."

Dart could not count on her determination lasting until sunrise. "I'll knock . . . announce us." She took a deep breath and pictured Chrism's warm green eyes, his easy, lazy smile. She regretted bringing bad tidings to his door in the night. She remembered the haunted words, lost and concerned. *We must be watchful . . . all of us.*

She had no choice.

She slipped her fingers from Laurelle's and crossed to the doors. A sil-ver knocker, carved into a flowering branch of a wyldrose, hung on the door. As she reached, she sensed movement beyond the door, a shift of shadows at her toes. Someone had moved across the hearth.

Lord Chrism.

Her fingers hesitated, trepidation flaring.

In the silence, the unhitching of a latch rang sharply.

Off to the left.

Dart flew back. A door opened.

Her door.

Laurelle stared, mouth open. Dart grabbed her arm and drew her down behind the brazier. Two figures stepped from her doorway. The first was a woman, her lithe figure decked in leather from boots to waist-length riding cape, the only dab of color, a blouse of ruby silk. The ruddy glow from the brazier lit her face as she glanced up the hall.

Dart recognized her.

Mistress Naff.

She served as the Hand of Chrism's Seed.

Behind her came a taller figure, outfitted in shades of green, wearing brown boots. About his shoulders was a cape of tanned leather framed in black fur. His eyes glowed in the darkness, full of Grace.

It was Lord Chrism.

"She must be bedded down again with your Hand of Tears," Mistress Naff said as Lord Chrism pulled closed the door.

Both glanced in their direction, not toward the brazier but toward Laurelle's door. Dart ducked fully away, ears craned to hear every word.

"She should be safe enough for the moment," Lord Chrism said.

"So how long do we dare wait?"

"Until all show their true colors," Chrism said.

The scuff of boots sounded, moving away.

Dart risked a glance around a corner of the brazier. The pair headed down the length of the High Wing. She watched until they vanished through a door that opened to the lower stair, taking a lamp with them.

Dart turned to the side. Laurelle had also watched them depart, peeking through the legs of a fanciful animal sculpted from the iron of the brazier.

Dart stood up, drawing her friend's eye.

"Why did we hide?" Laurelle whispered, her voice tremulous. "It was Lord Chrism . . . whom we had come to find."

Dart had no cause for such caution, except simple habit. "Maybe we should leave our own accusations until the morning," Dart said.

Laurelle nodded, her features pale even in the reddish glow.

Pupp sniffed at the brazier, slowly checking out each sculpted beast.

Dart stepped away when another bolt slid free of a lock. This time, Laurelle needed no encouragement to dive behind the far side of the brazier. The door to Chrism's rooms pulled open as they ducked away.

Dart peered under the brazier and spotted a pair of black boots. Only now did she remember the movement beyond the door to Chrism's chambers. If Lord Chrism had been in Dart's room, who was this other?

She risked sliding to the side to spy around the edge of the brazier.

The interloper headed down the hall, aiming to follow Lord Chrism and Mistress Naff. His figure was indistinct, fading into and out of the gloom, appearing as ghostly as Pupp. It took a moment for Dart to recognize the reason why. She watched the shadows seem to swim around the retreating form. A shadowcloak. During Dart's schooling, knights periodically visited the Conclave. She had witnessed their blessed ability to move through shadows unseen.

The figure pulled up the hood to the shadowcloak, vanishing completely for a breath, swallowed by the gloom, then reappeared briefly on the far side of the High Wing. He vanished down the same stair, following after the earlier two.

Despite the shadowplay, Dart had gotten a good look at the man's face before it disappeared under the hood of the shadowcloak. She could not mistake the ebony hair split by a shock of white.

"Yaellin de Mar," Laurelle mumbled at her side, aghast.

He had been in Chrism's room while the god had been in Dart's.

Why? What was the meaning of all this?

Dart stood up. All she knew for sure was that she had to follow after them all. She started down the High Wing. Pupp danced after her.

Laurelle hung back. "Dart, what are you doing?"

"I must warn Lord Chrism," she said, her steps hurried.

"Wait," Laurelle urged. "We don't know what's going on."

Dart could not argue. All she knew was what she had spotted in Yaellin's hand as he crept down the hall, before he vanished into the shadows.

A blade.

A *black* blade.

The same as had murdered the woman Jacinta.

"I must go," Dart said.

Dart climbed down the stairs, moving as cautiously as a titmouse, staying close to the wall. She hiked up the edge of her robe to keep the hem from brushing the stone and alerting the others of her presence.

Laurelle followed after, moving in Dart's footsteps, mimicking her careful progress.

Pupp continued ahead of them both, blazing a path onward. His fiery form illuminated their path, at least to Dart's eyes. Laurelle kept one hand on Dart's shoulder. Distantly the meager glow of the retreating lamp carried by Chrism and Naff flowed back to them.

Where were the guards posted to this doorway and stair? After the assassination of Master Willym, the High Wing was under constant guard. But none were at this door.

Dart continued onward, ready for living shadow to rush out and nab her. How had Yaellin obtained a shadowcloak? And how did he work its Grace to hide in the shadows? She had been taught that such blessed cloth would respond only to a knight.

She prayed the meager light cast by Pupp's molten body would be enough to expose a hidden assassin like Yaellin. Because that certainly must be his purpose. Surely the blade could not kill Lord Chrism, but Mistress Naff had no defense against its curse.

Then again, what was Yaellin doing in Chrism's rooms? Had he gone to harm the god? And what were Lord Chrism and Mistress Naff doing in *her* room? They had been searching for her, expressing concern for her safety. Did they already know of her nighttime intruder? Or maybe they were the ones who had come in the middle of the night, casting some blessing of protection upon her that she mistook for dark alchemies.

Her mind whirled with various scenarios.

They wound down and around the stairwell, then struck another hallway heading toward the southern half of the castillion. Where were they going? Occasionally a snippet of voice would carry back to them. Lord Chrism or Mistress Naff. But the words were unintelligible at this distance. So the two continued their pursuit.

Finally, another stair—an even *darker* stair—led downward again. It was narrow and dusty with disuse. Dart considered retreating back to the High Wing, but after coming so far, she had no choice but to continue.

The stair wound deeper and deeper.

"We must be well below the streets now," Laurelle whispered. "I've never been down this far."

Neither had Dart. Even the subterranean Graced Cache that stored Lord Chrism's repostilaries was not buried this deep. The air smelled dank, of river water and muck. And a chill had grown around them. Even the stairs had become cruder, hewn roughly from the rock, the edges crumbling.

Laurelle slipped on a stair and clutched Dart's shoulder to keep from falling. She gained her footing with care, but a slight limp marked her step.

"Are you all right?" Dart whispered.

"Bent my ankle a bit. But I can walk."

"Are you sure? Maybe we should turn back." A part of Dart hoped Laurelle would need to return. Determination could be sustained only so long. Fear had worn it thin.

"No," Laurelle said, her voice struggling for firmness and failing. "We've come this far. And besides, right now, *down* is easier than up with my ankle."

Dart nodded and slowly crept down the narrowing stairs. They had to proceed one after the other now. Laurelle kept behind.

"It's dark as pitch now," Laurelle said. "I can see no glow of the other's lamp."

Dart peered ahead. Laurelle was right. She had not noticed that the distant light had faded away.

A full flight ahead of them, Pupp continued downward, a ruddy ember rolling down the stairs. Rounding another turn in the stairs, firelight revealed the end of the staircase.

"There's a door ahead," Dart said.

"Where? How can you see?"

"I . . . I have good night sight," she lied and guided her friend. "It's this way."

Taking Laurelle by the hand, she crossed down the last stairs and approached the door. It was made of stone. Markings etched the door's surface. Ancient Littick from the look of the writing. And wound throughout, an intricate relief of a flowering wyldrose, the symbol of Chrism and Chrismferry.

Dart placed her hand on the door and felt a tingle under her palm. The door had been warded with Grace, sealed against intrusion. But now it stood ajar—surely left that way by the assassin who followed Lord Chrism. Yaellin must have broken the ward and kept the way open for a fast retreat. There was just enough room to slip through without moving the door. Dart feared the scrape of stone might alert Yaellin.

"This way," she urged the blind Laurelle. She waved Pupp ahead of her. His ruddy form illuminated a tunnel beyond the door.

The passage was high and narrow, appearing almost to be a natural fissure in the rock. Dart entered first, followed by Laurelle. Bits of silvery quartz caught every trace of light and glistened like tiny stars.

Again the echoed murmur of a pair of voices reached them.

"Oh, I can see a bit of glow again," Laurelle said, her feet growing steadier, less hesitant. "Where are they all going?"

Dart had no idea. They continued down the passage for a long stretch, chasing after the lamplight. Surely their destination could not be too much farther. In Pupp's glow, Dart noted flashes of white in the walls. She peered closer at one, then pulled back.

Bones . . .

A tiny rib cage and skull of an ancient fish. More and more appeared around them, a veritable school of dead fishes . . . and some larger creatures among them, with pointed toothy jaws. Dart had seen fossilites before, but their presence now boded ill. It was as if they were treading through some haunted sea, frozen in time, populated by skeletal denizens.

At last, the tunnel seemed to climb. Roots began to appear, knotted and thick, frilled by tiny hairs. More and more draped from the high roof or kneed out from the walls. Rock vanished under the mass of vinelike rootlets and thick taproots, forming a leafless forest around them, festooned with hanging falls of moss.

From haunted sea to haunted forest . . .

"We must be under the Eldergarden," Dart whispered. She pictured the massive myrrwood tree that graced the oldest section of the gardens. From its spreading limbs, roots dropped to the rich soil and grew into secondary trunks. New limbs then stretched farther, dropping more trunks, until one tree became a forest, filling most of the gardens.

Dart stared around her. She sensed they were under the spread of the myrrwood, with its dark bowers and sweet glens. The path had begun to angle upward, slowly wending back toward the surface. As she walked, she considered the warded door and the direction of the tunnel. She finally understood what path they must be walking, where it was taking them.

Into the heart of the myrrwood.

The tunnel must be Chrism's secret passage, leading to his private sanctuary, a region of the myrrwood reserved for the god alone.

Dart's feet slowed as they continued through the subterranean grove of roots and vines. It was not just fear of where she trespassed that heightened her caution. The growing tangle offered too many hiding places, too many cubbies in which assassins might conceal themselves. Furthering Dart's unease, the hairy rootlets that fringed all the surfaces waved in strange dances, contrary to the breeze that had begun to whisper down the tunnel. When she brushed against them, they clung and snagged, tugging hems and hair, as if trying to pull them away.

Even Pupp seemed uneasy, sniffing the air, pausing there, dropping back closer to them. He kept to the center of the tangled pathway. Dart slowed in turn, needing Pupp's glow to light her way.

"What's wrong?" Laurelle asked, noting her caution.

Dart shook her head.

As Pupp edged around a bend in the tunnel, he brushed too closely against a hanging corkscrew of a root—or maybe it had reached for him.

Either way, Pupp suddenly jerked away, darting forward, ripping away tiny root hairs . . . and yanking part of the root down.

It took half a heartbeat for Dart to realize the root had *touched* Pupp. His body flared brighter, eyes flashing with fire. In the brightness, she saw the reason why. An oily wetness seeped from the torn root. It dripped to the floor and glowed against the dark stone. The crimson color could not be mistaken.

Blood . . . blood imbued with Grace.

Before she could react, Laurelle stepped around the bend. A small cry sounded. Dart glanced back. Laurelle's eyes were huge, shining in Pupp's radiance. Horror paled her features. Laurelle stumbled back, catching herself up among the roots. Tendrils snagged into her robe, nightclothes, hair. One long feathery root wrapped full around her stretched neck.

A scream strangled from her, coming out as a mewl.

Dart rushed to her, tearing, ripping, clawing at the clinging roots. She tugged Laurelle free, both of them tumbling to the center of the tunnel. Pupp hurried toward them, eyes shining with fury and concern.

Laurelle scrambled and fought to free herself from Dart's tangled limbs. Dart searched around for what so terrified her friend. Had she seen Yaellin? Was he coming for them?

But the passage, well lit by Pupp, was empty.

"A daemon . . ." Laurelle cried, still sounding strangled. She gained her feet and backed away, one arm out toward Dart, trying to draw her, too.

On the ground, Dart finally noted the source of her terror. Laurelle's gaze was fixed upon Pupp. She could see him. The blood from the root must have splattered over him.

"There's nothing to fear," Dart said hurriedly and reached out for Pupp. Her fingertips found substance again. He pushed his muzzle happily into her palm, needing reassurance. His bright glow faded with his relief. "He's my friend."

Laurelle remained standing, but ready to bolt. "What . . . how . . . ?"

Dart stared up, pleading with her eyes. "He's Pupp."

Laurelle's brow pinched in confusion, then drew even tighter. "Pupp . . . I remember . . . Margarite told me . . . laughed . . . some imaginary friend of yours . . . You used to speak of it when you were a first-floorer."

"Not imaginary," Dart said.

Laurelle stared from girl to daemon. She slowly lowered herself to her knees. The horror faded from her face and something bordering on curiosity replaced it. "What is he?"

Dart glanced to Pupp, who sat on his haunches, glowering at the arch of roots. She remembered bits and pieces of her dream a few nights back. She had been a babe. Pupp had been suckling at her navel. "I don't know," she said softly. "He's always been with me. A shadow no one could see or touch."

"He's fading," Laurelle said.

"Is he?" Dart still felt his bronze shell, smooth, as warm as a mug of steaming bitternut. Then her fingers fell through him again.

"He's gone." Laurelle searched the passage, blind to Pupp, who continued to sit on his haunches.

Dart waved her fingers through his body. "No, he's still here."

"Truly? Then what made him plain to the eye just now?"

Dart pointed to the glowing ichor on the floor, still dripping from the torn root. "Blood . . . blood rich in Grace," she answered, then added quietly, ". . . or my own blood."

"We must show him to Lord Chrism," Laurelle said, renewing her resolve to continue. "Perhaps Pupp has something to do with Yaellin's interest in you."

"I don't see how. No one but me has ever seen Pupp."

"Lord Chrism will sort it all out." Laurelle nodded forward. "I think the others have stopped. The light has stopped moving away."

They continued together. Dart sidestepped the bleeding root and waved Pupp away from the pool below it. He seemed happy to oblige, though he did sniff at it. Could he smell the Grace?

As Dart continued, she eyed the knots of roots with raw suspicion. *Blood roots.* If these were indeed the roots of the myrrwood tree, why did they bleed? She recalled the history lesson given by Jasper Cheek, the magister of the grounds and towers. His words repeated in her head. She could still hear the pride in his voice. *Lord Chrism was the first god to marry himself to the land and share his Grace with all. His own hand laid the first seed, watered with his own blessed blood.*

Dart shivered. Was that why the roots bled even now?

She kept well away from the tangled root briers. The tiny hairs continued their ominous waving, seeking purchase.

"Do you smell that?" Laurelle asked.

Dart noted a sweetness to the air, a blend of honey and loam. She drew in a deeper breath.

"That's myrr," Laurelle said. "I have some sweetwater scented with it, a gift from my mother."

Dart felt a slightly warmer breeze wafting to them, the exhalation of spring, warming away the damp, winter chill of the passage. They were drawn toward it. Their pace increased. The lamplight grew brighter, plainly having stopped not far ahead.

They hiked the last few bends in the passage.

A short stair appeared, leading up, lit well.

They cautiously approached. There were only ten steps.

At the top, the lamp appeared in view, hanging on a peg and shining upon another stone door. This was carved like the first: twining rose vines amid a smattering of Littick letters. Warded, too, Dart noted. And like the other, it was ajar.

A murmur of voices could be heard now. More than two. A gathering.

Laurelle glanced to Dart, then back to the door. Together they both cautiously mounted the stairs and crept to the door. There was enough room for both to peek out. Pupp simply walked through the door and out into the open glade beyond.

From the doorway, Dart spotted the limbs and trunks of the ancient myrrwood, lit from below by small fires dotting the edges of a glade. Trunks were so thick that it would take a dozen men linking arms to measure around them. Heavy limbs climbed so high even moonlight failed to shine through. The glade appeared more like a giant raftered court than a forest glen.

Voices could be heard, talking in low tones, but clearly urgent.

The speakers were not in plain view.

Laurelle urged Dart out with a nudge. They slipped out the open door and hurried to a patch of bushes at the edge of the glade. They ducked down. The bushes were unknown to Dart but appeared more thorny than leafy. They could peer through them with ease.

Beyond, lit by the fires, a strange group of people gathered in the center near a raised mound surmounted by a pair of twin stone pillars. The stone columns were plainly ancient, hoary with lichen, half-wrapped in brown vines.

Lord Chrism climbed the mound, arms raised. He was bare-chested now. Both wrists had been cut and bled down the length of his arms.

The others gathered at the foot of the mound, a score of men and women. She recognized not only Mistress Naff, but also Jasper Cheek, and several guardsmen who served the High Wing.

Chrism faced the others, standing between the two pillars. When he spoke, it was in his softly assured, sad tones. "Here is where I first settled the land." He pointed to the mound at his feet, blood dripping to the soil. "I allowed myself to be tied here, strung between these two pillars. I had my body cut at the throat, at the wrist, and the groin. That is how a god settles a land, tying place to blood and flesh."

A murmur passed through the crowd.

"No longer." Chrism stepped back and spat at his feet. "I have broken free of my place, severing my connection, freeing the land and returning it to my people."

Dart tensed at these words. Laurelle and Dart shared a frightened glance. Was what Lord Chrism claiming true? Had he unsettled himself from the very land he had blessed? Dart remembered Jacinta's last words before falling upon the cursed blade, expressing a similar sentiment: *Myrillia will be free.*

Chrism continued. "As I was the first to bring peace to Myrillia, so now I will bring it true freedom. You are my chosen. Together we are the Cabal. Others across Myrillia already join our ranks. Let us once again, as we do with each new moon, swear our allegiance. Raise your cups. Be blessed and draw strength from my Grace."

All around the mound, the gathered men and women lifted their cups and drank. Dart noted the glow about the cups, the same as seeped from Chrism's wrists.

Blood . . . they were drinking his blood.

"No," Laurelle moaned under her breath.

Blood drinking was an abomination, used in black rites. A god's Grace was too strong. It took only a touch to the skin, a single drop, to pass on a blessing. To consume blood risked the loss of both will and body. It enslaved and deformed.

Chrism raised his arms out to his minions. A glow spread over the god's form, starting at the wrist and spreading outward. He was calling down a blessing.

"Be free."

The men and women gasped and let out small screams. They fell to the soil, on their sides, backs, facedown. They writhed and racked. Dart could hear bones breaking. Cries turned to howls. Across the glade, men became beasts, rising up on misshapen legs. Women crouched and hissed, faces stretched into bestial visages. All eyes, now aglow with wicked Grace, stared toward Chrism.

"As your flesh has changed, so will the world."

There was only one figure untouched by the transformation.

Mistress Naff climbed the hill to join Chrism. She slipped an arm around his naked waist and pulled him down into a kiss. It was a savage, bloody kiss, less passion than violence. As they parted, a dark smoky tendril connected their lips, a black umbilicus. It pulsed and roiled, seeming to almost take form, but not quite.

From that mass of darkness, fiery eyes opened and stared toward their hiding place. A keening wail filled the glade, sounding like the scream of slaughtered rabbits.

Laurelle pushed back into the wood. A misstep snapped a branch.

The noise was as loud as a clap.

Eyes . . . all eyes swung in their direction: beast, god, daemon.

Dart stood up, knowing they were found. She turned and fled with Laurelle. But in three steps, shadows swept down from the branches above, falling about them like water. She was blind, choked, panicked.

From the heart of the darkness, words reached Dart. "If you wish to live, move swiftly."

Dart knew the speaker.

Yaellin de Mar.

18

PAST AND PRESENT

TYLAR KEPT HIS BACK TO THE FIRE, BUT HE FELT NONE OF ITS HEAT. He stared at Kathryn. Her auburn hair had been plaited into a single braid. Her form was clothed in black. A shadowcloak lay swept behind one shoulder and draped to her ankles. He stared, unblinking. She hadn't changed. How could that be? Even now her blue eyes carried the same mix of doubt and confusion as when last he had seen her, seated before Tashijan's court.

Tylar was unprepared for his reaction. He had never intended to come across her. He had planned on avoiding the upper reaches of the Citadel where the warden and castellan kept their rooms. But here Kathryn was, standing before him.

Met with those eyes, Tylar could not move. A part of him wanted to lunge out, pull her into an embrace, kiss those lips, taste the woman to whom he'd pledged his heart . . . but another wanted to simply lash out. How could she have doubted him? Hadn't she known him better than any woman? And still even deeper down, a final part of him wanted to drop to his knees and beg her forgiveness for all he had done, all he had cost them both.

He tried speaking. "Kathryn . . ." But any further words died to ash in his mouth.

She turned her eyes away. Tylar found he could move again and stepped toward her. She stepped farther away. He relented and spoke the words that needed to be declared. "I didn't slay Meeryn."

"I know," Kathryn mumbled, her back to him. "And I know you didn't murder that family of cobblers five years ago."

Tylar stumbled at this. "How—?"

Kathryn cut him off. "The story is long." She glanced to the door. "It's not safe for you here, Tylar. Why did you return?"

"To clear my name. To expose the true slayer of Meeryn."

She glanced quickly back at him and away, but Tylar caught the flash of pain in her eyes. Her gaze dropped to the floor. Anger fired her words. "How does coming here help you?"

"A burden was placed upon me by Meeryn," Tylar said, and he briefly recounted Meeryn's death and her final words to him. "She cured my broken body but left me with this duty, this mystery."

"*Rivenscryr?* What does that mean?"

Tylar frowned. "According to Fyla of Tangled Reef, the word is a name in ancient Littick, the god's name for the talisman that sundered their world four thousand years ago."

Kathryn swung back around. "You mean the Godsword?"

He nodded.

"Why mention such a dread thing?"

"That's the answer I came here to find. Tashijan's libraries are the best in all of Myrillia. I've brought others to help me search." He motioned to the dark doorway to the neighboring bedroom. His companions appeared at his signal, stepping out of hiding, all draped in shadowcloaks. One carried a sword in hand.

"May I present Krevan," Tylar said, "formerly known as the Raven Knight."

Kathryn's eyes widened in shock. Her eyes traveled to the ancient sword in his hand. Serpentfang could not be mistaken.

There was no time for lengthier introductions as the others pushed into the small room, crowding it. Tylar named each in turn. "This is Rogger, a scholar turned thief. And Delia, one of Meeryn's former Hands."

Delia bowed her head. "Castellan Vail," she said formally.

"And lastly Eylan, Wyr-mistress from the Lair." The tall woman in leathers eyed Kathryn up and down, apprising her as a threat.

Once finished, Kathryn stared about the group. She'd been so focused on Tylar, she'd not considered that their might be others hiding in the next room. "How did you all get in here? Why are you in Perryl's rooms? And what's become of Perryl?"

Rogger nodded to Kathryn. "The last is as much a mystery to us as it is to you, my dear castellan. As to entering Tashijan, it was not hard when you're accompanied by a cadre of knights." He picked at the edge of the cloak he wore about his shoulders. "Though we can't use the Grace in them, a cloak is a cloak. Hiding the ordinary just as well as the extraordinary."

Tylar waved him back. "Perryl was the only person I knew I could trust here," he explained.

Kathryn winced at these words, but remained silent.

"It took only a few discreet inquiries to find our way to Perryl's domicile. We'd only just arrived and found him gone when you came knocking."

"You mentioned blood on his bed." Kathryn glanced to the back bedroom.

"Not much. A splattering of drops across his sheets. But a table was overturned. There had clearly been a struggle."

Kathryn paled visibly. "They've taken him."

"Who?"

"The Fiery Cross."

Tylar scrunched his brow, remembering rumors of such a clandestine order within the ranks of the Shadowknights. "How do you know this?"

A knock interrupted any further words.

"Castellan Vail," a voice said at the door.

Kathryn waved them to silence. "What is it, Lorr?"

"I just wanted to make sure you were secure."

"I'm fine, Lorr. Perryl and I are just finishing up."

"Very good."

Kathryn backed farther into the room. Her voice lowered. "I have no time to explain more. We have to get you away. I'll see to Perryl, but I know who might help you with your research into the Godsword."

"Who?"

"Master Gerrod Rothkild. A friend. I can give you directions to his rooms and will leave a note bearing my seal introducing you." She turned to a table by the hearth and found a piece of parchment. She quickly scribbled a note.

Tylar watched over her shoulder, making sure what she wrote wasn't a betrayal. The content of the note was brief with a promise to explain more. It asked the master to extend his trust of Kathryn to Tylar's party. She sealed it with melted wax and impressed the castellan's seal into it using her ring.

She handed the note to Tylar. "Stay hidden. I'll leave first and take my guard and his hounds away."

"Hounds?" Rogger asked. "What hounds?"

Kathryn glanced to the thief. "Warden Fields knew Tylar was coming here. He mistook his intentions. He thought . . . that Tylar was coming for me."

Rogger grinned. "Baiting a trap." He glanced to Eylan. "It seems everyone's been doing that lately with Tylar."

"Yes," Kathryn mumbled, "but I guess the bait here wasn't attractive enough for the godslayer."

Before Tylar could respond, Kathryn headed to the door. "Wait a quarter bell to be sure," she said. "Then follow my directions down to Gerrod's room."

Tylar met her at the door, stopping her from leaving. He whispered his words. "We're placing all our trust in you."

"You did that once before . . . and look what happened."

Tylar stared again into her eyes. He saw none of the doubt of a moment before, just sorrow.

"Keep hidden," she repeated. "And move swiftly. All of Tashijan is alerted."

Tylar fell back behind the door as she pulled the latch.

With the release, the door flew open, throwing Kathryn back and knocking Tylar against the wall.

Across the threshold, a great shaggy beast lunged into the room, as tall as a man and as massive as a bull. It roared, claws digging, hackles raised. Saliva sizzled through the threadbare rug.

On the floor, Kathryn crabbed out of its way, but her cloak tangled her.

Heart pounding, Tylar leaped off the wall, dagger in hand, and flew to stand between the beast and Kathryn. It snapped at him. Tylar twisted to the side. It caught the edge of his cloak, yanking. Before losing balance, he raised the dagger and plunged it into the hound's eye.

The beast howled and tossed its head, ripping the dagger from his fingers and whipping Tylar away. He struck the wall again, hard, hitting his head. Lights dazzled. He sank to the floor.

Krevan appeared along with Eylan at the bedroom door, swords in hand. At the door, a beastly looking man stepped behind the haunches of the hound. He bore daggers in both hands, his eyes aglow with Grace.

A wyld tracker.

Head aching, Tylar watched Kathryn rise to her feet, arms out, warding away both friend and foe.

"Stop!" Kathryn shouted, her voice firm with command. She had to end this.

The man claiming to be the Raven Knight kept his wary stance, as did the Wyr-woman at his side.

"No one move!" she ordered.

Barrin crouched low to the floor, lips rippled back, baring fangs in pain and fury. The dagger's hilt still protruded from his left eye.

Lorr's features matched the ferocity of his wounded bullhound, but he kept his stance at the door. "Castellan, come to me," he said through gritted teeth.

Kathryn held her place. "Lorr, call off Barrin and Hern."

The tracker's eyes narrowed in suspicion.

"Lorr, do as I say!"

With an angry grunt, he coaxed Barrin to drop to his belly. The bullhound moaned, rubbing its impaled eye with the edge of a paw, but the blade had been embedded deep, into bone and nerve. A whimpering flowed from it as the pain worsened.

"Wait," said Tylar. He pushed up from the wall and rubbed the back of his head. He moved toward the bullhound. "There's no reason to continue its suffering."

Lorr stepped toward Tylar. "If anyone is to end Barrin's misery, it will be me." He raised a dagger.

"No," Tylar warned sharply. "That's not necessary."

Kathryn joined them. "Lorr, do as he says."

Tylar crept slowly up to the wounded side of the bullhound. He reached toward the dagger's hilt. Barrin snapped at him, coming close to taking off Tylar's arm. A slather of tossed saliva struck Tylar's cloak, burning holes clean through.

"Can you hold him still?" Tylar asked Lorr.

"Be quick." The tracker swore under his breath but moved to Barrin's other side. He bent and whispered in his ear. Barrin's head rolled toward Lorr, wanting reassurance.

Tylar used the moment to dart forward. But rather than driving the dagger into the hound's brain, he snatched the dagger free and jumped back.

Barrin jerked his head up and pawed again at his eye. Kathryn expected blood and ichor to pour from the pierced globe. But when Barrin stared back at Lorr, his eye was unharmed, as if it had never been stabbed.

"How could this be?" the tracker gasped.

"A bale dagger," Tylar said. "A gift from Lord Balger. It heals as fast as it cuts. There should be no lasting harm."

Lorr's eyes remained narrowed, but their edge of fury slowly faded. Still, he kept both daggers in hand and his beasts at ready. The bullhounds fully blocked the only exit, waiting for their master's whistle to tear into those trapped here.

"You are the godslayer," Lorr said, staring hard at Tylar.

"I slew no god," he said with exasperation.

"He speaks the truth," Kathryn said.

Doubt still shone there. Tylar's compassion had bought them a moment, but nothing more. Kathryn sought some way to convince the tracker, but they didn't have much time. With all the commotion here, word would soon reach Argent or one of his cronies. But how to convince Lorr to let them all go?

Help came from an unusual source. A figure pushed between the Raven Knight and the Wyr-woman. It was the handmaiden to Meeryn. A slim young woman. Kathryn had forgotten her name.

Lorr had not. "Delia . . ." He stumbled forward a step. "It can't be . . ."

"We are ill-met here, Tracker Lorr."

"How did you . . . ?" He glanced to Tylar, then back to the handmaiden. "What are you doing here?"

"Helping my friends," she said with a sad smile. "Like I did with you and your wolf pups when I was a child. I still remember the one named Eyesore, the runt with the twisted back leg."

Something between a smile and a grimace formed on the tracker's face. "The tough old ranger died four years back. During a campaign with your father."

"Oh, no . . ." Genuine sorrow echoed in her voice.

Kathryn glanced to Tylar.

"She's Argent's daughter," he said.

Kathryn studied the slip of a girl. Brought to her attention, she now noted the similarity in features.

Lorr continued. "Delia, you were a chosen of Meeryn. I remember, when I first heard, I was right near to bursting with pride."

Now it was Delia's turn to widen her eyes in surprise. "How . . . You knew?"

"Though your father may have forgotten you, I have not. Not my little wolf girl."

Tears rose and brimmed the maiden's eyes.

Lorr seemed uncomfortable by the raw emotion. He glanced around the room. "But now you serve those accused of Meeryn's death."

"Falsely accused." Delia wiped at her eyes brusquely. "The true murderer is whom we seek to expose."

Lorr stared hard at the handmaiden, as if he were trying to use his keen sight and altered senses to read the truth, to search for enchantment upon the girl he once knew.

Kathryn knew she'd best press the matter. "Lorr, we must be away. They came for information that I think Master Gerrod might supply. We must not keep them."

Lorr shook his head. "They'll never make it. All the passages down to the master's levels have been barricaded tight with guards. None can pass from the upper levels to the lower without a full search."

"What if Kathryn goes herself?" Tylar asked. "She can inquire about Rivenscryr from her friend."

"Lorr would have to come with me," Kathryn said. "His absence would be noted. And what about you all? You can't stay here."

As proof to her words, shouts sounded distantly, coming from the main stair.

Lorr stirred. "Castellan, do you truly trust these folks?"

Kathryn stared at Tylar. Though he wore the same face, much had changed in him—then again much had not. She looked at him now with eyes aged by years and heartache, no longer so naive. He had always been a caring and generous man. In the past, she had let herself doubt this in a moment of panic, confusion, and shock. But she was no longer that woman either.

"I do trust him," she mumbled and turned to Lorr.

The tracker nodded. "Then there might be a way. But we'll all have to go together. I can show them a passage that is surely unguarded. A passage that isn't a passage."

"What about Perryl?" Tylar said.

Kathryn clenched a fist on the hilt of her sword. She pictured the young knight's straw hair and easy manner. She had a hard decision to make. "If what you say is true," she said, "then there's too much at stake. Lorr and I will search for him after you're gone. Until then, all we can do is pray he's safe."

Tylar hesitated, but finally nodded. Like Kathryn, he knew the weight of duty.

Kathryn turned to the doorway. "Show us, Lorr."

Tylar and the others pulled their cloaks and hoods back up. Lorr backed Barrin and Hern out into the hallway.

The noise of approaching boots grew louder. A call reached them. "What's all this uproar?"

Lorr shoved through the bullhounds to face the leader of a cadre of guards. Kathryn held her breath. What if he betrayed them?

"Just a tussle between a couple of hungry dogs," Lorr grumbled. "So unless you feel like joining them for dinner, you'd best clear on out." At a hand signal from the tracker, Hern growled with a great show of teeth.

The leader backed away several steps.

Lorr continued. "What is it about you skaggin' knights?" He waved back to Tylar and the other cloaked figures. "Always come running when you hear a dog bark, but you need some real fighting done and you're nowhere to be found."

The guard leader scowled at the insult. "You'd best watch your tongue, tracker."

Hern growled again.

"And you and your knights better watch *more* than your tongues."

The knight waved him off. "Take your beasts out of my halls."

Lorr sneered and shoved through his dogs. "Continue to the hall's back stair," he hissed as he passed Tylar. "The main stair will be too crowded."

"But don't we want to get *down* to the Masterlevels?" Tylar asked. "Those back stairs only lead up."

"Exactly."

❖

Tylar marched behind Kathryn as she followed Lorr up the stairs. One of the tracker's bullhounds led the way, the other trailed behind. Despite the tracker's willingness to help, he refused to drop his guard. He kept them all pinned between his beasts.

Rogger climbed behind Tylar. Delia kept to his side. Beyond them trailed Krevan and Eylan. Before entering Tashijan, they had left Corram, along with Krevan's six other Shadowknights, to guard their mounts in case a quick escape proved necessary. They had dared not move too large a group into Tashijan, lest they turn too many an eye, and the other Shadowknights' cloaks were needed to disguise Tylar, Rogger, Delia, and Eylan.

Tylar now regretted not bringing a few more knights.

They climbed past another three landings. Where was this tracker taking them? The muscles of Tylar's neck ached from the strain of this night. The fetid breath of the two bullhounds filled the narrow passage. Still, the beasts did succeed in driving other knights off the stairs and out of their way.

At last, Lorr grunted. "We'll head out here." The tracker checked the landing, then continued their parade through Tashijan. The halls widened at last.

Rogger moved up to one side of Tylar, Delia the other.

The thief nodded to Kathryn. He dropped his voice to a whisper. "So? How does it feel to see your betrothed again?"

Tylar had no desire to discuss such matters with Rogger—not until he could sort out his own feelings. But he was also conscious of Delia's presence at his side. She had avoided his eye ever since Kathryn had walked through the door. He remembered Delia's whispered words back in the Lair. *It's no oath that binds me . . .*

Though neither of them had firmed their feelings beyond tentative motions, he owed Delia an honest answer to Rogger's question as much as himself. "I . . . I don't know."

Before more could be said, Lorr waved. "Hurry now."

All had noted the many eyes following their passage. The bullhounds were difficult to miss. Someone would surely raise some inquiries. Word would eventually rise like smoke to the warden's chambers far overhead.

The hall ended a short ways ahead at a set of double doors.

Tylar recognized where they had been led. He frowned in confusion.

Beyond the doors lay the Grand Court of Tashijan, the giant amphitheater that served as the major gathering place for both knight and master.

Kathryn shook her head. "How does this help us? There's no exit to the Masterlevels through here."

Lorr ignored her and tried the door. He tugged without success. "Locked . . ."

"All the doors into the court will be," Kathryn said. "The last they were opened was for Argent's naming ceremony."

Lorr tried the door again, finally kicking it in frustration. The doors were made of stout oak, banded in iron, strong enough to blunt even an ax blade. The bronze lock required a key from Keeper Ryngold.

Rogger moved from Tylar's side. "Allow me." He slipped a slender pick knife and a bent fork from an inner pocket. Using his tools, he tinkered with the lock's inner workings.

At the entrance to the hallway, a group of knights and house staff had stopped to watch. Kathryn nodded to them, arms crossed. As castellan, few would question her actions directly. At the door, Rogger's labors were hidden behind the bulk of the bullhounds. The thief finally proved his skill. A tumble sounded from the doors. Rogger stood and pulled the latch. The wide doors easily swung open.

As the few knights at the other end of the hall moved on, one tarried a bit longer, eyes narrowed. Surely everyone had been alerted to watch for anything suspicious . . . and their activities, along with the presence of the bullhounds, were certainly out of the ordinary.

Word would spread.

Lorr grabbed one of the oil lamps from its hanger in the outside hall and swung it toward the door. "Inside . . . hurry."

Tylar and the others pushed into the dark amphitheater.

The dome of the roof stretched far overhead, beyond the reach of the lone lamp. Closer at hand, rings of tiered seating spread outward and climbed forty levels, disappearing into the gloom.

Lorr led the way down the few stairs to the main floor. His two bullhounds spread to either side, moving low to the ground, suspicious of the giant open space.

Tylar gaped upward. He remembered gatherings here in the past: the raucous crowd of knights, the laughter, the arguments. The empty hall now seemed haunted, and with the darkness closed around them, somehow smaller. But more than anything, Tylar felt how little he belonged here now. It wasn't just the stripping of his knighthood. What had once filled him with pride and a sense of purpose, now seemed pale and false. He had seen too much to ever wear the cloak as easily as he once had.

Kathryn glanced at him. Did she sense that about him? Did more than time and pain separate them? On the way up the stairs, Kathryn had briefly told him about her fears concerning the Fiery Cross, about Argent's connection, about some bloody sacrifice she had stumbled upon, pointing toward the Cross's involvement in some dark rites. Did her cloak still rest well on her shoulders?

Ahead, a dim glow shone from the floor, the only other source of light. Tylar knew what it marked. *The Hearthstone.* The heart and hearth of Tashijan. The flames of the fire pit had lit ceremonies dating back to before the coming of the gods, to the barbarous times of human kings. Grace kept its fires always glowing. It was quiet now, waiting to be stoked again.

Reaching the central dais, they circled around the Hearthstone. Kathryn eyed it with a sickly look on her face. Clearly she was remembering another pit, full of knights' bones, charred and broken. Tylar also felt a twinge of unease. Was Perryl already among those bones?

Lorr led them past the arch of seats on the dais and continued to the back wall.

"Where are we going?" Krevan asked, irritated at the tracker's reticence to explain.

The tracker reached the wall and held up his lamp. It shone off a plate of bronze that stood the height of a man.

The Shield Gong.

It was struck to summon all of Tashijan to the court. Its voice traveled throughout Tashijan.

Tylar finally understood Lorr's purpose.

Of course . . .

The gong covered the opening to a funneling tunnel. This narrow passage was not meant for the tread of knight nor master. Its maze of corkscrewing channels echoed the gong's ringing throughout Tashijan . . . from the tower tops to the subterranean warrens of the masters.

Lorr grabbed an edge of the bronze gong and pulled it back, exposing the unguarded tunnel.

Rogger nodded with respect. "A passage that isn't a passage," he said, repeating Lorr's earlier cryptic message. "How did you think of this?"

"Before undertaking Castellan Vail's guardianship," Lorr said, "I studied the maps of Tashijan. The first thing a tracker learns is the lay of the land, whether forest, mountain, or castle."

Without further ceremony, they all pushed into the tunnel. Krevan and Lorr shoved the gong back with their shoulders, raising it enough for the bullhounds to enter. They dared not leave the hounds behind. If anyone should come to investigate, the presence of the bullhounds would expose them.

Taking care, Krevan and Lorr lowered the gong back in place. It would not serve them to have the gong sound now, awaking all of Tashijan.

Lorr squeezed ahead with the lamp. The low ceiling kept them all crouched. He led the way. The echo tunnel twisted and turned, branching and forking. They had to trust Lorr's sense of direction and memory, but wyld trackers were well known for their ability to keep to a trail.

No one spoke, and they all walked as softly as possible, fearful that their tread or voice would echo outward.

Lorr continued his determined pace. Finally he took a left fork and followed its spiraling path. Light appeared ahead, and they soon found themselves at a grate. By now the tunnel had squeezed to the point that they were half-crawling. The bullhounds slunk on their bellies.

"This should be the third descended level of the masters," Lorr said.

Tylar helped the tracker lift the grate free and set it aside. They all gladly stumbled out into the regular hallway.

"I know where I am," Kathryn said, sounding surprised. "Master Gerrod's quarters are down another level. It's not far."

Kathryn now led the way, moving swiftly. The halls were thankfully all but empty. The masters were sticking to their quarters. With a godslayer afoot, the guarding of Tashijan had been left to the knights. Still, a few maids and the occasional baldpated master did widen their eyes at their passage. Kathryn nodded in a perfunctory manner.

At last, they reached a door. Kathryn knocked.

A small peek window opened in the door. All Tylar saw was a flash of bronze.

"Kathryn?" a muffled voice said.

"Gerrod, open the door."

The small window closed and a bar was thrown back. The door swung open.

Tylar stared at the squat, bronze figure. It took half a breath to hear the whir of the mekanicals. An articulated suit. All he could see of the man inside were a pair of moist eyes that surveyed the party with Kathryn, then settled to Tylar.

"I think you all should come inside," the master said, stepping aside.

Kathryn took comfort from the familiar surroundings and the stolid companionship of her friend. The room's braziers—sculpted into eagle, skreewyrm, wolfkit, and tyger—all burned brightly. Myrr and winterroot scented the air.

Gerrod offered her his chair by the fire, but she refused, still too agitated to sit.

Lorr kept watch with the bullhounds outside. Tylar and his four companions stood warily.

Gerrod paced the length of his room. "The Godsword," he said after hearing Tylar's story. "It is indeed named Rivenscryr, but only in the most ancient of Littick texts. If Meeryn used this word, then she meant you to know the truth behind the sword. Its oldest stories and legends."

"What do you mean?"

Gerrod sighed—or maybe it was just his mekanicals—as he faced Tylar. "Most stories say that Rivenscryr was destroyed when the home of the gods was sundered. This is not true."

Tylar frowned. "It still exists."

"In a form, yes. It had not been so much *destroyed* as *exhausted* after the Sundering."

"Go on," Tylar said. "Explain yourself."

"There is much I don't know. A great war occurred among the gods. Someone forged Rivenscryr as a weapon. But it was too potent. Something went wrong. It shattered all, friend and foe alike. Even their world."

"The Sundering," the handmaiden mumbled.

"Yes, but Rivenscryr survived and was carried here with the gods as they fell to Myrillia. Echoes of themselves were cast high and low. The gods lost parts of themselves. All that was dark went down to the naether, while all that was light went up to the aether, forming the *naethryn* and *aethryn*."

"And what were we left with here in Myrillia?" Rogger asked.

"Gods made flesh, as gray as any man."

"And the Godsword?" Kathryn asked.

"Rivenscryr fell with the gods to Myrillia, but it was spent, empty, exhausted. Nothing more than a dire talisman of the war that ended all, destroyed all. It left no victors, only the defeated."

"But if it fell here," Tylar asked, "how come no one's ever seen it? What does it look like?"

Gerrod stared into the hearth. "There is only one text that mentions its appearance. It was written by Pryde Manthion, the last of the ancient kings of Myrillia. The hide parchment is vaulted in the Bylantheum in the Ninth Land. It is written in the dead language of that country. Only a small handful of scholars can still read it. Titled *Shadowfall,* it recounts the coming of the gods to Myrillia. In the text, Pryde Manthion tells of a god who came to ground, bearing a great sword. 'Of light and shadow,' he describes it. 'Borne by a figure of blood and bone.' "

Gerrod grew silent.

Kathryn had learned to read the subtleties of expression in a man of bronze. Gerrod's head hung, his chin resting on his collarbone. One arm was half-raised toward the flames, not to warm them, but in a warding gesture. Gerrod was reluctant to speak.

Kathryn stepped beside him. She kept her voice low, meant for his ears only. "Gerrod, if you know more, please speak it. A dark time is upon all of Myrillia. Now is not the time for more secrets."

His arm lowered, relenting. "Manthion tried to steal the sword at this weak moment, but his fingers passed clean through. When he described the blade as light and shadow, it was not poetic. That was all the blade appeared to be to his hand. But as his fingers brushed this strange blade, he heard the screaming of a shattered world. It unmanned him. He fled in terror."

"And you think this sword is Rivenscryr?" Tylar asked. "Why is this tale any more substantive than the other thousand legends about the Godsword?"

Gerrod kept his face to the hearth. "Because in the ancient tongue of the Ninth Land, light and shadow are *ryvan* and *screer.*"

"Rivenscryr," Kathryn said.

Gerrod nodded. "Pryde Manthion may be the only mortal man ever to truly see the sword. *He* named it, not the gods."

Silence spread throughout the room. Kathryn still sensed something that Gerrod was afraid to speak. But before she could press him, Tylar moved closer.

"What became of the sword? Did this ancient tome say?"

A slow shake of the head answered Tylar.

"What else?" Kathryn asked, laying a hand on Gerrod's shoulder. He shuddered under her touch. "You know something else."

"*Know* is a strong word among scholars. It is fraught with hubris. The best to describe what I will say next is *suspect*." Gerrod took another few breaths. "I fear to speak it aloud."

"Truth is often gray," Tylar said softly. "But it's still the truth." He glanced at Kathryn. She understood this all too well.

"Tell us what you suspect," she said. "It will be up to us to act or not."

Gerrod turned to face the group. "Pryde Manthion saw a god with a sword, a blade he described as *ryvan* and *screer,* light and shadow. The gods took this name for their own, Rivenscryr. But what of the bearer of this sword, the one who came to Myrillia with it? Manthion described the figure as one of *blood* and *bone.*" He took another deep breath. "In ancient Manth, the words are *krys* and *ymm.*"

Stunned silence met his words.

"The first god seen by man," Gerrod said. "If this god took Pryde Manthion's name for the sword, did he take his own name, too? *Krys* and *ymm.*"

"Chrism . . ." Tylar said, more a moan.

Gerrod stared at Tylar. "To find Rivenscryr, you know where you must go next."

"If Chrism arrived with the Godsword, he may still possess it . . . or know where to find it."

"But be warned," Gerrod finished. "If Chrism arrived in Myrillia with the sword, could he also be the one who wielded it, who shattered their world?"

Tylar shook his head. "The answers will be found only in Chrismferry."

Gerrod stepped from the fire. "Then I'll help you get there. But first we need to draw off the wolves."

❖

Tylar stood two steps below the landing that separated the masters' subterranean realm from the upper Citadel. The others gathered below him, all wrapped in shadowcloaks and masklins. A wall of Shadowknights blocked their way.

Kathryn faced them, flanked by the bullhounds and backed by Lorr.

"Castellan Vail," the knight in charge said, a bulky fellow with porcine eyes. "All faces must be bared. None may pass from upper to lower without inspection."

"Ser Balyn, we are *not* passing from upper to lower, but the reverse. Do you believe the godslayer has burrowed into the Masterlevels, through solid rock, and now rises to attack Tashijan?"

The knight hesitated. "I have my orders."

"From Warden Fields . . . or the Fiery Cross?" Kathryn jabbed a finger at the badge pinned boldly on the knight's chest.

"They are one and the same."

"Not all follow the Cross. And those who have volunteered to protect me . . . against all . . . wish to stay anonymous. I have given my word, and I won't let it be broken upon your stiffness." Kathryn waved to Lorr. "I'm sure Warden Fields has informed you of Tracker Lorr's assignation to me, by his own writ, a man loyal to the warden. If he vouches for my guardians, then that is as good as the warden's, is it not?"

Ser Balyn shifted his feet.

Tylar grinned behind his masklin. Over his years with Kathryn, he had been the brunt of her clever tongue and sharp wit. It could tangle the best of men.

Kathryn pried the chink in the other's armor. "We *will* proceed, Ser Balyn. Feel free to inform Warden Fields. But we will pass unmolested."

She waved to Lorr. He whistled his hounds forward, wedging and forcing a phalanx through the wall of Shadowknights. The bullhounds snarled and dripped acid from their rippling lips.

Knights fell back.

Ser Balyn stood his ground.

Kathryn met his gaze, unblinking. "Would you raise a sword against the castellan of Tashijan?"

He finally stepped aside. "Warden Fields will know of this immediately."

Kathryn strode past him. "Do your duty," she said with an icy coldness. "And I'll do mine."

Tylar followed Kathryn's lead. He and Krevan flanked the others, showing their knighted stripes above the masklin. The others kept their faces lowered from sight. They moved past the line of guards on the landing and continued up the stairs.

Glancing back, Tylar saw Ser Balyn elbow aside another knight, off to send a fast dispatch up to the warden. Tylar turned forward and continued after the others. He glanced to a high window and caught a glitter of starshine. Dawn was not far off. Timing would be critical.

Earlier, Master Gerrod had gone ahead of them, to dispatch two wynd-ravens, birds blessed in fire and air. The ravens would race with fire under their wings. No bird was faster, homing upon their targets with the speed of Grace. One had been addressed by Kathryn, the other by Tylar. They needed allies in the coming storm.

Tylar increased his pace to join Lorr and Kathryn.

"We should separate now. Ser Balyn will have the Warden's Eyrie stirred up. They will be upon us like a flock of crows."

"And we dare wait no longer in the search for Perryl," Kathryn agreed.

Tylar reached out and took Lorr by the elbow. "Watch after her. Keep her from harm."

Lorr nodded. "She'll be safe. Warden Fields would not dare lay a hand on her. Now, as for you . . ." The tracker chuckled roughly.

Tylar knew a swift death awaited him if he was caught.

"Keep your track light and your path unmarked," Lorr warned, using an old wyldman adage.

"I'll do my best."

❖

Argent ser Fields raced with a cadre of knights, his best and most loyal. In the lead ran Symon ser Jaklar, whom many called his Wolf. Argent kept a step behind him. They all fed shadows into their cloaks, quickening their pace, sweeping through the halls, down stairs.

It wouldn't be long.

The godslayer is here. He knew it in his bones. They would have to be swift and merciless.

Earlier, he had heard word of Kathryn and Lorr. They had broken into the Grand Court. He had dispatched men to the amphitheater, but a search turned up no sign of them. Then again, there were a hundred doors that led out from the court. It was a clever way to lose any trackers upon their tail. In one door, out any of a hundred.

But why was Lorr cooperating with Kathryn?

And just a quarter bell ago, word again reached him in his Eyrie. Kathryn had bulled her way past the guards stationed between the sub-terranean Masterlevels and the upper Citadel. She had been in the lower levels, but how had she gotten there? He had left word with the guards to alert him if Kathryn should leave the Citadel for the Masterlevels. He had wanted her movements under constant scrutiny. But none could say how she suddenly appeared from below.

And with a handful of cloaked knights, folks who refused to show their faces.

Argent raced with his knights. He had faced monsters and hinter-kings. But no greater glory would come to him than to carry the head of the godslayer upon a pike. After this, all obstacles to his plans here at Tashijan would fall away. He would spread the Fiery Cross throughout Myrillia. A new age would dawn . . . and he would lead the way.

He slid out his sword. Blessed in Dark Alchemies of loam and fire, just a poke of it would turn flesh to stone. Such a weapon was forbidden, of course, but such a transgression would be forgiven when he brought the godslayer to justice.

Ahead, a knight enfolded from the darkness of another passage. He dropped to one knee.

"She moves swiftly," he reported. "Into the unoccupied areas of Tashijan."

"Are all still with her?" Argent commanded.

"She and the tracker lead five knights, all cloaked."

"Show me," Argent ordered.

The knight rose and joined their party, sweeping ahead, drawing speed from the shadowed halls. All of Tashijan converged upon Kathryn. Her party was easy to follow, what with two bullhounds at their lead. Scouts were left behind, like this one, to lead Argent toward her and the god-slayer.

Under orders, she and the others were not to be touched.

He would make the kill.

All of Tashijan would witness it.

Argent and his men stormed ahead. He felt the Black Grace coursing along the length of his sword. There was no greater swordsman in all of Myrillia. And not even a godslayer would survive the curse upon the blade.

They sped ahead, collecting scouts along the way, growing in size like a raging flood of snowmelt.

"She went through that way!"

"She crossed down that stair!"

"She circles back around this hall!"

Argent could almost smell her. Once Tylar was slain, Kathryn would be his. She would have a choice between the gallows and his wedding bed. And if she still refused, the blood of her friends would seal the arrangement. To save them, she would have to take his ring.

Another scout dropped to a knee ahead. "She's stopped," he said, voice trembling. "Trapped herself in a room without an exit. But something has excited her party."

Argent motioned Symon ser Jaklar to his side. They both pulled up their hoods and marched down a narrow passage. Other knights followed, two score, and more filled halls and passages around them. There would be no escape.

Light appeared ahead. A flickering torch.

Voices reached them. Argent recognized Lorr's thick cadence.

"The body were here," he said heatedly. "A slain knight . . . a pit of bones. Now nothing. I can't even scent the blood."

"The Fiery Cross must have known of your discovery," a gruff voice said. "Cleaned the place with curse and acid."

"So where's Perryl?" Lorr asked.

Argent frowned at these strange words.

With cursed blade in hand, he flowed into the room, drawing shadows to him, swelling with power. Ever his personal shadow, Symon swept to his side. More knights followed, billowing with darkness.

Bullhounds met them, crouched down, growling.

"Call off your dogs!" Argent bellowed, taking in the scene with a glance. They were in a domed chamber, crumbling seats circling the walls.

On the room's far side, Lorr perched at the edge of a pit, staring down. When he glanced up, he seemed unsurprised.

Near him, a slimmer figure leaned over the same pit.

The shadowcloak didn't fully obscure the body of the woman beneath. It must be Kathryn.

Between them stood a phalanx of Shadowknights, led by one man, looming and full of menace, fully masked.

It had to be Tylar, come for his woman.

Triumphant, Argent raced forward, sword raised. One of the bull-hounds lunged at him. But with reflexes borne of shadow, he sidestepped its teeth as Symon drove the beast away. A bloody howl of pain erupted as Symon stabbed the dog.

"Don't!" Lorr cried out.

The scream from the hound suddenly cut off. Argent allowed himself a grimace of satisfaction. Symon was second only to Argent in skill with a blade.

The leader of the knights glowered at him. Did Tylar recognize the man who had sent him into slavery? Argent pulled more speed, wicking it to his sword arm. Blade became a blur, impossible to parry.

He lunged.

All it will take is a nick.

Then the man shifted, not so much movement as the flicker of a shadow. A blade appeared, flashing silver. It met Argent's blade with a resounding clang.

Though surprised, Argent slipped the point of his blade along the other's sword and thrust for the man's forearm.

Just a mere cut . . .

But his point found only shadow.

The godslayer swirled away. A spark of silver glinted at the corner of Argent's eye. He ducked and rolled from the sudden dagger thrust. The blade held in Tylar's other hand.

Argent gained his feet, noting the fierce melee erupting around the room. Shadowknight fought Shadowknight. The second bullhound blocked the narrow entrance, snarling and snapping. It guarded over the remains of its companion. Blood pooled on the floor, making footing treacherous.

Argent continued his dance with his opponent. Parrying, lunging, sweeping. He had a dagger in his own hand now. None had ever withstood him so fiercely.

"Who are you?" Argent asked as their swords momentarily locked. Tylar could never fight this well.

The figure turned his blade ever so slightly, straining both men's muscles. A glitter of lamplight lit the length of the sword. A golden wyrm bloomed on the blade, unnoticed until now.

Argent gasped. "Serpentfang . . ."

Shock dropped his guard. The other took the advantage and turned Argent's blade. The Raven Knight kicked out at Argent's knee, knocking him off his footing. Argent fell forward, his sword thrusting straight ahead. The blade passed under his combatant's armpit and continued its plunge—into Symon ser Jaklar's chest as the Wolf tried to sneak up on the other's back.

The Raven Knight twirled away.

Symon stared at the blade in his chest, then up at Argent. A cry rose to his lips, but never came, his face twisted in agony, going gray, then black. Knight became statue, rooted to the stone floor.

Argent stumbled back, trying to free his blade, but the stone held it fast. He suddenly felt pressure against the hollow of his throat. He stared down the length of Serpentfang. The point bit into his neck.

"Call down your knights, Warden." The command was spoken calmly but resounded across the chamber.

Attention drew to them. The ringing of steel went silent. The two forces retreated to either side, the wounded and dead between them. The Raven Knight continued to hold the sword to Argent's throat.

"Have them stand down," the Raven Knight commanded. "The god-slayer is not with us."

Argent lowered his fingers from the hilt of the cursed blade. He saw the truth as the knights at the man's side dropped their masklins and threw back their hoods. Tylar was not among them.

Argent closed his eyes. He had been tricked. Kathryn had purposefully lured him away.

Knowing there was no gain, he faced his knights. "Stand down," he said. He noted the many eyes on the stone figure of Symon ser Jaklar. His own blade impaled through it. Cursed. His guilt plain by sword and witness.

Movement drew his eye. Lorr led Kathryn before him. Or at least the woman he'd assumed was Kathryn.

The figure tossed back her hood. Argent stared in disbelief.

"Hello, Father," Delia said.

❖

Tylar watched Stormwatch Tower fall away beneath him. The large, pot-bellied flippercraft had lifted smoothly from its cradle, its aeroskimmers glowing with Grace as it rose into the dark skies. Off to the east, the barest glimmer promised dawn, but sunrise was still a full two bells away. If all went well, by the time the sun showed its full face, they would be landing in Chrismferry.

Rogger sat in the seat across from him, staring out his own window. "Storm clouds are coming from the south."

Tylar twisted and spotted a few spats of lightning flickering.

Rogger leaned back. "Will I ever be dry?"

Kathryn and Gerrod shared their small compartment, one of ten private passenger cabins. Their two heads were bent in whispers.

Their only other companion was the stoic Eylan. The Wyr-woman studied Tylar from across the way, sitting stiffly, ever vigilant. She had spoken no more than three words since first joining them. And those words were *Leave me be*, to Rogger. Tylar suspected Rogger had heard those words often enough, but never with more command or more disdain. The two were posing as husband and wife, from Tashijan's cook staff, off to visit relatives in Chrismferry.

"I don't know why I married that woman," Rogger had griped at her rebuke.

The others had boarded the craft separately. With all of Tashijan's attention turned elsewhere, none of the guards had given the ship's passengers more than a cursory glance. The Citadel was more concerned about the godslayer *entering* Tashijan, not *leaving* it. Gerrod already had his cabin paid and reserved. Tylar had played the master's servant, hooded, his knight's tattoos wiped over with face paint. He had also acted the cripple, not a difficult ruse. Kathryn had entered in secret, using her considerable gift for shadowplay. She kept hidden until all had gathered in Gerrod's cabin.

Kathryn stirred from her discussion with Gerrod and turned to Tylar. "Both ravens we sent have been dispatched. Hopefully they'll reach their intended in time." She pulled out a letter from her cloak. It bore the castellan's seal, her seal.

Tylar leaned over and read the name.

Kathryn looked into his eyes. "This had been for Perryl. A cover for him to join Gerrod in his trip to Chrismferry."

He reached out and touched her hand, lowering the letter. "They'll find him in time."

"You can't know that."

Attempting to distract her from her worry, Tylar pointed to the letter. It was addressed to the same man to whom the wyndraven had been dispatched. "Will your man be able to aid us in gaining access to Chrism's castillion?"

"He should. Yaellin de Mar is one of Chrism's Hands."

"Do you trust him?"

"Fully."

"But with all that's going on, how can you be so sure?"

Kathryn glanced past him and out the window. "Because Yaellin is Ser Henri's bastard son."

19

THE FIRST GOD

"**K**EEP RUNNING," YAELLIN SNARLED.

Dart held Laurelle's hand as they fled through the dark myrrwood. Thorns tugged and scraped, branches slapped and stung. Dart's breath rasped ragged in her panicked flight. Laurelle let out soft moans.

Behind them, cries and shrieks grew ever closer. Ilk-beasts, once men and women, pursued them, crashing through the underbrush.

Dart remembered her dream of a few nights back. She had been chased then, as a babe, carried away by the old headmistress of the Conclave. *Why?*

Yaellin kept behind, urging them onward through bower and glade. The myrrwood seemed without end. Dart risked a glance over her shoulder. She saw nothing but a flowing wall of shadow.

He's keeping us hidden with his billowing cloak.

Ahead, Pupp raced through the wood, passing ghostly through bush and scrub without a rustle. Dart watched him bump against a bole of the myrrwood and bounce off of it. The trunk was solid to him, like the blood roots below.

She had no time for this mystery and chased after him. His glow helped light her path.

They passed crumbled walls, a moss-covered well, a tiny wooden arbor fallen to ruin. And still the wood continued onward. Grown from a single seed, sown with Chrism's own blood, the myrrwood's branches had stretched for four thousand years.

Would they ever escape its shadow?

At they ran, Dart noted the trunks grew thicker. They were not heading back toward the castillion, toward light and people, but deeper into the heart of the myrrwood.

"Where . . . ?" Dart gasped.

"To the back wall of the Eldergarden," Yaellin answered. "And over. We must reach the city."

As if hearing their words, a keening shriek erupted to the left. A large form crashed toward them.

"Behind me!" Yaellin called.

Dart twisted. Laurelle froze. With her hand gripping Laurelle's, Dart tugged her friend back around. Shadows swept over and past them. Pupp wheeled around and raced toward them.

Dart dropped to her knees, sheltered by a bole of the myrrwood.

A dark shape flung itself into their path. Eyes glowing crimson, it ran on all fours, fingers and toes twisted into razored claws. A row of bony spikes pierced through the skin of its arched back. It howled at Yaellin, its jaws hinging its entire head, and leaped at the man.

Yaellin's cloak sailed to a branch overhead, a flow of living shadow. Snagging purchase, Yaellin flew upward. The beast passed below him, snapping and spitting. With a hiss and a slash, it whirled.

But Yaellin had already dropped beside it. He struck out with his fist—no, not just a fist. He held a dagger with a shining black blade. He struck the ilk-beast in the side, then rolled backward. A lick of fire chased him, like a splash of blood, from the beast.

The creature reared up, claws extended—then collapsed into ash, faintly ruddy, like wood embers from a dying fire.

Yaellin waved to them with his dagger. "Hurry . . ."

Dart knew the weapon he had employed: the cursed blade from Jacinta. Dart was now glad Yaellin had stolen it. She and Laurelle fled to his side, and the chase continued.

But the pause to dispatch the lone beast had cost them. The howls had drawn closer.

"I . . . I can't go on," Laurelle moaned. Her feet began to trip.

Yaellin was there, scooping her up in arm and cloak. He reached for Dart with the other.

"I can still run," she said, not wishing to burden Yaellin. Besides, she had the wind for this. She had been running her entire life.

She turned to flee, Pupp at her side.

They dodged around boles as wide as carriage carts. The scent of myrrh grew stifling, trapped under the dense leafy canopy where wind, rain, and sunshine never reached. The underbrush turned skeletal, thorny, with strange red berries aglow in the gloom. Through the upper branches, luminescent butterflits of azure and crimson fluttered lazily, hanging and gliding in the too-still air.

Ahead a wall appeared, lit by the ruddy glow of Pupp's molten form.

Dart hurried ahead, sensing salvation. What had terrified her before— the empty streets of Chrismferry at night—now seemed a welcome place. At least their pursuers seemed to fall back, losing their track, or maybe they had come upon the smoldering ashes of their fellow beast and now proceeded with more caution.

Either way, they had to find a way over the wall.

Pupp had stopped ahead. Over the millennia, a thick deadfall had blown against the wall, tangled and dark in the night.

"Caution," Yaellin warned behind her, farther back than she expected.

"Where can we cross the wall?" Dart asked. The deadfall looked treacherous and unstable.

"It's no wall, Dart." Yaellin hurried to her, his voice dropped to the barest whisper.

Her foot crunched through brittle twigs and branches as she joined Pupp. She saw Yaellin was right. What she had thought was wall was instead a tree of such immensity that the curve of its trunk could not be easily discerned, appearing more like a wall of smooth, gray bark.

"Quiet now," Yaellin whispered. "Around to the left. Keep out of the bones."

Dart frowned, then saw where Yaellin pointed. She stumbled back with a strangled cry, crackling a mouse's rib cage under her heel. She gaped toward the tree. The snarl of deadfall showed itself to be bones, piled and broken: slender leg bones of deer, cracked skulls of rabbits, ribs of giant woodland slothkins, ivory horns of lothicorns.

"The true heart of the myrrwood," Yaellin intoned. "The one trunk from which all else spread."

"The Heartwood," Dart said, remembering the stories told. She stared around her. Here was Lord Chrism's private sanctuary, a forbidden, sacred place. None but the god was allowed to enter. Even the sun hid its face from this soil. "What happened?"

"Corruption . . . like with the men and women."

They circled its bole, keeping wide of the ring of bones. As they ran, a soft skittering sounded. A skull of a slothkin rose from the pile, lifted by a writhing root. Its empty eye sockets bloomed with a sickly yellow flame.

Yaellin guided them to the side, skirting bushes and trunks. "It wakes."

More skulls rose, igniting with fire. Riding roots, they pushed out of the pile and snaked outward. Piled bones toppled with a hollow wooden sound as the roots quested into the surrounding wood.

They ran, keeping hidden.

Movement to Dart's left drew her eye. A cracked skull of a deer, still antlered, teetered up from a beach of bone. It swung around, meeting her gaze. She found the blaze in the sockets fixing to her.

Her feet slowed.

A trilling filled her head, sweet and high. The wood grew darker at the edges. The skull and eyes glowed brighter. Words grew in her head, speaking with her own voice: *come, sleep, rest, come . . .*

Fingers gripped her chin and turned her face. "No," Yaellin said. He had placed Laurelle down. "Don't look."

She nodded, but still felt drawn to glance over. Her feet drifted her back toward the deadfall. Motion snaked throughout the pile. Bones skittered and rolled. New fires lit the night as more eyes opened, a dance of fireflits.

Pretty . . .

She turned to see—but a sweep of darkness dropped like a curtain across the sight.

"No," Yaellin repeated behind her. "Only a little farther."

Laurelle stumbled up to her, her face bled of all color.

A shape leaped before them. Both girls yelped, falling into each other's arms. But it was only a dwarf deerling, no taller than Dart's waist. Its ears quivered. It stopped on tiny hooves, blind to the three of them, then bounded forward, toward the deadfall.

Dart glanced after it.

It landed, knee deep in the bone pile. The treacherous footing stumbled its perch. It fell forward. Only then did it seem to note where it was. Its head snapped up, neck taut, a confused bleat escaping.

Then a snarl of roots tangled up out of the bones. It lifted the deerling high and swamped over its body. The animal fought, but the roots penetrated flesh as easily as water. A sharp wail squealed forth, but it ended in one heartbeat as yellow flames sprouted from the deerling's mouth and nose. More fires spat out from its ears and rear quarters.

Flesh roasted from the inside out, falling to ash as the body was shaken and jerked by the roots. All that was left of the deerling were bones, raining down upon the pile, growing the deadfall.

Aghast, Dart stumbled ahead. Through the darkness, other animals came to the call of the Heartwood. Cries rose all around the immense tree.

"This way," Yaellin said, finally reaching the far side of the tree. "The others must have herded us here, hoping we'd succumb to the tree."

"What is it?" Laurelle asked.

"Another ilk-beast. Trees are living creatures, like man or beast. As those who served Chrism drank his blood, so the first god once fed this tree. Its Grace was his to corrupt if and when he chose."

Dart remembered the blood roots in the tunnel. She risked a glance back toward the horror. She now knew where all that blood had come from, sucked by Grace from the woodland creatures.

Yaellin guided them onward. The howl of the other ilk-beasts had grown silent. Dart found the quiet more disturbing than their hunting cries. Were they lying in wait for an ambush?

For another full bell, they fled through the woods, no end in sight.

"Dawn is not far," Yaellin said. "We'd best be out of these woods and lost into the streets before the sun shows her face."

"Why are you helping us?" Dart finally asked. She eyed his cloak of shadows. "Who . . . who are you really?"

He glanced down to her. He had lowered his cloak's hood. His black hair, though, remained enough of a cowl, loose to the shoulder and as dark as the night. The only break was the streak of silver from brow to behind his right ear. "It seems, little Dart, we are half siblings in a way."

Dart frowned. Though the Hand had clearly saved them, she still felt wary.

"The headmistress of the Conclave was my mother," he said. "Melinda mir Mar. And you were the little one she rescued and raised so long ago. The little stray sheep hidden among a flock of others."

Dart shook her head in disbelief.

"It's true, little sister." A glimmer of a sad smile graced his face. "All was told to me by my father when I was about your age. He set a duty upon me like no other."

"What was that?"

"To keep watch over the Godsword."

"This is what Ser Henri told me," Kathryn said. She leaned closer to Tylar to keep their words private. The flippercraft's mekanicals chugged in rhythmic fashion. For a moment, his storm-gray eyes caught her gaze and her breath. She glanced down. "He . . . he told me once . . . a half-moon after you were shipped away. He was deep into his cups, of sour and sanguine a mood. Over you. Over my loss."

"Your loss?" Tylar asked.

"My loss of you . . ." she mumbled, speaking a half-truth. She was not ready to speak of the other yet.

He nodded. "I'm sorry."

The anguish in his words drew her eyes up. "I'm as much to blame. Before the adjudicators, I should've been more of a lover, less of a knight."

"The soothmancers would've had the truth out of you either way."

"But what was the truth?" she said, hating herself for sounding so bitter. "I was so distraught. So shaken by the accusations." She turned away. "You did come to bed bloody that night. Your sword was found at the home of the murdered cobblers."

"I know. I barely remember even waking that morning . . ."

"Castellan Mirra said you were fed a draft of drowsing alchemy. Probably in wine." Kathryn explained what the former castellan had related to her and Perryl, how Tylar was a pawn in a game of power among factions in Tashijan.

"Ser Henri knew my innocence?" Tylar asked at the end, clearly shaken, his voice hardening. "Even as I was sent away?"

"Do not judge him too harshly. He came to that knowledge late, and to speak it aloud at that time would have exposed too many others. Even Henri's wardenship would have been threatened, and Argent ser Fields and his Fiery Cross would have assumed the Warden's Eyrie much earlier."

Tylar seemed little settled, breathing hard. Kathryn knew this mood. She smelled the heat of his skin. It awakened other unwanted memories, but she shoved these down. "Tylar, if Ser Henri had laid this all out, given you the choice of sacrifice or freedom, which would you have chosen?"

He remained silent, staring out the windows. The craft's aeroskimmers glowed against the night sky. "It was not just *my* life in that balance," he mumbled and turned back to her.

Those eyes again . . . she felt her heart tremble.

"But perhaps you are right . . ." He released her, glancing down. "At the end, I may have walked of my own volition onto that slave ship. I was not without guilt. I had dealings with the Gray Traders. I placed myself into position to be that pawn."

Kathryn heard the pain in his voice, but her heart still echoed with his earlier words: *It was not just* my *life in that balance.* What if Tylar had known about the child . . . or even if Ser Henri had known at that time . . . would matters have changed? Would decisions have been made differently by all? Tears rose to her eyes. They came so fast, a surprise.

"Kathryn . . ." Tylar said.

"There is something I must speak to you about," she finally said, "but not here." She motioned to the cabin door. She needed to move. Though the others had offered some privacy by surreptitiously glancing elsewhere or murmuring in their own conversation, she still felt exposed.

Standing, she led Tylar out the cabin door. The axis hall of the craft led forward to the captain's deck and backward to a communal room with a viewing window. Checking to ensure the hallway was free of prying eyes, they headed toward the stern.

Once in the vacant back cabin, Kathryn crossed to the curve of blessed glass that opened onto a vista below. A railing bounded a gallery overlooking the lower window. She grabbed it firmly. Below a small village slid by, lit by a central bonfire.

"What is it?" Tylar asked.

"There is one more thing you must know about those awful days." She girded herself for what she must say. Tylar must have sensed her distress and placed his hand over hers on the railing. It was too much. She slid her hand away, perhaps jerking it too quickly.

"There was a child," she said, speaking woodenly, trying to be dispassionate. "Our child."

"What . . . ?" Tylar stiffened.

"A babe . . . a son. I was to tell you the night you came drunk—what I thought was drunk—and bloody to our bed." She shook her head. "Then the guards, pounding on the door in the morning . . . there was no time to tell."

"Tell me now," he said in a low voice, thunderous in its depths.

"The trial . . . the accusations . . . my testimony . . . it was too much." A sob bubbled out of her. She had been holding it in for half a decade. "I was not strong enough."

Tears flowed. She felt her knees go weak, her entire form trembling. The night coming back to her in full horror. "I lost the baby . . . my . . . our little baby boy."

She was blind now to the view below. All she could see was so much blood, on her, on the sheets, everywhere. She tried to wash it up, alone in her room, so no one would know. Then more cramping, more blood . . .

"I was not strong enough," she sobbed.

Tylar tried to put his arm around her, but she shoved him back.

"Not strong enough . . . not for you, not for our baby."

Tylar again pulled her to him, with both arms now, hugging her tight. "No one's that strong," he whispered in her ear.

She barely heard. She cried into his chest. Words escaped her like frightened birds. "Would you have . . . would you have . . . ?" She choked.

He pulled her tighter. "I wouldn't have left. Not for anything."

She nodded into his chest, continuing to sob, but it was less an aching, wrenching thing and more a release. He held her like that for a long time. She let him. Though too much time had passed between them, though they were not the same young man and woman from before, in this moment, they mourned as one, for a baby . . . and a larger part for themselves.

Finally Kathryn found she could breathe. She slowly extracted herself from Tylar's embrace.

"If I had known . . ." he offered.

Kathryn turned to the window, still blind to the panorama and too tired but knowing there was much still to do. She wiped the last of her tears. "I think that was why Ser Henri told me about Yaellin," she said slowly. "I don't even think he ever told Castellan Mirra. I think he sensed the wrong he did to you, to the baby, to the both of us, and sought some peace, sharing his own pain of family lost, of a son born out of wedlock, born out of passion."

"And this Yaellin was chosen to be a Hand to Chrism?"

"Not exactly."

"What do you mean?"

"Over many cups of mulled spice wine, Ser Henri told me much. More than he perhaps meant to. But who can say?" Kathryn turned from the rail. "He told me of his love for a woman named Melinda mir Mar, then the headmistress of the Conclave of Chrismferry."

"I remember her," Tylar said, surprised. "A tall woman of chestnut hair and comely of feature. She had visited a few times to Tashijan when I was squiring."

Kathryn nodded. "He was vague on how it all started. He was the warden of Tashijan, she the head of one of Myrillia's finest schools. The Conclave grounds still holds one of the largest libraries and scholariums. Henri's interest in alchemy had him visiting its stacks. The two had long talks into the night on a thousand matters large and small. To quote Ser Henri, 'We were like of mind and spirit.' "

Tylar nodded. "Is that not the way it always starts . . ."

Kathryn glanced to him, realizing that once the same words could have described them. But that was long ago. Was it still true? She cleared her throat and continued. "Though Henri didn't say it aloud, I think what drew them was a shared passion that went beyond lust. Each was burdened by the responsibility to guide and raise the young of Myrillia, both wanting the best for all. And at some point, they crossed that line from close companions to something warmer. They kept their trysts in secret. He visiting her, she him. Then, despite precautions, she grew with child. She bore a son. She never told anyone who the father was. Henri wanted to marry her, but she had refused. It seemed her duty to the Conclave and Myrillia's future surpassed all else in her heart. But Henri understood. He would not have given up his wardenship either."

"And the child? Young Yaellin?"

"His mother raised him in the school, even trained him in the ways to serve a god as a Hand. Then when he was old enough, at eleven birth years, she and Henri told him of his parentage. He was angry, lashed out against his mother. Henri ended up taking him back to Tashijan to learn the ways of the Shadowknight."

"He trained at Tashijan?"

"For three years," Kathryn answered. "Then something happened. I don't know what. Even deep in his cups, Ser Henri would not divulge it. Henri and Melinda took a journey together to the hinterlands."

Tylar glanced sharply at her. "The hinterlands? Why?"

"They had some duty there, something done in utmost secrecy. In the telling, Henri's face turned dark and shadowed of brow, clearly remembering that journey. A year after returning from their sojourn, Henri returned Yaellin to his mother."

"Why?"

Kathryn turned to Tylar. "Henri swore me to secrecy on this next matter, but I think it bears telling now. Whatever happened in the hinterlands required Henri and Melinda to commit an act of great heresy."

"What?"

"Henri took his son, not even marked with his first stripe, and trained him in secret. He then blessed him with alchemies to give him the full Grace of an ordained knight."

"Yaellin was knighted?"

"In secret. None knew. Henri was skilled enough in alchemies to gift the boy with shadowplay but still keep the gift hidden. After the boy was ready, Henri sent him back to Melinda and the Conclave. He was presented to the next moon ceremony and was chosen by Chrism's Oracle."

"Then what did you mean before that he was *not exactly* chosen?"

Kathryn licked her lips. "They paid to have him chosen."

Tylar shook his head—not in denial, but in shock that Henri would participate in such deceit. He knew it was not totally uncommon for a rich family to arrange a position for a son or daughter. While an Oracle, blinded by blood alchemies, served as the eyes of his god, such men were not without a will of their own, without their own vices. Including greed. They could sometimes be plied by gold to sway a choosing.

"So Henri bought a position in Chrism's court for his son," Tylar said. "A son secretly blessed into knighthood. Why?"

"Like I said before, some secrets Henri would not divulge. All he would say was that his son was set to guard something, to serve as Henri's eyes and ears at the castillion, a duty that tied back to that journey to the hinterlands."

"And Henri offered no reason for such a journey or why he had ensconced his son in Chrism's court?"

"He would speak no further. But now I wonder. If Meeryn's dying mention of Rivenscryr guides us to Chrism, perhaps Yaellin might know more. We'll have to hope he gets the raven I sent to him."

Tylar nodded and turned to face her. "I hope—"

Kathryn heard the characteristic snap of bowstring. The crossbow bolt grazed Tylar's shoulder and struck the back wall of the flippercraft.

Reacting on instinct, she cast her shadowcloak high, protecting both Tylar and herself. But she was too late. Another two bolts struck Tylar square in the chest, knocking him back. He made a small coughing noise. A third cut his ear, intended for his eye. Her cloak had blocked this killing shot.

From behind them, darkness flowed. Kathryn discerned three shapes, all Shadowknights. One with a sword, flanked by two bearing crossbows.

Tylar had fallen back against the rail, holding himself up by his arms. Feathered bolts sprouted from his chest and shoulder like bloody flowers. His eyes were fixed on the centermost knight, the one with the sword.

"Darjon . . ." he gasped.

❖

At long last, the wall appeared ahead. The end of the Eldergarden. The myrrwood spread to the ancient bricks. Roots dug at the wall's foundation, while branches shadowed its top.

Dart and Laurelle stumbled up to it, exhausted, worn, bleeding from a thousand scrapes. Dart stared up at the immense wall. How could they climb it?

Laurelle gently started to sob.

Yaellin appeared behind them, sweeping out of the gloom. "They know we escaped the Heartwood. We must not tarry."

Off in the distance, a howl echoed to them.

Dart wished she could sprout wings and fly. She wanted nothing more than to wing over the walls, past Chrismferry, out of the First Land. Her world, hardly secure and safe before, had never seemed so dark and full of menace.

"To me," Yaellin said and opened his arms.

Dart allowed Yaellin to hook an arm around her waist. Laurelle did the same. Still, Dart felt strange to have the man holding her. He had been such a source of personal terror and worry for so many days. A tremble of that fear iced her skin. Or maybe it was the sudden intimacy, his fingers digging deep into her chest, mingled with the long night's terror. It all harkened back to the horrible day in the rookery. Dart fought against thrashing from Yaellin's grip. He was not Master Willet.

"Hold fast," he said.

The cape of his cloak fluttered upward, fringed in shadows. Those shadows found purchase in the pitted, crumbling wall. Yaellin drew them upward, scaling the giant bricks. They flew up the wall with the speed of shadow.

Down below, Pupp glowed in the gloom, a tiny ember. He watched Dart fly away. He raised up on his hind legs, paws on the lowest brick, clearly distressed. While Pupp could pass through almost anything, he had one weakness. *Stone.* If Dart crossed over the wall, Pupp could not follow. The wall would block him.

"No," she moaned.

From out of the woods, two forms . . . then a third . . . burst forth, striking the wall with claws and nails. Ilk-beasts. They yowled and sought to climb the stone, but quickly fell back. The wall was too steep and high.

Pupp raced among them, unseen, invisible, insubstantial.

Yaellin reached the wall's top, perched there a breath, then swung his legs over and descended the far side. As Dart's view of Pupp vanished, she felt an immediate panic strike her. Always her companion, Pupp had never been far from her side. Her heart thudded heavily in her chest. Her fingers tightened on Yaellin.

They swept down the wall.

Desperate and frantic, Dart's gaze searched for some answer. The city of Chrismferry spread out before her. Though the skies glowed with dawn, the city was mostly illuminated by the many lamps and torches of the waking city. Its breadth spread to all horizons, split by the silvery shine of the Tigre River. The waterway disappeared under the span of the massive castillion. Closer, Dart spotted the towers of the Conclave. A few lights glowed from its many windows. Her life there seemed another world.

She glanced back up the wall.

Pupp . . .

In moments, Yaellin dropped and landed lightly on the cobbles of High Street. His cloak fell about him in liquid ripples, settling to his shoulders and ankles.

Dart and Laurelle were released.

"What now?" Laurelle asked, teeth chattering slightly. She held her arms snugged tight to her chest. She seemed to have also shrunken into herself, grown smaller.

Dart felt shaky herself. Her knees wobbled like winterfest pudding. The morning breeze chilled her heated skin. Gooseflesh pebbled her arms. Even her breathing seemed out of step. She had to force herself to draw air in and out, like she had forgotten her natural rhythm.

Yaellin answered Laurelle's question. "We must find a place to hide, where neither hound nor tracker can find us. With the coming of the sun, all manner of guard will be searching, surely with a concocted tale of some villainy committed by our persons. We must be away."

He started off down High Road, heading toward the river. He stuck to the deeper shadows beneath the Eldergarden wall.

"We must tell someone what we saw," Laurelle said, following.

"Tell them what?" Yaellin asked. "That Lord Chrism has gone mad of mind and heart? That he has taken to Dark Arts and plans to wreak havoc on all? We'd be hung and gutted before the first accusation could be made. Chrism has hid his corruption well. None will believe the impossible."

Dart walked, grazing a palm along the wall to support her. "Believe what? What have we witnessed?"

Yaellin stared back toward the cliff of bricks as if his vision could pierce it. "My father sent me here as a spy against the Cabal. I was sequestered here as a secret defender to the Godsword. To keep it from the clutches of the Cabal. Only in these last days had I come to suspect Chrism had been corrupted, a part of the Cabal himself."

Dart recalled the name. *The Cabal.* She had heard it spoken both in the grove and in her recent dream. "What is this group . . . this Cabal?"

Yaellin studied her. "It is a story best told after we're secure. I've friends in the city, those loyal to my father. For now, let it be known that all of Myrillia is threatened. And you, little Dart, may be the key all seek."

Dart stumbled. "What do you—?"

"This way," Yaellin said and darted across High Street. He aimed for one of the side streets, a narrow course between rich homes.

They had no choice but to chase after him. A wagon trundled up the road, rising from the river streets below. Not wanting to be seen, they hurried.

Yaellin kept a fast pace, twisting one way, then another. The narrow upper roads and stairs outlined the villas, terraced homes, and *palacios* of the city's nobility and rich gentlefolk. All sought homes close to the first god's castillion, and over the millennia, such land had become crowded and stacked with residences. The homes were tall and narrow. Some sections of the streets were even spanned by wings of various *palacios,* creating tunnels through the jumble of buildings.

With each step, Dart felt the terror of the long night begin to weigh on her, the toll finally striking. Her breath gasped. Her legs shook. She found herself needing support against the walls.

"Dart," Laurelle asked, "are you all right?"

Dart licked her lips, finding them too dry, her tongue thick. She shook her head and waved onward.

Laurelle drew to a stop. "Yaellin, she . . . we can't continue like this."

Yaellin drew to them. He studied their faces, then nodded. "It's probably best to get our feet off the streets anyway. We don't want to make our track too easy to follow. Come. Only a little farther." He set off again, moving a bit more slowly.

Still, to Dart, it felt like a full run. She did her best to keep up.

As last, Yaellin pointed to a wait-carriage, drawn by two horses, and led them up to it. The coachman was currying one of his two mounts. Yaellin had fixed his masklin in place to hide his face and used folds of shadow to cloak Dart and Laurelle from direct view.

"Good ser," the coachman said, straightening as Yaellin drew beside him.

"We would borrow your carriage if it's unencumbered," Yaellin said.

"Certainly, ser. I was about to start my day. Where'bouts can I carry you?"

Yaellin stepped to the door of the enclosed carriage. "I shall tell you once we're away." He ushered the two girls inside, then followed, taking the opposite bench.

The coachman closed the door, then clambered into his seat in front. A jingle of a belled lead announced their departure. The team drew the wagon with a creak of wheels.

"Keep low," Yaellin whispered to Dart and Laurelle. He opened the tiny hatch to speak to the coachman. The exchange was muffled, but Dart heard a bit. They were heading for the far side of the city, a half-day's journey. Yaellin passed up a heavy pouch of coin. Dart wondered how much of it was for their travel and how much was to buy the man's silence.

After Yaellin closed the hatch, he fished into an inner pocket of a cloak and removed a tiny vessel of crystal. "Hold out your hands," he told them. "Palms up."

Dart trembled, arms shaking. Even this was a strain.

Yaellin removed the jar's glass stopper. A dipping wand was attached to it, wet with the vessel's contents. He touched it once to Dart's left palm, then her right. She felt an itchy tingle. Yaellin anointed Laurelle's palms the same way, then his own.

"Wave the air," he instructed and demonstrated by wafting his arms a bit. Dart mimicked him. She smelled a slight stench to the air.

"It's an alchemy of air and black bile," Yaellin said. "A nulling recipe concocted by my father. It hides one's path from all who seek it with Grace. It works only if one is not touching soil." He wiped his palms on his cloak. "The blessing lasts for only a quarter bell. Hopefully that'll be long enough to break our trail so we can clear the inner city."

He leaned back into his seat.

Dart did the same. Her head felt full of butterflits. The growing light of the dawn stung her eyes, and her stomach churned. The bounce and pop of the carriage over broken cobbles did not help settle matters.

Yaellin noted her unease. "Dart, what's wrong?"

She shook her head, fanning the ache behind her eyes. A new twinge rose from her navel, a dull tugging as if her innards sought a way to escape her belly.

"I think she's taken ill," Laurelle said, taking her hand. "Her skin is cold."

Yaellin reached over and felt her brow. His eyes narrowed.

Dart pushed his hand away. The effort narrowed her vision, sparking lights at the corners. The tugging throb behind her navel grew worse. A moan rose to her lips. She rubbed at her belly.

Yaellin kneeled before Dart.

"Something's wrong," Laurelle said.

Dart barely heard her. She curled in on herself, bent double in her seat. "Stop . . ." she gasped. By now, her navel felt as if it were ripping open. She hugged her arms tight over her belly, as if to hold her guts inside. She retched, but nothing came out.

"What's wrong with her?" Laurelle asked.

The world darkened. Dawn receded back toward night. Dart slipped away to another time, another place. She had been in a wagon, then a boat.

Rocking, rocking, rocking . . .

All alone.

No, not alone.

She pictured a tiny form nested against her belly, nuzzling, suckling. Where it ached now.

"Pupp . . ." she moaned aloud. "No . . ."

Yaellin's voice sounded far away. "What's this delirium?"

"A creature. I saw it." Laurelle's words fluttered in and out of Dart's hollow head. ". . . claimed . . . always with her."

"And it's still with her?" Yaellin hissed. "Why didn't someone tell me?"

"Gone . . ." Dart murmured. "Trapped by stone . . . wall . . ."

"The Eldergarden!" Laurelle exclaimed. "The creature must still be back there."

"Trapped," Dart gasped, knowing she had to make herself understood. But her world had gone black, laced with agony. "Need . . ."

A hatch grated open, and Yaellin yelled, ordering the carriage stopped and turned about.

It happened too slowly. Dart faded, slipping into oblivion.

Then the carriage was around. Dart felt a syrupy warmth suffuse her. The pain remained, but it ebbed ever so slightly. The carriage trundled forward, heading back upward. Though Dart could not see it, she felt it with every strand of her being. The taut pull on her navel slackened. The world remained dark and painful, but she could breathe again.

Yaellin returned to her, his hand on her knee. "I saw the creature in your dream," he said. "I never imagined it was still with you."

"Saw it in her dreams?" Laurelle asked a question Dart was too agonized to voice.

"After I heard your tale of the shattered illuminaria," Yaellin said, addressing Laurelle, "I thought Dart might be the one. Impossibly brought here, to the one place she must not be. I had to be sure. So I snuck into Dart's room two nights back and cast a blessing of dreamsight upon her."

Dart groaned. So it *had* been Yaellin. He had been in her room.

"I wakened her earliest memories. I saw my mother . . . my father . . . stealing her away. I saw it all through her dream eyes. Even the tiny form of the creature."

"Is it some daemonspawn?" Laurelle asked. "Was she cursed?"

"I . . . I'm not sure."

Despite the agony, Dart heard the obfuscation behind Yaellin's words. He knew more than he was willing to speak, but she did not have the strength to confront him.

"If it's separated from her now, the loss must be causing her this pain. We must head back." Worry etched his words.

The carriage continued back the way they had just come. Dart felt strength return to her with every turn of the cart's wheel. The world slowly returned in shades of gray.

"Where will we go?" Laurelle asked. "Not back to the Eldergarden."

"No, we can't risk that. We'll have to find someplace close to the castillion as refuge. Then I need time to think."

"Where—?"

Something struck the side window, startling all. Dart lifted her aching head enough to look. A large bird perched on the window's sill. It cocked its head one way, then the other. A raven.

Dart gasped and pulled away from it. Her most intimate fears were tied to ravens. She pictured another set of ravens, flocked above her, staring down. She again felt rough hands pinning her, hot breath at her throat.

The dark bird pecked at the window, drawing her back.

"It's a messenger," Laurelle said, pointing to the white tube tied to the bird's foot.

Yaellin reached to the window latch, releasing the pane.

"No," Dart moaned.

Ignoring her, Yaellin pushed the window open. The bird hopped to his arm. "Air blessed," he said, noting the glow to the bird's eyes. "Homed to me."

"Is it from Chrism?" Laurelle asked, frightened.

"No. It bears the mark of Tashijan." He pointed out the sigil painted upon its right wing. The raven breathed rapidly, panting through an open beak. "It must have been searching the upper city until the null blessing we cast faded."

Yaellin worked loose the message tube. Dart still felt a deep unease at the raven's black presence. She kept well back.

"This is the seal of the castellan of Tashijan," Yaellin said with a frown. He broke the wax on the message tube and shook out the tiny scroll. He uncurled it and read the note silently. The raven took the moment to leap toward the window, wings snapping out.

Dart was happy to see it depart.

Finished reading, Yaellin rerolled the message. His brow had furrowed even deeper. "It seems we are not the only ones in flight this night. A meeting has been requested. It is with someone I trust . . . and my father trusted. It should be safe and may give us a place to hide that lies near Chrism's castillion."

"Where are you to meet?" Laurelle asked.

"At the Conclave," Yaellin answered. He turned to the coachman's hatch to inform him of the change.

Laurelle relaxed, obviously relieved to go to a place where she'd felt safe for so long. "Back to the school."

Dart remained still. Yaellin spoke to the coachman, but all Dart heard was the flapping of raven wings.

20

BURNING BLOOD

"DARJON . . ." TYLAR PUSHED UP FROM THE RAILING. HIS CHEST AND shoulder burned from the two impaled crossbow bolts. Each breath tore his insides further, flaming his lungs.

The three Shadowknights rushed his position. The flanking pair dropped their bows and yanked swords free. The center knight, Darjon ser Hightower, swept at Tylar, his own blade held low and menacingly.

There was no artistry in the attack, no nobility. It was a brutal and swift ambush. Darjon must have anticipated Tylar's escape from Tashijan, identifying the dawn flippercraft as a point of escape. Tylar recalled a similar ambush as he, Rogger, and Delia had fled the Summer Mount. Darjon had come close to killing Tylar then.

From the glow in his eyes, Darjon meant to finish what he'd started.

Kathryn rushed to block all three knights, swirling out with cloak and shadow. She met Darjon's sword with a clash of steel.

"Kathryn . . ." Tylar called, tasting blood on his lips. He shoved from the rail. He had to go to her aid.

"Stay there," she ordered stonily.

The other two knights closed upon them. Tylar dared not call forth his naethryn daemon. All along the wall and roof ran the intricate steel-and-glass mekanicals that flew the flippercraft. Even a brush of the daemon risked shattering and melting all to ruin, sending the craft to a flaming death.

Instead, Tylar grabbed a dagger from his belt and flung it with a skilled flip of his wrist. The blade struck one knight in the throat. He fell down, gagging on his own blood.

Kathryn continued a deadly dance of shadow and steel with Darjon. She was one of the most skilled knights at shadowplay. Her sword, while not as strong as some men's, was still swifter than most. She fought with cloak and blade, creating complex feints and lightning-fast parries.

Tylar turned his attention to the other knight as the man lunged at him. Tylar twisted. The man's blade sliced the air, drawing a line of fire along Tylar's belly. He fell back to the rail, a vulnerable position.

The sword stabbed again, swung from the side. The tall knight had a long reach. Tylar had no choice but to fall back over the railing that over-looked the flippercraft's view window. He dropped with enough skill to land on his feet, but the curve of blessed glass was slick. His legs went out from under him. He landed on his backside.

His attacker vaulted over the rail, hooking the edge of his shadowcloak to it. He flew deftly and landed as easily as a skeeterfly on a still pond. His sword struck at Tylar's floundering form.

Tylar kicked against the slick glass and slid away from the point of the sword. Blood ran down his arm from his wounded shoulder, smearing the glass. While he could not call the daemon, he could employ Meeryn's gift to him. He touched his right palm to the bloody glass and willed through his sweat the fiercest fire, picturing steam rising from volcanic vents. Blood bubbled around his fingertips; then the blessing passed into the glass. The window's surface heated. The blessing wasn't enough to melt the thick glass. It would take much more blood for that . . . and probably some tears to heighten the effect.

But his attacker didn't know that.

The knight felt the rising heat and slowed his attack. He stared be-tween his toes at the passing landscape far below, etched in the first light of the day. He seemed suddenly less sure of his footing, falling to one knee.

Tylar scooted to the frame of the glass. He had to move quickly. He slapped his other hand down upon the window and held the bloody palm firm against the hot glass. He narrowed his eyes and imagined the worst winter storm, freezing rain and icy hail, a wind so cold its kissed burned flesh. Deep in his bones, Tylar felt the blessing sink into the glass.

He jumped up, springing with all the force left in his legs, and grabbed the lip of the upper deck.

The hot glass, so suddenly and fiercely cooled, broke with a resound-ing pop. A thousand cracks skittered its surface. The knight, still on one knee atop the window, drew up fearfully, a skater on deadly ice.

Tylar hung by one hand from the lip of the upper deck. The knight stepped toward him. His cloak billowed upward to snag a purchase. The shift in the man's weight was all it took. The broken glass shattered under his boots, falling away. Wind tore up through the small hole and more of the window collapsed.

The knight had failed to secure a grip with his cloak in time. He fell with a shout.

Tylar turned away. Hanging above the glass, he reached up to grab one of the railings support posts, meaning to pull himself up.

Then something snagged his ankle.

He stared down. The knight had flung out the edge of his cloak and grabbed Tylar's leg. Tylar, weak from blood loss and agonized by the two bolts in his chest, almost lost his hold.

Below, the knight hauled himself back out of the hole in the glass, drawn upward by the Grace in his cloak. Tylar let go with one arm and snatched another dagger from his belt. He dragged up his burdened leg with a strength borne of desperation and fury. His body screamed, but he had lived with pain. He found strength in its fire.

He had to cut himself free before the knight used his body as a ladder to reach the rail above. Tylar hacked at the cloak, but its shadows knit back together as fast as he cut.

Trembling with the effort, his entire body strained to keep his snagged ankle in reach. But he could not cut himself free. The knight flew upward now.

The flippercraft passed over the wide Tigre River. The morning light cast the mighty channel below into bright silver. Light reflected upward through the broken window and bathed the area with blinding light. Shadows dispersed—leaving only cloth.

Tylar hacked one last time at the cloak's edge, wrapped tight to his ankle. The knight was almost upon him, a hand reaching out for his leg. Tylar saw the knight's face. His masklin had been ripped away by the sudden winds as the window had shattered. He was young, fresh faced, eyes wide with panic. He was no older than Perryl, and perhaps as innocent.

Tylar had no choice. The fingers that gripped the support post overhead were losing their strength. His breath was thick with wheezed blood. He reached down and sliced the cloak from his ankle. The young knight fell with a piercing scream, fingers still reaching. He tumbled out of the broken window and vanished.

Tylar sheathed his dagger, grabbed with his other arm, then used his legs and the last of his strength to pull himself back up. He rolled onto the upper deck.

Freeing his dagger again, he searched the space.

Halfway across the deck, two shadowed figures were locked in a tumbled embrace, writhing in a hand-to-hand battle.

Kathryn . . .

A final wrench of shadows and the outcome became clear. Rising to his feet, Darjon ser Hightower clutched a fistful of Kathryn's hair. He held her at his knees, head bent back, face bared. His sword lay at her throat.

"Move and she dies," Darjon yelled to Tylar.

Behind the bastard, the door to the common room shook with pounding. But it was barred. There would be no rescue. Tylar stared at Kathryn. Her lower lip had been split. Blood ran from both nostrils. Still, a fierceness met his gaze. *Don't give in,* she seemed to will him.

"What do you want?" Tylar asked.

"It was lucky you cracked that window. That sudden gust and bobble of the flippercraft saved my life. Your old witch here proved more skilled with a sword than I expected. But she's not as skilled with a fist, alas. Easy to catch off guard." He tightened his grip, his blade digging into her neck. Blood dribbled. "Now I want you to step over to that rail and fling yourself through that broken window. Do that and this sell-wench will live."

"Why?" Tylar asked, needing time to think. "Whose justice do you serve?"

"My own," Darjon snapped back.

Tylar shook his head. "To what end, then?"

A new fire flamed up in the man's eyes, sensing he had the upper hand. He sneered, circling more slowly. "For too long, man has been subservient to the Hundred, but a new order rises, a new day. Power shall be returned to the people, to mankind! No longer will we be the playthings, the raw clay, of the gods. The Cabal will set us free. What was settled, will be unsettled. What was stolen, will be returned. What ended so long ago, starts anew."

Tylar heard the cadence of fervor behind his words. "And the death of Meeryn?" he pressed, buying time.

"The first to fall. But she will not be the last! At long last, the War of the Gods is upon us."

"And I'm to be the goat for this first kill. If you're so proud of the death done in the Summering Isles, then why doesn't the Cabal take credit for it?"

Darjon's eyes narrowed, irritated. "The time is not yet right. Meeryn discovered the Cabal too soon. She had to be stopped. The naethryn assassin was called forth by one loyal to our cause. Not all gods wish to rule mankind. Some wish for our freedom. We work together—god and man—to free us both."

Tylar recognized madness when it was bared so plainly.

Pounding continued behind them. The characteristic chop of an ax echoed. Could Tylar stall Darjon enough for the others to break through?

"No more talk," Darjon said, as if reading his thoughts. "You have until the count of ten to hurl yourself over the railing, or I'll kill this woman."

"You made one mistake, Darjon," Tylar said coldly.

"And what's that?" he said with a sneer.

"You assumed I still have a fondness for this woman."

The satisfied sneer faltered.

"This is the woman who damned me with her own testimony," Tylar said, putting steel into his voice. "She broke her marital vow to me. She swore against me. Upon her words, I was broken on the wheel and sent into the slave circuses. She means nothing to me."

"You lie."

"Words are breath," Tylar conceded. "But actions are flesh." He turned the dagger in his hand and threw it with all the force in his arm.

Darjon shielded himself with a ward of shadowcloak, but the knight had not been Tylar's intended target. The blade struck Kathryn in the hollow of her exposed throat, burying itself to the hilt. A killing strike.

The force of the blow threw her back. Darjon held her up by a fistful of hair. Kathryn's eyes were wide with pain and shock. She gasped like a fish flopping on the bottom of a boat, soundless, yet agonized.

Darjon dropped her with disgust.

Tylar stood. He sidestepped to the first knight he had dispatched and collected the man's abandoned sword.

Darjon billowed out his cloak, folding darkness into shield, drawing power and speed.

Tylar widened his stance. Blood flowed from the two impaled bolts. He tasted and smelled it with every agonized breath. He was no match for Darjon. Still, he lifted his sword.

"Let's end this."

❖

Dart stepped from the carriage. Laurelle followed. Both girls kept behind Yaellin. He paid the coachman and spoke in low tones, menace and warning inflecting his quiet words. The man nodded and remounted his carriage seat. As the horses set off down the street, Yaellin's cloak soaked up the shadows in the alleyway, stirring the darkness like water.

"Will he tell anyone about us?" Laurelle asked.

"Gold will quiet a tongue for only so long," Yaellin said. "And fear of reprisal for aiding us may buy us another day. But I expect the bounty on the three of us will be high. The lure will draw him out. Before that happens, we must clear the upper city."

Dart, like the others, had noted the number of castillion guards out on the street, easy to spot in their gold-and-crimson livery. They were knocking on doors and questioning every wagon. Their own carriage had taken this alley to avoid a patrol. Chrism would soon have every garrison alerted from one end of Chrismferry to the other.

"What now?" she asked. Her eyes stared at the two towers of the Conclave. Yaellin had them dropped off several streets from its doors.

"We go on foot. We move swiftly. We stick to shadows."

Yaellin drew them across the street and down an alley. Dart ran to keep up. She still ached deep in her belly, her head raced with a thousand questions, and her heart pounded in terror and worry. She wanted to lie down, cover her face, and cry. But Yaellin's earlier words kept her moving.

And you, little Dart, may be the key all seek.

She prayed it wasn't so.

And what of Pupp? Where was he? He must be terrified, all alone. Was he suffering from their separation, too? Love for him welled through her, gave her some strength to continue running. The three of them, while heading toward the Conclave, were also moving in the direction of the walled Eldergarden. Each step helped steady her. She would find Pupp. He had protected her at her most dire moment. She could do no less for him, regardless of the risk.

They fled down another street, staying on the shadowed side. Gates to the Conclave lay around the next corner and down a block. "Not much farther," Yaellin promised them.

The pound of boot steps on cobbles sounded from ahead. The churlish voice of a captain reached them. "Check every doorway, every home, every stall."

Yaellin searched around them. The street offered no hiding place. "Back," he said with hushed urgency.

Dart turned around. The closest alley lay too far away. They'd never escape in time.

"Hurry," Yaellin urged.

"No," Laurelle said. "This way."

She ran ahead, toward the nearby corner, toward the approaching guards. Dart hesitated, then raced after Laurelle. She had lost one friend this morning. She'd not lose another.

Yaellin followed with a grumble.

Laurelle reached a shop at the corner and ducked inside. Dart knew the establishment. A wooden rolling pin hung above the lintel. It was Havershym's Bakery and Sweets. Girls and boys had been coming here for generations to buy or pinch bits of brittlesyrup, gingersnaps, or honeycakes. Laurelle was seldom without a bag of sweets from the shop, passing them out to her dearest friends.

Dart had never been the recipient of such largesse. In fact, she had been in the shop only once, when she was awarded two brass pinches for helping Mistress Grannice spin some raw wool. She had bought four pieces of karamellow, doling them out as a treat to herself once a month.

The brass bell rang as they rushed inside. The smell of sugar and rising bread filled their noses. The heat from the fired ovens in the back room warmed the chill of the streets off them.

The portly baker, Havershym himself, yelled from the back. "Bread's a-baking. Hold fast. I'll be up in a breath." Dart caught a glimpse of his backside as he bent with a long wooden bread peel. The knock and block of pans and utensils echoed from farther back, apprentices mixing and kneading. Laughter chimed out.

Laurelle did not stop. She ducked under the counter and ran past the short rows of sweets and alongside the steaming baskets of loafed breads. She reached a low, narrow door and pushed inside.

"Quickly," she said.

The space was filled with barrels of dry flour and casks of rock sugar. Bags hung from the rafters on iron hooks, smelling of seed and yeast.

Laurelle stooped under the bags and hurried toward the back door. She yanked it open. A dark alley lay beyond it. Dart and Yaellin caught up with Laurelle, and they headed down the alley to where it crossed with another. Dart suddenly knew where she was. She stared up. The towers of the Conclave climbed into the morning sky. They were in the back alley behind the school's courtyard.

Yaellin had the same realization. "We're here."

Dart glanced to Laurelle.

Her friend shrugged. "I spent so much time going to and from the shop, spending fistfuls of coin, that Havershym eventually allowed me to shorten my steps by using his back door. And I knew at this hour they'd still be busy with their ovens. If we moved swiftly enough, we could pass through their shop unseen."

They approached the back gate to the school's courtyard. Mostly used by carts and wagons to deliver goods, seldom did anyone give it any attention.

"Keep with me," Yaellin said as they neared the ironwork gate. He swept out his cloak and helped hide the girls. "Surely Chrism has sent ravens throughout the city to warn all to watch for us. He wouldn't have neglected the Conclave."

"Then where are we to go?" Dart asked.

"To whom we were called to meet. We'll hole up there until the others arrive."

"Hole up where?" Dart pressed.

Yaellin nodded to the open gate, sweeping shadows over Dart's head like gigantic raven's wings. "With Healer Paltry."

❖

Tylar waited for Darjon. The knight circled him, clearly suspicious. Or perhaps the knight was simply allowing Tylar to weaken further from his wounds.

Pounding and chopping continued at the door to the flippercraft's common room. Such ships were built of stubborn stoutoak and ironwood. Rescue would not be swift.

"Why don't you call your daemon?" Darjon taunted. "Or has it abandoned you?"

Tylar glowered. Darjon clearly had intended to dispatch him in the initial attack. He had been surprised by Kathryn's skill. And now he was wondering why Tylar hadn't summoned his daemon. Darjon's eyes sparked brighter, more confident.

Tylar stepped around, matching Darjon's dance, one circling the other. "Why forsake your cloak?" Tylar called out. "Why join the Cabal?"

Darjon kept his sword steady but slipped his masklin free with the point of his dagger. He exposed his pale features.

"It was a god's blood that did this to me," he spat. "I was to be a soothmancer, but the blessing went awry. It turned my skin at birth so pale that the sun burns with the slightest touch. It can hold no pigment, not even the tattoos of knighthood."

Tylar stared into those red eyes. He saw as much madness as Grace in that glow.

"Yet still, I sought to serve Myrillia honorably," Darjon continued, circling with cautious steps. "I trained hard and earned my right to don a shadowcloak. I was distinguished among my peers. But who would have a disfigured knight? One without stripes?" His voice hardened. "They placed me far from all else. In a god-realm of burning sunlight and eternally clear skies, where I dared never to shed my cloak lest my skin be burned or my eyes blinded. The day was forbidden me. Such a cruel assignment was as much a curse as my birth."

"We go where we are needed," Tylar said. "We serve who we must. That's a knight's duty."

"And such a condition is no better than slavery. I'm sure you of all people could understand that. Imagine being confined *not* to a cell or circus, like you were, but imprisoned in one's own cloak, forever unable to escape its shelter." He shook his sword at Tylar. "When the Cabal approached me, told me of another way to live, free of gods and enslavement to duty, I knew their cause was just. The Hundred have ruled for far too long. Now is the time for the rule of man."

Tylar had heard similar complaints in the past. "The Hundred do not rule us. They share their Graces. We honor their duty by offering service to them. It is through their humours that Myrillia has dragged itself out of barbarism and into a time of peace and prosperity. Men are free to live their own lives."

"And swine are just as free to rut and roll in the mud," Darjon said. "Blind and oblivious to the killing floor to come."

Tylar sighed. It was time to end this. He lifted his sword. "The Cabal will be stopped. We will find its head and chop it off."

Laughter, harsh and cruel, answered him. "The Cabal is legion. It thrives everywhere. Cut once and thrice will you be struck down. Like so . . ."

Darjon leaped at him.

Caught by surprise, Tylar stumbled back. He parried the knight's first thrust by brute force, feinted with his shoulders, and attempted a slice to the man's arm. But his blade found only shadow.

From out of a fold of cloak, a dagger stabbed at Tylar's side. He could not avoid it, only lessen the injury. He met the dagger with his arm, catching the blade's point with his forearm. The knife cut to bone.

Tylar twisted away, falling backward. He fled a few staggering steps until he was forced once again against the rail. Winds from the shattered window below rushed against his backside, threatening to buffet him forward onto Darjon's blade.

The knight closed upon him.

Enough . . .

Tylar had heard all he needed to hear. He nodded past Darjon's shoulder. At his signal, a flow of shadow whisked up. A flash of silver broke through the dark cloud. A sword lanced out and struck Darjon in the shoulder, piercing fully through.

Darjon glanced down in surprise. Before he could react further, the blade was yanked back out, unsheathed from his body. Released, he spun to face his attacker, half-falling.

Kathryn shed her cloak, revealing herself alive and unharmed.

"How . . . ?" Darjon mumbled.

Kathryn cocked back her free arm and struck the man in the teeth with a fist wrapped around a dagger's hilt. Darjon fell backward, hitting the rail hard and going down on one knee.

"I can fight with *fist* as well as sword," she said fiercely and kicked out with a heel. "Not to mention leg."

Caught in the chin, his head snapped back, then forward. He fell to his hands. Tylar held his sword to the man's neck. He supported himself on the rail with his other arm.

"The game is over, Darjon," Tylar said. "While you never were blessed as a soothmancer, others were. You will be exposed. As will your Cabal allies."

Darjon lifted his face to Tylar. "Myrillia will be free!" A fold of shadowcloak parted. Something dropped into the man's palm as he sat back.

Tylar pressed his sword into the man's neck, but he was too late. Darjon crushed the thin crystal vial against the floorboards under his palm. The tinkle of glass sounded.

Tylar kicked the man in the side, rolling him over. Kathryn guarded him with her sword.

Darjon held up a hand, showing Tylar his bloody palm, pierced by glass. "The Cabal lives!"

The man's palm and fingers melted to slag, losing all form, like warmed wax. The curse spread quickly, down the arm, over the shoulder and neck. The left side of Darjon's face drooped and sagged. His eye rolled down his flowing cheek.

Tylar and Kathryn both backed a step, fearful of the curse leaping to them. Darjon, still of some mind, took advantage. A snap of shadowcloak whipped out, snagged the rail, and contracted, yanking Darjon off the boards and over the rail.

Tylar lunged at him, striking the railing hard. One of the crossbow bolts snapped. A rib, grazed by the bolt, cracked with a flare of agony.

No . . .

Below, Darjon plummeted through window, tumbling past the belly of the flippercraft. Still wrapped in his shadowcloak, darkness shredded from his form, burned away by the brightness of the morning.

Tylar shoved backward, clutching his side. Darjon was no longer a concern.

"Tylar . . . ?" Kathryn came toward him.

"Get back!" he yelled.

Agony flared outward from the snapped rib. Bones broke and broke again: wrist, elbow, fingers. He crashed to the floor as both legs shattered under him. He writhed on the floor for two breaths.

The beast inside shook free of its broken cage, rising from his chest, burning through his shirt and cloak, a fountain of smoky darkness. It fled from his form, stirring and drawing the bones together in its wake, healing with callus and spur.

He saw the look of horror on Kathryn's face. He lifted a crooked arm toward her. The horror on her face deepened as she stumbled farther away.

Above him, the font of darkness spread its wings. Its shadow-maned head snaked outward. Flaming eyes opened, seeking the danger for which it had been summoned. It found only one target.

Kathryn continued her startled retreat.

The naethryn lunged at her, wings sweeping wide, eyes blazing.

Tylar had to stop it. He smeared his hands on his blood-soaked shirt and grabbed hold of the smoky umbilicus that linked the daemon to the black print on his chest. The Grace in his blood ignited like fire on contact. The cord throbbed and twisted under his fingers. Flames of Grace spread out over it, as swift as flowing water.

The naethryn, in midlunge, contorted as the wash of fire swamped it. Wings snapped wide. Neck whipped up. Then it was consumed. Flame and form lashed back toward Tylar. He braced for it. The kick as it struck knocked him on his rear. Blinded for a breath, he rolled back to his feet. He found his body healed again. Even his cuts. The bolts had vanished. He patted out the smoldering edges of the circle burned through his cloak and shirt.

Kathryn stared across the cabin, still stunned.

But she was safe.

Tylar felt a sudden lurch under him. The flippercraft hove up on its starboard side. The floor tilted. Tylar fell again to hands and knees. Kathryn tumbled backward, landing hard herself.

Tylar then smelled it. An acrid and familiar stench to the air.

Burning blood.

He craned upward. A large swath of crystal piping dripped molten glass. Crimson fluid, the air alchemies, dripped and sizzled through the slagged tubings, raining and flaming from above. The naethryn's wing must have brushed through the piping.

Gods above . . .

The flippercraft shuddered. Somewhere under the floorboards, the ship's mekanicals ground with the sound of tearing metal.

The floor tipped again, this time nose first.

The craft rattled and bucked.

As the angle steepened, both Tylar and Kathryn skidded down the tilted floor, striking the bow wall. She stared at him in raw fear.

They were going down.

❖

Buried in shadow, Dart climbed the familiar stairs. Laurelle kept beside her. They gripped each other's hands. Yaellin led the way, his cloak draping both girls.

"The eighth level?" Yaellin asked. "Is that correct?"

"Yes," Laurelle whispered from the nest of shadows. "That's where Healer Paltry keeps his chambers."

Dart clutched tighter to her friend. The stair smelled of boiling oats and frying griddle cakes. The homey scent, rising from the kitchens below, triggered memories of a simpler life, where her worst fears were to have a boy see her petties as she climbed these same stairs. Before all the blood and the terror . . .

Bright laughter flowed down to them. A flurry of thirdfloorers cascaded down the staircase, heading to break their fast in the commons.

Yaellin motioned Dart and Laurelle into the next landing, shielding them fully from sight.

The parade of girls rushed past, all bundled in skirts, hair tucked under caps. Peeking past an edge of shadowcloak, Dart recognized all the faces: Sissup, Hessy, Sharyn, Pallia. Tears welled in her eyes at their chatter and easy manner. Had she ever been so light of thought?

Excitement coursed through the air, carried like a wind about the girls.

"I heard they were Dark Alchemists," Pallia said, her voice frosted with frightened delight.

"No, I bet they were hinterland spies," Gerdie countered. "Cursed by rogue blood."

Only when they noted the Shadowknight posted on the landing did their voices grow hushed, eyes widening. Shadowknights were not an uncommon sight, but with the Conclave stirred up by black tidings, the presence of one drew curious stares. Once past the landing, the chatter resumed more excited than before, whispered behind hands, but still carrying to them.

"Did you see that knight?" Kylee said. "He was looking right at me. I was like to swoon."

"Me, too," Sissup said. "His eyes were dreamy."

As the last thirdfloorers passed, a voice called from above. "Hurry, girls!" Though stern, it was as familiar as a warm hug. Matron Grannice appeared. Her portly form waddled down the steps like a mother goose, herding her goslings ahead of her. "Enough chatter! Jenine, how many times must I tell you to get your fingers from your mouth? What god will choose a girl with fingernails chewed to nubbins? Now get . . ."

The matron finally noted the stranger on the landing. She stopped, tucked a stray lock of gray hair under her bonnet. "Ser knight, you'll have to forgive my girls. They are an excitable lot."

"Not at all, Matron."

Dart had to suppress an urge to climb out of Yaellin's cloak and into Matron Grannice's arms. She wanted to confess all, unburden herself.

Laurelle must have had similar thoughts. But both had seen too much horror in one night. Their only safety had been found in Yaellin's cloak. So they remained where they were, hidden from sight.

"Have you come from the castillion?" Grannice asked.

"Yes, I've been assigned to search every floor, from top to bottom. I pray the intrusion will not be too burdensome, good matron."

"Certainly not," the matron said. "I've heard all about the uproar. An attack by Dark Alchemists in the Eldergarden. Can these black days get any blacker? Is it true two of Chrism's Hands were abducted, possibly even corrupted?"

"Such matters I can't speak of directly, goodly lady."

She nodded sagely. "A silent tongue is a wise man's best feature."

"Indeed."

"Well, I won't keep you any longer from your duties. May the gods and shadows lighten your way."

Yaellin bowed his head.

Matron Grannice departed, waving her arms. "Off with you girls."

Several of the thirdfloorers had gathered several steps below, watching on, whispering to one another. But under the matron's glare, they turned and fled down the stairs.

With the way clear, Yaellin stepped back out and continued the climb toward the eighth level. Dart and Laurelle followed, though Laurelle kept glancing back over her shoulder. Dart read her thoughts. How easy it would be to run down those stairs, join her fellow thirdfloorers, and pretend all this never happened. But it had. That life was dead to them . . . to both of them.

Still, Dart glanced back, too.

Before she could turn around, a figure stepped from the dormitory hall of the thirdfloorers. She was in a hurry, tugging down her skirt over her petties with one hand, pulling her cap on with the other. She must be the head girl of the floor, assigned to douse the lamps and secure the floor. An honor once bestowed upon Laurelle. Plainly the girl was frightened to be alone on the stair . . . especially after all the dread rumors.

Dart recognized the girl as she straightened from spreading her skirt over her ankles. Laurelle knew her, too, and stopped. "Margarite . . ."

The girl stiffened, hearing her name whispered. She whirled around.

Yaellin had continued up a few steps, unaware Laurelle had stopped. Shadows stripped from her shoulders.

Margarite stared at Laurelle, as if seeing a ghost. She froze.

Laurelle stepped toward her. "Margarite," she said again.

The girl clutched her arms around her belly, scared, confused. She even backed away a step. "Laurelle . . . how . . . why . . . ?"

"Oh, Margarite," Laurelle said and rushed down, closing the distance. She hugged her friend. After a moment, Margarite did the same. They clung to each other.

Yaellin moved back down the steps, looming over the pair. Dart pushed free of the cloak. Margarite, still embraced, noted Dart's presence over Laurelle's shoulder. The girl's eyes narrowed. She pulled free of Laurelle's arms.

"What are you both doing here?" Margarite asked. The girl eyed Dart up and down, as if offended by her soiled appearance, though Laurelle was no better clothed.

Laurelle still held her old friend's hand. "We're here because—"

Yaellin cut her off. "As you must know," he said haughtily, "Healer Paltry is the personal physik to the High Wing of Chrism. We've come here to make sure these two Hands were not harmed by the attack. We will shelter here until this foul matter is dealt with."

Margarite stared at his dark form.

"None must know of our presence here," he continued in commanding tones. "Other Hands are being sequestered elsewhere. It is a matter of utmost secrecy. Can you bear this burden?"

Margarite continued to stare, wide-eyed. Then she seemed to realize the question had been directed at her and nodded.

"Swear upon it." He held out an edge of cloak. "In the way of Shadowknights, touch the blessed cloak and swear."

Margarite reached a trembling hand and brushed her fingertips upon the cloak. "I . . . I swear."

"You are very brave," Yaellin said with a nod, dropping his cloak. "Now you'd best return to the others lest you be missed."

Color blushed Margarite's cheeks. She offered a quick curtsy, then headed out, but not before Laurelle rushed to her and again hugged her.

"I miss you so," she whispered in her friend's ear.

Margarite nodded, but her eyes were on Yaellin's shadowed form.

They broke their embrace, and Margarite hurried down the stairs, casting many glances back at them.

Once out of sight, they set off again, climbing the stairs.

"Will she keep silent?" Yaellin asked.

"She's our friend," Laurelle said sternly.

Dart didn't bother to mention that such friendship did not extend to herself. She had noted the familiar look of disgust in Margarite's eyes. Dart trusted more in Margarite's fear and awe of the Shadowknight than old friendships.

At last they reached the eighth landing. Yaellin led them off the stair and down the main hall to a door carved with oak leaves and acorns on its lintel.

"Stay behind me," Yaellin said.

Dart needed no prompting to push deeper into the man's shadows. Laurelle huddled with her.

Yaellin knocked on the door.

Footsteps approached on the far side. A latch snicked. The door pulled open, sucking some of the shadows over the threshold.

"Who calls so—?" The voice rang with irritation, then cut off.

"Healer Paltry," Yaellin said. "I've come from the High Wing. Your presence is requested at the castillion. I'm to escort you on this black day."

Dart remained hidden, but she heard the satisfaction in the other's voice. "Of course. I've heard word. I'll gather my bag and be right with you. Step inside. I won't be more than a quarter bell."

Yaellin followed the healer into his chamber. Dart and Laurelle stepped after him. Past the entryway, the chamber opened into the healing ward. A hearth glowed with a morning fire, and lamps shone upon the empty cots, lined around the circular chamber's edges. In the center, a small brazier burned and smoked.

Yaellin closed the door and secured the latch.

Healer Paltry glanced back at the sound. "There's no need—"

Yaellin let his shadows and cloak drop from him. Dart and Laurelle stood on either side of him.

Healer Paltry's gaze fell upon Dart. Confusion crinkled his brow, and deep down something darker shone. Still, he kept his voice light. "What is all this?"

Yaellin pulled out his sword with a flash of silver. "I must ask you to keep us company, Healer Paltry. It seems that there is some matter of urgency that must be discussed."

Healer Paltry ignored the sword. His eyes still fixed upon Dart. "The Hand of Blood," he said. "And the Hand of Tears. The very ones wanted by the castillion guard. Ravens fly to every corner of Chrismferry. And you come here. I assume for my help."

Dart stared into the man's blue eyes, his handsome face. How could such beauty hide such a black heart? She met Paltry's gaze, sensing his attempt to intimidate her with the weight of his attention, to hold her quiet. Before, Dart had left the healer's presence trembling and panicked. She was not that girl any longer.

"Do not trust him," Dart said with a firmness that surprised her, finding strength from the night's terror to face the horror here. Eyes drew to her. "His vile wickedness runs to the marrow."

"Dart?" Laurelle said, surprised.

Yaellin glanced to Paltry. "What do you know of him? Do you know why Tashijan seeks him out?"

Paltry's eyes narrowed to sharp points, threatening.

Dart shook her head, keeping her gaze locked on the healer. "All I know . . . all I know is he took *all* from me . . ." The words came out, dragged up by sheer necessity, but still tearing, too large for her throat. Her vision blurred with tears, but she did not look away. Laurelle appeared at her side, taking her hand. Dart felt the warmth of her friend's touch.

Walls broke inside her. Reservoirs of bile and bitterness, sorrow and terror, anger and misery burst their holds. She felt lifted and dragged down. She squeezed tightly to Laurelle.

"He sent Master Willet . . . to the rookery." Dart began to shake. Tears took her vision, replaced it with flashes of the past, to a place of pain. "I . . . I couldn't stop him. He took me by force, broke me, turned brightness to blood. I . . . I . . . I . . ." Her voice turned to a low keening cry of pain and grief.

Laurelle drew her tight. "Oh, Dart . . ."

She gasped and choked.

"You could've told me," Laurelle consoled.

Dart shook her head, a bit too violently. "Spoiled . . . I was broken and impure. I had no other home."

"She lies," Paltry spat out. "She is corrupted, but not by my hand. She is foul where none can touch. I know!"

Dart felt a fury build in her that had no bounds, not even her own skin.

Laurelle must have felt it. She loosed her hold on Dart.

"Abomination," Paltry said, pointing a finger at her.

"Quiet!" Yaellin boomed. His sword found the healer's heart, poking through cloth to skin.

Paltry winced, dropping his arm.

"Do not speak of matters you know nothing about," Yaellin said harshly. "She is stronger and purer of heart than any who stand in this room. What was done to her . . ." His voice filled with cold promise. "You shall suffer a thousandfold."

Paltry glared at him. "That will be seen, ser knight. Not all in Tashijan share your sweet sentiment."

"Is that so?" Yaellin said. "Then perhaps you'll share your view with the new castellan. She comes this morning to question you."

Paltry blanched. "What . . . how . . . why . . . ?"

"Yes, I'm sure they'll be asking you the very same."

Dart took comfort from Paltry's sick look, the fear in his eyes.

"Now all we have to do is wait for our new guests." Yaellin nodded to one of the cots. "If you'd be so kind. We might as well be comfortable."

Yaellin backed Paltry upon the point of his sword. "Laurelle, will you also bar the door back there? We don't want to be disturbed while we wait."

Laurelle nodded and hurried to obey.

Yaellin dropped Paltry to the cot, then motioned Dart forward. He kept his sword at the healer's throat, but turned his attention to Dart. He reached a hand out. A dagger rested in his palm. "Take it."

Dart stared. The black blade could not be mistaken. It was the cursed dagger. She shook her head.

"Take it," he repeated, more commanding.

She obeyed, fingering its hilt with care.

"Here is its sheath." He passed her a belt.

She accepted it, confused, feeling as empty as the leather sheath.

"Some call this blade cursed, impure, vile, but it is only a dagger. It is only steel. How it is employed is the true character of a blade." He stared deep into Dart's eyes. "Remember that. What was done to your flesh does not soil you or defile you. Your heart is still yours. It is still innocent and pure."

Dart listened, but his words fell on stony soil. She could not . . . did not believe them.

Yaellin seemed to understand. He sighed and nodded to the dagger. "It is yours. Wear it well."

Dart backed up a few steps. She set the dagger down and tied the belt under her robe, over her nightclothes. She worked without looking down. Her gaze remained hard upon Paltry. He watched her. She retrieved the dagger. Its blade ate the light.

Slowly . . . very slowly she sheathed it.

If not comforted by Yaellin's words, she was a tiny bit less empty.

She snugged the dagger tight, fingers on the bone hilt.

Cursed or not, she *would* wear it well.

She still had promises to keep.

21

FREEFALL

TYLAR CLUNG TO KATHRYN AS THE FLIPPERCRAFT PLUMMETED. SMOKE filled the cabin, steaming from the slagged mekanicals as the blood alchemies burned. Beneath the floorboards, the grind and scream of strained iron and steel shook through the ship. Shouts and cries echoed to them from the forward sections.

Slowly the steep cant of the deck rolled slightly more even. The ship turned, attempting a slow spiral. The captain and his helmsman must be wresting the craft by sheer muscle and will.

But it was Tylar's chance to move.

He clutched Kathryn's elbow. "We must get to the others . . . to the captain's deck!" he yelled to be heard above the howl of the winds through the broken stern window. He had no plan, but they could do nothing here.

She nodded.

He helped haul her to her feet—and she helped him. The freeing of the naethryn daemon had healed his wounds, but it hadn't replaced the blood he'd lost. He found his vision narrowing.

"The daemon . . ." Kathryn glanced back to the smoky deck.

Earlier, Tylar had explained about the naether-spawn. Kathryn had studied the black palm print with interest. But to see the naethryn rip from his body, shattering its way out, had transformed mere words into true horror.

"What it did to you . . ." she said as they reached the door.

Tylar grabbed the door's locking bar. "That broken man you saw was not the work of the daemon, but the slave pits and circuses." He could not keep the bitterness from his words, even when he caught the wounded look in Kathryn's eyes. "The daemon keeps me whole."

Tylar freed the bar that Darjon had set. The door fell open under him. They tumbled through into the main passage . . . into chaos. Smoke wafted here, a pall lit by fires licking up from cracks in the floorboards. The lower ship, the mekanical spaces, must be on fire.

Travelers crowded the passage, abandoning cabins. They tangled and fought in panic. Orders were shouted, prayers raised, cries echoed.

"There!" Kathryn pointed.

Tylar spotted the flash of bronze. It was Master Gerrod, brilliant in his armor. He stood braced in a doorway a few spaces down the tilted passageway. One metal hand gripped Rogger by the shirt collar, keeping him in place.

Across the passage, Eylan shoved several folks out of her way with the handle of a long ax. The Wyr-mistress's dark eyes found Tylar and narrowed. Her efforts grew fiercer. Her duty had been to act as his bodyguard, to keep his valuable seed safe from harm. She seemed furious at how difficult he was making her chore.

Tylar and Kathryn hurried to the others.

He turned to Rogger and Gerrod. "We must get to the captain's deck."

Another explosion bucked the ship savagely. It rolled to port, throwing everyone to the wall. Cries grew sharper in alarm. Tylar snatched Kathryn around the waist. He felt her heartbeat pounding. He stared through the open door of a passenger's cabin and out its window.

With the ship rolled over, the city appeared beneath the flippercraft. Tall towers stretched close. He spotted townsmen on the streets, near enough to see their faces staring up. He knew what they were seeing. A flippercraft, trailing a tail of smoke and fire, about to strike the city.

Then the ship swung back even, taking away the view below—only now the craft's nose dipped more steeply.

A hand grabbed his elbow, as hard as any shackle.

He turned to find Eylan hauling him up.

Tylar attempted to shake free. "My seed will have to wait."

She scowled at him. Using her free arm, she stopped one of the crewmen with the butt of her ax handle, pinning the young man to the wall. "Take us to the foredeck," she demanded in a voice that offered no mercy.

The crewman balked, near blind with panic.

Not a good sign.

"I may be able to help the captain." Tylar grabbed the man by the shoulder, shoving the ax handle away. "I have Grace that may serve to save the ship."

The man's eyes fixed to him, to any hope, then nodded.

Gerrod and Rogger joined them. With Eylan in the lead, roughly knocking folks aside with the flat of her ax, they forced their way forward.

The crewman unlocked the hatch of the captain's deck. "We've lost all aeroskimmers. We're riding on the dregs of Grace. If you can do anything . . ."

Tylar led the others into a mirror of the stern common room. A deck overlooked a curved wall of glass, the *captain's eye*. But instead of open decking, the space was occupied by an arc of control seats. To the right and left, men fought to wield the starboard and port aeroskimmers. Smoke poured from one side, flames lapped on the other.

In the center, directly ahead, the helmsman sat, strapped to a chair that protruded out over the window, like the bowsprit of a ship. The position gave the man a full view of the city hurtling toward them. His feet worked a set of pedals, his hands a vast wheel. Smoke framed his form. A spat of flames danced under his toes.

It was deathly quiet as the team worked to save the flippercraft, to save the passengers, to save themselves. The captain stood behind his helmsman at the foot of the bowsprit. His brows darkened at the sight of the newcomers.

Tylar had no time for pleasantries. He hurried forward.

Below, the city filled the window.

Tylar recognized immediately the desperation of the captain's plan. The Tigre River lay directly below them. The captain was dropping the flippercraft into the river, plainly hoping to cushion their crash, and in turn, spare the lives of the townsfolk below.

But there was a problem with his plan.

Directly ahead, a massive structure blocked the river. Nine towers and a keep. Chrism's castillion. They were falling too fast. With the aeroskimmers out, they could not swing around. It was a dead man's drop. They might strike the river, but like a skipped stone on a flat pond, they would crash headlong into the keep itself. Though the castillion was raised up on giant pillars to allow river barges to pass beneath, it was not high enough to accommodate the bulk of the flippercraft.

"Captain," Tylar said, "where's your main plumb to the alchemical tank?"

The captain pointed to the left. "We used all our reserves. We have nothing left."

Tylar was already moving. Kathryn followed, along with the captain. They reached the plumb feed used to fill the tanks. It was a column of thick glass, sealed at the top. The entire crew's eyes were on them.

Tylar ordered the captain, "Open the plumb." He turned to Kathryn and bared his wrists. "Your sword. Cut deep."

To her credit, she did not balk. The blade slid free with a flash of silver. With a speed borne of desperation, she thrust her blade's edge across both wrists. She was not gentle. She sliced to bone. Tendons severed. Blood poured.

Tylar swung his arms over the open feeding tube. His blood flowed down the glass, heading for the mekanicals in the ship's belly.

Rogger appeared at his side. "Your Grace's aspect is *water*. Not air. This is no Fin."

"It's about to become one." Tylar nodded to the window, hugging the tube, wrists on fire. The Tigre River swelled out the window. The castillion lay an arrow's shot away.

Tylar closed his eyes and willed his streaming blood. He pictured the crimson river reaching the main mekanicals that flew the ship. He recalled the explosive effect his raw blood had on the Fin as they fled Tangle Reef.

Pure, undiluted power.

He prayed it was enough.

He cast his will along with his blood to the heart of the flippercraft. He flowed his Grace through the mekanicals and over the keel of the craft.

Water . . .

Into an ocean he had been born, birthed as his mother drowned in a sinking scuttlecraft off the Greater Coast. He touched that place, drew upon half memories buried deep within. Water flowed back with his first sensations of this world. He was pushed from warm womb to cold sea.

Falling, falling, falling . . .

He wailed, babe and man. His mouth filled with water, his lungs. Deep in his chest, beyond blood and bone, he felt the daemon respond, stirring and waking. Here, too, water swelled.

Once again, he drowned in it, lived in it, breathed it.

This was his Grace, gifted by Meeryn.

He opened his eyes and stared out at the window. Water filled the world. A moment from striking. But they were one and the same: ship, river, and man.

"Hold fast!" the helmsman screamed.

There was no need. The river accepted its own, opening beneath them, drawing them to its flowing bosom.

The flippercraft fell smoothly into the river's embrace, sinking rather than striking, drawn beneath its waves, joining the strength of its currents.

"The wheel's responding!" the helmsman choked out, trapped between horror and hope.

Rogger yelled back at him. "The castillion!"

Though they had landed, caught by the river itself, Lord Chrism's keep still rushed toward them. The window was three-quarters submerged, but there was enough view out its upper section to see the castillion's massive stone pylons and the lower half of the keep.

"Take the ship *down!*" Rogger screamed, running for the helmsman.

Tylar nodded, too weak to respond . . . or stand. Hugging the plumb tube, he slid down its length, smearing blood. He felt arms catch him. A warm breath touched his ear.

"I have you," Kathryn said.

He nodded again. *Yes, once you did . . .*

Vision narrowing, he saw Rogger yelling at the helmsman, but no words reached him. Still, he watched the waterline climb the window. The flippercraft submerged toward the bottom of the deep river.

The castillion pillars swept toward them, dark shadows in the river. The ship hoved over, turning slightly in the current. The pillars passed to either side. Sunlit waters became murky depths as they dove under the castillion. A grinding scrape shook the ship, coming from topside, as if the upper skin of the flippercraft were being sheared away.

The craft shook and rattled.

Then sunlight bathed down over the hurtling ship.

A cry pierced the pounding in Tylar's ear: "We're under and through!" Cheers followed.

Tylar closed his eyes. He still felt arms around him. He fell into them, gratefully and fully—then slipped away.

"Help me with him!" Kathryn screamed.

She lifted Tylar into her arms, drawing on shadows to give her strength. But she was surprised at how light he was, an empty shell of his former self. Blood ran down his arms, soaking through her cloak.

The captain had beached the flippercraft into a section of docklands, crashing through a few small ferryboats, riding up over a stone pier, and burying its nose onto the shore. Its stern still lay in the water, pulled by the currents. The river threatened to carry the craft back out again.

They did not have much time.

The captain shouted orders, attempting to rein in the growing chaos. A jam of passengers blocked the exit from the captain's deck. Passengers pushed forward from the sinking stern. Some carried baggage in their arms or atop their heads. Others simply clawed and cried their way forward, attempting to reach one of the two flank doors.

Behind them, water flooded in from the shattered rear window, climbing higher and higher, washing up the ship as the river pushed into all compartments. All that had kept them from drowning earlier had been the air trapped inside the flippercraft. And now smoke choked the air, thicker since their landing in the Tigre. River water had doused the flames in the lower holds, but smoke still rose from the smolders and flaming oil slicks.

Kathryn hugged Tylar to her breast, his head hung back, neck exposed. So pale, so pale . . .

She needed to get him to safety. There was no time even to bandage his wrists.

Eylan came to Kathryn's aid. Using the haft of her ax like a cudgel, she forged a brutal path out the captain's cabin and into the hallway. Rogger fell in tow. Gerrod already stood at the hold's doorway, gripped fast with the strength of his mekanicals, a boulder in a river. Once Kathryn reached him, he joined Eylan in wading through the crowd, aiming for the starboard hatch. Sunlight blazed there.

"We must reach the streets as swiftly as possible," Gerrod said. "The entire garrison will be down here to investigate."

Kathryn followed in the pair's wake. Rogger came behind her.

But still the crowds resisted. The water grew deeper, climbing to midthigh. Kathryn did not know when she started crying. But the tears were hot against her cold cheeks. *Don't die . . . not now . . .*

Tylar still breathed, but raspy and coarse, too shallow.

They needed to hurry.

The ship rolled, pushed by the current. Wood ground on stone. Water sloshed, folk fell, some going under, trod on by others. Gerrod helped a little girl, pulling her out of the water by the scruff of her collar. Her father gratefully accepted her back, eyes wide with the panic they all felt. None wanted to be aboard the flippercraft if it should be dragged back and under the river.

The doorway was packed tight with the press of bodies.

It seemed they would never get through.

Then men appeared to either side of Kathryn. They were the ship's crew, armed with staves and poles. She recognized the leader of the men who had guarded the captain's deck.

"Stay with us," he hissed at her.

With barked yells and much poking and striking, the crowd was beaten aside. The crew reached the starboard door and set up a post there. They forced order upon the point of their staves. The way opened. Kathryn and the others were waved through. With some semblance of calm established, the flow of escaping passengers quickened.

Kathryn glanced to the leader of the crewmen.

He met her eyes. "We're in your debt. All of you." His eyes settled to the slack form of Tylar. When he looked back up, there was only sorrow there. He, like Kathryn, knew death.

But Kathryn didn't have to believe it or accept it. She jumped into the river. Waist-deep in its current, she trudged toward shore. By now, half the city seemed to have gathered along the levy.

Off to the left, a glint of armor shone through the rambling crowd.

A troop of castillion guards.

Gerrod led their party away, drifting down the river to the right. They reached shore and climbed out. "Quickly. This way," he said and set off at a fast pace, heading into the dark and narrows of the wharfs.

Eylan stepped to Kathryn's side. "I can take him," she said in a soft voice, very unlike her usual brusqueness.

Still Kathryn shook her head. "I can't . . ." She continued with Tylar, held up by shadow and sorrow.

"We need to find an alchemist," Rogger said. The thief, soaked from crown to heel, looked like a drowned river rat. "Firebalm will heal his wounds in a heartbeat."

"Where?" Kathryn gasped. She did not know the city well.

"No," Gerrod said, stopping in the shadows of an alley. "We've no time." He reached up and pulled down a shirt drying from a window line. His mekanical fingers ripped strips. "Bind his wounds. That will hold for now. And we don't want to leave a blood trail for any hunters to track."

As they packed and cinched the wounds, Gerrod's caution proved warranted. A troop of castillion guards swept down the neighboring street. Kathryn used the alley's shadows and cast her cloak over their huddled party.

"Something has the city stirred up," Gerrod said after the guards passed. "The response to the crash was too swift. All the city's garrisons must have already been on the street."

"Why the activity?" Rogger asked.

Gerrod gained his feet. "Word of the godslayer's arrival must have reached the wrong ears."

Kathryn agreed. They had no way of knowing how things had fared back at Tashijan. Once she was found to be missing, it would take Argent ser Fields only a short time to discern they had fled by the dawn flippercraft.

With Tylar's wounds bound, they set off again.

"Where now?" Rogger asked.

"To where we were originally headed," Gerrod answered. He pointed upward, to a pair of towers a quarter reach away. It was the Conclave of Chrismferry. "We came to question a healer . . . now we need him even more."

❖

Dart crowded the window with Laurelle. They stared off toward the castillion and the Tigre River. A trail of smoke rose from the near shore. Moments ago, all had heard a deep low boom, thunder in sunlight. Dart had been nearest the window. A quick glance out revealed a geyser of water exploding up from the Tigre, not far from where the river disappeared under Chrism's castillion.

A distant crash of stone echoed.

From their height and position, Dart watched something massive shoot out from under the main keep, a huge boat, nothing like she had ever seen, a wooden whale. It trailed fire and smoke, rocketing forth. Then it vanished behind the dockworks on this side of the river. The subsequent crash could not be mistaken, billowing up with fresh smoke. The strange craft had struck the wharf area.

"A flippercraft," Yaellin had said dourly.

Dart scrunched her brow. A flippercraft? What was one of the air ships doing in the river? Had it fallen out of the skies?

Laurelle stayed close to Dart. For too long, both had been jangled by the terror and hopelessness of their plight. Holing up here offered no comfort. Now stopped, tensions grew as their reality sunk home. They were outcasts, fugitives. A life of easy luxury and respect had been shattered in one night.

Dart pushed open the window, needing fresh air. Laurelle leaned against her. Her fingers found Dart's.

Across the short way to the river, shouts reached them, along with the shrill whistles of the water wagons. A pair of mekanical flutterseats whisked out from under the castillion and sped over the water. They bore the gold and crimson of Chrism's guard.

"What do you think happened?" Laurelle asked.

"A crash," Yaellin said behind them. His voice had hardened.

Laurelle glanced to him, hearing his worry. "What . . . do you think it concerns us?"

Yaellin answered with a darkened countenance. He kept his sword upon Paltry, even though the man's hands had been bound behind his back and tied to the bed's head rails.

Dart kept her vigil at the window. It was as if now the very skies were falling.

Paltry stirred on the bed, working his shoulders. "It was the flipper-craft bearing the contingent from Tashijan, wasn't it?" he said with thick disdain. "Your friends. Your allies. Those who came to help you."

Dart glanced back at Yaellin, praying he would discount Paltry's words. Instead, Yaellin remained silent.

Paltry laughed, but with no humor, only satisfaction. He took strength from their despair and glanced to Dart. "The abomination will be slain. I failed once in my duty. But now the great weight and wheel of Chrismferry will crush you."

As his words sank home, Dart's heart stopped beating. *I failed once in my duty.* She pictured kindly Master Willym falling atop her, his blood washing hotly over her. Murdered. A bolt meant for her.

Laurelle realized the same. Fire entered her voice. "*You!* You hired the assassin."

"And it was gold poorly spent. I took great care to hire the best black-foot, to get him placed in the shadows, to arrange his flight afterward. And what did I get for my efforts? The abomination still lives." His gaze poisoned upon Dart.

"You killed Master Willym," Dart said coldly.

"An unfortunate consequence. But the old man had been burned by Grace for so long, he didn't have long to live."

Dart remembered the former Hand's last word.

Beware . . .

Had Willym known about Chrism, suspected something? Had he tried to warn her? She remembered, as she struggled from beneath him, a last glimpse into the dying man's eyes. A sudden clarity and horror. She had thought it was the sight of his own death—but now she knew what it was. It was the break of some charm, a curse lifted, a yoke shattered. Willym had been ensorcelled, his will and memories bent. Such black alchemies were not beyond the corrupted. Only his death had set him free.

Had the same been intended for her? She pictured Chrism and Mistress Naff sneaking from her room and shuddered.

"You'll never escape," Paltry continued, drawing back Dart's gaze. "There's nowhere you can hide for long."

A sudden knocking proved his words, firm and hard, shaking the door. "Open the way!" a voice commanded, ringing with authority.

Laurelle clutched Dart.

Paltry smiled. "It's already too late."

Yaellin crossed to the door. He pulled up his hood and hooked his masklin back in place, completing his disguise as a Shadowknight. "One word," he spat at Paltry, "and it will be the last to fall from your lips." Yaellin bared a throwing dagger. He held it with deadly competence.

The pounding repeated. "Open for the injured! A great mishap has struck the river!"

Dart glanced to the open window and back to the barred door. Of all the times for broken men and women to fall at the Conclave's door. They couldn't refuse care. But how could they untie Paltry to ministrate?

They were trapped.

Paltry's grin widened.

Yaellin reached the door and slid back a tiny spy hole to peer out into the hall. Dart saw him stiffen in surprise. Shadows, quiet a moment ago, billowed out anew about his form in agitation. Yaellin turned his masked face back to Paltry. His eyes narrowed. The blade was lifted higher, the threat plain.

Not a word.

Yaellin nodded to Dart. "Help me with the bar."

Dart hesitated, legs locked in terror. Then she hurried forward. Laurelle hung back, a fist clutched to her throat. Dart lifted the stoutoak bar with both hands, then stepped aside at Yaellin's urging.

She crept back, still holding the bar. She would use it if necessary as a club.

Yaellin slipped the latch, then pulled the door open a short space. He spent a moment searching the hall, blocking the way.

Dart heard Matron Grannice's voice.

"Healer Paltry will take good care of your man," the matron promised.

"Thank you most kindly," a woman answered, sounding strained.

"It is an honor, Castellan Vail."

Yaellin opened the door wider, plainly having waited for Matron Grannice to step away and return below. A motley group pushed into the room.

Dart fell back.

In the lead, a man of solid bronze entered the room. A soft purring accompanied his every step. The torchlight ran over his form like liquid fire. He led another Shadowknight, cloaked and masked, but obviously a woman. She wore a diadem at her throat, bright as a star in the night sky.

But Dart's attention fell more upon the man whom she carried in her arms like a babe. He wore a simple brown servant's robe, the hood thrown back. Blood soaked both arms. His wrists were tied with soiled red rags. His face, pale as soapstone, looked like that of a porcelain doll: fragile, drained. The only assurance that he still lived was the ragged, wet rattle of his breath.

Yaellin followed her. "Kathryn . . . what happened?"

Dart noted the last two figures to enter the room. Opposites in the extreme. A young woman and a bearded older man, one tall, one slight, one fierce and stolid in countenance, the other hiding an edge of wry amusement.

The bearded stranger closed the door. His eyes fell on Dart. He held out a hand.

She didn't know what he wanted.

"The door's bar, little lass. We mustn't let anyone wander in here."

Dart jumped and passed him the length of stoutoak. He secured the door with a wink toward Dart. She found herself warming to the man, surprised at herself.

Voices drew their attention to the room's center.

The woman lowered her charge to an empty bed. He sprawled boneless on the down mattress. "We need the healer's attention," she said. "He's lost most of his blood."

The woman stepped back and revealed a strange sight. The man's robe had a blackened hole in the center, down to the bare skin. Centered in the hole, tattooed on the man's chest, was a black handprint. A strange glow marked its edges. And if Dart stared long enough, she could almost see the surface of the print stirring, as if something rippled past, under the dark surface, disturbing the black well there.

Dart found it hard to look away. Her feet drew her closer. One of her hands even reached out.

"Who is he?" Yaellin asked

The woman's answer stayed Dart's hand.

"He's the godslayer."

❖

"Firebalm won't stop the bleeding from a slash this deep," the healer said darkly, plainly reluctant to touch a man with such a dreaded reputation.

Kathryn shoved the man. "Do it." She'd already heard a threadbare account of Healer Paltry's crimes and duplicity and had no time for his hesitation or tongue.

He stumbled to Tylar's bedside. He bore a pot of firebalm in one hand. Yaellin kept a sword to the man's back. Rogger had cut away Tylar's old bandages, exposing the raw wounds. Blood again flowed from them, but pumping weaker than before. Tylar's heart had fallen to a fluttering beat.

Paltry scooped a dab of balm.

"More," Rogger said from across the bed. "Like you said, this is no scratch."

The healer glowered, then dug a more generous amount. He cradled Tylar's gaping wrist in one hand, then smeared the balm with the other. With its touch, a fierce glow erupted, shining with familiar Grace.

Paltry jerked his hands away in surprise. A soft moan escaped Tylar, sounding more pleasurable than the usual reaction to the sting of firebalm.

The glow quickly faded, vanishing away as the peeled edges of skin, muscle, and tendon drew together like so much molded clay. In a moment, the wrist had closed without even a scar.

"The other," Kathryn said.

Paltry grabbed more balm, no longer reluctant. His eyes shone with natural curiosity. Monster or not, he was still a healer.

"Impressive, is it not?" Rogger said as the other wrist mended. "The gifted Grace in his blood does much to protect him. But it can't replace what he left behind at the flippercraft."

"Blessed bloodroot," Gerrod said, straightening after studying the miraculous healing with keen eyes. "Its curative Grace will flush the bone's marrow and encourage new humour to fill his heart and veins."

Paltry nodded. "But it will only—"

Yaellin silenced him with a poke of his sword point. The healer needed no other encouragement. He crossed to the apothecary cabinet mounted along one wall of the circular healing chamber. He lifted the crystal lid and shook free a few dried stalks into a glass crucible.

"Where did you obtain this bloodroot?" Yaellin asked.

Paltry set about grinding the root with a glass pestle. A faint bluish glow rose along with a scent of copper and mint. "It comes from the Eldergarden. I harvested it myself."

"Where?"

"From the healer's garden. In the shadow of the sacred myrrwood."

Yaellin knocked aside the crucible with the back of his hand. It shattered against the wall.

Kathryn frowned. "What?"

"It might be corrupted, like the tree in the garden. I don't think it would be wise to expose the godslayer to it."

Yaellin had already given an abbreviated account of his escape with the girls . . . and of Lord Chrism's corruption. The world seemed to grow darker with each breath. Kathryn waved the healer away.

"Fine," Paltry said. "I have some older vine from the Ninth Land. Is that far enough away from the Eldergarden?"

"Fetch it," Yaellin commanded. "And be quick about it."

As the healer set to work again, using a smaller set of wan-looking vines, Yaellin explained. "The corruption in Myrillia is more deeply rooted than any suspected, even my own father."

Gerrod joined them. "Maybe we'd all best discover what each knows. It seems multiple threads are woven to this same spot. But where to begin?"

Kathryn nodded to Yaellin. "I think your story is the oldest, the closest to the beginning."

He sighed. "Yes, my story may be the oldest . . . with threads that stretch even farther, back to before any of us. But what I know personally started twelve years ago."

"What?"

"An emissary arrived in Tashijan, sent to my father in secret. Sent from the hinterlands. A call for help."

"From whom?" Gerrod asked.

"From one of the rogue gods that roam that unsettled land."

"A rogue?" Kathryn stirred. The gods of the hinterlands were little more than raving beasts, committing horrible acts upon those who should cross their paths. Few lived who ever met a rogue god. The Shadow-knights themselves had first been established as border guards to keep the taint of the rogues from passing out of their lands and into the settled realms. Why would a rogue be contacting their enemy?

Yet even this curiosity could not keep Kathryn from watching the healer crush the root to a powder, then pour it into a cup of water. Her concern for Tylar weighed too heavily on her heart. With the elixir prepared, Eylan helped lift Tylar up while Paltry poured the contents down Tylar's throat.

He did not resist. Half the elixir spilled over Tylar's chin and down his chest. Once finished, Tylar was laid back to his bed.

Kathryn settled to the cot's edge.

The talk had quieted. All watched.

"I can't help more here," Paltry said after there appeared to be no response. The miracle of the firebalm did not seem to be shared by the bloodroot. "He'll have to be moved to the main physik in the Cobbleshores district. They have blessed swine in their pens for blood drafting. That's where he should be."

Kathryn watched Tylar's chest rise and fall. At some point, she had taken his hand, but she couldn't say when. Was he breathing slightly more deeply? Did his lips have a touch more color? Or was it merely her heart wanting it to be true?

"While we keep watch," Gerrod said, turning back to Yaellin, "tell us more about this visitor to your father."

Yaellin nodded. "The emissary came to my father's room in the dead of night, bearing disturbing tidings. Three pieces of information that would set my father on a course that I believe has led us all here."

Everyone gathered closer. Even the two young girls watched from the room's corner.

"First, the rogue's emissary was one of the Wyr," Yaellin said, nodding to Eylan. "They of all people still occasionally made contact with the maddened ones. She came with a secret kept hidden for millennia, a secret known only to the rogues. Unlike our settled gods who are bound to their realms, unable to leave their lands, rogues still roam. It is such lack of rooting that leads to the raving found among the rogues. Their Grace burns through them. They have no outlet for release. No land in which to ground their Grace. It maddens them."

Kathryn nodded, still focused on Tylar.

"But what the rogues have kept hidden deep in their hinterlands is a secret none suspected. Free to roam, both male and female gods, they have borne children."

Kathryn glanced hard at Yaellin, attempting to read the man. "Impossible. Grace destroys such seeds in the womb."

Yaellin shook his head. "In a coupling between god and man, yes. But not so with two gods. Such children do sometimes survive, though it is a rarity. Only a couple times each millennia. The last child was born over four hundred years ago. And that is the crux of the problem. Most of these children were slain at birth, first in fear, then in envy."

"Envy?" Rogger asked.

"Such children are not like the other Myrillian gods. They are born, but they were never sundered. They are purer than either sire or dam.

They are of flesh, but also carry with them those parts all others lost to the naether and aether. They are whole . . . in a manner."

"Unsundered," Gerrod whispered, dread and awe in his voice.

"Almost." Yaellin said. "But it was enough for all such offspring to be slain. Savaged and hacked beyond healing. Then four hundred years ago, one of their children, a boy, was stolen, kidnapped, before it could be slain. It took the rogues a full year, as maddened as they are at most times, to discover the child's fate. The boy's desiccated and mummified remains were discovered in the hinterlands of the Fourth Lands. His heart was missing."

"Who did this?" Kathryn asked. "Who performed such a black rite?" She could not help but picture the young knight sprawled in a circle of his own blood, his chest cleaved open.

"All the hinterland rogues could discover was a name: *the Cabal.*"

"What did they want with the boy?" Gerrod asked.

Yaellin shook his head. "It was never discovered for certain. But the rogue who sent the emissary had a suspicion. She believed the boy's murder was tied back to the Godsword."

"Rivenscryr," Rogger said.

"The old Littick name for the sword," Yaellin agreed. "The emissary revealed a second black secret concerning the Godsword. The weapon that shattered their world had been forged in their own *blood.* According to the rogue, the sword, once wielded and spent, needed fresh blood, the blood of an *intact* god, a god from their original kingdom, someone unsundered. Blood from a sundered god lacked something vital to enliven the sword. So after the Sundering, when the gods came to Myrillia, the weapon proved useless. No sundered god could whet it back into existence. It became a weapon without substance."

"A sword of light and shadow," Gerrod intoned, repeating the words Pryde Manthion used to describe and name the great weapon.

Yaellin nodded. "The rogue who sent the warning believed that the Cabal had stolen the infant godling in an attempt to forge anew the Godsword. The boy's body had been drained of all blood. Such blood could bring Rivenscryr back into this world, a weapon that could shatter worlds."

Silence settled over the room.

"But there was a last warning from this rogue god," Yaellin continued, voice lowering. "A new babe had been born to the rogues, a babe born to the same god who sent the emissary. She could not see her child slain. Although half-maddened by wild Grace, she was still a mother. She feared for her infant's safety. So she asked my father to come for her baby. To steal the child away before anyone knew of its existence. To keep her baby safe among the settled god-realms of Myrillia."

"And he did that?" Kathryn asked, aghast.

"He took a cadre of knights and a woman who knew the hinterlands well, my own mother, the mistress of this school. They had a harrowing journey. It seemed word had leaked to the Cabal. My father and mother barely escaped with the child, losing all their guards to the fell beasts of the Cabal."

"What became of the child?" Gerrod asked.

Yaellin turned and faced one of the two girls, the smaller of the two, with straw-colored hair. Her eyes were wide with dawning horror. "My father hid her here."

Dart stared back at Yaellin. *No . . . it was all a lie . . . impossible.*

Laurelle stepped from her side, stumbling back.

"I'm only a girl," Dart answered in a squeaky tight voice.

Yaellin came to her, dropping to a knee. "Yes, you are." He took her hand. She barely felt his touch. "You are flesh like any other girl." He squeezed to emphasize it. "Never let anyone tell you otherwise. But I'm afraid you must know deep in your heart that you're different. Not worse, not better even. Just different."

She attempted to pull her hand free—not so much to escape him as his words. But she couldn't so easily escape her heart. He was right. She had always known she was different. And it wasn't just the presence of Pupp, her ghostly companion. She always felt the outsider, the girl looking in through a window at the simple lives of the other girls. Still, how could she be a god?

Yaellin continued his explanation. "Dart was hidden at the school, in plain sight. Only two folks ever knew about her. My father and mother. I don't know when they were planning on revealing her true heritage to her." He glanced at Dart with sorrow. "Ser Henri did not reveal himself to be my father until I was about your age. I suppose he was not very good at . . . revealing difficult truths. I'm sorry you had to learn of your own parentage in such an ill manner as this."

Dart simply shook her head, still denying, waiting to wake up from this unending nightmare. A tear rolled down her cheek. Then fingers wrapped around her hand. She turned. It was Laurelle, returned to her side. Fingers squeezed. She drew great comfort, but the tears flowed heavier.

Yaellin continued, facing the others again. "Knowledge of the girl's identity and location died with my mother and father. But when I heard of the explosion of the illuminaria during the testing of Dart, I knew the girl must be someone special. None but a god could cause such a reaction. So I investigated with dream alchemies and discovered the truth."

Master Gerrod stirred from his station. "And I suspect you were not the only one investigating the incident." He glanced to Healer Paltry. "Another's curiosity was aroused."

Paltry had been standing near the back, watched by the tall swordswoman. He seemed to shrink in on himself.

The bronze figure stepped toward the healer. "You sent her blood to Tashijan, to Castellan Mirra. You came in the thick of the night, in secret. Why?"

Paltry had a sick pall to his face by now. "I . . . I made inquiries after what happened here. I dared not be too bold because . . . because . . ."

"Because of your complicity in raping young children," the master said bluntly.

Dart felt a surge of raw fury, drying the flow of her tears. One hand still held Laurelle's, but her other fell to the hilt of the dagger Yaellin had given her.

Paltry looked away. "After the girl was chosen, I sent word to the Council at Tashijan, asking the masters a theoretical question about what might have happened. I was surprised to hear back from the castellan. But then again, she was once a master herself. She asked me to bring a test of the girl's blood. So I stole one of her soiled undergarments. The girl claimed she was bleeding from her menstra, but . . . but . . ."

"You knew better," Gerrod said. "You knew of the harm done to her."

Dart's fingers tightened on her dagger's hilt.

Paltry ignored the accusation and spoke to the floor. "I took the soiled garment to Castellan Mirra, following her order of secrecy."

Master Gerrod turned to the woman seated beside the godslayer. "It is no wonder I could not match the blood to any of the Hundred, yet it tested like that of a god."

His gaze fell upon Dart's figure. Though he was cased in bronze, there was a kind concern in his eyes. She wanted to run into his arms, to have those armored arms protect her. Or maybe it was just that his bronze form reminded her of Pupp, of his security. The loss of her friend ached inside her.

But Gerrod was not done with Paltry. "What happened after that?"

"I . . . I heard back from Castellan Mirra. She claimed the girl was an abomination. She expressed fear of some plot against Chrism."

"If Henri had not informed her of the girl," Master Gerrod said, "I could see Mirra making that mistake, the same as I did with the blood. And with Henri's recent death, she must have assumed the worst."

Yaellin stirred. "So you attempted to kill Dart. Why?"

"I was so ordered. Castellan Mirra sent gold and names among the blackfeet. She asked me to stay my hand until she could investigate further. She seemed to fear some faction at Tashijan."

"The Fiery Cross," Castellan Vail mumbled.

Gerrod fixed Paltry with a cold stare. "Did Mirra ever contact you again?"

"No, she disappeared . . . vanished at Tashijan. I assumed something had happened. I had no choice but to continue with her plan to kill the abomination. It was for the good of Myrillia." Paltry puffed up at this last bit.

The master made a rude noise. "Rather, it fit *your* plans just fine. You didn't want the young girl's rape being discovered. What if she talked? So you carried forward the assassination anyway."

Dart's head spun with the stories being told.

"But she lived," Yaellin said. "And the story of the illuminaria did not escape the attention of Mistress Naff. She must have told Chrism of the incident. They must have started to suspect the truth."

"And they didn't know before this," the bearded man said, turning toward Dart. "Seems strange that a child Ser Henri hid from the Cabal ends up back on their doorstep, and they're none the wiser."

"Perhaps not so strange," Master Gerrod said. "Remember, it was an Oracle that chose her. Such men and women are tied to the deepest desires of the gods they serve. The one who chose Dart must have made his choice based on Chrism's deep-seated craving for the blood of a godling. The Oracle must have blindly sensed something about the girl with his Grace-blessed senses. Especially as it was the Hand of Blood for which she was picked. A very appropriate choice, considering the circumstances and his master's desires."

Again a heavy silence weighed upon the room.

The man with the beard tugged at his whiskers. "According to Master Gerrod's ancient texts, Chrism arrived here with the Godsword. And we came here hoping he still had it or knew where to find it. But now we discover he's corrupted, a part of this Cabal, if not its leader." He turned to Yaellin. "When did you begin to suspect Chrism?"

"Only seven days ago. He hides himself well. But over the past few moons, I had noted strange happenings at the High Wing. Hands seemed to be burning faster, aging quicker. Strange dreams plagued us all. At first,

I attributed it to the same malaise spreading over Myrillia. But then I discovered more and more Cabalists appearing near the castillion, acting more boldly, hardly hiding their allegiances. They seemed to be focused on the Eldergarden. Fearing some foul mischief, I ventured into the deep wood, all the way to the Heartwood. As the Hand of Black Bile, it was an easy thing to anoint myself with nullifying alchemies and move past Chrism's wards unseen. There, to my horror, I discovered the corruption. With my father dead and Castellan Mirra gone, I didn't know whom to trust."

Yaellin glanced to Castellan Vail. "And when Argent ser Fields, my father's enemy, chose you as the new castellan, I feared you might have been corrupted. I was seeing Cabalists everywhere. So instead, I pursued my dead father's wishes. To protect the Godsword from the Cabal. I watched Chrism closely, dogging his steps in secret. I hoped to discover where the Godsword might be hidden. To steal it if I could. I've even searched his rooms twice." He shook his head. "To no avail."

Dart remembered Yaellin sneaking out of Chrism's chambers. He had been seeking the sword. If they hadn't followed him . . .

Master Gerrod paced around the circular room, slowly, methodically. "Which brings us to the death of Meeryn. She must have learned about Chrism. He must have sent that black naether-spawn to slay her, to silence her. But how did it kill her?"

The answer came from an unexpected source. "With the Godsword," the man in the bed said, pushing up on one elbow. He opened eyes a startling storm-gray in color. How long had he been feigning sleep?

Dart took a worried step backward.

"Tylar . . ." Castellan Vail said with relief.

He held her back with a nod, a silent assurance that he was all right. "The beast had a weapon," he continued. "I saw it. A lance of silver that seemed ghostly yet potent."

"Rivenscryr," Yaellin said. "Chrism must have been able to forge it."

"With the blood of the infant boy," Tylar said, demonstrating how much he had overheard. "They must have a small cache still left."

"But the source is too meager for them to show themselves," Master Gerrod said. "They still move in secret."

"For now." Tylar's gray eyes found Dart. "I think that was why Ser Henri kept this child alive . . . in secret. He could've slain her to keep her blood from ever falling into the Cabal's hands, but he knew eventually a war would arise, a new War of the Gods here on Myrillia. And he wanted our side to have a way to wield the Godsword. So he placed a guard upon the one god who had knowledge of the sword." Tylar nodded to Yaellin, then turned to Dart. "And he locked away a source of blood to fuel the sword."

Dart felt a growing horror at his words. Tylar continued to stare at her, sorrowfully yet fiercely.

"So what do we do?" Castellan Vail asked.

"We do what we all must. I was named a godslayer. Now I must become one in truth." He finally faced the others. "We must kill Lord Chrism."

FIFTH

War of the Gods

"There came a grate splitting of the sky. A thunderclap felled all to their knays. The rott'd trees cracked. The birds of the aer did stryke the ground, which did shake and growl like a beast in payn. Waters flooded their banks and drown'd the land. The sun did flare with grate fyre and fury. And the blue sky went the black of a bruise.

"And in that trembling light, he fell to the mount, to his knays, a grate lord of blood and bone, bearing a sword of light and shadow. He sayd unto me, 'Lo, all is at an end.'"

—Pryde Manthion, the last human king
Shadowfall [Book of Fyre, lin. 103–104]

22

UNDER THE RAVEN'S EYE

TYLAR SIPPED THE DRAFT OF BLOODVINE, BITTER BUT SWEETENED WITH honey. It was his third dousing. He held the mug with two hands, needing both. A shiver from his bones threatened to shake his frame, but he contained it.

Kathryn sat on the neighboring bed. He felt her eyes on him, a steady watch, as if expecting him to swoon at any moment. Upon his waking, she had tried to comfort him with her soothing hands and whispered words, but it grew too difficult for them both. Such intimacy was still beyond them, confused by old familiarity and new awkwardness.

And for the moment, more important matters had to be settled.

It was nigh on midday and a plan had yet to be worked that held any chance of victory. They had debated and strategized. How did one reach Lord Chrism with untold legions of ilk-beasts guarding his grounds and an entire castillion garrison roused to alert? And once cornered, how did one slay a god corrupted by Dark Grace and wielding untold power?

Tylar studied the room over his mug. They were too few: a thief, a warrior woman, a wise man in bronze, two Shadowknights . . . and two frightened girls.

Gerrod knelt with Dart. He peered into her eyes with a dark lens. Earlier he had pricked her finger and dabbed her blood upon a crystal wafer. He, with the assistance of the healer, had tested the girl as bell after bell chimed the passing morning.

He lowered his scope. "Thank you, Dart. That'll be all."

She nodded and scooted to the other end of the bed. Her friend sat down next to her. They leaned close to each other, like two frightened rabbits, eyes fixed and glassy. Tylar could only imagine such terror. His upbringing among the orphanages of Akkabak Harbor had not been easy, but it was nothing compared to the experiences of the two girls here.

Gerrod stepped over to Tylar. Kathryn sat straighter on the next cot.

The master shook his head. "Most strange. I can detect Grace in her blood, faint yet certainly present. But it is oddly and persistently inert. No alchemies can stir it or react to it. I've searched for any trace of quickening in her body, some faint glow at the back of the eyes, any sign that Grace manifests in the girl. But I've discovered nothing. It's as if she has no ability to bless or utilize her Grace, not within herself and certainly not without."

"So is she a god or not?" Kathryn asked.

"Not as we know a god to be. It is said that the gods, before the great Sundering of their own kingdom, bore no special Grace. That only after their naethryn and aethryn aspects were stripped from them did the remaining flesh quicken with humoral Graces. Masters have debated the reason for this over the many centuries. It is supposed that a god's Grace manifests from some ethereal connection that persists between the gods of Myrillia and their torn counterparts, a bleeding of power that still flows through all three."

"And the girl?" Rogger asked, joining them. He settled next to Kathryn on the cot.

"She is unsundered," Gerrod said. "Whole. I think that is why she does not manifest with any significant Grace. But I would know more about this creature that accompanies her."

"Pupp," the girl, Dart, said from the neighboring bed. Despite her frightened countenance, she had been listening intently. "His name is Pupp."

Gerrod shifted. "What can you tell me about him?" Tylar noted his calm demeanor and lack of condescension when dealing with the girl.

She licked her lips. "He's always been with me." She glanced over to Yaellin. He guarded the door, periodically checking the hallway, while Eylan kept a watchful eye on the healer. "Even as a babe, he was with me."

Yaellin nodded. "I saw him in her dreams. Ugly fellow. Fiery eyes. All molten and barely formed."

Dart's eyes hardened.

"He's not ugly," the second girl declared, coming to her friend's defense. "He's . . . he's . . . *fearsome*."

"I thought no one could see this creature?" Kathryn said.

Dart glanced to Kathryn. The girl's gaze was steady. There was certainly a well of strength in her small frame. "Only I can see him at most times. And even I can't touch him then. Only stone seems to block him."

"And he's trapped in the Eldergarden?" Tylar asked, having heard their story.

The girl nodded with a pained look of worry.

"And when was the first time, this creature . . . this Pupp . . . revealed himself to other than yourself?" Gerrod asked.

The girl's steadiness faltered. Her eyes sank to the floor. She seemed to collapse into herself.

Gerrod continued with reassuring tones. "You're among friends, Dart. We wouldn't ask this of you unless it was important."

She kept her eyes down. Her voice was a whisper. "It was with Master Willet . . . up . . . up in the rookery."

Dart swallowed. She let go her last secret reluctantly. Fury had given her strength before to accuse Paltry, to tell what had happened to her, but now she must reveal the end. "Master Willet . . ."

She spotted Healer Paltry leaning forward. His eyes were sharp, his lips thin. How long must he have wondered what had become of his cohort? His face shone with oil. How had she ever considered him handsome?

She turned away and took a deeper breath. "Pupp attacked him, protecting me."

"I thought—"

She cut off Master Gerrod. If she stopped her words now, she might never finish them. "It was my blood . . . my virginal blood." She choked on this last. So much had been stolen from her, more than she could measure. Would the pain ever end? "Pupp bathed himself in it. I think he knew the touch of my blood gave substance to his form. He blazed with fire and tore into Willet."

Dart was drawn back to the rookery, to the blood, to the break of bone, to the sear of flesh, to the boil of blood . . . "All was consumed," she said. "Gone. Not even blood stained the planks."

No one spoke.

The silence drew Dart back to the room. She saw the look of horror on Paltry's face. She found no satisfaction in it.

"And Pupp?" Gerrod asked.

Dart shook her head. "Once the blood dried from him, he became a ghost again."

Yaellin spoke from the door. "My father, Ser Henri, knew of Pupp. Dart used to speak of her ghostly pet, before others ridiculed and chided her into silence and secrets. My father believed her companion might be some amalgam of Dart's naethryn and aethryn selves. Born whole, Dart was not stripped of these parts. Yet they remain not fully of this world either. They cling to her."

Dart listened, balanced between horror and understanding. She and Pupp had always been one, but she never suspected how much of a *one* they were. If the others were right, Pupp was as much a part of her as her leg or arm.

Gerrod nodded. "And her blood has the Grace to pull this part of her fully into our world."

"Not just *her* blood," Yaellin countered. Dart had already told him about the drop of Chrism's blood striking Pupp, and the blood roots down in the subterranean passage. "*Any* blood rich enough with Grace. Pupp just needs fuel to cross the barrier into substance."

"Such strangeness abounds," Gerrod concluded.

The castellan rose from the cot. "Which does not settle the matter of Chrism and what we might do about this Cabal. We cannot hide forever in this cell."

Dart listened with half an ear as more discussions and plans were weighed, balanced, and discarded. She found tears coming again to her eyes. She could not say why. They rose from the hollowness inside her. She did not fully know who she was any more: girl, god, or monster.

She stared at her hands, blurred by her tears. They seemed a stranger's now.

A second pair of hands covered hers, grasping. She lifted her gaze to find Laurelle close to her, staring back at her. "It doesn't matter," her friend said. There was no horror in her eyes. "None of this matters. I know you." She squeezed her fingers. "This is the Dart I know. You've shown your heart in the past and now. The rest is just shadow and light."

Dart sniffed and took Laurelle's hand in her own. She so wanted it to be true. But she had only to hear the others discuss slaying a god to know that there were matters greater than flesh . . . even her own. And she had a role to play. Dart had no say in her birth, even her years in the Conclave were ordered and orchestrated by others. But no longer. From here, she would have to forge her own path. It was for her to decide.

Girl, god, or monster.

❖

Kathryn shook her head. "This is madness. We must wait on others. Bring full forces to bear. We can't lay siege on the castillion with just the handful here."

Tylar stood. Kathryn noted the wobble in his knees, though Tylar tried to hide it with a wave of his arm.

"Chrism will not wait," he argued. "He knows he's been exposed. If he has not found us by sunset, there is no accounting of what he might do. He could unleash all manner of horror in the city. Or he could merely escape with his Cabal, hiding away, disappearing with the Godsword. He'd be a thousandfold more difficult to root out."

"You propose going in on our own?" she said. "With no knowledge of what may lay in wait?"

"If we could only find the Godsword . . ." Tylar grumbled.

Yaellin spoke from the doorway. "I've searched everywhere for the weapon. It's nowhere to be—"

Distant shouts silenced the man. All eyes turned to the door.

Yaellin swung to the spy hole. "It's coming from down the stairs. I'll check." He lifted the bar and pulled the latch. He vanished in a whirl of cloak and shadow.

With the door cracked, the heavy tread of boots on stone echoed up from below. Surely it was the castillion guard. Orders were shouted to search every floor. This was no random search.

"We've been found," Tylar said.

Kathryn slid free her sword. Others did the same. There was no escape up the tower. They'd have to fight their way to the streets.

Kathryn called up the power in her cloak, billowing darkness around her form. They had to get Tylar safely away . . . and the girl. The child could not be captured, returned to Chrism's reach. With such a source of blood, the Godsword would be Chrism's to wield. That must not happen.

Glancing over a shoulder, Kathryn spotted the girl crouched with her friend. She had a dagger in hand and a fierce set to her eyes.

Shadows suddenly shifted behind the girl's shoulders.

Oh no . . .

❖

Darkness fell across Dart, drawing her eye to the sunlit window nearby. She had left the window open after watching the flippercraft crash earlier. A naked shape crept over the sill, claws digging into stone, eyes glowing with grace. Smoke steamed its form.

An ilk-beast.

The creature leaped into the room—toward Laurelle, the closest to the window.

Dart screamed as the creature struck her friend, knocking her to the bed. Another pair of creatures filled the window, crawling in from either side, misshapen horrors. At the same time, windows shattered around the room. More ilk-beasts boiled in from all sides.

Dart lunged toward the nearest, the one tangled with Laurelle. Her friend kicked and bit, turning as feral as the creature that attacked her. But a swipe of claws ripped her robe and drew bloody furrows across her chest. Laurelle cried out.

Dart already had her cursed dagger in hand. She plunged it to the hilt in the monster's back. It reared up, tearing the blade from Dart's grasp. The beast struggled for the impaled dagger, writhing to reach it. It screamed, but all that came out was fire. Its body stiffened with pain, a statue of agony.

Laurelle kicked out at it from the bed. Her heel struck its form and it shattered to ash, blowing outward. A reek of charred flesh whelmed over them.

Dart joined Laurelle, dropping behind the edge of the bed, ducking almost under it.

Around the room, a dance of blades held the ilk-beasts in check. The castellan swirled in and out of shadow, dealing death with swift skill. The tall Wyr-mistress had a sword in each fist, lunging and stabbing in all directions, seeming to have eyes in the back of her head. Even the godslayer wielded a blade in one hand and a dagger in the other, his back to the bearded man who fought with a broken chair leg, sharp as a spear.

But more and more beasts crawled and scrambled into the chamber.

Dart blindly searched the hot ash pile for her dagger. Despite her terror, she dug with care. It would not do to prick her finger on its black tip.

"Make for the door!" Master Gerrod called to them. His bronze form had sprouted sharp blades at elbows and knees. He held the legion at bay from Dart's corner.

Laurelle grabbed Dart's arm. She pointed under the bed.

Dart abandoned her search and belly-crawled with Laurelle beneath the bed to its other side. They waited for a clear moment, then shoved across the open space to the next cot, diving beneath it and crawling toward the far door. They waited until the fighting ebbed away from the entry.

"Now," Dart urged.

The two girls rolled out and to their feet. Hand in hand, they raced for the door and through it. The hallway echoed with the fighting, but it was thankfully empty. They fled down its length, realizing that the clash of swords grew louder again only as they neared the stairwell.

Their feet slowed.

More fighting ahead. Yaellin must be holding the stairs.

The scrape of claw on stone drew their attention behind them. Laurelle let out a small whimper.

Climbing down the corridor, a lone ilk-beast had followed them into the hallway, a cat chasing two fleeing mice. On all fours, it was massively muscled, naked of all clothing. Its skin ran with black mottles. Its muzzled face held a fixed snarl, revealing daggered fangs. Fiery eyes stared at them.

Trapped between the two battles—stair and chamber—there was nowhere to run. Dart pawed her belted sheath. They had no weapons.

The beast let out a growl and stalked toward them.

Tylar stabbed a beast through the eye. From the bared breasts, it was once a woman. But her skin had hardened to scale, her fingers to bony claws. Oil cast the nails in a poisonous sheen. But the worst was her face: slitted eyes aglow with a yellowish flame, nostrils flared for scenting, jaws shaped like an adder, full of fangs.

With a grunt, Tylar yanked his blade free. The beast fell, convulsing on the stone floor. A hissing wail flowed forth. Even in death, the creature remained a monster, its human self burned away forever by corrupted Grace.

Tylar felt a mix of sorrow and fury. What could drive someone to yield all of themselves to such a defilement? He remembered Darjon's shout. *Myrillia will be free!* He stepped over the dead body. She was certainly free now.

The battle raged. The air reeked of burst bowels and blood. The room echoed with wails and shrieks of the raving.

But Tylar dared not call forth his daemon. With fighting in such close quarters, friend as well as foe could find themselves brushed with the deadly touch of the naethryn. So he fought, Rogger on one side, Kathryn on the other. Gerrod and Eylan were another island of resistance across the room.

"Make for the door!" he yelled. "We'll hold them off better in the hall!"

But his order was understood by the ilk-beasts, too. Though the men and woman had forsaken themselves to this fate, some semblance of human cognition remained. The pack of beasts surged toward the door, cutting off their retreat. The way was slammed shut.

More beasts clawed and crawled through the windows. Was there no end to Chrism's slavering army? How many had given themselves to this false god?

With a grunt, Rogger went down on one knee, his shoulder ripped to shreds by a lash of claw, his stave knocked from his fingers.

Tylar used a backhanded blow with the hilt of his sword to crack the ilk-beast in the face. It fell back.

Rogger gained his feet. Kathryn passed him a dagger.

"We can't hold them," she said. "We're being swamped."

With each death, the floor grew slicker with blood, each step more treacherous. And it was not only the beasts' blood that stained it. They all bore cuts and scrapes.

Tylar found his vision narrowing. Fear and fury had helped fuel his fight, but there were limits. He had lost too much blood earlier, had had too little time to recover. His heel slipped in a pool of blood. He fell into the arms of one of the beasts, a squat toadish man with bony spines growing from his skin. Tylar felt himself speared across arms and chest.

As he struggled to free himself, the creature suddenly jerked, spasmed, and released Tylar. He fell to Tylar's toes, a dagger hilt protruding from the back of his neck, impaled to the brain.

Tylar matched gazes with Eylan. Even while fighting her own host of monsters, she had thrown the dagger with unerring accuracy, protecting her charge, doing her duty.

He nodded his thanks and raised his blade as another beast lunged for his throat. He struck out with his elbow, catching the creature across the nose. Then stabbed upward with his other hand, fingers wrapped around his dagger. He shoved the blade under the beast's rib cage, driving through to the heart. It gasped and choked. He kneed the beast away from him.

Enough.

"To the walls!" he called out. "Backs to the walls!"

The beasts could not block such a general order.

Tylar and the others cut a swath, retreating to the stone walls. Tylar, Rogger, and Kathryn found spots on one side of the room, Eylan and Gerrod on the other.

"I must loose the beast," Tylar said to Kathryn and Rogger. "Stay as low as possible."

" 'Bout time," Rogger grumbled.

Kathryn cast out shadows to shield them.

Working quickly, Tylar sheathed his dagger, grabbed his smallest finger with his other hand, braced himself, then snapped the digit clean backward. Agony flamed his hand like a hammer strike.

Nothing else happened.

Rogger looked on. "Only popped it out of place. Let me help."

Tylar glanced up in time to see the hilt of Rogger's dagger aiming for his face. He could've ducked, but didn't. The iron hilt struck him square in the nose. He heard the crush of bone at the back of his skull.

It echoed outward, rattling through his body.

Though he was prepared, the agony was no less than before. Each break was fresh, each snap ripped flesh. He fell to his knees, which broke before even striking stone.

"Get clear!" he screamed as he felt the buildup behind his rib cage. Then those bones broke, too.

The daemon sailed forth, through the same hole it had burned in his clothes earlier. With its escape, bones reset and healed, callused and misaligned.

Tylar's vision opened enough to see Kathryn and Rogger falling to the walls on either side. The naethryn smoked from his body, spreading wings and stretching its neck.

Ilk-beasts still had enough humanity in them to know terror. The creatures fled from the daemon's path as it settled to the stone floor on smoky claws and legs. Fiery eyes scanned the room.

Across the way, even those beasts that had been attacking Eylan and Gerrod gave pause, backing in panic from the dark newcomer. Several fled back out the window.

Tylar straightened, sensing a change in the tide of battle. "Make for the door," he urged.

They all began sliding along the walls.

Not all the ilk-beasts were cowed by the naether-spawn's appearance. Several leaped with piercing shrieks. Tylar smiled grimly. Their deaths would not be pleasant.

But the beasts crashed through the naethryn as if the daemon were ordinary woodsmoke. They came out the far side, unharmed. The yellowish fire in their eyes remained just as fierce.

Gerrod called from across the way as the two parties converged on the door. "Their corrupted Grace shields them! The naethryn's Grace is a match to their own. It cannot harm them!"

"Now he tells us," Rogger griped.

All around the room, the pack of ilk-beasts took heart from their braver few. They rushed at the party pinned to the walls, with little ma-neuverability.

Tylar tried to raise his sword, but his misshapen curl of fingers could not grip it. The sword fell and clanged against the stone floor. He couldn't defend himself.

Beasts closed upon them, swamping them.

❖

Dart shoved Laurelle behind her as the ilk-beast stalked down the hall. "Get to the stairs!"

"But—"

"Get Yaellin!" she yelled.

Dart knew they couldn't both flee. The beast would be upon them be-fore they could reach the stair. Someone had to hold it off.

Laurelle must've understood this, too. She didn't argue further and ran down the hall.

The mottle-skinned beast twitched, watching Laurelle flee. But it did not pursue. There was easier prey. It lowered its head, snarling, revealing a maw of sharp fangs. A slight black pall steamed from its pores, along with the scent of burning blood. Black Grace burned through its flesh.

Dart sought any weapon, any means to escape. The only objects in the halls were a row of chairs along either wall. Dart had sat in those same chairs as she waited for her purity to be tested. Then, too, she had been terrified.

Creeping backward, Dart kicked and shoved the chairs into the hall-way. But the monster simply bulled through them.

Distantly, she heard Laurelle's cry for help. Aid would never reach Dart in time.

The monster knew this, too—and leaped.

It flew headlong through the air.

With no retreat, Dart dove forward.

Under the beast. Under one of the scattered chairs.

The beast, ill prepared for such an unexpected move, twisted in midair. Its hindquarters smashed atop the chair. Dart scrambled free as the wooden legs snapped like saplings. She rolled past the creature's rear.

The beast thrashed around, kicking and slashing at the tangle of chairs.

Dart glanced back to the healing chamber. Its door had been slammed closed moments ago. And even if it had not, there was no sanctuary to be found in that room. She heard the shrieks and wails from inside.

The ilk-beast regained its footing.

It slunk toward her again, shoving through the chairs. It would not make the same mistake twice. Despite its ravening appearance, its eyes glowed with keen intelligence. Somewhere inside its twisted form was the man who had consumed Chrism's blood. Both beast and man burned with fury.

A howling wail escaped its throat.

Dart felt her knees weaken. She trembled from crown to heel.

With one last growl, it ran at her, low this time, but bulked at the shoulder. Claws scraped stone.

Dart stumbled backward, tripped on a broken chair, and fell hard to her backside.

The beast lunged up, claws raised, fangs bared. It crashed down upon its cowering prey.

Dart dropped to her back. Her fingers scrabbled for any weapon. Her palm found a shattered chair leg and raised it, braced with both arms now.

The beast landed on her, impaling itself on her sharpened stave of wood. Through the throat. Blood splashed over Dart. It burned like acid, blinded her eyes.

But the beast was far from dead. The mortal wound would take time to kill, and the beast intended to take Dart with it.

It shoved up enough to bring a claw to Dart's shoulder. Skin tore, muscle, down to bone, pinning her. Dart screamed. Her mouth filled with the blood. She spat and choked, fearing to consume it, fearing she'd become what attacked her.

Panic fired her arms. The weight, the blood, the hot breath . . . all brought back a deeper terror. She struggled against the violation.

No!

The scream ripped up through her, yelled against all that tormented her, past and present. She shoved her stave deeper. The beast wailed and bucked backward. Its claws tore from her shoulder and she lost her stave.

The beast snarled and fell upon her again. It raised its muzzle to rip into Dart's throat.

Then its left eye exploded with blood and gore.

The point of an arrow protruded out of the socket.

Shot from behind.

The body crashed atop Dart, knocking the last of the wind from her. She kicked and clawed her way from under it, gaining her freedom.

With her left shoulder on fire, Dart shoved to her feet. Down the hall, she spotted a whirl of shadow turning away.

With crossbow in hand, Yaellin returned to his defense of the stairs, vanishing down a few steps.

Laurelle appeared out of the cloak of his shadows. "Hurry, Dart!"

Dart stumbled past the ilk-beast, then gained her footing. She fled the length of the hall and reached Laurelle.

"Up!" Yaellin yelled from down a bend in the spiral stairs. Bodies draped the closest steps. "Get to hiding!"

Laurelle grabbed Dart's uninjured arm and urged her upward.

They fled together. Each step jarred Dart's clawed shoulder and drew hot tears.

They ran with no plan but to escape, to put as much distance as possible between them and the horrors below.

A door appeared, blocking the way.

It wasn't until then that Dart realized where they had reached.

The top of the tower.

The rookery.

Her feet slowed. Her head shook. "No . . ."

"We must hide," Laurelle said. She grabbed the handle and yanked the door open.

A flutter of wings sounded inside the dark chamber. The air stung of guano. A few beams of light illuminated the dusty space, but succeeded only in highlighting the darker shadows.

"Come. We can hide here."

Laurelle drew Dart inside. She closed the door behind them.

Dart could not breathe as they stumbled deeper into the rookery. Eyes shone down from above. Dart searched the floor for blood. She knew the spot. By the back window, on the floor . . . bare planks, speckled with droppings. How could such horror leave no lasting mark?

"We'll be safe here."

Dart slowly shook her head. There was no safety to be found here.

The snick of a thrown latch sounded behind them.

Dart didn't need to turn. It was happening all over again.

"So we come full circle," the voice said at the door.

Laurelle stiffened. "Healer Paltry . . ."

Dart slowly turned. The man stalked from the shadows. He bore a long sword in one hand. He carried it deftly. He must have escaped when the fighting first occurred, sneaking out the door and slipping past Yaellin as he defended the stairs, choosing the same place to hide.

Paltry came forward, fully into the light.

"Now to put an end to the abomination."

❖

Kathryn defended Tylar. She kept her eyes from his broken form. She could not balance the knight from a moment ago with the crippled wreck at her feet. Her heart ached, as if she'd lost Tylar all over again.

In fury, she stabbed and hacked to keep him safe. The naether daemon had no effect on the ilk-beasts. If anything, it made the fighting more difficult. Their party had to be careful of its shadowy form. While its touch might not harm the corrupted creatures, they had no such protection.

A slip of her cloak had accidentally brushed through the smoky umbilicus that connected Tylar to his leashed beast. The brief contact sucked all Grace from her, dropping shadows and cloak to her shoulders. All the speed borne of Grace died. It would take time to draw shadows back into her cloak. In the meantime, she felt as if she were fighting in mud.

Tylar understood the danger. He bloodied his palms and readied to call back the beast. "To the door," he urged.

If nothing else, at least the appearance of the daemon had cleared the beasts blocking the room's only exit. Gerrod and the Wyr-mistress had already reached the door and held it for them.

Kathryn hacked the last few steps to join them.

Gerrod manned the door, his armor stained from head to toe with blood and gore. "Rein in your daemon," he called to Tylar.

With a nod, Tylar brought his bloody palms to the black umbilicus. His touch ignited a burst of fire. It raced out from him, consuming the naethryn before it. Wings burned away. Details blurred to smoke. The flash of fire startled the ilk-beasts, buying them all time to slip from the room.

Tylar waved them through as the fires reached the tip of his daemon's nose and whipped back again. "Stand clear!"

The flames raged back toward Tylar.

He was the last, standing in the doorway. When the fiery wave struck him, he was knocked backward through the door. Eylan caught him and kept him from falling. Gerrod slammed the door.

Ilk-beasts struck and dug at the planking.

Gerrod shouldered the door, but the fight rattled the frame.

Tylar returned. Hale again. He wiped his sweated brow, then jabbed a fingertip on his dagger. "Back," he warned Gerrod.

Tylar reached a bloody finger to one of the door's hinges. A crackle of frost snapped from his touch. The iron took on a bluish cast. He did the same to the other two hinges.

"Frozen," Tylar said. He stepped back and waved Gerrod off.

The ilk-beasts still fought the door, but the hinges refused to bend.

"I don't know how long it will hold, but we'd best not wait and see."

Tylar led the way down the hall. Kathryn noted the snowy pallor to his features. Though healed again, he was far from hale. A body, even one blessed by a god, had limits that would break it. And Tylar was nearing his end.

They reached the stairway. Yaellin awaited them. He stood with his back to the curve of the stairs. Two bodies were sprawled on the nearest steps, and a pile blocked the way down.

"Keep clear," he warned.

A crossbow bolt sparked off the stones and ricocheted up the stairwell from below.

"None dare come closer on foot," Yaellin said. "But they won't let us down either."

Gerrod stared around the space. "Where are the girls?"

❖

Dart held her place in the rookery. She watched Paltry stride across the planks. She felt the oddest sense of finality in this moment. As if she were meant to be here. A calmness settled into her, filling corners that had recently been empty.

The same could not be said for Laurelle. "You . . . you'd best stay back," she warned. She clearly wanted to retreat farther into the rookery, but the space was open. No place to hide. The only true escape from here was to plunge through one the chamber's many windows.

Paltry smiled. "The monsters below will either kill your defenders or chase them off. Either way, none will question your guilt . . . or my killing of you both."

Laurelle fell back toward one of the walls. Dart followed, but only three steps.

Paltry continued. "And once slain, I will lay your bodies at Chrism's feet. What does it matter if one's god is corrupted or righteous? In the end, it matters only if one has pleased him or not. From such pleasure, riches will flow."

A splatter of guano struck Paltry's cheek. He flinched, clearly edgy despite his easy words. Still, his sword did not falter. Dart stopped and held her place. She knew where she stood. On these planks, all was ripped from her: her innocence, her safety, her sense of self. Above, the dark rafters glowed with the hundred eyes of the ravens, silent spectators then and now.

Paltry approached, sword pointed. "Which to kill first? Will it be worse for you, Dart, to see your friend die before you?"

Dart merely stared. In the silence, she felt a string, previously taut, relaxing inside her. A sense of security braced her.

She glanced to the planks. She had left here hollow, left a part of herself behind, but now she could reclaim it . . . with a little help.

She glanced up to Paltry. He sensed the diamond in her gaze, cold and hard. His footsteps faltered.

Dart waited for the tightness inside her to fully loosen, then spoke three words. "To me, Pupp."

He came through the door, passing like a ghost. He must have finally found a break in the stones, or a place to climb, or a gate. Perhaps he had even backtracked the long path back to the High Wing, then down again . . . returning to the only home both had known. But ultimately she knew what drew him.

She reached to her lacerated shoulder. She wet her fingers.

Blood.

Pupp raced to her, a shining coal in the darkness. They were one and the same. Blood for blood.

Paltry stopped his approach, plainly confused by her words, disturbed by her countenance.

Dart bent to one knee. She had once pondered what she was: girl, god, or monster. For the moment, she made her choice.

Monster.

Her bloody fingers touched Pupp. She felt the heat of his flesh. His form grew brighter. She smeared him with her blood and lifted her eyes to Paltry.

He stared in horror at the figure of flaming bronze, spiked and razor edged. Flames glowed in Pupp's eyes and lapped from his muzzle.

Paltry stumbled away.

Dart waited.

Finally, Paltry met her gaze.

Dart did not smile. She said one last word. "Fetch."

❖

Tylar heard the scream from a full two flights away. He rushed up the last of the steps, followed by Eylan and Kathryn. Rogger, Gerrod, and Yaellin remained below, plotting some strategy to escape, pinned as they were between ilk-beasts and castillion guards.

Above, the scream changed pitch into a wail of horror and pain. It was not a child's scream. It ripped from the throat of a man.

Ahead a door appeared.

Tylar rushed to it.

"Careful," Kathryn warned. "It could be more ilk-beasts."

Tylar's fingers fought the latch, but it was secured from inside. "Dart! Laurelle!" he called out as the wail died to a moan.

There was only one last place the girls could be hiding.

Behind this door.

Tylar pounded on it.

A small cry answered, full of horror, but plainly a girl's voice this time. "We . . . we're here."

A flutter of footsteps sounded. The latch inside was thrown back. Before Tylar could even touch the door, it was flung wide and the black-haired girl flew out. She collapsed into Tylar's arms, hugging him tight, clinging, sobbing.

Inside the dark chamber, plainly a rookery from the smell, a pool of light lit the center. It illuminated the wreck of a body on the floor, torn limb from limb. Blood reflected the light, spreading into a wide lake.

The source of the illumination climbed from the wreckage of the body. It glowed with a fierce light, standing shorter than a man's knee. It was bulked and spiked, muzzled and flamed, covered in gore. It seemed to meet Tylar's gaze. An intelligence shone there, a match to what he saw in the flaming gaze of the naethryn inside him.

"Pupp . . ." he said, naming the beast and knowing it to be true.

It shook its spiky mane, flared brighter for a breath, then vanished away, taking its glow with it. Darkness closed over the center of the room. A hundred ravens suddenly took wing, screaming and flying for all the open windows, leaving shadow behind.

A second figure stepped out of the deeper gloom. It was the other girl.

"Dart," Tylar mumbled.

She trembled, plainly unable to move farther.

Tylar passed Laurelle to Kathryn. "Watch her."

Unburdened, Tylar hurried into the room. Dart didn't seem to see him. Her eyes were glazed. Bending down, he took her into his arms and pulled her to his chest. "You're safe," he said.

Something like a laugh escaped the child. It was a sound too old for one so young, full of mirthless disbelief. And she was right. They were far from safe.

Still, she burrowed into him. He felt the tears through his thin shirt. He let her cry, rocking her slightly. He could guess what had happened here. He had noted the shirt on the macerated body. Soaked in blood, the hatching of oak leaf and acorn was still evident in silver thread.

The healer must have trapped the girls here, threatened them. Dart had defended herself with the only weapon at hand.

"I . . . I . . . killed him."

"Hush," he whispered. "I know you didn't mean it."

She glanced up from his chest. Her eyes reminded Tylar of the gaze of Wyr-lord Bennifren, a babe with ancient eyes. But this was no Grace of longevity. It was simply the gaze of a girl who had seen too much.

She shook her head. "I wanted him dead. I . . . I sent Pupp."

Tylar remembered her story. Before, Pupp had killed in her defense, coming to her aid unbidden. But this time, Dart must have been more directly involved. Now she was waking to the horror of such a committed act.

Still, she kept her feet. Her sobbing slowly settled to intermittent quakes. Tylar knew the brutality perpetrated upon her. She might be a godling, but the flesh and heart was that of a young girl. Though she was stricken by the bloodshed, he suspected it also helped return a part of what was stolen from her. Blood for blood.

"Come," he said softly. "We must clear from here."

She nodded. She kept one hand in his. But her eyes were on his chest. She pointed to the black print there.

"You also carry something with you," she said. "I can see it stir."

Tylar stared down at the mark. It seemed no more than tattooed flesh. Plainly her eyes saw more than his did. As she could see Pupp, her sight must also allow her to peer more deeply into him. Uncomfortable with that, he shifted his shirt to cover his mark.

She glanced to his eyes. "Does it make you any less a man?"

Tylar met her gaze, knowing she wondered the same of herself. He again saw the age behind those young eyes. He knew they deserved an honest answer, rather than one that falsely comforted.

"I don't know."

❖

Dart kept behind the others on the stair. The occasional crossbow bolt struck the stones and rattled at them.

"It's not much of a plan," Tylar said.

"And we're not much of an army," the bearded man answered.

Tylar sighed. Dart watched him, sensing an odd connection to him. She remembered his arms around her, his sweat. She had feared the god-slayer when she had first heard about the murder in the Summering Isles. Now she wanted him close. Even Pupp sniffed at his heels, hovering around him.

Dart sat on a step, arms tight around her knees. The terror of the rookery had ebbed with each step down from above. She knew the slaughter was justified, but she had yet to balance the horror of the act with the gut-level satisfaction she also felt.

Laurelle also remained quiet, staring without a blink. She kept to Dart's side, but she did not offer her hand as before. Dart knew her friend was still seeing Paltry torn asunder by the fiery Pupp. Though the act saved them both, the blood was hard to clear from one's eyes.

"We must open the stairs," Rogger repeated. "It's the only way."

"Fine. Let's try it. But it still seems too simple to work."

"The more complicated a plan, the more likely it will fail," Master Gerrod countered.

With no other argument, the group retreated up the stairs, winding around a bend and out of direct sight from the lower landing. Only Rogger remained below.

The bearded man cupped his mouth and shouted. "Dark knight," he called. Dart was startled by the bass tenor bursting forth from his thin frame. "Retreat to the healer's cell! We'll hole up there until nightfall!"

With those words and much clatter of boots, Rogger ran several steps down the hallway in the direction of Paltry's room, then kicked his boots into his hands and ran barefooted back to the landing and up to them.

Tylar simply shook his head at the simple diversion.

Rogger kept a watch at the bend in the stairs.

A few more crossbow bolts cracked up to them.

Rogger ducked back around. "Here they come," he mouthed.

Whispers and the tread of boots sounded.

"Door's shut at the other end," one of the guards called from the landing.

"Get those axes up here," another answered. "Now's our chance to flush the bastards."

More commotion and the trot of boots followed. Guards raced from the landing and down the hallway. Upon reaching the far door, one of the men shouted back, "I can hear them inside!"

A final rush of guards pounded past the landing below. After a moment of silence, Rogger and Tylar both peeked around the bend.

"Way's clear," Tylar said, sounding vaguely bothered that the plan had succeeded. "There's sure to be a few strays on the stairs, but nothing we shouldn't be able to handle. We push all the way to the streets and away."

They fled silently. The two knights, Yaellin and Kathryn, led the way, utilizing the shadows. With the guards focused on the healer's door, their party slipped past the landing without being spotted. As they descended, the crash of an ax into wood echoed behind them.

They did not have much time until their ruse was discovered.

They raced downward.

As Tylar had guessed, a few guards still manned the stairs, but Yaellin and the castellan swept down upon them, shrouded in shadows. The guards were swiftly dispatched and left sprawled on the stairs.

They had no time to mourn their acts. There was no telling the innocent from the guilty. But all of Myrillia was at stake.

Cringing at each death, Dart fled with the others, Laurelle at her side.

Rogger dropped back to Dart and held something in his hand. "You left this behind."

Dart stared at the black blade. It was the cursed dagger Yaellin had given her. She had thought it lost forever. If she'd had it earlier . . . with Paltry . . .

Rogger winked at her. "As a thief, I know better than to leave a weapon behind."

Dart took the blade with a nod of thanks and returned it to her sheath.

They descended floor after floor.

A shout erupted as they crossed one floor's landing. Dart turned to see a tall man in the neighboring hall. He was dressed in the gold and crimson of the castillion guard, but from the finery of his dress, he was clearly the captain of this guard.

Before the captain could shout a second time, Rogger threw a dagger. It struck the man in the throat and tossed him back, gurgling. His fall revealed a girl behind him.

Dart and Laurelle met her gaze. The girl's guilt was plain.

Here was the one who had alerted the guards, who had betrayed them. Margarite.

Before a word could be spoken, Master Gerrod hurried Dart and Laurelle down the final two flights. They broke into the open courtyard. A handful of guards were posted here, but they were too few to block their escape through the back gate and out to the alleys beyond.

Shouts followed, but they quickly faded away among the maze of alleyways and side streets.

Laurelle glanced to Dart. The pain of Margarite's betrayal still shone brightly in Laurelle's eyes.

Friends had become enemies. Whom could they trust?

At last Laurelle reached for Dart again.

Dart took her hand, gladly, gratefully.

It would have to be enough.

23

SWORD IN SHADOW

RELEASING HOLD OF THE SCALING ROPE, TYLAR DROPPED TO THE SOIL beside Kathryn and Gerrod. The tree limbs overhead creaked and shivered from the winds gusting over the crumbled wall of ancient stones. The sky had darkened with lowering clouds. The air smelled wet and heavy.

A storm was coming.

Tylar stepped aside as Yaellin flew down a second rope with the two girls. Dart carried Pupp under one arm. She had used a touch of her blood to give him substance, so the wall would not separate them again. Landing, Dart lowered her strange companion and stood. As Pupp faded, neither child looked pleased to find themselves back in the Eldergarden.

Yaellin touched Dart's shoulder, attempting to reassure her.

With the entire upper city scouted by guards—both castillion forces and footmen brought up from the lower garrisons—it was no longer safe in the streets.

A handful of Shadowknights, in service to Chrism, haunted dark corners. But Kathryn and Yaellin had no trouble sidestepping or dispatching them. They were young, fresh to their cloaks. Still, it was lucky Chrism kept so few knights in residence, what with the city so close to Tashijan.

Kathryn looked grim as Rogger and Eylan descended the stone wall, the last of their group. Tylar knew her worry. He had also noted the patch worn by one of the knights, knocked senseless by Yaellin. It had been sewn to his inner cloak. A crimson circle bisected by a cross of flames.

The Fiery Cross.

Kathryn had grown silent since the discovery. Still, Tylar could read her fears. How far had the Cross spread? How deeply in collusion were they with all these dark happenings?

For now, Tashijan would have to wait.

Gerrod, who had been studying the gloomy myrrwood, turned to Yaellin. "You're sure you can find your way back to where the blood ritual took place?"

The knight nodded and pointed.

Gerrod had proposed using this time, while attention was diverted to the search of the streets, to investigate Chrism's sanctuary in the wood. His plan seemed wise. None would suspect they'd hole up in the dark woods, under Chrism's very nose. Still, now faced with the myrrwood and knowing the corruption at its heart, doubts rose. It was plain in all their faces. Perhaps this wasn't the safest place to hide.

But Gerrod was right. They needed to learn more about what had happened to Chrism before they confronted or exposed him. Knowledge was their best weapon.

Once gathered, the group set off into the wood, led by Yaellin.

Tylar paced Gerrod. The master's armor whirred and one knee had begun to squeak. "What do you hope to find at that site?" Tylar asked.

"I don't suppose to guess," he answered slowly. "But from the story told, the blood ritual took place at the spot where Chrism first settled to this land. I think that's significant."

Tylar frowned. "Why?"

Like everyone else, Tylar knew the history of Chrism's settlement of the first god-realm. In an attempt to end the ravings that plagued him, as all the gods suffered, Chrism had bled himself into the land, fully and completely, drained empty, attempting to end his life. But death did not come. Instead, as his living blood bonded to the region, he discovered peace from the ravenings. He was the first to find such solace, but word spread. Others quickly followed, staking out their own realms. Only the rogues remained unfettered, preferring madness to confinement to one realm. But even they found themselves eventually pushed and isolated among the many stretches of raw hinterland.

"Chrism was the first to settle," Gerrod answered. "Yet at this site, he commits dark acts. He speaks of being free, of unfettering himself from his own realm. Could such a thing be possible? Did Chrism break his bond to the land? Has he reverted back to a rogue? Is it madness or corruption? We must search this site for any answers."

Tylar nodded. It was a chilling thought. *Chrism gone rogue.*

They continued the trek in silence. Winds shook the upper tree limbs. Dried leaves fell with whispery rattles, putting everyone on edge, making it seem like the forest itself gasped and wheezed. The darkness grew to a midnight gloom. The only light came from strange luminescent berries decorating thorny bushes and palm-sized butterflits resting among the branches.

After a time, Yaellin lifted an arm and waved them to an even quieter tread. "We skirt the Heartwood. Take care we don't wake it."

The knight led them around in a wide arc. Tylar caught glimpses of the massive bole of the tree, the heart of the wood, corrupted and ilked like the men and women who served Chrism. Very faintly, the rustle of dried wood . . . or bone . . . whispered from that direction.

No one spoke.

They slowly passed the Heartwood and continued farther into the myrrwood. A light rain began to patter the canopy, but few drops reached the ground. They might as well have been indoors.

"Not much farther," Yaellin said.

They paused to take a short break. Bandages were checked. All of them bore wounds, except for Gerrod, who worked on the creaking joints of his armor.

Then they set off again, moving more slowly, eyes wary for any ilk-beasts still lurking here after the ritual. But the woods appeared empty. The hunt out in the streets still occupied Chrism's minions.

But for how long?

"There!" Yaellin said.

He pointed toward a pair of stone pillars in the middle of a glade of massive trunks. The branches overhead wove together to form a massive raftered roof. A few drizzling streams wormed through the canopy and tinkled to small pools of rainwater.

They waited at the edge for Kathryn and Yaellin to make a complete circuit of the glade. All seemed quiet. A faint smell of old woodsmoke hung in the air. Tylar spotted a circle of fire pits, dug into the ground, gone cold.

Yaellin and Kathryn reappeared.

"No one's about," Kathryn said.

"I found some spoor," Yaellin said with thick distaste. "Ilk-beast. But nothing fresher than two bells. I think we're alone."

"For the moment," Kathryn said. "We'd best make a fast inspection, then find a less conspicuous place to ride out the storm and decide what course to pursue next."

As if agreeing with her, thunder grumbled distantly.

Tylar led the others into the glade, aiming for the twin pillars. They were white granite, etched with yellow lichen, and half overgrown with vines that were now brown and dead.

Despite all that had occurred, Tylar could not help but feel a bit of reverence for this site. Here is where the present age of Myrillia had begun, the longest stretch of sustained order and relative peace. Chrism might be corrupted now, but his great sacrifice here four thousand years ago could neither be dismissed nor belittled.

Tylar walked around the pillars. Here Chrism had himself bound, cut at throat, groin, and wrist. He bled himself in despair, refusing the very madness that now consumed him. He sought an end, but instead found a beginning.

What had happened?

Gerrod knelt between the pillars. He dug up a handful of soil. Tylar twinged a bit at the violation of the sacred ground. Gerrod sniffed at the soil, then replaced it with a pat.

"Fresh loam," Gerrod mumbled. "I don't understand. I smell no corruption."

Tylar heard the disappointment in his voice.

"Maybe if I had more time . . . my alchemy tools . . ." He straightened up with a creak. "Nothing's here."

"What did you hope to find?" Tylar asked.

"Proof for what we must claim. Who will believe Chrism is corrupt? You heard on the street. Those who saw the ilk-beasts believe we are their masters. We're also blamed for the flippercraft's crash and the subsequent damage to the lower holds of the castillion. But if we could've shown this spot to be corrupted . . ." He shook his head. "I'm sorry. I led you all out here for nothing."

Kathryn laid a hand on his shoulder. "We needed to hide, to regroup. No harm is done."

"I had hoped maybe the Godsword was here," Gerrod continued, crestfallen. "If Yaellin could find no sign of it in the High Wing, maybe it had been sequestered here."

"I searched here, too," Yaellin said. "There is no sword."

"Chrism must keep it with him," Tylar said.

A new voice interrupted them, coming from around the edge of Kathryn's cloak. "I . . . I don't understand."

Kathryn turned, revealing Dart. She stood near one of the pillars.

"What is it?" Tylar asked.

She pointed to the ground. "There's a sword stuck in the dirt right there."

Tylar saw nothing.

She shooed her fingers at the ground. "Pupp, get away from there."

Tylar glanced to Kathryn, then Gerrod.

Rogger spoke aloud what they all suddenly understood. "She can see it! Just like her dog creature."

" 'A sword of shadow and light,' " Gerrod said. "No wonder it's never been seen or found."

"Rivenscryr," Tylar gasped. "The Godsword."

Dart frowned at all their reactions. They had to be mistaken. The sword appeared be ordinary dull bronze, even its unadorned hilt. Surely this was no dire weapon to shatter worlds.

But all eyes were upon her. From their expressions, they failed to see what was evident to her. She watched Pupp again nose up to the embedded sword. His bronze form was almost a match to the blade and hilt, except his form glowed with a molten sheen. The sword appeared cold and somehow ancient.

"Can you describe what you see?" Gerrod asked.

She did, knowing they were mistaken. There must be some blessing or curse placed upon the blade, hiding its form, but it could not possibly be the dreaded Godsword. ". . . and it's shoved into the dirt, almost to the hilt. A handspan of blade still shows." She held out her hand, fingers splayed to indicate.

"Are there any markings?" the master asked.

Dart stepped closer to be sure. Everyone else had backed from the space between the pillars. She leaned down. One hand reached out.

"No!" a firm voice commanded.

She yanked her arm back. The order had come from Eylan. Few words had ever been spoken by the Wyr-mistress, but these now had the force of familiar command. She was used to being obeyed.

"She mustn't touch the Godsword," Eylan said, her voice dropping slightly upon the others' sudden attention.

"Why's that?" Rogger asked.

Eylan's eyes, black already, darkened further. She turned to Tylar. "The sword is meant only for the god-bearer."

Tylar frowned. "Me?"

Rogger harrumphed. "It's a better name than god*slayer*."

"What do you know that you've not told us?" Tylar asked.

The Wyr-mistress glanced from Dart to Tylar. "We were not sure. When you came to the Wyr, you came with Grace. You came alone. But in the tower, I bore witness to the god inside you. And in the same tower, you found your sheath."

"I found my *what*?"

The Wyr-mistress again glanced down to Dart. "She is the sheath." Eylan faced Tylar again. "And you are the sword."

Tylar pinched his brows.

Gerrod spoke up. "I believe Wyr-mistress Eylan is referring to Dart's blood. As the child of two gods, she alone has the ability to whet the sword from shadow to substance. But apparently, *you* are the one meant to wield the sword."

"According to whom?" Castellan Vail asked.

Again attention focused to Eylan. Still, Dart's breathing remained labored. She glanced to Laurelle. Her friend had her arms crossed tightly about her chest. Yaellin guarded over her. Dart dropped back to them, fearing what would be spoken next.

"Who spoke of this *sheath* and *sword*?" Tylar asked.

Eylan met his gaze, but nodded toward Dart. "This one's mother."

"What?" Dart gasped.

Yaellin bent down to her. "It's all right, Dart," he whispered.

She leaned in to him. It was all too much for her. For so many years, she had wondered about her mother and father, fantasized about them, been plagued with questions. But the truth was worse than never knowing. Yaellin held her and wrapped her up in shadow, offering what comfort he could.

Gerrod shifted toward the Wyr-mistress, understanding glowing in his eyes. "It was *you* who carried the message to Tashijan from the hinterland god, the child's mother. You were the emissary who told Ser Henri about the child and urged her rescue."

Eylan did not disagree.

"But there was more that was never told to Ser Henri," Gerrod said. "Wasn't there?"

A slow nod answered him. "The god and mother raved. Such creatures are sometimes so flamed by Grace that all moorings to the present are burned away. They travel to the past . . . and to places yet to come. The godmother saw the great war of the ancient past . . . and an even greater war to come to Myrillia." Eylan stared hard at Tylar. "And they were the *same* war."

"What does that mean?" Castellan Vail asked.

It was Gerrod who answered. "Another War of the Gods."

Eylan turned to the armored master. "No, not another war . . . the *same* war. The old enmities still exist, shoved deep into the naether. But they will rise again to bring their ancient war to our soil."

Tylar took a deep breath. "And it's already begun." He touched the black mark on his bare chest.

Dart feared his fingers would fall through that stirring void. Something drew to the surface as his fingers neared. But the man seemed ignorant of it. His fingers found only his own flesh. Dart glanced from Pupp, to the sword, to the stirring darkness centered on Tylar's chest. They were all the same. Barely connected to this world.

Only she could see them.

Eylan's words repeated in her head. *She is the sheath. And you are the sword.* A shiver passed through Dart, rising from places she didn't know existed inside her.

"Why was all this not told to Ser Henri?" Castellan Vail asked.

"The god-mother forbade it. She saw strings of continuity and lines of force. 'I am a spider,' she told me, 'in a web without end.' Only certain strings could be enlightened. The rest needed to remain dark. Only the Wyr knew the truth. Because the god-bearer would come to us. And as Tashijan protected the sheath, I must protect the sword."

"And all that about needing his seed?" Rogger asked. "That was all a ruse?"

Eylan arched a brow at the thief. "No. We will still have his seed. We of the Wyr have our own goals that are independent of great wars. In this one matter here, our thread and the gods' thread cross."

"In other words," Rogger said, "why not take advantage of the situation?"

Eylan shrugged.

Rogger pursed his lips and tugged his beard. "I can respect that."

Gerrod, though, was not finished with Eylan. "What else did Dart's mother see in the future? What will happen in this war?"

Eylan shook her head, looking concerned for the first time. "According to the god-mother, too many lines intersected at this moment. 'A dark tangle of webs, shrouded in mists.' Details beyond the joining of the sword and sheath are unknown."

"There's no hint about what we must do?" Tylar asked. "With Rivenscryr? With ourselves?"

Eylan remained silent for a long breath. Her voice dropped from its stolid demeanor to softer, sadder tones. "The Wyr don't believe in the preordained. Prophecy is a path walked by fools."

"Yet here we all are," Gerrod said. "The sword and the sheath."

"Yes, but were the words of the god ordained or only supposed? She knew the Godsword still existed. She knew her child bore the blood to wield it. She knew the old enemies still lurked in the naether. Is it so much to suppose a return to war? Is such a thing prophecy?" Eylan's eyes drifted to Dart. "The Wyr have their own idea why the child was sent into the settled lands."

"And what idea is that?" Tylar asked.

Eylan kept her gaze fixed to Dart. "We think she was sent here to start the war, a flame set to a very long wick."

Dart fell back from her words. But Yaellin still held her.

No . . . it couldn't be true . . .

Tylar watched the poor girl sink into Yaellin's shadows, saw the horror in her eyes. He understood what she must be feeling. He had only to glance to his own chest. Could it be true? Were they both just pawns in a greater war?

Gerrod covered his eyes. "For four thousand years, the two sides of the ancient war have been held in check. All that kept them apart was this vanished sword." He waved to the empty ground between the pillars, to the ghost blade. "But if a way to forge the sword again was loosed, and both sides knew of its existence, then both could no longer stay idle."

"Blood dripped into a skorpion's nest," Rogger said. "Stirring all into a frenzy."

"All the dire happenings across Myrillia," Tylar said. *The rise of strange beasts, the spat of skirmishes along the hinterlands, the increases in dark rites, the disturbing behavior of some gods . . .*

"Stirrings of the coming war," Eylan said.

"And Meeryn's death . . ."

Tylar remembered Darjon's words as they fought aboard the flippercraft. *The first to fall. But she will not be the last! At long last, the War of the Gods is upon us.*

At last, Tylar began to fathom Meeryn's death. The resurgence of old enmities. No one spoke as the rain continued to patter atop the bower's roof. Streams of drizzle tinkled too brightly in the darkness. It seemed suddenly much colder.

"And Chrism?" Gerrod asked. "It was he who brought the sword to Myrillia. Now it's planted here. Why? What role is he playing?"

Tylar shook his head. "Only one person can answer that." He stared in the direction of the dark castillion, lost behind the branches of the corrupted myrrwood. "We'll have to ask him."

"And how do you propose doing that?" Rogger asked. "Knock on the front door and ask him to tea?"

Tylar turned to Dart. He hated to ask this of her, but he had no choice. None of them did. They had a role to play. Sword and sheath. And even if they were both pawns in some greater game, it didn't mean they could not make their own choices.

"Dart," he began, "I'm sorry. I must—"

"I know," she said with surprising firmness. She stepped out of Yaellin's shadows and peeled back the bandage that bound her clawed shoulder. Wincing, she tugged the dried cloth, tearing away scabbing and causing blood to flow fresh. She dabbed her fingertips in it. "I don't know how much blood . . ."

"Touch and see," Tylar said. "That's all I ask."

She nodded and moved forward. Tylar accompanied her, keeping to her shoulder. It was much to require of one so young. Then again, he had seen her eyes up in the rookery. She was a child no longer.

After a final glance up to him, she reached out to the empty air. Her fingers quested—then something ignited her fingertips, glowing so brightly that the bones of her hand could be discerned through her flesh.

She yanked her arm, tripping back into him.

He caught her and hugged her to his waist, but his eyes were on the ground ahead of them.

Gasps rose around them.

A handspan above the leaf-strewn loam floated the golden hilt of a sword. But there was no blade. Tylar bent down. The hilt simply hovered in the air. It seemed made more of sunlight than metal. Tylar waved his hand under the hilt. "Nothing," he said.

"It's still there," Dart said. "The blade."

"It must take more blood," Gerrod said. "The hilt and blade must be two pieces of a whole. I suspect the entire blade's length must be smeared in blood."

Tylar reached for the hilt. "I'll pull it free."

"Wait!" Gerrod urged. "It was planted here for a reason, at the site where Chrism poured his own blood and settled this realm. So intimately connected to this plot of land, he may know if anyone removes the sword."

"Then so be it," Tylar said. "Let him *fear* for once." He reached again for the blade.

"Wait!" This time, the command came from Dart.

"What is it?"

"Master Gerrod says *all* the blade needs blood." Dart wet both palms with the blood dripping from her left shoulder. She then sprawled atop the leafy loam and positioned a palm on either side of the hilt.

"You tell me when," he said.

Dart nodded and settled her hands. She took a rattling, deep breath. "Grab the hilt."

Tylar obeyed, though he heard the terror in her voice. He gripped the hilt. It felt warm to the touch, almost as if he could sink his fingers into its surface. But it wasn't a pleasant warmth, more like sticking your hands in a raw belly wound. There was a sickly fleshy feel to the grip, as if the hilt were trying to hold him. "I . . . I've got it."

"Pull!" Dart said, bringing her palms together. Again a brightness erupted, limning all in silver, shoving the myrrwood shadows far away. He drew the blade up between her palms.

She cried out but held her place, hands pressed.

Tylar watched the blade unsheathe between her palms, ablaze with the same silver light. It blinded the eye. He drew it to its full length from her hands. It stretched the length of his arm, solid moonlight, in contrast with the hilt's sunlight.

Tylar gaped at the sword. He suddenly recognized what he held. He had seen the weapon before. On the streets of Punt. Wielded by the black naether beast, the assassin of Meeryn. The same blade had plunged through Meeryn's breast and heart.

"It killed her," he gasped. He felt the certainty stir deep inside him, smoky and black. Meeryn's naethryn knew the weapon. Tylar faced the others. "Here is the blade that slew Meeryn."

At his feet, Dart again cried out. She rolled away. Her hands smoked as if seared . . . but her flesh appeared untouched.

Then something ranker welled through the air, coming up from below. It reeked of black bile and the rot of poisoned flesh.

Kathryn grabbed Tylar's shoulder. "Get back."

Tylar stumbled away with her. The others retreated in all directions.

Up from the wound in the soil, where the blade had been planted, a black snake of smoky darkness coiled upward.

"Gloom," Tylar said, recognizing the steaming stack.

The naether bled into this world, substanceless but deadly. The stench worsened. Distantly, heard in the bones rather than the ear, a sound issued forth, not of this world. It keened with a piercing cry that threatened to shatter teeth.

Ears were covered. Feet fled.

But the font of darkness slowly dissipated. The land closed over the rent. The wound, free of the sword, healed.

Still no one spoke.

Tylar held the Godsword, feeling its oily embrace of his palm and fingers. He wanted to toss the sword and run . . . and keep running. Instead, he squeezed his fingers tighter. He was the *sword*.

"What was that?" Rogger finally asked, the first to find his tongue.

"The naether," Gerrod mumbled. "The sword pierced clean through from our world to the other."

Tylar pictured the blade doing the same to Meeryn. Had she been pierced, not just through the heart, but all the way down to the naether? If so, perhaps it was a stream of Gloom, rather than the sword, that burned away her heart.

Reaching up, Tylar placed a hand to his own chest. Had Meeryn used the last of her dying Grace to reach into that same naether and drag forth her naethryn undergod and bind it to Tylar? Was it all she could do? Some way to continue her own battle in this war? Had she marked Tylar as her avatar and set him loose with a piece of herself?

He gripped the sword. *If so . . . so be it.* He had seen what killed Meeryn. And at the point of an ordinary sword, he had witnessed the corruption that turned ordinary men and women into ilk-beasts, the humanity burned from them. He lifted the blade. He knew which side of the war he wished to lend his sword, *this* sword . . . and himself.

The Gloom faded away, swallowed by the greater shadows of the myrrwood. The pillars stood as before, only their encrusted brown vines had turned to ash, the yellow lichen blackened. A stench still clung to the glade.

The woods seemed somehow darker. A grumbling, felt in the soles of the feet, threatened, and the bower overhead shivered. More rain drizzled through the disturbed canopy.

"The myrrwood felt the passage of the Gloom," Gerrod said. "Certainly Chrism will have, too. It is no longer safe here. He will know about the sword."

Tylar nodded in the direction of the castillion. "Then let us return what is his."

"How do you propose to get to him?" Kathryn asked.

"The subterranean route," Yaellin said. "The entrance is over here."

They all followed the knight out the dark glade and through a short section of forest. A stone door appeared in the side of a small hummock. Its surface bore an etching of tangled wyldroses. Littick symbols glowed through the thorns and petals.

" 'Blood and bone' " Gerrod read. "*Krys* and *ymm*."

"Warded with Chrism's own name," Kathryn said.

"And blood," Yaellin said. He reached into a pocket of his cloak and removed a small crystal repostilary. "But the god's own black bile will nullify the blessing."

The knight removed the stopper. It had a small glass wand attached to its underside, like a woman's sweetwater bottle, used to dab scent to throat and wrist. Only this was not so pleasant. Tylar whiffed the stench of black bile. It seemed even a god's shite did not smell like roses.

Yaellin painted the bile along the lines of Littick lettering. The glow died under each stroke, smearing away the warding. Once done, a crack of stone sounded. Yaellin reached to draw the door open.

It slammed wide on its own.

A black snarl of roots burst forth, like the tentacles of a miiodon—and just as deadly. Yaellin was snatched and torn from his place, dragged into the tunnel's entrance. Roots choked and tore. Blood spurted. His form disappeared without a sound. Even his scream was strangled away.

Other roots grabbed and tangled into the gathered party.

Dart fell to her backside, her ankle wrapped in vine. Tylar lunged at her, but she grabbed her dagger from its sheath and stabbed it into the root. The squirming vine blackened, cracking with flame. She tumbled away as the root fell to ash, releasing her.

Others fared worse. Dart's friend Laurelle had been in Yaellin's shadow. With the knight ripped from her side, she was seized at waist and leg.

Tylar twisted at the hip and swung his sword in a broad stroke. The shining blade cleaved through a mass of roots near the entrance. It passed as if through air. The severed roots writhed, spewing black blood. Laurelle fell free, as did Eylan, who had lunged to the girl's aid and become entangled herself.

At the tunnel entrance, the stumped ends of the root, sliced by Rivenscryr, burst into flame, as if the blood inside were oil and the sword a tinder match. Coiling roots exploded from the inside, casting forth gouts of fiery debris. The flames raced deeper down the tunnel. More blasts echoed.

The party tumbled away.

"Yaellin . . ." Dart moaned.

He was gone.

Smoke and flames billowed out. The ground shook as the fires spread down the subterranean tunnel. A few roots writhed and twisted, but these also blew apart as the blood inside them torched.

"Away!" Tylar called with a pained expression.

He led them off through the myrrwood. He knew no path, but simply fled in the direction of the castillion.

A brilliant explosion lit the night behind them. Tylar turned in time to see one of the massive trunks of the myrrwood burst into flame, becoming a giant torch. Another, deeper in the forest, shattered with flames.

"The myrrwood is all *one* tree," Gerrod said. "You've set its roots on fire. And it continues to spread, flaming through the channels of blood. From one tree to another."

Tylar gaped.

"You lit the wick," Rogger said. "Now all we can do is run!"

More trees exploded into living torches, all around them, behind and in front. The ground shook underfoot.

They fled as the forest continued its immolation. Trunks shattered, debris rained down. Smoke rolled and choked.

They had no choice but to keep fleeing—toward the castillion.

But they had no delusions for what awaited them.

"If Chrism didn't know you were coming," Rogger coughed out, "he does now. All of Chrismferry will be looking this way."

Laurelle spoke, her face smeared with soot, tear tracks traced through the ash. "You . . . your sword." She pointed.

Tylar raised the weapon, still gripping the warm hilt. Only that was all he held. In the mad flight, he hadn't noticed.

The sword's blade had vanished.

"One stroke," Gerrod said as they paused in their flight, cowering in a dark section of forest momentarily free of flames. "That must be all the sword can bear before needing to be replenished."

Kathryn watched Dart again lay her bloody hands upon the sword and draw them along its length. Smoke rose from between her pressed palms, and from that blood and smoke, the silver sword appeared once again, whetted by the girl's Grace.

Tylar stepped back.

"You two are indeed sword and sheath," Rogger mumbled. "Both of you had better keep close."

More blasts echoed from the deeper forest behind them. Ahead lay patches of fire. The heat grew worse with each breath. They dared not tarry in the fiery woods any longer.

"Let's go," Tylar said.

Dart glanced back. Kathryn followed. She caught the haunted look in the young girl's eyes. She had seen too much death for one day.

Kathryn recognized the sorrow. She placed a hand on the girl's shoulder. "He did his duty," she said softly. "There will be time to mourn Yaellin later."

Dart nodded and turned, but her eyes shone brighter with tears.

It was easy to say . . . harder to do.

Kathryn also glanced back. First the father and now the son. She prayed Ser Henri and Yaellin's sacrifices had not been in vain. With the last strength of her arms, she would make it so.

The woods finally grew thinner around them. The eternal night of the heavy bower lightened to gray skies and stiff winds. Rain broke the canopy. After the heat and stifle of the deeper wood, its coolness was a relief.

Distantly, thunder rumbled.

They paused to rest one last time.

Ahead the towers of the castillion peeked between the weave of branches. It was afire with torches. At windows, along battlements. The castillion awaited them.

Kathryn sought any other path. She faced the fiery woods behind them. Despite the downpour, the woods glowed and flamed, steamed and smoked. There was no escape that way. There was not enough water across all of Myrillia to douse that fire. To Kathryn, it seemed all the elements had gathered for this coming night: loam, air, fire, and water.

A tree ahead of them burst, engulfed in a spiral of flame.

Tylar lifted the quickened blade and pointed his arm.

Though set by their own hand, the fires drove them forward.

They had no choice.

She remembered Eylan's tale of prophecy and ordainment. Perhaps they never had a choice.

She stared at Tylar. *Traitor, godslayer, sword-bearer.* But all she could see was the man she once loved . . . perhaps still loved. She could not deny this last. The heart did not forget.

Still, she remembered the broken man, the smoky daemon. Tylar was no longer the knight she knew. He had been broken and re-formed. Who was he now? Did she have the strength to find out? Would they ever have the time?

The woods opened before them. More of the castillion appeared in bits and pieces. The rain fell harder.

Reaching the edge of the myrrwood, they saw what lay ahead of them. Torches sputtered throughout the Eldergarden, illuminating brighter pools in the stormy gloom and shivering shadows. The far side of the Eldergarden stirred with dark shapes. Some wore the livery of the castillion guard, but such finery was shredded and torn. Most were naked to the rain.

Ilk-beasts.

All of them.

"He's transformed the entire guard," Gerrod said. "Even the house staff."

"An ilk legion," Rogger mumbled.

Tylar faced them with his one sword. Kathryn read the despair in his eyes. His daemon was useless against the writhing throng that awaited them. His sword could strike only once before it vanished back to shadow and light. And in the thick of battle, there would be no chance to replenish the blade. How could Tylar even defend the god-child?

Still, behind the despair, a weary determination shone through.

Then the skies over the castillion opened, the clouds parted. A dark shape lowered from the storm, aglow with soft Grace. Then another appeared . . . and another. Flippercrafts. A half dozen dropped around the towers of castillion. Lightning crackled along the clouds, highlighting the flags mounted atop each ship.

Kathryn stared and knew all was lost.

The flags were black. Each emblem crimson.

The Fiery Cross.

Kathryn pictured the slain young knight on the stone floor. His heart cut out, his blood spilled. She smelled again the burned bones of the charnel pit.

Lit by the fires below, the belly of each flippercraft opened above the towers. Ropes tumbled out, uncoiling, snaking to battlements and terraces.

Figures flowed down the ropes, ravens in a storm.

"Tashijan must have been summoned," Gerrod said.

Kathryn slowly nodded.

And the Fiery Cross answered.

24

FALL FROM ON HIGH

THE SIX FLIPPERCRAFTS EMPTIED OVER THE TOWERS AND BATTLEMENTS. Shadowknights flew down scores of ropes, dropping to stations throughout the castillion and grounds.

Tylar lost count of the number. Over two hundred.

"The Fiery Cross has come to defend Chrism," Gerrod said.

Lightning crackled in a mighty arc across the belly of the clouds, threatening the airships. It was foolhardy to ride a lightning storm. But such was the determination of Tashijan.

The winds gusted harder. Rain pelted like hail. One flippercraft brushed too near a tower. Starboard skimmer paddles snapped, sheared away. The ship hove up on its side, fighting for balance.

The damaged flippercraft swung away from the castillion—toward them. It wobbled. A pair of unlucky knights fell from the dangling ropes, jostled loose by the sudden canting. The two plummeted into the gardens, wings of shadow billowing out. They disappeared, their fates unknown.

The ship fared no better, dropping swiftly. It belly crashed through an old garden wall. The cracking splinter of wood sounded like thunder.

"Seems a bad day for flippercrafts," Rogger mumbled at Tylar's side.

The ship skidded between their party and the castillion, rolled half on its side, port aeroskimmers high. Bluish fires spat up from the stern end. Rain turned to steam, shrouding the craft.

But not enough to hide the rush of knights and crew escaping the ship.

Behind Tylar, another of the myrrwood trees erupted, gouting flames high. The heat rolled over them. Too near. Fiery branches rained down around them and out into the main gardens.

They had to move or be burned.

"This way," Tylar said and led them from the flaming forest. "Stay low."

"Where are we going?" Rogger asked as they headed into the gardens.

"To the stoved ship," Tylar said. "We're too few. We need to convince those others to aid us."

"And how are you going to do that?" the thief asked. "Your face isn't that pretty."

Tylar nodded to Kathryn. "She's still castellan of Tashijan, second only to Argent. Shaken up, the few knights here may listen to her." He lifted his sword. "And if they don't, we have this."

Rogger shrugged. "Don't mind me if I hide behind you, then."

Tylar took the thief's words to heart. Their chances were poor.

The group marched through the gardens, trudging a direct route through bushes and flower patches. The rain continued to pour, turning dirt to mud. The crashed flippercraft towered ahead of them.

Tylar stopped by a low stone fence. There was no reason to risk all. "Everyone else stay hidden here. Kathryn and I will go forward alone."

No one objected. Only Eylan met his gaze.

"Keep the others safe," Tylar said to her, letting his concern for them ring clear. "That will serve us all best."

Eylan glanced to the two girls, then nodded. The others had already sunk down and leaned against the wall, seeking some shelter from the wind and rain.

Tylar glanced to Kathryn. She nodded her readiness.

They set off down a gravel path, bordered by hedges and pocked with dancing pools of rainwater. They moved swiftly, falling into an easy rhythm, as if this were any rainy night and they were returning from some engagement together. Still, Kathryn fingered her diadem, the symbol of her station. It might be all that stood between them and a sword through the heart.

She glanced to Tylar, eyes shining with powers drawn from the shadows. There were words behind that gaze.

Tylar feared for them to be spoken aloud and turned away.

He gripped his sword. Its hilt remained warm, flowing to fit his fingers, throbbing slightly under his palm like a heartbeat. He stared down at it. What was he carrying? What was this Godsword?

Lightning crackled brilliantly, drawing his attention. The gardens flashed in stark silver. Darkness shifted. A shadowy shape rose, as if from the path itself, blocking them. A sword threatened.

"Hold!" Kathryn boomed out.

Tylar jumped, surprised at her firm authority.

The knight's sword lowered slightly.

"I am Castellan Vail," she continued, not letting the other collect himself. "Take me to your foreknight or whoever's in charge."

The sword lowered farther.

But before more could be managed, a deep growl erupted from the left. Something huge ripped through a thorny tangle of elderwytch.

Ilk-beast.

Tylar flew back, sword ready.

It crashed through the neighboring hedgerow, thrusting right through it, hardly slowing. Nothing could be discerned but its dark muscled bulk.

Tylar lunged out with his sword. No matter its size, the Godsword would surely kill it. But before he could strike, a clang of steel knocked his sword high.

Caught by surprise, Tylar stumbled.

Lightning burst overhead, revealing the beast, limned in silver. It was a steaming, slavering monster—but a *familiar* monster.

"Barrin!" Kathryn called.

The bullhound skidded to a stop, paws sliding in the mud. Its tongue, as wide as a hearthside rug, lolled out. Its rear end wiggled with all the enthusiasm of its stumped tail.

The knight who had blocked Tylar's sword shed his shadows. He reached to his masklin and let it drop.

"Krevan," Tylar said, relieved.

The other knight on the path stepped nearer. It was Krevan's right-hand man, the older knight, Corram.

Kathryn joined them. "I don't understand."

"Come see," Krevan said.

He walked them through the ruined hedge. The view opened again. The smoking flippercraft was a mountain to the right, but an arrow's shot ahead rose the castillion. Its battlements still glowed with torches, as did the terraces and windows. It blazed in the stormy gloom.

In the bright illumination, Shadowknights swept along parapets and flew from terraces down to the garden grounds. The dark wave struck the mass of ilk-beasts in the gardens. Wails and shrieks erupted. A pitched battle began.

"More knights still come by windmares," Krevan assured them. He turned to Tylar. "We come to aid the godslayer."

"How . . . the Warden . . . the Fiery Cross . . . ?" Kathryn seemed unable to rein in her thoughts. She waved at the other flippercrafts and their flags.

Tylar frowned, no less confused.

"Warden Fields was *convinced* to listen," Krevan said. The knight lifted his sword, Serpentfang. "Even someone as well regarded as Argent ser Fields is no match for the Raven Knight returned." This last was spoken sourly.

Tylar stared up at the flippercrafts. Krevan must have used his notoriety to sway Tashijan to his cause. There must certainly be more story to tell, but it would have to wait.

On the far side of the gardens, screams pierced the low thunder, rising from both beast and knight.

"While we were flying here, a raven arrived from Lord Chrism," Krevan said. "He warned of a curse that had transformed his troops into monstrous beasts. He claimed the guards were still loyal. Only their appearances had been altered by the curse. A curse placed upon him by the godslayer . . . and some daemon child."

"No daemon," a voice said behind them. Rogger stepped out of hiding. Plainly the thief had been trailing after them, abandoning his hiding place. He waved an arm, and the others appeared, too.

Tylar frowned at them all.

Rogger placed an arm around Dart. "She's more like a god, actually. A very tiny god."

Dart stared, gaping at the massive bullhound. It looked capable of swallowing her in one bite.

Krevan's brow bunched. He studied the group for answers.

"There's too much to tell," Tylar said. "First, we must reach Chrism."

"I have enough men and women to form a phalanx," Krevan said. "We might be able to forge a path to the castillion."

"Gather them," Tylar ordered.

Krevan led them back to the flippercraft, trailed by the bullhound.

They met Lorr on the way back. The tracker bowed his head toward Kathryn. "The big kank still has a nose for you," Lorr said, cuffing Barrin by the ear. "As soon as he got ground under his paws, he was mewling and drooling. I knew he had your scent."

Krevan spoke. "When we saw the fire spreading in the woods, we figured you all were somewhere in the gardens. We had planned to land after off-loading our men and search for your group."

"We landed a bit harder than we intended," Corram said.

They reached the stoved flippercraft. Krevan sent Corram to gather a dozen knights. A sharp cry erupted from the lee side of the grounded ship.

Tylar turned.

A shape flew at him. He barely got his sword out of the way in time.

Delia threw her arms around him, hugging tight, all but climbing atop him. "Tylar . . . I knew you still lived."

He carefully returned her embrace. He felt the tears on his neck . . . and her lips. Tylar met Kathryn's eyes over the young woman's shoulder. She glanced away.

Delia finally seemed to collect herself, shedding from him like water. She smoothed her cloak and backed away. "I'm sorry . . ."

Tylar had no words. He still felt her lips on his neck, the heat of her tears. He was saved from responding to Delia's apology or Kathryn's silence by Corram's arrival with a shadowed mass of knights.

"The weakest flank is off by the southeast tower," Corram said. "We may be able to break through there to the keep."

Tylar prayed he was right. He stared across at the others. "There's no need for all to go. The remaining knights here can protect you." It was no surprise that Eylan stepped forward. The Wyr-mistress had an interest in his surviving . . . or at least part of him.

Rogger followed her. He pointed to a bare spot under his elbow, among the branded sigils of the gods. "I still have Chrism's sigil to collect."

Kathryn joined them. "Tashijan must be represented."

"As should the Council of Masters," Gerrod said, stepping up. "And I know the castillion well. It's easy to get lost."

The last stood alone, arms tight around her chest, trembling. "The sword may need to be replenished," Dart said.

Tylar knelt down to meet her eye. "Brave words, but it's best you and your friend stay here."

"Mayhap we'll need her," Rogger said. "That sword of yours might need a bit more blood."

He shook his head. "No. It's risky enough to bring the sword near Chrism. If something goes wrong, I won't hand him the girl, too." He stared across the group. "I have Meeryn's Grace and daemon. You have your swords and shadows. That will have to do until we reach Chrism. If I can't take him out in the first stroke of the sword, I doubt I'll ever have a chance for a second."

Rogger slowly nodded.

"Dart stays here," Tylar said. With the matter settled, he turned to Delia and Lorr. "Keep the girls safe. No harm can befall them."

They both nodded.

Dart fell back with the others. Laurelle wrapped her in an embrace. They had seen too much horror. Tylar prayed it would end now.

He faced his knights and companions. "Let nothing stop us."

❖

Dart watched them set off, sheltered in the lee of the crashed ship. Its fires had been put out. For the moment, it offered security. But Dart knew how tentative such safety could be.

Across the way, the knights formed a wedge of shadow and sword. The godslayer and the others sheltered between, ready to aid with dagger and blade. They moved swiftly away, a black arrow sweeping low across the gardens, skirting ponds and walls, aiming for the southeast tower.

She followed their strike into the flank of the besieged ilk-beast legion. All that could be discerned were a few flashes of silver, like lightning on the ground.

The muzzled man, plainly a wyld tracker from his leather and double belts of knives and daggers, drew alongside Dart. He held something out for her. It was a spyglass. He had a second for Laurelle.

Laurelle shook her head, backing up a step.

Dart took the glass and raised it to her eye. She wanted to watch. It took a moment to center on the fighting. Though drawn closer to the battle, it was still difficult for her to see. Shadows obscured detail as knight fought beast with blade and darkness. She was surprised to hear words whisper at her ear. She heard Tylar's voice ring out clearly.

"Make for the terrace! We'll hold them there, then at the door!" Screams and shrieks drowned the rest.

Dart lowered the glass to study it. The din of battle diminished.

"Air blessed," Tracker Lorr said. "The lens brings both sight and *sound* closer. Great for hunting dark woods."

Dart nodded, lifting the glass again.

The woman who had hugged Tylar earlier joined them. Lorr turned to her. "This child here is not much older than you were, Delia, when your father sent you away."

"He may regret that now," she answered. "The soothmancers will be running their bloody hands over him for days before they're done with him."

Dart followed none of this. Instead, she concentrated on the fighting. Sounds again reached her. Strangled cries, death rattles, and the clash of steel. But it appeared Tylar and the others had broken through the ranks.

A clutch of knights burst from the writhing bulk of ilk-beasts, flying up the steps to the terraces below the southeast tower. They were a ragged bunch compared to the orderly wedge of before—but they had escaped. The group reached the door.

"Krevan!" Tylar again shouted. "Hold here! Let none pass!"

The party filtered through the door, leaving behind a knot of shadows at the threshold.

The others vanished away.

"They're inside," Lorr said.

Dart glanced to him, lowering her spyglass. The tracker had watched without the need of a lens.

The woman Delia stared, too, but Dart sensed she watched more with her heart than her eyes. Her embrace with Tylar had been a close one.

"I expect the castillion has been emptied out," Lorr said to Delia. "They'll make for the High Wing."

Dart lifted her glass again. She searched the castillion. She sought out the centermost tower, the one over the river.

The High Wing.

Dart wondered what had befallen the other Hands: the rotund Master Pliny, the diminutive Master Munchcryden, the twins Master Fairland and Mistress Tre. Not to mention Matron Shashyl. Had they all been ilked? Were they among the legion?

She heard the cries of the beastly army, punctuated by racking booms of thunder. The storm fell worse atop the castillion. Rains spattered into their shelter now, whipped up by growing winds.

The flippercrafts were forced to retreat, drifting away to settle in neighboring fields or elsewhere in the Eldergarden. The storm drove them to ground.

Droplets struck her lens, sparkling and watering her view of the highest tower of Tashijan.

Still, a voice reached her, dreadful and familiar. "The godslayer comes with the sword," Mistress Naff said.

"You know what you must do." The voice still sounded as warm as sun-baked loam. It invited one to listen. It reminded Dart of when she first met Chrism, here in the same gardens, mistaking him for a groundskeep. And though she had witnessed it with her own eyes, she could not balance that memory with what had transpired off in the myrrwood. "Is all in readiness to welcome the godslayer?"

Dart heard the hard smile behind Mistress Naff's next words. "The trap is set. There will be no escape. For any of them. It will end here."

❖

Tylar climbed the stairs of the center tower. They approached the High Wing. He led the way with Kathryn at his side. Eylan followed with Gerrod and Rogger. Krevan and Corram guarded their rear.

The only sound was the tread of their own steps. Even the cries of battle in the gardens had disappeared, swallowed by the heavy stone. All that interrupted their footsteps was the occasional hollow rumble of thunder.

Where were the folk of the keep?

Surely not all had been corrupted into beasts.

Yet not a single person moved in the halls. The entire keep had become a crypt, haunted and empty. Torches hissed in sconces and braziers crackled. The castillion seemed to be holding its breath, waiting.

The tension dragged their steps. Each crack of thunder stopped them until it echoed away. They had slowly traversed the lower halls from the southeast tower. In the lower holds, they discovered sections of the floor had fallen away, into the river below.

"Our flippercraft must have ripped through some of the castillion's old underpinnings as it crashed through here," Rogger had said, peering down into the river. The waters below had churned and roiled with the storm.

But such damage was slight compared to the true blow struck here.

The corruption of a god, the heart of an entire realm.

Tylar stared upward, toward the High Wing.

They climbed another four flights, moving in silence. None dared speak. Tylar rounded the last bend in the stair. The main double doors to the High Wing were not only unguarded, they lay open.

He stopped, suspicious.

They waited, listening for any sign of an ambush.

All that was heard was the rumble of thunder.

Tylar met Kathryn's eyes. He sheathed his ordinary blade and slid free Rivenscryr. The snick of metal sounded loud on the stair.

He stepped around the bend, hugging the wall, his blade held ready. He moved up one step, then another.

The rest followed.

In this steady manner, they climbed to the top of the stairs. Tylar tried his best to scan the hall beyond the open doors. Like all the halls, the High Wing appeared deserted. Had Chrism fled?

This worry drove Tylar over the threshold and into the great hall.

Windows lined one side, doors the other. Halfway down the hallway, the central brazier still glowed in the dimness. The crack of a log in the great furnace startled Tylar. It sounded like the break of a bone. A sound he knew too well.

He pushed farther into the hall.

Nothing. .

He waved the others to check the closest rooms. All the doors were open, as if they had been left ajar in a mad rush to escape. Kathryn and Gerrod tried the first chamber. Eylan and Rogger the next. Tylar led Krevan and Corram to the third.

Kathryn and Gerrod were already returning. "Empty," whispered Kathryn, wearing a deep frown of worry.

Rogger appeared at his door. He waved. "Come see this."

Tylar, Kathryn, and Gerrod followed the thief into the chamber. The air in the room smelled of burned rye and something sickly sweet, like honey gone bad.

Eylan waited for them in the back bedchamber. A figure lay atop the bed, arms folded over the rise of an ample belly. He looked to be in gentle repose, eyes closed. His chest rose and fell evenly. A brazier smoldered in one corner, the source of the room's reek.

"Master Pliny, one of Chrism's Hands," Rogger introduced.

"He won't wake," Eylan said.

"Spellcast," Gerrod said. "Thralled by black Grace."

A stern voice interrupted them. "Another lies in the same state in the next room," Krevan said.

They backed out to the main hall.

"Apparently Chrism spared his Hands from the ilking," Rogger said. "I guess he's too lazy to train new ones. Good Hands are hard to find."

The other rooms were quickly checked. Two other Hands were discovered enthralled and slumbering.

"Mistress Naff is still missing," Gerrod said. He stared around at the others.

All had heard Dart's accounting of the ceremony in the myrrwood, the chosen few. The remainder of the castillion had not been spared. Chrism must have blood fed the keep staff and guards in secret, drafting all in some hidden manner. Perhaps in wine, perhaps in food. Afterward, they all went about their duties unaware that at a moment's call all would be lost: their forms, their minds, their humanity.

Tylar felt no real sympathy for those who went willingly to the torch, but so many others had had no choice. He stared up and down the hall. Even the Hands had become puppets.

Everyone gathered again in the hall.

There was only one room left to be searched.

The golden doors to Chrism's chambers stood closed, lit by the glow of the brazier before them.

Tylar stepped forward, flanked by Krevan and Kathryn. He clutched the Godsword in hand, fingers squeezing the throbbing hilt. The blade seemed to eat the light coming off the brazier and shone brighter for it.

He reached a hand toward the doors' latch.

Their surface was plated in gold. If locked, it would take time to chop their way inside. Perhaps the closed doors were a ruse. To distract them, while Chrism made his true escape.

Tylar's fingers touched the latch and the twin doors fell open on their own, swinging inside.

A lone figure stood at the threshold.

She was stunning, slim of waist, generous of curve and breast, auburn hair trailing in lazy curves over one shoulder and down to midback. She leaned slightly to one side, a palm resting on a hip, an inviting glint to her eyes.

"The godslayer," she whispered, her lips, rouged red and full, barely moving. "Welcome to the High Wing."

Tylar froze, transfixed—not so much by her beauty, but her nakedness. She stood unabashed, her nipples bared. Below her throat, no hair marred her smooth white skin.

But it was not unmarked.

Centered on her chest, a black handprint stood out starkly.

A twin to his own.

❖

"They must be warned," Delia insisted.

"I can send a cadre of knights," a cloaked figure said, "but that would strip our defenses. I was ordered to keep you all under guard."

Dart listened to the exchange from the shadow of the downed ship. She had related what she'd overheard in the High Wing, of a trap being set, but nothing was being done. Nothing but talking. Her fists balled up.

She glanced back out into the rain.

She spotted one hope to break this deadlock. She turned to Laurelle. "Can you distract those others?" She waved to Delia and the clutch of bantering knights.

Laurelle stirred, her brows frowned. "Why? What are you going to do?"

"I'm going to strike for the castillion."

Laurelle's eyes widened. "Are you mad? What about what Ser Tylar said? To keep you and the sword apart?"

"There are two daemons up there." Dart remembered the kiss she had witnessed in the Eldergardens between Mistress Naff and Chrism. She remembered the smoky darkness that linked the pair's lips. "The godslayer will need more than one strike. I'm the only one who can help him."

Laurelle wrung her hands, but she nodded, her eyes firming with the plan. "I'll do my best here. But how are you going to get there?"

She reached and hugged Laurelle tight. "Pupp is not the only dog here." With those words, she set off into the rain.

Laurelle waited a moment, then headed in the opposite direction.

Dart rushed through the pelting rain. It stung now like bee stings, whipped by the winds. But she pushed on. She reached her only hope.

"Tracker Lorr," she said.

The wyldman seemed unsurprised by her sudden appearance but confused for the reason behind it. "Child?"

She spoke in a rush. "Can your hound carry me to the castillion? I heard before . . . when you came . . . that he could smell Castellan Vail."

"Aye, the big kank can, but that's not a trip for a mite like you."

Dart grabbed the edge of his buckskin coat. "I must get there."

"Because of the trap?" Lorr asked. "Best leave that to your elders."

Dart sensed time passing too swiftly. She filled her voice with firm conviction. A wyld tracker's senses were supposed to be acute enough to tell lie from truth. "All will be lost unless I can reach them in time. I know it. Now is not the moment for caution or half steps. I know it's risky for me to go. But I'm the only one who can help. If we lose now, we lose everything."

He stared down at her, his eyes slightly aglow.

Dart met his gaze. "I must go."

A commotion rose by the flippercraft. Laurelle was sobbing, panicked and throwing herself among the knights. They gathered about her, concerned.

"Turning the other's noses, I see," Lorr asked.

Dart nodded. "I can't let them stop me. If you won't help, I'll do it myself." She stalked toward the mountain of dog flesh.

The beast turned its massive head toward her, tongue lolling. Standing full in the storm, he seemed oblivious to the wind and downpour. A pool of saliva had dripped between his paws. The matt of ivy at his feet had gone brown from the poisoned touch of his drool. Plainly the blood on the wind had the dog stirred mightily.

The bullhound shook his mane as she reached him, dousing her with dirty rainwater. The stench of wet fur welled.

Lorr came to her side and knelt down. His voice had grown gruffer, but somehow warmer, too. "I once knew a girl with your spirit." He glanced to the others. His eyes seemed to fix on the woman Delia. "Back then I had been too cautious, taken half steps to stand up for her, to demand better for her. I knew better." He shook his head. "I knew better."

Lorr stood back up and turned to his bullhound. He grabbed him by the nose, pushed his face down, and stared into his eyes. A single nip could take off the tracker's arm. But the bullhound responded to the dominant manner and dropped to his forepaws, submitting.

"Listen, you ol' kank. You go find the mistress." He leaned closer. Lorr's eyes seemed to glow brighter. "Understand. Find *Kathryn*," he said the name slowly. Lorr did not take his eyes from Barrin. "Child, climb on his back."

Dart faced the hill of hound and balked. Even Pupp shied around the great beast, hackles raised.

"Hurry now," the tracker urged. "Up on the bent knee, then over his withers. Before I change my mind."

Goosed by his threat, Dart mounted the dog. It was like climbing a sopping rug. A growl flowed as she hooked a leg and pulled herself over. The rumble was felt in her belly.

"Quiet down, Barrin," Lorr said firmly.

The growl lowered below hearing level, but Dart still felt it in the pit of her stomach.

"Grab his leather collar," Lorr said. "And hold tight."

Dart obeyed, clenching her fingers.

"All right, then." Lorr backed, then dropped his arm. "Off with you! Find the mistress!"

Muscles surged under Dart. The hound leaped fully to his feet and bounded off. She was thrown high, hanging by her hands. She landed hard between the hound's shoulders.

Barrin grunted and raced across the gardens.

Shouts erupted behind her.

Dart ignored them. She concentrated on her mount. Every one of her bones rattled, including her teeth, but the hound kept his gait even, allowing her at least to keep her seat. Dart pulled up enough to peer forward over the dog's head. They raced through the gardens, splashing through shallow ponds, bounding over low shrubs. A hedgeline appeared, taller than she stood.

She lowered herself and closed her eyes.

She felt Barrin's muscles harden under her. He sped faster. She waited for his leap or his plunge through the woody hedge. Which was worse?

A surge of muscle and they were flying. She opened her eyes. Barrin sailed over the hedge and landed in a smooth curve on the far side, catching her up.

"Good dog," she said, bouncing only a little.

She stared ahead. They were almost to the battle line. It had mired to large patches of fighting. Barrin sniffed at the bloodshed. He was a war hound. His head stared longingly toward the battle. He slowed.

"Find . . . find Kathryn," Dart reminded him, not knowing if he could hear her squeak.

But his ears were sharp. He focused back on the castillion. He bounded through the edge of the battlefield. Bodies were sprawled everywhere. Barrin simply padded over them and away. He avoided the patches of fighting, but the screeches and shouts kept his ears pricked.

"Kathryn," Dart whispered. "Kathryn . . ." She was now repeating it over and over. Not so much to guide the dog, as to calm herself, to distract herself from the blood and torn bodies.

At last they reached the castillion. Barrin flew up a set of stairs to a wide terrace. The dead found their way here, too. The tiles were black with blood. Too much for even the storm to wash away. Ahead, the windows had been smashed during the fighting.

Barrin leaped through the widest.

Dart ducked low to his back to avoid the jagged shards poking down from the top frame. Then they were through, racing down empty halls. Dart stayed low, fingers crimped tight to the hound's collar. Only now did she spare a worry for Tylar and the others.

Was she too late?

Tylar stared at the black handprint resting between Mistress Naff's breasts. He found himself unable to move, gripped by shock. What did it mean?

That momentary pause proved his undoing.

From the dark print, a jet of oily darkness poured forth, too fast for the eye to follow. It struck him square in the chest. But there was no impact. The darkness shot through him—no, *into* him, through his own mark.

He felt the swell behind his rib cage. Bones snapped outward. Flesh tore. And as before, once one bone broke, the rest followed. Agony flamed through him. He knew it would end. The shadowbeast would rise and he would cripple again. But at least the pain would go away.

Until then, agony trapped his breath.

Cries rose around him, but they sounded far away now, muffled by an unknown depth of water. He felt himself sinking deeper.

The pain did not end. What was broken, stayed broken. There was no healing.

Through unblinking eyes, he watched smoky black tentacles sprout from the jet of darkness. They shot and coiled in all directions, flailing out. Some struck him, but to no effect. The darkness draped around them, tangling. He and Naff became caged at the heart of a weaving tangle of smoky tendrils.

Tylar knew what trapped him.

Gloom, a tangle of naether.

But as his own daemon's smoky form caused him no harm, neither could this darkness. Still, he was caught, a fly in a web, a *broken* fly, unable to move.

Darkness continued to snake into him.

He swelled, filled from the inside.

Too much . . .

Finally, something woke in Tylar, lashing out. He felt his body wrenched deep inside. His daemon rose to fight the trespasser. He felt the clash, beyond blood and bone. They writhed and tore. Tylar could not breathe. If the fighting continued much longer, he'd be unmoored. Nothing would be left of him.

Perhaps sensing this, the naethryn inside him pushed outward, dragging the other daemon with it. Smoke billowed thicker between Naff and Tylar. Darkness boiled as daemon fought daemon. Vague shapes took form.

An edge of wing, a glimpse of muzzle, smoky claws.

All belonging to his own daemon.

But that was not all. Other apparitions stirred and roiled in the smoky storm: a lash of snaking tail, a tongue of forked flame, a maw of black teeth. Though caught in glimpses, Tylar recognized the shapes.

From Punt.

Here, fighting his own daemon, was the beast who had murdered Meeryn. It lived inside Mistress Naff.

Mirth seemed to rise like steam.

"I was rewarded after I slew Meeryn," Mistress Naff said. "Given this skin to wear and walk this world. Now it's your time to follow."

Darkness closed around Tylar. The hall dissolved away—but not sight. An inner eye opened. He watched, experienced, lived as someone else. He found himself struggling against someone.

The attacker was impossibly strong.

A tangle of brown hair, stubbled chin, hungry green eyes . . .

Chrism.

No, she mouthed. *Why . . . ?*

It was Mistress Naff.

She was struck in the mouth, but Tylar tasted the blood. Chrism thrust into her, rough, tearing. Tylar was unprepared. The pain tore his belly, his legs, his groin. She screamed. He screamed.

It stretched endlessly, then the burn of seed spilled into her. He felt it like a wash of fire. It seared through her, through him. They were one. Memories locked.

Raped . . . by Chrism.

His corrupted seed ate her from the inside. Hollowed her out. All that was once a woman was eaten away. Nothing was left. He felt himself going, too, following.

. . . No . . .

A ring of command shot through him.

. . . THAT IS NOT YOUR PATH . . .

The words came from outside, from inside.

. . . IT IS ECHOES . . . NOT TO BE FOLLOWED . . . HERE IS YOUR BODY . . .

Agony flared anew . . . a more familiar agony. He knew the break of bones . . . *his* bones. He took the pain and claimed it for his own.

. . . DO NOT LOSE YOUR PATH . . .

Tylar recognized now the voice of his naethryn daemon.

Vision returned, tunneled and distant.

Corram lunged with a sword, attempting to cut him free. But the naether could not be harmed by mere steel. A lash of Gloom snapped forth, striking Corram in the face. He stumbled back, dropping his sword. He reached for his face. But it was too late. It was already gone.

Corram fell backward, blood pouring from the hollow that was once chin, lips, and nose. He struck the floor, dead.

A dagger flew with deadly accuracy at Mistress Naff's throat. Thrown by Rogger. But a flow of Gloom turned it to slag in midair. It splattered to the floor. Harmless.

No weapon could pierce the naether tangle.

Save one.

Tylar could not see the Godsword in his hand. But he felt it. The hilt clung to his broken hand, refusing to let go. Tylar willed his body to move, to strike out at the daemon wearing Mistress Naff's skin, the one who slew Meeryn and won this body. Tylar knew the real woman was long gone. All that was left were shadows and light, meant to trick him, to lure him astray like a will-o'-the-wisp in a dark wood.

Echoes, as his naethryn had claimed.

He struggled to raise the weapon, but he found no strength in his broken limbs. All he had was will. And that wasn't enough.

Laughter met his struggle.

"We will have the sword . . . and you," the daemon promised. A slim arm rose and reached for Rivenscryr. "With it, we will tear open this world, like this shell I wear now, and claim it for our own! We will be free!"

Tylar struggled, broken and hopeless.

There was no escape.

Fingers closed on the Godsword's hilt.

Dart heard Mistress Naff's voice from a landing away.

We will have the sword!

Dart hopped from the hound's back, almost breaking her leg on the stairs. The sudden loss of his rider stopped the bullhound. Dart did not want to be dragged unwilling into the same trap as the others.

She left the hound below. She hoped her command to *stay* was obeyed.

Reaching the open doors, she crouched and studied the hall.

We will be free!

Dart ignored Mistress Naff. She spotted one knight down on the floor, blood pooling around his head. The others seemed at a loss on how to penetrate a tangled web that locked Tylar and Mistress Naff together. From her hiding place, Dart searched for Lord Chrism, but he was nowhere to be seen.

She returned her study to Tylar . . . and his sword.

He had to be broken free.

But how?

Kathryn despaired as she watched the daemon woman's fingers close upon the hilt of the Godsword. She had heard the woman's mad claim.

But how could they stop her?

Rogger circled the pair, seeking any means to penetrate the snarl of

Gloom. He had tried striking from behind, but still the Gloom had thwarted him, burning his dagger to molten steel that dripped and steamed to the stones.

Krevan hovered by his fallen friend. His face was a mask of fury, but there was no outlet for his anger. Eylan and Gerrod stood to the side. Eylan pointed to a torch on the wall, then to the rug at her feet. Plainly she was thinking to set it on fire.

Gerrod wisely shook his head. Even if they could light the rug, it was doubtful flames would fare any better than steel.

Krevan stirred from his vigil and pointed his sword back to the door.

Kathryn turned, dropping lower, wary.

A small figure ran toward them.

It was the child. Dart. What was she doing here?

Kathryn closed upon her, intending to keep her back. The godling must not fall into Chrism's hands. Especially if the monster recovered the sword. Kathryn's fingers tightened on her own hilt. She could not let the child be taken alive.

Still, Kathryn stared down at the girl's small flushed face as she joined her. *Do I have the strength to slay this girl if I must?*

"Castellan Vail," Dart gasped. "You must throw your dagger!"

She grabbed the girl's arm as she tried to move closer. "We already tried. No blade can reach her."

Dart fought her grip. "Not *her*." She freed her arm and jabbed it forward. *"Him!"*

"Tylar?"

Dart bent and touched Kathryn's calf. "Strike him here. She may not expect that."

"But—?"

"Do it!" The small voice chimed with a mix of command and desperation.

Kathryn twisted around, trusting the girl for now. She slipped a dagger free. "Rogger!" she called out. "Strike from behind again! All of you! On my command! Attack together!"

Kathryn pushed Dart behind her. She hoped the additional distraction might allow a blade to slip by the smoky defenses and strike Tylar's calf.

"Now!"

Blades fell from all sides, aimed for the woman.

Kathryn swiped her dagger low, swinging from the hip. She put all the force of muscle and shadow into her throw.

The blade flew from her fingertips, sent with a prayer.

Elsewhere, steel exploded into fiery, molten splashes.

All done to protect Naff.

Not Tylar.

Kathryn's blade slipped through a break in the tangle. The dagger struck Tylar's calf, spearing completely through it.

Kathryn straightened. Nothing happened. The stalemate continued. Tylar did not even seem to notice the blow, too racked in pain already.

She stared down at the girl.

If Tylar lost this battle . . .

Kathryn lifted her sword. The girl did not even notice. She continued her focus on the two in the smoky tangle.

Dart's lips moved, a whisper. "Go, Pupp . . ."

Frowning, Kathryn turned back to Tylar.

At his knee, something formed. A misshapen, molten chunk of bronze. It moved, defining itself into some four-legged creature of sharp points and razored edges. Its nose was pressed to Tylar's calf, to the dagger.

To his blood!

"Tylar's Grace!" Gerrod gasped, stepping to them, laying a hand on Dart's shoulder. "It ignites her creature!"

"Pupp," Dart corrected.

The bronze creature stalked around Tylar's leg. Unseen and without substance before, it must have slipped in and waited for a source of Grace.

It found it in Tylar's blood.

The daemoness finally noted the monster in her midst and jerked back. But it was too late.

Pupp leaped, flying high, all four claws extended. He latched onto Nass's belly, flaring brighter. She screamed.

Flames shot out her back as Pupp buried his fiery muzzle into her flesh. She fell backward, tumbling out of her protective tangle and into Chrism's rooms.

As she fell, the web shattered, releasing Tylar. He toppled back, sprawling without strength.

From both their chests, the dark streams receded, sucked back into the void from which they came. Tylar sat up, shaking away the residual shock. He tested his limbs, as if making sure they were still his.

He stood up, but almost fell as he put weight on his impaled leg. He glanced to the dagger, then back up again. He hobbled to Naff.

"That's enough, Pupp," Tylar said.

He motioned with his sword. It shone brightly.

Pupp backed away.

The ruin that was Mistress Naff steamed and bled. The reek of charred flesh wafted heavily. But she was still alive. Eyes moved, tracking Tylar. Feeble tendrils of Gloom wormed from her chest print.

Words bubbled with blood. "What you carry is no blessing. It'll eat you, too. From the inside!"

Ignoring the threat, Tylar lifted his sword and held it high in both arms. "This is for Meeryn . . . and Mistress Naff."

The creature at his feet struggled, but its spine had been shattered.

Tylar drove the blade down, through the center of the black mark. It slid to the hilt, despite the stone under the body. Tylar yanked it back. Flames followed the sword up, but the blade was gone.

A wail tore through the hall, issuing from the black well.

Kathryn dropped her sword and clamped her ears. She and the others fell to their knees. The keening ripped at the edges of her mind—then it was gone.

On the floor, Mistress Naff's body burned away quickly, flaming to ash.

"Only a shell," Tylar mumbled. He touched his own mark. Kathryn read the fear in his eyes. Was he anything more himself?

She gained her feet and hurried to him. He began to slump, wasted and worn. She caught him, pulled him to her.

Off to the side, Pupp faded again, the blood and Grace burned away.

Rogger clapped Dart on the shoulder. "Clever girl. You'd make a good thief someday. With the proper training, of course."

Krevan joined them. "And where is Chrism?"

From up and down the hall, laughter echoed forth, tinkling in a handful of voices. Kathryn turned. From doors along the hall, figures stepped forth, moving woodenly, eyes blazing brighter than stars.

Chrism's Hands.

Laughter flowed from their throats. But it was plainly not their own. Enthralled, the Hands had become Chrism's eyes and tongue, too.

Their words echoed up and down the hall.

"I will face the godslayer alone . . . or all of Chrismferry will perish!"

25

CABAL

"Y OU CAN'T GO ALONE," KATHRYN PRESSED.

"You heard Chrism," Tylar said and waved at the Hands. Their eyes blazed. The creatures watched their every move. Tylar wondered how much humanity was left in them. "I have to go alone or he'll tear down the entire castillion and dump it in the river. And all of Chrismferry will follow."

They had all heard Chrism's order and command.

It was no idle threat.

A moment ago, Krevan had attempted to use the outer stairs. None of the Hands tried to stop him, but their eyes watched. Upon setting a foot on the top step, a mighty crack sounded to the south, followed by a crash of heavy stone, louder than thunder. The entire castillion shook.

"Chrism is still master of loam," Gerrod had warned. "Perhaps he couldn't tear all his realm apart, but certainly he could shatter this castle, pull down the river's dikes and levies, flooding the entire city."

So they had no choice. They were trapped in the High Wing. Only one person could descend.

The godslayer.

"It's a trap," Rogger said. "You know that, of course?"

Tylar did not even bother answering the thief's question.

"This is wrong," Eylan said stiffly and nodded to Dart. "Chrism seeks to separate you from your sheath. He knows therein lies your strength. He will divide and conquer."

"We could still run," Krevan said. "Attempt to escape the castillion before it falls. Stand to fight another day."

"No," Gerrod answered. The master was kneeling on the floor, marking in charcoal a rough layout of Tigre Hall, where Tylar was to meet

Chrism. The grand hall at the base of the tower was where the god normally conducted his affairs of the realm.

Gerrod leaned back. "Even if we escape, if Chrismferry falls, so falls the First Land. And in such chaos, all of Myrillia will be threatened."

Tylar nodded. "Right or wrong, we make a stand here."

"*You* make a stand," Kathryn said sourly.

"This is my battle," Tylar said. "You all know it. From the moment Meeryn touched my chest, it was to prepare me for this fight."

Silence met his words.

Finally Krevan stirred. "If you must go alone, then take a part of me with you." He stepped forward and held out his sword. The golden wyrm glowed along the length of silver. "Serpentfang is only steel, but there is no stronger blade or one as finely balanced. Perhaps what Grace can't defeat, steel may."

Tylar accepted the sword and Krevan's scabbard. He belted it in place.

Rogger came next, shrugging out of his belt of daggers. "I guess these are only going to gather rust."

Tylar snugged the belt across his chest.

"But I want those back when you're done," the thief added. "It's not like I'm givin' the blades for keeps or nothing."

Gerrod waved Tylar over. "All I have is my knowledge." He pointed to the charcoal sketch. "Best to know the lay of the land when engaging battle." He quickly went over the map.

Tylar nodded when done.

"There's a back stair," Gerrod said, pointing to the far side of the High Wing. "It leads directly to Tigre Hall through a small anteroom."

Eylan stood next to him. "I have nothing to give but my sworn word," she said. "I'll forsake my duty for now. Let you leave with your seed."

Tylar nodded his awkward thanks.

Dart came up next. "And all I have is my blood, which I've given freely." She had already ignited his sword. "And Pupp won't leave my side. Not here."

Tylar knelt and touched Dart's cheek. "He's done enough, as have you."

Dart glanced to her toes. "But there is still one thing left for me to do." She met his eyes. Again they seemed so much older than the face that held them. The girl's fingers touched the dagger worn at her belt. Yaellin's cursed dagger. Her voice was a whisper. "I won't be captured."

Tylar opened his mouth to object, but she was already backing away. The girl knew the truth. False hope would only insult her.

Tylar stood as Kathryn stepped to him. She shimmered out of her Shadowcloak and held it out to him. "It's ripe with power."

"But I'm no blessed knight."

"Still, it will serve you for a short time, until it's bled of Grace. Use the shadows wisely."

She attempted to help him into it, but it became too awkward. His elbow struck hers. She stepped on his toe. They no longer moved well together. She backed away.

Tylar settled into the cloak on his own, relying on old habit.

Kathryn met his eyes. Tears welled. Again she seemed unable to say something. It was as if they were locked behind some door, waiting for a key. Tylar did not have it. He wasn't even sure he could find the lock. Too much guilt and grief clouded everything. It was hard to say where hers began and his ended.

And what, in the end, did he have to offer? He touched his chest. He had seen the horror in her eyes when she had viewed the broken form that was his true shape. The body he wore now was only memory, a shell of who he once was. Illusions, echoes, shadows, and light.

He turned away, knowing all was suspect.

Even his heart.

The Hands stirred. Voices raised in that eerie cadence, rising from all the throats together.

"Bring the sword now." The castillion shook again. Stones toppled deep in the keep. "I will wait no longer."

Tylar took a steadying breath. He faced the others.

The time for words was over. He gripped the sword and headed for the back door. The others followed, as did the Hands, moving woodenly. Puppets manipulated by the god below. Were any of them freer?

Tylar reached the door, opened it, and without glancing back, he headed down the narrow stair.

Kathryn watched him depart, disappearing down the dark throat. She flashed back to the docks below Tashijan, spying upon Tylar in chains, leaving her life, broken and stripped. Tears finally flowed. She turned away.

The Hands simply stared, eyes on fire.

Kathryn wanted to take a sword to each, to savage them completely. Her shoulders shook. Her fingers clenched on the hilt of her blade. But the folk here were not to blame. To put them to the blade would serve no end.

She stared at the others, her companions.

It was difficult to meet anyone's eyes.

To do so was to read the hopelessness in each.

Kathryn fell to her knees on the stones. She covered her face, bowing her head to the floor. She had not allowed herself to break down. Not in front of Tylar. Pain wrenched through her. He had left her again, with nothing but her guilt. Her belly ached, remembering an old pain . . . and blood.

She hated him at that moment.

But as before, on her knees, she wanted only one thing.

Come back.

❖

Tylar stalked down the stairs. The way was narrow. Only a few torches lit it. He kept his mind fixed to what he must face, but at the edges of his perception, he felt the shadow Graces flowing throughout his cloak.

As he swept past a torch, the power ebbed to the deepest folds, and as he descended into darkness again, it flushed anew. This tidal rhythm was as familiar as his own heartbeat . . . yet it was muffled. He was cut off from it fully. It felt more like memory than reality.

And in many ways, it was.

He descended swiftly, tasting the power, remembering a time when he wore such a cloak without ever feeling it. It was a second skin. But this was not his skin, he reminded himself.

It was Kathryn's cloak.

She had worn this same cloth when she had sat and denied him in court. Expressed her doubts of him. But then again, how honest had he been with her? She had known nothing of his dealings with the Gray Traders.

At the time, he had been brash enough to believe he could slip between the black and the white. It had all started to raise funds for the orphanages of Akkabak Harbor, where he had grown up. He didn't want others to face the same cold streets and rough peddling that he had. Few survived. And he'd still had contacts among the Traders from his own days among the alleys.

But slowly things changed. Coins began to find their way into his own pocket. A few at first, then a bit more. It seemed a minor thing, done for the greater good.

Tylar felt old bile rising. It was hard to recognize when gray darkened to black, when twilight became true night.

But it did.

Then there was Kathryn. They were to be one. Her light finally opened his eyes to the darkness. He tried to break away. But mistrust was the coin of the Gray Traders. Murders were laid at his doorstep.

Old anger flared. Old injustices.

If only he had never met her . . .

He closed his eyes, knowing it wasn't fair. But the anger still burned, deeper than he cared to admit. And mixed amid it all was a new, rawer guilt. His child. Lost in blood and heartbreak. How could she ever forgive him?

And somehow that guilt, that question, only fueled the anger inside him. His steps began to hurry.

He found the cloak suddenly cloying.

But at last, he reached the end of the stairs. There was nowhere else to run. He forced his feet to slow, his breathing to even.

He halted on the bottom step and took a deep breath.

It was time to stop running.

Stepping down, he moved to the door. It led to a small antechamber, the walls lined with benches and pillows. He inspected the room from the doorway, ready for another trap. It was empty. The far door was grander. According to Gerrod's sketch, it opened to the main hall.

He approached the door, Rivenscryr in hand.

Thunder echoed.

He waited for it to pass, then leaned an ear to the door. He heard nothing, except for a rumble of rushing water under his feet. The Tigre River flowed under this bottommost level. It must be flood high by now.

Stepping back, he gripped the Godsword and reached to the latch with his other hand. He pulled the door open and flowed into the hall, touching the Grace in his cloak to hide his entry. He kept crouched and slid to the neighboring wall.

Tigre Hall spread before him, half in ruins.

He gaped at the destruction. The churn of water burbled louder, echoing up from ragged holes in the floor. It seemed the grand hall had not been spared when the flippercraft tore beneath the keep.

But that was not all the damage.

Torches lit the space sparingly, hanging from sconces, illuminating broken benches, tables, and splintered chairs. It looked as if some mad whirlwind had torn through the hall. The broken floor could not have done all this damage.

Then Tylar smelled it.

A residual odor of burned blood.

Here was where Chrism must have gathered his guard and underfolk, where the humanity was burned from them by corrupted Grace. The destruction was the aftermath of that foul birthing.

"Do not tarry at the door, Godslayer."

The soft voice came from the far side of the room, where tables and chairs still stood upright. A raised dais was lit by two torches atop poles. They blazed merrily, brighter than those along the walls. Their flickering flames shone upon a row of nine chairs atop the dais. Four smaller seats flanked each side of a taller chair. It had been carved from myrrwood, gone black by age.

The throne of Chrism.

It was empty.

The figure rose from the steps of the dais. He had been righting an overturned pot that supported a dwarf sedge-wood tree. Its fronded crown shook slightly as the pot settled on the floor.

Lord Chrism stood back, staring at it, fists on his hips. Then he reached forward and touched the spindly trunk. The small buds, buried amid the leaves, opened, peeling back opalescent petals.

Satisfied, Chrism lifted his other arm and motioned Tylar to join him. "This way, Godslayer."

Chrism climbed the dais and dropped to his throne. He lounged comfortably and waited.

Tylar waded out of shadows and edged warily across the room. He skirted the edges of a hole. The rush of water below sounded like a heavy wind.

He glanced down.

Deeper in the water, a slight glow shone. Perhaps a glowpike working against the stream. Then it vanished, swept away.

Tylar cleared the ruined sections of the hall and continued forward. Behind the dais, another hole cracked the floor, spewing up a bit of spray that scintillated in the torchlight. It was too bright for such a dark moment.

Chrism's eyes fixed on the Godsword as Tylar stepped forward. Tylar read the desire behind his dispassionate features.

The god waved to a chair by the sedge-wood tree.

Tylar remained standing.

Chrism sighed, a soft, pleasant sound. "I've called you down here to make you an offer, Tylar."

Tylar winced at the god's familiarity.

Chrism continued. "The Cabal could use someone of your . . . unique talents. It would be a shame to waste such an opportunity, but we will if we must. Join us freely, turn over the sword, and we'll spare all your companions in the High Wing."

Tylar stared at the god before him. He was plainly handsome, unassuming in greens and browns. But Tylar remembered another Chrism. He again touched Mistress Naff's memories, of Chrism attacking her, abusing her, destroying her with his corrupted seed. Tylar still felt the stubble of his cheek at his throat. He remembered the agony.

There was no kindness or mercy to be had here.

His fingers tightened.

Chrism noted the strain of his muscles. "A shame."

"Who are you?" Tylar asked. He would know more. From the easy carriage of the god, there was a trap hidden here. He wanted time to discern it, to let it show itself, to let the god drop his guard. He needed every advantage.

But mostly he wanted answers.

"I am still Chrism," the god answered. "Or rather as much of Chrism as once filled this skin. We are one and the same. Or rather one part of three. Except our aethryn selves have vanished to the aether. Unknowable, untouchable, uncaring of flesh and things beneath it."

"You're a naethryn," Tylar said, realizing the deeper truth behind the god's words. Disgust filled his words. "You're Chrism's undergod."

Chrism shrugged. "This cloth is as much mine to wear as the one before."

"How . . . ?" Tylar asked. "What became of the other?"

"Gone. Burned away by the sword you carry with you now."

"You killed a part of yourself?"

"It was no matter. The Sundering shivered away all that was soft and merciful from me, left it in flesh here. The greater purpose was set aside, forgotten. But not in the naether! We still remembered. Those who served He Who Comes still survived. We banded together."

"The Cabal," Tylar mumbled.

A nod answered. "When the time was ripe, the Cabal stole the Godsword, whetted the blade, and buried it into the spot where Chrism bled and settled this land. He knew it, of course, felt its poison in his precious garden, and came to the pillars, to the sword. He was so easily trapped . . . *again.*"

"What do you mean?"

Chrism sat straighter. "That's right. You never knew the truth." Laughter flowed, darkly complexioned. "The story of Chrism's settling of this First Land. His great sacrifice. It was not as your illustrious historicals describe. Do you wish to know how your lands *truly* started?"

Tylar noted the furtive movements behind Chrism's shoulders. *I must keep the god distracted, focused on me.*

"What happened?" Tylar asked stiffly, but he shifted the Godsword to catch Chrism's eye.

Chrism settled back. "It was a dark time when the gods first came to this world. Atrocities were committed across Myrillia, by god and man alike. Chrism was no different. He raved. Did horrible things. He was eventually captured by your folk. Chained between the pillars here. His throat, wrists, and groin were sliced to the bone. They meant to kill the daemon who had slain a hundred children among their villages. But Chrism bled and bled. Undying, he fed the land. His Grace took root here, and his ravings died away. He pledged himself to the land and spent another hundred years chained to that pillar, in servitude, until finally being freed."

Tylar's skin went cold at that thought. A century in chains.

"Only after he was freed was his discovery shared among the other gods. Others settled to escape the ravings. But the first . . . Chrism's settling was not done by choice or even despair, but by force. A savage and bloody beginning of Myrillia's new age."

Tylar shook his head, refusing to believe.

"And the Godsword," Chrism continued. "Why do you think Chrism slew those children? He was trying to revive our sword. When we were whole, in our own kingdom, we forged it for He Who Comes. Some sense of this persisted in his ravings. He struggled to revive the sword. But once settled, such desire faded. He hid the sword, but others knew of it."

"Your Cabal."

Chrism nodded. "For millennia we sought some way to break from the naether and into this world. Rivenscryr was our only hope. And there were those among your people who used Dark Grace to thin our world from yours. We broke through in tiny seepages. Enough to set a foothold here. We lured others to us. We set them on a path to free Myrillia."

Tylar remembered the screams of freedom by Darjon. Such human Cabalists had been duped, believing they fought for some greater purpose, some illusory freedom that would benefit all of Myrillia, not realizing the Cabal's darker purpose.

Chrism leaned forward. "Who do you think finally released Chrism from his chains after a hundred years? Who allowed Chrism to spread his peaceful message and start this age?"

Curiosity burned in Tylar. Yet he had to maintain focus. Not let his eyes wander to the silent writhing that rose behind the throne. It had not been a glowpike in the waters under the keep. Tylar's eyes narrowed.

"It was the Cabal who freed Chrism from his chains. Those first to wear human skin. But not the last."

"If . . . if you freed Chrism from his chains then why murder him now?"

"At that place in history, peace served the Cabal. Time was needed to study this land and the odd Graces born to us here. It took millennia to spread ourselves, to root ourselves, to corrupt those of weak mind. But four centuries ago, a new way to whet Rivenscryr was discovered."

"The godling boy."

Chrism smiled, a predatory gleam. "Much was wasted until we discovered how to use the boy's gifts. It was difficult without possessing the sword at the time. The boy died too soon. He did not have our natural ability to heal from mortal wounds. Who would've known that? The offspring of gods was not immortal. So much was wasted. We won't make that same mistake again."

Tylar pictured Dart. He couldn't let this monster have her.

Chrism continued. "But the Cabal did preserve enough of the boy's blood, saved in crystal. We bided our time. We chose where best to strike first. Two centuries ago, the castillion here was infiltrated, the sword stolen and whetted and planted as a trap in the Eldergarden. The god came, sensing the poisoned touch of the sword in his midst. He found the sword, yanked it free. The fool."

"The sword had pierced into the naether," Tylar said.

"And I was there, waiting. When he pulled the blade, I swept forth and into Chrism. Bathed in Gloom, he had no defenses. I burned the quick from his flesh, hollowing him out. Then I slipped into him like one slips into a well-worn boot."

Tylar touched his chest, forgetting himself.

Chrism noted his movement. "Not like you, Godslayer. Or even like the creature you slew in the High Wing, wearing Mistress Naff's skin. That underling, of low mind and station, served us, carried the whetted sword and slew Meeryn. It was unfortunate Meeryn had learned of the Cabal's infiltration of Chrismferry; even she did not know how high it had spread. But such knowledge could not be allowed to survive."

"So you had Meeryn killed," Tylar said.

"The Cabal will have this world. We will possess it like I do this skin. We will pave the way once again for He Who Comes. Nothing will stop us this time. We acted too hastily in the past, in our own kingdom. We did not understand fully what I had forged." Chrism stared at the sword again, eyes shining. "But now we do. As before, we will bring a new age to Myrillia. But not one of peace for the crawling vermin of these lands. Such a time has ended. You shall become our chattel and clay. Your blood and flesh will open the way for His coming."

"Who—?"

Chrism sneered. "Even his name you are not worthy to hear."

Chrism finally stood. A black mist steamed from his skin. Tylar had seen such a sheen in gods when they were worked up, like when Meeryn had fled her assassin. But while Meeryn's glow was sunlight and petals, the pall rising from Chrism ate the light and stirred with the winds of the naether. It made his form shimmer, as across baked sands.

"I am not like you or the creature you slew," he repeated. "You are possessed by smoke and shadow. But as I forged Rivenscryr, it forged me. *You* are possession. *I* am fruition, culmination, perfection."

He lifted his arms. His true form pierced out of his flesh.

"See the face of the Cabal!"

❖

Locked in dark thoughts, Dart stood by the windows of the High Wing. She kept one hand on the dagger at her belt. Tylar had been gone so long. What was happening? She could see the others reflected in the windows. They all seemed lost to their private dungeons. Kathryn had finally risen from the floor, her eyes haunted and empty. Krevan and Eylan, warriors both, seemed boneless now, sunken in. Gerrod had gone very still, becoming a bronze statue, unmoving.

And among them stood the Hands, eyes blazing, watching them all. Two of the Hands stood, sentinels of flesh and Dark Grace. But the other two wandered the hall, keeping a blazing eye on all.

Dart watched for them, keeping away in a slow dance. She didn't want herself being grabbed and pinned before she could wield the dagger and end her life. Her blood would never be Chrism's. Pupp kept to her side. He was clearly disturbed by the Hands, too.

So she kept a watch on the room's reflection while staring out at the storm. The windows of the High Wing faced across all of Chrismferry. The Tigre River snaked outward from the castillion, splitting the city in half.

True night neared, though it was hard to discern through the dark clouds. Lights dotted the city below.

How many went about their ordinary day, oblivious of the terror and bloodshed being waged at the city's heart? Dart wished for such oblivion, to live a simple life. But wishes would not help her now.

Lightning flashed in a forking display across the skies. For a moment, night became day again. The city appeared in stark, silvery relief. The river below ignited, reflecting the brilliance.

Thunder followed as darkness swept back over Chrismferry. Dart blinked away the flash of the lightning, dazzled. But the brightness would not go away. The river below continued to shine in patches as if the waters had trapped some of the brilliance and refused to let it go.

She leaned closer, her forehead on the cold glass. Her brow wrinkled.

The tiny glows in the water moved as she watched, streaming toward the castillion, against the current. These were no reflections.

"Lights . . ." Dart mumbled.

Lights under the water.

Fingers closed on her shoulder. She jumped, fearing it was one of the Hands.

"Hush," Rogger said, a faint whisper at her ear. "Back away."

Dart, though confused, obeyed. She stared questioningly at Rogger. The thief simply shook his head.

"Help me," he said as he drew her to the opposite side of the hall, away from the bank of windows. "We need to keep the Hands' attention away."

Though she did not fully understand, Dart nodded. She had asked similar of Laurelle earlier. To draw the eyes from what must not be seen.

Dart pulled her dagger. "Struggle with me," she whispered. "If there is one person here who Chrism is most concerned about, it's *me*. He will not wish me to come to harm."

Rogger seemed to understand her intent and reached for her hand.

"But be careful of the blade," Dart added.

"Naturally," Rogger said, taking hold of her hand. "Shall we dance?"

Dart nodded, raised her voice for all to hear, and feigned a struggle. "I . . . I can't stand it anymore! I will take my own life!"

"No, you mustn't!" Rogger answered.

She and Rogger began their dance, drawing all eyes away from the windows, away from the glow moving against the current.

❖

"See the true face of the Cabal!"

Tylar gaped as Chrism stepped down from the dais. His flesh was pierced by hard black spines. His eyes went black, but still glowed with some inner fire.

"I am no smoky phantom," he said. His voice quaked at the edges with the keening wail of the naether. "I am naethryn given flesh and form in this world."

He stepped lower, arms outstretching, spines shattering out his finger-tips into great claws. His knees broke as he stepped to the stone floor, bending backward inhumanly. Shining black spurs sprouted from the backs of his legs. They dripped with oil that ate through the stone.

Tylar fell backward, knowing now why Chrism had been so relaxed. He was no daemon, but something greater and deadlier.

Chrism stalked toward him. From either side of his head, behind his ears, a pair of horns spiraled out, winding back in a fierce sweep. He opened his mouth and black fangs uprooted teeth. His tongue burned away to flame.

"Do you think to stand against us, little man?" A laugh as harsh as braided steel burst forth. "Not even your sword can slay me. Why do you think it was left in the gardens, untended, unguarded? Rivenscryr forged me. It cannot unmake me."

Tylar balked. Was it true?

"WHO ARE YOU TO FACE ME?" Chrism boomed, his words racking through the wail. "YOU ARE NO GODSLAYER!"

Tylar stood before the onslaught. "You know I'm not," he answered quietly. "Because you took everything from me. My honor, my body, even my humanity."

"THEN WHAT IS LEFT? WHAT ARE YOU TO DEFY ME?"

Tylar sheathed Rivenscryr and pulled forth Krevan's sword. "I am a knight."

He lunged toward the beast, firing all the Grace in his cloak, igniting shadow to speed and strength. He fed it into his one arm, sweeping at the naether monster.

"Now!" he shouted.

By then, the writhing wall of tangleweed had climbed the wall behind the throne, reaching to the ceiling. It had risen silently, growing thicker, bending leaf and vine to sluice the river water. Not even a drip spattered to alert Chrism.

This was no growth of loam, but of *water.*

Chrism was blind to it.

Upon Tylar's shout, the wall of tangleweed burst out and crashed over the daemon, ripe with Fyla's Grace.

Tangleweed wrapped and bound, coiled and snarled.

The poisonous touch of the naethryn burned vine and leaf, but more weed surged to take its place. And there was still flesh that moored the naethryn, Chrism's old shell. Tendril and stalk rooted deep for purchase.

Still, Chrism bucked and tore. Neither god nor weed could get the upper hand.

Tylar tipped the balance, striking with his borrowed sword. He cleaved into the beast's shoulder. Steel clanged, like striking rock. The sword was knocked from his grip. But Chrism's attention was diverted long enough for a ropy vine to snare his claw on one side.

Tylar dove away as the other claw swiped at his belly, ready to rip him in half. But the years in the slave pits had taught him how to roll and dodge. He landed on his shoulder and flipped back to his feet.

Rogger's daggers rested in both palms.

He threw one, then the other. The first struck Chrism in the throat. The other in his belly. Tylar grabbed another pair from his belt and whipped them, hitting upper arm and lower thigh.

Vines followed, winding out to grab the embedded daggers, finding good purchase to further wrap up the naethryn. A thick trunk lashed around Chrism's throat.

A ripping howl escaped the creature's maw.

Chrism was lifted bodily from the floor, dragged up by the neck. Legs kicked, poisoned spurs sliced through the weeds under them.

"Strike now!" a voice rang behind him. Fyla, the Mistress of Tangle Reef, had come, rising through another of the broken holes. "Strike with the Godsword!"

Tylar ran at the writhing naethryn. He dragged Rivenscryr from its sheath and lifted it high, cradling its hilt in both fists.

One strike. That would be all he had.

Tylar tapped the last of the Grace in Kathryn's cloak. With a will borne of blood and shadow, Tylar leaped at the naethryn. Chrism's legs attempted to kick him away. Tylar twisted in midair. A spur caught him in the thigh, but it was too late.

Tylar struck the monster and drove the blade clean through the monster's chest, through the heart of the naethryn.

Chrism racked, throwing Tylar back.

He tumbled away, hitting the stone hard.

A wail shattered through the room. Torches were blown out. Darkness fell. Tylar scrambled backward.

But glow pods quickly rose from the many holes and cracks in the floor. It was one of those same pods that Tylar had spotted in the river's current earlier.

Light returned.

Chrism still hung among the weeds, panting heavily, wrapped tight in vines. The beast no longer fought. The sword hilt rested square in the center of the chest.

His fiery black eyes sought Tylar, then Fyla.

"Meeryn's lover," Chrism spat, blood flowing from his lips.

Fyla remained silent. She stood naked, resting atop one of her weed pads.

Instead, Tylar, gaining his feet, spoke. His left thigh was on fire, but he ignored it. "It is not only man that will hold this line," he said coldly and certainly. "We are not alone. Bring this war if you will, but it will not be only a War of Gods . . . but a War of Gods *and Man.*"

Chrism writhed again, but the weeds dug deeper into to his flesh. "You have not slain me. Rivenscryr cannot harm me."

"But it can rend your flesh," Fyla said calmly. A tiny tendril of weed spiraled out, glowing with Grace. It reached across Chrism's shoulder.

Chrism's eyes widened with fear.

The fragile sprout touched the tip of the hilt.

Fires blasted outward from the impaled sword. Flesh seared and blackened. Chrism arched backward, screaming flames. His body blazed among the weeds.

Tylar watched as flesh turned to ash, falling fully away, revealing the full extent of the black naethryn. It was the form of a mighty wyrm, clawed and horned. It screamed one last time; then shape without substance dissolved, collapsing in on itself.

With a mighty clap of thunder, it was gone.

The sword tumbled from on high and clattered against the floor. It bounced and rattled, then settled to the stones.

Tylar walked up to it. The blade was still present. It had not vanished. He stared from the intact sword, to Fyla, frowning.

Her weedy pad carried her closer, dropping to the stone.

"The naethryn spoke the truth," she said.

Tylar bent and retrieved the sword. He stared at the blade. "It did not kill him."

"No, but he has been banished back to the naether. Without his toehold in flesh here, he could not remain in our world. And with Chrism's body destroyed, his naethryn will never find a host that will allow him to take such perfect form again. It is a blow that the Cabal will find hard to recover from."

Tylar stared at the flowing weed, wondering at her arrival. "How . . . ?"

"The raven you sent upon departing Tashijan reached me, calling me to Chrismferry. I was already nearby, hugging the coast of the First Land, hoping to be of use."

Tylar had forgotten the raven he had sent. Kathryn had sent hers to Yaellin, to alert him to meet them at the school. But his raven had been sent out to sea, to seek out Fyla.

"I had wanted you to come here only to support my claims," Tylar said. "To speak on my behalf when I met with Chrism."

She nodded. "But I have ears in many places. I heard of the battle as I was already flowing up the Tigre River from the coast. I came to lend my strength to this war."

"And that you did." Tylar held out Rivenscryr to Fyla, resting the blade across his palms. "This is the sword of the gods. You must take it."

She raised a palm. "That was the past. Like you said to Chrism, this is no longer a war of gods alone. Man has as much stake here in Myrillia as any of us. More so, in fact. Rivenscryr now belongs to the world of man. It is yours to bear."

"Why me?"

Fyla moved closer. She leaned out from her pad. This was not her realm. Weed and water were her home. Only the river channel allowed her to delve so far into the First Land.

She tenderly brushed Tylar's lips, sighing between them, then pulled away. "Thank you. For Meeryn. For myself."

Her pad lifted her up and began to slide away.

Tylar followed a step, lifting the blade. "Why me?"

She met his gaze, eyes shining with Grace, and answered him. "Because you were chosen. Because there is no other." Her eyes glowed with sadness and sympathy. "Because you must."

26

DOORS

DART RACED DOWN THE HIGH WING HALL. SUNLIGHT BLAZED WITH the dawn of a new day. It seemed a full year had passed since that awful, bloody day, but it had been only a full moonpass. Twenty-eight days. Dart reached Laurelle's door and knocked briskly. There was no immediate answer, so she knocked harder.

"Hold!" a shout answered her. "You'll rattle the door right off its hinges!"

"What is taking you so long?" Dart squirmed in her new leather boots.

Pupp danced around her, matching her excitement.

Dart smoothed the lay of her velvet brown pants and snowy silk blouse. But it was the cloak she was most proud of. It was as black as any Shadowcloak and hung perfectly to her ankles. It was pinned at her throat by a black diamond.

Laurelle finally opened the door. Dart had to blink, taken aback. Laurelle was resplendent in a silver gown and a tiara of kryst jewels. Each jewel shone brilliantly against the ebony of her friend's straight locks.

"There's plenty of time," Laurelle said, but even her cheeks were flushed.

"But you must be in your seat before the ceremony begins," Dart said. "The other Hands have already left."

Dart led the way down the hall to the back stair. The girls hurried, but a firm voice struck out behind them.

"Children! I'll not have one of you tripping on a gown's hem or a cloak's edge. You'll tumble all the way down to Tigre Hall."

Dart slowed her step. "Sorry, Matron Shashyl." She turned and curtsied to the portly woman. Dart had to hide a smile. Thankfully Shashyl had been away from the keep when Chrism had ilked the guards and underfolk. She had been visiting her sick sister in Cobbleshores. She was spared, one of the few.

Matron Shashyl stepped to the door to the private stair and held it open. "Grace is not only found in humours," she said sagely, "but also in the bearing of a young woman."

"Yes, Matron," Laurelle said with a perfectly serene face.

But once the door closed behind them, Laurelle burst with laughter. They fled down the stairs, as if late for their morning meal. They wound around and around the narrow stairs. Pupp lit the way, racing ahead. They finally reached the bottom and burst into the antechamber.

They almost collided with the bulk of Master Pliny. He had been bent over, securing a bootlace. He straightened, his jowled face flushed. "There you are, Mistress Laurelle. I was to wait for you so we can enter, arm in arm."

"I'd be honored," Laurelle said and leaned out an elbow. But she winked past his shoulder to Dart.

Dart hid a giggle behind a fist. The Hands had no recollection of their enthrallment by Chrism. Once the monster had been vanquished, the blaze of fire had died in their eyes, and they had all collapsed. Each slept for a full day, then woke as if from a regular slumber.

But they had all heard the tale afterward.

Each still held a haunted look in the eye.

Guards at the doors, new to their posts, opened the way. The muffled voices of the crowds filling the grand hall rose to a din. Laurelle and Master Pliny set off into the arched chamber.

Dart watched from the doorway. Tigre Hall was in the midst of repair. Temporary planks covered the holes in the floor, but the rush of the river could still be heard below.

Laurelle and Pliny slowly traversed the aisle between the curved benches that fronted the grand dais. The wood smiths had built most of the seating in only the past few days, working through all the bells.

Laurelle finally reached the dais and climbed with Pliny. They each took their seats, filling their proper places as Hands of the realm. Dart glanced to the chair to the immediate right of the center myrrwood throne. It had been her place. Hand of Blood. But another sat there now.

Delia.

It was her right as Meeryn's original Hand of Blood.

But others were empty. Yet to be filled.

The smile on her lips faded as she remembered Yaellin, fallen to save her. She would honor him as best she could. She reached and clutched the black diamond at her throat.

"There you are," a firm voice cracked behind her.

Dart jumped and turned. She curtsied again. "Castellan Vail."

"A page does not curtsy," Kathryn said sternly. "They bow, first the head, then at the waist."

Dart licked her lips. She was to leave in the next day or so for Tashijan, to train as a knight. She would serve as page to the castellan herself. The clothes she wore now were reflective of her station. It had taken a bit of convincing to fight for this opportunity.

Tylar and the others had refused at first.

But Dart had not backed down. Yaellin had been both knight and Hand. To honor his sacrifice, she would become the same.

Surprisingly, Kathryn had come to her defense.

"None know the girl there," the castellan had said. "Only those loyal to us, like Krevan and Gerrod, know the secret of her godhood. Not even Argent is aware. What better place to keep her safe than at the heart of Tashijan, surrounded by knights? And perhaps it's still best to keep you and Dart apart for now."

Tylar had finally relented, bowing to the wisdom of it.

So Dart had been bled almost daily by Delia, the new Hand of Blood. Her humour was stored in secret, available for Tylar to ignite Rivenscryr whenever necessary. Dart was no longer needed here, not as Hand, nor as sheath.

Dart attempted to bow now as the castellan directed.

Kathryn watched. "Much better." Then she leaned down and faced Dart. "Is this something you truly want? To come with me to Tashijan? You are safe here."

Dart met her gaze. Nowhere was truly safe. She had learned that too well. True security could be found only in one's own heart. She would learn to defend herself, to find a place for herself.

"I want to be a knight," Dart said solemnly. "I *will* be a knight."

Kathryn stared at her and nodded. "Then come with me." She crossed to the door. "Stay by my side."

Dart fell in step with Kathryn as she traversed the hall. Cloaked knights and tattooed masters filled all the benches to the right. It was as if all of Tashijan had come.

Kathryn stepped to the very front bench. She sidled over and sat next to a tall man with a plate of bone over one eye.

"Warden Fields," Kathryn said icily.

"Castellan Vail," he answered with as much warmth. His one good eye settled to Dart. Pupp gave the man a wide berth.

"My new page," Kathryn said and patted the open seat next to her.

The man nodded. His interest glazed over, and he turned away.

Dart fell into her seat, sitting straight, clutching the front edge of the bench.

She stared across to the other side of the hall. Nobles throughout the First Land and beyond had come to attend, as had Hands from realms throughout Myrillia. Each god had sent at least one Hand. Most gods from the First Land had sent all their handservants.

As Dart gawked, she spotted a face staring back at her. Her brow crinkled with recognition. It was one of her fellow thirdfloorers from the Conclave. A dark boy. His bronzed face was easy to pick out among the older, paler Hands of his retinue. She had never learned his name. He had been chosen the same night as Dart and Laurelle, chosen by Jessup of Oldenbrook, a distinguished house of the First Land. But Dart also remembered how he had spoken up for her when the others had ridiculed · her.

His eyes met hers. He nodded.

She was surprised to feel heat suffuse her face.

A trumpet sounded, startling her back around.

Drums beat at the rear of the room.

Folk throughout the hall stood. Dart rose with the tide.

Doors opened at the back, and a march of castillion guards entered Tigre Hall. Stepping in beat to the drums, they crossed down the center aisle, taking up stations to either side, forming an alley. Swords were raised, forming an archway.

Another trumpet blasted—and he appeared, stepping into the hall.

Kathryn stiffened at Dart's side. Tylar strode down the tunnel of swords. His black hair had been oiled straight back. His face had been shaved to polished smoothness. As he marched, his gray eyes shone with the storm inside him. This was not a role he cared to play. He wore a solid outfit of black: boots, pants, shirt, and cloak. The only color was the silver scabbard worn at the waist.

It bore the Godsword.

Rivenscryr.

He marched down the long aisle toward the chair that awaited him. Since that bloody day, ravens had been flying throughout Myrillia. The skies were thick with their wings. Gods were consulted across the Nine Lands. It was decided that Chrismferry could not be left fallow after the slaying of Chrism. It was the city around which all of Myrillia turned.

A regent was needed.

Someone with Grace to share, to keep commerce flowing.

Still bearing Meeryn's blessings, Tylar had been chosen.

He strode up to the tall myrrwood seat, faced the crowd, and pulled forth Rivenscryr.

He had no choice.

At the end, the godslayer had become a god.

Tylar stood by the central brazier in the High Wing.

"It's about time you returned these," Rogger said and strapped on his belt of daggers. "I expect I'll be needing them."

"Are you leaving already?" Tylar asked. "The sun's almost setting."

He snugged the belt. "That's the beginning of a new day for a thief."

Tylar clapped him on the shoulder. "Watch yourself. Where will you head first?"

Rogger touched the side of his nose. "Perhaps I'd best leave my path unknown for now."

Tylar nodded. He clasped Rogger in a firm embrace. The thief was heading off to investigate how far the Cabal's corruption had spread in other god's households. He would be traveling under the guise of his interrupted pilgrimage. In fact, he wore a fresh brand, Chrism's sigil, on his backside. "Seemed the best place," Rogger had commented.

"When will I hear from you?" Tylar asked now as they both separated.

"When you least expect it," Rogger said with a wink. "I'll send word through Krevan and the Black Flaggers."

With a final few words of parting, the two separated. Rogger headed away. Tylar turned to face his next obstacle.

The doors to Chrism's rooms.

As regent, they were now *his* rooms. But he was not sure he was ready to step through those doors. He glanced over his shoulder. Beyond the windows, the sun descended into the flow of the Tigre River, painting the skies in rosy hues and violet splashes.

A brilliant sunset.

But Tylar knew most of the beauty came from the pall of smoke that continued to steam from the smoldering myrrwood forest. The fires had yet to die away fully. Deep embers still glowed, buried among the piles of ashes. A forest that lived for four thousand years did not expire easily.

A door closed to the left, drawing his attention.

Kathryn stepped through it. Both of them froze, caught by surprise.

"Kathryn . . ." he finally choked out.

For the past many days, they had been missing each other, each busy with a thousand details and questions, drawn in opposite directions. He fell more and more into his duties here. Her attentions were drawn to Tashijan.

Or was it simply that they were each avoiding the other, unsure what to do? How to face a past . . . and a future?

"I . . . I was just picking up something Dart left in Laurelle's room." Kathryn nodded to the room she just left. "We head out for Tashijan in the morning."

"So soon?" It was like everyone was fleeing from his side.

"There is much to settle at Tashijan," Kathryn said. "Argent has already headed back. He hurries to firm those still loyal to him. After he passed the soothmancer's test, clearing his name of any of the bloodiness that occurred at the Citadel, he seeks to reestablish his position."

"Argent still refuses to step down? Even after he admits to employing a cursed sword?"

Kathryn shook her head. "There is still enough support for him both among the Fiery Cross members and the Council to keep his seat."

"And what of the Fiery Cross?" Tylar asked. He drew her closer to the golden doors, away from direct sight.

Kathryn frowned. "I don't know how Argent passed his soothing, but I know what I saw. Perhaps he knows nothing about the dead knight and the bloody sacrifice, but someone in the Fiery Cross does. There is foulness afoot, and I will root it out."

Tylar's brow crinkled with concern. Perryl still remained missing, vanished from his room. "And what of Dart? Is it safe to bring her into such a house?"

"I don't think your house is any safer," Kathryn said with a glint of irritation. "I'm not sure all the gods are as satisfied as they claim with your regency. And we don't know where the Cabal will strike next, but your neck is sticking out there."

Tylar nodded, conceding the point. He had his own house to clean. Stray ilk-beasts were still showing up throughout the city, having escaped to the gardens during the aftermath of the battle. And any face could hide a Cabalist.

"I'll keep the girl safe," Kathryn assured him.

Words suddenly died between them. Kathryn seemed to be waiting for something from him. Her eyes drifted down and away.

"I must go," she finally mumbled.

A part of him wanted to ask her to stay. But how could he? She was needed at Tashijan. There were few over there he could truly trust, and as castellan, she could do the most good. And what could he offer to make her stay? The discomfort between them, born of old bitterness and guilt, only seemed to worsen with time spent in each other's company.

Neither had the words to heal . . . if it could ever be done.

It was too complicated, too wounded, too bloodied.

He nodded. "Travel safe."

She hesitated, glancing up at him, a breath away from saying something else.

A neighboring door opened to the right. Delia stepped out. Her eyes widened to find Kathryn and Tylar huddled together.

"Excuse me," she said shyly.

Delia wore a simple shift of white linen belted at the waist with a black cord, a match to her dark hair. She carried her tools in her hands.

Her eyes found Tylar. "You . . . you mentioned wanting to complete the day's bloodletting before final bells."

Tylar stared at her. After watching the shifting shadows of Kathryn's cloak, Delia seemed somehow crisper, more vivid, and lighter of spirit.

"Of course," he said. "I had forgotten."

He glanced to Kathryn. She backed away, turned, and stepped toward the main hallway. But not before he noted the pain in her eyes.

"Kathryn . . ."

She glanced back at him and shook her head.

No more words. They each had their own path to follow from here.

She marched down the hall.

Tylar watched until she vanished out the far door. She was right. He turned to the wide golden doors, grabbed the handle, and shoved into his new chambers.

Here was his path.

In Darkness . . .

MIRRA MOVED SLOWLY DOWN THE BLACK STAIR, WRAPPED IN A FURRED cloak and leaning on a stout cane. She took care to open the wards before her and close them after.

Precautions must be taken . . . even down here.

She moved far beneath Tashijan, as deep as Stormwatch Tower thrust high. None knew of these old tunnels and caverns. They were ancient even in the times of the human kings, burial crypts of the primitive el'rayn, a race before man. Not even their bones remained, just piles of dust and a few teeth.

Such is the impermanence of flesh . . .

She continued deeper. She needed no torch to guide her steps. She knew the way. Light was not welcome here. It threatened the barrier between this world and the naether below. Only in such sunless places did the naether come close enough to cross without the Godsword.

Still, she paused on the stair to rest her knees and back. She stared up. All was set. Her duty was almost done: to spread dissent, to corrupt, to confuse. Ser Henri had been too pliant a fool, so easy to flail his fears, to beset him with suspicions. She had set him against the Fiery Cross, playing one side upon the other. And the linchpin had been Henri's golden boy, Tylar ser Noche. How simple it had been to tease the mistrust of the Gray Traders, to get them to plant murder at Tylar's feet, then have him stripped and broken. It also broke poor Henri, made him even more compliant to her whispered words of conspiracies and dark covenants within the order.

The schism had been set.

All that was left was to widen the crack, to bring Tashijan down.

As Tashijan falls, so falls Myrillia.

Despite this thought, an irritated frown drew her lips back down. Henri had managed to keep one secret from her. Who could have known he had such strength? The abomination had lived, hidden so close. Even torture had not loosened Henri's tongue.

The secret had threatened everything.

Still, Mirra drew strength as she remembered Henri's screams, warded into silence, for their ears only. It was no matter in the end. With Henri's death, the Fiery Cross occupied the Eyrie now. And such an assignation continued to ring with discomfort throughout Tashijan. Argent ser Fields sat uncomfortably upon his throne. He would prove an even greater ally than Ser Henri.

It would not be long.

With a sigh, she continued down the stairs, passing tunnel after tunnel, each lined by niche after niche, ancient el'rayn crypts. But new residences had taken roost, the ancient dust swept clean.

In each cubicle, they waited, naether bound, and black blooded. A thousand strong. New knights to occupy Tashijan. Darker than any shadow, more powerful than any Grace.

The Black Ghawl.

She heard them breathe around her in the darkness, ageless, collected for four centuries and stored here, awaiting their rise.

Soon.

Mirra wended the last few steps to the deepest cavern.

She touched the last ward and a glow finally rose about the chamber ahead. Not a natural light, but the shine of putrefaction and decay. She walked gladly into its embrace.

The cavern was empty, except for a ripple of volcanic flowstone that had hardened into an altar. Upon the black stone rested a pale figure. Naked. Staring blindly upward.

She approached the altar. It was time to add one more to her legion.

It had been a shame to waste her last subject. To abandon his body on the floor, cold and emptied of blood. But he had served his purpose. To cast suspicion upon the Fiery Cross, to plant yet another seed of suspicion, sowed this time into the hearts of the new castellan . . . and in turn, into the godslayer.

She cursed under her breath at this last.

Tylar had cost them much.

But there were ways of handling a godslayer.

And Tylar *had* forged Rivenscryr.

This thought stirred the shadows around her. The naethryn waited at the gates. It would not be long. Myrillia was far from settled. Already the wheel turned.

Soon.

She turned her attention back to the pale figure sprawled upon the flowstone altar. Littick sigils marked his flesh, drawn in her own blood. She dabbed her fingers in a bowl and dripped the cursed alchemies into the boy's eyes.

Blindness dissolved like crusts from his gaze. The Littick symbols burst into flame.

He blinked. Then screamed.

"Hush," Mirra whispered. "It is time to bend a knee to a new master, Ser Perryl."

She lifted the dagger.

The boy could not move. So fair of features, so blue of eye.

But not for long.

She lifted the dagger high, far enough for the frozen boy to see.

Terror was an important element of alchemy.

With the strength of both shoulders, she plunged the dagger deep into Perryl's chest. The cursed blade passed easily through his ribs to the fist of red muscle that lay beneath. She let the dagger rest there, dropping her hands.

The hilt vibrated with each failing beat of the boy's heart.

Once, twice, thrice . . .

She waited. No more.

She reached forward and uncapped the top of the hilt. The hollow handle had been carved from an infant's leg bone, taken from the godling child stolen by the Cabal four centuries ago.

With all ready, Mirra climbed atop the flowstone altar. She straddled the boy, one leg on each side of his chest. She lifted the hem of her robe and squatted over the open handle of the dagger. She removed the plug of linen from between her legs. She allowed her menstra blood to flow and drip into the hollow handle.

Menstra to bless . . . she recited. *Or in this case . . . curse.*

It did not take long. It never did.

The bone hilt twitched.

The beat of a new heart, black and poisoned.

Once, twice, thrice . . .

APPENDIX TO MYRILLIA

The Four Aspects of the Gods

1. AIR
2. FIRE
3. WATER
4. LOAM

Litany of Nine Graces

BLOOD to open the way
SEED or MENSES to bless
SWEAT to imbue
TEARS to swell
SALIVA to ebb
PHLEGM to manifest
YELLOW BILE to gift
and BLACK to take it all away

The Nine Humoral Graces of the Gods

(PRIMARY QUADRICLES)

1. BLOOD defines the character of the blessing.
2. MASCULINE SEED will pass a sustained blessing upon a *living* creature.
3. FEMININE MENSES does the same as "seed."
4. SWEAT lays a blessing upon *nonliving* objects.

(SECONDARY QUINTRANGLES)

5. TEARS will *heighten* a blessing for short periods of time.
6. SALIVA will *weaken* the blessing for short periods of time.
7. PHLEGM will allow manifestations of the Grace beyond a body or object, useful in mixing alchemies.
8. YELLOW BILE (the waters passed by a God) will pass a blessing of *brief* duration.
9. BLACK BILE (the solids passed by a God) will *nullify* a Grace.